DATE DUE

VLADIMIR NABOKOV

VLADIMIR NABOKOV

NOVELS 1969–1974

Ada
or Ardor: A Family Chronicle

Transparent Things

Look at the Harlequins!

THE LIBRARY OF AMERICA

Manufactured in the United States of America

BRIAN BOYD
ADVISED ON TEXTUAL MATTERS AND
WROTE THE NOTES FOR THIS VOLUME

Contents

ADA

OR ARDOR:
A FAMILY CHRONICLE

*Family
Tree*

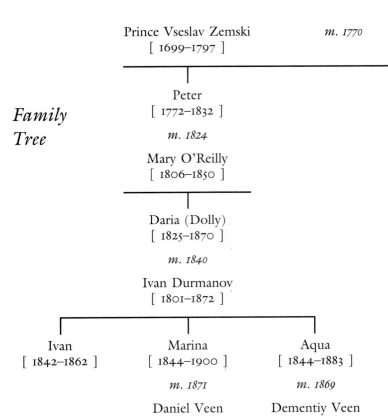

Prince Vseslav Zemski
[1699–1797]   *m. 1770*

Peter
[1772–1832]

m. 1824

Mary O'Reilly
[1806–1850]

Daria (Dolly)
[1825–1870]

m. 1840

Ivan Durmanov
[1801–1872]

Ivan   Marina   Aqua
[1842–1862]   [1844–1900]   [1844–1883]

                    m. 1871   *m. 1869*

                    Daniel Veen   Dementiy Veen

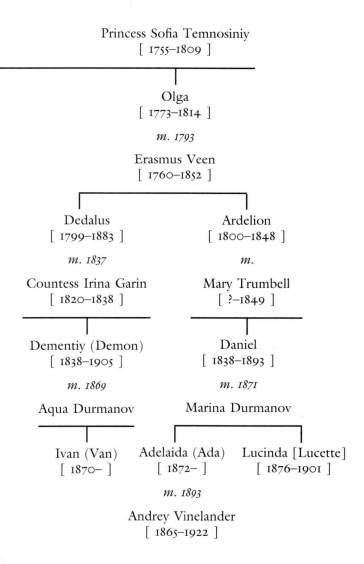

Princess Sofia Temnosiniy
[1755–1809]

Olga
[1773–1814]

m. 1793

Erasmus Veen
[1760–1852]

Dedalus
[1799–1883]

m. 1837

Countess Irina Garin
[1820–1838]

Ardelion
[1800–1848]

m.

Mary Trumbell
[?–1849]

Dementiy (Demon)
[1838–1905]

m. 1869

Aqua Durmanov

Daniel
[1838–1893]

m. 1871

Marina Durmanov

Ivan (Van)
[1870–]

Adelaida (Ada)
[1872–]

Lucinda [Lucette]
[1876–1901]

m. 1893

Andrey Vinelander
[1865–1922]

To Véra

With the exception of Mr. and Mrs. Ronald Oranger,
a few incidental figures,
and some non-American citizens, all the persons
mentioned by name in this book are dead.

[Ed.]

Part One

I

"ALL happy families are more or less dissimilar; all unhappy ones are more or less alike," says a great Russian writer in the beginning of a famous novel (*Anna Arkadievitch Karenina*, transfigured into English by R. G. Stonelower, Mount Tabor Ltd., 1880). That pronouncement has little if any relation to the story to be unfolded now, a family chronicle, the first part of which is, perhaps, closer to another Tolstoy work, *Detstvo i Otrochestvo* (*Childhood and Fatherland*, Pontius Press, 1858).

Van's maternal grandmother Daria ("Dolly") Durmanov was the daughter of Prince Peter Zemski, Governor of Bras d'Or, an American province in the Northeast of our great and variegated country, who had married, in 1824, Mary O'Reilly, an Irish woman of fashion. Dolly, an only child, born in Bras, married in 1840, at the tender and wayward age of fifteen, General Ivan Durmanov, Commander of Yukon Fortress and peaceful country gentleman, with lands in the Severn Tories (Severnïya Territorii), that tesselated protectorate still lovingly called "Russian" Estoty, which commingles, granoblastically and organically, with "Russian" Canady, otherwise "French" Estoty, where not only French, but Macedonian and Bavarian settlers enjoy a halcyon climate under our Stars and Stripes.

The Durmanovs' favorite domain, however, was Raduga near the burg of that name, beyond Estotiland proper, in the Atlantic panel of the continent between elegant Kaluga, New Cheshire, U.S.A., and no less elegant Ladoga, Mayne, where they had their town house and where their three children were born: a son, who died young and famous, and a pair of difficult female twins. Dolly had inherited her mother's beauty and temper but also an older ancestral strain of whimsical, and not seldom deplorable, taste, well reflected, for instance, in the names she gave her daughters: Aqua and Marina ("Why not Tofana?" wondered the good and sur-royally antlered general with a controlled belly laugh, followed by a small

7

closing cough of feigned detachment—he dreaded his wife's flares).

On April 23, 1869, in drizzly and warm, gauzy and green Kaluga, Aqua, aged twenty-five and afflicted with her usual vernal migraine, married Walter D. Veen, a Manhattan banker of ancient Anglo-Irish ancestry who had long conducted, and was soon to resume intermittently, a passionate affair with Marina. The latter, some time in 1871, married her first lover's first cousin, also Walter D. Veen, a quite as opulent, but much duller, chap.

The "D" in the name of Aqua's husband stood for Demon (a form of Demian or Dementius), and thus was he called by his kin. In society he was generally known as Raven Veen or simply Dark Walter to distinguish him from Marina's husband, Durak Walter or simply Red Veen. Demon's twofold hobby was collecting old masters and young mistresses. He also liked middle-aged puns.

Daniel Veen's mother was a Trumbell, and he was prone to explain at great length—unless sidetracked by a bore-baiter—how in the course of American history an English "bull" had become a New England "bell." Somehow or other he had "gone into business" in his twenties and had rather rankly grown into a Manhattan art dealer. He did not have—initially at least—any particular liking for paintings, had no aptitude for any kind of salesmanship, and no need whatever to jolt with the ups and downs of a "job" the solid fortune inherited from a series of far more proficient and venturesome Veens. Confessing that he did not much care for the countryside, he spent only a few carefully shaded summer weekends at Ardis, his magnificent manor near Ladore. He had revisited only a few times since his boyhood another estate he had, up north on Lake Kitezh, near Luga, comprising, and practically consisting of, that large, oddly rectangular though quite natural body of water which a perch he had once clocked took half an hour to cross diagonally and which he owned jointly with his cousin, a great fisherman in his youth.

Poor Dan's erotic life was neither complicated nor beautiful, but somehow or other (he soon forgot the exact circumstances as one forgets the measurements and price of a fondly made topcoat worn on and off for at least a couple of seasons) he fell comfortably in love with Marina, whose family he had known when they still had their Raduga place (later sold to Mr. Eliot, a Jewish businessman). One afternoon in the spring of 1871, he proposed to Marina in the Up elevator of Manhattan's first ten-floor building, was indignantly rejected at the seventh stop (Toys), came down alone and, to air his feelings, set off in a counter-Fogg direction on a triple trip round the globe, adopting, like an animated parallel, the same itinerary every time. In November 1871, as he was in the act of making his evening plans with the same smelly but nice cicerone in a *café-au-lait* suit whom he had hired already twice at the same Genoese hotel, an aerocable from Marina (forwarded with a whole week's delay via his Manhattan office which had filed it away through a new girl's oversight in a dove hole marked RE AMOR) arrived on a silver salver telling him she would marry him upon his return to America.

According to the Sunday supplement of a newspaper that had just begun to feature on its funnies page the now long defunct Goodnight Kids, Nicky and Pimpernella (sweet siblings who shared a narrow bed), and that had survived with other old papers in the cockloft of Ardis Hall, the Veen-Durmanov wedding took place on St. Adelaida's Day, 1871. Twelve years and some eight months later, two naked children, one dark-haired and tanned, the other dark-haired and milk-white, bending in a shaft of hot sunlight that slanted through the dormer window under which the dusty cartons stood, happened to collate that date (December 16, 1871) with another (August 16, same year) anachronistically scrawled in Marina's hand across the corner of a professional photograph (in a raspberry-plush frame on her husband's kneehole library table) identical in every detail—including the commonplace sweep of a bride's ectoplasmic veil, partly blown by a parvis breeze athwart the groom's trousers—to the newspaper reproduction. A girl was born on July 21, 1872, at Ardis, her putative father's seat in Ladore County, and for some obscure mnemonic reason was registered as Adelaida. Another daughter, this time Dan's very own, followed on January 3, 1876.

Besides that old illustrated section of the still existing but rather gaga *Kaluga Gazette*, our frolicsome Pimpernel and Nicolette found in the same attic a reel box containing what

turned out to be (according to Kim, the kitchen boy, as will
be understood later) a tremendous stretch of microfilm taken
by the globetrotter, with many of its quaint bazaars, painted
cherubs and pissing urchins reappearing three times at different points, in different shades of heliocolor. Naturally, at a
time one was starting to build a family one could not display
very well certain intérieurs (such as the group scenes in Da-
mascus starring him and the steadily cigar-smoking archeol-
ogist from Arkansas with the fascinating scar on his liver side,
and the three fat whores, and old Archie's premature squit-
teroo, as the third male member of the party, a real British
brick, drolly called it); yet most of the film, accompanied by
purely factual notes, not always easy to locate—because of the
elusive or misleading bookmarks in the several guidebooks
scattered around—was run by Dan many times for his bride
during their instructive honeymoon in Manhattan.

The two kids' best find, however, came from another carton
in a lower layer of the past. This was a small green album with
neatly glued flowers that Marina had picked or otherwise obtained at Ex, a mountain resort, not far from Brig, Switzerland, where she had sojourned before her marriage, mostly in
a rented chalet. The first twenty pages were adorned with a
number of little plants collected at random, in August, 1869,
on the grassy slopes above the chalet, or in the park of the
Hotel Florey, or in the garden of the sanatorium near it ("my
nusshaus," as poor Aqua dubbed it, or "the Home," as Marina more demurely identified it in her locality notes). Those
introductory pages did not present much botanical or psychological interest; and the fifty last pages or so remained blank;
but the middle part, with a conspicuous decrease in number
of specimens, proved to be a regular little melodrama acted
out by the ghosts of dead flowers. The specimens were on one
side of the folio, with Marina Dourmanoff (*sic*)'s notes *en
regard*.

Ancolie Bleue des Alpes, Ex en Valais, i.ix.69. From Englishman in hotel. "Alpine Columbine, color of your eyes."
Epervière auricule. 25.x.69, Ex, *ex* Dr. Lapiner's walled alpine garden.
Golden [ginkgo] leaf: fallen out of a book "The Truth

about Terra" which Aqua gave me before going back to her Home. 14.XII.69.

Artificial edelweiss brought by my new nurse with a note from Aqua saying it came from a "*mizernoe* and bizarre" Christmas Tree at the Home. 25.XII.69.

Petal of orchid, one of 99 orchids, if you please, mailed to me yesterday, Special Delivery, *c'est bien le cas de le dire*, from Villa Armina, Alpes Maritimes. Have laid aside ten for Aqua to be taken to her at her Home. Ex en Valais, Switzerland. "Snowing in Fate's crystal ball," as he used to say. (Date erased.)

Gentiane de Koch, rare, brought by *lapochka* [darling] Lapiner from his "mute gentiarium" 5.I. 1870.

[blue-ink blot shaped accidentally like a flower, or improved felt-pen deletion] *Compliquaria compliquata* var. *aquamarina*. Ex, 15.I.70.

Fancy flower of paper, found in Aqua's purse. Ex, 16.II.1870, made by a fellow patient, at the Home, which is no longer hers.

Gentiana verna (*printanière*). Ex, 28.III.1870, on the lawn of my nurse's cottage. Last day here.

The two young discoverers of that strange and sickening treasure commented upon it as follows:

"I deduce," said the boy, "three main facts: that not yet married Marina and her married sister hibernated in my *lieu de naissance*; that Marina had her own Dr. Krolik, *pour ainsi dire*; and that the orchids came from Demon who preferred to stay by the sea, his dark-blue great-grandmother."

"I can add," said the girl, "that the petal belongs to the common Butterfly Orchis; that my mother was even crazier than her sister; and that the paper flower so cavalierly dismissed is a perfectly recognizable reproduction of an early-spring sanicle that I saw in profusion on hills in coastal California last February. Dr. Krolik, our local naturalist, to whom you, Van, have referred, as Jane Austen might have phrased it, for the sake of rapid narrative information (you recall Brown, don't you, Smith?), has determined the example I brought back from Sacramento to Ardis, as the Bear-Foot, B,E,A,R, my love, not my foot or yours, or the Stabian flower girl's—an allusion, which your father, who, according to Blanche, is also mine, would understand like this" (American finger-snap). "You will be grateful," she continued, embracing him, "for my not mentioning its scientific name. Incidentally the other foot—the *Pied de Lion* from that poor little Christmas larch, is by the same hand—possibly belonging to a very sick Chinese boy who came all the way from Barkley College."

"Good for you, Pompeianella (whom *you* saw scattering her flowers in one of Uncle Dan's picture books, but whom *I* admired last summer in a Naples museum). Now don't you think we should resume our shorts and shirts and go down, and bury or burn this album at once, girl. Right?"

"Right," answered Ada. "Destroy and forget. But we still have an hour before tea."

Re the "dark-blue" allusion, left hanging:

A former viceroy of Estoty, Prince Ivan Temnosiniy, father of the children's great-great-grandmother, Princess Sofia Zemski (1755–1809), and a direct descendant of the Yaroslav rulers of pre-Tartar times, had a millennium-old name that meant in Russian "dark blue." While happening to be immune to the sumptuous thrills of genealogic awareness, and indifferent to the fact that oafs attribute both the aloofness and the fervor to snobbishness, Van could not help feeling esthetically moved by the velvet background he was always able to distinguish as a comforting, omnipresent summer sky through the black foliage of the family tree. In later years he had never been able to reread Proust (as he had never been able to enjoy again the perfumed gum of Turkish paste) without a roll-wave of surfeit and a rasp of gravelly heartburn; yet his favorite purple passage remained the one concerning the name "Guermantes," with whose hue his adjacent ultramarine merged in the prism of his mind, pleasantly teasing Van's artistic vanity.

Hue or who? Awkward. Reword! (marginal note in Ada Veen's late hand).

2

Marina's affair with Demon Veen started on his, her, and Daniel Veen's birthday, January 5, 1868, when she was twenty-four and both Veens thirty.

As an actress, she had none of the breath-taking quality that makes the skill of mimicry seem, at least while the show lasts, worth even more than the price of such footlights as insomnia, fancy, arrogant art; yet on that particular night, with soft snow falling beyond the plush and the paint, *la Durmanska* (who paid the great Scott, her impresario, seven thousand gold dollars a week for publicity alone, plus a bonny bonus for every engagement) had been from the start of the trashy ephemeron (an American play based by some pretentious hack on a famous Russian romance) so dreamy, so lovely, so stirring, that Demon (not *quite* a gentleman in amorous matters) made a bet with his orchestra-seat neighbor, Prince N., bribed a series of green-room attendants, and then, in a *cabinet reculé* (as a French writer of an earlier century might have mysteriously called that little room in which the broken trumpet and poodle hoops of a forgotten clown, besides many dusty pots of colored grease, happened to be stored) proceeded to possess her between two scenes (Chapter Three and Four of the martyred novel). In the first of these she had undressed in graceful silhouette behind a semitransparent screen, reappeared in a flimsy and fetching nightgown, and spent the rest of the wretched scene discussing a local squire, Baron d'O., with an old nurse in Eskimo boots. Upon the infinitely wise countrywoman's suggestion, she goose-penned, from the edge of her bed, on a side table with cabriole legs, a love letter and took five minutes to reread it in a languorous but loud voice for nobody's benefit in particular since the nurse sat dozing on a kind of sea chest, and the spectators were mainly concerned with the artificial moonlight's blaze upon the lovelorn young lady's bare arms and heaving breasts.

Even before the old Eskimo had shuffled off with the message, Demon Veen had left his pink velvet chair and proceeded to win the wager, the success of his enterprise being assured by the fact that Marina, a kissing virgin, had been in love with him since their last dance on New Year's Eve. Moreover, the tropical moonlight she had just bathed in, the penetrative sense of her own beauty, the ardent pulses of the imagined maiden, and the gallant applause of an almost full house made her especially vulnerable to the tickle of Demon's moustache. She had ample time, too, to change for the next scene, which started with a longish intermezzo staged by a ballet company whose services Scotty had engaged, bringing the Russians all the way in two sleeping cars from Belokonsk, Western Estoty. In a splendid orchard several merry young gardeners wearing for some reason the garb of Georgian tribesmen were popping raspberries into their mouths, while several equally implausible servant girls in sharovars (somebody had goofed—the word "samovars" may have got garbled in the agent's aerocable) were busy plucking marshmallows and peanuts from the branches of fruit trees. At an invisible sign of Dionysian origin, they all plunged into the violent dance called *kurva* or "ribbon boule" in the hilarious program whose howlers almost caused Veen (tingling, and light-loined, and with Prince N.'s rose-red banknote in his pocket) to fall from his seat.

His heart missed a beat and never regretted the lovely loss, as she ran, flushed and flustered, in a pink dress into the orchard, earning a claque third of the sitting ovation that greeted the instant dispersal of the imbecile but colorful transfigurants from Lyaska—or Iveria. Her meeting with Baron O., who strolled out of a side alley, all spurs and green tails, somehow eluded Demon's consciousness, so struck was he by the wonder of that brief abyss of absolute reality between two bogus fulgurations of fabricated life. Without waiting for the end of the scene, he hurried out of the theater into the crisp crystal night, the snowflakes star-spangling his top hat as he returned to his house in the next block to arrange a magnificent supper. By the time he went to fetch his new mistress in his jingling sleigh, the last-act ballet of Caucasian generals and metamorphosed Cinderellas had come to a sudden close, and Baron d'O., now in black tails and white gloves, was kneeling in the middle of an empty stage, holding the glass slipper that his fickle lady had left him when eluding his belated advances. The claqueurs were getting tired and looking at their watches when Marina in a black cloak slipped into Demon's arms and swan-sleigh.

They reveled, and traveled, and they quarreled, and flew back to each other again. By the following winter he began to suspect she was being unfaithful to him, but could not determine his rival. In mid-March, at a business meal with an art expert, an easy-going, lanky, likeable fellow in an old-fashioned dress-coat, Demon screwed in his monocle, unclicked out of its special flat case a small pen-and-wash and said he thought (did not doubt, in fact, but wished his certitude to be admired) that it was an unknown product of Parmigianino's tender art. It showed a naked girl with a peach-like apple cupped in her half-raised hand sitting sideways on a convolvulus-garlanded support, and had for its discoverer the additional appeal of recalling Marina when, rung out of a hotel bathroom by the phone, and perched on the arm of a chair, she muffled the receiver while asking her lover something that he could not make out because the bath's voice drowned her whisper. Baron d'Onsky had only to cast one glance at that raised shoulder and at certain vermiculated effects of delicate vegetation to confirm Demon's guess. D'Onsky had the reputation of not showing one sign of esthetic emotion in the presence of the loveliest masterpiece; this time, nonetheless, he laid his magnifier aside as he would a mask, and allowed his undisguised gaze to caress the velvety apple and the nude's dimpled and mossed parts with a smile of bemused pleasure. Would Mr. Veen consider selling it to him there and then, Mr. Veen, please? Mr. Veen would not. Skonky (a one-way nickname) must content himself with the proud thought that, as of today, he and the lucky owner were the sole people to have ever admired it *en connaissance de cause*. Back it went into its special integument; but after finishing his fourth cup of cognac, d'O. pleaded for one last peep. Both men were a little drunk, and Demon secretly wondered if the rather banal resemblance of that Edenic girl to a young actress, whom his visitor had no doubt seen on the stage in "Eugene and Lara" or "Lenore Raven" (both painfully panned by a "disgustingly incorruptible" young critic), should be, or would be, commented upon. It was not: such nymphs were really very much

alike because of their elemental limpidity since the similarities
of young bodies of water are but murmurs of natural innocence and double-talk mirrors, that's my hat, his is older, but
we have the same London hatter.

Next day Demon was having tea at his favorite hotel with
a Bohemian lady whom he had never seen before and was
never to see again (she desired his recommendation for a job
in the Glass Fish-and-Flower department in a Boston museum) when she interrupted her voluble self to indicate Marina and Aqua, blankly slinking across the hall in modish
sullenness and bluish furs with Dan Veen and a *dackel* behind,
and said:

"Curious how that appalling actress resembles 'Eve on the
Clepsydrophone' in Parmigianino's famous picture."

"It is anything but famous," said Demon quietly, "and you
can't have seen it. I don't envy you," he added; "the naïve
stranger who realizes that he or she has stepped into the mud
of an alien life must experience a pretty sickening feeling. Did
you get that small-talk information directly from a fellow
named d'Onsky or through a friend of a friend of his?"

"Friend of his," replied the hapless Bohemian lady.

Upon being questioned in Demon's dungeon, Marina,
laughing trillingly, wove a picturesque tissue of lies; then
broke down, and confessed. She swore that all was over; that
the Baron, a physical wreck and a spiritual Samurai, had gone
to Japan forever. From a more reliable source Demon learned
that the Samurai's real destination was smart little Vatican, a
Roman spa, whence he was to return to Aardvark, Massa, in
a week or so. Since prudent Veen preferred killing his man in
Europe (decrepit but indestructible Gamaliel was said to be
doing his best to forbid duels in the Western Hemisphere—a
canard or an idealistic President's instant-coffee caprice, for
nothing was to come of it after all), Demon rented the fastest
petroloplane available, overtook the Baron (looking very fit)
in Nice, saw him enter Gunter's Bookshop, went in after him,
and in the presence of the imperturbable and rather bored
English shopkeeper, back-slapped the astonished Baron across
the face with a lavender glove. The challenge was accepted;
two native seconds were chosen; the Baron plumped for
swords; and after a certain amount of good blood (Polish and

Irish—a kind of American "Gory Mary" in barroom parlance)
had bespattered two hairy torsoes, the white-washed terrace,
the flight of steps leading backward to the walled garden in
an amusing Douglas d'Artagnan arrangement, the apron of a
quite accidental milkmaid, and the shirtsleeves of both seconds, charming Monsieur de Pastrouil and Colonel St. Alin,
a scoundrel, the latter gentlemen separated the panting com-
batants, and Skonky died, not "of his wounds" (as it was
viciously rumored) but of a gangrenous afterthought on the
part of the least of them, possibly self-inflicted, a sting in the
groin, which caused circulatory trouble, notwithstanding
quite a few surgical interventions during two or three years of
protracted stays at the Aardvark Hospital in Boston—a city
where, incidentally, he married in 1869 our friend the Bohemian lady, now keeper of Glass Biota at the local museum.

Marina arrived in Nice a few days after the duel, and tracked
Demon down in his villa Armina, and in the ecstasy of reconciliation neither remembered to dupe procreation, whereupon started the extremely *interesnoe polozhenie* ("interesting
condition") without which, in fact, these anguished notes
could not have been strung.

(Van, I trust your taste and your talent but are we *quite
sure* we should keep reverting so *zestfully* to that wicked world
which after all may have existed only oneirologically, Van?
Marginal jotting in Ada's 1965 hand; crossed out lightly in her
latest wavering one.)

That reckless stage was not the last but the shortest—a matter of four or five days. He pardoned her. He adored her. He
wished to marry her very much—on the condition she
dropped her theatrical "career" at once. He denounced the
mediocrity of her gift and the vulgarity of her entourage, and
she yelled he was a brute and a fiend. By April 10 it was Aqua
who was nursing him, while Marina had flown back to her
rehearsals of "Lucile," yet another execrable drama heading
for yet another flop at the Ladore playhouse.

"Adieu. Perhaps it is better thus," wrote Demon to Marina
in mid-April, 1869 (the letter may be either a copy in his calligraphic hand or the unposted original), "for whatever bliss
might have attended our married life, and however long that
blissful life might have lasted, one image I shall not forget and

will not forgive. Let it sink in, my dear. Let me repeat it in such terms as a stage performer can appreciate. You had gone to Boston to see an old aunt—a cliché, but the truth for the nonce—and I had gone to *my* aunt's ranch near Lolita, Texas. Early one February morning (around noon *chez vous*) I rang you up at your hotel from a roadside booth of pure crystal still tear-stained after a tremendous thunderstorm to ask you to fly over at once because I, Demon, rattling my crumpled wings and cursing the automatic dorophone, could not live without you and because I wished you to see, with me holding you, the daze of desert flowers that the rain had brought out. Your voice was remote but sweet; you said you were in Eve's state, hold the line, let me put on a *penyuar*. Instead, blocking my ear, you spoke, I suppose, to the man with whom you had spent the night (and whom I would have dispatched, had I not been overeager to castrate him). Now *that* is the sketch made by a young artist in Parma, in the sixteenth century, for the fresco of *our* destiny, in a prophetic trance, and coinciding, except for the apple of terrible knowledge, with an image repeated in two men's minds. Your runaway maid, by the way, has been found by the police in a brothel here and will be shipped to you as soon as she is sufficiently stuffed with mercury."

3

The details of the L disaster (and I do not mean Elevated) in the *beau milieu* of last century, which had the singular effect of both causing and cursing the notion of "Terra," are too well-known historically, and too obscene spiritually, to be treated at length in a book addressed to young laymen and lemans—and not to grave men or gravemen.

Of course, today, after great anti-L years of reactionary delusion have gone by (more or less!) and our sleek little machines, Faragod bless them, hum again after a fashion, as they did in the first half of the nineteenth century, the mere geographic aspect of the affair possesses its redeeming comic side, like those patterns of brass marquetry, and bric-à-Braques, and the ormolu horrors that meant "art" to our humorless forefathers. For, indeed, none can deny the presence of something highly ludicrous in the very configurations that were solemnly purported to represent a varicolored map of Terra. *Ved'* ("it is, isn't it") sidesplitting to imagine that "Russia," instead of being a quaint synonym of Estoty, the American province extending from the Arctic no longer vicious Circle to the United States proper, was on Terra the name of a country, transferred as if by some sleight of *land* across the ha-ha of a doubled ocean to the opposite hemisphere where it sprawled over all of today's Tartary, from Kurland to the Kuriles! But (even more absurdly), if, in Terrestrial spatial terms, the Amerussia of Abraham Milton was split into its components, with tangible water and ice separating the political, rather than poetical, notions of "America" and "Russia," a more complicated and even more preposterous discrepancy arose in regard to time—not only because the history of each part of the amalgam did not quite match the history of each counterpart in its discrete condition, but because a gap of up to a hundred years one way or another existed between the two earths; a gap marked by a bizarre confusion of directional signs at the crossroads of passing time with not *all* the no-longers of one world corresponding to the not-yets of the other. It was owing, among other things, to this "scientifically ungraspable" concourse of divergences that minds *bien rangés* (not apt to unhobble hobgoblins), rejected Terra as a fad or a fantom, and deranged minds (ready to plunge into any abyss) accepted it in support and token of their own irrationality.

As Van Veen himself was to find out, at the time of his passionate research in terrology (then a branch of psychiatry) even the deepest thinkers, the purest philosophers, Paar of Chose and Zapater of Aardvark, were emotionally divided in their attitude toward the possibility that there existed "a distortive glass of our distorted glebe" as a scholar who desires to remain unnamed has put it with such euphonic wit. (Hm! Kveree-kveree, as poor Mlle L. used to say to Gavronsky. In Ada's hand.)

There were those who maintained that the discrepancies and "false overlappings" between the two worlds were too

numerous, and too deeply woven into the skein of successive
events, not to taint with trite fancy the theory of essential
sameness; and there were those who retorted that the dissim-
ilarities only confirmed the live organic reality pertaining to
the other world; that a perfect likeness would rather suggest
a specular, and hence speculatory, phenomenon; and that two
chess games with identical openings and identical end moves
might ramify in an infinite number of variations, on *one* board
and in *two* brains, at any middle stage of their irrevocably
converging development.

The modest narrator has to remind the rereader of all this,
because in April (my favorite month), 1869 (by no means a
mirabilic year), on St. George's Day (according to Mlle Larivière's maudlin memoirs) Demon Veen married Aqua Durmanov—out of spite and pity, a not unusual blend.

Was there some additional spice? Marina, with perverse
vainglory, used to affirm in bed that Demon's senses must
have been influenced by a queer sort of "incestuous" (whatever that term means) pleasure (in the sense of the French
plaisir, which works up a lot of supplementary spinal vibrato),
when he fondled, and savored, and delicately parted and de-
filed, in unmentionable but fascinating ways, flesh (*une chair*)
that was both that of his wife and that of his mistress, the
blended and brightened charms of twin peris, an Aquamarina
both single and double, a mirage in an emirate, a geminate
gem, an orgy of epithelial alliterations.

Actually, Aqua was less pretty, and far more dotty, than Marina. During her fourteen years of miserable marriage she
spent a broken series of steadily increasing sojourns in sana-
toriums. A small map of the European part of the British
Commonwealth—say, from Scoto-Scandinavia to the Riviera,
Altar and Palermontovia—as well as most of the U.S.A., from
Estoty and Canady to Argentina, might be quite thickly prick-
led with enameled red-cross-flag pins, marking, in her War of
the Worlds, Aqua's bivouacs. She had plans at one time to
seek a modicum of health ("just a little grayishness, please,
instead of the solid black") in such Anglo-American protec-
torates as the Balkans and Indias, and might even have tried
the two Southern Continents that thrive under our joint do-
minion. Of course, Tartary, an independent inferno, which at

the time spread from the Baltic and Black seas to the Pacific Ocean, was touristically unavailable, though Yalta and Altyn Tagh sounded strangely attractive . . . But her real destination was Terra the Fair and thither she trusted she would fly on libellula long wings when she died. Her poor little letters from the homes of madness to her husband were sometimes signed: Madame Shchemyashchikh-Zvukov ("Heart rending-Sounds").

After her first battle with insanity at Ex en Valais she returned to America, and suffered a bad defeat, in the days when Van was still being suckled by a very young wet nurse, almost a child, Ruby Black, born Black, who was to go mad too: for no sooner did all the fond, all the frail, come into close contact with him (as later Lucette did, to give another example) than they were bound to know anguish and calamity, unless strengthened by a strain of his father's demon blood.

Aqua was not quite twenty when the exaltation of her nature had begun to reveal a morbid trend. Chronologically, the initial stage of her mental illness coincided with the first decade of the Great Revelation, and although she might have found just as easily another theme for her delusion, statistics show that the Great, and to some Intolerable, Revelation caused more insanity in the world than even an over-preoccupation with religion had in medieval times.

Revelation can be more perilous than Revolution. Sick minds identified the notion of a Terra planet with that of another world and this "Other World" got confused not only with the "Next World" but with the Real World in us and beyond us. *Our* enchanters, *our* demons, are noble iridescent creatures with translucent talons and mightily beating wings; but in the eighteen-sixties the New Believers urged one to imagine a sphere where our splendid friends had been utterly degraded, had become nothing but vicious monsters, disgusting devils, with the black scrota of carnivora and the fangs of serpents, revilers and tormentors of female souls; while on the opposite side of the cosmic lane a rainbow mist of angelic spirits, inhabitants of sweet Terra, restored all the stalest but still potent myths of old creeds, with rearrangement for melodeon of all the cacophonies of all the divinities and divines ever spawned in the marshes of this our sufficient world.

Sufficient for your purpose, Van, *entendons-nous*. (Note in the margin.)

Poor Aqua, whose fancies were apt to fall for all the fangles of cranks and Christians, envisaged vividly a minor hymnist's paradise, a future America of alabaster buildings one hundred stories high, resembling a beautiful furniture store crammed with tall white-washed wardrobes and shorter fridges; she saw giant flying sharks with lateral eyes taking barely one night to carry pilgrims through black ether across an entire continent from dark to shining sea, before booming back to Seattle or Wark. She heard magic-music boxes talking and singing, drowning the terror of thought, uplifting the lift girl, riding down with the miner, praising beauty and godliness, the Virgin and Venus, in the dwellings of the lonely and the poor. The unmentionable magnetic power denounced by evil lawmakers in this our shabby country—oh, everywhere, in Estoty and Canady, in "German" Mark Kennensie, as well as in "Swedish" Manitobogan, in the workshop of the red-shirted Yukonets as well as in the kitchen of the red-kerchiefed Lyaskanka, and in "French" Estoty, from Bras d'Or to Ladore— and very soon throughout both our Americas, and all over the other stunned continents—was used on Terra as freely as water and air, as bibles and brooms. Two or three centuries earlier she might have been just another consumable witch.

In her erratic student years Aqua had left fashionable Brown Hill College, founded by one of her less reputable ancestors, to participate (as was also fashionable) in some Social Improvement project or another in the Severnïya Territorii. She organized with Milton Abraham's invaluable help a Phree Pharmacy in Belokonsk, and fell grievously in love there with a married man, who after one summer of parvenu passion dispensed to her in his Camping Ford *garçonnière* preferred to give her up rather than run the risk of endangering his social situation in a philistine town where businessmen played "golf" on Sundays and belonged to "lodges." The dreadful sickness, roughly diagnosed in her case, and in that of other unfortunate people, as an "extreme form of mystical mania combined with existalienation" (otherwise plain madness), crept over her by degrees, with intervals of ecstatic peace, with skipped areas of precarious sanity, with sudden dreams of eternity-certainty, which grew ever rarer and briefer.

After her death in 1883, Van computed that in the course of thirteen years, counting every presumed moment of presence, counting the dismal visits to her various hospitals, as well as her sudden tumultuous appearances in the middle of the night (wrestling with her husband or the frail but agile English governess all the way upstairs, wildly welcomed by the old *appenzeller*—and finally making the nursery, wigless, slipperless, with bloodied fingernails), he had actually seen her, or been near her, all in all, for a length of time hardly exceeding that of human gestation.

The rosy remoteness of Terra was soon veiled for her by direful mists. Her disintegration went down a shaft of phases, every one more racking than the last; for the human brain can become the best torture house of all those it has invented, established and used in millions of years, in millions of lands, on millions of howling creatures.

She developed a morbid sensitivity to the language of tap water—which echoes sometimes (much as the bloodstream does predormitarily) a fragment of human speech lingering in one's ears while one washes one's hands after cocktails with strangers. Upon first noticing this immediate, sustained, and in her case rather eager and mocking but really quite harmless replay of this or that recent discourse, she felt tickled at the thought that she, poor Aqua, had accidentally hit upon such a simple method of recording and transmitting speech, while technologists (the so-called Eggheads) all over the world were trying to make publicly utile and commercially rewarding the extremely elaborate and still very expensive hydrodynamic telephones and other miserable gadgets that were to replace those that had gone *k chertyam sobach'im* (Russian "to the devil") with the banning of an unmentionable "lammer." Soon, however, the rhythmically perfect, but verbally rather blurred volubility of faucets began to acquire too much pertinent sense. The purity of the running water's enunciation grew in proportion to the nuisance it made of itself. It spoke soon after she had listened, or been exposed, to somebody talking—not necessarily to her—forcibly and expressively, a

person with a rapid characteristic voice, and very individual or
very foreign phrasal intonations, some compulsive narrator's
patter at a horrible party, or a liquid soliloquy in a tedious
play, or Van's lovely voice, or a bit of poetry heard at a lecture,
my lad, my pretty, my love, take pity, but especially the more
fluid and *flou* Italian verse, for instance that ditty recited between knee-knocking and palpebra-lifting, by a half-Russian,
half-dotty old doctor, doc, toc, ditty, dotty, ballatetta, debo-
letta . . . tu, voce sbigottita . . . spigotty e diavoletta . . . de
lo cor dolente . . . con ballatetta va . . . va . . . della strutta,
destruttamente . . . mente . . . mente . . . stop that record,
or the guide will go on demonstrating as he did this very
morning in Florence a silly pillar commemorating, he said, the
"elmo" that broke into leaf when they carried stone-heavy-
dead St. Zeus by it through the gradual, gradual shade; or the
Arlington harridan talking incessantly to her silent husband as
the vineyards sped by, and even in the tunnel (they can't do
this to you, you tell them, Jack Black, you just tell them . . .).
Bathwater (or shower) was too much of a Caliban to speak
distinctly—or perhaps was too brutally anxious to emit the hot
torrent and get rid of the infernal ardor to bother about small
talk; but the burbly flowlets grew more and more ambitious
and odious, and when at her first "home" she heard one of
the most hateful of the visiting doctors (the Cavalcanti
quoter) garrulously pour hateful instructions in Russian-
lapped German into her hateful bidet, she decided to stop
turning on tap water altogether.

But that phase elapsed too. Other excruciations replaced her
namesake's loquacious quells so completely that when, during
a lucid interval, she happened to open with her weak little
hand a lavabo cock for a drink of water, the tepid lymph replied in its own lingo, without a trace of trickery or mimicry:
Finito! It was now the forming of soft black pits (*yamï,
yamïshchi*) in her mind, between the dimming sculptures of
thought and recollection, that tormented her phenomenally;
mental panic and physical pain joined black-ruby hands, one
making her pray for sanity, the other, plead for death. Man-
made objects lost their significance or grew monstrous connotations; clothes hangers were really the shoulders of
decapitated Tellurians, the folds of a blanket she had kicked

off her bed looked back at her mournfully with a stye on one drooping eyelid and dreary reproof in the limp twist of a livid lip. The effort to comprehend the information conveyed somehow to people of genius by the hands of a timepiece, or piece of time, became as hopeless as trying to make out the sign language of a secret society or the Chinese chant of that young student with a non-Chinese guitar whom she had known at the time she or her sister had given birth to a mauve baby. But her madness, the majesty of her madness, still retained a mad queen's pathetic coquetry: "You know, Doctor, I think I'll need glasses soon, I don't know" (lofty laugh), "I just can't make out what my wrist watch says . . . For heaven's sake, tell me what it says! Ah! Half-past for—for what? Never mind, never mind, 'never' and 'mind' are twins, I have a twin sister and a twin son. I know you want to examine my pudendron, the Hairy Alpine Rose in *her* album, collected ten years ago" (showing her ten fingers gleefully, proudly, ten is ten!).

Then the anguish increased to unendurable massivity and nightmare dimensions, making her scream and vomit. She wanted (and was allowed, bless the hospital barber, Bob Bean) to have her dark curls shaved to an aquamarine prickle, because they grew *into* her porous skull and curled inside. Jigsaw pieces of sky or wall came apart, no matter how delicately put together, but a careless jolt or a nurse's elbow can disturb so easily those lightweight fragments which became incomprehensible blancs of anonymous objects, or the blank backs of "Scrabble" counters, which she could not turn over sunny side up, because her hands had been tied by a male nurse with Demon's black eyes. But presently panic and pain, like a pair of children in a boisterous game, emitted one last shriek of laughter and ran away to manipulate each other behind a bush as in Count Tolstoy's *Anna Karenin*, a novel, and again, for a while, a little while, all was quiet in the house, and their mother had the same first name as hers had.

At one time Aqua believed that a stillborn male infant half a year old, a surprised little fetus, a fish of rubber that she had produced in her bath, in a *lieu de naissance* plainly marked X in her dreams, after skiing at full pulver into a larch stump, had somehow been saved and brought to her at the Nusshaus, with her sister's compliments, wrapped up in blood-soaked cotton wool, but perfectly alive and healthy, to be registered as her son Ivan Veen. At other moments she felt convinced that the child was her sister's, born out of wedlock, during an exhausting, yet highly romantic blizzard, in a mountain refuge on Sex Rouge, where a Dr. Alpiner, general practitioner and gentian-lover, sat providentially waiting near a rude red stove for his boots to dry. Some confusion ensued less than two years later (September, 1871—her proud brain still retained dozens of dates) when upon escaping from *her* next refuge and somehow reaching her husband's unforgettable country house (imitate a foreigner: "*Signor Konduktor, ay vant go Lago di Luga, hier geld*") she took advantage of his being massaged in the solarium, tiptoed into their former bed-room—and experienced a delicious shock: *her* talc powder in a half-full glass container marked colorfully Quelques Fleurs still stood on *her* bedside table; *her* favorite flame-colored nightgown lay rumpled on the bedrug; to her it meant that only a brief black nightmare had obliterated the radiant fact of her having slept with her husband all along—ever since Shakespeare's birthday on a green rainy day, but for most other people, alas, it meant that Marina (after G. A. Vronsky, the movie man, had left Marina for another long-lashed *Khristosik* as he called all pretty starlets) had conceived, *c'est bien le cas de le dire*, the brilliant idea of having Demon divorce mad Aqua and marry Marina who thought (happily and correctly) she was pregnant again. Marina had spent a *rukuliruyushchiy* month with him at Kitezh but when she smugly divulged her intentions (just before Aqua's arrival) he threw her out of the house. Still later, on the last short lap of a useless existence, Aqua scrapped all those ambiguous recollections and found herself reading and rereading, busily, blissfully, her son's letters in a luxurious "sanastoria" at Centaur, Arizona. He invariably wrote in French calling her *petite maman* and describing the amusing school he would be living at after his thirteenth birthday. She heard his voice through the nightly tinnitus of her new, planful, last, last insomnias and it consoled her. He called her usually mummy, or mama, accenting the last syllable in English, the first, in Russian; somebody had said that triplets and heraldic dracunculi often occurred in trilingual families; but there was absolutely no doubt *whatsoever* now (except, perhaps, in hateful long-dead Marina's hell-dwelling mind) that Van was *her*, *her*, Aqua's, beloved son.

Being unwilling to suffer another relapse after this blessed state of perfect mental repose, but knowing it could not last, she did what another patient had done in distant France, at a much less radiant and easygoing "home." A Dr. Froid, one of the administerial centaurs, who may have been an émigré brother with a passport-changed name of the Dr. Froit of Signy-Mondieu-Mondieu in the Ardennes or, more likely, the same man, because they both came from Vienne, Isère, and were only sons (as her son was), evolved, or rather revived, the therapistic device, aimed at establishing a "group" feeling, of having the finest patients help the staff if "thusly inclined." Aqua, in her turn, repeated exactly clever Eleonore Bonvard's trick, namely, opting for the making of beds and the cleaning of glass shelves. The astorium in St. Taurus, or whatever it was called (who cares—one forgets little things very fast, when afloat in infinite non-thingness) was, perhaps, more modern, with a more refined desertic view, than the Mondefroid bleak-house horsepittle, but in both places a demented patient could outwit in one snap an imbecile pedant.

In less than a week Aqua had accumulated more than two hundred tablets of different potency. She knew most of them—the jejune sedatives, and the ones that knocked you out from eight P.M. till midnight, and several varieties of superior soporifics that left you with limpid limbs and a leaden head after eight hours of non-being, and a drug which was in itself delightful but a little lethal if combined with a draught of the cleansing fluid commercially known as Morona; and a plump purple pill reminding her, she had to laugh, of those with which the little gypsy enchantress in the Spanish tale (dear to Ladore schoolgirls) puts to sleep all the sportsmen and all their bloodhounds at the opening of the hunting season. Lest some busybody resurrect her in the middle of the float-away process, Aqua reckoned she must procure for herself a maximum period of undisturbed stupor elsewhere than in a glass house, and the carrying out of that second part of the project was simplified and encouraged by another agent or double of the Isère Professor, a Dr. Sig Heiler whom every-

body venerated as a great guy and near-genius in the usual
sense of near-beer. Such patients who proved by certain
twitchings of the eyelids and other semi-private parts under
the control of medical students that Sig (a slightly deformed
but not unhandsome old boy) was in the process of being
dreamt of as a "papa Fig," spanker of girl bottoms and spunky
spittoon-user, were assumed to be on the way to haleness and
permitted, upon awakening, to participate in normal outdoor
activities such as picnics. Sly Aqua twitched, simulated a yawn,
opened her light-blue eyes (with those startlingly contrasty
jet-black pupils that Dolly, her mother, also had), put on
yellow slacks and a black bolero, walked through a little
pinewood, thumbed a ride with a Mexican truck, found a suitable gulch in the chaparral and there, after writing a short
note, began placidly eating from her cupped palm the multicolored contents of her handbag, like any Russian country girl
lakomyashchayasya yagodami (feasting on berries) that she had
just picked in the woods. She smiled, dreamily enjoying the
thought (rather "Kareninian" in tone) that her extinction
would affect people about as deeply as the abrupt, mysterious,
never explained demise of a comic strip in a Sunday paper one
had been taking for years. It was her last smile. She was discovered much sooner, but had also died much faster than expected, and the observant Siggy, still in his baggy khaki shorts,
reported that Sister Aqua (as for some reason they all called
her) lay, as if buried prehistorically, in a *fetus-in-utero* position,
a comment that seemed relevant to his students, as it may be
to mine.

Her last note, found on her and addressed to her husband
and son, might have come from the sanest person on this or
that earth.

> *Aujourd'hui* (*heute*-toity!) I, this eye-rolling toy, have
> earned the psykitsch right to enjoy a landparty with Herr
> Doktor Sig, Nurse Joan the Terrible, and several "pa-
> tients," in the neighboring *bor* (piney wood) where I
> noticed exactly the same skunk-like squirrels, Van, that
> your Darkblue ancestor imported to Ardis Park, where
> you will ramble one day, no doubt. The hands of a
> clock, even when out of order, must know and let the

dumbest little watch know where they stand, otherwise neither is a dial but only a white face with a trick mustache. Similarly, *chelovek* (human being) must know where he stands and let others know, otherwise he is not even a *klok* (piece) of a *chelovek*, neither a he, nor she, but "a tit of it" as poor Ruby, my little Van, used to say of her scanty right breast. I, poor *Princesse Lointaine, très lointaine* by now, do not know where I stand. Hence I must fall. So adieu, my dear, dear son, and farewell, poor Demon, I do not know the date or the season, but it is a reasonably, and no doubt seasonably, fair day, with a lot of cute little ants queuing to get at my pretty pills.

> [Signed] My sister's sister who *teper'*
> *iz ada* ("now is out of hell")

"If we want life's sundial to show its hand," commented Van, developing the metaphor in the rose garden of Ardis Manor at the end of August, 1884, "we must always remember that the strength, the dignity, the delight of man is to spite and despise the shadows and stars that hide their secrets from us. Only the ridiculous power of pain made her surrender. And I often think it would have been so much more plausible, esthetically, ecstatically, Estotially speaking—if she were really my mother."

4

When, in the middle of the twentieth century, Van started to reconstruct his deepest past, he soon noticed that such details of his infancy as really mattered (for the special purpose the reconstruction pursued) could be best treated, could not seldom be *only* treated, when reappearing at various later stages of his boyhood and youth, as sudden juxtapositions that revived the part while vivifying the whole. This is why his first love has precedence here over his first bad hurt or bad dream.

He had just turned thirteen. He had never before left the comforts of the paternal roof. He had never before realized that such "comforts" might not be taken for granted, only occurring in some introductory ready-made metaphor in a book about a boy and a school. A few blocks from the school-grounds, a widow, Mrs. Tapirov, who was French but spoke English with a Russian accent, had a shop of objets d'art and more or less antique furniture. He visited it on a bright winter day. Crystal vases with crimson roses and golden-brown asters were set here and there in the fore part of the shop—on a gilt-wood console, on a lacquered chest, on the shelf of a cabinet, or simply along the carpeted steps leading to the next floor where great wardrobes and flashy dressers semi-encircled a singular company of harps. He satisfied himself that those flowers were artificial and thought it puzzling that such imitations always pander so exclusively to the eye instead of also copying the damp fat feel of live petal and leaf. When he called next day for the object (unremembered now, eighty years later) that he wanted repaired or duplicated, it was not ready or had not been obtained. In passing, he touched a half-opened rose and was cheated of the sterile texture his finger-tips had expected when cool life kissed them with pouting lips. "My daughter," said Mrs. Tapirov, who saw his surprise, "always puts a bunch of real ones among the fake *pour attraper le client*. You drew the joker." As he was leaving she came in, a schoolgirl in a gray coat with brown shoulder-length ringlets and a pretty face. On another occasion (for a certain part of the thing—a frame, perhaps—took an infinite time to heal or else the entire article proved to be unobtainable after all) he saw her curled up with her schoolbooks in an armchair—a domestic item among those for sale. He never spoke to her. He loved her madly. It must have lasted at least one term.

That was love, normal and mysterious. Less mysterious and considerably more grotesque were the passions which several generations of schoolmasters had failed to eradicate, and which as late as 1883 still enjoyed an unparalleled vogue at Riverlane. Every dormitory had its catamite. One hysterical lad from Upsala, cross-eyed, loose-lipped, with almost abnormally awkward limbs, but with a wonderfully tender skin texture and the round creamy charms of Bronzino's Cupid (the big one, whom a delighted satyr discovers in a lady's bower), was much prized and tortured by a group of foreign boys, mostly Greek and English, led by Cheshire, the rugby ace; and partly out of bravado, partly out of curiosity, Van surmounted his disgust and coldly watched their rough orgies. Soon, however, he abandoned this surrogate for a more natural though equally heartless divertissement.

The aging woman who sold barley sugar and Lucky Louse magazines in the corner shop, which by tradition was not strictly out of bounds, happened to hire a young helper, and Cheshire, the son of a thrifty lord, quickly ascertained that this fat little wench could be had for a Russian green dollar. Van was one of the first to avail himself of her favors. These were granted in semi-darkness, among crates and sacks at the back of the shop after hours. The fact of his having told her he was sixteen and a libertine instead of fourteen and a virgin proved a source of embarrassment to our hell-raker when he tried to bluster his inexperience into quick action but only succeeded in spilling on the welcome mat what she would have gladly helped him to take indoors. Things went better six minutes later, after Cheshire and Zographos were through; but only at the next mating party did Van really begin to enjoy her gentleness, her soft sweet grip and hearty joggle. He knew she was nothing but a fubsy pig-pink whorelet and would elbow her face away when she attempted to kiss him after he had finished and was checking with one quick hand, as he had seen Cheshire do, if his wallet was still in his hip pocket; but somehow or other, when the last of some forty convulsions had come and gone in the ordinary course of collapsing time, and his train was bowling past black and green fields to Ardis, he found himself endowing with unsuspected poetry her poor image, the kitchen odor of her arms, the humid eyelashes in the sudden gleam of Cheshire's lighter and even the creaky steps of old deaf Mrs. Gimber in her bedroom upstairs.

In an elegant first-class compartment, with one's gloved hand in the velvet side-loop, one feels very much a man of the world as one surveys the capable landscape capably skimming by. And every now and then the passenger's roving eyes paused for a moment as he listened inwardly to a nether itch, which he supposed to be (correctly, thank Log) only a minor irritation of the epithelium.

5

In the early afternoon he descended with his two suitcases into
the sunny peace of the little rural station whence a winding
road led to Ardis Hall, which he was visiting for the first time
in his life. In a miniature of the imagination, he had seen a
saddled horse prepared for him; there was not even a trap.
The station master, a stout sunburnt man in a brown uniform,
was sure they expected him with the evening train which was
slower but had a tea car. He would ring up the Hall in a
moment, he added as he signaled to the anxious engine driver.
Suddenly a hackney coach drove up to the platform and a red-
haired lady, carrying her straw hat and laughing at her own
haste, made for the train and just managed to board it before
it moved. So Van agreed to use the means of transportation
made available to him by a chance crease in the texture of
time, and seated himself in the old calèche. The half-hour
drive proved not unpleasant. He was taken through pine-
woods and over rocky ravines, with birds and other animals
singing in the flowering undergrowth. Sunflecks and lacy
shadows skimmed over his legs and lent a green twinkle to
the brass button deprived of its twin on the back of the coachman's coat. They passed through Torfyanka, a dreamy hamlet
consisting of three or four log izbas, a milkpail repair shop
and a smithy smothered in jasmine. The driver waved to an
invisible friend and the sensitive runabout swerved slightly to
match his gesture. They were now spinning along a dusty
country road between fields. The road dipped and humped
again, and at every ascent the old clockwork taxi would slow
up as if on the brink of sleep and reluctantly overcome its
weakness.

They bounced on the cobblestones of Gamlet, a half-Russian village, and the chauffeur waved again, this time to a boy
in a cherry tree. Birches separated to let them pass across an
old bridge. Ladore, with its ruinous black castle on a crag,
and its gay multicolored roofs further downstream were
glimpsed—to be seen again many times much later in life.

Presently the vegetation assumed a more southern aspect as
the lane skirted Ardis Park. At the next turning, the romantic
mansion appeared on the gentle eminence of old novels. It

was a splendid country house, three stories high, built of pale
brick and purplish stone, whose tints and substance seemed
to interchange their effects in certain lights. Notwithstanding
the variety, amplitude and animation of great trees that had
long replaced the two regular rows of stylized saplings
(thrown in by the mind of the architect rather than observed
by the eye of a painter) Van immediately recognized Ardis
Hall as depicted in the two-hundred-year-old aquarelle that
hung in his father's dressing room: the mansion sat on a rise
overlooking an abstract meadow with two tiny people in
cocked hats conversing not far from a stylized cow.

None of the family was at home when Van arrived. A servant in waiting took his horse. He entered the Gothic archway
of the hall where Bouteillan, the old bald butler who unpro-
fessionally now wore a mustache (dyed a rich gravy brown)
met him with gested delight—he had once been the valet of
Van's father—"*Je parie*," he said, "*que Monsieur ne me recon-
naît pas*," and proceeded to remind Van of what Van had
already recollected unaided, the farmannikin (a special kind of
box kite, untraceable nowadays even in the greatest museums
housing the toys of the past) which Bouteillan had helped him
to fly one day in a meadow dotted with buttercups. Both
looked up: the tiny red rectangle hung for an instant askew
in a blue spring sky. The hall was famous for its painted ceil-
ings. It was too early for tea: Would Van like him or a maid
to unpack? Oh, one of the maids, said Van, wondering briefly
what item in a schoolboy's luggage might be supposed to
shock a housemaid. The picture of naked Ivory Revery (a
model)? Who cared, now that he was a man?

Acting upon the butler's suggestion he went to make a *tour
du jardin*. As he followed a winding path, soundlessly stepping on its soft pink sand in the cloth gumshoes that were
part of the school uniform, he came upon a person whom he
recognized with disgust as being his former French governess
(the place swarmed with ghosts!). She was sitting on a green
bench under the Persian lilacs, a parasol in one hand and in
the other a book from which she was reading aloud to a small
girl who was picking her nose and examining with dreamy
satisfaction her finger before wiping it on the edge of the
bench. Van decided she must be "Ardelia," the eldest of the

two little cousins he was supposed to get acquainted with. Actually it was Lucette, the younger one, a neutral child of eight, with a fringe of shiny reddish-blond hair and a freckled button for nose: she had had pneumonia in spring and was still veiled by an odd air of remoteness that children, especially impish children, retain for some time after brushing through death. Mlle Larivière suddenly looked at Van over her green spectacles—and he had to cope with another warm welcome. In contrast to Albert, she had not changed at all since the days she used to come three times a week to Dark Veen's house in town with a bagful of books and the tiny, tremulous poodlet (now dead) that could not be left behind. It had glistening eyes like sad black olives.

Presently they all strolled back, the governess shaking in reminiscent grief her big-chinned, big-nosed head under the moiré of her parasol, Lucy gratingly dragging a garden hoe she had found, and young Van in his trim gray suit and flowing tie, with his hands behind his back, looking down at his neatly stepping mute feet—trying to place them in line, for no special reason.

A victoria had stopped at the porch. A lady, who resembled Van's mother, and a dark-haired girl of eleven or twelve, preceded by a fluid dackel, were getting out. Ada carried an untidy bunch of wild flowers. She wore a white frock with a black jacket and there was a white bow in her long hair. He never saw that dress again and when he mentioned it in retrospective evocation she invariably retorted that he must have dreamt it, she never had one like that, never could have put on a dark blazer on such a hot day, but he stuck to his initial image of her to the last.

Some ten years ago, not long before or after his fourth birthday, and toward the end of his mother's long stay in a sanatorium, "Aunt" Marina had swooped upon him in a public park where there were pheasants in a big cage. She advised his nurse to mind her own business and took him to a booth near the band shell where she bought him an emerald stick of peppermint candy and told him that if his father wished she would replace his mother and that you could not feed the birds without Lady Amherst's permission, or so he understood.

They now had tea in a prettily furnished corner of the otherwise very austere central hall from which rose the grand staircase. They sat on chairs upholstered in silk around a pretty table. Ada's black jacket and a pink-yellow-blue nosegay she had composed of anemones, celandines and columbines lay on a stool of oak. The dog got more bits of cake than it did ordinarily. Price, the mournful old footman who brought the cream for the strawberries, resembled Van's teacher of history, "Jeejee" Jones.

"He resembles my teacher of history," said Van when the man had gone.

"I used to love history," said Marina, "I loved to identify myself with famous women. There's a ladybird on your plate, Ivan. Especially with famous beauties—Lincoln's second wife or Queen Josephine."

"Yes, I've noticed—it's beautifully done. We've got a similar set at home."

"*Slivok* (some cream)? I hope you speak Russian?" Marina asked Van, as she poured him a cup of tea.

"*Neohotno no sovershenno svobodno* (reluctantly but quite fluently)," replied Van, *slegka ulïbnuvshis'* (with a slight smile). "Yes, lots of cream and three lumps of sugar."

"Ada and I share your extravagant tastes. Dostoevski liked it with raspberry syrup."

"Pah," uttered Ada.

Marina's portrait, a rather good oil by Tresham, hanging above her on the wall, showed her wearing the picture hat she had used for the rehearsal of a Hunting Scene ten years ago, romantically brimmed, with a rainbow wing and a great drooping plume of black-banded silver; and Van, as he recalled the cage in the park and his mother somewhere in a cage of her own, experienced an odd sense of mystery as if the commentators of his destiny had gone into a huddle. Marina's face was now made up to imitate her former looks, but fashions had changed, her cotton dress was a rustic print, her auburn locks were bleached and no longer tumbled down her temples, and nothing in her attire or adornments echoed the dash of her riding crop in the picture and the regular pattern of her brilliant plumage which Tresham had rendered with ornithological skill.

There was not much to remember about that first tea. He
noticed Ada's trick of hiding her fingernails by fisting her hand
or stretching it with the palm turned upward when helping
herself to a biscuit. She was bored and embarrassed by everything her mother said and when the latter started to talk about
the Tarn, otherwise the New Reservoir, he noted that Ada
was no longer sitting next to him but standing a little way off
with her back to the tea table at an open casement with the
slim-waisted dog on a chair peering over splayed front paws
out into the garden too, and she was asking it in a private
whisper what it was it had sniffed.

"You can see the Tarn from the library window," said Marina. "Presently Ada will show you all the rooms in the house.
Ada?" (She pronounced it the Russian way with two deep,
dark "*a*"s, making it sound rather like "ardor.")

"You can catch a glint of it from here too," said Ada, turning her head and, *pollice verso*, introducing the view to Van
who put his cup down, wiped his mouth with a tiny embroidered napkin, and stuffing it into his trouser pocket, went up
to the dark-haired, pale-armed girl. As he bent toward her (he
was three inches taller and the double of that when she married a Greek Catholic, and his shadow held the bridal crown
over her from behind), she moved her head to make him
move his to the required angle and her hair touched his neck.
In his first dreams of her this re-enacted contact, so light, so
brief, invariably proved to be beyond the dreamer's endurance
and like a lifted sword signaled fire and violent release.

"Finish your tea, my precious," called Marina.

Presently, as Marina had promised, the two children went
upstairs. "Why do stairs creak so desperately, when two children go upstairs," she thought, looking up at the balustrade
along which two left hands progressed with strikingly similar
flips and glides like siblings taking their first dancing lesson.
"After all, we were twin sisters; everybody knows that." The
same slow heave, she in front, he behind, took them over the
last two steps, and the staircase was silent again. "Old-fashioned qualms," said Marina.

6

Ada showed her shy guest the great library on the second floor, the pride of Ardis and her favorite "browse," which her mother never entered (having her own set of a Thousand-and-One Best Plays in her boudoir), and which Red Veen, a sentimentalist and a poltroon, shunned, not caring to run into the ghost of his father who had died there of a stroke, and also because he found nothing so depressing as the collected works of unrecollected authors, although he did not mind an occasional visitor's admiring the place's tall bookcases and short cabinets, its dark pictures and pale busts, its ten chairs of carved walnut, and two noble tables inlaid with ebony. In a slant of scholarly sunlight a botanical atlas upon a reading desk lay open on a colored plate of orchids. A kind of divan or daybed covered in black velvet, with two yellow cushions, was placed in a recess, below a plate-glass window which offered a generous view of the banal park and the man-made lake. A pair of candlesticks, mere phantoms of metal and tallow, stood, or seemed to stand, on the broad window ledge.

A corridor leading off the library would have taken our silent explorers to Mr. and Mrs. Veen's apartments in the west wing, had they pursued their investigations in that direction. Instead, a semi-secret little staircase spiraled them from behind a rotatory bookcase to the upper floor, she, pale-thighed, above him, taking longer strides than he, three steep steps behind.

The bedchambers and adjacent accommodations were more than modest, and Van could not help regretting he was too young, apparently, to be assigned one of the two guest rooms next to the library. He recalled nostalgically the luxuries of home as he considered the revolting objects that would close upon him in the solitude of summer nights. Everything struck him as being intended for a cringing cretin, the dismal poorhouse bed with a medieval headboard of dingy wood, the self-creaking wardrobe, the squat commode of imitation mahogany with chain-linked knobs (one missing), the blanket chest (a sheepish escape from the linen room), and the old bureau whose domed front flap was locked or stuck: he found the knob in one of its useless pigeonholes and handed it to

Ada who threw it out of the window. Van had never encountered a towel horse before, never seen a washstand made specially for the bathless. A round looking-glass above it was ornamented with gilt gesso grapes; a satanic snake encircled the porcelain basin (twin of the one in the girls' washroom across the passage). An elbow chair with a high back and a bedside stool supporting a brass candlestick with a greasepan and handle (whose double he had seemed to have seen mirrored a moment ago—where?) completed the worst and main part of the humble equipment.

They went back to the corridor, she tossing her hair, he clearing his throat. Further down, a door of some playroom or nursery stood ajar and stirred to and fro as little Lucette peeped out, one russet knee showing. Then the doorleaf flew open—but she darted inside and away. Cobalt sailing boats adorned the white tiles of a stove, and as her sister and he passed by that open door a toy barrel organ invitingly went into action with a stumbling little minuet. Ada and Van returned to the ground floor—this time all the way down the sumptuous staircase. Of the many ancestors along the wall, she pointed out her favorite, old Prince Vseslav Zemski (1699–1797), friend of Linnaeus and author of *Flora Ladorica*, who was portrayed in rich oil holding his barely pubescent bride and her blond doll in his satin lap. An enlarged photograph, soberly framed, hung (rather incongruously, Van thought) next to the rosebud-lover in his embroidered coat. The late Sumerechnikov, American precursor of the Lumière brothers, had taken Ada's maternal uncle in profile with upcheeked violin, a doomed youth, after his farewell concert.

On the first floor, a yellow drawing room hung with damask and furnished in what the French once called the Empire style opened into the garden and now, in the late afternoon, was invaded across the threshold by the large leaf shadows of a paulownia tree (named, by an indifferent linguist, explained Ada, after the patronymic, mistaken for a second name or surname of a harmless lady, Anna Pavlovna Romanov, daughter of Pavel, nicknamed Paul-minus-Peter, why she did not know, a cousin of the non-linguist's master, the botanical Zemski, I'm going to scream, thought Van). A china cabinet encaged a whole zoo of small animals among which the oryx and the okapi, complete with scientific names, were especially recommended to him by his charming but impossibly pretentious companion. Equally fascinating was a five-fold screen with bright paintings on its black panels reproducing the first maps of four and a half continents. We now pass into the music room with its little-used piano, and a corner room called the Gun Room containing a stuffed Shetland pony which an aunt of Dan Veen's, maiden name forgotten, thank Log, once rode. On the other, or some other, side of the house was the ballroom, a glossy wasteland with wallflower chairs. "Reader, ride by" ("*mimo, chitatel'*," as Turgenev wrote). The "mews," as they were improperly called in Ladore County, were architecturally rather confusing in the case of Ardis Hall. A latticed gallery looked across its garlanded shoulder into the garden and turned sharply toward the drive. Elsewhere, an elegant loggia, lit by long windows, led now tonguetied Ada and intolerably bored Van into a bower of rocks: a sham grotto, with ferns clinging to it shamelessly, and an artificial cascade borrowed from some brook or book, or Van's burning bladder (after all that confounded tea).

The servants' quarters (except those of two painted and powdered maids who had rooms upstairs) were on the courtyard side of the ground floor and Ada said she had visited them once in the explorative stage of her childhood but all she remembered was a canary and an ancient machine for grinding coffee beans which settled the matter.

They zoomed upstairs again. Van popped into a water-closet—and emerged in much better humor. A dwarf Haydn again played a few bars as they walked on.

The attic. This is the attic. Welcome to the attic. It stored a great number of trunks and cartons, and two brown couches one on top of the other like copulating beetles, and lots of pictures standing in corners or on shelves with their faces against the wall like humiliated children. Rolled up in its case was an old "jikker" or skimmer, a blue magic rug with Arabian designs, faded but still enchanting, which Uncle Daniel's father had used in his boyhood and later flown when drunk. Because of the many collisions, collapses and other accidents, especially numerous in sunset skies over idyllic fields, jikkers were banned by the air patrol; but four years later Van who loved that sport bribed a local mechanic to clean the thing, reload its hawking-tubes, and generally bring it back into magic order and many a summer day would they spend, his Ada and he, hanging over grove and river or gliding at a safe ten-foot altitude above surfaces of roads or roofs. How comic the wobbling, ditch-diving cyclist, how weird the arm-flailing and slipping chimney sweep!

Vaguely impelled by the feeling that as long as they were inspecting the house they were, at least, doing *something*—keeping up a semblance of consecutive action which, despite the brilliant conversational gifts both possessed, would degenerate into a desperate vacuum of self-conscious loafing with no other resource than affected wit followed by silence, Ada did not spare him the basement where a big-bellied robot throbbed, manfully heating the pipes that meandered to the huge kitchen and to the two drab bathrooms, and did their poor best to keep the castle habitable on festive visits in winter.

"You have not seen anything yet!" cried Ada. "There is still the roof!"

"But that is going to be our last climb today," said Van to himself firmly.

Owing to a mixture of overlapping styles and tiles (not easily explainable in non-technical terms to non-roof-lovers), as well as to a haphazard continuum, so to speak, of renovations, the roof of Ardis Manor presented an indescribable confusion of angles and levels, of tin-green and fin-gray surfaces, of scenic ridges and wind-proof nooks. You could clip and kiss, and survey in between, the reservoir, the groves, the meadows, even the inkline of larches that marked the boundary of the nearest estate miles away, and the ugly little shapes of more or less legless cows on a distant hillside. And one could easily hide behind some projection from inquisitive skimmers or picture-taking balloons.

A gong bronzily boomed on a terrace.

For some odd reason both children were relieved to learn that a stranger was expected to dinner. He was an Andalusian architect whom Uncle Dan wanted to plan an "artistic" swimming pool for Ardis Manor. Uncle Dan had intended to come, too, with an interpreter, but had caught the Russian "hrip"

(Spanish flu) instead, and had phoned Marina asking her to be very nice to good old Alonso.

"You must help me!" Marina told the children with a worried frown.

"I could show him a copy, perhaps," said Ada, turning to Van, "of an absolutely fantastically lovely *nature morte* by Juan de Labrador of Extremadura—golden grapes and a strange rose against a black background. Dan sold it to Demon, and Demon has promised to give it to me on my fifteenth birthday."

"We also have some Zurbarán fruit," said Van smugly. "Tangerines, I believe, and a fig of sorts, with a wasp upon it. Oh, we'll dazzle the old boy with shop talk!"

They did not. Alonso, a tiny wizened man in a double-breasted tuxedo, spoke only Spanish, while the sum of Spanish words his hosts knew scarcely exceeded half a dozen. Van had *canastilla* (a little basket), and *nubarrones* (thunderclouds), which both came from an *en regard* translation of a lovely Spanish poem in one of his schoolbooks. Ada remembered, of course, *mariposa*, butterfly, and the names of two or three birds (listed in ornithological guides) such as *paloma*, pigeon, or *grévol*, hazel hen. Marina knew *aroma* and *hombre*, and an anatomical term with a "j" hanging in the middle. In consequence, the table-talk consisted of long lumpy Spanish phrases pronounced very loud by the voluble architect who thought he was dealing with very deaf people, and of a smatter of French, intentionally but vainly italianized by his victims. Once the difficult dinner was over, Alonso investigated by the light of three torches held by two footmen a possible site for an expensive pool, put the plan of the grounds back into his brief-case, and after kissing by mistake Ada's hand in the dark, hastened away to catch the last southbound train.

7

Van had gone to bed, sandpaper-eyed, soon after "evening tea," a practically tea-less summertime meal which came a

couple of hours after dinner and the occurrence of which
seemed to Marina as natural and inevitable as that of a sunset
before night. This routine Russian feast consisted in the Ardis
household of *prostokvasha* (translated by English governesses
as curds-and-whey, and by Mlle Larivière as *lait caillé*, "cur-
dled milk"), whose thin, cream-smooth upper layer little Miss
Ada delicately but avidly (Ada, those adverbs qualified many
actions of yours!) skimmed off with her special V monogrammed silver spoon and licked up, before attacking the
more amorphous junkety depths of the stuff; with this came
coarse black peasant bread; dusky *klubnika* (*Fragaria elatior*),
and huge, bright-red garden strawberries (a cross between two
other *Fragaria* species). Van had hardly laid his cheek on his
cool flat pillow when he was violently aroused by a clamorous
caroling—bright warbles, sweet whistles, chirps, trills, twitters,
rasping caws and tender chew-chews—which he assumed, not
without a non-Audubon's apprehension, Ada could, and
would, break up into the right voices of the right birds. He
slipped into loafers, collected soap, comb and towel, and, containing his nudity in a terry-cloth robe, left his bedroom with
the intention of going for a dip in the brook he had observed
on the eve. The corridor clock tocked amid an auroral silence
broken indoors only by the snore coming from the governess'
room. After a moment of hesitation he visited the nursery
water closet. There, the mad aviary and rich sun got at him
through a narrow casement. He was quite well, quite well! As
he descended the grand staircase, General Durmanov's father
acknowledged Van with grave eyes and passed him on to old
Prince Zemski and other ancestors, all as discreetly attentive
as those museum guards who watch the only tourist in a dim
old palace.

The front door proved to be bolted and chained. He tried
the glassed and grilled side door of a blue-garlanded gallery;
it, too, did not yield. Being still unaware that under the stairs
an inconspicuous recess concealed an assortment of spare keys
(some very old and anonymous, hanging from brass hooks)
and communicated through a toolroom with a secluded part
of the garden, Van wandered through several reception rooms
in search of an obliging window. In a corner room he found,

standing at a tall window, a young chambermaid whom he had glimpsed (and promised himself to investigate) on the preceding evening. She wore what his father termed with a semi-assumed leer "soubret black and frissonet frill"; a tortoiseshell comb in her chestnut hair caught the amber light; the French window was open, and she was holding one hand, starred with a tiny aquamarine, rather high on the jamb as she looked at a sparrow that was hopping up the paved path toward the bit of baby-toed biscuit she had thrown to him. Her cameo profile, her cute pink nostril, her long, French, lily-white neck, the outline, both full and frail, of her figure (male lust does not go very far for descriptive felicities!), and especially the savage sense of opportune license moved Van so robustly that he could not resist clasping the wrist of her raised tight-sleeved arm. Freeing it, and confirming by the coolness of her demeanor that she had sensed his approach, the girl turned her attractive, though almost eyebrowless, face toward him and asked him if he would like a cup of tea before breakfast. No. What was her name? Blanche—but Mlle Larivière called her "Cendrillon" because her stockings got so easily laddered, see, and because she broke and mislaid things, and confused flowers. His loose attire revealed his desire; this could not escape a girl's notice, even if color-blind, and as he drew up still closer, while looking over her head for a suitable couch to take shape in some part of this magical manor—where *any* place, as in Casanova's remembrances could be dream-changed into a sequestered seraglio nook—she wiggled out of his reach completely and delivered a little soliloquy in her soft Ladoran French:

"*Monsieur a quinze ans, je crois, et moi, je sais, j'en ai dix-neuf. Monsieur* is a nobleman; I am a poor peat-digger's daughter. *Monsieur a tâté, sans doute, des filles de la ville; quant à moi, je suis vierge, ou peu s'en faut. De plus,* were I to fall in love with you—I mean really in love—and I might, alas, if you possessed me *rien qu'une petite fois*—it would be, for me, only grief, and infernal fire, and despair, and even death, *Monsieur. Finalement,* I might add that I have the whites and must see *le Docteur Chronique,* I mean Crolique, on my next day off. Now we have to separate, the sparrow has disappeared, I see, and Monsieur Bouteillan has entered the next room, and can perceive us clearly in that mirror above the sofa behind that silk screen."

"Forgive me, girl," murmured Van, whom her strange, tragic tone had singularly put off, as if he were taking part in a play in which he was the principal actor, but of which he could only recall that one scene.

The butler's hand in the mirror took down a decanter from nowhere and was withdrawn. Van, reknotting the cord of his robe, passed through the French window into the green reality of the garden.

8

On the same morning, or a couple of days later, on the terrace:

"*Mais va donc jouer avec lui*," said Mlle Larivière, pushing Ada, whose young hips disjointedly jerked from the shock. "Don't let your cousin *se morfondre* when the weather is so fine. Take him by the hand. Go and show him the white lady in your favorite lane, and the mountain, and the great oak."

Ada turned to him with a shrug. The touch of her cold fingers and damp palm and the self-conscious way she tossed back her hair as they walked down the main avenue of the park made him self-conscious too, and under the pretext of picking up a fir cone he disengaged his hand. He threw the cone at a woman of marble bending over a stamnos but only managed to frighten a bird that had perched on the brim of her broken jar.

"There is nothing more banal in the world," said Ada, "than pitching stones at a hawfinch."

"Sorry," said Van, "I did not intend to scare that bird. But then, I'm not a country lad, who knows a cone from a stone. What games, *au fond*, does she expect us to play?"

"*Je l'ignore*," replied Ada. "I really don't care very much how her poor mind works. *Cache-cache*, I suppose, or climbing trees."

"Oh, I'm good at that," said Van, "in fact, I can even brachiate."

"No," she said, "we are going to play *my* games. Games I have invented all by myself. Games Lucette, I hope, will be able to play next year with me, the poor pet. Come, let us start. The present series belongs to the shadow-and-shine group, two of which I'm going to show you."

"I see," said Van.

"You will in a moment," rejoined the pretty prig. "First of all we must find a nice stick."

"Look," said Van, still smarting a bit, "there goes another haw-haw finch."

By then they had reached the *rond-point*—a small arena encircled by flowerbeds and jasmine bushes in heavy bloom. Overhead the arms of a linden stretched toward those of an oak, like a green-spangled beauty flying to meet her strong father hanging by his feet from the trapeze. Even then did we both understand that kind of heavenly stuff, even then.

"Something rather acrobatic about those branches up there, no?" he said, pointing.

"Yes," she answered. "I discovered it long ago. The teil is the flying Italian lady, and the old oak aches, the old lover aches, but still catches her every time" (impossible to reproduce the right intonation while rendering the entire sense— after eight decades!—but she did say something extravagant, something quite out of keeping with her tender age as they looked up and then down).

Looking down and gesturing with a sharp green stake borrowed from the peonies, Ada explained the first game.

The shadows of leaves on the sand were variously interrupted by roundlets of live light. The player chose his roundlet—the best, the brightest he could find—and firmly outlined it with the point of his stick; whereupon the yellow round light would appear to grow convex like the brimming surface of some golden dye. Then the player delicately scooped out the earth with his stick or fingers within the roundlet. The level of that gleaming *infusion de tilleul* would magically sink in its goblet of earth and finally dwindle to one precious drop. That player won who made the most goblets in, say, twenty minutes.

Van asked suspiciously if that was all.

No, it was not. As she dug a firm little circle around a particularly fine goldgout, Ada squatted and moved, squatting,
with her black hair falling over her ivory-smooth moving
knees while her haunches and hands worked, one hand holding the stick, the other brushing back bothersome strands of
hair. A gentle breeze suddenly eclipsed her fleck. When that
occurred, the player lost one point, even if the leaf or the
cloud hastened to move aside.

All right. What was the other game?

The other game (in a singsong voice) might seem a little
more complicated. To play it properly one had to wait for
P.M. to provide longer shadows. The player—

"Stop saying 'the player.' It is either you or me."

"Say, you. You outline my shadow behind me on the sand.
I move. You outline it again. Then you mark out the next
boundary (handing him the stick). If I now move back—"

"You know," said Van, throwing the stick away, "personally I think these are the most boring and stupid games anybody has ever invented, anywhere, any time, A.M. or P.M."

She said nothing but her nostrils narrowed. She retrieved
the stick and stuck it back, furiously, where it belonged, deep
into the loam next to a grateful flower to which she looped
it with a silent nod. She walked back to the house. He wondered if her walk would be more graceful when she grew up.

"I'm a rude brutal boy, please forgive me," he said.

She inclined her head without looking back. In token of
partial reconciliation, she showed him two sturdy hooks
passed into iron rings on two tulip-tree trunks between which,
before she was born, another boy, also Ivan, her mother's
brother, used to sling a hammock in which he slept in midsummer when the nights became really sultry—this was the
latitude of Sicily, after all.

"A splendid idea," said Van. "By the way, do fireflies burn
one if they fly into you? I'm just asking. Just a city boy's silly
question."

She showed him next where the hammock—a whole set of
hammocks, a canvas sack full of strong, soft nets—was stored:
this was in the corner of a basement toolroom behind the
lilacs, the key was concealed in this hole here which last year

was stuffed by the nest of a bird—no need to identify it. A pointer of sunlight daubed with greener paint a long green box where croquet implements were kept; but the balls had been rolled down the hill by some rowdy children, the little Erminins, who were now Van's age and had grown very nice and quiet.

"As we all are at that age," said Van and stooped to pick up a curved tortoiseshell comb—the kind that girls use to hold up their hair behind; he had seen one, exactly like that, quite recently, but when, in whose hairdo?

"One of the maids," said Ada. "That tattered chapbook must also belong to her, *Les Amours du Docteur Mertvago*, a mystical romance by a pastor."

"Playing croquet with you," said Van, "should be rather like using flamingoes and hedgehogs."

"Our reading lists do not match," replied Ada. "That *Palace in Wonderland* was to me the kind of book everybody so often promised me I would adore, that I developed an insurmountable prejudice toward it. Have you read any of Mlle Larivière's stories? Well, you will. She thinks that in some former Hindooish state she was a boulevardier in Paris; and writes accordingly. We can *squirm* from here into the front hall by a secret passage, but I think we are supposed to go and look at the *grand chêne* which is really an elm." Did he like elms? Did he know Joyce's poem about the two washerwomen? He did, indeed. Did he like it? He did. In fact he was beginning to like very much arbors and ardors and Adas. They rhymed. Should he mention it?

"And now," she said, and stopped, staring at him.

"Yes?" he said, "and now?"

"Well, perhaps, I ought not to try to divert you—after you trampled upon those circles of mine; but I'm going to relent and show you the real marvel of Ardis Manor; my larvarium, it's in the room next to mine" (which he never saw, never—how odd, come to think of it!).

She carefully closed a communicating door as they entered into what looked like a glorified rabbitry at the end of a marble-flagged hall (a converted bathroom, as it transpired). In spite of the place's being well aired, with the heraldic stained-glass windows standing wide open (so that one heard the

screeching and catcalls of an undernourished and horribly
frustrated bird population), the smell of the hutches—damp
earth, rich roots, old greenhouse and maybe a hint of goat—
was pretty appalling. Before letting him come nearer, Ada fid-
dled with little latches and grates, and a sense of great
emptiness and depression replaced the sweet fire that had been
consuming Van since the beginning of their innocent games
on that day.

"*Je raffole de tout ce qui rampe* (I'm crazy about everything
that crawls)," she said.

"Personally," said Van, "I rather like those that roll up in
a muff when you touch them—those that go to sleep like old
dogs."

"Oh, they don't go to *sleep*, *quelle idée*, they *swoon*, it's a
little syncope," explained Ada, frowning. "And I imagine it
may be quite a little shock for the younger ones."

"Yes, I can well imagine that, too. But I suppose one gets
used to it, by-and-by, I mean."

But his ill-informed hesitations soon gave way to esthetic
empathy. Many decades later Van remembered having much
admired the lovely, naked, shiny, gaudily spotted and streaked
sharkmoth caterpillars, as poisonous as the mullein flowers
clustering around them, and the flat larva of a local catocalid
whose gray knobs and lilac plaques mimicked the knots and
lichens of the twig to which it clung so closely as to practically
lock with it, and, of course, the little Vaporer fellow, its black
coat enlivened all along the back with painted tufts, red, blue,
yellow, of unequal length, like those of a fancy toothbrush
treated with certified colors. And that kind of simile, with
those special trimmings, reminds me today of the entomological entries in Ada's diary—which we must have somewhere,
mustn't we, darling, in that drawer there, no? you don't think
so? Yes! Hurrah! Samples (your round-cheeked script, my
love, was a little larger, but otherwise nothing, nothing, nothing has changed):

"The retractile head and diabolical anal appendages of the
garish monster that produces the modest Puss Moth belong
to a most uncaterpillarish caterpillar, with front segments
shaped like bellows and a face resembling the lens of a folding

camera. If you gently stroke its bloated smooth body, the sensation is quite silky and pleasant—until the irritated creature ungratefully squirts at you an acrid fluid from a slit in its throat."

"Dr. Krolik received from Andalusia and kindly gave me five young larvae of the newly described very local Carmen Tortoiseshell. They are delightful creatures, of a beautiful jade nuance with silvery spikes, and they breed only on a semi-extinct species of high-mountain willow (which dear Crawly also obtained for me)."

(At ten or earlier the child had read—as Van had—*Les Malheurs de Swann*, as the next sample reveals):

"I think Marina would stop scolding me for my hobby ('There's something indecent about a little girl's keeping such revolting pets . . . ,' 'Normal young ladies should loathe snakes and worms,' et cetera) if I could persuade her to overcome her old-fashioned squeamishness and place simultaneously on palm and pulse (the hand alone would not be roomy enough!) the noble larva of the Cattleya Hawkmoth (mauve shades of Monsieur Proust), a seven-inch-long colossus, flesh colored, with turquoise arabesques, rearing its hyacinth head in a stiff 'Sphinxian' attitude."

(Lovely stuff! said Van, but *even* I did not quite assimilate it, when I was young. So let us not bore the boor who flips through a book and thinks: "what a hoaxer, that old V.V.!")

At the end of his so remote, so near, 1884 summer Van, before leaving Ardis, was to make a visit of adieu to Ada's larvarium.

The porcelain-white, eye-spotted Cowl (or "Shark") larva, a highly prized gem, had safely achieved its next metamorphosis, but Ada's unique Lorelei Underwing had died, paralyzed by some ichneumon that had not been deceived by those clever prominences and fungoid smudges. The multicolored toothbrush had comfortably pupated within a shaggy cocoon, promising a Persian Vaporer later in the autumn. The two Puss Moth larvae had assumed a still uglier but at least more vermian and in a sense venerable aspect: their pitchforks

now limply trailing behind them, and a purplish flush dulling
the cubistry of their extravagant colors, they kept "ramping"
rapidly all over the floor of their cage in a surge of prepupa-
tional locomotion. Aqua had walked through a wood and into
a gulch to do it last year. A freshly emerged *Nymphalis carmen*
was fanning its lemon and amber-brown wings on a sunlit
patch of grating, only to be choked with one nip by the nimble fingers of enraptured and heartless Ada; the Odettian
Sphinx had turned, bless him, into an elephantoid mummy
with a comically encased trunk of the guermantoid type; and
Dr. Krolik was swiftly running on short legs after a very special
orange-tip above timberline, in another hemisphere, *Antocharis ada* Krolik (1884)—as it was known until changed to
A. prittwitzi Stümper (1883) by the inexorable law of taxonomic priority.

"But, afterwards, when all these beasties have hatched,"
asked Van, "what do you do with them?"

"Oh," she said, "I take them to Dr. Krolik's assistant who
sets them and labels them and pins them in glassed trays in a
clean oak cabinet, which will be mine when I marry. I shall
then have a big collection, and continue to breed all kinds of
leps—my dream is to have a special Institute of Fritillary larvae
and violets—all the special violets they breed on. I would have
eggs or larvae rushed to me here by plane from all over North
America, with their foodplants—Redwood Violets from the
West Coast, and a Pale Violet from Montana, and the Prairie
Violet, and Egglestone's Violet from Kentucky, and a rare
white violet from a secret marsh near an unnamed lake on an
arctic mountain where Krolik's Lesser Fritillary flies. Of
course, when the things emerge, they are quite easy to mate
by hand—you hold them—for quite a while, sometimes—like
this, in folded-wing profile" (showing the method, ignoring
her poor fingernails), "male in your left hand, female in your
right, or vice versa, with the tips of their abdomens touching,
but they must be quite fresh and *soaked* in their favorite violet's reek."

9

Was she really pretty, at twelve? Did he want—would he ever want to caress her, to really caress her? Her black hair cascaded over one clavicle and the gesture she made of shaking it back and the dimple on her pale cheek were revelations with an element of immediate recognition about them. Her pallor shone, her blackness blazed. The pleated skirts she liked were becomingly short. Even her bare limbs were so free from suntan that one's gaze, stroking her white shins and forearms, could follow upon them the regular slants of fine dark hairs, the silks of her girlhood. The iridal dark-brown of her serious eyes had the enigmatic opacity of an Oriental hypnotist's look (in a magazine's back-page advertisement) and seemed to be placed higher than usual so that between its lower rim and the moist lower lid a cradle crescent of white remained when she stared straight at you. Her long eyelashes seemed blackened, and in fact were. Her features were saved from elfin prettiness by the thickish shape of her parched lips. Her plain Irish nose was Van's in miniature. Her teeth were fairly white, but not very even.

Her poor pretty hands—one could not help cooing with pity over them—rosy in comparison to the translucent skin of the arm, rosier even than the elbow that seemed to be blushing for the state of her nails: she bit them so thoroughly that all vestige of free margin was replaced by a groove cutting into the flesh with the tightness of wire and lending an additional spatule of length to her naked fingertips. Later, when he was so fond of kissing her cold hands she would clench them, allowing his lips nothing but knuckle, but he would fiercely pry her hand open to get at those flat blind little cushions. (But, oh my, oh, the long, languid, rose-and-silver, painted and pointed, delicately stinging onyxes of her adolescent and adult years!)

What Van experienced in those first strange days when she showed him the house—and those nooks in it where they were to make love so soon—combined elements of ravishment and exasperation. Ravishment—because of her pale, voluptuous, impermissible skin, her hair, her legs, her angular movements, her gazelle-grass odor, the sudden black stare of her

wide-set eyes, the rustic nudity under her dress; exasperation—because between him, an awkward schoolboy of genius,
and that precocious, affected, impenetrable child there extended a void of light and a veil of shade that no force could
overcome and pierce. He swore wretchedly in the hopeless-
ness of his bed as he focused his swollen senses on the glimpse
of her he had engulfed when, on their second excursion to
the top of the house, she had mounted upon a captain's trunk
to unhasp a sort of illuminator through which one acceded to
the roof (even the dog had once gone there), and a bracket
or something wrenched up her skirt and he saw—as one sees
some sickening miracle in a Biblical fable or a moth's shocking
metamorphosis—that the child was darkly flossed. He noticed
that she seemed to have noticed that he had or might have
noticed (what he not only noticed but retained with tender
terror until he freed himself of that vision—much later—and
in strange ways), and an odd, dull, arrogant look passed across
her face: her sunken cheeks and fat pale lips moved as if she
were chewing something, and she emitted a yelp of joyless
laughter when he, big Van, slipped on a tile after wriggling
in his turn through the skylight. And in the sudden sun, he
realized that until then, he, small Van, had been a blind virgin,
since haste, dust and dusk had obscured the mousy charms of
his first harlot, so often possessed.

His sentimental education now went on fast. Next morning,
he happened to catch sight of her washing her face and arms
over an old-fashioned basin on a rococo stand, her hair knotted on the top of her head, her nightgown twisted around
her waist like a clumsy corolla out of which issued her slim
back, rib-shaded on the near side. A fat snake of porcelain
curled around the basin, and as both the reptile and he
stopped to watch Eve and the soft woggle of her bud-breasts
in profile, a big mulberry-colored cake of soap slithered out
of her hand, and her black-socked foot hooked the door shut
with a bang which was more the echo of the soap's crashing
against the marble board than a sign of pudic displeasure.

IO

Weekday lunch at Ardis Hall. Lucette between Marina and
the governess; Van between Marina and Ada; Dack, the
golden-brown stoat, under the table, either between Ada and
Mlle Larivière, or between Lucette and Marina (Van secretly
disliked dogs, especially at meals, and especially that smallish
longish freak with a gamey breath). Arch and grandiloquent,
Ada would be describing a dream, a natural history wonder,
a special belletristic device—Paul Bourget's "*monologue
intérieur*" borrowed from old Leo—or some ludicrous blunder in the current column of Elsie de Nord, a vulgar literary
demimondaine who thought that Lyovin went about Moscow
in a *nagol'nïy tulup*, "a muzhik's sheepskin coat, bare side
out, bloom side in," as defined in a dictionary our commen-
tator produced like a conjurer, never to be procurable by El-
sies. Her spectacular handling of subordinate clauses, her
parenthetic asides, her sensual stressing of adjacent monosyllables ("Idiot Elsie simply *can't read*")—all this somehow
finished by acting upon Van, as artificial excitements and
exotic torture-caresses might have done, in an aphrodisiac
sinistral direction that he both resented and perversely
enjoyed.

"My precious" her mother called her, punctuating Ada's
discourse with little ejaculations: "Terribly funny!" "Oh, I
adore that!" but also indulging in more admonitory remarks,
such as "Do sit a wee bit straighter" or "*Eat*, my precious"
(accenting the "eat" with a motherly urge very unlike the
malice of her daughter's spondaic sarcasms).

Ada, now sitting straight, incurving her supple spine in her
chair, then, as the dream or adventure (or whatever she was
relating) reached a climax, bending over the place from which
Price had prudently removed her plate, and suddenly all elbows, sprawling forward, invading the table, then leaning
back, extravagantly making mouths, illustrating "long, long"
with both hands up, up!

"My precious, you haven't tried the—oh, Price, bring the—"

The what? The rope for the fakir's bare-bottomed child to
climb up in the melting blue?

"It was sort of long, long. I mean (interrupting herself)

. . . like a tentacle . . . no, let me see" (shake of head, jerk of features, as if unknotting a tangled skein with one quick tug).

No: enormous purple pink plums, one with a wet yellow burst-split.

"And so there I was—" (the tumbling hair, the hand flying to the temple, sketching but not terminating the brushing-off-strand stroke; then a sudden peal of rough-rippled laughter ending in a moist cough).

"No, but seriously, Mother, you must imagine me utterly speechless, *screaming* speechlessly, as I realized—"

At the third or fourth meal Van also realized something. Far from being a bright lass showing off for the benefit of a newcomer, Ada's behavior was a desperate and rather clever attempt to prevent Marina from appropriating the conversation and transforming it into a lecture on the theater. Marina, on the other hand, while awaiting a chance to trot out her troika of hobby horses, took some professional pleasure in playing the hackneyed part of a fond mother, proud of her daughter's charm and humor, and herself charmingly and humorously lenient toward their brash circumstantiality: *she* was showing off—not Ada! And when Van had understood the true situation, he would take advantage of a pause (which Marina was on the point of filling with some choice Stanislavskiana) to launch Ada upon the troubled waters of Botany Bay, a voyage which at other times he dreaded, but which now proved to be the safest and easiest course for his girl. This was particularly important at dinner, since Lucette and her governess had an earlier evening meal upstairs, so that Mlle Larivière was not there, at those critical moments, and could not be relied on to take over from lagging Ada with a breezy account of her work on a new novella of her composition (her famous *Diamond Necklace* was in the last polishing stage) or with memories of Van's early boyhood such as those eminently acceptable ones concerning his beloved Russian tutor, who gently courted Mlle L., wrote "decadent" Russian verse in sprung rhythm, and drank, in Russian solitude.

Van: "That yellow thingum" (pointing at a floweret prettily depicted on an Eckercrown plate) "—is it a buttercup?"

Ada: "No. That yellow flower is the common Marsh Marigold, *Caltha palustris*. In this country, peasants miscall it 'Cowslip,' though of course the true Cowslip, *Primula veris*, is a different plant altogether."

"I see," said Van.

"Yes, indeed," began Marina, "when I was playing Ophelia, the fact that I had once collected flowers—"

"Helped, no doubt," said Ada. "Now the Russian word for marsh marigold is *Kuroslep* (which muzhiks in Tartary misapply, poor slaves, to the buttercup) or else *Kaluzhnitsa*, as used quite properly in Kaluga, U.S.A."

"Ah," said Van.

"As in the case of many flowers," Ada went on, with a mad scholar's quiet smile, "the unfortunate French name of our plant, *souci d'eau*, has been traduced or shall we say transfigured—"

"Flowers into bloomers," punned Van Veen.

"*Je vous en prie, mes enfants!*" put in Marina, who had been following the conversation with difficulty and now, through a secondary misunderstanding, thought the reference was to the undergarment.

"By chance, this very morning," said Ada, not deigning to enlighten her mother, "our learned governess, who was also yours, Van, and who—"

(First time she pronounced it—at that botanical lesson!)

"—is pretty hard on English-speaking transmongrelizers—monkeys called 'ursine howlers'—though I suspect her reasons are more chauvinistic than artistic and moral—drew my attention—my wavering attention—to some really gorgeous bloomers, as you call them, Van, in a Mr. Fowlie's *soi-disant* literal version—called 'sensitive' in a recent Elsian rave—sensitive!—of *Mémoire*, a poem by Rimbaud (which she fortunately—and farsightedly—made me learn by heart, though I suspect she prefers Musset and Coppée)"—

". . . *les robes vertes et déteintes des fillettes* . . ." quoted Van triumphantly.

"Egg-zactly" (mimicking Dan). "Well, Larivière allows me to read him only in the Feuilletin anthology, the same you have apparently, but I shall obtain his *oeuvres complètes* very soon, oh very soon, much sooner than anybody thinks. Incidentally, she will come down after tucking in Lucette, our darling copperhead who by now should be in her green night-gown—''

"*Angel moy*," pleaded Marina, "I'm sure Van cannot be interested in Lucette's nightdress!"

"—the nuance of willows, and counting the little sheep on her *ciel de lit* which Fowlie turns into 'the *sky's bed*' instead of 'bed ceiler.' But, to go back to our poor flower. The forged *louis d'or* in that collection of fouled French is the transformation of *souci d'eau* (our marsh marigold) into the asinine 'care of the water'—although he had at his disposal dozens of synonyms, such as mollyblob, marybud, maybubble, and many other nicknames associated with fertility feasts, whatever those are."

"On the other hand," said Van, "one can well imagine a similarly bilingual Miss Rivers checking a French version of, say, Marvell's *Garden*—"

"Oh," cried Ada, "I can recite 'Le jardin' in my own trans-version—let me see—

> *En vain on s'amuse à gagner*
> *L'Oka, la Baie du Palmier . . ."*

". . . to win the Palm, the Oke, or Bayes!" shouted Van.

"You know, children," interrupted Marina resolutely with calming gestures of both hands, "when I was your age, Ada, and my brother was *your* age, Van, we talked about croquet, and ponies, and puppies, and the last *fête-d'enfants*, and the next picnic, and—oh, millions of nice normal things, but never, never of old French botanists and God knows what!"

"But you just said you collected flowers?" said Ada.

"Oh, just one season, somewhere in Switzerland. I don't remember when. It does not matter now."

The reference was to Ivan Durmanov: he had died of lung cancer years ago in a sanatorium (not far from Ex, somewhere in Switzerland, where Van was born eight years later). Marina often mentioned Ivan who had been a famous violinist at eighteen, but without any special show of emotion, so that Ada now noted with surprise that her mother's heavy make-up had started to thaw under a sudden flood of tears (maybe some allergy to flat dry old flowers, an attack of hay fever, or gentianitis, as a slightly later diagnosis might have shown retrospectively). She blew her nose, with the sound of an elephant, as she said herself—and here Mlle Larivière came down for coffee and recollections of Van as a *bambin angélique* who adored *à neuf ans*—the precious dear!—Gilberte Swann *et la Lesbie de Catulle* (and who had learned, all by himself, to release the adoration as soon as the kerosene lamp had left the mobile bedroom in his black nurse's fist).

II

A few days after Van's arrival Uncle Dan came by the morning train from town for his habitual weekend stay with his family.

Van happened to run into him as Uncle Dan was crossing the hall. The butler very charmingly (thought Van) signaled to his master *who* the tall boy was by setting one hand three feet from the ground and then notching it up higher and higher—an altitudinal code that our young six-footer alone understood. Van saw the little red-haired gentleman glance with perplexity at old Bouteillan, who hastened to whisper Van's name.

Mr. Daniel Veen had a curious manner, when advancing toward a guest, of dipping the fingers of his stiffly held right hand into his coat pocket and holding them there in a kind of purifying operation until the exact moment of the handshake came.

He informed Van that it was going to rain in a few minutes "because it had started to rain at Ladore," and the rain, he said, "took about half-an-hour to reach Ardis." Van thought this was a quip and chuckled politely but Uncle Dan looked perplexed again and, staring at Van with pale fish-eyes, inquired if he had familiarized himself with the environs, how many languages he knew, and would he like to buy for a few kopecks a Red Cross lottery ticket?

"No, thank you," said Van, "I have enough of my own lotteries"—and his uncle stared again, but sort of sideways.

Tea was served in the drawing room, and everybody was rather silent and subdued, and presently Uncle Dan retired to his study, pulling a folded newspaper out of an inner pocket, and no sooner had he left the room than a window flew open all by itself, and a powerful shower started to drum upon the liriodendron and imperialis leaves outside, and the conversation became general and loud.

Not long did the rain last—or rather stay: it continued on its presumable way to Raduga or Ladoga or Kaluga or Luga, shedding an uncompleted rainbow over Ardis Hall.

Uncle Dan in an overstuffed chair was trying to read, with the aid of one of the dwarf dictionaries for undemanding tourists which helped him to decipher foreign art catalogues, an article apparently devoted to oystering in a Dutch-language illustrated paper somebody on the train had abandoned opposite him—when an abominable tumult started to spread from room to room through the whole house.

The sportive dackel, one ear flapping, the other upturned and showing its gray-mottled pink, rapidly moving his comical legs, and skidding on the parquetry as he executed abrupt turns, was in the act of carrying away, to a suitable hiding place where to worry it, a sizable wad of blood-soaked cottonwool, snatched somewhere upstairs. Ada, Marina and two maids were pursuing the merry animal but he was impossible to corner among all the baroque furniture as he tore through innumerable doorways. Suddenly the whole chase veered past Uncle Dan's armchair and shot out again.

"Good Lord!" he exclaimed, on catching sight of the gory trophy, "somebody must have chopped off a thumb!" Patting his thighs and his chair, he sought and retrieved—from under the footstool—the vestpocket wordbook and went back to his paper, but a second later had to look up "*groote*," which he had been groping for when disturbed.

The simplicity of its meaning annoyed him.

Through an open french door Dack led his pursuers into the garden. There, on the third lawn, Ada overtook him with the flying plunge used in "American football," a kind of Rugby game cadets played at one time on the wet turfy banks of the Goodson River. Simultaneously, Mlle Larivière rose from the bench where she had been paring Lucette's fingernails, and pointing her scissors at Blanche who had rushed up with a paper bag, she accused the young slattern of a glaring precedent—namely of having once dropped a hairpin in Lucette's cot, *un machin long comme ça qui faillit blesser l'enfant à la fesse*. Marina, however, who had a Russian noblewoman's morbid fear of "offending an inferior," declared the incident closed.

"*Nehoroshaya, nehoroshaya sobaka*," crooned Ada with great aspiratory and sibilatory emphasis as she gathered into her arms the now lootless, but completely unabashed, "bad dog."

12

Hammock and honey: eighty years later he could still recall with the young pang of the original joy his falling in love with Ada. Memory met imagination halfway in the hammock of his boyhood's dawns. At ninety-four he liked retracing that first amorous summer not as a dream he had just had but as a recapitulation of consciousness to sustain him in the small gray hours between shallow sleep and the first pill of the day. Take over, dear, for a little while. Pill, pillow, billow, billions. Go on from here, Ada, please!

(She). Billions of boys. Take one fairly decent decade. A billion of Bills, good, gifted, tender and passionate, not only spiritually but physically well-meaning Billions, have bared the jillions of their no less tender and brilliant Jills during that decade, at stations and under conditions that have to be controlled and specified by the worker, lest the entire report be choked up by the weeds of statistics and waist-high generalizations. No point would there be, if we left out, for example, the little matter of prodigious individual awareness and young genius, which makes, in some cases, of this or that particular gasp an *unprecedented and unrepeatable event* in the continuum of life or at least a thematic anthemia of such events in a work of art, or a denouncer's article. The details that shine through or shade through: the local leaf through the hyaline skin, the green sun in the brown humid eye, *tout ceci, vsyo eto*, in tit and toto, must be taken into account, now prepare to take over (no, Ada, go on, *ya zaslushalsya*: I'm all enchant-

ment and ears), if we wish to convey the fact, the fact, the
fact—that among those billions of brilliant couples in one
cross section of what you will allow me to call spacetime (for
the convenience of reasoning), one couple is a unique super-
imperial couple, *sverhimperatorskaya cheta*, in consequence of
which (to be inquired into, to be painted, to be denounced,
to be put to music, or to the question and death, if the decade
has a scorpion tail after all), the particularities of their love-
making influence in a special unique way two long lives and
a few readers, those pensive reeds, and their pens and mental
paintbrushes. Natural history indeed! Unnatural history—because that precision of senses and sense must seem unpleasantly peculiar to peasants, and because the detail is all: The
song of a Tuscan Firecrest or a Sitka Kinglet in a cemetery
cypress; a minty whiff of Summer Savory or Yerba Buena on
a coastal slope; the dancing flitter of a Holly Blue or an Echo
Azure—combined with other birds, flowers and butterflies:
that has to be heard, smelled and seen through the transparency of death and ardent beauty. And the most difficult:
beauty itself as perceived through the there and then. The
males of the firefly (now it's really your turn, Van).

The males of the firefly, a small luminous beetle, more like
a wandering star than a winged insect, appeared on the first
warm black nights of Ardis, one by one, here and there, then
in a ghostly multitude, dwindling again to a few individuals
as their quest came to its natural end. Van watched them with
the same pleasurable awe he had experienced as a child, when,
lost in the purple crepuscule of an Italian hotel garden, in an
alley of cypresses, he supposed they were golden ghouls or the
passing fancies of the garden. Now as they softly flew, apparently straight, crossing and recrossing the darkness around
him, each flashed his pale-lemon light every five seconds or
so, signaling in his own specific rhythm (quite different from
that of an allied species, flying with *Photinus ladorensis*, according to Ada, at Lugano and Luga) to his grass-domiciled
female pulsating in photic response after taking a couple of
moments to verify the exact type of light code he used. The
presence of those magnificent little animals delicately illuminating, as they passed, the fragrant night, filled Van with a
subtle exhilaration that Ada's entomology seldom evoked in

him—maybe in result of the abstract scholar's envy which a naturalist's immediate knowledge sometimes provokes. The hammock, a comfortable oblong nest, reticulated his naked body either under the weeping cedar that sprawled over one corner of a lawn, and granted a partial shelter in case of a shower, or, on safer nights, between two tulip trees (where a former summer guest, with an opera cloak over his clammy nightshirt, had awoken once because a stinkbomb had burst among the instruments in the horsecart, and striking a match, Uncle Van had seen the bright blood blotching his pillow).

The windows in the black castle went out in rows, files, and knight moves. The longest occupant of the nursery water closet was Mlle Larivière, who came there with a rose-oil lampad and her *buvard*. A breeze ruffled the hangings of his now infinite chamber. Venus rose in the sky; Venus set in his flesh.

All that was a little before the seasonal invasion of a certain interestingly primitive mosquito (whose virulence the not-too-kind Russian contingent of our region attributed to the diet of the French winegrowers and bogberry-eaters of Ladore); but even so the fascinating fireflies, and the still more eerie pale cosmos coming through the dark foliage, balanced with new discomforts the nocturnal ordeal, the harassments of sweat and sperm associated with his stuffy room. Night, of course, *always* remained an ordeal, throughout the near-century of his life, no matter how drowsy or drugged the poor man might be—for genius is not all gingerbread even for Billionaire Bill with his pointed beardlet and stylized bald dome, or crusty Proust who liked to decapitate rats when he did not feel like sleeping, or *this* brilliant or obscure V.V. (depending on the eyesight of readers, also poor people despite our jibes and their jobs); but at Ardis, the intense life of the star-haunted sky troubled the boy's night so much that, on the whole, he felt grateful when foul weather or the fouler gnat—the *Kamargsky Komar* of our *muzhiks* and the *Moustique moscovite* of their no less alliterative retaliators—drove him back to his bumpy bed.

In this our dry report on Van Veen's early, too early love, for Ada Veen, there is neither reason, nor room for metaphysical digression. Yet, let it be observed (just while the lucifers fly and throb, and an owl hoots—also most

rhythmically—in the nearby park) that Van, who at the time
had still not really tasted the Terror of Terra—vaguely attrib-
uting it, when analyzing his dear unforgettable Aqua's torments, to pernicious fads and popular fantasies—even then, at
fourteen, recognized that the old myths, which willed into
helpful being a whirl of worlds (no matter how silly and mystical) and situated them within the gray matter of the star-
suffused heavens, contained, perhaps, a glowworm of strange
truth. His nights in the hammock (where that other poor
youth had cursed his blood cough and sunk back into dreams
of prowling black spumas and a crash of symbols in an orchal
orchestra—as suggested to him by career physicians) were
now haunted not so much by the agony of his desire for Ada,
as by that meaningless space overhead, underhead, everywhere, the demon counterpart of divine time, tingling about
him and through him, as it was to retingle—with a little more
meaning fortunately—in the last nights of a life, which I do
not regret, my love.

He would fall asleep at the moment he thought he would
never sleep again, and his dreams were young. As the first
flame of day reached his hammock, he woke up another
man—and very much of a man indeed. "Ada, our ardors and
arbors"—a dactylic trimeter that was to remain Van Veen's
only contribution to Anglo-American poetry—sang through
his brain. Bless the starling and damn the stardust! He was
fourteen and a half; he was burning and bold; he would have
her fiercely some day!

One such green resurrection he could particularize when
replaying the past. Having drawn on his swimming trunks,
having worked in and crammed in all that intricate, reluctant
multiple machinery, he had toppled out of his nest and forthwith endeavored to determine whether her part of the house
had come alive. It had. He saw a flash of crystal, a fleck of
color. She was having *sa petite collation du matin* alone on a
private balcony. Van found his sandals—with a beetle in one
and a petal in the other—and, through the toolroom, entered
the cool house.

Children of her type contrive the purest philosophies. Ada
had worked out her own little system. Hardly a week had
elapsed since Van's arrival when he was found worthy of being

initiated in her web of wisdom. An individual's life consisted of certain classified things: "real things" which were unfrequent and priceless, simply "things" which formed the routine stuff of life; and "ghost things," also called "fogs," such as fever, toothache, dreadful disappointments, and death. Three or more things occurring at the same time formed a "tower," or, if they came in immediate succession, they made a "bridge." "Real towers" and "real bridges" were the joys of life, and when the towers came in a series, one experienced supreme rapture; it almost never happened, though. In some circumstances, in a certain light, a neutral "thing" might look or even actually become "real" or else, conversely, it might coagulate into a fetid "fog." When the joy and the joyless happened to be intermixed, simultaneously or along the ramp of duration, one was confronted with "ruined towers" and "broken bridges."

The pictorial and architectural details of her metaphysics made her nights easier than Van's, and that morning—as on most mornings—he had the sensation of returning from a much more remote and grim country than she and her sunlight had come from.

Her plump, stickily glistening lips smiled.

(When I kiss you *here*, he said to her years later, I always remember that blue morning on the balcony when you were eating a *tartine au miel*; so much better in French.)

The classical beauty of clover honey, smooth, pale, translucent, freely flowing from the spoon and soaking my love's bread and butter in liquid brass. The crumb steeped in nectar.

"Real thing?" he asked.

"Tower," she answered.

And the wasp.

The wasp was investigating her plate. Its body was throbbing.

"We shall try to eat one later," she observed, "but it must be *gorged* to taste good. Of course, it can't sting your tongue. No animal will touch a person's tongue. When a lion has finished a traveler, bones and all, he *always* leaves the man's tongue lying like that in the desert" (making a negligent gesture).

"I doubt it."

"It's a well-known mystery."

Her hair was well brushed that day and sheened darkly in contrast with the lusterless pallor of her neck and arms. She wore the striped tee shirt which in his lone fantasies he especially liked to peel off her twisting torso. The oilcloth was divided into blue and white squares. A smear of honey stained what remained of the butter in its cool crock.

"All right. And the third Real Thing?"

She considered him. A fiery droplet in the wick of her mouth considered him. A three-colored velvet violet, of which she had done an aquarelle on the eve, considered him from its fluted crystal. She said nothing. She licked her spread fingers, still looking at him.

Van, getting no answer, left the balcony. Softly her tower crumbled in the sweet silent sun.

13

For the big picnic on Ada's twelfth birthday and Ida's forty-second *jour de fête*, the child was permitted to wear her lolita (thus dubbed after the little Andalusian gipsy of that name in Osberg's novel and pronounced, incidentally, with a Spanish "t," not a thick English one), a rather long, but very airy and ample, black skirt, with red poppies or peonies, "deficient in botanical reality," as she grandly expressed it, not yet knowing that reality and natural science are synonymous in the terms of this, and only this, dream.

(Nor did you, wise Van. Her note.)

She had stepped into it, naked, while her legs were still damp and "piney" after a special rubbing with a washcloth (morning baths being unknown under Mlle Larivière's regime) and pulled it on with a brisk jiggle of the hips which provoked her governess's familiar rebuke: *mais ne te trémousse pas comme ça quand tu mets ta jupe! Une petite fille de bonne maison*, etc. *Per contra*, the omission of panties was ignored by Ida Larivière, a bosomy woman of great and repulsive beauty (in nothing but corset and gartered stockings at the moment) who was not above making secret concessions to the heat of the dog-days herself; but in tender Ada's case the practice had deprecable effects. The child tried to assuage the rash in the soft arch, with all its accompaniment of sticky, itchy, not altogether unpleasurable sensations, by tightly straddling the cool limb of a Shattal apple tree, much to Van's disgust as we shall see more than once. Besides the lolita, she wore a short-sleeved white black-striped jersey, a floppy hat (hanging behind her back from an elastic around her throat), a velvet hairband and a pair of old sandals. Neither hygiene, nor sophistication of taste, were, as Van kept observing, typical of the Ardis household.

She tumbled out of her tree like a hoopoe when they all were ready to start. Hurry, hurry, my bird, my angel. The English coachman, Ben Wright, was still stone-sober (having had for breakfast only one pint of ale). Blanche, who had been to a big picnic at least once (when rushed to Pineglen to unlace Mademoiselle, who had fainted), now performed the less glamorous duty of carrying away snarling and writhing Dack to her little room in the turret.

A charabanc had already conveyed two footmen, three armchairs and a number of hampers to the site of the picnic. The novelist, wearing a white satin dress (made by Vass of Manhattan for Marina who had lately lost ten pounds), with Ada sitting beside her, and Lucette, *très en beauté* in a white sailor blouse, perched next to sullen Wright, drove there in the *calèche*. Van rode behind on one of his uncle's or grand-uncle's bicycles. The forest road remained reasonably smooth if you kept to its middle run (still sticky and dark after a rainy dawn) between the sky-blue ruts, speckled with the reflections of the same birch leaves whose shadows sped over the taut nacrine silk of Mlle Larivière's open sunshade and the wide brim of Ada's rather rakishly donned white hat. Now and then Lucette from beside blue-coated Ben looked back at Van and made slacken-speed little signals with the flat of one hand as she had seen her mother do to Ada when fearing she would crash with her pony or bicycle into the back of the carriage.

Marina came in a red motorcar of an early "runabout" type, operated by the butler very warily as if it were some fancy variety of corkscrew. She looked unwontedly smart in a man's gray flannels and sat holding the palm of her gloved hand on the knob of a clouded cane as the car, wobbling a little, arrived at the very edge of the picnic site, a picturesque glade in an old pinewood cut by ravishingly lovely ravines. A strange pale butterfly passed from the opposite side of the woods, along the Lugano dirt road, and was followed presently by a landau from which emerged one by one, nimbly or slowly, depending on age and condition, the Erminin twins, their young pregnant aunt (narrationally a great burden), and a governess, white-haired Mme Forestier, the school friend of Mathilde in a forthcoming story.

Three adult gentlemen, moreover, were expected but never turned up: Uncle Dan, who missed the morning train from town; Colonel Erminin, a widower, whose liver, he said in a note, was behaving like a *pecheneg*; and his doctor (and chess partner), the famous Dr. Krolik, who called himself Ada's court jeweler, and indeed brought her his birthday present early on the following day—three exquisitely carved chrysalids ("Inestimable gems," cried throatily Ada, tensing her brows), all of which were to yield, before long, specimens of a disappointing ichneumon instead of the Kibo Fritillary, a recently discovered rarity.

Stacks of tender crustless sandwiches (perfect rectangles five inches by two), the tawny corpse of a turkey, black Russian bread, pots of Gray Bead caviar, candied violets, little raspberry tarts, half a gallon of Goodson white port, another of ruby, watered claret in thermos flasks for the girls, and the cold sweet tea of happy childhoods—all this is more readily imagined than described. One found it instructive [thus in the MS. Ed.].

One found it instructive to place side by side Ada Veen and Grace Erminin: the skimmed-milk pallor of Ada and her coeval's healthy hot flush; the straight black witchwench-hair of the one and the brown bob of the other; my love's lackluster grave eyes and the blue twinkle behind Grace's horn-rimmed glasses; the former's naked thigh and the latter's long red stockings; the gipsy skirt and the sailor suit. Still more instructive, perhaps, was to note how Greg's plain features had been transposed practically intact into his sister's aura where they acquired a semblance of girlish "good looks" without impairing the close resemblance between sailor boy and maiden.

The ruins of the turkey, the port wine which only the governesses had touched, and a broken Sèvres plate were quickly removed by the servants. A cat appeared from under a bush, stared in a shock of intense surprise, and, despite a chorus of "kitty-kitty," vanished.

Presently Mlle Larivière asked Ada to accompany her to a secluded spot. There, the fully clad lady, with her voluminous dress retaining its stately folds but grown as it were an inch longer so that it now hid her prunella shoes, stood stock-still over a concealed downpour and a moment later reverted to her normal height. On their way back, the well-meaning pedagogue explained to Ada that a girl's twelfth birthday was a suitable occasion to discuss and foresee a thing which, she said, was going to make a *grande fille* of Ada any day now. Ada, who had been sufficiently instructed about it by a schoolteacher six months earlier, and who in fact had had it already twice, now astounded her poor governess (who could never cope with Ada's sharp and strange mind) by declaring that it was all bluff and nuns' nonsense; that those things hardly ever happened to normal girls today and would certainly not occur in her case. Mlle Larivière, who was a remarkably stupid person (in spite or perhaps because of her propensity for novelizing), mentally passed in review her own experience and wondered for a few dreadful minutes if perhaps, while she indulged in the arts, the progress of science had not changed that of nature.

The early afternoon sun found new places to brighten and old places to toast. Aunt Ruth dozed with her head on an ordinary bed pillow provided by Mme Forestier, who was knitting a tiny jersey for her charges' future half-sibling. Lady Erminin, through the bothersome afterhaze of suicide, was, reflected Marina, looking down, with old wistfulness and an infant's curiosity, at the picnickers, under the glorious pine verdure, from the Persian blue of her abode of bliss. The children displayed their talents: Ada and Grace danced a Russian fling to the accompaniment of an ancient music box (which kept halting in mid-bar, as if recalling other shores, other, radial, waves); Lucette, one fist on her hip, sang a St. Malô fisher-song; Greg put on his sister's blue skirt, hat and glasses, all of which transformed him into a very sick, mentally retarded Grace; and Van walked on his hands.

Two years earlier, when about to begin his first prison term at the fashionable and brutal boarding school, to which other Veens had gone before him (as far back as the days "when Washingtonias were Wellingtonias"), Van had resolved to study some striking stunt that would give him an immediate and brilliant ascendancy. Accordingly, after a conference with Demon, King Wing, the latter's wrestling master, taught the strong lad to walk on his hands by means of a special play of the shoulder muscles, a trick that necessitated for its acquirement and improvement nothing short of a dislocation of the caryatics.

What pleasure (thus in the MS.). The pleasure of suddenly discovering the right knack of topsy-turvy locomotion was rather like learning to man, after many a painful and ignominious fall, those delightful gliders called Magicarpets (or "jikkers") that were given a boy on his twelfth birthday in the adventurous days before the Great Reaction—and then what a breathtaking long neural caress when one became airborne for the first time and managed to skim over a haystack, a tree, a burn, a barn, while Grandfather Dedalus Veen, running with upturned face, flourished a flag and fell into the horsepond.

Van peeled off his polo shirt and took off his shoes and socks. The slenderness of his torso, matching in tint if not in texture, the tan of his tight shorts, contrasted with the handsome boy's abnormally developed deltoids and sinewy forearms. Four years later Van could stun a man with one blow of either elbow.

His reversed body gracefully curved, his brown legs hoisted like a Tarentine sail, his joined ankles tacking, Van gripped with splayed hands the brow of gravity, and moved to and fro, veering and sidestepping, opening his mouth the wrong way, and blinking in the odd bilboquet fashion peculiar to eyelids in his abnormal position. Even more extraordinary than the variety and velocity of the movements he made in imitation of animal hind legs was the effortlessness of his stance; King Wing warned him that Vekchelo, a Yukon professional, lost it by the time he was twenty-two; but that summer afternoon, on the silky ground of the pineglade, in the magical heart of Ardis, under Lady Erminin's blue eye, fourteen-year-old Van treated us to the greatest performance we have ever seen a brachiambulant give. Not the faintest flush showed on his face or neck! Now and then, when he detached his organs of locomotion from the lenient ground, and seemed actually to clap his hands in midair, in a miraculous parody of a ballet jump, one wondered if this dreamy indolence of levitation was not a result of the earth's canceling its pull in a fit of absentminded benevolence. Incidentally, one curious consequence of certain muscular changes and osteal "reclicks" caused by the special training with which Wing had racked him was Van's inability in later years to shrug his shoulders.

Questions for study and discussion:

1. Did *both* palms leave the ground when Van, while reversed, seemed actually to "skip" on his hands?

2. Was Van's adult incapacity to "shrug" things off only physical or did it "correspond" to some archetypal character of his "undersoul"?

3. Why did Ada burst into tears at the height of Van's performance?

Finally Mlle Larivière read her *La Rivière de Diamants*, a story she had just typed out for *The Quebec Quarterly*. The pretty and refined wife of a seedy clerk borrows a necklace from a wealthy woman friend. On the way home from the office party she loses it. For thirty or forty horrible years the unfortunate husband and wife labor and economize to repay the debts they accumulated in the purchase of a half-million-franc necklace which they had secretly substituted for the lost one when returning the jewelbox to Mme F. Oh, how Mathilde's heart fluttered—would Jeanne open the box? She did not. When decrepit but victorious (he, half-paralyzed by a half-century of *copie* in their *mansarde*, she, unrecognizably coarsened by the washing of floors *à grand eau*), they confess everything to a white-haired but still young-looking Mme F. the latter tells them, in the last phrase of the tale: "But, my poor Mathilde, the necklace was false: it cost only five hundred francs!"

Marina's contribution was more modest, but it too had its

charm. She showed Van and Lucette (the others knew all
about it) the exact pine and the exact spot on its rugged red
trunk where in old, very old days a magnetic telephone
nested, communicating with Ardis Hall. After the banning of
"currents and circuits," she said (rapidly but freely, with an
actress's *désinvolture* pronouncing those not quite proper
words—while puzzled Lucette tugged at the sleeve of Van, of
Vanichka, who could explain everything), her husband's
grandmother, an engineer of great genius, "tubed" the Red-
mont rill (running just below the glade from a hill above
Ardis). She made it carry vibrational *vibgyors* (prismatic
pulsations) through a system of platinum segments. These
produced, of course, only one-way messages, and the instal-
lation and upkeep of the "drums" (cylinders) cost, she said,
a Jew's eye, so that the idea was dropped, however tempting
the possibility of informing a picnicking Veen that his house
was on fire.

As if to confirm many people's discontent with national and
international policies (old Gamaliel was by now pretty gaga),
the little red car came chugging back from Ardis Hall and the
butler jumped out with a message. Monsieur had just arrived
with a birthday present for Mademoiselle Ada, but nobody
could figure out how the complicated object worked, and Madame must help. The butler had brought a letter which he
now placed on a pocket tray and presented to Marina.

We cannot reconstitute the exact wording of the message,
but we know it said that this thoughtful and very expensive
gift was a huge beautiful doll—unfortunately, and strangely,
more or less naked; still more strangely, with a braced right
leg and a bandaged left arm, and a boxful of plaster jackets
and rubber accessories, instead of the usual frocks and frills.
Directions in Russian or Bulgarian made no sense because
they were not in the modern Roman, but in the old Cyrillitsa,
a nightmare alphabet which Dan had never been able to master. Could Marina come over at once to have suitable doll
clothes cut out of some nice silk discards her maid had collected in a drawer he had discovered and wrap the box again
in fresh tissue paper?

Ada, who had been reading the note over her mother's
shoulder, shuddered and said:

"You tell him to take a pair of tongs and carry the whole business to the surgical dump."

"*Bednyachok!* Poor, poor little man," exclaimed Marina, her eyes brimming with pity. "Of course I'll come. Your cruelty, Ada, is sometimes, sometimes, I don't know—satanic!"

Briskly walking her long cane, her face twitching with nervous resolution, Marina marched toward the vehicle, which presently moved, turning and knocking over an empty half-gallon bottle as its fender leafed through an angry burnberry bush in order to avoid the parked *calèche*.

But whatever wrath there hung in the air, it soon subsided. Ada asked her governess for pencils and paper. Lying on his stomach, leaning his cheek on his hand, Van looked at his love's inclined neck as she played anagrams with Grace, who had innocently suggested "insect."

"Scient," said Ada, writing it down.

"Oh no!" objected Grace.

"Oh yes! I'm sure it exists. He is a great scient. Dr. Entsic was scient in insects."

Grace meditated, tapping her puckered brow with the eraser end of the pencil, and came up with:

"Nicest!"

"Incest," said Ada instantly.

"I give up," said Grace. "We need a dictionary to check your little inventions."

But the glow of the afternoon had entered its most oppressive phase, and the first bad mosquito of the season was resonantly slain on Ada's shin by alert Lucette. The charabanc had already left with the armchairs, the hampers and the munching footmen, Essex, Middlesex and Somerset; and now Mlle Larivière and Mme Forestier were exchanging melodious adieux. Hands waved, and the twins with their ancient governess and sleepy young aunt were carried away in the landau. A pale diaphanous butterfly with a very black body followed them and Ada cried "Look!" and explained it was closely related to a Japanese Parnassian. Mlle Larivière said suddenly she would use a pseudonym when publishing the story. She led her two pretty charges toward the calèche and poked *sans façons* in his fat red neck with the point of her parasol Ben Wright, grossly asleep in the back under the low-hanging

festoons of foliage. Ada tossed her hat into Ida's lap and ran
back to where Van stood. Being unfamiliar with the itinerary
of sun and shade in the clearing, he had left his bicycle to
endure the blazing beams for at least three hours. Ada
mounted it, uttered a yelp of pain, almost fell off, googled,
recovered—and the rear tire burst with a comic bang.

The discomfitured machine was abandoned under a shrub
to be fetched later by Bouteillan Junior, yet another household character. Lucette refused to give up her perch (accepting with a bland little nod the advice of her drunken boxfellow
who was seen to touch her bare knees with a good-natured
paw); and there being no *strapontin*, Ada had to content herself with Van's hard lap.

It was the children's first bodily contact and both were embarrassed. She settled down with her back to Van, resettled as
the carriage jerked, and wriggled some more, arranging her
ample pine-smelling skirt, which seemed to envelop him airily,
for all the world like a barber's sheet. In a trance of awkward
delight he held her by the hips. Hot gouts of sun moved fast
across her zebra stripes and the backs of her bare arms and
seemed to continue their journey through the tunnel of his
own frame.

"Why did you cry?" he asked, inhaling her hair and the
heat of her ear. She turned her head and for a moment looked
at him closely, in cryptic silence.

(Did I? I don't know—it upset me somehow. I can't explain
it, but I felt there was something dreadful, brutal, dark, and,
yes, dreadful, about the whole thing. A later note.)

"I'm sorry," he said as she looked away, "I'll never do it
again in your presence."

(By the way, that "for all the world," I detest the phrase.
Another note in Ada's late hand.)

With his entire being, the boiling and brimming lad relished
her weight as he felt it responding to every bump of the road
by softly parting in two and crushing beneath it the core of
the longing which he knew he had to control lest a possible
seep perplex her innocence. He would have yielded and
melted in animal laxity had not the girl's governess saved the
situation by addressing him. Poor Van shifted Ada's bottom
to his right knee, blunting what used to be termed in the

jargon of the torture house "the angle of agony." In the mournful dullness of unconsummated desire he watched a row of izbas straggle by as the *calèche* drove through Gamlet, a hamlet.

"I can never get used (*m'y faire*)," said Mlle Laparure, "to the contrast between the opulence of nature and the squalor of human life. See that old moujik *décharné* with that rent in his shirt, see his miserable *cabane*. And see that agile swallow! How happy, nature, how unhappy, man! Neither of you told me how you liked my new story? Van?"

"It's a good fairy tale," said Van.

"It's a fairy tale," said careful Ada.

"*Allons donc!*" cried Mlle Larivière. "On the contrary— every detail is realistic. We have here the drama of the petty bourgeois, with all his class cares and class dreams and class pride."

(True; that might have been the intent—apart from the *pointe assassine*; but the story lacked "realism" *within its own terms*, since a punctilious, penny-counting employee would have found out, first of all, no matter how, *quitte à tout dire à la veuve*, what exactly the lost necklace had cost. *That* was the fatal flaw in the Larivière pathos-piece, but at the time young Van and younger Ada could not quite grope for that point although they felt instinctively the falsity of the whole affair.)

A slight commotion took place on the box. Lucette turned around and spoke to Ada.

"I want to sit with you. *Mne tut neudobno, i ot nego neho-rosho pakhnet* (I'm uncomfortable here, and he does not smell good)."

"We'll be there in a moment," retorted Ada, "*poterpi* (have a little patience)."

"What's the matter?" asked Mlle Larivière.

"Nothing. *Il pue.*"

"Oh dear! I doubt strongly he ever was in that Rajah's service."

14

Next day, or the day after the next, the entire family was having high tea in the garden. Ada, on the grass, kept trying to make an anadem of marguerites for the dog while Lucette looked on, munching a crumpet. Marina remained for almost a minute wordlessly stretching across the table her husband's straw hat in his direction; finally he shook his head, glared at the sun that glared back and retired with his cup and the *Toulouse Enquirer* to a rustic seat on the other side of the lawn under an immense elm.

"I ask myself who can that be," murmured Mlle Larivière from behind the samovar (which expressed fragments of its surroundings in demented fantasies of a primitive genre) as she slitted her eyes at a part of the drive visible between the pilasters of an open-work gallery. Van, lying prone behind Ada, lifted his eyes from his book (Ada's copy of *Atala*).

A tall rosy-faced youngster in smart riding breeches dismounted from a black pony.

"It's Greg's beautiful new pony," said Ada.

Greg, with a well-bred boy's easy apologies, had brought Marina's platinum lighter which his aunt had discovered in her own bag.

"Goodness, I've not even had time to miss it. How is Ruth?"

Greg said that both Aunt Ruth and Grace were laid up with acute indigestion—"not because of your wonderful sandwiches," he hastened to add, "but because of all those burnberries they picked in the bushes."

Marina was about to jingle a bronze bell for the footman to bring some more toast, but Greg said he was on his way to a party at the Countess de Prey's.

"Rather soon (*skorovato*) she consoled herself," remarked Marina, alluding to the death of the Count killed in a pistol duel on Boston Common a couple of years ago.

"She's a very jolly and handsome woman," said Greg.

"And ten years older than me," said Marina.

Now Lucette demanded her mother's attention.

"What are Jews?" she asked.

"Dissident Christians," answered Marina.

"Why is Greg a Jew?" asked Lucette.

"Why-why!" said Marina; "because his parents are Jews."

"And his grandparents? His *arrière* grandparents?"

"I really wouldn't know, my dear. Were your ancestors Jews, Greg?"

"Well, I'm not sure," said Greg. "Hebrews, yes—but not Jews in quotes—I mean, not comic characters or Christian businessmen. They came from Tartary to England five centuries ago. My mother's grandfather, though, was a French marquis who, I know, belonged to the Roman faith and was crazy about banks and stocks and jewels, so I imagine people may have called him *un juif*."

"It's not a very old religion, anyway, as religions go, is it?" said Marina (turning to Van and vaguely planning to steer the chat to India where she had been a dancing girl long before Moses or anybody was born in the lotus swamp).

"Who cares—" said Van.

"And Belle" (Lucette's name for her governess), "is she also a dizzy Christian?"

"Who cares," cried Van, "who cares about all those stale myths, what does it matter—Jove or Jehovah, spire or cupola, mosques in Moscow, or bronzes and bonzes, and clerics, and relics, and deserts with bleached camel ribs? They are merely the dust and mirages of the communal mind."

"How did this idiotic conversation start in the first place?" Ada wished to be told, cocking her head at the partly ornamented dackel or *taksik*.

"*Mea culpa*," Mlle Larivière explained with offended dignity. "All I said, at the picnic, was that Greg might not care for ham sandwiches, because Jews and Tartars do not eat pork."

"The Romans," said Greg, "the Roman colonists, who crucified Christian Jews and Barabbits, and other unfortunate people in the old days, did not touch pork either, but I certainly do and so did my grandparents."

Lucette was puzzled by a verb Greg had used. To illustrate it for her, Van joined his ankles, spread both arms horizontally, and rolled up his eyes.

"When I was a little girl," said Marina crossly, "Mesopotamian history was taught practically in the nursery."

"Not all little girls can learn what they are taught," observed Ada.

"Are we Mesopotamians?" asked Lucette.

"We are Hippopotamians," said Van. "Come," he added, "we have not yet ploughed today."

A day or two before, Lucette had demanded that she be taught to hand-walk. Van gripped her by her ankles while she slowly progressed on her little red palms, sometimes falling with a grunt on her face or pausing to nibble a daisy. Dack barked in strident protest.

"*Et pourtant*," said the sound-sensitive governess, wincing, "I read to her twice Ségur's adaptation in fable form of Shakespeare's play about the wicked usurer."

"She also knows my revised monologue of his mad king," said Ada:

> *Ce beau jardin fleurit en mai,*
> *Mais en hiver*
> *Jamais, jamais, jamais, jamais, jamais*
> *N'est vert, n'est vert, n'est vert, n'est vert,*
> *n'est vert.*

"Oh, that's good," exclaimed Greg with a veritable sob of admiration.

"Not so *energichno*, children!" cried Marina in Van- and Lucette's direction.

"*Elle devient pourpre*, she is getting crimson," commented the governess. "I sustain that these indecent gymnastics are no good for her."

Van, his eyes smiling, his angel-strong hands holding the child's cold-carrot-soup legs just above the insteps, was "ploughing around" with Lucette acting the sullow. Her bright hair hung over her face, her panties showed from under the hem of her skirt, yet she still urged the ploughboy on.

"*Budet, budet*, that'll do," said Marina to the plough team.

Van gently let her legs down and straightened her dress. She lay for a moment, panting.

"I mean, I would love lending him to you for a ride any time. For any amount of time. Will you? Besides, I have another black."

But she shook her head, she shook her bent head, while still twisting and twining her daisies.

"Well," he said, getting up, "I must be going. Good-bye, everybody. Good-bye, Ada. I guess it's your father under that oak, isn't it?"

"No, it's an elm," said Ada.

Van looked across the lawn and said as if musing—perhaps with just a faint touch of boyish show-off:

"I'd like to see that Two-Lice sheet too when Uncle is through with it. I was supposed to play for my school in yesterday's cricket game. Veen sick, unable to bat, Riverlane humbled."

15

One afternoon they were climbing the glossy-limbed shattal tree at the bottom of the garden. Mlle Larivière and little Lucette, screened by a caprice of the coppice but just within earshot, were playing grace hoops. One glimpsed now and then, above or through foliage, the skimming hoop passing from one unseen sending stick to another. The first cicada of the season kept trying out its instrument. A silver-and-sable skybab squirrel sat sampling a cone on the back of a bench.

Van, in blue gym suit, having worked his way up to a fork just under his agile playmate (who naturally was better acquainted with the tree's intricate map) but not being able to see her face, betokened mute communication by taking her ankle between finger and thumb as *she* would have a closed butterfly. Her bare foot slipped, and the two panting youngsters tangled ignominiously among the branches, in a shower of drupes and leaves, clutching at each other, and the next moment, as they regained a semblance of balance, his expressionless face and cropped head were between her legs and a last fruit fell with a thud—the dropped dot of an inverted exclamation point. She was wearing his wristwatch and a cotton frock.

("Remember?"

"Yes, of course, I remember: you kissed me here, on the inside—"

"And you started to strangle me with those devilish knees of yours—"

"I was seeking some sort of support.")

That might have been true, but according to a later (considerably later!) version they were still in the tree, and still glowing, when Van removed a silk thread of larva web from his lip and remarked that such negligence of attire was a form of hysteria.

"Well," answered Ada, straddling her favorite limb, "as we all know by now, Mlle La Rivière de Diamants has nothing against a hysterical little girl's not wearing pantalets during *l'ardeur de la canicule*."

"I refuse to share the ardor of your little canicule with an apple tree."

"It is really the Tree of Knowledge—this specimen was imported last summer wrapped up in brocade from the Eden National Park where Dr. Krolik's son is a ranger and breeder."

"Let him range and breed by all means," said Van (her natural history had long begun to get on his nerves), "but I swear no apple trees grow in Iraq."

"Right, but that's not a true apple tree."

("Right and wrong," commented Ada, again much later: "We did discuss the matter, but you could not have permitted yourself such vulgar repartees then. At a time when the chastest of chances allowed you to snatch, as they say, a first shy kiss! Oh, for shame. And besides, there was no National Park in Iraq eighty years ago." "True," said Van. "And no caterpillars bred on that tree in our orchard." "True, my lovely and larveless." Natural history was past history by that time.)

Both kept diaries. Soon after that foretaste of knowledge, an amusing thing happened. She was on her way to Krolik's house with a boxful of hatched and chloroformed butterflies and had just passed through the orchard when she suddenly stopped and swore (*chort!*). At the same moment Van, who had set out in the opposite direction for a bit of shooting practice in a nearby pavilion (where there was a bowling alley and other recreational facilities, once much used by other

Veens), also came to an abrupt standstill. Then, by a nice co-incidence, both went tearing back to the house to hide their diaries which both thought they had left lying open in their respective rooms. Ada, who feared the curiosity of Lucette and Blanche (the governess presented no threat, being patholog-ically unobservant), found out she was wrong—she had put away the album with its latest entry. Van, who knew that Ada was a little "snoopy," discovered Blanche in his room feigning to make the made bed, with the unlocked diary lying on the stool beside it. He slapped her lightly on the behind and re-moved the shagreen-bound book to a safer place. Then Van and Ada met in the passage, and would have kissed at some earlier stage of the Novel's Evolution in the History of Lit-erature. It might have been a neat little sequel to the Shattal Tree incident. Instead, both resumed their separate ways—and Blanche, I suppose, went to weep in her bower.

16

Their first free and frantic caresses had been preceded by a brief period of strange craftiness, of cringing stealth. The masked offender was Van, but her passive acceptance of the poor boy's behavior seemed tacitly to acknowledge its disrep-utable and even monstrous nature. A few weeks later both were to regard that phase of his courtship with amused con-descension; at the time, however, its implicit cowardice puz-zled her and distressed him—mainly because he was keenly conscious of her being puzzled.

Although Van had never had the occasion to witness any-thing close to virginal revolt on the part of Ada—not an easily frightened or overfastidious little girl ("*Je raffole de tout ce qui rampe*"), he could rely on two or three dreadful dreams to imagine her, in real, or at least responsible, life, recoiling with a wild look as she left his lust in the lurch to summon her governess or mother, or a gigantic footman (not existing in the house but killable in the dream—punchable with sharp-ringed knuckles, puncturable like a bladder of blood), after which he knew he would be expelled from Ardis—

(In Ada's hand: I vehemently object to that "not overfastidious." It is unfair in fact, and fuzzy in fancy. Van's marginal note: Sorry, puss; that must stay.)

—but even if he were to will himself to mock that image so as to blast it out of all consciousness, he could not feel proud of his conduct: in those actual undercover dealings of his with Ada, by doing what he did and the way he did it, with that unpublished relish, he seemed to himself to be either taking advantage of her innocence or else inducing her to conceal from him, the concealer, her awareness of what he concealed.

After the first contact, so light, so mute, between his soft lips and her softer skin had been established—high up in that dappled tree, with only that stray ardilla daintily leavesdropping—nothing seemed changed in one sense, all was lost in another. Such contacts evolve their own texture; a tactile sensation is a blind spot; we touch in silhouette. Henceforth, at certain moments of their otherwise indolent days, in certain recurrent circumstances of controlled madness, a secret sign was erected, a veil drawn between him and her—

(Ada: They are now practically extinct at Ardis. Van: Who? Oh, I see.)

—not to be removed until he got rid of what the necessity of dissimulation kept degrading to the level of a wretched itch.

(Och, Van!)

He could not say afterwards, when discussing with her that rather pathetic nastiness, whether he really feared that his *avournine* (as Blanche was to refer later, in her bastard French, to Ada) might react with an outburst of real or well-feigned resentment to a stark display of desire, or whether a glum, cunning approach was dictated to him by considerations of pity and decency toward a chaste child, whose charm was too compelling not to be tasted in secret and too sacred to be openly violated; but something went wrong—that much was clear. The vague commonplaces of vague modesty so dreadfully in vogue eighty years ago, the unsufferable banalities of shy wooing buried in old romances as arch as Arcady, those moods, those modes, lurked no doubt behind the hush of his ambuscades, and that of her toleration. No record has remained of the exact summer day when his wary and elaborate coddlings began; but simultaneously with her sensing that at certain moments he stood indecently close behind her, with his burning breath and gliding lips, she was aware that those silent, exotic approximations must have started long ago in some indefinite and infinite past, and could no longer be stopped by her, without her acknowledging a tacit acceptance of their routine repetition in that past.

On those relentlessly hot July afternoons, Ada liked to sit on a cool piano stool of ivoried wood at a white-oilcloth'd table in the sunny music room, her favorite botanical atlas open before her, and copy out in color on creamy paper some singular flower. She might choose, for instance, an insect-mimicking orchid which she would proceed to enlarge with remarkable skill. Or else she combined one species with another (unrecorded but possible), introducing odd little changes and twists that seemed almost morbid in so young a girl so nakedly dressed. The long beam slanting in from the french window glowed in the faceted tumbler, in the tinted water, and on the tin of the paintbox—and while she delicately painted an eyespot or the lobes of a lip, rapturous concentration caused the tip of her tongue to curl at the corner of her mouth, and as the sun looked on, the fantastic, black-blue-brown-haired child seemed in her turn to mimic the mirror-of-Venus blossom. Her flimsy, loose frock happened to be so deeply cut out behind that whenever she concaved her back while moving her prominent scapulae to and fro and tilting her head—as with air-poised brush she surveyed her damp achievement, or with the outside of her left wrist wiped a strand of hair off her temple—Van, who had drawn up to her seat as close as he dared, could see down her sleek *ensellure* as far as her coccyx and inhale the warmth of her entire body. His heart thumping, one miserable hand deep in his trouser pocket—where he kept a purse with half a dozen ten-dollar gold pieces to disguise his state—he bent over her, as she bent over her work. Very lightly he let his parched lips travel down her warm hair and hot nape. It was the sweetest, the strongest, the most mysterious sensation that the boy had ever experienced; nothing in his sordid venery of the past winter could duplicate that downy tenderness, that despair of desire. He would have lingered forever on the little middle knob of rounded delight on the back of her neck, had she kept it inclined forever—and had the unfortunate fellow been able to endure much longer the ecstasy of its touch under his wax-still mouth without rubbing against her with mad abandon. The vivid crimsoning of an exposed ear and the gradual torpor invading her paintbrush were the only signs—fearful signs—of her feeling the increased pressure of his caress. Silently he would slink away to his room, lock the door, grasp a towel, uncover himself, and call forth the image he had just left behind, an image still as safe and bright as a hand-cupped flame—carried into the dark, only to be got rid of there with savage zeal; after which, drained for a while, with shaky loins and weak calves, Van would return to the purity of the sun-suffused room where a little girl, now glistening with sweat, was still painting her flower: the marvelous flower that simulated a bright moth that in turn simulated a scarab.

If the relief, any relief, of a lad's ardor had been Van's sole concern; if, in other words, no love had been involved, our young friend might have put up—for one casual summer—with the nastiness and ambiguity of his behavior. But since Van loved Ada, that complicated release could not be an end in itself; or, rather, it was only a dead end, because unshared; because horribly hidden; because not liable to melt into any subsequent phase of incomparably greater rapture which, like a misty summit beyond the fierce mountain pass, promised to be the true pinnacle of his perilous relationship with Ada. During that midsummer week or fortnight, notwithstanding those daily butterfly kisses on that hair, on that neck, Van felt even farther removed from her than he had been on the eve of the day when his mouth had accidentally come into contact with an inch of her skin hardly perceived by him sensually in the maze of the shattal tree.

But nature is motion and growth. One afternoon he came up behind her in the music room more noiselessly than ever before because he happened to be barefooted—and, turning her head, little Ada shut her eyes and pressed her lips to his in a fresh-rose kiss that entranced and baffled Van.

"Now run along," she said, "quick, quick, I'm busy," and as he lagged like an idiot, she anointed his flushed forehead with her paintbrush in the semblance of an ancient Estotian "sign of the cross." "I have to finish this," she added, pointing with her violet-purple-soaked thin brush at a blend of *Ophrys scolopax* and *Ophrys veenae*, "and in a minute we must dress up because Marina wants Kim to take our picture—holding hands and grinning" (grinning, and then turning back to her hideous flower).

17

The hugest dictionary in the library said under Lip: "Either of a pair of fleshy folds surrounding an orifice."

Mileyshiy Emile, as Ada called Monsieur Littré, spoke thus: "*Partie extérieure et charnue qui forme le contour de la bouche . . . Les deux bords d'une plaie simple*" (we simply speak with our wounds; wounds procreate) " . . . *C'est le membre qui lèche.*" Dearest Emile!

A fat little Russian encyclopedia was solely concerned with *guba*, lip, as meaning a district court in ancient Lyaska or an arctic gulf.

Their lips were absurdly similar in style, tint and tissue. Van's upper one resembled in shape a long-winged sea bird coming directly at you, while the nether lip, fat and sullen, gave a touch of brutality to his usual expression. Nothing of that brutality existed in the case of Ada's lips, but the bow shape of the upper one and the largeness of the lower one with its disdainful prominence and opaque pink repeated Van's mouth in a feminine key.

During our children's kissing phase (a not particularly healthy fortnight of long messy embraces), some odd pudibund screen cut them off, so to speak, from each other's raging bodies. But contacts and reactions to contacts could not help coming through like a distant vibration of desperate signals. Endlessly, steadily, delicately, Van would brush his lips against hers, teasing their burning bloom, back and forth, right, left, life, death, reveling in the contrast between the airy tenderness of the open idyll and the gross congestion of the hidden flesh.

There were other kisses. "I'd like to taste," he said, "the inside of your mouth. God, how I'd like to be a goblin-sized Gulliver and explore that cave."

"I can lend you my tongue," she said, and did.

A large boiled strawberry, still very hot. He sucked it in as far as it would go. He held her close and lapped her palate. Their chins got thoroughly wet. "Hanky," she said, and informally slipped her hand into his trouser pocket, but withdrew it quickly, and had him give it himself. No comment.

("I appreciated your tact," he told her when they recalled, with amusement and awe that rapture and that discomfort. "But we lost a lot of time—irretrievable opals.")

He learned her face. Nose, cheek, chin—all possessed such a softness of outline (associated retrospectively with keepsakes, and picture hats, and frightfully expensive little courtesans in Wicklow) that a mawkish admirer might well have imagined the pale plume of a reed, that unthinking man—*pascal-trezza*—shaping her profile, while a more childish and sensual digit would have liked, and did like, to palpate that nose, cheek, chin. Remembrance, like Rembrandt, is dark but festive. Remembered ones dress up for the occasion and sit still. Memory is a photo-studio de luxe on an infinite Fifth Power Avenue. The fillet of black velvet binding her hair that day (the day of the mental picture) brought out its sheen at the silk of the temple and along the chalk of the parting. It hung lank and long over the neck, its flow disjoined by the shoulder; so that the mat white of her neck through the black bronze stream showed in triangular elegancy.

Accentuating her nose's slight tilt turned it into Lucette's; smoothing it down, into Samoyed. In both sisters, the front teeth were a trifle too large and the nether lip too fat for the ideal beauty of marble death; and because their noses were permanently stuffed, both girls (especially later, at fifteen and twelve) looked a little dreamy or dazed in profile. The lusterless whiteness of Ada's skin (at twelve, sixteen, twenty, thirty-three, et cetera) was incomparably rarer than Lucette's golden bloom (at eight, twelve, sixteen, twenty-five, finis). In both, the long pure line of the throat, coming straight from Marina, tormented the senses with unknown, ineffable promises (not kept by the mother).

The eyes. Ada's dark brown eyes. What (Ada asks) are eyes anyway? Two holes in the mask of life. What (she asks) would they mean to a creature from another corpuscle or milk bubble whose organ of sight was (say) an internal parasite resembling the written word "deified"? What, indeed, would a pair of beautiful (human, lemurian, owlish) eyes mean to anybody if found lying on the seat of a taxi? Yet I have to describe yours. The iris: black brown with amber specks or spokes placed around the serious pupil in a dial arrangement of identical hours. The eyelids: sort of pleaty, *v skladochku* (rhyming in Russian with the diminutive of her name in the accusative case). Eye shape: languorous. The procuress in Wicklow, on that satanic night of black sleet, at the most tragic, and almost fatal point of my life (Van, thank goodness, is ninety now—in Ada's hand) dwelt with peculiar force on the "long eyes" of her pathetic and adorable grandchild. How I used to seek, with what tenacious anguish, traces and tokens of my unforgettable love in all the brothels of the world!

He discovered her hands (forget that nail-biting business). The pathos of the carpus, the grace of the phalanges demanding helpless genuflections, a mist of brimming tears, agonies of unresolvable adoration. He touched her wrist, like a dying doctor. A quiet madman, he caressed the parallel strokes of the delicate down shading the brunette's forearm. He went back to her knuckles. Fingers, please.

"I am sentimental," she said. "I could dissect a koala but not its baby. I like the words damozel, eglantine, elegant. I love when you kiss my elongated white hand."

She had on the back of her left hand the same small brown spot that marked his right one. She was sure, she said—either disingenuously or giddily—it descended from a birthmark Marina had had removed surgically from that very place years ago when in love with a cad who complained it resembled a bedbug.

On very still afternoons one could hear the pre-tunnel toot of the two-two to Toulouse from the hill, where that exchange can be localized.

"Cad is too strong," remarked Van.

"I used it fondly."

"Even so. I think I know the man. He has less heart than wit, that's a fact."

As he looks, the palm of a gipsy asking for alms fades into that of the almsgiver asking for a long life. (When will film-makers reach the stage *we* have reached?) Blinking in the green sunshine under a birch tree, Ada explained to her passionate fortuneteller that the circular marblings she shared with Turgenev's Katya, another innocent girl, were called "waltzes" in California ("because the señorita will dance all night").

On her twelfth birthday, July 21, 1884, the child had stopped biting her fingernails (but not her toenails) in a grand act of will (as her quitting cigarettes was to be, twenty years later). True, one could list some compensations—such as a blessed lapse into delicious sin at Christmas, when *Culex chateaubriandi* Brown does not fly. A new and conclusive resolution was taken on New Year's Eve after Mlle Larivière had threatened to smear poor Ada's fingertips with French mustard and tie green, yellow, orange, red, pink riding hoods of wool around them (the yellow index was a *trouvaille*).

Soon after the birthday picnic, when kissing the hands of his little sweetheart had become a tender obsession with Van, her nails, although still on the squarish side, became strong enough to deal with the excruciating itch that local children experienced in midsummer.

During the last week of July, there emerged, with diabolical regularity, the female of Chateaubriand's mosquito. Chateaubriand (Charles), who had not been the first to be bitten by it . . . but the first to bottle the offender, and with cries of vindictive exultation to carry it to Professor Brown who wrote the rather slap-bang Original Description ("small black palpi . . . hyaline wings . . . yellowy in certain lights . . . which should be extinguished if one keeps open the kasements [German printer!] . . . " The *Boston Entomologist* for August, quick work, 1840) was not related to the great poet and memoirist born between Paris and Tagne (as he'd better, said Ada, who liked crossing orchids).

> Mon enfant, ma soeur,
> Songe à l'épaisseur
> Du grand chêne à Tagne;
> Songe à la montagne,
> Songe à la douceur—

—of scraping with one's claws or nails the spots visited by that fluffy-footed insect characterized by an insatiable and reckless appetite for Ada's and Ardelia's, Lucette's and Lucile's (multiplied by the itch) blood.

The "pest" appeared as suddenly as it would vanish. It settled on pretty bare arms and legs without the hint of a hum, in a kind of *recueilli* silence, that—by contrast—caused the sudden insertion of its absolutely hellish proboscis to resemble the brass crash of a military band. Five minutes after the attack in the crepuscule, between porch step and cricket-crazed garden, a fiery irritation would set in, which the strong and the cold ignored (confident it would last a mere hour) but which the weak, the adorable, the voluptuous took advantage of to scratch and scratch and scratch scrumptiously (canteen cant). "*Sladko!* (Sweet!)" Pushkin used to exclaim in relation to a different species in Yukon. During the week following her birthday, Ada's unfortunate fingernails used to stay garnet-stained and after a particularly ecstatic, lost-to-the-world session of scratching, blood literally streamed down her shins— a pity to see, mused her distressed admirer, but at the same time disgracefully fascinating—for we are visitors and investigators in a strange universe, indeed, indeed.

The girl's pale skin, so excitingly delicate to Van's eye, so vulnerable to the beast's needle, was, nevertheless, as strong as a stretch of Samarkand satin and withstood all self-flaying attempts whenever Ada, her dark eyes veiled as in the erotic trances Van had already begun to witness during their immoderate kissing, her lips parted, her large teeth lacquered with saliva, scraped with her five fingers the pink mounds caused by the rare insect's bite—for it *is* a rather rare and interesting mosquito (described—not quite simultaneously— by two angry old men—the second was Braun, the Philadelphian dipterist, a much better one than the Boston professor), and rare and rapturous was the sight of my beloved trying to quench the lust of her precious skin, leaving at first pearly, then ruby, stripes along her enchanting leg and briefly attaining a drugged beatitude into which, as into a vacuum, the ferocity of the itch would rush with renewed strength.

"Look here," said Van, "if you do not stop *now* when I say one, two, three, I shall open this knife" (opening the knife) "and slash my leg to match yours. Oh, please, devour your fingernails! Anything is more welcome."

Because, perhaps, Van's lifestream was too bitter—even in those glad days—Chateaubriand's mosquito never cared much for him. Nowadays it seems to be getting extinct, what with the cooler climate and the moronic draining of the lovely rich marshes in the Ladore region as well as near Kaluga, Conn., and Lugano, Pa. (A short series, all females, replete with their fortunate captor's blood, has recently been collected, I am told, in a secret habitat quite far from the above-mentioned stations. Ada's note.)

18

Not only in ear-trumpet age—in what Van called their dot-dot-dotage—but even more so in their adolescence (summer, 1888), did they seek a scholarly excitement in establishing the past evolution (summer, 1884) of their love, the initial stages of its revelations, the freak discrepancies in gappy chronographies. She had kept only a few—mainly botanical and entomological—pages of her diary, because on rereading it she had found its tone false and finical; he had destroyed his entirely because of its clumsy schoolboyish style combined with heedless, and false, cynicism. Thus they had to rely on oral tradition, on the mutual correction of common memories. "And do you remember, *a ti pomnish', et te souviens-tu*" (invariably with that implied codetta of "and," introducing the bead to be threaded in the torn necklace) became with them, in their intense talks, the standard device for beginning every other sentence. Calendar dates were debated, sequences sifted and shifted, sentimental notes compared, hesitations and resolutions passionately analyzed. If their recollections now and then did not tally, this was often owing to sexual differences rather than to individual temperament. Both were diverted by life's young fumblings, both saddened by the wisdom of time. Ada tended to see those initial stages as an extremely gradual and diffuse growth, possibly unnatural, probably unique, but wholly delightful in its smooth unfolding which precluded any brutish impulses or shocks of shame. Van's memory could not help picking out specific episodes branded forever with abrupt and poignant, and sometimes regrettable, physical thrills. She had the impression that the insatiable delectations she arrived at, without having expected or summoned them, were experienced by Van only by the time she attained them: that is, after weeks of cumulative caresses; her first physiological reactions to them she demurely dismissed as related to childish practices which she had indulged in before and which had little to do with the glory and tang of individual happiness. Van, on the contrary, not only could tabulate every informal spasm he had hidden from her before they became lovers, but stressed philosophic and moral distinctions between the shattering force of self-abuse and the overwhelming softness of avowed and shared love.

When we remember our former selves, there is always that little figure with its long shadow stopping like an uncertain belated visitor on a lighted threshold at the far end of an impeccably narrowing corridor. Ada saw herself there as a wonder-eyed waif with a bedraggled nosegay; Van saw himself as a nasty young satyr with clumsy hooves and an ambiguous flue pipe. "But I was only twelve," Ada would cry when some indelicate detail was brought up. "I was in my fifteenth year," sadly said Van.

And did the young lady recall, he asked, producing metaphorically some notes from his pocket, the very first time she guessed that her shy young "cousin" (their official relationship) was physically excited in her presence, though decently swathed in layers of linen and wool and not in contact with the young lady?

She said, frankly no, she did not—indeed, could not—because at eleven, despite trying numberless times to unlock with every key in the house the cabinet in which Walter Daniel Veen kept "Jap. & Ind. erot. prints" as seen distinctly labeled through the glazed door (the key to which Van found for her in a twinkle—taped to the back of the pediment), she had still been rather hazy about the way human beings mated. She was very observant, of course, and had closely examined various insects *in copula*, but at the period discussed clear examples of mammalian maleness had rarely come to her notice and had remained unconnected with any idea or possibility of sexual function (such as for example the time she had contemplated the soft-looking beige beak of the Negro janitor's boy who sometimes urinated in the girls' water closet at her first school in 1883).

Two other phenomena that she had observed even earlier proved ridiculously misleading. She must have been about nine when that elderly gentleman, an eminent painter whom she could not and would not name, came several times to dinner at Ardis Hall. Her drawing teacher, Miss Wintergreen, respected him greatly, though actually her *natures mortes* were considered (in 1888 and again 1958) incomparably superior to the works of the celebrated old rascal who drew his diminutive nudes invariably from behind—fig-picking, peach-buttocked nymphets straining upward, or else rock-climbing girl scouts in bursting shorts—

"I know exactly," interrupted Van angrily, "whom you mean, and would like to place on record that even if his delicious talent is in disfavor today, Paul J. Gigment had every right to paint schoolgirls and poolgirls from any side he pleased. Proceed."

Every time (said unruffled Ada) Pig Pigment came, she cowered when hearing him trudge and snort and pant upstairs, ever nearer like the Marmoreal Guest, that immemorial ghost, seeking her, crying for her in a thin, querulous voice not in keeping with marble.

"Poor old chap," murmured Van.

His method of contact, she said, "*puisqu'on aborde ce thème-là*, and I'm certainly *not* making offensive comparisons," was to insist, with maniacal force, that he help her reach for something—anything, a little gift he had brought, bonbons, or simply some old toy that he'd picked up from the floor of the nursery and hung up high on the wall, or a pink candle burning blue that he commanded her to blow out on an arbre de Noël, and despite her gentle protests he would raise the child by her elbows, taking his time, pushing, grunting, saying: ah, how heavy and pretty she was—this went on and on until the dinner gong boomed or Nurse entered with a glass of fruit juice and what a relief it was, for everybody concerned, when in the course of that fraudulent ascension her poor little bottom made it *at last* to the crackling snow of his shirtfront, and he dropped her, and buttoned his dinner jacket. And she remembered—

"Stupidly exaggerated," commented Van. "Also, I suppose, artificially recolored in the lamplight of later events as revealed still later."

And she remembered blushing painfully when somebody said poor Pig had a very sick mind and "a hardening of the artery," that is how she heard it, or perhaps "heartery"; but she also knew, even then, that the artery could become awfully long, for she had seen Drongo, a black horse, looking, she must confess, most dejected and embarrassed by what was happening to it right in the middle of a rough field with all the daisies watching. She thought, arch Ada said (how truthfully, was another question), that a foal was dangling, with one black rubber leg free, out of Drongo's belly because she did not understand that Drongo was not a mare at all and had not got a pouch as the kangaroo had in an illustration she worshipped, but then her English nurse explained that Drongo was a very sick horse and everything fell into place.

"Fine," said Van, "that's certainly fascinating; but I was thinking of the first time you might have suspected I was also a sick pig or horse. I am recalling," he continued, "the round table in the round rosy glow and you kneeling next to me on a chair. I was perched on the chair's swelling arm and you were building a house of cards, and your every movement was magnified, of course, as in a trance, dream-slow but also tremendously vigilant, and I positively reveled in the girl odor of your bare arm and in that of your hair which now is murdered by some popular perfume. I date the event around June 10—a rainy evening less than a week after my first arrival at Ardis."

"I remember the cards," she said, "and the light and the noise of the rain, and your blue cashmere pullover—but nothing else, nothing odd or improper, *that* came later. Besides, only in French love stories *les messieurs hument* young ladies."

"Well, I did while you went on with your delicate work. Tactile magic. Infinite patience. Fingertips stalking gravity. Badly bitten nails, my sweet. Forgive these notes, I cannot really express the discomfort of bulky, sticky desire. You see I was hoping that when your castle toppled you would make a Russian splash gesture of surrender and sit down on my hand."

"It was not a castle. It was a Pompeian Villa with mosaics and paintings inside, because I used only court cards from Grandpa's old gambling packs. Did I sit down on your hot hard hand?"

"On my open palm, darling. A pucker of paradise. You remained still for a moment, fitting my cup. Then you rearranged your limbs and reknelt."

"Quick, quick, quick, collecting the flat shining cards again to build again, again slowly? We were abominably depraved, weren't we?"

"All bright kids are depraved. I see you do recollect—"

"Not that particular occasion, but the apple tree, and when you kissed my neck, *et tout le reste*. And then—*zdravstvuyte: apofeoz*, the Night of the Burning Barn!"

19

A sort of hoary riddle (*Les Sophismes de Sophie* by Mlle Stopchin in the Bibliothèque Vieux Rose series): did the Burning Barn come before the Cockloft or the Cockloft come first. Oh, first! We had long been kissing cousins when the fire started. In fact, I was getting some Château Baignet cold cream from Ladore for my poor chapped lips. And we both were roused in our separate rooms by her crying *au feu*! July 28? August 4?

Who cried? Stopchin cried? Larivière cried? Larivière? Answer! Crying that the barn *flambait*?

No, she was fast ablaze—I mean, asleep. I know, said Van, it was she, the hand-painted handmaid, who used your watercolors to touch up her eyes, or so Larivière said, who accused her and Blanche of fantastic sins.

Oh, of course! But not Marina's poor French—it was our little goose Blanche. Yes, she rushed down the corridor and lost a miniver-trimmed slipper on the grand staircase, like Ashette in the English version.

"And do you remember, Van, how warm the night was?"

"*Eshchyo bï!* (as if I did not!). That night because of the blink—"

That night because of the bothersome blink of remote sheet lightning through the black hearts of his sleeping-arbor, Van had abandoned his two tulip trees and gone to bed in his room. The tumult in the house and the maid's shriek interrupted a rare, brilliant, dramatic dream, whose subject he was unable to recollect later, although he still held it in a saved jewel box. As usual, he slept naked, and wavered now between pulling on a pair of shorts, or draping himself in his tartan lap robe. He chose the second course, rattled a matchbox, lit his bedside candle, and swept out of his room, ready to save Ada and all her larvae. The corridor was dark, somewhere the dachshund was barking ecstatically. Van gleaned from subsiding cries that the so-called "baronial barn," a huge beloved structure three miles away, was on fire. Fifty cows would have been without hay and Larivière without her midday coffee cream had it happened later in the season. Van felt slighted. They've all gone and left me behind, as old Fierce mumbles at the end of the *Cherry Orchard* (Marina was an adequate Mme Ranevski).

With the tartan toga around him, he accompanied his black double down the accessory spiral stairs leading to the library. Placing a bare knee on the shaggy divan under the window, Van drew back the heavy red curtains.

Uncle Dan, a cigar in his teeth, and kerchiefed Marina with Dack in her clutch deriding the watchdogs, were in the process of setting out between raised arms and swinging lanterns in the runabout—as red as a fire engine!—only to be overtaken at the crunching curve of the drive by three English footmen on horseback with three French maids *en croupe*. The entire domestic staff seemed to be taking off to enjoy the fire (an infrequent event in our damp windless region), using every contraption available or imaginable: telegas, teleseats, roadboats, tandem bicycles and even the clockwork luggage carts with which the stationmaster supplied the family in memory of Erasmus Veen, their inventor. Only the governess (as Ada, not Van, had by then discovered) slept on through everything, snoring with a wheeze and a harkle, in the room adjacent to the old nursery where little Lucette lay for a minute awake before running after her dream and jumping into the last furniture van.

Van, kneeling at the picture window, watched the inflamed eye of the cigar recede and vanish. That multiple departure . . . Take over.

That multiple departure really presented a marvelous sight against the pale star-dusted firmament of practically subtropical Ardis, tinted between the black trees with a distant flamingo flush at the spot where the Barn was Burning. To reach it one had to drive round a large reservoir which I could make out breaking into scaly light here and there every time some adventurous hostler or pantry boy crossed it on water skis or in a Rob Roy or by means of a raft—typical raft ripples like fire snakes in Japan; and one could now follow with an artist's eye the motorcar's lamps, fore and aft, progressing east along the AB bank of that rectangular lake, then turning sharply upon reaching its B corner, trailing away up the short side and creeping back west, in a dim and diminished aspect, to a middle point on the far margin where they swung north and disappeared.

As two last retainers, the cook and the night watchman, scurried across the lawn toward a horseless trap or break, that stood beckoning them with erected thills (or was it a rickshaw? Uncle Dan once had a Japanese valet), Van was delighted and shocked to distinguish, right there in the inky shrubbery, Ada in her long nightgown passing by with a lighted candle in one hand and a shoe in the other as if stealing after the belated ignicolists. It was only her reflection in the glass. She dropped the found shoe in a wastepaper basket and joined Van on the divan.

"Can one see anything, oh, can one see?" the dark-haired child kept repeating, and a hundred barns blazed in her amber-black eyes, as she beamed and peered in blissful curiosity. He relieved her of her candlestick, placing it near his own longer one on the window ledge. "You are naked, you are dreadfully indecent," she observed without looking and without any emphasis or reproof, whereupon he cloaked himself tighter, Ramses the Scotsman, as she knelt beside him. For a moment they both contemplated the romantic night piece framed in the window. He had started to stroke her, shivering, staring ahead, following with a blind man's hand the dip of her spine through the batiste.

"Look, gipsies," she whispered, pointing at three shadowy forms—two men, one with a ladder, and a child or dwarf—circumspectly moving across the gray lawn. They saw the candle-lit window and decamped, the smaller one walking *à reculons* as if taking pictures.

"I stayed home on purpose, because I hoped you would too—it was a contrived coincidence," she said, or said later she'd said—while he continued to fondle the flow of her hair, and to massage and rumple her nightdress, not daring yet to go under and up, daring, however, to mold her nates until, with a little hiss, she sat down on his hand and her heels, as the burning castle of cards collapsed. She turned to him and next moment he was kissing her bare shoulder, and pushing against her like that soldier behind in the queue.

First time I hear about him. I thought old Mr. Nymphobottomus had been my only predecessor.

Last spring. Trip to town. French theater matinée. Mademoiselle had mislaid the tickets. The poor fellow probably thought "Tartuffe" was a tart or a stripteaser.

Ce qui n'est pas si bête, au fond. Which was not so dumb after all. Okay. In that scene of the Burning Barn—

Yes?

Nothing. Go on.

Oh, Van, that night, that moment as we knelt side by side in the candlelight like Praying Children in a very bad picture, showing two pairs of soft-wrinkled, once arboreal-animal, soles—not to Grandma who gets the Xmas card but to the surprised and pleased Serpent, I remember wanting so badly to ask you for a bit of purely scientific information, because my sidelong glance—

Not now, it's not a nice sight right now and it will be worse in a moment (or words to that effect).

Van could not decide whether she really was utterly ignorant and as pure as the night sky—now drained of its fire color—or whether total experience advised her to indulge in a cold game. It did not really matter.

Wait, not right now, he replied in a half-muffled mutter.

She insisted: I wannask, I wannano—

He caressed and parted with his fleshy folds, *parties très charnues*, in the case of our passionate siblings, her lank loose, nearly lumbus-length (when she threw back her head as now) black silks as he tried to get at her bed-warm splenius. (It is not necessary, here or elsewhere, there was another similar passage, to blotch a reasonably pure style with vague anatomical terms that a psychiatrist remembers from his student days. In Ada's late hand.)

"I wannask," she repeated as he greedily reached his hot pale goal.

"I want to ask you," she said quite distinctly, but also quite beside herself because his ramping palm had now worked its way through at the armpit, and his thumb on a nipplet made her palate tingle: ringing for the maid in Georgian novels—inconceivable without the presence of elettricità—

(I protest. You cannot. It is banned even in Lithuanian and Latin. Ada's note.)

"—to ask you . . ."

"Ask," cried Van, "but don't spoil everything" (such as feeding upon you, writhing against you).

"Well, why," she asked (demanded, challenged, one flame crepitated, one cushion was on the floor), "why do you get so fat and hard there when you—"

"Get where? When I what?"

In order to explain, tactfully, tactually, she belly-danced against him, still more or less kneeling, her long hair getting in the way, one eye staring into his ear (their reciprocal positions had become rather muddled by then).

"Repeat!" he cried as if she were far away, a reflection in a dark window.

"You will show me at once," said Ada firmly.

He discarded his makeshift kilt, and her tone of voice changed immediately.

"Oh, dear," she said as one child to another. "It's all skinned and raw. Does it hurt? Does it hurt horribly?"

"Touch it quick," he implored.

"Van, poor Van," she went on in the narrow voice the sweet girl used when speaking to cats, caterpillars, pupating puppies, "yes, I'm sure, it smarts, would it help if I'd touch, are you sure?"

"You bet," said Van, "*on n'est pas bête à ce point*" ("there are limits to stupidity," colloquial and rude).

"Relief map," said the primrose prig, "the rivers of Africa." Her index traced the blue Nile down into its jungle and traveled up again. "Now what's this? The cap of the Red Bolete is not half as plushy. In fact" (positively chattering), "I'm reminded of geranium or rather pelargonium bloom."

"God, we all are," said Van.

"Oh, I like this texture, Van, I like it! Really I do!"

"Squeeze, you goose, can't you see I'm dying."

But our young botanist had not the faintest idea how to handle the thing properly—and Van, now in extremis, driving it roughly against the hem of her nightdress, could not help groaning as he dissolved in a puddle of pleasure.

She looked down in dismay.

"Not what you think," remarked Van calmly. "This is *not* number one. Actually it's as clean as grass sap. Well, now the Nile is settled stop Speke."

(I wonder, Van, *why* you are doing your best to transform our poetical and unique past into a dirty farce? Honestly, Van! Oh, I *am* honest, that's how it went. I wasn't sure of my ground, hence the sauciness and the simper. *Ah, parlez pour vous: I*, dear, can affirm that those famous fingertrips up your Africa and to the edge of the world came considerably later when I knew the itinerary by heart. Sorry, no—if people remembered the same they would not be different people. That's-how-it-went. But we are not "different"! Think and dream are the same in French. Think of the *douceur*, Van! Oh, I am thinking of it, of course, I am—it was all *douceur*, my child, my rhyme. That's better, said Ada.)

Please, take over.

Van stretched himself naked in the now motionless candlelight.

"Let us sleep here," he said. "They won't be back before dawn relights Uncle's cigar."

"My nightie is *trempée*," she whispered.

"Take it off, this plaid sleeps two."

"Don't look, Van."

"That's not fair," he said and helped her to slip it up and over her hair-shaking head. She was shaded with a mere touch of coal at the mystery point of her chalk-white body. A bad boil had left a pink scar between two ribs. He kissed it, and lay back on his clasped hands. She was inspecting from above his tanned body the ant caravan to the oasis of the navel; he was decidedly hirsute for so young a boy. Her young round breasts were just above his face. I denounce the philistine's postcoital cigarette both as a doctor and an artist. It is, however, true that Van was not unaware of a glass box of Turkish Traumatis on a console too far to be reached with an indolent stretch. The tall clock struck an anonymous quarter, and Ada was presently watching, cheek on fist, the impressive, though oddly morose, stirrings, steady clockwise launch, and ponderous upswing of virile revival.

But the shag of the couch was as tickly as the star-dusted sky. Before anything new happened, Ada went on all fours to rearrange the lap robe and cushions. Native girl imitating rabbit. He groped for and cupped her hot little slew from behind, then frantically scrambled into a boy's sandcastle-molding position; but she turned over, naively ready to embrace him the way Juliet is recommended to receive her Romeo. She was right. For the first time in their love story, the blessing, the genius of lyrical speech descended upon the rough lad, he murmured and moaned, kissing her face with voluble tenderness, crying out in three languages—the three greatest in all the world—pet words upon which a dictionary of secret diminutives was to be based and go through many revisions till the definitive edition of 1967. When he grew too loud, she shushed, shushingly breathing into his mouth, and now her four limbs were frankly around him as if she had been lovemaking for years in all our dreams—but impatient young passion (brimming like Van's overflowing bath while he is reworking this, a crotchety gray old wordman on the edge of a hotel bed) did not survive the first few blind thrusts; it burst at the lip of the orchid, and a bluebird uttered a warning warble, and the lights were now stealing back under a rugged dawn, the firefly signals were circumscribing the reservoir, the dots of the carriage lamps became stars, wheels rasped on the gravel, all the dogs returned well pleased with the night treat, the cook's niece Blanche jumped out of a pumpkin-hued police van in her stockinged feet (long, long after midnight, alas)—and our two naked children, grabbing lap robe and nightdress, and giving the couch a parting pat, pattered back with their candlesticks to their innocent bedrooms.

"And do you remember," said gray-moustached Van as he took a Cannabina cigarette from the bedside table and rattled a yellow-blue matchbox, "how reckless we were, and how Larivière stopped snoring but a moment later went on shaking the house, and how cold the iron steps were, and how disconcerted I was—by your—how shall I put it?—lack of restraint."

"Idiot," said Ada, from the wall side, without turning her head.

Summer 1960? Crowded hotel somewhere between Ex and Ardez?

Ought to begin dating every page of the manuscript: Should be kinder to my unknown dreamers.

20

Next morning, his nose still in the dreambag of a deep pillow contributed to his otherwise austere bed by sweet Blanche (with whom, by the parlor-game rules of sleep, he had been holding hands in a heartbreaking nightmare—or perhaps it was just her cheap perfume), the boy was at once aware of the happiness knocking to be let in. He deliberately endeavored to prolong the glow of its incognito by dwelling on the last vestiges of jasmine and tears in a silly dream; but the tiger of happiness fairly leaped into being.

That exhilaration of a newly acquired franchise! A shade of it he seemed to have kept in his sleep, in that last part of his recent dream in which he had told Blanche that he had learned to levitate and that his ability to tread air with magic

ease would allow him to break all records for the long jump
by strolling, as it were, a few inches above the ground for a
stretch of say thirty or forty feet (too great a length might be
suspicious) while the stands went wild, and Zambovsky of
Zambia stared, arms akimbo, in consternation and disbelief.

Tenderness rounds out true triumph, gentleness lubricates
genuine liberation: emotions that are not diagnostic of glory
or passion in dreams. One half of the fantastic joy Van was to
taste from now on (forever, he hoped) owed its force to the
certainty that he could lavish on Ada, openly and at leisure,
all the puerile petting that social shame, male selfishness, and
moral apprehension had prevented him from envisaging before.

On weekends, all three meals of the day were heralded by
three gongs, small, medium and big. The first now announced
breakfast in the dining room. Its vibration suscitated the
thought that in twenty-six steps Van would join his young
accomplice, whose delicate musk he still preserved in the hollow of his hand—and affected Van with a kind of radiant
amazement: Had it *really* happened? Are we *really* free?
Certain caged birds, say Chinese amateurs shaking with fat-
man mirth, knock themselves out against the bars (and lie
unconscious for a few minutes) every blessed morning, right
upon awakening, in an automatic, dream-continuing, dream-
lined dash—although they are, those iridescent prisoners,
quite perky and docile and talkative the rest of the time.

Van thrust his bare toe into a sneaker, retrieving the while
its mate from under the bed; he hurried down, past a pleased-
looking Prince Zemski and a grim Vincent Veen, Bishop of
Balticomore and Como.

But she was not down yet. In the bright dining room, full
of yellow flowers in drooping clusters of sunshine, Uncle Dan
was feeding. He wore suitable clothes for a suitably hot day
in the country—namely, a candy-striped suit over a mauve
flannel shirt and piqué waistcoat, with a blue-and-red club tie
and a safety-goldpinned very high soft collar (all his trim
stripes and colors were a little displaced, though, in the process of comic strip printing, because it was Sunday). He had
just finished his first buttered toast, with a dab of ye-old Orange Marmalade and was making turkey sounds as he rinsed

his dentures orally with a mouthful of coffee prior to swallowing it and the flavorous flotsam. Being, as I had reason to
believe, plucky, I could make myself suffer a direct view of the
man's pink face with its (rotating) red "tashy," but I was not
obliged (mused Van, in 1922, when he saw those *baguenaudier* flowers again) to stand his chinless profile with its curly
red sideburn. So Van considered, not without appetite, the
blue jugs of hot chocolate and baton-segments of bread prepared for the hungry children. Marina had her breakfast in
bed, the butler and Price ate in a recess of the pantry (a pleasing thought, somehow) and Mlle Larivière did not touch any
food till noon, being a doom-fearing "*midinette*" (the sect,
not the shop) and had actually made her father confessor join
her group.

"You could have taken us to see the fire, Uncle dear," remarked Van, pouring himself a cup of chocolate.

"Ada will tell you all about it," replied Uncle Dan, lovingly
buttering and marmalading another toast. "She greatly enjoyed the excursion."

"Oh, she went with you, did she?"

"Yes—in the black charabanc, with all the butlers. Jolly
good fun, rally" (pseudo-British pronunciation).

"But that must have been one of the scullery maids, not
Ada," remarked Van. "I didn't realize," he added, "we had
several here—I mean, butlers."

"Oh, I imagine so," said Uncle Dan vaguely. He repeated
the internal rinsing process, and with a slight cough put on
his spectacles, but no morning paper had come—and he took
them off again.

Suddenly Van heard her lovely dark voice on the staircase
saying in an upward direction, "*Je l'ai vu dans une des cor-
beilles de la bibliothèque*"—presumably in reference to some
geranium or violet or slipper orchid. There was a "bannister
pause," as photographers say, and after the maid's distant glad
cry had come from the library Ada's voice added: "*Je me de-
mande*, I wonder *qui l'a mis là*, who put it there." *Aussitôt
après* she entered the dining room.

She wore—though not in collusion with him—black shorts,
a white jersey and sneakers. Her hair was drawn back from
her big round brow and thickly pigtailed. The rose of a rash

under her lower lip glistened with glycerine through the patchily dabbed-on powder. She was too pale to be really pretty. She carried a book of verse. My eldest is rather plain but has nice hair, and my youngest is pretty, but foxy red, Marina used to say. Ungrateful age, ungrateful light, ungrateful artist, but *not* ungrateful lover. A veritable wave of adoration buoyed him up from the pit of the stomach to heaven. The thrill of seeing her, and knowing she knew, and knowing nobody else knew what they had so freely, and dirtily, and delightfully indulged in, less than six hours ago, turned out to be too much for our green lover despite his trying to trivialize it with the moral corrective of an opprobrious adverb. Fluffing badly a halfhearted "hello," not a habitual morning greeting (which, besides, she ignored), he bent over his breakfast while watching with a secret polyphemic organ her every movement. She slapped lightly Mr. Veen's bald head with her book in passing behind him and noisily moved the chair next to him on the other side from Van. Blinking, doll-lashing daintily, she poured herself a big cup of chocolate. Though it had been thoroughly sweetened, the child placed a lump of sugar on her spoon and eased it into the cup, relishing the way the hot brown liquid suffused and dissolved one crystal-grained crumbling corner and then the entire piece.

Meanwhile, Uncle Dan, in delayed action, chased an imaginary insect off his pate, looked up, looked around, and at last acknowledged the newcomer.

"Oh yes, Ada," he said, "Van here is anxious to know something. What were you doing, my dear, while he and I were taking care of the fire?"

Its reflection invaded Ada. Van had never seen a girl (as translucently white-skinned as she), or indeed anybody else, porcelain or peach, blush so substantially and habitually, and the habit distressed him as being much more improper than any act that might cause it. She stole a foolish glance at the somber boy and began saying something about having been fast ablaze in her bedroom.

"You were not," interrupted Van harshly, "you were with me looking at the blaze from the library window. Uncle Dan is all wet."

"*Ménagez vos américanismes*," said the latter—and then

opened his arms wide in paternal welcome as guileless Lucette trotted into the room with a child's pink, stiff-bagged butter-fly net in her little fist, like an oriflamme.

Van shook his head disapprovingly at Ada. She showed him the sharp petal of her tongue, and with a shock of self-indignation her lover felt himself flushing in his turn. So much for the franchise. He ringed his napkin and retired to the *mestechko* ("little place") off the front hall.

After she too had finished breakfasting, he waylaid her, gorged with sweet butter, on the landing. They had one moment to plan things, it was all, historically speaking, at the dawn of the novel which was still in the hands of parsonage ladies and French academicians, so such moments were precious. She stood scratching one raised knee. They agreed to go for a walk before lunch and find a secluded place. She had to finish a translation for Mlle Larivière. She showed him her draft. François Coppée? Yes.

> Their fall is gentle. The woodchopper
> Can tell, before they reach the mud,
> The oak tree by its leaf of copper,
> The maple by its leaf of blood.

"*Leur chute est lente,*" said Van, "*on peut les suivre du regard en reconnaissant*—that paraphrastic touch of 'chopper' and 'mud' is, of course, pure Lowden (minor poet and translator, 1815–1895). Betraying the first half of the stanza to save the second is rather like that Russian nobleman who chucked his coachman to the wolves, and then fell out of his sleigh."

"I think you are very cruel and stupid," said Ada. "This is not meant to be a work of art or a brilliant parody. It is the ransom exacted by a demented governess from a poor overworked schoolgirl. Wait for me in the Baguenaudier Bower," she added. "I'll be down in exactly sixty-three minutes."

Her hands were cold, her neck was hot; the postman's boy had rung the doorbell; Bout, a young footman, the butler's bastard, crossed the resonant flags of the hall.

On Sunday mornings the mail came late, because of the voluminous Sunday supplements of the papers from Balticomore, and Kaluga, and Luga, which Robin Sherwood, the old postman, in his bright green uniform, distributed on horseback throughout the somnolent countryside. As Van, humming his school song—the only tune he could ever carry—skipped down the terrace steps, he saw Robin on his old bay holding the livelier black stallion of his Sunday helper, a handsome English lad whom, it was rumored behind the rose hedges, the old man loved more vigorously than his office required.

Van reached the third lawn, and the bower, and carefully inspected the stage prepared for the scene, "like a provincial come an hour too early to the opera after jogging all day along harvest roads with poppies and bluets catching and twinkle-twining in the wheels of his buggy" (Floeberg's *Ursula*).

Blue butterflies nearly the size of Small Whites, and likewise of European origin, were flitting swiftly around the shrubs and settling on the drooping clusters of yellow flowers. In less complex circumstances, forty years hence, our lovers were to see again, with wonder and joy, the same insect and the same bladder-senna along a forest trail near Susten in the Valais. At the present moment he was looking forward to collecting what he would recollect later, and watched the big bold Blues as he sprawled on the turf, burning with the evoked vision of Ada's pale limbs in the variegated light of the bower, and then coldly telling himself that fact could never quite match fancy. When he returned from a swim in the broad and deep brook beyond the bosquet, with wet hair and tingling skin, Van got the rare treat of finding his foreglimpse of live ivory accurately reproduced, except that she had loosened her hair and changed into the curtal frock of sunbright cotton that he was so fond of and had so ardently yearned to soil in the so recent past.

He had resolved to deal first of all with her legs which he felt he had not feted enough the previous night; to sheathe them in kisses from the A of arched instep to the V of velvet; and this Van accomplished as soon as Ada and he got sufficiently deep in the larchwood which closed the park on the steep side of the rocky rise between Ardis and Ladore.

Neither could establish in retrospect, nor, indeed, persisted in trying to do so, how, when and where he actually "deflowered" her—a vulgarism Ada in Wonderland had happened to find glossed in *Phrody's Encyclopedia* as: "to break a virgin's vaginal membrane by manly or mechanical means," with the example: "The sweetness of his soul was deflowered (Jeremy Taylor)." Was it that night on the lap robe? Or that day in the larchwood? Or later in the shooting gallery, or in the attic, or on the roof, or on a secluded balcony, or in the bathroom, or (not very comfortably) on the Magic Carpet? We do not know and do not care.

(You kissed and nibbled, and poked, and prodded, and worried me there so much and so often that my virginity was lost in the shuffle; but I do recall definitely that by midsummer the machine which our forefathers called "sex" was working as smoothly as later, in 1888, etc., darling. Marginal note in red ink.)

21

Ada was denied the free use of the library. According to the latest list (printed May 1, 1884), it contained 14,841 items, and even that dry catalogue her governess preferred not to place in the child's hands—"*pour ne pas lui donner des idées.*" On her own shelves, to be sure, Ada had taxonomic works on botany and entomology as well as her schoolbooks and a few innocuous popular novels. But not only was she not supposed to browse in the library unsupervised, but every book she took out to read in bed or bower had to be checked by her mentor and charged "*en lecture*" with name and stamped date in the index-card files kept in a careful mess by Mlle Larivière and in a kind of desperate order (with the insertion of queries, calls of distress, and even imprecations, on bits of pink, red or purple paper) by a cousin of hers, Monsieur Philippe Verger, a diminutive old bachelor, morbidly silent and shy, who moused in, every other week, for a few hours of quiet work— so quiet, in fact, that one afternoon when a tallish library ladder suddenly went into an eerie backward slow-motion swoon with him high up on it embracing a windmill of volumes, he reached the floor, supine, with his ladder and books, in such a hush that guilty Ada, who had thought she was alone (pulling out and scanning the utterly unrewarding *Arabian Nights*), mistook his fall for the shadow of a door being stealthily opened by some soft-fleshed eunuch.

Her intimacy with her *cher, trop cher René*, as she sometimes called Van in gentle jest, changed the reading situation entirely—whatever decrees still remained pinned up in mid-air. Soon upon his arrival at Ardis, Van warned his former governess (who had reasons to believe in his threats) that if he were not permitted to remove from the library at any time, for any length of time, and without any trace of "*en lecture*," any volume, collected works, boxed pamphlets or incunabulum that he might fancy, he would have Miss Vertograd, his father's librarian, a completely servile and infinitely accommodative spinster of Verger's format and presumable date of publication, post to Ardis Hall trunkfuls of eighteenth-century libertines, German sexologists, and a whole circus of Shastras and Nefsawis in literal translation with apocryphal addenda. Puzzled Mlle Larivière would have consulted the Master of Ardis, but she never discussed with him anything serious since the day (in January, 1876) when he had made an unexpected (and rather halfhearted, really—let us be fair) pass at her. As to dear, frivolous Marina, she only remarked, when consulted, that at Van's age she would have poisoned her governess with anti-roach borax if forbidden to read, for example, Turgenev's *Smoke*. Thereafter, anything Ada wanted or might have wanted to want was placed by Van at her disposal in various safe nooks, and the only visible consequence of Verger's perplexities and despair was an increase in the scatter of a curious snow-white dust that he always left here and there, on the dark carpet, in this or that spot of plodding occupation—such a cruel curse on such a neat little man!

At a nice Christmas party for private librarians arranged under the auspices of the Braille Club in Raduga a couple of years earlier, empathic Miss Vertograd had noticed that she and giggling Verger, with whom she was in the act of sharing a quiet little cracker (tugged apart with no audible result— nor did the gold paper frilled at both ends yield any bonbon or breloque or other favor of fate), shared also a spectacular skin disease that had been portrayed recently by a famous American novelist in his *Chiron* and described in side-splitting style by a co-sufferer who wrote essays for a London weekly. Very delicately, Miss Vertograd would transmit through Van library slips to the rather unresponsive Frenchman with this or that concise suggestion: "Mercury!" or "*Höhensonne* works wonders." Mademoiselle, who was in the know, too, looked up "Psoriasis" in a one-volume medical encyclopedia, which her late mother had left her and which had not only helped her and her charges on various minor occasions but had suggested suitable illnesses for the characters in the stories she contributed to the *Québec Quarterly*. In the present case, the cure optimistically advised was to "take a warm bath at least twice a month and avoid spices"; this she typed out and passed on to her cousin in a Get-Well envelope. Finally, Ada showed Van a letter from Dr. Krolik on the same subject; it said (English version): "Crimson-blotched, silver-scaled, yellow-crusted wretches, the harmless psoriatics (who cannot communicate their skin trouble and are otherwise the healthiest of people—actually, their *bobo*'s protect them from bubas and buboes, as my teacher used to observe) were confused with lepers—yes, lepers—in the Middle Ages, when thousands if not millions of Vergers and Vertograds crackled and howled bound by enthusiasts to stakes erected in the public squares of Spain and other fire-loving countries." But this note they decided not to plant in the meek martyr's index under PS as they had first intended: lepidopterists are overeloquent on lepidosis.

Novels, poems, scientific and philosophical works wandered out unnoticed after the poor librarian gave his *démission éplorée* on the first of August, 1884. They crossed lawns and traveled along hedges somewhat in the manner of the objects carried away by the Invisible Man in Wells' delightful tale, and landed in Ada's lap wherever she and Van had their trysts. Both sought excitement in books as the best readers always do; both found in many renowned works pretentiousness, tedium and facile misinformation.

In a story by Chateaubriand about a pair of romantic siblings, Ada had not quite understood when she first read it at nine or ten the sentence "*les deux enfants pouvaient donc s'abandonner au plaisir sans aucune crainte.*" A bawdy critic in a collection of articles which she now could gleefully con-

sult (*Les muses s'amusent*) explained that the "*donc*" referred
both to the infertility of tender age and to the sterility of
tender consanguinity. Van said, however, that the writer and
the critic erred, and to illustrate his contention, drew his
sweetheart's attention to a chapter in the opus "Sex and
Lex" dealing with the effects on the community of a disastrous caprice of nature.

In those times, in this country "incestuous" meant not only
"unchaste"—the point regarded linguistics rather than legal-
istics—but also implied (in the phrase "incestuous cohabitation," and so forth) interference with the continuity of human
evolution. History had long replaced appeals to "divine law"
by common sense and popular science. With those considerations in mind, "incest" could be termed a crime only inas-
much as inbreeding might be criminal. But as Judge Bald
pointed out already during the Albino Riots of 1835, practically
all North American and Tartar agriculturists and animal farmers used inbreeding as a method of propagation that tended
to preserve, and stimulate, stabilize and even create anew favorable characters in a race or strain unless practiced too rigidly. If practiced rigidly incest led to various forms of decline,
to the production of cripples, weaklings, "muted mutates"
and, finally, to hopeless sterility. Now *that* smacked of
"crime," and since nobody could be supposed to control judiciously orgies of indiscriminate inbreeding (somewhere in
Tartary fifty generations of ever woolier and woolier sheep had
recently ended abruptly in one hairless, five-legged, impotent
little lamb—and the beheading of a number of farmers failed
to resurrect the fat strain), it was perhaps better to ban "incestuous cohabitation" altogether. Judge Bald and his follow-
ers disagreed, perceiving in "the deliberate suppression of a
possible benefit for the sake of avoiding a probable evil" the
infringement of one of humanity's main rights—that of enjoying the liberty of its evolution, a liberty no other creature
had ever known. Unfortunately after the rumored misadven-
ture of the Volga herds and herdsmen a much better documented *fait divers* happened in the U.S.A. at the height of
the controversy. An American, a certain Ivan Ivanov of Yukonsk, described as an "habitually intoxicated laborer" ("a
good definition," said Ada lightly, "of the true artist"), man-

aged somehow to impregnate—in his sleep, it was claimed by him and his huge family—his five-year-old great-granddaughter, Maria Ivanov, and, then, five years later, also got Maria's daughter, Daria, with child, in another fit of somnolence. Photographs of Maria, a ten-year-old granny with little Daria and baby Varia crawling around her, appeared in all the newspapers, and all kinds of amusing puzzles were provided by the genealogical farce that the relationships between the numerous living—and not always clean-living—members of the Ivanov clan had become in angry Yukonsk. Before the sixty-year-old somnambulist could go on procreating, he was clapped into a monastery for fifteen years as required by an ancient Russian law. Upon his release he proposed to make honorable amends by marrying Daria, now a buxom lass with problems of her own. Journalists made a lot of the wedding, and the shower of gifts from well-wishers (old ladies in New England, a progressive poet in residence at Tennesee Waltz College, an entire Mexican high school, et cetera), and on the same day Gamaliel (then a stout young senator) thumped a conference table with such force that he hurt his fist and demanded a retrial and capital punishment. It was, of course, only a temperamental gesture; but the Ivanov affair cast a long shadow upon the little matter of "favorable inbreeding." By mid-century not only first cousins but uncles and grandnieces were forbidden to intermarry; and in some fertile parts of Estoty the izba windows of large peasant families in which up to a dozen people of different size and sex slept on one *blin*-like mattress were ordered to be kept uncurtained at night for the convenience of petrol-torch-flashing patrols—"Peeping Pats," as the anti-Irish tabloids called them.

Another hearty laugh shook Van when he unearthed for entomologically-minded Ada the following passage in a reliable *History of Mating Habits*. "Some of the perils and ridicule which attend the missionary position adopted for mating purposes by our puritanical intelligentsia and so justly derided by the 'primitive' but healthy-minded natives of the Begouri Islands are pointed out by a prominent French orientalist [thick footnote, skipped here] who describes the mating habits of the fly *Serromyia amorata* Poupart. Copulation takes place with both ventral surfaces pressed together and the mouths touching. When the last throb (*frisson*) of intercourse is terminated the female sucks out the male's body content through the mouth of her impassioned partner. One supposes (see Pesson *et al.*) [another copious footnote] that the titbits, such as the juicy leg of a bug enveloped in a webby substance, or even a mere token (the frivolous dead end or subtle beginning of an evolutionary process—*qui le sait!*) such as a petal carefully wrapped up and tied up with a frond of red fern, which certain male flies (but apparently not the *femorata* and *amorata* morons) bring to the female before mating, represent a prudent guarantee against the misplaced voracity of the young lady."

Still more amusing was the "message" of a Canadian social worker, Mme de Réan-Fichini, who published her treatise, *On Contraceptive Devices*, in Kapuskan patois (to spare the blushes of Estotians and United Statians; while instructing hardier fellow-workers in her special field). "*Sole sura metoda*," she wrote, "*por decevor natura, est por un strong-guy de contino-contino-contino jusque le plesir brimz; et lors, a lultima instanta, svitchera a l'altra gropa* [groove]; *ma perquoi una femme ardora andor ponderosa ne se retorna kvik enof, la transita e facilitata per positio torovago*"; and that term an appended glossary explained in blunt English as "the posture generally adopted in rural communities by all classes, beginning by the country gentry and ending with the lowliest farm animals throughout the United Americas from Patagony to Gasp." *Ergo*, concluded Van, our missionary goes up in smoke.

"Your vulgarity knows no bounds," said Ada.

"Well, I prefer to burn than to be slurped up alive by the Cheramie—or whatever you call her—and have my widow lay a lot of tiny green eggs on top of it!"

Paradoxically, "scient" Ada was bored by big learned works with woodcuts of organs, pictures of dismal medieval whorehouses, and photographs of this or that little Caesar in the process of being ripped out of the uterus as performed by butchers and masked surgeons in ancient and modern times; whereas Van, who disliked "natural history" and fanatically denounced the existence of physical pain in all worlds, was infinitely fascinated by descriptions and depictions of harrowed human flesh. Otherwise, in more flowery fields, their tastes and titters proved to be much the same. They liked Rabelais and Casanova; they loathed *le sieur* Sade and Herr Masoch and Heinrich Müller. English and French pornographic poetry, though now and then witty and instructive, sickened them in the long run, and its tendency, especially in France before the invasion, of having monks and nuns perform sexual feats seemed to them as incomprehensible as it was depressing.

The collection of Uncle Dan's Oriental Erotica prints turned out to be artistically second-rate and inept calisthenically. In the most hilarious, and expensive, picture, a Mongolian woman with an inane oval face surmounted by a hideous hair-do was shown communicating sexually with six rather plump, blank-faced gymnasts in what looked like a display window jammed with screens, potted plants, silks, paper fans and crockery. Three of the males, contorted in attitudes of intricate discomfort, were using simultaneously three of the harlot's main orifices; two older clients were treated by her manually; and the sixth, a dwarf, had to be contented with her deformed foot. Six other voluptuaries were sodomizing her immediate partners, and one more had got stuck in her armpit. Uncle Dan, having patiently disentangled all those limbs and belly folds directly or indirectly connected with the absolutely calm lady (still retaining somehow parts of her robes), had penciled a note that gave the price of the picture and identified it as: "Geisha with 13 lovers." Van located, however, a fifteenth navel thrown in by the generous artist but impossible to account for anatomically.

That library had provided a raised stage for the unforgettable scene of the Burning Barn; it had thrown open its glazed doors; it had promised a long idyll of bibliolatry; it might have become a chapter in one of the old novels on its own shelves; a touch of parody gave its theme the comic relief of life.

22

My sister, do you still recall
The blue Ladore and Ardis Hall?

Don't you remember any more
That castle bathed by the Ladore?

*Ma soeur, te souvient-il encore
Du château que baignait la Dore?*

My sister, do you still recall
The Ladore-washed old castle wall?

*Sestra moya, tï pomnish' goru,
I dub vïsokiy, i Ladoru?*

My sister, you remember still
The spreading oak tree and my hill?

*Oh! qui me rendra mon Aline
Et le grand chêne et ma colline?*

Oh, who will give me back my Jill
And the big oak tree and my hill?

*Oh! qui me rendra, mon Adèle,
Et ma montagne et l'hirondelle?*

*Oh! qui me rendra ma Lucile,
La Dore et l'hirondelle agile?*

Oh, who will render in our tongue
The tender things he loved and sung?

They went boating and swimming in Ladore, they followed
the bends of its adored river, they tried to find more rhymes
to it, they walked up the hill to the black ruins of Bryant's
Castle, with the swifts still flying around its tower. They traveled to Kaluga and drank the Kaluga Waters, and saw the
family dentist. Van, flipping through a magazine, heard Ada
scream and say "*chort*" (devil) in the next room, which he
had never heard her do before. They had tea at a neighbor's,
Countess de Prey—who tried to sell them, unsuccessfully, a
lame horse. They visited the fair at Ardisville where they es-

pecially admired the Chinese tumblers, a German clown, and a sword-swallowing hefty Circassian Princess who started with a fruit knife, went on to a bejeweled dagger and finally engulfed, string and all, a tremendous salami sausage.

They made love—mostly in glens and gullies.

To the average physiologist, the energy of those two youngsters might have seemed abnormal. Their craving for each other grew unbearable if within a few hours it was not satisfied several times, in sun or shade, on roof or in cellar, anywhere. Despite uncommon resources of ardor, young Van could hardly keep pace with his pale little *amorette* (local French slang). Their immoderate exploitation of physical joy amounted to madness and would have curtailed their young lives had not summer, which had appeared in prospect as a boundless flow of green glory and freedom, begun to hint hazily at possible failings and fadings, at the fatigue of its fugue—the last resort of nature, felicitous alliterations (when flowers and flies mime one another), the coming of a first pause in late August, a first silence in early September. The orchards and vineyards were particularly picturesque that year; and Ben Wright was fired after letting winds go free while driving Marina and Mlle Larivière home from the *Vendange* Festival at Brantôme near Ladore.

Which reminds us. Catalogued in the Ardis library under "Exot Lubr" was a sumptuous tome (known to Van through Miss Vertograd's kind offices) entitled "Forbidden Masterpieces: a hundred paintings representing a private part of Nat. Gal. (Sp. Sct.), printed for H.R.M. King Victor." This was (beautifully photographed in color) the kind of voluptuous and tender stuff that Italian masters allowed themselves to produce in between too many pious Resurrections during a too long and lusty Renaissance. The volume itself had been either lost or stolen or lay concealed in the attic among Uncle Ivan's effects, some of them pretty bizarre. Van could not recollect whose picture it was that he had in mind, but thought it might have been attributed to Michelangelo da Caravaggio in his youth. It was an oil on unframed canvas depicting two misbehaving nudes, boy and girl, in an ivied or vined grotto or near a small waterfall overhung with bronze-tinted and dark emerald leaves, and great bunches of translucent grapes, the shadows and limpid reflections of fruit and foliage blending magically with veined flesh.

Anyway (this may be purely a stylistic transition), he felt himself transferred into that forbidden masterpiece, one afternoon, when everybody had gone to Brantôme, and Ada and he were sunbathing on the brink of the Cascade in the larch plantation of Ardis Park, and his nymphet had bent over him and his detailed desire. Her long straight hair that seemed of a uniform bluish-black in the shade now revealed, in the gem-like sun, strains of deep auburn alternating with dark amber in lanky strands which clothed her hollowed cheek or were gracefully cleft by her raised ivory shoulder. The texture, gloss and odor of those brown silks had once inflamed his senses at the very beginning of that fatal summer, and continued to act upon him, strongly and poignantly, long after his young excitement had found in her other sources of incurable bliss. At ninety, Van remembered his first fall from a horse with scarcely less breathlessness of thought than that first time she had bent over him and he had possessed her hair. It tickled his legs, it crept into his crotch, it spread all over his palpitating belly. Through it the student of art could see the summit of the *trompe-l'oeil* school, monumental, multicolored, jutting out of a dark background, molded in profile by a concentration of caravagesque light. She fondled him; she entwined him: thus a tendril climber coils round a column, swathing it tighter and tighter, biting into its neck ever sweeter, then dissolving strength in deep crimson softness. There was a crescent eaten out of a vine leaf by a sphingid larva. There was a well-known microlepidopterist who, having run out of Latin and Greek names, created such nomenclatorial items as Marykisme, Adakisme, Ohkisme. She did. Whose brush was it now? A titillant Titian? A drunken Palma Vecchio? No, she was anything but a Venetian blonde. Dosso Dossi, perhaps? Faun Exhausted by Nymph? Swooning Satyr? Doesn't that new-filled molar hurt your own tongue? It bruised me. I'm joking, my circus Circassian.

A moment later the Dutch took over: Girl stepping into a pool under the little cascade to wash her tresses, and accompanying the immemorial gesture of wringing them out by making wringing-out mouths—immemorial too.

My sister, do you recollect
That turret, "Of the Moor" yclept?

My sister, do you still recall
The castle, the Ladore, and all?

23

All went well until Mlle Larivière decided to stay in bed for
five days: she had sprained her back on a merry-go-round at
the Vintage Fair, which, besides, she needed as the setting for
a story she had begun (about a town mayor's strangling a
small girl called Rockette), and knew by experience that nothing kept up the itch of inspiration so well as *la chaleur du lit*.
During that period, the second upstairs maid, French, whose
moods and looks did not match the sweet temper and limpid
grace of Blanche, was supposed to look after Lucette, and
Lucette did her best to avoid the lazy servant's surveillance in
favor of her cousin's and sister's company. The ominous
words: "Well, if Master Van lets you come," or "Yes, I'm
sure Miss Ada won't mind your mushroom-picking with her,"
became something of a knell in regard to love's freedom.

While the comfortably resting lady was describing the bank
of a brook where little Rockette liked to frolic, Ada sat reading
on a similar bank, wistfully glancing from time to time at an
inviting clump of evergreens (that had frequently sheltered
our lovers) and at brown-torsoed, barefooted Van, in turned-
up dungarees, who was searching for his wristwatch that he
thought he had dropped among the forget-me-nots (but
which Ada, he forgot, was wearing). Lucette had abandoned
her skipping rope to squat on the brink of the brook and float
a fetus-sized rubber doll. Every now and then she squeezed
out of it a fascinating squirt of water through a little hole that
Ada had had the bad taste to perforate for her in the slippery
orange-red toy. With the sudden impatience of inanimate
things, the doll managed to get swept away by the current.
Van shed his pants under a willow and retrieved the fugitive.
Ada, after considering the situation for a moment, shut her

book and said to Lucette, whom usually it was not hard to enchant, that she, Ada, felt she was quickly turning into a dragon, that the scales had begun to turn green, that now she *was* a dragon and that Lucette must be tied to a tree with the skipping rope so that Van might save her just in time. For some reason, Lucette balked at the notion but physical strength prevailed. Van and Ada left the angry captive firmly attached to a willow trunk, and, "prancing" to feign swift escape and pursuit, disappeared for a few precious minutes in the dark grove of conifers. Writhing Lucette had somehow torn off one of the red knobbed grips of the rope and seemed to have almost disentangled herself when dragon and knight, prancing, returned.

She complained to her governess who, completely misconstruing the whole matter (which could also be said of her new composition), summoned Van and from her screened bed, through a reek of embrocation and sweat, told him to refrain from turning Lucette's head by making of her a fairy-tale damsel in distress.

On the following day Ada informed her mother that Lucette badly needed a bath and that she would give it to her, whether her governess liked it or not. "*Horosho*," said Marina (while getting ready to receive a neighbor and his protégé, a young actor, in her best Dame Marina style), "but the temperature should be kept at exactly twenty-eight (as it had been since the eighteenth century), and don't let her stay in it longer than ten or twelve minutes."

"Beautiful idea," said Van as he helped Ada to heat the tank, fill the old battered bath and warm a couple of towels.

Despite her being only in her ninth year and rather underdeveloped, Lucette had not escaped the delusive pubescence of red-haired little girls. Her armpits showed a slight stipple of bright floss and her chub was dusted with copper.

The liquid prison was now ready and an alarm clock given a full quarter of an hour to live.

"Let her soak first, you'll soap her afterwards," said Van feverishly.

"Yes, yes, yes," cried Ada.

"I'm Van," said Lucette, standing in the tub with the mulberry soap between her legs and protruding her shiny tummy.

"You'll turn into a boy if you do that," said Ada sternly, "and that won't be very amusing."

Warily, the little girl started to sink her buttocks in the water.

"Too hot," she said, "much too horribly hot!"

"It'll cool," said Ada, "plop down and relax. Here's your doll."

"Come on, Ada, for goodness' sake, let her soak," repeated Van.

"And remember," said Ada, "don't you dare get out of this nice warm water until the bell rings or you'll die, because that's what Krolik said. I'll be back to lather you, but don't call me; we have to count the linen and sort out Van's hankies."

The two elder children, having locked the door of the L-shaped bathroom from the inside, now retired to the seclusion of its lateral part, in a corner between a chest of drawers and an old unused mangle, which the sea-green eye of the bathroom looking-glass could not reach; but barely had they finished their violent and uncomfortable exertions in that hidden nook, with an empty medicine bottle idiotically beating time on a shelf, when Lucette was already calling resonantly from the tub and the maid knocking on the door: Mlle Larivière wanted some hot water too.

They tried all sorts of other tricks.

Once, for example, when Lucette had made of herself a particular nuisance, her nose running, her hand clutching at Van's all the time, her whimpering attachment to his company turning into a veritable obsession, Van mustered all his persuasive skill, charm, eloquence, and said with conspiratory undertones: "Look, my dear. This brown book is one of my most treasured possessions. I had a special pocket made for it in my school jacket. Numberless fights have been fought over it with wicked boys who wanted to steal it. What we have here" (turning the pages reverently) "is no less than a collection of the most beautiful and famous short poems in the English language. This tiny one, for example, was composed in tears forty years ago by the Poet Laureate Robert Brown, the old gentleman whom my father once pointed out to me up in the air on a cliff under a cypress, looking down on the

foaming turquoise surf near Nice, an unforgettable sight for
all concerned. It is called 'Peter and Margaret.' Now you have,
say" (turning to Ada in solemn consultation), "forty minutes"
("Give her a full hour, she can't even memorize *Mironton,
mirontaine*")—"all right, a full hour to learn these eight lines
by heart. You and I" (whispering) "are going to prove to your
nasty arrogant sister that stupid little Lucette can do anything.
If" (lightly brushing her bobbed hair with his lips), "if, my
sweet, you can recite it and confound Ada by not making one
single slip—you must be careful about the 'here-there' and
the 'this-that,' and every other detail—*if* you can do it then I
shall give you this valuable book for keeps." ("Let her try the
one about finding a feather and seeing Peacock plain," said
Ada drily—"it's a bit harder.") "No, no, she and I have already chosen that little ballad. All right. Now go in here"
(opening a door) "and don't come out until I call you. Otherwise, you'll forfeit the reward, and will regret the loss all
your life."

"Oh, Van, how lovely of you," said Lucette, slowly entering her room, with her bemused eyes scanning the fascinating
flyleaf, his name on it, his bold flourish, and his own wonderful drawings in ink—a black aster (evolved from a blot), a
doric column (disguising a more ribald design), a delicate leafless tree (as seen from a classroom window), and several pro-
files of boys (Cheshcat, Zogdog, Fancytart, and Ada-like Van
himself).

Van hastened to join Ada in the attic. At that moment he
felt quite proud of his stratagem. He was to recall it with a
fatidic shiver seventeen years later when Lucette, in her last
note to him, mailed from Paris to his Kingston address on
June 2, 1901, "just in case," wrote:

"I kept for years—it must be in my Ardis nursery—the anthology you once gave me; and the little poem you wanted
me to learn by heart is still word-perfect in a safe place of my
jumbled mind, with the packers trampling on my things, and
upsetting crates, and voices calling: time to go, time to go.
Find it in Brown and praise me again for my eight-year-old
intelligence as you and happy Ada did that distant day, that
day somewhere tinkling on its shelf like an empty little bottle.
Now read on:

"Here, said the guide, was the field,
There, he said, was the wood.
This is where Peter kneeled,
That's where the Princess stood.

No, the visitor said,
You are the ghost, old guide.
Oats and oaks may be dead,
But *she* is by my side."

24

Van regretted that because Lettrocalamity (Vanvitelli's old joke!) was banned all over the world, its very name having become a "dirty word" among upper-upper-class families (in the British and Brazilian sense) to which the Veens and Durmanovs happened to belong, and had been replaced by elaborate surrogates only in those very important "utilities"—telephones, motors—what else?—well a number of gadgets for which plain folks hanker with lolling tongues, breathing faster than gundogs (for it's quite a long sentence), such trifles as tape recorders, the favorite toys of his and Ada's grandsires (Prince Zemski had one for every bed of his harem of schoolgirls) were not manufactured any more, except in Tartary where they had evolved "*minirechi*" ("talking minarets") of a secret make. Had our erudite lovers been allowed by common propriety and common law to knock into working order the mysterious box they had once discovered in their magic attic, they might have recorded (so as to replay, eight decades later) Giorgio Vanvitelli's arias as well as Van Veen's conversations with his sweetheart. Here, for example, is what they might have heard today—with amusement, embarrassment, sorrow, wonder.

(Narrator: on that summer day soon after they had entered the kissing phase of their much too premature and in many ways fatal romance, Van and Ada were on their way to the Gun Pavilion *alias* Shooting Gallery, where they had located, on its upper stage, a tiny, Oriental-style room with bleary glass cases that had once lodged pistols and daggers—judging by the shape of dark imprints on the faded velvet—a pretty and melancholy recess, rather musty, with a cushioned window seat and a stuffed Parluggian Owl on a side shelf, next to an empty beer bottle left by some dead old gardener, the year of the obsolete brand being 1842.)

"Don't jingle them," she said, "we are watched by Lucette, whom I'll strangle some day."

They walked through a grove and past a grotto.

Ada said: "Officially we are maternal cousins, and cousins can marry by special decree, *if* they promise to sterilize their first five children. But, moreover, the father-in-law of my mother was the brother of your grandfather. Right?"

"That's what I'm told," said Van serenely.

"Not sufficiently distant," she mused, "or is it?"

"Far enough, fair enough."

"Funny—I saw that verse in small violet letters before you put it into orange ones—just one second before you spoke. Spoke, smoke. Like the puff preceding a distant cannon shot.

"Physically," she continued, "we are more like twins than cousins, and twins or even siblings can't marry, of course, or will be jailed and 'altered,' if they persevere."

"Unless," said Van, "they are specially decreed cousins."

(Van was already unlocking the door—the green door against which they were to bang so often with boneless fists in their later separate dreams.)

Another time, on a bicycle ride (with several pauses) along wood trails and country roads, soon after the night of the Burning Barn, but before they had come across the herbarium in the attic, and found confirmation of something both had forefelt in an obscure, amusing, bodily rather than moral way, Van casually mentioned he was born in Switzerland and had been abroad twice in his boyhood. She had been once, she said. Most summers she spent at Ardis; most winters in their Kaluga town home—two upper stories in the former Zemski *chertog* (palazzo).

In 1880, Van, aged ten, had traveled in silver trains with showerbaths, accompanied by his father, his father's beautiful secretary, the secretary's eighteen-year-old white-gloved sister (with a bit part as Van's English governess and milkmaid), and his chaste, angelic Russian tutor, Andrey Andreevich Aksakov ("AAA"), to gay resorts in Louisiana and Nevada. AAA explained, he remembered, to a Negro lad with whom Van had scrapped, that Pushkin and Dumas had African blood, upon which the lad showed AAA his tongue, a new interesting trick which Van emulated at the earliest occasion and was slapped by the younger of the Misses Fortune, put it back in your face, sir, she said. He also recalled hearing a cummerbunded Dutchman in the hotel hall telling another that Van's father, who had just passed whistling one of his three tunes, was a famous "camler" (camel driver—shamoes having been imported recently? No, "gambler").

Before his boarding-school days started, his father's pretty house, in Florentine style, between two vacant lots (5 Park Lane in Manhattan), had been Van's winter home (two giant guards were soon to rise on both sides of it, ready to frog-march it away), unless they journeyed abroad. Summers in Radugalet, the "other Ardis," were so much colder and duller than those here in *this*, Ada's, Ardis. Once he even spent both winter *and* summer there; it must have been in 1878.

Of course, of course, because that was the first time, Ada recalled, she had glimpsed him. In his little white sailor suit and blue sailor cap. (*Un régulier angelochek*, commented Van in the Raduga jargon.) He was eight, she was six. Uncle Dan had unexpectedly expressed the desire to revisit the old estate. At the last moment Marina had said she'd come too, despite Dan's protests, and had lifted little Ada, hopla, with her hoop, into the calèche. They took, she imagined, the train from La-doga to Raduga, for she remembered the way the station man with the whistle around his neck went along the platform, past the coaches of the stopped local, banging shut door after door, all six doors of every carriage, each of which consisted of six one-window carrosses of pumpkin origin, fused to-gether. It was, Van suggested, a "tower in the mist" (as she called any good recollection), and then a conductor walked on the running board of every coach with the train also running and opened doors all over again to give, punch, collect tickets, and lick his thumb, and change money, a hell of a job, but another "mauve tower." Did they hire a motor landaulet to Radugalet? Ten miles, she guessed. Ten versts, said Van.

She stood corrected. He was out, he imagined, *na progulke* (promenading) in the gloomy firwood with Aksakov, his tutor, and Bagrov's grandson, a neighbor's boy, whom he teased and pinched and made horrible fun of, a nice quiet little fellow who quietly massacred moles and anything else with fur on, probably pathological. However, when they arrived, it became instantly clear that Demon had not expected ladies. He was on the terrace drinking goldwine (sweet whisky) with an orphan he had adopted, he said, a lovely Irish wild rose in whom Marina at once recognized an impudent scullery maid who had briefly worked at Ardis Hall, and had been ravished by an unknown gentleman—who was now well-known. In those days Uncle Dan wore a monocle in gay-dog copy of his cousin, and this he screwed in to view Rose, whom perhaps he had also been promised (here Van interrupted his interlocutor telling her to mind her vocabulary). The party was a disaster. The orphan languidly took off her pearl earrings for Marina's appraisal. Grandpa Bagrov hobbled in from a nap in the boudoir and mistook Marina for a *grande cocotte* as the enraged lady conjectured later when she had a chance to get at poor Dan. Instead of staying for the night, Marina stalked off and called Ada who, having been told to "play in the garden," was mumbling and numbering in raw-flesh red the white trunks of a row of young birches with Rose's purloined lipstick in the preamble to a game she now could not remember—what a pity, said Van—when her mother swept her back straight to Ardis in the same taxi leaving Dan—to his devices and vices, inserted Van—and arriving home at sunrise. But, added Ada, just before being whisked away and deprived of her crayon (tossed out by Marina *k chertyam sobach'im*, to hell's hounds—and it did remind one of Rose's terrier that had kept trying to hug Dan's leg) the charming glimpse was granted her of tiny Van, with another sweet boy, and blond-bearded, white-bloused Aksakov, walking up to the house, and, oh yes, she had forgotten her hoop—no, it was still in the taxi. But, personally, Van had not the slightest recollection of that visit or indeed of that particular summer, because his father's life, anyway, was a rose garden all the time, and he had been caressed by ungloved lovely hands more than once himself, which did not interest Ada.

Now what about 1881, when the girls, aged eight-nine and five, respectively, had been taken to the Riviera, to Switzerland, to the Italian lakes, with Marina's friend, the theatrical big shot, Gran D. du Mont (the "D" also stood for Duke, his mother's maiden name, *des hobereaux irlandais, quoi*), traveling discreetly on the next Mediterranean Express or next Simplon or next Orient, or whatever other *train de luxe* carried the three Veens, an English governess, a Russian nurse and two maids, while a semi-divorced Dan went to some place in equatorial Africa to photograph tigers (which he was surprised not to see) and other notorious wild animals, trained to cross the motorist's path, as well as some plump black girls in a traveling-agent's gracious home in the wilds of Mozambique. She could recollect, of course, when she and her sister played "note-comparing," much better than Lucette such things as itineraries, spectacular flora, fashions, the covered galleries with all sorts of shops, a handsome suntanned man with a black mustache who kept staring at her from his corner in the restaurant of Geneva's Manhattan Palace; but Lucette, though so much younger, remembered heaps of bagatelles, little "turrets" and little "barrels," *biryul'ki proshlago*. She was, *cette Lucette*, like the girl in *Ah, cette Line* (a popular novel), "a macédoine of intuition, stupidity, naïveté and cunning." By the way, she had confessed, Ada had *made* her confess, that it was, as Van had suspected, the other way round—that when they returned to the damsel in distress, she was in all haste, not freeing herself, but actually trying to tie herself up again after breaking loose and spying on them through the larches. "Good Lord," said Van, "that explains the angle of the soap!" Oh, what did it matter, who cared, Ada only hoped the poor little thing would be as happy at Ada's age as Ada was now, my love, my love, my love, my love. Van hoped the bicycles parked in the bushes did not show their sparkling metal through the leaves to some passenger on the forest road.

After that, they tried to settle whether their ways had merged somewhere or run closely parallel for a bit that year in Europe. In the spring of 1881, Van, aged eleven, spent a few months with his Russian tutor and English valet at his grandmother's villa near Nice, while Demon was having a much better time in Cuba than Dan was at Mocuba. In June,

Van was taken to Florence, and Rome, and Capri, where his father turned up for a brief spell. They parted again, Demon sailing back to America, and Van with his tutor going first to Gardone on Lake Garda, where Aksakov reverently pointed out Goethe's and d'Annunzio's marble footprints, and then staying for a while in autumn at a hotel on a mountain slope above Leman Lake (where Karamzin and Count Tolstoy had roamed). Did Marina suspect that Van was somewhere in the same general area as she throughout 1881? Probably no. Both girls had scarlet fever in Cannes, while Marina was in Spain with her Grandee. After carefully matching memories, Van and Ada concluded that it was not impossible that somewhere along a winding Riviera road they passed each other in rented victorias that both remembered were green, with green-harnessed horses, or perhaps in two different trains, going perhaps the same way, the little girl at the window of one sleeping car looking at the brown sleeper of a parallel train which gradually diverged toward sparkling stretches of sea that the little boy could see on the other side of the tracks. The contingency was too mild to be romantic, nor did the possibility of their having walked or run past each other on the quay of a Swiss town afford any concrete thrill. But as Van casually directed the searchlight of backthought into that maze of the past where the mirror-lined narrow paths not only took different turns, but used different levels (as a mule-drawn cart passes under the arch of a viaduct along which a motor skims by), he found himself tackling, in still vague and idle fashion, the science that was to obsess his mature years—problems of space and time, space versus time, time-twisted space, space as time, time as space—and space breaking away from time, in the final tragic triumph of human cogitation: I am because I die.

"But *this*," exclaimed Ada, "is certain, this is reality, this is pure fact—this forest, this moss, your hand, the ladybird on my leg, this cannot be taken away, can it? (it will, it was). *This* has all come together *here*, no matter how the paths twisted, and fooled each other, and got fouled up: they inevitably met here!"

"We must now find our bicycles," said Van, "we are lost 'in another part of the forest.' "

"Oh, let's not return yet," she cried, "oh, wait."

"But I want to make sure of our whereabouts and when-abouts," said Van. "It is a philosophical need."

The day was darkening; a beaming vestige of sunlight lingered in a western strip of the overcast sky: we have all seen the person who after gaily greeting a friend crosses the street with that smile still fresh on his face—to be eclipsed by the stare of the stranger who might have missed the cause and mistaken the effect for the bright leer of madness. Having worked out that metaphor, Van and Ada decided it was really time to go home. As they rode through Gamlet, the sight of a Russian *traktir* gave such a prod to their hunger that they dismounted and entered the dim little tavern. A coachman drinking tea from the saucer, holding it up to his loud lips in his large claw, came straight from a pretzel-string of old novels. There was nobody else in the steamy hole save a kerchiefed woman pleading with (*ugovarivayushchaya*) a leg-dangling lad in a red shirt to get on with his fish soup. She proved to be the *traktir*-keeper and rose, "wiping her hands on her apron," to bring Ada (whom she recognized at once) and Van (whom she supposed, not incorrectly, to be the little chatelaine's "young man") some small Russian-type "hamburgers" called *bitochki*. Each devoured half a dozen of them—then they retrieved their bikes from under the jasmins to pedal on. They had to light their carbide lamps. They made a last pause before reaching the darkness of Ardis Park.

By a kind of lyrical coincidence they found Marina and Mlle Larivière having evening tea in the seldom-used Russian-style glassed-in veranda. The novelist, who was now quite restored, but still in flowery négligé, had just finished reading her new story in its first fair copy (to be typed on the morrow) to Tokay-sipping Marina, who had *le vin triste* and was much affected by the suicide of the gentleman "*au cou rouge et puissant de veuf encore plein de sève*" who, frightened by his victim's fright, so to speak, had compressed too hard the throat of the little girl he had raped in a moment of «*gloutonnerie impardonnable.*»

Van drank a glass of milk and suddenly felt such a wave of delicious exhaustion invading his limbs that he thought he'd go straight to bed. "*Tant pis,*" said Ada, reaching voraciously for the *keks* (English fruit cake). "Hammock?" she inquired;

but tottering Van shook his head, and having kissed Marina's melancholy hand, retired.

"*Tant pis*," repeated Ada, and with invincible appetite started to smear butter all over the yolk-tinted rough surface and rich incrustations—raisins, angelica, candied cherry, cedrat—of a thick slice of cake.

Mlle Larivière, who was following Ada's movements with awe and disgust, said:

"*Je rêve. Il n'est pas possible qu'on mette du beurre par-dessus toute cette pâte britannique, masse indigeste et immonde.*"

"*Et ce n'est que la première tranche,*" said Ada.

"Do you want a sprinkle of cinnamon on your *lait caillé*?" asked Marina. "You know, Belle" (turning to Mlle Larivière), "she used to call it 'sanded snow' when she was a baby."

"She was never a baby," said Belle emphatically. "She could break the back of her pony before she could walk."

"I wonder," asked Marina, "how many miles you rode to have our athlete drained so thoroughly."

"Only seven," replied Ada with a munch smile.

25

On a sunny September morning, with the trees still green, but the asters and fleabanes already taking over in ditch and dalk, Van set out for Ladoga, N.A., to spend a fortnight there with his father and three tutors before returning to school in cold Luga, Mayne.

Van kissed Lucette on each dimple and then on the neck—and winked to prim Larivière who looked at Marina.

It was time to go. They saw him off: Marina in her *shlafrok*, Lucette petting (substitutionally) Dack, Mlle Larivière who did not know yet that Van had left behind an inscribed book she had given him on the eve, and a score of copiously tipped servants (among whom we noticed kitchen Kim with his camera)—practically the entire household, except Blanche who had the headache, and dutiful Ada who had asked to be excused, having promised to visit an infirm villager (she had a heart of gold, that child, really—as Marina so willingly, so wisely used to observe).

Van's black trunk and black suitcase, and black king-size dumbbells, were heaved into the back of the family motorcar; Bouteillan put on a captain's cap, too big for him, and grape-blue goggles; "*remouvez votre* bottom, I will drive," said Van—and the summer of 1884 was over.

"She rolls sweetly, sir," remarked Bouteillan in his quaint old-fashioned English. "*Tous les pneus sont neufs*, but, alas, there are many stones on the way, and youth drives fast. Monsieur should be prudent. The winds of the wilderness are indiscreet. *Tel un lis sauvage confiant au désert*—"

"Quite the old comedy retainer, aren't you?" remarked Van drily.

"*Non, Monsieur*," answered Bouteillan, holding on to his cap. "*Non. Tout simplement j'aime bien Monsieur et sa demoiselle.*"

"If," said Van, "you're thinking of little Blanche, then you'd better quote Delille not to me, but to your son, who'll knock her up any day now."

The old Frenchman glanced at Van askance, *pozheval gubami* (chewed his lips), but said nothing.

"One will stop here for a few minutes," said Van, as they reached Forest Fork, just beyond Ardis. "I intend to pick some boletes for Father to whom I shall certainly (Bouteillan having sketched a courteous gesture) transmit your salute. This handbrake must have been—damn it—in use before Louis the Sixteenth migrated to England."

"It needs to be greased," said Bouteillan and consulted his watch; "yes, we have ample time to catch the 9:04."

Van plunged into the dense undergrowth. He wore a silk shirt, a velvet jacket, black breeches, riding boots with star spurs—and this attire was hardly convenient for making *klv zdB AoyvBno wkh gwzxm dqg kzwAAqvo* a *gwttp vq wifhm* Ada in a natural bower of aspens; *xliC mujzikml*, after which she said:

"Yes—so as not to forget. Here's the formula for our correspondence. Learn this by heart and then eat it up like a good little spy."

"*Poste restante* both ways; and I want at least three letters a week, my white love."

It was the first time he had seen her in that luminous frock nearly as flimsy as a nightgown. She had braided her hair, and he said she resembled the young soprano Maria Kuznetsova in the letter scene in Tschchaikow's opera *Onegin and Olga.*

Ada, doing her feminine best to restrain and divert her sobs by transforming them into emotional exclamations, pointed out some accursed insect that had settled on an aspen trunk.

(Accursed? *Accursed?* It was the newly described, fantastically rare vanessian, *Nymphalis danaus* Nab., orange-brown, with black-and-white foretips, mimicking, as its discoverer Professor Nabonidus of Babylon College, Nebraska, realized, not the Monarch butterfly directly, but the Monarch *through* the Viceroy, one of the Monarch's best known imitators. In Ada's angry hand.)

"Tomorrow you'll come here with your green net," said Van bitterly, "my butterfly."

She kissed him all over the face, she kissed his hands, then again his lips, his eyelids, his soft black hair. He kissed her ankles, her knees, her soft black hair.

"When, my love, when again? In Luga? Kaluga? Ladoga? Where, when?"

"That's not the point," cried Van, "the point, the point, the point is—will you be faithful, will you be faithful to me?"

"You spit, love," said wan-smiling Ada, wiping off the P's and the F's. "I don't know. I adore you. I shall never love anybody in my life as I adore you, never and nowhere, neither in eternity, nor in terrenity, neither in Ladore, nor on Terra, where they say our souls go. But! But, my love, my Van, I'm physical, horribly physical, I don't know, I'm frank, *qu'y puis-je?* Oh dear, don't ask me, there's a girl in my school who is in love with me, I don't know what I'm saying—"

"The girls don't matter," said Van, "it's the fellows I'll kill if they come near you. Last night I tried to make a poem about it for you, but I can't write verse; it begins, it only begins: Ada, our ardors and arbors—but the rest is all fog, try to fancy the rest."

They embraced one last time, and without looking back he fled.

Stumbling on melons, fiercely beheading the tall arrogant fennels with his riding crop, Van returned to the Forest Fork.

Morio, his favorite black horse, stood waiting for him, held by young Moore. He thanked the groom with a handful of stellas and galloped off, his gloves wet with tears.

26

For their correspondence in the first period of separation, Van and Ada had invented a code which they kept perfecting during the next fifteen months after Van left Ardis. The entire period of that separation was to span almost four years ("our black rainbow," Ada termed it), from September, 1884 to June, 1888, with two brief interludes of intolerable bliss (in August, 1885 and June, 1886) and a couple of chance meetings ("through a grille of rain"). Codes are a bore to describe; yet a few basic details must be, reluctantly, given.

One-letter words remained undisguised. In any longer word each letter was replaced by the one succeeding it in the alphabet at such an ordinal point—second, third, fourth, and so forth—which corresponded to the number of letters in that word. Thus "love," a four-letter word, became "*pszi*" ("p" being the fourth letter after "l" in the alphabetic series, "s" the fourth after "o," et cetera), whilst, say, "lovely" (in which the longer stretch made it necessary, in two instances, to resume the alphabet after exhausting it) became "*ruBkrE*," where the letters overflowing into the new alphabetic series were capitalized: B, for instance, standing for "v" whose substitute had to be the sixth letter ("lovely" consists of six letters) coming after it: *wxyzAB*, and "y" going still deeper into that next series: *zABCDE*. There is an awful moment in popular books on cosmic theories (that breezily begin with plain straightforward chatty paragraphs) when there suddenly start to sprout mathematical formulas, which immediately blind one's brain. We do not go as far as that here. If he approaches the description of our lovers' code (the "our" may constitute a source of irritation in its own right, but never mind) with a little more attention and a little less antipathy, the simplest-minded reader will, one trusts, understand that "overflowing" into the next ABC business.

Unfortunately, complications arose. Ada suggested certain improvements, such as beginning every message in ciphered French, then, switching to ciphered English after the first two-letter word, switching back to French after the first three-letter word, and reshuffling the shuttle with additional variations. Owing to these improvements the messages became even harder to read than to write, especially as both correspondents, in the exasperation of tender passion, inserted afterthoughts, deleted phrases, rephrased insertions and reinstated deletions with misspellings and miscodings, owing as much to their struggle with inexpressible distress as to their overcomplicating its cryptogram.

In the second period of separation, beginning in 1886, the code was radically altered. Both Van and Ada still knew by heart the seventy-two lines of Marvell's "The Garden" and the forty lines of Rimbaud's "Mémoire." It was from those two texts that they chose the letters of the words they needed. For example, l2.11. l1.2.20. l2.8 meant "love," with "l" and the number following it denoting the line in the Marvell poem, and the next number giving the position of the letter in that line, l2.11, meaning "eleventh letter in second line." I hold this to be pretty clear; and when, for the sake of misleading variety, the Rimbaud poem was used, the letter denoting the line would simply be capitalized. Again, this is a nuisance to explain, and the explanation is fun to read only for the purpose (thwarted, I am afraid) of looking for errors in the examples. Anyway, it soon proved to have defects even more serious than those of the first code. Security demanded they should not possess the poems in print or script for consultation and however marvelous their power of retention was, errors were bound to increase.

They wrote to each other in the course of 1886 as often as before, never less than a letter per week; but, curiously enough, in their third period of separation, from January, 1887, to June, 1888 (after a very long long-distance call and a very brief meeting), their letters grew scarcer, dwindling to a mere twenty in Ada's case (with only two or three in the spring of 1888) and about twice as many coming from Van. No passages from the correspondence can be given here, since all the letters were destroyed in 1889.

(I suggest omitting this little chapter altogether. Ada's note.)

27

"Marina gives me a glowing account of you and says *uzhe chuvstvuetsya osen'*. Which is very Russian. Your grandmother would repeat regularly that 'already-is-to-be-felt-autumn' remark every year, at the same time, even on the hottest day of the season at Villa Armina: Marina never realized it was an anagram of the sea, not of her. You look splendid, *sinok moy*, but I can well imagine how fed up you must be with her two little girls. Therefore, I have a suggestion—"

"Oh, I liked them enormously," purred Van. "Especially dear little Lucette."

"My suggestion is, come with me to a cocktail party today. It is given by the excellent widow of an obscure Major de Prey—obscurely related to our late neighbor, a fine shot but the light was bad on the Common, and a meddlesome garbage collector hollered at the wrong moment. Well, that excellent and influential lady who wishes to help a friend of mine" (clearing his throat) "has, I'm told, a daughter of fifteen summers, called Cordula, who is sure to recompense you for playing Blindman's Buff all summer with the babes of Ardis Wood."

"We played mostly Scrabble and Snap," said Van. "Is the needy friend also in my age group?"

"She's a budding Duse," replied Demon austerely, "and the party is strictly a 'prof push.' You'll stick to Cordula de Prey, I, to Cordelia O'Leary."

"*D'accord*," said Van.

Cordula's mother, an overripe, overdressed, overpraised comedy actress, introduced Van to a Turkish acrobat with tawny hairs on his beautiful orang-utan hands and the fiery eyes of a charlatan—which he was not, being a great artist in his circular field. Van was so taken up by his talk, by the training tips he lavished on the eager boy, and by envy, ambition,

respect and other youthful emotions, that he had little time
for Cordula, round-faced, small, dumpy, in a turtle-neck
sweater of dark-red wool, or even for the stunning young lady
on whose bare back the paternal hand kept resting lightly as
Demon steered her toward this or that useful guest. But that
very same evening Van ran into Cordula in a bookshop and
she said, "By the way, Van—I can call you that, can't I? Your
cousin Ada is my schoolmate. Oh, yes. Now, explain, please,
what did you do to our difficult Ada? In her very first letter
from Ardis, she positively gushed—our Ada gushed!—about
how sweet, clever, unusual, irresistible—"

"Silly girl. When was that?"

"In June, I imagine. She wrote again later, but her reply—
because I was quite jealous of you—really I was!—and had
fired back lots of questions—well, her reply was evasive, and
practically void of Van."

He looked her over more closely than he had done before.
He had read somewhere (we might recall the precise title if
we tried, not Tiltil, that's in Blue Beard . . .) that a man can
recognize a Lesbian, young and alone (because a tailored old
pair can fool no one), by a combination of three characteristics: slightly trembling hands, a cold-in-the-head voice, and
that skidding-in-panic of the eyes if you happen to scan with
obvious appraisal such charms as the occasion might force her
to show (lovely shoulders, for instance). Nothing whatever of
all that (yes—*Mytilène, petite isle*, by Louis Pierre) seemed to
apply to Cordula, who wore a "garbotosh" (belted mackintosh) over her terribly unsmart turtle and held both hands
deep in her pockets as she challenged his stare. Her bobbed
hair was of a neutral shade between dry straw and damp. Her
light blue iris could be matched by millions of similar eyes in
pigment-poor families of French Estoty. Her mouth was doll-
pretty when consciously closed in a mannered pout so as to
bring out what portraitists call the two "sickle folds" which,
at their best, are oblong dimples and, at their worst, the
creases down the well-chilled cheeks of felt-booted apple-cart
girls. When her lips parted, as they did now, they revealed
braced teeth, which, however, she quickly remembered to
shutter.

"My cousin Ada," said Van, "is a little girl of eleven or

twelve, and much too young to fall in love with anybody, except people in books. Yes, I too found her sweet. A trifle on the blue-stocking side, perhaps, and, at the same time, impudent and capricious—but, yes, sweet."

"I wonder," murmured Cordula, with such a nice nuance of pensive tone that Van could not tell whether she meant to close the subject, or leave it ajar, or open a new one.

"How could I get in touch with you?" he asked. "Would you come to Riverlane? Are you a virgin?"

"I don't date hoodlums," she replied calmly, "but you can always 'contact' me through Ada. We are not in the same class, in more ways than one" (laughing); "she's a little genius, I'm a plain American ambivert, but we are enrolled in the same Advanced French group, and the Advanced French group is assigned the same dormitory so that a dozen blondes, three brunettes and one redhead, la Rousse, can whisper French in their sleep" (laughing alone).

"What fun. Okay, thanks. The even number means bunks, I guess. Well, I'll be seeing you, as the hoods say."

In his next coded letter to Ada Van inquired if Cordula might not be the *lezbianochka* mentioned by Ada with such unnecessary guilt. I would as soon be jealous of your own little hand. Ada replied, "What rot, leave what's-her-name out of it"; but even though Van did not know yet how fiercely untruthful Ada could be when shielding an accomplice, Van remained unconvinced.

The rules of her school were old-fashioned and strict to the point of lunacy, but they reminded Marina nostalgically of the Russian Institute for Noble Maidens in Yukonsk (where she had kept breaking them with much more ease and success than Ada or Cordula or Grace could at Brownhill). Girls were allowed to see boys at hideous teas with pink cakes in the headmistress's Reception Room three or four times per term, and any girl of twelve or thirteen could meet a gentleman's son in a certified milk-bar, just a few blocks away, every third Sunday, in the company of an older girl of irreproachable morals.

Van braced himself to see Ada thus, hoping to use his magic wand for transforming whatever young spinster came along into a spoon or a turnip. Those "dates" had to be approved

by the victim's mother at least a fortnight in advance. Soft-
toned Miss Cleft, the headmistress, rang up Marina who told
her that Ada could not possibly need a chaperone to go out
with a cousin who had been her sole companion on day-long
rambles throughout the summer. "That's exactly it," Cleft
rejoined, "two young ramblers are exceptionally prone to
intertwine, and a thorn is always close to a bud."

"But they are practically brother and sister," ejaculated Marina, thinking as many stupid people do that "practically"
works both ways—reducing the truth of a statement and making a truism sound like the truth. "Which only increases the
peril," said soft Cleft. "Anyway, I'll compromise, and tell dear
Cordula de Prey to make a third: she admires Ivan and adores
Ada—consequently can only add zest to the zipper" (stale
slang—stale even then).

"Gracious, what *figli-migli*" (mimsey-fimsey), said Marina,
after having hung up.

In a dark mood, unwarned of what to expect (strategic fore-
knowledge might have helped to face the ordeal), Van waited
for Ada in the school lane, a dismal back alley with puddles
reflecting a sullen sky and the fence of the hockey ground. A
local high-school boy, "dressed to kill," stood near the gate,
a little way off, a fellow waiter.

Van was about to march back to the station when Ada appeared—with Cordula. *La bonne surprise!* Van greeted them
with a show of horrible heartiness ("And how goes it with
you, sweet cousin? Ah, Cordula! Who's the chaperone, you,
or Miss Veen?"). The sweet cousin sported a shiny black raincoat and a down-brimmed oilcloth hat as if somebody was to
be salvaged from the perils of life or sea. A tiny round patch
did not quite hide a pimple on one side of her chin. Her
breath smelled of ether. Her mood was even blacker than his.
He cheerily guessed it would rain. It did—hard. Cordula remarked that his trench coat was chic. She did not think it
worth while to go back for umbrellas—their delicious goal was
just round the corner. Van said corners were never round, a
tolerable quip. Cordula laughed. Ada did not: there were no
survivors, apparently.

The milk-bar proved to be so crowded that they decided to
walk under The Arcades toward the railway station café. He

knew (but could do nothing about it) that all night he would regret having deliberately overlooked the fact—the main, agonizing fact—that he had not seen his Ada for close to three months and that in her last note such passion had burned that the cryptogram's bubble had burst in her poor little message of promise and hope, baring a defiant, divine line of uncoded love. They were behaving now as if they had never met before, as if this was but a blind date arranged by their chaperone. Strange, malevolent thoughts revolved in his mind. What exactly—not that it mattered but one's pride and curiosity were at stake—what exactly had they been up to, those two ill-groomed girls, last term, this term, last night, every night, in their pajama-tops, amid the murmurs and moans of their abnormal dormitory? Should he ask? Could he find the right words: not to hurt Ada, while making her bed-filly know he despised her for kindling a child, so dark-haired and pale, coal and coral, leggy and limp, whimpering at the melting peak? A moment ago when he had seen them advancing together, plain Ada, seasick but doing her duty, and Cordula, apple-cankered but brave, like two shackled prisoners being led into the conqueror's presence, Van had promised himself to revenge deceit by relating in polite but minute detail the latest homosexual or rather pseudo-homosexual row at his school (an upper-form boy, Cordula's cousin, had been caught with a lass disguised as a lad in the rooms of an eclectic prefect). He would watch the girls flinch, he would demand some story from them to match his. That urge had waned. He still hoped to get rid for a moment of dull Cordula and find something cruel to make dull Ada dissolve in bright tears. But that was prompted by his *amour-propre*, not by their *sale amour*. He would die with an old pun on his lips. And why "dirty"? Did he feel any Proustian pangs? None. On the contrary: a private picture of their fondling each other kept pricking him with perverse gratification. Before his inner bloodshot eye Ada was duplicated and enriched, twinned by entwinement, giving what he gave, taking what he took: Corada, Adula. It struck him that the dumpy little Countess resembled his first whorelet, and that sharpened the itch.

They talked about their studies and teachers, and Van said:

"I would like your opinion, Ada, and yours, Cordula, on the following literary problem. Our professor of French literature maintains that there is a grave philosophical, and hence artistic, flaw in the entire treatment of the Marcel and Albertine affair. It makes sense if the reader *knows* that the narrator is a pansy, and that the good fat cheeks of Albertine are the good fat buttocks of Albert. It makes none if the reader cannot be supposed, and should not be required, to know *anything* about this or any other author's sexual habits in order to enjoy to the last drop a work of art. My teacher contends that if the reader knows nothing about Proust's perversion, the detailed description of a heterosexual male jealously watchful of a homosexual female is preposterous because a normal man would be only amused, tickled pink in fact, by his girl's frolics with a female partner. The professor concludes that a novel which can be appreciated only by *quelque petite blanchisseuse* who has examined the author's dirty linen is, artistically, a failure."

"Ada, what on earth is he talking about? Some Italian film he has seen?"

"Van," said Ada in a tired voice, "you do not realize that the Advanced French Group at my school has advanced no farther than to Racan and Racine."

"Forget it," said Van.

"But *you*'ve had too much Marcel," muttered Ada.

The railway station had a semi-private tearoom supervised by the stationmaster's wife under the school's idiotic auspices. It was empty, save for a slender lady in black velvet, wearing a beautiful black velvet picture hat, who sat with her back to them at a "tonic bar" and never once turned her head, but the thought brushed him that she was a cocotte from Toulouse. Our damp trio found a nice corner table and with sighs of banal relief undid their raincoats. He hoped Ada would discard her heavy-seas hat but she did not, because she had cut her hair because of dreadful migraines, because she did not want him to see her in the rôle of a moribund Romeo.

(On fait *son grand Joyce* after doing one's *petit Proust*. In Ada's lovely hand.)

(But read on; it is pure V.V. Note that lady! In Van's bedbuvard scrawl.)

As Ada reached for the cream, he caught and inspected her dead-shamming hand. We remember the Camberwell Beauty that lay tightly closed for an instant upon our palm, and suddenly our hand was empty. He saw, with satisfaction, that her fingernails were now long and sharp.

"Not too sharp, are they, my dear," he asked for the benefit of *dura* Cordula, who should have gone to the "powder room"—a forlorn hope.

"Why, no," said Ada.

"You don't," he went on, unable to stop, "you don't scratch little people when you stroke little people? Look at your little girl friend's hand" (taking it), "look at those dainty short nails (cold innocent, docile little paw!). *She* could not catch them in the fanciest satin, oh, no, could you, Ardula—I mean, Cordula?"

Both girls giggled, and Cordula kissed Ada's cheek. Van hardly knew what reaction he had expected, but found that simple kiss disarming and disappointing. The sound of the rain was lost in a growing rumble of wheels. He glanced at his watch; glanced up at the clock on the wall. He said he was sorry—that was his train.

"Not at all," wrote Ada (paraphrased here) in reply to his abject apologies, "we just thought you were drunk; but I'll never invite you to Brownhill again, my love."

28

The year 1880 (Aqua was still alive—somehow, somewhere!) was to prove to be the most retentive and talented one in his long, too long, never too long life. He was ten. His father had lingered in the West where the many-colored mountains acted upon Van as they had on all young Russians of genius. He could solve an Euler-type problem or learn by heart Pushkin's "Headless Horseman" poem in less than twenty minutes. With white-bloused, enthusiastically sweating Andrey Andreevich, he lolled for hours in the violet shade of pink cliffs, studying major and minor Russian writers—and puzzling out the exaggerated but, on the whole, complimentary allusions to his father's volitations and loves in another life in Lermontov's diamond-faceted tetrameters. He struggled to keep back his tears, while AAA blew his fat red nose, when shown the peasant-bare footprint of Tolstoy preserved in the clay of a motor court in Utah where he had written the tale of Murat, the Navajo chieftain, a French general's bastard, shot by Cora Day in his swimming pool. What a soprano Cora had been! Demon took Van to the world-famous Opera House in Telluride in West Colorado and there he enjoyed (and sometimes detested) the greatest international shows— English blank-verse plays, French tragedies in rhymed couplets, thunderous German musical dramas with giants and magicians and a defecating white horse. He passed through various little passions—parlor magic, chess, fluff-weight boxing matches at fairs, stunt-riding—and of course those unforgettable, much too early initiations when his lovely young English governess expertly petted him between milkshake and bed, she, petticoated, petititted, half-dressed for some party with her sister and Demon and Demon's casino-touring companion, bodyguard and guardian angel, monitor and adviser, Mr. Plunkett, a reformed card-sharper.

Mr. Plunkett had been, in the summer of his adventurous years, one of the greatest *shuler*'s, politely called "gaming conjurers," both in England and America. At forty, in the middle of a draw-poker session he had been betrayed by a fainting fit of cardiac origin (which allowed, alas, a bad loser's dirty hands to go through his pockets), had spent several years in prison, had become reconverted to the Roman faith of his forefathers and, upon completing his term, had dabbled in missionary work, written a handbook on conjuring, conducted bridge columns in various papers and done some sleuthing for the police (he had two stalwart sons in the force). The outrageous ravages of time and some surgical tampering with his rugged features had made his gray face not more attractive but at least unrecognizable to all but a few old cronies, who now shunned his chilling company, anyway. To Van he was even more fascinating than King Wing. Gruff but kindly Mr. Plunkett could not resist exploiting that fascination (we all like to be liked) by introducing Van to the tricks of an art now become pure and abstract, and therefore genuine. Mr. Plunkett considered the use of all mechanical media, mirrors and vulgar "sleeve rakes" as leading inevitably to exposure, just as jellies, muslin, rubber hands and so on sully and shorten a professional medium's career. He taught Van what to look for when suspecting the cheater with bright objects around him ("Xmas tree" or "twinkler," as those amateurs, some of them respectable clubmen, are called by professionals). Mr. Plunkett believed only in sleight-of-hand; secret pockets were useful (but could be turned inside out and against you). Most essential was the "feel" of a card, the delicacy of its palming, and digitation, the false shuffle, deck-sweeping, pack-roofing, prefabrication of deals, and above all a finger agility that practice could metamorphose into veritable vanishing acts or, conversely, into the materialization of a joker or the transformation of two pairs into four kings. One absolute requisite, if using privately an additional deck, was memorizing discards when hands were not prearranged. For a couple of months Van practiced card tricks, then turned to other recreations. He was an apprentice who learned fast, and kept his labeled phials in a cool place.

In 1885, having completed his prep-school education, he went up to Chose University in England, where his fathers had gone, and traveled from time to time to London or Lute (as prosperous but not overrefined British colonials called that lovely pearl-gray sad city on the other side of the Channel).

Sometime during the winter of 1886–7, at dismally cold Chose, in the course of a poker game with two Frenchmen and a fellow student whom we shall call Dick, in the latter's smartly furnished rooms in Serenity Court, he noticed that the French twins were losing not only because they were happily and hopelessly tight, but also because *milord* was that "crystal cretin" of Plunkett's vocabulary, a man of many mirrors—small reflecting surfaces variously angled and shaped, glinting discreetly on watch or signet ring, dissimulated like female fireflies in the undergrowth, on table legs, inside cuff or lapel, and on the edges of ashtrays, whose position on adjacent supports Dick kept shifting with a negligent air—all of which, as any card-sharper might tell you, was as dumb as it was redundant.

Having bided his time, and lost several thousands, Van decided to put some old lessons into practice. There was a pause in the game. Dick got up and went to a speaking-tube in the corner to order more wine. The unfortunate twins were passing to each other a fountain pen, thumb-pressing and re-pressing it in disastrous transit as they calculated their losses, which exceeded Van's. Van slipped a pack of cards into his pocket and stood up rolling the stiffness out of his mighty shoulders.

"I say, Dick, ever met a gambler in the States called Plunkett? Bald gray chap when I knew him."

"Plunkett? Plunkett? Must have been before my time. Was he the one who turned priest or something? Why?"

"One of my father's pals. Great artist."

"Artist?"

"Yes, artist. I'm an artist. I suppose *you* think you're an artist. Many people do."

"What on earth is an artist?"

"An underground observatory," replied Van promptly.

"That's out of some modern novel," said Dick, discarding his cigarette after a few avid inhales.

"That's out of Van Veen," said Van Veen.

Dick strolled back to the table. His man came in with the wine. Van retired to the W.C. and started to "doctor the deck," as old Plunkett used to call the process. He remembered that the last time he had made card magic was when showing some tricks to Demon—who disapproved of their poker slant. Oh, yes, and when putting at ease the mad conjurer at the ward whose pet obsession was that gravity had something to do with the blood circulation of a Supreme Being.

Van felt pretty sure of his skill—and of *milord*'s stupidity— but doubted he could keep it up for any length of time. He was sorry for Dick, who, apart from being an amateur rogue, was an amiable indolent fellow, with a pasty face and a flabby body—you could knock him down with a feather, and he frankly admitted that if his people kept refusing to pay his (huge and trite) debts, he would have to move to Australia to make new ones there and forge a few checks on the way.

He now *constatait avec plaisir*, as he told his victims, that only a few hundred pounds separated him from the shoreline of the minimal sum he needed to appease his most ruthless creditor, whereupon he went on fleecing poor Jean and

Jacques with reckless haste, and then found himself with three honest aces (dealt to him lovingly by Van) against Van's nimbly mustered four nines. This was followed by a good bluff against a better one; and with Van's generously slipping the desperately flashing and twinkling young lord good but not good enough hands, the latter's martyrdom came to a sudden end (London tailors wringing their hands in the fog, and a moneylender, the famous St. Priest of Chose, asking for an appointment with Dick's father). After the heaviest betting Van had yet seen, Jacques showed a forlorn *couleur* (as he called it in a dying man's whisper) and Dick surrendered with a straight flush to his tormentor's royal one. Van, who up to then had had no trouble whatever in concealing his delicate maneuvers from Dick's silly lens, now had the pleasure of seeing him glimpse the second joker palmed in his, Van's, hand as he swept up and clasped to his bosom the "rainbow ivory"—Plunkett was full of poetry. The twins put on their ties and coats and said they had to quit.

"Same here, Dick," said Van. "Pity you had to rely on your crystal balls. I have often wondered why the Russian for it—I think we have a Russian ancestor in common—is the same as the German for 'schoolboy,' minus the umlaut"—and while prattling thus, Van refunded with a rapidly written check the ecstatically astonished Frenchmen. Then he collected a handful of cards and chips and hurled them into Dick's face. The missiles were still in flight when he regretted that cruel and commonplace bewgest, for the wretched fellow could not respond in any conceivable fashion, and just sat there covering one eye and examining his damaged spectacles with the other—it was also bleeding a little—while the French twins were pressing upon him two handkerchiefs which he kept good-naturedly pushing away. Rosy aurora was shivering in green Serenity Court. Laborious old Chose.

(There should be a sign denoting applause. Ada's note.)

Van fumed and fretted the rest of the morning, and after a long soak in a hot bath (the best adviser, and prompter and inspirer in the world, except, of course, the W.C. seat) decided to pen—pen is the word—a note of apology to the cheated cheater. As he was dressing, a messenger brought him a note from Lord C. (he was a cousin of one of Van's Riverlane schoolmates), in which generous Dick proposed to substitute for his debt an introduction to the Venus Villa Club to which his whole clan belonged. Such a bounty no boy of eighteen could hope to obtain. It was a ticket to paradise. Van tussled with his slightly overweight conscience (both grinning like old pals in their old gymnasium)—and accepted Dick's offer.

(I think, Van, you should make it clearer why you, Van, the proudest and cleanest of men—I'm not speaking of abject physicalities, we are all organized that way—but why you, pure Van, could accept the offer of a rogue who no doubt continued to "flash and twinkle" after that fiasco. I think you should explain, *primo*, that you were dreadfully overworked, and *secundo*, that you could not bear the thought that the rogue knew, that he being a rogue, you could not call him out, and were safe, so to speak. Right? Van, do you hear me? I think—.)

He did not "twinkle" long after that. Five or six years later, in Monte Carlo, Van was passing by an open-air café when a hand grabbed him by the elbow, and a radiant, ruddy, comparatively respectable Dick C. leaned toward him over the petunias of the latticed balustrade:

"Van," he cried, "I've given up all that looking-glass dung, congratulate me! Listen: the only safe way is to mark 'em! Wait, that's not all, can you imagine, they've invented a microscopic—and I mean microscopic—point of euphorion, a precious metal, to insert under your thumbnail, you can't see it with the naked eye, but one minuscule section of your monocle is made to magnify the mark you make with it, like killing a flea, on one card after another, as they come along in the game, that's the beauty of it, no preparations, no props, nothing! Mark 'em! Mark 'em!" good Dick was still shouting, as Van walked away.

29

In mid-July, 1886, while Van was winning the table-tennis tournament on board a "luxury" liner (that now took a whole week to reach in white dignity Manhattan from Dover!), Marina, both her daughters, their governess, and two maids were shivering in more or less simultaneous stages of Russian *influentsa* at various stops on their way by train from Los Angeles to Ladore. A hydrogram from Chicago awaiting Van at his father's house on July 21 (her dear birthday!) said: "dadaist impatient patient arriving between twenty-fourth and seventh call doris can meet regards vicinity."

"Which reminds me painfully of the *golubyanki* (*petits bleus*) Aqua used to send me," remarked Demon with a sigh (having mechanically opened the message). "Is tender Vicinity some girl I know? Because you may glare as much as you like, but this is *not* a wire from doctor to doctor."

Van raised his eyes to the Boucher plafond of the breakfast room and, shaking his head in derisive admiration, commented on Demon's acumen. Yes, that was right. He had to travel incontinently to Garders (anagram of "regards," see?) to a hamlet the opposite way from Letham (see?) to see a mad girl artist called Doris or Odris who drew only gee-gees and sugar daddies.

Van rented a room under a false name (Boucher) at the only inn of Malahar, a miserable village on Ladore River, some twenty miles from Ardis. He spent the night fighting the celebrated mosquito, or its *cousin*, that liked him more than the Ardis beast had. The toilet on the landing was a black hole, with the traces of a fecal explosion, between a squatter's two giant soles. At 7 A.M. on July 25 he called Ardis Hall from the Malahar post office and got connected with Bout who was connected with Blanche and mistook Van's voice for the butler's.

"Dammit, Pa," he said into his bedside dorophone, "I'm busy!"

"I want Blanche, you idiot," growled Van.

"*Oh, pardon,*" cried Bout, "*un moment, Monsieur.*"

A bottle was audibly uncorked (drinking hock at seven in the morning!) and Blanche took over, but scarcely had Van begun to deliver a carefully worded message to be transmitted to Ada, when Ada herself who had been on the *qui vive* all night answered from the nursery, where the clearest instrument in the house quivered and bubbled under a dead barometer.

"Forest Fork in Forty-Five minutes. Sorry to spit."

"Tower!" replied her sweet ringing voice, as an airman in heaven blue might say "Roger."

He rented a motorcycle, a venerable machine, with a saddle upholstered in billiard cloth and pretentious false mother-of-pearl handlebars, and drove, bouncing on tree roots along a narrow "forest ride." The first thing he saw was the star gleam of her dismissed bike: she stood by it, arms akimbo, the black-haired white angel, looking away in a daze of shyness, wearing a terrycloth robe and bedroom slippers. As he carried her into the nearest thicket he felt the fever of her body, but only realized how ill she was when after two passionate spasms she got up full of tiny brown ants and tottered, and almost collapsed, muttering about gipsies stealing their jeeps.

It was a beastly, but beautiful, tryst. He could not remember—

(That's right, I can't either. Ada.)

—one word they said, one question, one answer; he rushed her back as close to the house as he dared (having kicked her bike into the bracken)—and that evening when he rang up Blanche, she dramatically whispered that *Mademoiselle* had *une belle pneumonie, mon pauvre Monsieur.*

Ada was much better three days later, but he had to return to Man to catch the same boat back to England—and join a circus tour which involved people he could not let down.

His father saw him off. Demon had dyed his hair a blacker black. He wore a diamond ring blazing like a Caucasian ridge. His long, black, blue-ocellated wings trailed and quivered in the ocean breeze. *Lyudi oglyadïvalis'* (people turned to look). A temporary Tamara, all kohl, kasbek rouge, and flamingo-boa, could not decide what would please her daemon lover more—just moaning and ignoring his handsome son or acknowledging bluebeard's virility as reflected in morose Van, who could not stand her Caucasian perfume, Granial Maza, seven dollars a bottle.

(You know, that's my favorite chapter up to now, Van, I don't know why, but I love it. And you can keep your Blanche in her young man's embrace, even that does not matter. In Ada's fondest hand.)

30

On February 5, 1887, an unsigned editorial in *The Ranter* (the usually so sarcastic and captious Chose weekly) described Mascodagama's performance as "the most imaginative and singular stunt ever offered to a jaded music-hall public." It was repeated at the Rantariver Club several times, but nothing in the programme or in publicity notices beyond the definition "Foreign eccentric" gave any indication either of the exact nature of the "stunt" or of the performer's identity. Rumors, carefully and cleverly circulated by Mascodagama's friends, diverted speculations toward his being a mysterious visitor from beyond the Golden Curtain, particularly since at least half-a-dozen members of a large Good-will Circus Company that had come from Tartary just then (i.e., on the eve of the Crimean War)—three dancing girls, a sick old clown with his old speaking goat, and one of the dancers' husbands, a make-up man (no doubt, a multiple agent)—had already defected between France and England, somewhere in the newly constructed "Chunnel." Mascodagama's spectacular success in a theatrical club that habitually limited itself to Elizabethan plays, with queens and fairies played by pretty boys, made first of all a great impact on cartoonists. Deans, local politicians, national statesmen, and of course the current ruler of the Golden Horde were pictured as mascodagamas by topical humorists. A grotesque imitator (who was really Mascodagama himself in an oversophisticated parody of his own act!) was booed at Oxford (a women's college nearby) by local rowdies. A shrewd reporter, who had heard him curse a crease in the stage carpet, commented in print on his "Yankee twang." Dear Mr. "Vascodagama" received an invitation to Windsor Castle from its owner, a bilateral descendant of Van's own ancestors, but he declined it, suspecting (incorrectly, as it later transpired) the misprint to suggest that his incognito had been divulged by one of the special detectives at Chose—the same, perhaps, who had recently saved the psychiatrist P. O. Tyomkin from the dagger of Prince Potyomkin, a mixed-up kid from Sebastopol, Id.

During his first summer vacation, Van worked under Tyomkin, at the Chose famous clinic, on an ambitious dissertation he never completed, "Terra: Eremitic Reality or Collective Dream?" He interviewed numerous neurotics, among whom there were variety artists, and literary men, and at least three intellectually lucid, but spiritually "lost," cosmologists who either were in telepathic collusion (they had never met and did not even know of one another's existence) or had discovered, none knew how or where, by means, maybe, of forbidden "ondulas" of some kind, a green world rotating in space and spiraling in time, which in terms of matter-and-mind was like ours and which they described in the same specific details as three people watching from three separate windows would a carnival show in the same street.

He spent his free time in gross dissipation.

Sometime in August he was offered a contract for a series of matinées and nights in a famous London theater during the Christmas vacation and on weekends throughout the winter season. He accepted gladly, being badly in need of a strict distraction from his perilous studies: the special sort of obsession under which Tyomkin's patients labored had something about it that made it liable to infect its younger investigators.

Mascodagama's fame reached inevitably the backwoods of America: a photograph of him, masked, it is true, but unable to mislead a fond relative or faithful retainer, was reproduced by the Ladore, Ladoga, Laguna, Lugano and Luga papers in the first week of 1888; but the accompanying reportage was not. The work of a poet, and only a poet ("especially of the Black Belfry group," as some wit said), could have adequately described a certain macabre quiver that marked Van's extraordinary act.

The stage would be empty when the curtain went up; then, after five heartbeats of theatrical suspense, something swept out of the wings, enormous and black, to the accompaniment of dervish drums. The shock of his powerful and precipitous

entry affected so deeply the children in the audience that for
a long time later, in the dark of sobbing insomnias, in the
glare of violent nightmares, nervous little boys and girls relived, with private accretions, something similar to the "primordial qualm," a shapeless nastiness, the swoosh of nameless
wings, the unendurable dilation of fever which came in a cav-
ern draft from the uncanny stage. Into the harsh light of its
gaudily carpeted space a masked giant, fully eight feet tall,
erupted, running strongly in the kind of soft boots worn by
Cossack dancers. A voluminous, black shaggy cloak of the
burka type enveloped his *silhouette inquiétante* (according to
a female Sorbonne correspondent—we've kept all those cuttings) from neck to knee or what appeared to be those sec-
tions of his body. A Karakul cap surmounted his top. A black
mask covered the upper part of his heavily bearded face. The
unpleasant colossus kept strutting up and down the stage for
a while, then the strut changed to the restless walk of a caged
madman, then he whirled, and to a clash of cymbals in the
orchestra and a cry of terror (perhaps faked) in the gallery,
Mascodagama turned over in the air and stood on his head.

In this weird position, with his cap acting as a pseudopodal
pad, he jumped up and down, pogo-stick fashion—and suddenly came apart. Van's face, shining with sweat, grinned between the legs of the boots that still shod his rigidly raised
arms. Simultaneously his real feet kicked off and away the false
head with its crumpled cap and bearded mask. The magical
reversal "made the house gasp." Frantic ("deafening," "delirious," "a veritable tempest of") applause followed the gasp.
He bounded offstage—and next moment was back, now
sheathed in black tights, dancing a jig on his hands.

We devote so much space to the description of his act not
only because variety artists of the "eccentric" race are apt to
be forgotten especially soon, but also because one wishes to
analyze its thrill. Neither a miraculous catch on the cricket
field, nor a glorious goal slammed in at soccer (he was a College Blue in both those splendid games), nor earlier physical
successes, such as his knocking out the biggest bully on his
first day at Riverlane School, had ever given Van the satisfaction Mascodagama experienced. It was not directly related to
the warm breath of fulfilled ambition, although as a very old

man, looking back at a life of unrecognized endeavor, Van did welcome with amused delight—more delight than he had actually felt at the time—the banal acclaim and the vulgar envy that swirled around him for a short while in his youth. The essence of the satisfaction belonged rather to the same order as the one he later derived from self-imposed, extravagantly difficult, seemingly absurd tasks when V.V. sought to express something, which *until* expressed had only a twilight being (or even none at all—nothing but the illusion of the backward shadow of its imminent expression). It was Ada's castle of cards. It was the standing of a metaphor on its head not for the sake of the trick's difficulty, but in order to perceive an ascending waterfall or a sunrise in reverse: a triumph, in a sense, over the ardis of time. Thus the rapture young Mascodagama derived from overcoming gravity was akin to that of artistic revelation in the sense utterly and naturally unknown to the innocents of critical appraisal, the social-scene commentators, the moralists, the ideamongers and so forth. Van on the stage was performing organically what his figures of speech were to perform later in life—acrobatic wonders that had never been expected from them and which frightened children.

Neither was the sheer physical pleasure of maniambulation a negligible factor, and the peacock blotches with which the carpet stained the palms of his hands during his gloveless dance routine seemed to be the reflections of a richly colored nether world that he had been the first to discover. For the tango, which completed his number on his last tour, he was given a partner, a Crimean cabaret dancer in a very short scintillating frock cut very low on the back. She sang the tango tune in Russian:

> *Pod znóynïm nébom Argentíni,*
> *Pod strástnïy góvor mandolíni*

> 'Neath sultry sky of Argentina,
> To the hot hum of mandolina

Fragile, red-haired "Rita" (he never learned her real name), a pretty Karaite from Chufut Kale, where, she nostalgically said, the Crimean cornel, *kizil'*, bloomed yellow among the arid rocks, bore an odd resemblance to Lucette as she was to look ten years later. During their dance, all Van saw of her were her silver slippers turning and marching nimbly in rhythm with the soles of his hands. He recouped himself at rehearsals, and one night asked her for an assignation. She indignantly refused, saying she adored her husband (the make-up fellow) and loathed England.

Chose had long been as famous for the dignity of its regulations, as for the brilliancy of its pranksters. Mascodagama's identity could not escape the interest and then the knowledge of the authorities. His college tutor, a decrepit and dour homosexual, with no sense of humor whatever and an innate respect for all the conventions of academic life, pointed out to a highly irritated and barely polite Van that in his second year at Chose he was not supposed to combine his university studies with the circus, and that if he insisted on becoming a variety artist he would be sent down. The old gentleman also wrote a letter to Demon asking him to make his son forget Physical Stunts for the sake of Philosophy and Psychiatry, especially since Van was the first American to have won (at seventeen!) the Dudley Prize (for an essay on Insanity and Eternal Life). Van was not quite sure yet what compromise pride and prudence might arrive at, when he left for America early in June, 1888.

31

Van revisited Ardis Hall in 1888. He arrived on a cloudy June afternoon, unexpected, unbidden, unneeded; with a diamond necklace coiled loose in his pocket. As he approached from a side lawn, he saw a scene out of some new life being rehearsed for an unknown picture, without him, not for him. A big party seemed to be breaking up. Three young ladies in yellow-blue Vass frocks with fashionable rainbow sashes surrounded a stoutish, foppish, baldish young man who stood, a flute of champagne in his hand, glancing down from the drawing-room terrace at a girl in black with bare arms: an old runabout, shivering at every jerk, was being cranked up by a hoary chauffeur in front of the porch, and those bare arms, stretched wide, were holding outspread the white cape of Baroness von Skull, a grand-aunt of hers. Against the white cape Ada's new long figure was profiled in black—the black of her smart silk dress with no sleeves, no ornaments, no memories. The slow old Baroness stood groping for something under one armpit, under the other—for what? a crutch? the dangling end of tangled bangles?—and as she half-turned to accept the cloak (now taken from her grandniece by a belated new footman) Ada also half-turned, and her yet ungemmed neck showed white as she ran up the porch steps.

Van followed her inside, in between the hall columns, and through a group of guests, toward a distant table with crystal jugs of cherry *ambrozia*. She wore, unmodishly, no stockings; her calves were strong and pale, and (I have a note here, for the ghost of a novel) "the low cut of her black dress allowed the establishment of a sharp contrast between the familiar mat whiteness of her skin and the brutal black horsetail of her new hair-do."

Excluding each other, private swoons split him in two: the devastating certainty that as soon as he reached, in the labyrinth of a nightmare, a brightly remembered small room with a bed and a child's washstand, she would join him there in her new smooth long beauty; and, on the shade side, the pang and panic of finding her changed, hating what he wanted, condemning it as wrong, explaining to him dreadful new circumstances—that they both were dead or existed only as extras in a house rented for a motion picture.

But hands offering him wine or almonds or their open selves, impeded his dream quest. He pressed on, notwithstanding the swoops of recognition: Uncle Dan pointed him out with a cry to a stranger who feigned amazement at the singularity of the optical trick—and, next moment, a repainted, red-wigged, very drunk and tearful Marina was gluing cherry-vodka lips to his jaw and unprotected parts, with smothered mother-sounds, half-moo, half-moan, of Russian affection.

He disentangled himself and pursued his quest. She had now moved to the drawing room, but by the expression of

her back, by the tensed scapulae, Van knew she was aware of
him. He wiped his wet buzzing ear and acknowledged with a
nod the raised glass of the stout blond fellow (Percy de Prey?
Or did Percy have an older brother?). A fourth maiden in the
Canadian couturier's corn-and-bluet summer "creation"
stopped Van to inform him with a pretty pout that he did not
remember her, which was true. "I am exhausted," he said.
"My horse caught a hoof in a hole in the rotting planks of
Ladore Bridge and had to be shot. I have walked eight miles.
I think I am dreaming. I think you are Dreaming Too." "No,
I'm Cordula!" she cried, but he was off again.

Ada had vanished. He discarded the caviar sandwich that
he found himself carrying like a ticket and, turning into the
pantry, told Bout's brother, a new valet, to take him to his
old room and get him one of those rubber tubs he had used
as a child four years ago. Plus somebody's spare pajamas. His
train had broken down in the fields between Ladoga and Ladore, he had walked twenty miles, God knows when they'd
send up his bags.

"They have just come," said the real Bout with a smile both
confidential and mournful (Blanche had jilted him).

Before tubbing, Van craned out of his narrow casement to
catch sight of the laurels and lilacs flanking the front porch
whence came the hubbub of gay departures. He made out
Ada. He noticed her running after Percy who had put on his
gray topper and was walking away across a lawn which his
transit at once caused to overlap in Van's mind with the fleet-
ing memory of the paddock where he and Van had once happened to discuss a lame horse and Riverlane. Ada overtook
the young man in a patch of sudden sunlight; he stopped, and
she stood speaking to him and tossing her head in a way she
had when nervous or displeased. De Prey kissed her hand.
That was French, but all right. He held the hand he had kissed
while she spoke and then kissed it again, and that was not
done, that was dreadful, that could not be endured.

Leaving his post, naked Van went through the clothes he
had shed. He found the necklace. In icy fury, he tore it into
thirty, forty glittering hailstones, some of which fell at her feet
as she burst into the room.

Her glance swept the floor.

"What a shame—" she began.

Van calmly quoted the punchline from Mlle Larivière's famous story: "*Mais, ma pauvre amie, elle était fausse*"—which was a bitter lie; but before picking up the spilled diamonds, she locked the door and embraced him, weeping—the touch of her skin and silk was all the magic of life, but why does everybody greet me with tears? He also wanted to know was that Percy de Prey? It was. Who had been kicked out of Riverlane? She guessed he had. He had changed, he had grown swine-stout. He had, hadn't he just? Was he her new beau?

"And now," said Ada, "Van is going to stop being vulgar—I mean, stop forever! Because I had and have and shall always have only one beau, only one beast, only one sorrow, only one joy."

"We can collect your tears later," he said, "I can't wait."

Her open kiss was hot and tremulous, but when he tried to draw up her dress she flinched with a murmur of reluctant denial, because the door had come alive: two small fists could be heard drumming upon it from the outside, in a rhythm both knew well.

"Hi, Lucette!" cried Van: "I'm changing, go away."

"Hi, Van! They want Ada, not you. They want you downstairs, Ada!"

One of Ada's gestures—used when she had to express in a muted flash all the facets of her predicament ("See, I was right, that's how it is, *nichego ne podelaesh*'")—consisted of rounding by means of both hands an invisible bowl from rim to base, accompanied by a sad bow. This is what she did now before leaving the room.

The situation was repeated in a much more pleasing strain a few hours later. For supper Ada wore another dress, of crimson cotton, and when they met at night (in the old toolroom by the glow of a carbide lantern) he unzipped her with such impetuous force that he nearly tore it in two to expose her entire beauty. They were still fiercely engaged (on the same bench covered with the same tartan lap robe—thoughtfully brought) when the outside door noiselessly opened, and Blanche glided in like an imprudent ghost. She had her own key, was back from a rendezvous with old Sore the Burgundian night watchman, and stopped like a fool gaping at the young couple. "Knock next time," said Van with a grin, not bothering to pause—rather enjoying, in fact, the bewitching apparition: she wore a miniver cloak that Ada had lost in the woods. Oh, she had become wonderfully pretty, and *elle le mangeait des yeux*—but Ada slammed the lantern shut, and with apologetic groans, the slut groped her way to the inner passage. His true love could not help giggling; and Van resumed his passionate task.

They stayed on and on, quite unable to part, knowing any explanation would do if anybody wondered why their rooms had remained empty till dawn. The first ray of the morning dabbed a toolbox with fresh green paint, when, at last moved by hunger, they got up and quietly repaired to the pantry.

"*Chto, vispalsya, Vahn* (well, slept your fill, Van)?" said Ada, beautifully mimicking her mother's voice, and she continued in her mother's English: "By your appetite, I judge. And, I think, it is only the first *brekfest*."

"Okh," grumbled Van, "my kneecaps! That bench was cruel. And I am *hongry*."

They sat, facing each other, at a breakfast table, munching black bread with fresh butter, and Virginia ham, and slices of genuine Emmenthaler cheese—and here's a pot of transparent honey: two cheerful cousins, "raiding the icebox" as children in old fairy tales, and the thrushes were sweetly whistling in the bright-green garden as the dark-green shadows drew in their claws.

"My teacher," she said, "at the Drama School thinks I'm better in farces than in tragedy. If they only knew!"

"There is nothing to know," retorted Van. "Nothing, nothing has changed! But that's the general impression, it was too dim down there for details, we'll examine them tomorrow on our little island: 'My sister, do you still recall . . .' "

"Oh shut up!" said Ada. "I've given up all that stuff—*petits vers, vers de soie . . .* "

"Come, come," cried Van, "some of the rhymes were magnificent acrobatics on the part of the child's mind: '*Oh! qui me rendra, ma Lucile, et le grand chêne and zee big hill.*' Little Lucile," he added in an effort to dissipate her frowns with a joke, "little Lucile has become so peachy that I think I'll switch over to her if you keep losing your temper like that. I remember the first time you got cross with me was when I chucked a stone at a statue and frightened a finch. That's memory!"

She was on bad terms with memory. She thought the servants would be up soon now, and then one could have something hot. That fridge was all fudge, really.

"Why, suddenly sad?"

Yes, she was sad, she replied, she was in dreadful trouble, her quandary might drive her insane if she did not know that her heart was pure. She could explain it best by a parable. She was like the girl in a film he would see soon, who is in the triple throes of a tragedy which she must conceal lest she lose her only true love, the head of the arrow, the point of the pain. In secret, she is simultaneously struggling with three torments—trying to get rid of a dreary dragging affair with a married man, whom she pities; trying to nip in the bud—in the sticky red bud—a crazy adventure with an attractive young fool, whom she pities even more; and trying to keep intact the love of the only man who is all her life and who is above pity, above the poverty of her feminine pity, because as the script says, his ego is richer and prouder than anything those two poor worms could imagine.

What had she actually done with the poor worms, after Krolik's untimely end?

"Oh, set them free" (big vague gesture), "turned them out, put them back onto suitable plants, buried them in the pupal state, told them to run along, while the birds were not looking—or alas, feigning not to be looking.

"Well, to mop up that parable, because you have the knack of interrupting and diverting my thoughts, I'm in a sense also torn between three private tortures, the main torture being ambition, of course. I know I shall never be a biologist, my passion for creeping creatures is great, but not all-consuming. I know I shall always adore orchids and mushrooms and violets, and you will still see me going out alone, to wander alone in the woods and return alone with a little lone lily; but flowers, no matter how irresistible, must be given up, too, as soon as I have the strength. Remains the great ambition and the greatest terror: the dream of the bluest, remotest, hardest dramatic climbs—probably ending as one of a hundred old spider spinsters teaching drama students, knowing, that, as you insist, sinister insister, we can't marry, and having always before me the awful example of pathetic, second-rate, brave Marina."

"Well, that bit about spinsters is rot," said Van, "we'll pull it off somehow, we'll become more and more distant relations in artistically forged papers and finally dwindle to mere name-sakes, or at the worst we shall live quietly, you as my house-keeper, I as your epileptic, and then, as in your Chekhov, 'we shall see the whole sky swarm with diamonds.'"

"Did you find them all, Uncle Van?" she inquired, sighing, laying her dolent head on his shoulder. She had told him everything.

"More or less," he replied, not realizing she had. "Anyway, I made the best study of the dustiest floor ever accomplished by a romantic character. One bright little bugger rolled under the bed where there grows a virgin forest of fluff and fungi. I'll have them reassembled in Ladore when I motor there one of these days. I have lots of things to buy—a gorgeous bath-robe in honor of your new swimming pool, a cream called Chrysanthemum, a brace of dueling pistols, a folding beach mattress, preferably black—to bring you out not on the beach but on that bench, and on our *isle de Ladore*."

"Except," she said, "that I do not approve of your making a laughingstock of yourself by looking for pistols in souvenir shops, especially when Ardis Hall is full of old shotguns and rifles, and revolvers, and bows and arrows—you remember, we had lots of practice with them when you and I were children."

Oh, he did, he did. Children, yes. In point of fact, how puzzling to keep seeing that recent past in nursery terms. Be-cause nothing had changed—you are with me, aren't you?—nothing, not counting little improvements in the grounds and the governess.

Yes! Wasn't that a scream? Larivière blossoming forth, bo-soming forth as a great writer! A sensational Canadian best-selling author! Her story "The Necklace" (*La rivière de diamants*) had become a classic in girls' schools and her gor-geous pseudonym "Guillaume de Monparnasse" (the leaving out of the "t" made it more *intime*) was well-known from

Quebec to Kaluga. As she put it in her exotic English: "Fame struck and the roubles rolled, and the dollars poured" (both currencies being used at the time in East Estotiland); but good Ida, far from abandoning Marina, with whom she had been platonically and irrevocably in love ever since she had seen her in "Bilitis," accused herself of neglecting Lucette by overindulging in Literature; consequently she now gave the child, in spurts of vacational zeal, considerably more attention than poor little Ada (said Ada) had received at twelve, after *her* first (miserable) term at school. Van had been such an idiot: suspecting Cordula! Chaste, gentle, dumb, little Cordula de Prey, when Ada had explained to him, twice, thrice, in different codes, that she had *invented* a nasty tender schoolmate, at a time when she had been literally *torn* from him, and only assumed—in advance, so to speak—such a girl's existence. A kind of blank check that she wanted from him; "Well, you got it," said Van, "but now it's destroyed and will not be renewed; but why did you run after fat Percy, what was so important?"

"Oh, very important," said Ada, catching a drop of honey on her nether lip, "his mother was on the dorophone, and he said please tell her he was on his way home, and I forgot all about it, and rushed up to kiss you!"

"At Riverlane," said Van, "we used to call that a Doughnut Truth: only the truth, and the whole truth, with a hole in the truth."

"I hate you," cried Ada, and made what she called a warning frog face, because Bouteillan had appeared in the doorway, his mustache shaved, coatless, tieless, in crimson braces that were holding up to his chest his well-filled black trousers. He disappeared, promising to bring them their coffee.

"But let me ask you, dear Van, let me ask you something. How many times has Van been unfaithful to me since September, 1884?"

"Six hundred and thirteen times," answered Van. "With at least two hundred whores, who only caressed me. I've remained absolutely true to you because those were only 'ob-manipulations' (sham, insignificant strokings by unremembered cold hands)."

The butler, now fully dressed, arrived with the coffee and

toast. And the *Ladore Gazette*. It contained a picture of Marina being fawned upon by a young Latin actor.

"Pah!" exclaimed Ada. "I had quite forgotten. He's coming today, with a movie man, and our afternoon will be ruined. But I feel refreshed and fit," she added (after a third cup of coffee). "It is only ten minutes to seven now. We shall go for a nice stroll in the park; there are one or two places that you might recognize."

"My love," said Van, "my phantom orchid, my lovely bladder-senna! I have not slept for two nights—one of which I spent imagining the other, and this other turned out to be more than I had imagined. I've had enough of you for the time being."

"Not a very fine compliment," said Ada, and rang resonantly for more toast.

"I've paid you eight compliments, as a certain Venetian—"

"I'm not interested in vulgar Venetians. You have become so coarse, dear Van, so strange . . . "

"Sorry," he said, getting up. "I don't know what I'm saying, I'm dead tired, I'll see you at lunch."

"There will be no lunch today," said Ada. "It will be some messy snack at the poolside, and sticky drinks all day."

He wanted to kiss her on her silky head but Bouteillan at that moment came in and while Ada was crossly rebuking him for the meager supply of toast, Van escaped.

32

The shooting script was now ready. Marina, in dorean robe and coolie hat, reclined reading in a long-chair on the patio. Her director, G. A. Vronsky, elderly, baldheaded, with a spread of grizzled fur on his fat chest, was alternately sipping his vodka-and-tonic and feeding Marina typewritten pages from a folder. On her other side, crosslegged on a mat, sat Pedro (surname unknown, stagename forgotten), a repulsively handsome, practically naked young actor, with satyr ears,

slanty eyes, and lynx nostrils, whom she had brought from
Mexico and was keeping at a hotel in Ladore.

Ada, lying on the edge of the swimming pool, was doing
her best to make the shy dackel face the camera in a reasonably
upright and decent position, while Philip Rack, an insignificant but on the whole likable young musician who in his
baggy trunks looked even more dejected and awkward than
in the green velvet suit he thought fit to wear for the piano
lessons he gave Lucette, was trying to take a picture of the
recalcitrant chop-licking animal and of the girl's parted breasts
which her half-prone position helped to disclose in the opening of her bathing suit.

If one dollied now to another group standing a few paces
away under the purple garlands of the patio arch, one might
take a medium shot of the young maestro's pregnant wife in
a polka-dotted dress replenishing goblets with salted almonds,
and of our distinguished lady novelist resplendent in mauve
flounces, mauve hat, mauve shoes, pressing a zebra vest on
Lucette, who kept rejecting it with rude remarks, learned from
a maid but uttered in a tone of voice just beyond deafish Mlle
Larivière's field of hearing.

Lucette remained topless. Her tight smooth skin was the
color of thick peach syrup, her little crupper in willow-green
shorts rolled drolly, the sun lay sleek on her russet bob and
plumpish torso: it showed but a faint circumlocution of femininity, and Van, in a scowling mood, recalled with mixed
feelings how much more developed her sister had been at not
quite twelve years of age.

He had spent most of the day fast asleep in his room, and
a long, rambling, dreary dream had repeated, in a kind of
pointless parody, his strenuous "Casanovanic" night with Ada
and that somehow ominous morning talk with her. Now that
I am writing this, after so many hollows and heights of time,
I find it not easy to separate our conversation, as set down in
an inevitably stylized form, and the drone of complaints, turning on sordid betrayals that obsessed young Van in his dull
nightmare. Or was he dreaming now that he had been dreaming? Had a grotesque governess really written a novel entitled
Les Enfants Maudits? To be filmed by frivolous dummies, now
discussing its adaptation? To be made even triter than the

original Book of the Fortnight, and its gurgling blurbs? Did he detest Ada as he had in his dream? He did.

Now, at fifteen, she was an irritating and hopeless beauty; a rather unkempt one, too; only twelve hours ago, in the dim toolroom he had whispered a riddle in her ear: what begins with a "de" and rhymes more or less with a Silesian river ant? She was eccentric in habits and clothing. She cared nothing for sunbathing, and not a tinge of the tan that had californized Lucette could be traced on the shameless white of Ada's long limbs and scrawny shoulder blades.

A remote cousin, no longer René's sister, not even his half-sister (so lyrically anathematized by Monparnasse), she stepped over him as over a log and returned the embarrassed dog to Marina. The actor, who quite likely would run into somebody's fist in a forthcoming scene, made a filthy remark in broken French.

"*Du sollst nicht zuhören*," murmured Ada to German Dack before putting him back in Marina's lap under the "accursed children." "*On ne parle pas comme ça devant un chien*," added Ada, not deigning to glance at Pedro, who nevertheless got up, reconstructed his crotch, and beat her to the pool with a Nurjinski leap.

Was she really beautiful? Was she at least what they call attractive? She was exasperation, she was torture. The silly girl had heaped her hair under a rubber cap, and this gave an unfamiliar, vaguely clinical look to her neck, with its odd dark wisps and strags, as if she had obtained a nurse's job and would never dance again. Her faded, bluish-gray, one-piece swimsuit had a spot of grease and a hole above one hip—nibbled through, one might conjecture, by a tallow-starved larva—and seemed much too short for careless comfort. She smelled of damp cotton, axillary tufts, and nenuphars, like mad Ophelia. None of those minor matters would have annoyed Van, had she and he been alone together; but the presence of the all-male actor made everything obscene, drab and insupportable. We move back to the lip of the pool.

Our young man, being exceptionally *brezgliv* (squeamish, easily disgusted), had no desire to share a few cubic meters of chlorinated celestino ("blues your bath") with two other fellows. He was emphatically not Japanese. He always remem-

bered, with shudders of revulsion, the indoor pool of his prep
school, the running noses, the pimpled chests, the chance
contacts with odious male flesh, the suspicious bubble bursting like a small stink bomb, and especially, especially, the
bland, sly, triumphant and absolutely revolting wretch who
stood in shoulder-high water and secretly urinated (and, God,
how he had beaten him up, though that Vere de Vere was
three years older than he).

He now kept carefully out of reach of any possible splash
as Pedro and Phil snorted and fooled in their foul bath. Presently the pianist, floating up and showing his awful gums in
a servile grin, tried to draw Ada into the pool from her outstretched position on the tiled margin, but she evaded the
grab of his despair by embracing the big orange ball she had
just fished out and, pushing him away with that shield, she
then threw it toward Van, who slapped it aside, refusing the
gambit, ignoring the gambol, scorning the gambler.

And now hairy Pedro hoisted himself onto the brink and
began to flirt with the miserable girl (his banal attentions
were, really, the least of her troubles).

"Your leetle aperture must be raccommodated," he said.

"*Que voulez-vous dire*, for goodness sake?" she asked, instead of dealing him a backhand wallop.

"Permit that I contact your charming penetralium," the
idiot insisted, and put a wet finger on the hole in her swimsuit.

"Oh *that*" (shrugging and rearranging the shoulder strap
displaced by the shrug). "Never mind that. Next time, maybe,
I'll put on my fabulous new bikini."

"Next time, maybe, no Pedro?"

"Too bad," said Ada. "Now go and fetch me a Coke, like
a good dog."

"*E tu?*" Pedro asked Marina as he walked past her chair.
"Again screwdriver?"

"Yes, dear, but with grapefruit, not orange, and a little *zucchero*. I can't understand" (turning to Vronsky), "why do I
sound a hundred years old on this page and fifteen on the
next? Because if it is a flashback—and it is a flashback, I suppose" (she pronounced it *fleshbeck*), "Renny, or what's his
name, René, should not know what he seems to know."

"He does not," cried G.A., "it's only a half-hearted flashback. Anyway, this Renny, this lover number one, does not know, of course, that she is trying to get rid of lover number two, while she's wondering all the time if she can dare go on dating number three, the gentleman farmer, see?"

"*Nu, eto chto-to slozhnovato* (sort of complicated), Grigoriy Akimovich," said Marina, scratching her cheek, for she always tended to discount, out of sheer self-preservation, the considerably more *slozhnïe* patterns of her own past.

"Read on, read, it all becomes clear," said G.A., riffling through his own copy.

"Incidentally," observed Marina, "I hope dear Ida will not object to our making him not only a poet, but a ballet dancer. Pedro could do that beautifully, but he can't be made to recite French poetry."

"If she protests," said Vronsky, "she can go and stick a telegraph pole—where it belongs."

The indecent "telegraph" caused Marina, who had a secret fondness for salty jokes, to collapse in Ada-like ripples of rolling laughter (*pokativshis' so smehu vrode Adi*): "But let's be serious, I still don't see how and why his wife—I mean the second guy's wife—accepts the situation (*polozhenie*)."

Vronsky spread his fingers and toes.

"*Prichyom tut polozhenie* (situation-shituation)? She is blissfully ignorant of their affair and besides, she knows she is fubsy and frumpy, and simply cannot compete with dashing Hélène."

"I see, but some won't," said Marina.

In the meantime, Herr Rack swam up again and joined Ada on the edge of the pool, almost losing his baggy trunks in the process of an amphibious heave.

"Permit me, Ivan, to get you also a nice cold Russian *kok*?" said Pedro—really a very gentle and amiable youth at heart. "Get yourself a cocoanut," replied nasty Van, testing the poor faun, who did not get it, in any sense, and, giggling pleasantly, went back to his mat. Claudius, at least, did not court Ophelia.

The melancholy young German was in a philosophical mood shading into the suicidal. He had to return to Kalugano with his Elsie, who Doc Ecksreher thought "would present him with driplets in dry weeks." He hated Kalugano, his and her home town, where in a moment of "mutual aberration" stupid Elsie had given him her all on a park bench after a wonderful office party at Muzakovski's Organs where the oversexed pitiful oaf had a good job.

"When are you leaving?" asked Ada.

"Forestday—after tomorrow."

"Fine. That's fine. Adieu, Mr. Rack."

Poor Philip drooped, fingerpainting sad nothings on wet stone, shaking his heavy head, gulping visibly.

"One feels . . . One feels," he said, "that one is merely playing a role and has forgotten the next speech."

"I'm told many feel that," said Ada; "it must be a *furchtbar* feeling."

"Cannot be helped? No hope any more at all? I am dying, yes?"

"You are dead, Mr. Rack," said Ada.

She had been casting sidelong glances, during that dreadful talk, and now saw pure, fierce Van under the tulip tree, quite a way off, one hand on his hip, head thrown back, drinking beer from a bottle. She left the pool edge, with its corpse, and moved toward the tulip tree making a strategic detour between the authoress, who—still unaware of what they were doing to her novel—was dozing in a deckchair (out of whose wooden arms her chubby fingers grew like pink mushrooms), and the leading lady, now puzzling over a love scene where the young chatelaine's "radiant beauty" was mentioned.

"But," said Marina, "how can one act out 'radiant,' what does radiant beauty mean?"

"Pale beauty," said Pedro helpfully, glancing up at Ada as she passed by, "the beauty for which many men would cut off their members."

"Okay," said Vronsky. "Let us get on with this damned script. He leaves the pool-side patio, and since we contemplate doing it in color—"

Van left the pool-side patio and strode away. He turned into a side gallery that led into a grovy part of the garden, grading insensibly into the park proper. Presently, he noticed that Ada had hastened to follow him. Lifting one elbow, revealing the black star of her armpit, she tore off her bathing cap and with a shake of her head liberated a torrent of hair.

Lucette, in color, trotted behind her. Out of charity for the
sisters' bare feet, Van changed his course from gravel path to
velvet lawn (reversing the action of Dr. Ero, pursued by the
Invisible Albino in one of the greatest novels of English literature). They caught up with him in the Second Coppice.
Lucette, in passing, stopped to pick up her sister's cap and
sunglasses—the sunglasses of much-sung lasses, a shame to
throw them away! My tidy little Lucette (I shall never forget
you . . .) placed both objects on a tree stump near an empty
beer bottle, trotted on, then went back to examine a bunch
of pink mushrooms that clung to the stump, snoring. Double
take, double exposure.

"Are you furious, because—" began Ada upon overtaking
him (she had prepared a sentence about her having to be polite after all to a piano tuner, practically a servant, with an
obscure heart ailment and a vulgar pathetic wife—but Van
interrupted her).

"I object," he said, expelling it like a rocket, "to two
things. A brunette, even a sloppy brunette, should shave her
groin before exposing it, and a well-bred girl does not allow
a beastly lecher to poke her in the ribs even if she must wear
a moth-eaten, smelly rag much too short for her charms."
"*Ach!*" he added, "why the hell did I return to Ardis!"

"I promise, I promise to be more careful from now on and
not let lousy Pedro come near," she said with happy rigorous
nods—and an exhalation of glorious relief, the cause of which
was to torture Van only much later.

"Oh, wait for me!" yelped Lucette.

(Torture, my poor love! Torture! Yes! But it's all sunk and
dead. Ada's late note.)

The three of them formed a pretty Arcadian combination
as they dropped on the turf under the great weeping cedar,
whose aberrant limbs extended an oriental canopy (propped
up here and there by crutches made of its own flesh like this
book) above two black and one golden-red head as they had
above you and me on dark warm nights when we were reckless, happy children.

Van, sprawling supine, sick with memories, put his hands
behind his nape and slit his eyes at the Lebanese blue of the
sky between the fascicles of the foliage. Lucette fondly ad-

mired his long lashes while pitying his tender skin for the inflamed blotches and prickles between neck and jaw where shaving caused the most trouble. Ada, her keepsake profile inclined, her mournful magdalene hair hanging down (in sympathy with the weeping shadows) along her pale arm, sat examining abstractly the yellow throat of a waxy-white helleborine she had picked. She hated him, she adored him. He was brutal, she was defenseless.

Lucette, always playing her part of the clinging, affectionately fussy lassy, placed both palms on Van's hairy chest and wanted to know why he was cross.

"I'm not cross with *you*," replied Van at last.

Lucette kissed his hand, then attacked him.

"Cut it out!" he said, as she wriggled against his bare thorax. "You're unpleasantly cold, child."

"It's not true, I'm hot," she retorted.

"Cold as two halves of a canned peach. Now, roll off, please."

"Why two? Why?"

"Yes, why," growled Ada with a shiver of pleasure, and, leaning over, kissed him on the mouth. He struggled to rise. The two girls were now kissing him alternatively, then kissing each other, then getting busy upon him again—Ada in perilous silence, Lucette with soft squeals of delight. I do not remember what *Les Enfants Maudits* did or said in Monparnasse's novelette—they lived in Bryant's château, I think, and it began with bats flying one by one out of a turret's *oeil-de-boeuf* into the sunset, but *these* children (whom the novelettist did not really know—a delicious point) might also have been filmed rather entertainingly had snoopy Kim, the kitchen photo-fiend, possessed the necessary apparatus. One hates to write about those matters, it all comes out so improper, esthetically speaking, in written description, but one cannot help recalling in this ultimate twilight (where minor artistic blunders are fainter than very fugitive bats in an insect-poor wilderness of orange air) that Lucette's dewy little contributions augmented rather than dampened Van's invariable reaction to the only and main girl's lightest touch, actual or imagined. Ada, her silky mane sweeping over his nipples and navel, seemed to enjoy doing everything to jolt my present pencil and make, in that ridiculously remote past, her innocent little sister notice and register what Van could not control. The crushed flower was now being merrily crammed under the rubber belt of his black trunks by twenty tickly fingers. As an ornament it had not much value; as a game it was inept and dangerous. He shook off his pretty tormentors, and walked away on his hands, a black mask over his carnival nose. Just then, the governess, panting and shouting, arrived on the scene. "*Mais qu'est-ce qu'il t'a fait, ton cousin?*" she kept anxiously asking, as Lucette, shedding the same completely unwarranted tears that Ada had once shed, rushed into the mauve-winged arms.

33

The following day began with a drizzle; but cleared up after lunch. Lucette had her last piano lesson with gloomy Herr Rack. The repetitive tinkle-thump-tinkle reached Van and Ada during a reconnaissance in a second-floor passage. Mlle Larivière was in the garden, Marina had fluttered away to Ladore, and Van suggested they take advantage of Lucette's being "audibly absent" by taking refuge in an upstairs dressing room.

Lucette's first tricycle stood there in a corner; a shelf above a cretonne-covered divan held some of the child's old "untouchable" treasures among which was the battered anthology he had given her four years ago. The door could not be locked, but Van was impatient, and the music would surely endure, as firm as a wall, for at least another twenty minutes. He had buried his mouth in Ada's nuque, when she stiffened and raised a warning finger. Heavy slow steps were coming up the grand staircase. "Send him away," she muttered. "*Chort* (hell)," swore Van, adjusting his clothes, and went out on the landing. Philip Rack was trudging up, Adam's apple bobbing, ill-shaven, livid, gums exposed, one hand on his chest, the other clutching a roll of pink paper while the music continued to play on its own as if by some mechanical device.

"There's one downstairs in the hall," said Van, assuming, or feigning to assume, that the unfortunate fellow had stomach cramps or nausea. But Mr. Rack only wanted "to make his farewells"—to Ivan Demonovich (accented miserably on the second "o"), to Fraülein Ada, to Mademoiselle Ida, and of course to Madame. Alas, Van's cousin and aunt were in town, but Phil might certainly find his friend Ida writing in the rose garden. Was Van sure? Van was damned well sure. Mr. Rack shook Van's hand with a deep sigh, looked up, looked down, tapped the banisters with his mysterious pink-paper tube, and went back to the music room, where Mozart had begun to falter. Van waited for a moment, listening and grimacing involuntarily, and presently rejoined Ada. She sat with a book in her lap.

"I must wash my right hand before I touch you or anything," he said.

She was not really reading, but nervously, angrily, absently flipping through the pages of what happened to be that old anthology—*she* who at any time, if she picked up a book, would at once get engrossed in whatever text she happened to slip into "from the book's brink" with the natural movement of a water creature put back into its brook.

"I have never clasped a wetter, limper, nastier forelimb in all my life," said Van, and cursing (the music downstairs had stopped), went to the nursery W.C. where there was a tap. From its window he saw Rack put his lumpy black briefcase into the front basket of his bicycle and weave away, taking his hat off to an unresponsive gardener. The clumsy cyclist's balance did not survive his futile gesture: he brushed harshly against the hedge on the other side of the path, and crashed. For a moment or two Rack remained in tangled communion with the privet, and Van wondered if he should not go down to his aid. The gardener had turned his back on the sick or drunken musician, who, thank goodness, was now getting out of the bushes and replacing his briefcase in its basket. He rode away slowly, and a surge of obscure disgust made Van spit into the toilet bowl.

Ada had left the dressing room by the time he returned. He discovered her on a balcony, where she was peeling an apple for Lucette. The kind pianist would always bring her an apple, or sometimes an inedible pear, or two small plums. Anyway, that was his last gift.

"Mademoiselle is calling you," said Van to Lucette.

"Well, she'll have to wait," said Ada, leisurely continuing her "ideal peel," a yellow-red spiral which Lucette watched with ritual fascination.

"Have some work to do," Van blurted out. "Bored beyond words. Shall be in the library."

"Okay," limpidly responded Lucette without turning—and emitted a cry of pleasure as she caught the finished festoons.

He spent half an hour seeking a book he had put back in the wrong place. When he found it at last, he saw he had finished annotating it and so did not need it any more. For a while he lay on the black divan, but that seemed only to increase the pressure of passionate obsession. He decided to return to the upper floor by the cochlea. There he recalled with anguish, as something fantastically ravishing and hopelessly irretrievable, her hurrying up with her candlestick on the night of the Burning Barn, capitalized in his memory forever—he with his dancing light behind her hurdies and calves and mobile shoulders and streaming hair, and the shadows in huge surges of black geometry overtaking them, in their winding upward course, along the yellow wall. He now found the third-floor door latched on the other side, and had to return down to the library (memories now blotted out by trivial exasperation) and take the grand staircase.

As he advanced toward the bright sun of the balcony door he heard Ada explaining something to Lucette. It was something amusing, it had to do with—I do not remember and cannot invent. Ada had a way of hastening to finish a sentence before mirth overtook her, but sometimes, as now, a brief burst of it would cause her words to explode, and then she would catch up with them and conclude the phrase with still greater haste, keeping her mirth at bay, and the last word would be followed by a triple ripple of sonorous, throaty, erotic and rather cosy laughter.

"And now, my sweet," she added, kissing Lucette on her dimpled cheek, "do me a favor: run down and tell bad Belle it's high time you had your milk and *petit-beurre*. *Zhivo* (quick)! Meanwhile, Van and I will retire to the bathroom—

or somewhere where there's a good glass—and I'll give him
a haircut; he needs one badly. Don't you, Van? Oh, I know
where we'll go . . . Run along, run along, Lucette."

34

That frolic under the sealyham cedar proved to be a mistake.
Whenever not supervised by her schizophrenic governess,
whenever not being read to, or walked, or put to bed, Lucette
was now a pest. At nightfall—if Marina was not around, drinking, say, with her guests under the golden globes of the new
garden lamps that glowed here and there in the sudden green-
ery, and mingled their kerosene reek with the breath of helio-
trope and jasmine—the lovers could steal out into the deeper
darkness and stay there until the *nocturna*—a keen midnight
breeze—came tumbling the foliage, *"troussant la raimée,"* as
Sore, the ribald night watchman, expressed it. Once, with his
emerald lantern, he had stumbled upon them and several
times a phantom Blanche had crept past them, laughing softly,
to mate in some humbler nook with the robust and securely
bribed old glowworm. But waiting all day for a propitious
night was too much for our impatient lovers. More often than
not they had worn themselves out well before dinnertime, just
as they used to in the past; Lucette, however, seemed to lurk
behind every screen, to peep out of every mirror.

They tried the attic, but noticed, just in time, a rent in its
floor through which one glimpsed a corner of the mangle
room where French, the second maid, could be seen in her
corset and petticoat, passing to and fro. They looked
around—and could not understand how they had ever been
able to make tender love among splintered boxes and projecting nails, or wriggle through the skylight onto the roof,
which any green imp with coppery limbs could easily keep
under surveillance from a fork of the giant elm.

There still was the shooting gallery, with its Orientally
draped recess under the sloping roof. But it crawled now with
bedbugs, reeked of stale beer, and was so grimy and greasy

that one could not dream of undressing or using the little divan. All Van saw there of his new Ada were her ivorine thighs and haunches, and the very first time he clasped them she bade him, in the midst of his vigorous joy, to glance across her shoulder over the window ledge, which her hands were still clutching in the ebbing throbs of her own response, and note that Lucette was approaching—skipping rope, along a path in the shrubbery.

Those intrusions were repeated on the next two or three occasions. Lucette would come ever nearer, now picking a chanterelle and feigning to eat it raw, then crouching to capture a grasshopper or at least going through the natural motions of idle play and carefree pursuit. She would advance up to the center of the weedy playground in front of the forbidden pavilion, and there, with an air of dreamy innocence, start to jiggle the board of an old swing that hung from the long and lofty limb of Baldy, a partly leafless but still healthy old oak (which appeared—oh, I remember, Van!—in a century-old lithograph of Ardis, by Peter de Rast, as a young colossus protecting four cows and a lad in rags, one shoulder bare). When our lovers (you like the authorial possessive, don't you, Van?) happened to look out again, Lucette was rocking the glum dackel, or looking up at an imaginary woodpecker, or with various pretty contortions unhurriedly mounting the gray-looped board and swinging gently and gingerly as if never having done it yet, while idiot Dack barked at the locked pavilion door. She increased her momentum so cannily that Ada and her cavalier, in the pardonable blindness of ascending bliss, never once witnessed the instant when the round rosy face with all its freckles aglow swooped up and two green eyes leveled at the astounding tandem.

Lucette, the shadow, followed them from lawn to loft, from gatehouse to stable, from a modern shower booth near the pool to the ancient bathroom upstairs. Lucette-in-the-Box came out of a trunk. Lucette desired they take her for walks. Lucette insisted on their playing "leaptoad" with her—and Ada and Van exchanged dark looks.

Ada thought up a plan that was not simple, was not clever, and moreover worked the wrong way. Perhaps she did it on purpose. (Strike out, strike out, *please*, Van.) The idea was to have Van fool Lucette by petting her in Ada's presence, while kissing Ada at the same time, and by caressing and kissing Lucette when Ada was away in the woods ("in the woods," "botanizing"). This, Ada affirmed, would achieve two ends—assuage the pubescent child's jealousy and act as an alibi in case she caught them in the middle of a more ambiguous romp.

The three of them cuddled and cosseted so frequently and so thoroughly that at last one afternoon on the long-suffering black divan he and Ada could no longer restrain their amorous excitement, and under the absurd pretext of a hide-and-seek game they locked up Lucette in a closet used for storing bound volumes of *The Kaluga Waters* and *The Lugano Sun*, and frantically made love, while the child knocked and called and kicked until the key fell out and the keyhole turned an angry green.

More objectionable yet than those fits of vile temper were, to Ada's mind, the look of stricken ecstasy that Lucette's face expressed when she would tightly cling to Van with arms, and knees, and prehensile tail, as if he were a tree trunk, even an ambulating tree trunk, and could not be pried off him unless smartly slapped by big sister.

"I have to admit," said Ada to Van as they floated downstream in a red boat, toward a drape of willows on a Ladore islet, "I have to admit with shame and sorrow, Van, that the splendid plan is a foozle. I think the brat has a dirty mind. I think she is criminally in love with you. I think I shall tell her you are her uterine brother and that it is illegal and altogether abominable to flirt with uterine brothers. Ugly dark words scare her, I know; they scared me when I was four; but she is essentially a dumb child, and should be protected from nightmares and stallions. If she still does not desist, I can always complain to Marina, saying she disturbs us in our meditations and studies. But perhaps you don't mind? Perhaps she excites you? Yes? She excites you, confess?"

"This summer is so much sadder than the other," said Van softly.

35

We are now on a willow islet amidst the quietest branch of the blue Ladore, with wet fields on one side and on the other a view of Bryant's Castle, remote and romantically black on its oak-timbered hill. In that oval seclusion, Van subjected his new Ada to a comparative study; juxtapositions were easy, since the child he had known in minute detail four years before stood vividly illumined in his mind against the same backdrop of flowing blue.

Her forehead area seemed to have diminished, not only because she had become taller, but because she did her hair differently, with a dramatic swirl in front; its whiteness, now clear of all blemishes, had acquired a particularly mat tinge, and soft skinfolds crossed it, as if she had been frowning too much all those years, poor Ada.

The eyebrows were as regal and thick as ever.

The eyes. The eyes had kept their voluptuous palpebral creases; the lashes, their semblance of jet-dust incrustation; the raised iris, its Hindu-hypnotic position; the lids, their inability to stay alert and wide open during the briefest embrace; but those eyes' expression—when she ate an apple, or examined a found thing, or simply listened to an animal or a person—had changed, as if new layers of reticence and sadness had accumulated, half-veiling the pupil, while the glossy eyeballs shifted in their lovely long sockets with a more restless motion than of yore: Mlle Hypnokush, "whose eyes never dwell on you and yet pierce you."

Her nose had not followed Van's in the latter's thickening of Hibernian outline; but the bone was definitely bolder, and the tip seemed to turn up more strongly, and had a little vertical groove that he did not recall having seen in the twelve-year-old colleenette.

In a strong light, a suggestion of darkish silk down (related to that on her forearms) could be now made out between nose and mouth but was doomed, she said, to extinction at the first cosmetical session of the fall season. A touch of lipstick now gave her mouth an air of deadpan sullenness, which, by contrast, increased the shock of beauty when in gayety or greed she revealed the moist shine of her large teeth and the red riches of tongue and palate.

Her neck had been, and remained, his most delicate, most poignant delight, especially when she let her hair flow freely, and the warm, white, adorable skin showed through in chance separations of glossy black strands. Boils and mosquito bites had stopped pestering her, but he discovered the pale trace of an inch-long cut which ran parallel to her vertebrae just below the waist and which resulted from a deep scratch caused last August by an erratic hatpin—or rather by a thorny twig in the inviting hay.

(You are merciless, Van.)

On that secret islet (forbidden to Sunday couples—it belonged to the Veens, and a notice-board calmly proclaimed that "trespassers might get shot by sportsmen from Ardis Hall," Dan's wording) the vegetation consisted of three Babylonian willows, a fringe of alder, many grasses, cattails, sweetflags, and a few purple-lipped twayblades, over which Ada crooned as she did over puppies or kittens.

Under the shelter of those neurotic willows Van pursued his survey.

Her shoulders were intolerably graceful: I would never permit my wife to wear strapless gowns with such shoulders, but how could she be my wife? Renny says to Nell in the English version of Monparnasse's rather comic tale: "The infamous shadow of our unnatural affair will follow us into the low depths of the Inferno which our Father who is in the sky shows to us with his superb digit." For some odd reason the worse translations are not from the Chinese, but from plain French.

Her nipples, now pert and red, were encircled by fine black hairs which would soon go, too, being, she said, *unschicklich*. Where had she picked up, he wondered, that hideous word? Her breasts were pretty, pale and plump, but somehow he had preferred the little soft swellings of the earlier girl with their formless dull buds.

He recognized the familiar, individual, beautiful intake of her flat young abdomen, its wonderful "play," the frank and eager expression of the oblique muscles and the "smile" of her navel—to borrow from the vocabulary of the belly dancer's art.

One day he brought his shaving kit along and helped her to get rid of all three patches of body hair:

"Now I'm Scheher," he said, "and you are his Ada, and that's your green prayer carpet."

Their visits to that islet remained engraved in the memory of that summer with entwinements that no longer could be untangled. They saw themselves standing there, embraced, clothed only in mobile leafy shadows, and watching the red rowboat with its mobile inlay of reflected ripples carry them off, waving, waving their handkerchiefs; and that mystery of mixed sequences was enhanced by such things as the boat's floating back to them while it still receded, the oars crippled by refraction, the sunflecks now rippling the other way like the strobe effect of spokes counterwheeling as the pageant rolls by. Time tricked them, made one of them ask a remembered question, caused the other to give a forgotten answer, and once in a small alder thicket, duplicated in black by the blue stream, they found a garter which was certainly hers, she could not deny it, but which Van was positive she had never worn on her stockingless summer trips to the magic islet.

Her lovely strong legs had, maybe, grown longer but they still preserved the sleek pallor and suppleness of her nymphet years. She could still suck her big toe. The right instep and the back of her left hand bore the same small not overconspicuous but indelible and sacred birthmark, with which nature had signed his right hand and left foot. She attempted to coat her fingernails with Scheherazade's Lacquer (a very grotesque fad of the 'eighties) but she was untidy and forgetful in matters of grooming, the varnish flaked off, leaving unseemly blotches, and he requested her to revert to her "lackluster" state. In compensation, he bought her in the town of Ladore (that rather smart little resort) an ankle chain of gold but she lost it in the course of their strenuous trysts and unexpectedly broke into tears when he said never mind, another lover some day would retrieve it for her.

Her brilliance, her genius. Of course, she had changed in four years, but he, too, had changed, by concurrent stages, so that their brains and senses stayed attuned and were to stay thus always, through all separations. Neither had remained the brash *Wunderkind* of 1884, but in bookish knowledge both surpassed their coevals to an even more absurd extent than in childhood; and in formal terms Ada (born on July 21, 1872) had already completed her private school course while Van, her senior by two years and a half, hoped to get his master's degree at the end of 1889. Her conversation might have lost some of its sportive glitter, and the first faint shadows of what she would later term "my acarpous destiny" (*pustotsvetnost'*) could be made out—at least, in back view; but the quality of her innate wit had deepened, strange "metempirical" (as Van called them) undercurrents seemed to double internally, and thus enrich, the simplest expression of her simplest thoughts. She read as voraciously and indiscriminately as he, but each had evolved a more or less "pet" subject—he the terrological part of psychiatry, she the drama (especially Russian), a "pet" he found "pat" in her case but hoped would be a passing vagary. Her florimania endured, alas; but after Dr. Krolik died (in 1886) of a heart attack in his garden, she had placed all her live pupae in his open coffin where he lay, she said, as plump and pink as *in vivo*.

Amorously, now, in her otherwise dolorous and irresolute adolescence, Ada was even more aggressive and responsive than in her abnormally passionate childhood. A diligent student of case histories, Dr. Van Veen never quite managed to match ardent twelve-year-old Ada with a non-delinquent, non-nymphomaniac, mentally highly developed, spiritually happy and normal English child in his files, although many similar little girls had bloomed—and run to seed—in the old châteaux of France and Estotiland as portrayed in extravagant romances and senile memoirs. His own passion for her Van found even harder to study and analyze. When he recollected caress by caress his Venus Villa sessions, or earlier visits to the riverhouses of Ranta or Livida, he satisfied himself that his reactions to Ada remained beyond all that, since the merest touch of her finger or mouth following a swollen vein produced not only a more potent but essentially different *delicia* than the slowest "winslow" of the most sophisticated young harlot. What, then, was it that raised the animal act to a level higher than even that of the most exact arts or the wildest flights of pure science? It would not be sufficient to say that in his love-making with Ada he discovered the pang, the *ogon'*, the agony of supreme "reality." Reality, better say, lost the quotes it wore like claws—in a world where independent and original minds must cling to things or pull things apart in order to ward off madness or death (which is the master madness). For one spasm or two, he was safe. The new naked reality needed no tentacle or anchor; it lasted a moment, but could be repeated as often as he and she were physically able to make love. The color and fire of that instant reality depended solely on Ada's identity as perceived by him. It had nothing to do with virtue or the vanity of virtue in a large sense—in fact it seemed to Van later that during the ardencies of that summer he knew all along that she had been, and still was, atrociously untrue to him—just as she knew long before he told her that he had used off and on, during their separation, the live mechanisms tense males could rent for a few minutes as described, with profuse woodcuts and photographs, in a three-volume *History of Prostitution* which she had read at the age of ten or eleven, between *Hamlet* and Captain Grant's *Microgalaxies.*

For the sake of the scholars who will read *this* forbidden memoir with a secret tingle (they are human) in the secret chasms of libraries (where the chatter, the lays and the fannies of rotting pornographers are piously kept)—its author must add in the margin of galley proofs which a bedridden old man heroically corrects (for those slippery long snakes add the last touch to a writer's woes) a few more [the end of the sentence cannot be deciphered but fortunately the next paragraph is scrawled on a separate writing-pad page. Editor's Note].

. . . about the rapture of her identity. The asses who might really think that in the starlight of eternity, *my*, Van Veen's, and *her*, Ada Veen's, conjunction, somewhere in North America, in the nineteenth century represented but one trillionth of a trillionth part of a pinpoint planet's significance can bray *ailleurs, ailleurs, ailleurs* (the English word would not supply the onomatopoeic element; old Veen is kind), because the rapture of her identity, placed under the microscope of reality (which is the only reality), shows a complex system of those subtle bridges which the senses traverse—laughing, embraced, throwing flowers in the air—between membrane and brain, and which always was and is a form of memory, even at the moment of its perception. I am weak. I write badly. I may die tonight. My magic carpet no longer skims over crown canopies and gaping nestlings, and her rarest orchids. Insert.

36

Pedantic Ada once said that the looking up of words in a lexicon for any other needs than those of expression—be it instruction or art—lay somewhere between the ornamental assortment of flowers (which could be, she conceded, mildly romantic in a maidenly headcocking way) and making collage-pictures of disparate butterfly wings (which was always vulgar and often criminal). *Per contra*, she suggested to Van that verbal circuses, "performing words," "poodle-doodles," and so forth, might be redeemable by the quality of the brain work required for the creation of a great logogriph or inspired pun and should not preclude the help of a dictionary, gruff or complacent.

That was why she admitted "Flavita." The name came from *alfavit*, an old Russian game of chance and skill, based on the scrambling and unscrambling of alphabetic letters. It was fashionable throughout Estoty and Canady around 1790, was revived by the "Madhatters" (as the inhabitants of New Amsterdam were once called) in the beginning of the nineteenth century, made a great comeback, after a brief slump, around 1860, and now a century later seems to be again in vogue, so I am told, under the name of "Scrabble," invented by some genius quite independently from its original form or forms.

Its chief Russian variety, current in Ada's childhood, was played in great country houses with 125 lettered blocks. The object was to make rows and files of words on a board of 225 squares. Of these, 24 were brown, 12 black, 16 orange, 8 red, and the rest golden-yellow (i.e., flavid, in concession to the game's original name). Every letter of the Cyrillic alphabet rated a number of points (the rare Russian *F* as much as 10, the common *A* as little as 1). Brown doubled the basic value

of a letter, black tripled it. Orange doubled the sum of points
for the whole word, red tripled the sum. Lucette would later
recall how her sister's triumphs in doubling, tripling, and even
nonupling (when passing through two red squares) the numerical value of words evolved monstrous forms in her delirium during a severe streptococcal ague in September, 1888, in
California.

For each round of the game each player helped himself to
seven blocks from the container where they lay face down,
and arrayed in turn his word on the board. In the case of the
opening coup, on the still empty field, all he had to do was
to align any two or all of his seven letters in such a way as to
involve the central square, marked with a blazing heptagon.
Subsequently, the catalyst of one of the letters already on the
board had to be used for composing one's word, across or
down. That player won who collected the greatest number of
points, letter by letter and word by word.

The set our three children received in 1884 from an old
friend of the family (as Marina's former lovers were known),
Baron Klim Avidov, consisted of a large folding board of saffian and a boxful of weighty rectangles of ebony inlaid with
platinum letters, only one of which was a Roman one, namely
the letter J on the two joker blocks (as thrilling to get as a
blank check signed by Jupiter or Jurojin). It was, incidentally,
the same kindly but touchy Avidov (mentioned in many racy
memoirs of the time) who once catapulted with an uppercut
an unfortunate English tourist into the porter's lodge for his
jokingly remarking how clever it was to drop the first letter of
one's name in order to use it as a *particule*, at the Gritz, in
Venezia Rossa.

By July the ten *A*'s had dwindled to nine, and the four *D*'s
to three. The missing *A* eventually turned up under an
Aproned Armchair, but the *D* was lost—faking the fate of its
apostrophizable double as imagined by a Walter C. Keyway,
Esq., just before the latter landed, with a couple of unstamped
postcards, in the arms of a speechless multilinguist in a frock
coat with brass buttons. The wit of the Veens (says Ada in a
marginal note) knows no bounds.

Van, a first-rate chess player—he was to win in 1887 a match
at Chose when he beat the Minsk-born Pat Rishin (champion

of Underhill and Wilson, N.C.)—had been puzzled by Ada's inability to raise the standard of her, so to speak, damsel-errant game above that of a young lady in an old novel or in one of those anti-dandruff color-photo ads that shows a beautiful model (made for other games than chess) staring at the shoulder of her otherwise impeccably groomed antagonist across a preposterous traffic jam of white and scarlet, elaborately and unrecognizably carved Lalla Rookh chessmen, which not even cretins would want to play with—even if royally paid for the degradation of the simplest thought under the itchiest scalp.

Ada did manage, now and then, to conjure up a combinational sacrifice, offering, say, her queen—with a subtle win after two or three moves if the piece were taken; but she saw only one side of the question, preferring to ignore, in the queer lassitude of clogged cogitation, the obvious counter combination that would lead inevitably to her defeat if the grand sacrifice were *not* accepted. On the Scrabble board, however, this same wild and weak Ada was transformed into a sort of graceful computing machine, endowed, moreover, with phenomenal luck, and would greatly surpass baffled Van in acumen, foresight and exploitation of chance, when shaping appetizing long words from the most unpromising scraps and collops.

He found the game rather fatiguing, and toward the end played hurriedly and carelessly, not deigning to check "rare" or "obsolete" but quite acceptable possibilities provided by a loyal dictionary. As to ambitious, incompetent and temperamental Lucette, she had to be, even at twelve, discreetly advised by Van who did so chiefly because it saved time and brought a little closer the blessed moment when she could be bundled off to the nursery, leaving Ada available for the third or fourth little flourish of the sweet summer day. Especially boring were the girls' squabbles over the legitimacy of this or that word: proper names and place names were taboo, but there occurred borderline cases, causing no end of heartbreak, and it was pitiful to see Lucette cling to her last five letters (with none left in the box) forming the beautiful ARDIS which her governess had told her meant "the point of an arrow"—but only in Greek, alas.

A particular nuisance was the angry or disdainful looking

up of dubious words in a number of lexicons, sitting, standing and sprawling around the girls, on the floor, under Lucette's chair upon which she knelt, on the divan, on the big round table with the board and the blocks and on an adjacent chest of drawers. The rivalry between moronic Ozhegov (a big, blue, badly bound volume, containing 52,872 words) and a small but chippy Edmundson in Dr. Gerschizhevsky's reverent version, the taciturnity of abridged brutes and the unconventional magnanimity of a four-volume Dahl ("My darling dahlia," moaned Ada as she obtained an obsolete cant word from the gentle long-bearded ethnographer)—all this would have been insupportably boring to Van had he not been stung as a scientist by the curious affinity between certain aspects of Scrabble and those of the planchette. He became aware of it one August evening in 1884 on the nursery balcony, under a sunset sky the last fire of which snaked across the corner of the reservoir, stimulated the last swifts, and intensified the hue of Lucette's copper curls. The morocco board had been unfolded on a much inkstained, monogrammed and notched deal table. Pretty Blanche, also touched, on earlobe and thumbnail, with the evening's pink—and redolent with the perfume called Miniver Musk by handmaids—had brought a still unneeded lamp. Lots had been cast, Ada had won the right to begin, and was in the act of collecting one by one, mechanically and unthinkingly, her seven "luckies" from the open case where the blocks lay face down, showing nothing but their anonymous black backs, each in its own cell of flavid velvet. She was speaking at the same time, saying casually: "I would much prefer the Benten lamp here but it is out of *kerosin*. Pet (addressing Lucette), be a good scout, call her—Good Heavens!"

The seven letters she had taken, S,R,E,N,O,K,I, and was sorting out in her *spektrik* (the little trough of japanned wood each player had before him) now formed in quick and, as it were, self-impulsed rearrangement the key word of the chance sentence that had attended their random assemblage.

Another time, in the bay of the library, on a thundery evening (a few hours before the barn burned), a succession of Lucette's blocks formed the amusing VANIADA, and from this she extracted the very piece of furniture she was in the

act of referring to in a peevish little voice: "But I, too, perhaps, would like to sit on the divan."

Soon after that, as so often occurs with games, and toys,
and vacational friendships, that seem to promise an eternal
future of fun, Flavita followed the bronze and blood-red trees
into the autumn mists; then the black box was mislaid, was
forgotten—and accidentally rediscovered (among boxes of table silver) four years later, shortly before Lucette's visit to
town where she spent a few days with her father in mid-July,
1888. It so happened that this was to be the last game of Flavita
that the three young Veens were ever to play together. Either
because it happened to end in a memorable record for Ada,
or because Van took some notes in the hope—not quite un-
fulfilled—of "catching sight of the lining of time" (which, as
he was later to write, is "the best informal definition of por-
tents and prophecies"), the last round of that particular game
remained vividly clear in his mind.

"*Je ne peux rien faire*," wailed Lucette, "*mais rien*—with
my idiotic *Buchstaben*, REMNILK, LINKREM . . ."

"Look," whispered Van, "*c'est tout simple*, shift those two
syllables and you get a fortress in ancient Muscovy."

"Oh, no," said Ada, wagging her finger at the height of
her temple in a way she had. "Oh, no. That pretty word does
not exist in Russian. A Frenchman invented it. There is no
second syllable."

"Ruth for a little child?" interposed Van.

"Ruthless!" cried Ada.

"Well," said Van, "you can always make a little cream,
KREM or KREME—or even better—there's KREMLI, which
means Yukon prisons. Go through her ORHIDEYa."

"Through her silly orchid," said Lucette.

"And now," said Ada, "Adochka is going to do something
even sillier." And taking advantage of a cheap letter recklessly
sown sometime before in the seventh compartment of the up-
permost fertile row, Ada, with a deep sigh of pleasure, composed the adjective TORFYaNUYu which went through a
brown square at F and through two red squares ($37 \times 9 =$
333 points) and got a bonus of 50 (for placing all seven blocks
at one stroke) which made 383 in all, the highest score ever

obtained for one word by a Russian scrambler. "There!" she said, "Ouf! *Pas facile.*" And brushing away with the rosy knuckles of her white hand the black-bronze hair from her temple, she recounted her monstrous points in a smug, melodious tone of voice like a princess narrating the poison-cup killing of a superfluous lover, while Lucette fixed Van with a mute, fuming appeal against life's injustice—and then looking again at the board emitted a sudden howl of hope:

"It's a place name! One can't use it! It's the name of the first little station after Ladore Bridge!"

"That's right, pet," sang out Ada. "Oh, pet, you are so right! Yes, Torfyanaya, or as Blanche says, *La Tourbière*, is, indeed, the pretty but rather damp village where our *cendrillon*'s family lives. But, *mon petit*, in our mother's tongue—*que dis-je*, in the tongue of a maternal grandmother we all share—a rich beautiful tongue which my pet should not neglect for the sake of a Canadian brand of French—this quite ordinary adjective means 'peaty,' feminine gender, accusative case. Yes, that one coup has earned me nearly 400. Too bad—*ne dotyanula* (didn't quite make it)."

"*Ne dotyanula!*" Lucette complained to Van, her nostrils flaring, her shoulders shaking with indignation.

He tilted her chair to make her slide off and go. The poor child's final score for the fifteen rounds or so of the game was less than half of her sister's last masterstroke, and Van had hardly fared better, but who cared! The bloom streaking Ada's arm, the pale blue of the veins in its hollow, the charred-wood odor of her hair shining brownly next to the lampshade's parchment (a translucent lakescape with Japanese dragons), scored infinitely more points than those tensed fingers bunched on the pencil stub could ever add up in the past, present or future.

"The loser will go *straight* to bed," said Van merrily, "and *stay* there, and we shall go down and fetch her—in exactly ten minutes—a big cup (the dark-blue cup!) of cocoa (sweet, dark, skinless Cadbury cocoa!)."

"I'm not going anywhere," said Lucette, folding her arms. "First, because it is only half-past eight, and, second, because I know perfectly well *why* you want to get rid of me."

"Van," said Ada, after a slight pause, "will you please summon Mademoiselle; she's working with Mother over a script which cannot be more stupid than this nasty child is."

"I would like to know," said Van, "the meaning of her interesting observation. Ask her, Ada dear."

"She thinks we are going to play Scrabble without her," said Ada, "or, go through those Oriental gymnastics which, you remember, Van, you began teaching me, as you remember."

"Oh, I remember! You remember I showed you what my teacher of athletics, you remember his name, King Wing, taught me."

"You remember a lot, ha-ha," said Lucette, standing in front of them in her green pajamas, sun-tanned chest bare, legs parted, arms akimbo.

"Perhaps the simplest—" began Ada.

"The simplest answer," said Lucette, "is that you two *can't* tell me why exactly you want to get rid of me."

"Perhaps the simplest answer," continued Ada, "is for you, Van, to give her a vigorous, resounding spanking."

"I dare you!" cried Lucette, and veered invitingly.

Very gently Van stroked the silky top of her head and kissed her behind the ear; and, bursting into a hideous storm of sobs, Lucette rushed out of the room. Ada locked the door after her.

"She's an utterly mad and depraved gipsy nymphet, of course," said Ada, "yet we must be more careful than ever . . . oh terribly, terribly, terribly . . . oh, careful, my darling."

37

It was raining. The lawns looked greener, and the reservoir grayer, in the dull prospect before the library bay window. Clad in a black training suit, with two yellow cushions propped under his head, Van lay reading Rattner on Terra, a difficult and depressing work. Every now and then he glanced at the autumnally tocking tall clock above the bald pate of tan Tartary as represented on a large old globe in the fading light of an afternoon that would have suited early October better than early July. Ada, wearing an unfashionable belted macintosh that he disliked, with her handbag on a strap over one shoulder, had gone to Kaluga for the whole day—officially to try on some clothes, unofficially to consult Dr. Krolik's cousin, the gynecologist Seitz (or "Zayats," as she transliterated him mentally since it also belonged, as Dr. "Rabbit" did, to the leporine group in Russian pronunciation). Van was positive that not once during a month of love-making had he failed to take all necessary precautions, sometimes rather bizarre, but incontestably trustworthy, and had lately acquired the sheath-like contraceptive device that in Ladore county only barbershops, for some odd but ancient reason, were allowed to sell. Still he felt anxious—and was cross with his anxiety—and Rattner, who halfheartedly denied any objective existence to the sibling planet in his text, but grudgingly accepted it in obscure notes (inconveniently placed between chapters), seemed as dull as the rain that could be discerned slanting in parallel pencil lines against the darker background of a larch plantation, borrowed, Ada contended, from Mansfield Park.

At ten minutes to five, Bout quietly came in with a lighted kerosene lamp and an invitation from Marina for a chat in her room. As Bout passed by the globe he touched it and looked with disapproval at his smudged finger. "The world is dusty," he said. "Blanche should be sent back to her native village. *Elle est folle et mauvaise, cette fille.*"

"Okay, okay," muttered Van, going back to his book. Bout left the room, still shaking his silly cropped head, and Van, yawning, allowed Rattner to slide down from the black divan on to the black carpet.

When he looked up again at the clock, it was gathering its strength to strike. He hastily got up from his couch recalling that Blanche had just come in to ask him to complain to Marina that Mlle Ada had again refused to give her a lift to "Beer Tower," as local jokers called her poor village. For a few moments the brief dim dream was so closely fused with the real event that even when he recalled Bout's putting his finger on the rhomboid peninsula where the Allies had just landed (as proclaimed by the Ladore newspaper spread-eagled on the library table), he still clearly saw Blanche wiping Crimea clean with one of Ada's lost handkerchiefs. He swarmed up the cochlea to the nursery water-closet; heard from afar the governess and her wretched pupil recite speeches from the horrible "Berenice" (a contralto croak alternating with a completely expressionless little voice); and decided that Blanche or rather Marina probably wished to know if he had been serious when he said the other day he would enlist at nineteen, the earliest volunteer age. He also gave a minute's thought to the sad fact that (as he well knew from his studies) the confusion of two realities, one in single, the other in double, quotes, was a symptom of impending insanity.

Naked-faced, dull-haired, wrapped up in her oldest kimono (her Pedro had suddenly left for Rio), Marina reclined on her mahogany bed under a golden-yellow quilt, drinking tea with mare's milk, one of her fads.

"Sit down, have a spot of *chayku*," she said. "The cow is in the smaller jug, I *think*. Yes, it is." And when Van, having kissed her freckled hand, lowered himself on the *ivanilich* (a kind of sighing old hassock upholstered in leather): "Van, dear, I wish to say something to you, because I know I shall never have to repeat it again. Belle, with her usual flair for the right phrase, has cited to me the *cousinage-dangereux-voisinage adage*—I mean 'adage,' I always fluff that word—and complained *qu'on s'embrassait dans tous les coins*. Is that true?"

Van's mind flashed in advance of his speech. It was, Marina, a fantastic exaggeration. The crazy governess had observed it once when he carried Ada across a brook and kissed her because she had hurt her toe. I'm the well-known beggar in the saddest of all stories.

"*Erunda* (nonsense)," said Van. "She once saw me carrying Ada across the brook and misconstrued our stumbling huddle (*spotïkayushcheesya sliyanie*)."

"I do not mean Ada, silly," said Marina with a slight snort, as she fussed over the teapot. "Azov, a Russian humorist, derives *erunda* from the German *hier und da*, which is neither here nor there. Ada is a big girl, and big girls, alas, have their own worries. Mlle Larivière meant Lucette, of course. Van, those soft games must stop. Lucette is twelve, and naive, and I know it's all clean fun, yet (*odnako*) one can never behave too *delikatno* in regard to a budding little woman. *A propos de coins:* in Griboedov's *Gore ot uma*, 'How stupid to be so clever,' a play in verse, written, I think, in Pushkin's time, the hero reminds Sophie of their childhood games, and says:

> How oft we sat together in a corner
> And what harm might there be in that?

but in Russian it is a little ambiguous, have another spot, Van?" (he shook his head, simultaneously lifting his hand, like his father), "because, you see,—no, there is none left anyway—the second line, *i kazhetsya chto v etom*, can be also construed as 'And in *that* one, meseems,' pointing with his finger at a corner of the room. Imagine—when I was rehearsing that scene with Kachalov at the Seagull Theater, in Yukonsk, Stanislavski, Konstantin Sergeevich, actually wanted him to make that cosy little gesture (*uyutnen'kiy zhest*)."

"How very amusing," said Van.

The dog came in, turned up a brimming brown eye Vanward, toddled up to the window, looked at the rain like a little person, and returned to his filthy cushion in the next room.

"I could never stand that breed," remarked Van. "Dackelophobia."

"But girls—do you like girls, Van, do you have many girls? You are not a pederast, like your poor uncle, are you? We have had some dreadful perverts in our ancestry but— Why do you laugh?"

"Nothing," said Van. "I just want to put on record that I adore girls. I had my first one when I was fourteen. *Mais qui me rendra mon Hélène?* She had raven black hair and a skin like skimmed milk. I had lots of much creamier ones later. *I kazhetsya chto v etom?*"

"How strange, how sad! Sad, because I know hardly anything about your life, my darling (*moy dushka*). The Zemskis were terrible rakes (*razvratniki*), one of them loved small girls, and another *raffolait d'une de ses juments* and had her tied up in a special way—don't ask me how" (double-hand gesture of horrified ignorance) "—when he dated her in her stall. *Kstati* (*à propos*), I could never understand how heredity is transmitted by bachelors, unless genes can jump like chess knights. I almost beat you, last time we played, we must play again, not today, though—I'm too sad today. I would have liked so much to know everything, *everything*, about you, but now it's too late. Recollections are always a little 'stylized' (*stilizovani*), as your father used to say, an irresistible and hateful man, and now, even if you showed me your old diaries, I could no longer whip up any real emotional reaction to them, though all actresses can shed tears, as I'm doing now. You see (rummaging for her handkerchief under her pillow), when children are still quite tiny (*takie malyutki*), we cannot imagine that we can go without them, for even a couple of days, and later we do, and it's a couple of weeks, and later it's months, gray years, black decades, and then the *opéra bouffe* of the Christians' eternity. I think even the shortest separation is a kind of training for the Elysian Games—who said that? I said that. And your costume, though very becoming, is, in a sense, *traurniy* (funerary). I'm spouting drivel. Forgive me these idiotic tears . . . Tell me, is there *anything* I could do for you? Do think up something! Would you like a beautiful, practically new Peruvian scarf, which he left behind, that crazy boy? No? It's not your style? Now go. And remember—not a word to poor Mlle Larivière, who means well!"

Ada came back just before dinnertime. Worries? He met her as she climbed rather wearily the grand staircase, trailing her vanity bag by its strap up the steps behind her. Worries? She smelled of tobacco, either because (as she said) she had spent an hour in a compartment for smokers, or had smoked (she added) a cigarette or two herself in the doctor's waiting room, or else because (and this she did not say) her unknown lover was a heavy smoker, his open red mouth full of rolling blue fog.

"Well? *Tout est bien?*" asked Van after a sketchy kiss. "No worries?"

She glared, or feigned to glare, at him.

"Van, you should not have rung up Seitz! He does not even know my name! You promised!"

Pause.

"I did not," answered Van quietly.

"*Tant mieux*," said Ada in the same false voice, as he helped her out of her coat in the corridor. "*Oui, tout est bien.* Will you stop sniffing me over, dear Van? In fact the blessed thing started on the way home. Let me pass, please."

Worries of her own? Of her mother's automatic making? A casual banality? "We all have our troubles"?

"Ada!" he cried.

She looked back, before unlocking her (always locked) door. "What?"

"Tuzenbakh, not knowing what to say: 'I have not had coffee today. Tell them to make me some.' Quickly walks away."

"Very funny!" said Ada, and locked herself up in her room.

38

In mid-July Uncle Dan took Lucette to Kaluga where she was to stay, with Belle and French, for five days. The Lyaskan Ballet and a German circus were in town, and no child would want to miss the schoolgirls' field-hockey and swimming matches which old Dan, a child at heart, attended religiously at that time of the year; moreover she had to undergo a series of "tests" at the Tarus Hospital to settle what caused her weight and temperature to fluctuate so abnormally despite her eating so heartily and feeling so well.

On the Friday afternoon when her father planned to return with her, he also expected to bring a Kaluga lawyer to Ardis where Demon was to come too, an unusual occurrence. The business to be discussed was the sale of some "blue" (peat-bog) land which belonged to both cousins and which both, for different reasons, were anxious to get rid of. As usually happened with Dan's most carefully worked-out plans, something misfired, the lawyer could not promise to come till late in the evening, and just before Demon arrived, his cousin aerogrammed a message asking Marina to "dine Demon" without waiting for Dan and Miller.

That *kontretan* (Marina's humorous term for a not necessarily nasty surprise) greatly pleased Van. He had seen little of his father that year. He loved him with light-hearted devotion, had worshipped him in boyhood, and respected him staunchly now in his tolerant but better informed youth. Still later a tinge of repulsion (the same repulsion he felt in regard to his own immorality) became admixed to the love and the esteem; but, on the other hand, the older he grew the more firmly he felt that he would give his life for his father, at a moment's notice, with pride and pleasure, in any circumstance imaginable. When Marina, in the late Eighteen-Nineties, in her miserable dotage, used to ramble on, with embarrassing and disgusting details, about dead Demon's "crimes," he felt pity for him and her, but his indifference to Marina and his adoration for his father remained unchanged—to endure thus even now, in the chronologically hardly believable Nineteen-Sixties. No accursed generalizer, with a half-penny mind and dry-fig heart, would be able to explain (and this is my sweetest revenge for all the detractions my lifework has met with) the individual vagaries evolved in those and similar matters. No art and no genius would exist without such vagaries, and this is a final pronouncement, damning all clowns and clods.

When had Demon visited Ardis in recent years? April 23, 1884 (the day Van's first summer stay there had been suggested, planned, promised). Twice in the summer of 1885 (while Van was climbing mountains in the Western states, and the Veen girls were in Europe). A dinner in 1886, in June or July (where was Van?). In 1887 for a few days in May (Ada was botanizing with a German woman in Estotia or California. Van was whoring in Chose).

Taking advantage of Larivière's and Lucette's absence, Van had long dallied with Ada in the comfortable nursery, and was now hanging from the wrong window, which did not give a clear view of the drive, when he heard the rich purr of his father's motorcar. He dashed downstairs—the speed of his descent causing the heat of the banisters to burn the palm of his hand in a merry way remindful of similar occasions in his boyhood. There was nobody in the hall. Demon had entered the house from a side gallery and was now settled in the sun-dusted music room, wiping his monocle with a special *zamshinka* ("shammy") as he awaited his "prebrandial" brandy (an ancient quip). His hair was dyed a raven black, his teeth were houndwhite. His smooth glossy brown face with its trimly clipped black mustache and humid dark eyes beamed at his son, expressing the radiant love which Van reciprocated, and which both vainly tried to camouflage with habitual pleasantry.

"Hullo, Dad."

"Oh, hullo, Van."

Très Américain. Schoolyard. There he slams the car door, there he comes through the snow. Always gloves, no overcoat ever. Want to go to the "bathroom," Father? My land, sweet land.

"D'you want to go to the 'bathroom'?" asked Van, with a twinkle.

"No thanks, I had my bath this morning." (Quick sigh acknowledging the passage of time: he, too, remembered every detail of those father-and-son dinners at Riverlane, the immediate dutiful offer of the W.C., the hearty masters, the ignoble meal, creamed hash, God save America, embarrassed sons, vulgar fathers, titled Britisher and Greek grandee matching yachts, and yacs, and yoickfests in the Bahamudas. May I transfer inconspicuously this delicious pink-frosted synthesis from my plate to yours, son? "You don't *like* it, Dad!" (acting horribly hurt). God save their poor little American tastebuds.

"Your new car sounds wonderful," said Van.

"Doesn't it? Yes." (Ask Van about that *gornishon*—Franco-Russian slang of the meanest grade for a cute *kameristochka*). "And how is everything, my dear boy? I saw you last the day you returned from Chose. We waste life in separations! We are the fools of fate! Oh let's spend a month together in Paris or London before the Michaelmas term!"

Demon shed his monocle and wiped his eyes with the modish lace-frilled handkerchief that lodged in the heart pocket of his dinner jacket. His tear glands were facile in action when no real sorrow made him control himself.

"You look quite satanically fit, Dad. Especially with that fresh oeillet in your lapel eye. I suppose you have not been much in Manhattan lately—where did you get its last syllable?"

Homespun pun in the Veenish vein.

"I offered myself *en effet* a trip to Akapulkovo," answered Demon, needlessly and unwillingly recollecting (with that special concussion of instant detail that also plagued his children) a violet-and-black-striped fish in a bowl, a similarly striped couch, the subtropical sun bringing out the veins of an onyx ashtray astray on the stone floor, a batch of old, orange-juice-stained *Povesa* (playboy) magazines, the jewels he had brought, the phonograph singing in a dreamy girl's voice "*Petit nègre, au champ qui fleuronne,*" and the admirable abdomen of a very expensive, and very faithless, and altogether adorable young Créole.

"Did what's-her-name go with you?"

"Well, my boy, frankly, the nomenclature is getting more and more confused every year. Let us speak of plainer things. Where are the drinks? They were promised me by a passing angel."

(Passing angel?)

Van pulled a green bell-cord which sent a melodious message pantryward and caused the old-fashioned, bronze-framed little aquarium, with its lone convict cichlid, to bubble antiphonally in a corner of the music room (an eerie, perhaps self-aerating reaction, which only Kim Beauharnais, the kitchen boy, understood). "Should he ring her up after dinner," wondered Demon. What time would it be there? Not much use, bad for the heart.

"I don't know if you know," said Van, resuming his perch on the fat arm of his father's chair. "Uncle Dan will be here with the lawyer and Lucette only after dinner."

"Capital," said Demon.

"Marina and Ada should be down in a minute—*ce sera un dîner à quatre.*"

"Capital," he repeated. "You look splendid, my dear, dear fellow—and I don't have to exaggerate compliments as some do in regard to an aging man with shoe-shined hair. Your dinner jacket is very nice—or, rather, it's very nice recognizing one's old tailor in one's son's clothes—like catching oneself repeating an ancestral mannerism—for example, this (wagging his left forefinger three times at the height of his temple), which my mother did in casual, pacific denial; that gene missed you, but I've seen it in my hairdresser's looking-glass when refusing to have him put Crêmlin on my bald spot; and you know who had it too—my aunt Kitty, who married the banker Bolenski after divorcing that dreadful old wencher Lyovka Tolstoy, the writer.''

Demon preferred Walter Scott to Dickens, and did not think highly of Russian novelists. As usual, Van considered it fit to make a corrective comment:

"A fantastically artistic writer, Dad.''

"You are a fantastically charming boy,'' said Demon, shedding another sweet-water tear. He pressed to his cheek Van's strong shapely hand. Van kissed his father's hairy fist which was already holding a not yet visible glass of liquor. Despite the manly impact of their Irishness, all Veens who had Russian blood revealed much tenderness in ritual overflows of affection while remaining somewhat inept in its verbal expression.

"I say,'' exclaimed Demon, "what's happened—your shaftment is that of a carpenter's. Show me your other hand. Good gracious'' (muttering:) "Hump of Venus disfigured, Line of Life scarred but monstrously long . . .'' (switching to a gipsy chant:) "You'll live to reach Terra, and come back a wiser and merrier man'' (reverting to his ordinary voice:) "What puzzles me as a palmist is the strange condition of the Sister of your Life. And the roughness!''

"Mascodagama,'' whispered Van, raising his eyebrows.

"Ah, of course, how blunt (dumb) of me. Now tell me—you like Ardis Hall?''

"I adore it,'' said Van. "It's for me the *château que baignait la Dore*. I would gladly spend all my scarred and strange life here. But that's a hopeless fancy.''

"Hopeless? I wonder. I know Dan wants to leave it to Lucile, but Dan is greedy, and my affairs are such that I can satisfy great greed. When I was your age I thought that the sweetest word in the language rhymes with 'billiard,' and now I know I was right. If you're really keen, son, on having this property, I might try to buy it. I can exert a certain pressure upon my Marina. She sighs like a hassock when you sit upon her, so to speak. Damn it, the servants here are not Mercuries. Pull that cord again. Yes, maybe Dan could be made to sell.''

"That's very black of you, Dad,'' said pleased Van, using a slang phrase he had learned from his tender young nurse,

Ruby, who was born in the Mississippi region where most magistrates, public benefactors, high priests of various so-called "denominations," and other honorable and generous men, had the dark or darkish skin of their West-African ancestors, who had been the first navigators to reach the Gulf of Mexico.

"I wonder," Demon mused. "It would cost hardly more than a couple of millions minus what Cousin Dan owes me, minus also the Ladore pastures, which are utterly mucked up and should be got rid of gradually, if the local squires don't blow up that new kerosene distillery, the *stüd i sram* (shame) of our county. I am not *particularly* fond of Ardis, but I have nothing against it, though I detest its environs. Ladore Town has become very honky-tonky, and the gaming is not what it used to be. You have all sorts of rather odd neighbors. Poor Lord Erminin is practically insane. At the races, the other day, I was talking to a woman I preyed upon years ago, oh long before Moses de Vere cuckolded her husband in my absence and shot him dead in my presence—an epigram you've heard before, no doubt from these very lips—"

(The next thing will be "paternal repetitiousness.")

"—but a good son should put up with a little paternal repetitiousness— Well, she tells me her boy and Ada see a lot of each other, et cetera. Is that true?"

"Not really," said Van. "They meet now and then—at the usual parties. Both like horses, and races, but that's all. There is no et cetera, that's out of the question."

"Good! Ah, the portentous footfall is approaching, I hear. Prascovie de Prey has the worst fault of a snob: overstatement. *Bonsoir*, Bouteillan. You look as ruddy as your native vine— but we are not getting any younger, as the amerlocks say, and that pretty messenger of mine must have been waylaid by some younger and more fortunate suitor."

"*Proshu, papochka* (please, Dad)," murmured Van, who always feared that his father's recondite jests might offend a menial—while sinning himself by being sometimes too curt.

But—to use a hoary narrational turn—the old Frenchman knew his former master too well to be bothered by gentlemanly humor. His hand still tingled nicely from slapping Blanche's compact young bottom for having garbled Mr. Veen's simple request and broken a flower vase. After placing his tray on a low table he retreated a few steps, his fingers remaining curved in the tray-carrying position, and only then acknowledged Demon's welcome with a fond bow. Was Monsieur's health always good? Indeed it was.

"I'll want," said Demon, "a bottle of your Château Latour d'Estoc for dinner"; and when the butler, having removed *en passant* a crumpled little handkerchief from the piano top, had left the room with another salute: "How do you get along with Ada? She's what—almost sixteen now? Very musical and romantic?"

"We are close friends," said Van (who had carefully prepared his answer to a question he had expected to come in one form or another). "We have really more things in common than, for instance, ordinary lovers or cousins or siblings. I mean, we are really inseparable. We read a lot, she is spectacularly self-educated, thanks to her granddad's library. She knows the names of all the flowers and finches in the neighborhood. She is altogether a very amusing girl."

"Van . . . ," began Demon, but stopped—as he had begun and stopped a number of times before in the course of the last years. Some day it would have to be said, but this was not the right moment. He inserted his monocle and examined the bottles: "By the way, son, do you crave any of these aperitifs? My father allowed me Lilletovka and that Illinois Brat—awful bilge, *antranou svadi*, as Marina would say. I suspect your uncle has a cache behind the solanders in his study and keeps there a finer whisky than this *usque ad Russkum*. Well, let us have the cognac, as planned, unless you are a *filius aquae*?"

(No pun intended, but one gets carried away and goofs.)

"Oh, I prefer claret. I'll concentrate (*nalyagu*) on the Latour later on. No, I'm certainly no T-totaler, and besides the Ardis tap water is not recommended!"

"I must warn Marina," said Demon after a gum-rinse and a slow swallow, "that her husband should stop swilling tittery, and stick to French and Califrench wines—after that little stroke he had. I met him in town recently, near Mad Avenue, saw him walking toward me quite normally, but then as he caught sight of me, a block away, the clockwork began slowing

down and he stopped—oh, helplessly!—before he reached
me. That's hardly normal. Okay. Let our sweethearts never
meet, as we used to say, up at Chose. Only Yukonians think
cognac is bad for the liver, because they have nothing but
vodka. Well, I'm glad you get along so well with Ada. That's
fine. A moment ago, in that gallery, I ran into a remarkably
pretty soubrette. She never once raised her lashes and answered in French when I— Please, my boy, move that screen
a little, that's right, the stab of a sunset, especially from under
a thunderhead, is not for my poor eyes. Or poor ventricles.
Do you like the type, Van—the bowed little head, the bare
neck, the high heels, the trot, the wiggle, you do, don't you?"

"Well, sir—"

(Tell him I'm the youngest Venutian? Does he belong, too?
Show the sign? Better not. Invent.)

"—Well, I'm resting after my torrid affair, in London, with
my tango-partner whom you saw me dance with when you
flew over for that last show—remember?"

"Indeed, I do. Curious, you calling it that."

"I think, sir, you've had enough brandy."

"Sure, sure," said Demon, wrestling with a subtle question
which only the ineptitude of a kindred conjecture had
crowded out of Marina's mind, granted it could have entered
by some back door; for ineptitude is always synonymous with
multitude, and nothing is fuller than an empty mind.

"Naturally," continued Demon, "there is a good deal to
be said for a restful summer in the country . . ."

"Open-air life and all that," said Van.

"It is incredible that a young boy should control his father's
liquor intake," remarked Demon, pouring himself a fourth
shallow. "On the other hand," he went on, nursing the thin-
stemmed, gold-rimmed cup, "open-air life may be pretty
bleak without a summer romance, and not many decent girls
haunt the neighborhood, I agree. There was that lovely Erminin girl, *une petite juive très aristocratique*, but I understand
she's engaged. By the way, the de Prey woman tells me her
son has enlisted and will soon be taking part in that deplorable
business abroad which our country should have ignored. I
wonder if he leaves any rivals behind?"

"Goodness no," replied honest Van. "Ada is a serious young lady. She has no beaux—except me, *ça va seins durs.* Now who, who, who, Dad, who said that for *'sans dire'*?"

"Oh! King Wing! When I wanted to know how he liked his French wife. Well, that's fine news about Ada. She likes horses, you say?"

"She likes," said Van, "what all our belles like—balls, orchids, and *The Cherry Orchard.*"

Here Ada herself came running into the room. Yes-yes-yes-yes, here I come. Beaming!

Old Demon, iridescent wings humped, half rose but sank back again, enveloping Ada with one arm, holding his glass in the other hand, kissing the girl in the neck, in the hair, burrowing in her sweetness with more than an uncle's fervor. "Gosh," she exclaimed (with an outbreak of nursery slang that affected Van with even more *umilenie, attendrissement,* melting ravishment, than his father seemed to experience). "How lovely to see you! Clawing your way through the clouds! Swooping down on Tamara's castle!"

(Lermontov paraphrased by Lowden.)

"The last time I enjoyed you," said Demon, "was in April when you wore a raincoat with a white and black scarf and simply reeked of some arsenic stuff after seeing your dentist. Dr. Pearlman has married his receptionist, you'll be glad to know. Now to business, my darling. I accept your dress" (the sleeveless black sheath), "I tolerate your romantic hairdo, I don't care much for your pumps *na bosu nogu* (on bare feet), your Beau Masque perfume—*passe encore*, but, my precious, I abhor and reject your livid lipstick. It may be the fashion in good old Ladore. It is not done in Man or London."

"*Ladno* (Okay)," said Ada and, baring her big teeth, rubbed fiercely her lips with a tiny handkerchief produced from her bosom.

"That's also provincial. You should carry a black silk purse. And now I'll show what a diviner I am: your dream is to be a concert pianist!"

"It is not," said Van indignantly. "What perfect nonsense. She can't play a note!"

"Well, no matter," said Demon. "Observation is not always

the mother of deduction. However, there is nothing improper about a hanky dumped on a Bechstein. You don't have, my love, to blush so warmly. Let me quote for comic relief

> *"Lorsque son fi-ancé fut parti pour la guerre*
> *Irène de Grandfief, la pauvre et noble enfant*
> *Ferma son pi-ano . . . vendit son éléphant*

"The gobble *enfant* is genuine, but the elephant is mine."

"You don't say so," laughed Ada.

"Our great Coppée," said Van, "is awful, of course, yet he has one very fetching little piece which Ada de Grandfief here has twisted into English several times, more or less successfully."

"Oh, Van!" interjected Ada with unusual archness, and scooped up a handful of salted almonds.

"Let's hear it, let's hear it," cried Demon as he borrowed a nut from her cupped hand.

The neat interplay of harmonious motions, the candid gayety of family reunions, the never-entangling marionette strings—all this is easier described than imagined.

"Old storytelling devices," said Van, "may be parodied only by very great and inhuman artists, but only close relatives can be forgiven for paraphrasing illustrious poems. Let me preface the effort of a cousin—anybody's cousin—by a snatch of Pushkin, for the sake of rhyme—"

"For the *snake* of rhyme!" cried Ada. "A paraphrase, even my paraphrase, is like the corruption of 'snakeroot' into 'snagrel'—all that remains of a delicate little birthwort."

"Which is amply sufficient," said Demon, "for my little needs, and those of my little friends."

"So here goes," continued Van (ignoring what he felt was an indecent allusion, since the unfortunate plant used to be considered by the ancient inhabitants of the Ladore region not so much as a remedy for the bite of a reptile, as the token of a very young woman's easy delivery; but no matter). "By chance preserved has been the poem. In fact, I have it. Here it is: *Leur chute est lente* and one can know 'em . . ."

"Oh, *I* know 'em," interrupted Demon:

> *"Leur chute est lente. On peut les suivre*
> *Du regard en reconnaissant*

> *Le chêne à sa feuille de cuivre*
> *L'érable à sa feuille de sang*

"Grand stuff!"

"Yes, that was Coppée and now comes the cousin," said Van, and he recited:

> "Their fall is gentle. The leavesdropper
> Can follow each of them and know
> The oak tree by its leaf of copper,
> The maple by its blood-red glow."

"Pah!" uttered the versionist.

"Not at all!" cried Demon. "That 'leavesdropper' is a splendid trouvaille, girl." He pulled the girl to him, she landing on the arm of his *Klubsessel*, and he glued himself with thick moist lips to her hot red ear through the rich black strands. Van felt a shiver of delight.

It was now Marina's turn to make her entrée, which she did in excellent chiaroscuro circumstances, wearing a spangled dress, her face in the soft focus sought by ripe stars, holding out both arms and followed by Jones who carried two flambeaux and kept trying to keep within the limits of decorum the odd little go-away kicks he was aiming backwards at a brown flurry in the shadows.

"Marina!" cried Demon with perfunctory enthusiasm, and patted her hand as he joined her on a settee.

Puffing rhythmically, Jones set one of his beautiful dragon-entwined flambeaux on the low-boy with the gleaming drinks and was about to bring over its fellow to the spot where Demon and Marina were winding up affable preliminaries but was quickly motioned by Marina to a pedestal near the striped fish. Puffing, he drew the curtains, for nothing but picturesque ruins remained of the day. Jones was new, very efficient, solemn and slow, and one had to get used gradually to his ways and wheeze. Years later he rendered me a service that I will never forget.

"She's a *jeune fille fatale*, a pale, heart-breaking beauty," Demon confided to his former mistress without bothering to discover whether the subject of his praise could hear him (she did) from the other end of the room where she was helping

Van to corner the dog—and showing much too much leg in
the process. Our old friend, being quite as excited as the rest
of the reunited family, had scampered in after Marina with an
old miniver-furred slipper in his merry mouth. The slipper
belonged to Blanche, who had been told to whisk Dack to
her room but, as usual, had not incarcerated him properly.
Both children experienced a chill of *déjà-vu* (a twofold *déjà-
vu*, in fact, when contemplated in artistic retrospect).

"*Pozhalsta bez glupostey* (please, no silly things), especially
devant les gens," said deeply flattered Marina (sounding the
final "s" as her granddams had done); and when the slow fish-
mouthed footman had gone carrying away, supine, high-
chested Dack and his poor plaything, she continued: "Really,
in comparison to the local girls, to Grace Erminin, for example, or Cordula de Prey, Ada is a Turgenevian maiden or
even a Jane Austen miss."

"I'm Fanny Price, actually," commented Ada.

"In the staircase scene," added Van.

"Let's not bother about their private jokes," said Marina
to Demon. "I never can understand their games and little
secrets. Mlle Larivière, however, has written a wonderful
screenplay about mysterious children doing strange things in
old parks—but don't let her start talking of her literary successes tonight, that would be fatal."

"I hope your husband won't be *too* late," said Demon. "He
is not at his best after eight P.M., summertime, you know. By
the way, how's Lucette?"

At this moment both battants of the door were flung open
by Bouteillan in the grand manner, and Demon offered *ka-
lachikom* (in the form of a Russian crescent loaf) his arm to
Marina. Van, who in his father's presence was prone to lapse
into a rather dismal sort of playfulness, proposed taking Ada
in, but she slapped his wrist away with a sisterly *sans-gêne*, of
which Fanny Price might not have approved.

Another Price, a typical, too typical, old retainer whom Marina (and G. A. Vronsky, during their brief romance) had
dubbed, for unknown reasons, "Grib," placed an onyx ashtray
at the head of the table for Demon, who liked to smoke between courses—a puff of Russian ancestry. A side table supported, also in the Russian fashion, a collection of red, black,

gray, beige hors-d'oeuvres, with the serviette caviar (*salfeto-chnaya ikra*) separated from the pot of Graybead (*ikra sve-zhaya*) by the succulent pomp of preserved boletes, "white," and "subbetuline," while the pink of smoked salmon vied with the incarnadine of Westphalian ham. The variously fla-vored *vodochki* glittered, on a separate tray. The French cuisine had contributed its *chaudfroids* and *foie gras*. A window was open, and the crickets were stridulating at an ominous speed in the black motionless foliage.

It was—to continue the novelistic structure—a long, joyful, delicious dinner, and although the talk consisted mainly of family quips and bright banalities, that reunion was to remain suspended in one's memory as a strangely significant, not wholly pleasant, experience. One treasured it in the same way as when falling in love with a picture in a pinacoteca or re-membering a dream style, the dream detail, the meaningful richness of color and contour in an otherwise meaningless vi-sion. It should be observed that nobody, not even the reader, not even Bouteillan (who crumbled, alas, a precious cork), was at his or her best at that particular party. A faint element of farce and falsity flawed it, preventing an angel—if angels could visit Ardis—from being completely at ease; and yet it was a marvelous show which no artist would have wanted to miss.

The tablecloth and the candle blaze attracted timorous or impetuous moths among which Ada, with a ghost pointing them out to her, could not help recognizing many old "flut-terfriends." Pale intruders, anxious only to spread out their delicate wings on some lustrous surface; ceiling-bumpers in guildman furs; thick-set rake-hells with bushy antennae; and party-crashing hawkmoths with red black-belted bellies, sailed or shot, silent or humming, into the dining room out of the black hot humid night.

It was a black hot humid night in mid-July, 1888, at Ardis, in Ladore county, let us not forget, let us never forget, with a family of four seated around an oval dinner table, bright with flowers and crystal—not a scene in a play, as might have seemed—nay, *must* have seemed—to a spectator (with a cam-era or a program) placed in the velvet pit of the garden. Six-teen years had elapsed from the end of Marina's three-year affair with Demon. Intermissions of various length—a break of two months in the spring of 1870, another, of almost four, in the middle of 1871—had at the time only increased the tenderness and the torture. Her singularly coarsened features, her attire, that sequin-spangled dress, the glittering net over her strawberry-blond dyed hair, her red sunburnt chest and melodramatic make-up, with too much ochre and maroon in it, did not even vaguely remind the man, who had loved her more keenly than any other woman in his philanderings, of the dash, the glamour, the lyricism of Marina Durmanov's beauty. It aggrieved him—that complete collapse of the past, the dispersal of its itinerant court and music-makers, the logical impossibility to relate the dubious reality of the present to the unquestionable one of remembrance. Even these hors-d'oeuvres on the *zakusochniy stol* of Ardis Manor and its painted dining room did not link up with their *petits soupers*, although, God knows, the triple staple to start with was always much the same—pickled young boletes in their tight-fitting glossy fawn helmets, the gray beads of fresh caviar, the goose liver paste, pique-aced with Perigord truffles.

Demon popped into his mouth a last morsel of black bread with elastic samlet, gulped down a last pony of vodka and took his place at the table with Marina facing him across its oblong length, beyond the great bronze bowl with carved-looking Calville apples and elongated Persty grapes. The alcohol his vigorous system had already imbibed was instrumental, as usual, in reopening what he gallicistically called condemned doors, and now as he gaped involuntarily as all men do while spreading a napkin, he considered Marina's pretentious *ciel-étoilé* hair-dress and tried to *realize* (in the rare full sense of the word), tried to *possess* the reality of a fact by forcing it into the sensuous center, that here was a woman whom he had intolerably loved, who had loved him hysterically and skittishly, who insisted they make love on rugs and cushions laid on the floor ("as respectable people do in the Tigris-Euphrates valley"), who would woosh down fluffy slopes on a bobsleigh a fortnight after parturition, or arrive by the Orient Express with five trunks, Dack's grandsire, and a maid, to Dr. Stella Ospenko's *ospedale* where he was recovering from a scratch received in a sword duel (and still visible as a white weal under his eighth rib after a lapse of nearly seventeen years). How strange that when one met after a long separation a chum or fat aunt whom one had been fond of as a child the unimpaired human warmth of the friendship was rediscovered at once, but with an old mistress this never happened—the human part of one's affection seemed to be swept away with the dust of the inhuman passion, in a wholesale operation of demolishment. He looked at her and acknowledged the perfection of the potage, but she, this rather thick-set woman, goodhearted, no doubt, but restive and sour-faced, glazed over, nose, forehead and all, with a sort of brownish oil that she considered to be more "juvenizing" than powder, was more of a stranger to him than Bouteillan who had once carried her in his arms, in a feigned faint, out of a Ladore villa and into a cab, after a final, quite final row, on the eve of her wedding.

Marina, essentially a dummy in human disguise, experienced no such qualms, lacking as she did that *third sight* (individual, magically detailed imagination) which many otherwise ordinary and conformant people may also possess, but without which memory (even that of a profound "thinker" or technician of genius) is, let us face it, a stereotype or a tear-sheet. We do not wish to be too hard on Marina; after all, her blood throbs in our wrists and temples, and many of our megrims are hers, not his. Yet we cannot condone the grossness of her soul. The man sitting at the head of the table and joined to her by a pair of cheerful youngsters, the "juvenile" (in movie parlance) on her right, the "ingénue" on her left, differed in no way from the same Demon in much the same black jacket (minus perhaps the carnation he had evidently purloined from a vase Blanche had been told to bring from the gallery) who sat next to her at the Praslins' last Christmas. The dizzy chasm he felt every time he met her, that awful "wonder of life" with its extravagant jumble of geological faults, could not be bridged by what *she* accepted as a dotted line of humdrum encounters: "poor old" Demon (all her pillow mates being retired with that title) appeared before her like a harmless ghost, in the foyers of theaters "between mirror and fan," or in the drawing rooms of common friends, or once in Lincoln Park, indicating an indigo-buttocked ape with his cane and not saluting her, according to the rules of the *beau monde,* because he was with a courtesan. Somewhere, further back, much further back, safely transformed by her screen-corrupted mind into a stale melodrama was her three-year-long period of hectically spaced love-meetings with Demon, *A Torrid Affair* (the title of her only cinema hit), passion in *palaces,* the palms and larches, his Utter Devotion, his impossible temper, separations, reconciliations, Blue Trains, tears, treachery, terror, an insane sister's threats, helpless, no doubt, but leaving their tiger-marks on the drapery of dreams, especially when dampness and dark affect one with fever. And the shadow of retribution on the backwall (with ridiculous legal innuendoes). All this was mere scenery, easily packed, labeled "Hell" and freighted away; and only very infrequently some reminder would come—say, in the trick-work closeup of two left hands belonging to different sexes—doing what? Marina could no longer recall (though only *four* years had elapsed!)—playing *à quatre mains?*—no, neither took piano lessons—casting bunny-shadows on a wall?—closer, warmer, but still wrong; measuring something? But what? Climbing a tree? The polished trunk of a tree? But where, when? Someday, she mused, one's past must be put in order. Retouched, retaken. Certain "wipes" and "inserts" will have to be made in the picture; certain telltale abrasions in the emulsion will have to be corrected; "dissolves" in the sequence discreetly combined with the trimming out of unwanted, embarrassing "footage," and definite guarantees obtained; yes, someday—before death with its clapstick closes the scene.

Tonight she contented herself with the automatic ceremony of giving him what she remembered, more or less correctly, when planning the menu, as being his favorite food—*zelyonïya shchi,* a velvety green sorrel-and-spinach soup, containing slippery hard-boiled eggs and served with finger-burning, irresistibly soft, meat-filled or carrot-filled or cabbage-filled *pirozhki*—peer-rush-KEY, thus pronounced, thus celebrated here, for ever and ever. After that, she had decided, there would be bread-crumbed sander (*sudak*) with boiled potatoes, hazel-hen (*ryabchiki*) and that special asparagus (*bezukhanka*) which does not produce Proust's After-effect, as cookbooks say.

"Marina," murmured Demon at the close of the first course. "Marina," he repeated louder. "Far from me" (a locution he favored) "to criticize Dan's taste in white wines or the manners *de vos domestiques.* You know me, I'm above all that rot, I'm . . ." (gesture); "but, my dear," he continued, switching to Russian, "the *chelovek* who brought me the *pirozhki*—the new man, the plumpish one with the eyes (*s glazami*)—"

"Everybody has eyes," remarked Marina drily.

"Well, *his* look as if they were about to octopus the food he serves. But that's not the point. He pants, Marina! He suffers from some kind of *odïshka* (shortness of breath). He should see Dr. Krolik. It's depressing. It's a rhythmic pumping pant. It made my soup ripple."

"Look, Dad," said Van, "Dr. Krolik can't do much, because, as you know quite well, he's dead, and Marina can't tell her servants not to breathe, because, as you also know, they're alive."

"The Veen wit, the Veen wit," murmured Demon.

"Exactly," said Marina. "I simply refuse to do anything about it. Besides poor Jones is not at all asthmatic, but only nervously eager to please. He's as healthy as a bull and has rowed me from Ardisville to Ladore and back, and enjoyed it, many times this summer. You are cruel, Demon. I can't tell him '*ne pïkhtite*,' as I can't tell Kim, the kitchen boy, not to take photographs on the sly—he's a regular snap-shooting fiend, that Kim, though otherwise an adorable, gentle, honest boy; nor can I tell my little French maid to stop getting invitations, as she somehow succeeds in doing, to the most exclusive *bals masqués* in Ladore."

"That's interesting," observed Demon.

"He's a dirty old man!" cried Van cheerfully.

"Van!" said Ada.

"I'm a dirty *young* man," sighed Demon.

"Tell me, Bouteillan," asked Marina, "what other good white wine do we have—what can you recommend?" The butler smiled and whispered a fabulous name.

"Yes, oh, yes," said Demon. "Ah, my dear, you should not think up dinners all by yourself. Now about rowing—you mentioned rowing . . . Do you know that *moi, qui vous parle,*

was a Rowing Blue in 1858? Van prefers football, but he's only
a College Blue, aren't you Van? I'm also better than he at
tennis—not lawn tennis, of course, a game for parsons, but
'court tennis' as they say in Manhattan. What else, Van?''

"You still beat me at fencing, but I'm the better shot.
That's not real *sudak, papa*, though it's tops, I assure you.''

(Marina, having failed to obtain the European product in
time for the dinner, had chosen the nearest thing, wall-eyed
pike, or "dory," with Tartar sauce and boiled young potatoes.)

"Ah!" said Demon, tasting Lord Byron's Hock. "This re-
deems Our Lady's Tears.''

"I was telling Van a moment ago," he continued, raising
his voice (he labored under the delusion that Marina had
grown rather deaf), "about your husband. My dear, he over-
does the juniper vodka stuff, he's getting, in fact, a mite fuzzy
and odd. The other day I chanced to walk through Pat Lane
on the Fourth Avenue side, and there he was coming, at quite
a spin, in his horrid town car, that primordial petrol two-seater
he's got, with the tiller. Well, he saw me, from quite a distance, and waved, and the whole contraption began to shake
down, and finally stopped half a block away, and there he sat
trying to budge it with little jerks of his haunches, you know,
like a child who can't get his tricycle unstuck, and as I walked
up to him I had the definite impression that it was *his* mechanism that had stalled, not the Hardpan's.'' But what Demon,
in the goodness of his crooked heart, omitted to tell Marina
was that the imbecile, in secret from his art adviser, Mr. Aix,
had acquired for a few thousand dollars from a gaming friend
of Demon's, and with Demon's blessings, a couple of fake
Correggios—only to resell them by some unforgivable fluke
to an equally imbecile collector, for half a million which Demon considered henceforth as a loan his cousin should certainly refund him if sanity counted for something on this
gemel planet. And, conversely, Marina refrained from telling
Demon about the young hospital nurse Dan had been mon-
keying with ever since his last illness (it was, by the way, she,
busybody Bess, whom Dan had asked on a memorable occasion to help him get "something nice for a half-Russian child
interested in biology").

"*Vous me comblez*," said Demon in reference to the burgundy, "though, *pravda*, my maternal grandfather would have left the table rather than see me drinking red wine instead of champagne with *gelinotte*. Superb, my dear (blowing a kiss through the vista of flame and silver)."

The roast hazel-hen (or rather its New World representative, locally called "mountain grouse") was accompanied by preserved lingonberries (locally called "mountain cranberries"). An especially succulent morsel of one of those brown little fowls yielded a globule of birdshot between Demon's red tongue and strong canine: "*La fève de Diane*," he remarked, placing it carefully on the edge of his plate. "How is the car situation, Van?"

"Vague. I ordered a Roseley like yours but it won't be delivered before Christmas. I tried to find a Silentium with a side car and could not, because of the war, though what connection exists between wars and motorcycles is a mystery. But we manage, Ada and I, we manage, we ride, we bike, we even jikker."

"I wonder," said sly Demon, "why I'm reminded all at once our great Canadian's lovely lines about blushing Irène:

> "*Le feu si délicat de la virginité*
> *Qui* something *sur son front . . .*

"All right. You can ship mine to England, provided—"

"By the way, Demon," interrupted Marina, "where and how can I obtain the kind of old roomy limousine with an old professional chauffeur that Praskovia, for instance, has had for years?"

"Impossible, my dear, they are all in heaven or on Terra. But what would Ada like, what would my silent love like for her birthday? It's next Saturday, *po razschyotu po moemu* (by my reckoning), isn't it? *Une rivière de diamants?*"

"*Protestuyu!*" cried Marina. "Yes, I'm speaking *seriozno*. I object to your giving her *kvaka sesva* (*quoi que ce soit*), Dan and I will take care of all that."

"Besides you'll forget," said Ada laughing, and very deftly showed the tip of her tongue to Van who had been on the look-out for her conditional reaction to "diamonds."

Van asked: "Provided what?"

"Provided you don't have one waiting already for you in George's Garage, Ranta Road."

"Ada, you'll be jikkering alone soon," he continued, "I'm going to have Mascodagama round out his vacation in Paris. *Qui* something *sur son front, en accuse la beauté!*"

So the trivial patter went. Who does not harbor in the darkest gulf of his mind such bright recollections? Who has not squirmed and covered his face with his hands as the dazzling past leered at him? Who, in the terror and solitude of a long night—

"What was that?" exclaimed Marina, whom certicle storms terrified even more than they did the Antiamberians of Ladore County.

"Sheet lightning," suggested Van.

"If you ask me," said Demon, turning on his chair to consider the billowing drapery, "I'd guess it was a photographer's flash. After all, we have here a famous actress and a sensational acrobat."

Ada ran to the window. From under the anxious magnolias a white-faced boy flanked by two gaping handmaids stood aiming a camera at the harmless, gay family group. But it was only a nocturnal mirage, not unusual in July. Nobody was taking pictures except Perun, the unmentionable god of thunder. In expectation of the rumble, Marina started to count under her breath, as if she were praying or checking the pulse of a very sick person. One heartbeat was supposed to span one mile of black night between the living heart and a doomed herdsman, felled somewhere—oh, very far—on the top of a mountain. The rumble came—but sounded rather subdued. A second flash revealed the structure of the French window.

Ada returned to her seat. Van picked up her napkin from under her chair and in the course of his brief plunge and ascent brushed the side of her knee with his temple.

"Might I have another helping of Peterson's Grouse, *Tetrastes bonasia windriverensis*?" asked Ada loftily.

Marina jangled a diminutive cowbell of bronze. Demon placed his palm on the back of Ada's hand and asked her to pass him the oddly evocative object. She did so in a staccato arc. Demon inserted his monocle and, muffling the tongue of memory, examined the bell; but it was not the one that had once stood on a bed-tray in a dim room of Dr. Lapiner's chalet; was not even of Swiss make; was merely one of those sweet-sounding translations which reveal a paraphrast's crass counterfeit as soon as you look up the original.

Alas, the bird had not survived "the honor one had made to it," and after a brief consultation with Bouteillan a somewhat incongruous but highly palatable bit of saucisson d'Arles added itself to the young lady's fare of *asperges en branches* that everybody was now enjoying. It almost awed one to see the pleasure with which she and Demon distorted their shiny-lipped mouths in exactly the same way to introduce orally from some heavenly height the voluptuous ally of the prim lily of the valley, holding the shaft with an identical bunching of the fingers, not unlike the reformed "sign of the cross" for protesting against which (a ridiculous little schism measuring an inch or so from thumb to index) so many Russians had been burnt by other Russians only two centuries earlier on the banks of the Great Lake of Slaves. Van remembered that his tutor's great friend, the learned but prudish Semyon Afanasievich Vengerov, then a young associate professor but already a celebrated Pushkinist (1855–1954), used to say that the only vulgar passage in his author's work was the cannibal joy of young gourmets tearing "plump and live" oysters out of their "cloisters" in an unfinished canto of *Eugene Onegin*. But then "everyone has his own taste," as the British writer Richard Leonard Churchill mistranslates a trite French phrase (*chacun à son goût*) twice in the course of his novel about a certain Crimean Khan once popular with reporters and politicians, "A Great Good Man"—according, of course, to the cattish and prejudiced Guillaume Monparnasse about whose new celebrity Ada, while dipping the reversed corolla of one hand in a bowl, was now telling Demon, who was performing the same rite in the same graceful fashion.

Marina helped herself to an Albany from a crystal box of Turkish cigarettes tipped with red rose petal and passed the box on to Demon. Ada, somewhat self-consciously, lit up too.

"You know quite well," said Marina, "that your father disapproves of your smoking at table."

"Oh, it's all right," murmured Demon.

"I had Dan in view," explained Marina heavily. "He's very prissy on that score."

"Well, and I'm not," answered Demon.

Ada and Van could not help laughing. All that was banter—not of a high order, but still banter.

A moment later, however, Van remarked: "I think I'll take an Alibi—I mean an Albany—myself."

"Please note, everybody," said Ada, "how *voulu* that slip was! I like a smoke when I go mushrooming, but when I'm back, this horrid tease insists I smell of some romantic Turk or Albanian met in the woods."

"Well," said Demon, "Van's quite right to look after your morals."

The real *profitrol'* (very soft "l"") of the Russians, as first made by their cooks in Gavana before 1700, consists of larger puffs coated with creamier chocolate than the dark and puny "profit rolls" served in European restaurants. Our friends had finished that rich sweetmeat flooded with *chocolat-au-lait* sauce, and were ready for some fruit, when Bout followed by his father and floundering Jones made a sensational entry.

All the toilets and waterpipes in the house had been suddenly seized with borborygmic convulsions. This always signified, and introduced, a long-distance call. Marina, who had been awaiting for several days a certain message from California in response to a torrid letter, could now hardly contain her passionate impatience and had been on the point of running to the dorophone in the hall at the first bubbling spasm, when young Bout hurried in dragging the long green cord (visibly palpitating in a series of swells and contractions rather like a serpent ingesting a field mouse) of the ornate, brass-and-nacre receiver, which Marina with a wild "*A l'eau!*" pressed to her ear. It was, however, only fussy old Dan ringing her up to inform everybody that Miller could not make it that night after all and would accompany him to Ardis bright and early on the following morning.

"Early but hardly bright," observed Demon, who was now glutted with family joys and slightly annoyed he had missed the first half of a gambling night in Ladore for the sake of all that well-meant but not *quite* first-rate food.

"We'll have coffee in the yellow drawing room," said

Marina as sadly as if she were evoking a place of dreary exile. "Jones, *please*, don't walk on that phonecord. You have no idea, Demon, how I dread meeting again, after all those years, that dislikable Norbert von Miller, who has probably become even more arrogant and obsequious, and moreover does not realize, I'm sure, that Dan's wife is me. He's a Baltic Russian" (turning to Van) "but really *echt deutsch*, though his mother was born Ivanov or Romanov, or something, who owned a calico factory in Finland or Denmark. I can't imagine how he got his barony; when I knew him twenty years ago he was plain Mr. Miller."

"He is still that," said Demon drily, "because you've got two Millers mixed up. The lawyer who works for Dan is my old friend Norman Miller of the Fainley, Fehler and Miller law firm and physically bears a striking resemblance to Wilfrid Laurier. Norbert, on the other hand, has, I remember, a head like a *kegelkugel*, lives in Switzerland, knows perfectly well whom you married and is an unmentionable blackguard."

After a quick cup of coffee and a drop of cherry liqueur Demon got up.

"*Partir c'est mourir un peu, et mourir c'est partir un peu trop.* Do tell Dan and Norman I can give them tea-and-cake any time tomorrow at the Bryant. By the way, how's Lucette?"

Marina knitted her brows and shook her head acting the fond, worried mother though, in point of fact, she bore her daughters even less affection than she had for cute Dack and pathetic Dan.

"Oh, we had quite a scare," she replied finally, "quite a nasty scare. But now, apparently—"

"Van," said his father, "be a good scout. I did not have a hat but I did have gloves. Ask Bouteillan to look in the gallery, I may have dropped them there. No. Stay! It's all right. I left them in the car, because I recall the cold of this flower, which I took from a vase in passing . . ."

He now threw it away, discarding with it the shadow of his fugitive urge to plunge both hands in a soft bosom.

"I had hoped you'd sleep here," said Marina (not really caring one way or another). "What is your room number at the hotel—not 222 by any chance?"

She liked romantic coincidences. Demon consulted the tag on his key: 221—which was good enough, fatidically and anecdotically speaking. Naughty Ada, of course, stole a glance at Van, who tensed up the wings of his nose in a grimace that mimicked the slant of Pedro's narrow, beautiful nostrils.

"They make fun of an old woman," said Marina, not without coquetry, and in the Russian manner kissed her guest on his inclined brow as he lifted her hand to his lips: "You'll forgive me," she added, "for not going out on the terrace. I've grown allergic to damp and darkness; I'm sure my temperature has already gone up to thirty-seven and seven, at least."

Demon tapped the barometer next to the door. It had been tapped too often to react in any intelligible way and remained standing at a quarter past three.

Van and Ada saw him off. The night was very warm and dripping with what Ladore farmers called green rain. Demon's black sedan glinted elegantly among the varnished laurels in the moth-flaked porchlight. He tenderly kissed the children, the girl on one cheek, the boy on the other, then Ada again—in the hollow of the white arm that clasped his neck. Nobody paid much attention to Marina, who waved from a tangelo-colored oriel window a spangled shawl although all she could see was the sheen of the car's bonnet and the rain slanting in the light of its lamps.

Demon pulled on his gloves and sped away with a great growl of damp gravel.

"That last kiss went a little too far," remarked Van, laughing.

"Oh well—his lips sort of slipped," laughed Ada and, laughing, they embraced in the dark as they skirted the wing of the house.

They stopped for a moment under the shelter of an indulgent tree, where many a cigar-smoking guest had stopped after dinner. Tranquilly, innocently, side by side in their separately ordained attitudes, they added a trickle and a gush to the more professional sounds of the rain in the night, and then lingered, hand in hand, in a corner of the latticed gallery waiting for the lights in the windows to go out.

"What was faintly off-key, *ne tak*, about the whole eve-ning?" asked Van softly. "You noticed?"

"Of course, I did. And yet I adore him. I think he's quite crazy, and with no place or occupation in life, and far from happy, and philosophically irresponsible—and there is abso-lutely nobody like him."

"But what went wrong tonight? You were tongue-tied, and everything we said was *fal'shivo*. I wonder if some inner nose in him smelled you in me, and me in you. He tried to ask me . . . Oh it was not a nice family reunion. What exactly went wrong at dinner?"

"My love, my love, as if you don't know! We'll manage, perhaps, to wear our masks always, till dee do us part, but we shall never be able to marry—while they're both alive. We simply can't swing it, because he's more conventional in his own way than even the law and the social lice. One can't bribe one's parents, and waiting forty, fifty years for them to die is too horrible to imagine—I mean the mere thought of *anybody* waiting for such a thing is not in our nature, is mean and monstrous!"

He kissed her half-closed lips, gently and "morally" as they defined moments of depth to distinguish them from the de-spair of passion.

"Anyway," he said, "it's fun to be two secret agents in an alien country. Marina has gone upstairs. Your hair is wet."

"Spies from Terra? You believe, you believe in the existence of Terra? Oh, you do! You accept it. I know you!"

"I accept it as a state of mind. That's not quite the same thing."

"Yes, but you want to prove it *is* the same thing."

He brushed her lips with another religious kiss. Its edge, however, was beginning to catch fire.

"One of these days," he said, "I will ask you for a repeat performance. You will sit as you did four years ago, at the same table, in the same light, drawing the same flower, and I shall go through the same scene with such joy, such pride, such—I don't know—gratitude! Look, all the windows are dark now. I, too, can translate when I simply have to. Listen to this:

> Lights in the rooms were going out.
> Breathed fragrantly the *rozï*.
> We sat together in the shade
> Of a wide-branched *beryozï*."

"Yes, 'birch' is what leaves the translator in the 'lurch,' doesn't it? That's a terrible little poem by Konstantin Romanov, right? Just elected president of the Lyascan Academy of Literature, right? Wretched poet and happy husband. Happy husband!"

"You know," said Van, "I really think you should wear *something* underneath on formal occasions."

"Your hands are cold. Why formal? You said yourself it was a family affair."

"Even so. You were in peril whenever you bent or sprawled."

"I never *sprawl*!"

"I'm quite sure it's not hygienic, or perhaps it's a kind of jealousy on my part. Memoirs of a Happy Chair. Oh, my darling."

"At least," whispered Ada, "it pays off now, doesn't it? Croquet room? *Ou comme ça?*"

"*Comme ça*, for once," said Van.

39

Although fairly eclectic in 1888, Ladore fashions were not quite as free as taken for granted at Ardis.

For the grand picnic on her birthday sixteen-year-old Ada wore a plain linen blouse, maize-yellow slacks and scuffed moccasins. Van had wanted her to let her hair down; she demurred, saying it was too long for country comfort, but finally compromised by tying it midway behind with a rumpled ribbon of black silk. Van's only observance of summer elegancies consisted of a blue polo jersey, knee-length gray flannel trousers, and sport "creepers."

While the rustic feast was being prepared and distributed among the sun gouts of the traditional pine glade, the wild girl and her lover slipped away for a few moments of ravenous ardor in a ferny ravine where a rill dipped from ledge to ledge between tall burnberry bushes. The day was hot and breathless. The smallest pine had its cicada.

She said: "Speaking as a character in an old novel, it seems so long, long ago, *davnïm davno*, since I used to play wordgames here with Grace and two other lovely girls. 'Insect, incest, nicest.'"

Speaking as a botanist and a mad woman, she said, the most extraordinary word in the English language was "husked," because it stood for opposite things, covered and uncovered, tightly husked but easily husked, meaning they peel off quite easily, you don't have to tear the waistband, you brute. "Carefully husked brute," said Van tenderly. The passage of time could only enhance his tenderness for the creature he clasped, this adored creature, whose motion was now more supple, whose haunches had grown more lyrate, whose hair-ribbon he had undone.

As they crouched on the brink of one of the brook's crystal shelves, where, before falling, it stopped to have its picture taken and take pictures itself, Van, at the last throb, saw the reflection of Ada's gaze in the water flash a warning. Something of the sort had happened somewhere before: he did not have time to identify the recollection that, nonetheless, led him to identify at once the sound of the stumble behind him.

Among the rugged rocks they found and consoled poor little Lucette, whose foot had slipped on a granite slab in a tangle of bushes. Flushed and flustered, the child rubbed her thigh in much-overdone agony. Van and Ada gaily grasped one little hand each and ran Lucette back to the glade, where she laughed, where she flopped, where she made for her favorite tarts awaiting her on one of the unfolded tables. There she husked out of her sweat shirt, hitched up her green shorts and, asquat on the russet ground, attacked the food she had collected.

Ada had declined to invite anybody except the Erminin twins to her picnic; but she had had no intention of inviting the brother without the sister. The latter, it turned out, could not come, having gone to New Cranton to see a young drummer, her first boy friend, sail off into the sunrise with his regiment. But Greg had to be asked to come after all: on the previous day he had called on her bringing a "talisman" from his very sick father, who wanted Ada to treasure as much as his grandam had a little camel of yellow ivory carved in Kiev, five centuries ago, in the days of Timur and Nabok.

Van did not err in believing that Ada remained unaffected by Greg's devotion. He now met him again with pleasure—the kind of pleasure, immoral in its very purity, which adds its icy tang to the friendly feelings a successful rival bears toward a thoroughly decent fellow.

Greg, who had left his splendid new black Silentium motorcycle in the forest ride, observed:

"We have company."

"Indeed we do," assented Van. "*Kto sii* (who are they)? Do you have any idea?"

Nobody had. Raincoated, unpainted, morose, Marina came over and peered through the trees the way Van pointed.

After reverently inspecting the Silentium, a dozen elderly townsmen, in dark clothes, shabby and uncouth, walked into the forest across the road and sat down there to a modest *colazione* of cheese, buns, salami, sardines and Chianti. They were quite sufficiently far from our picnickers not to bother them in any way. They had no mechanical music boxes with them. Their voices were subdued, their movements could not have been more discreet. The predominant gesture seemed to be ritually limited to this or that first crumpling brown paper or coarse gazette paper or baker's paper (the very lightweight and inefficient sort), and discarding the crumpled bit in quiet, abstract fashion, while other sad apostolic hands unwrapped the victuals or for some reason or other wrapped them up again, in the noble shade of the pines, in the humble shade of the false acacias.

"How odd," said Marina, scratching her sunlit bald patch.

She sent a footman to investigate the situation and tell those Gipsy politicians, or Calabrian laborers, that Squire Veen would be *furious* if he discovered trespassers camping in his woods.

The footman returned, shaking his head. They did not speak English. Van went over:

"Please go away, this is private property," said Van in Vulgar Latin, French, Canadian French, Russian, Yukonian Russian, very low Latin again: *proprieta privata.*

He stood looking at them, hardly noticed by them, hardly shade-touched by the foliage. They were ill-shaven, blue-jowled men in old Sunday suits. One or two wore no collar but had kept the thyroid stud. One had a beard and a humid squint. Patent boots, with dust in the cracks, or orange-brown shoes either very square or very pointed had been taken off and pushed under the burdocks or placed on the old tree stumps of the rather drab clearing. How odd indeed! When Van repeated his request, the intruders started to mutter among themselves in a totally incomprehensible jargon, making small flapping motions in his direction as if half-heartedly chasing away a gnat.

He asked Marina—did she want him to use force, but sweet, dear Marina said, patting her hair, one hand on her hip, no, let us ignore them—especially as they were now drawing a little deeper into the trees—look, look—some dragging *à reculons* the various parts of their repast upon what resembled an old bedspread, which receded like a fishing boat pulled over pebbly sand, while others politely removed the crumpled wrappings to other more distant hiding places in keeping with the general relocation: a most melancholy and meaningful picture—but meaning what, what?

Gradually their presence dissolved from Van's mind. Everybody was now having a wonderful time. Marina threw off the pale raincoat or rather "dustcoat" she had put on for the picnic (after all, with one thing and another, her domestic gray dress with the pink fichu was quite gay enough, she declared, for an old lady) and raising an empty glass she sang, with brio and very musically, the Green Grass aria: "Replenish, replenish the glasses with wine! Here's a toast to love! To the rapture of love!" With awe and pity, and no love, Van kept reverting to that poor bald patch on Traverdiata's poor old head, to the scalp burnished by her hairdye an awful pine rust color much shinier than her dead hair. He attempted, as so many times before, to squeeze out some fondness for her but as usual failed and as usual told himself that Ada did not love her mother either, a vague and cowardly consolation.

Greg, assuming with touching simplicity that Ada would

notice and approve, showered Mlle Larivière with a thousand little attentions—helping her out of her mauve jacket, pouring out for her the milk into Lucette's mug from a thermos bottle, passing the sandwiches, replenishing, replenishing Mlle Larivière's wineglass and listening with a rapt grin to her diatribes against the English, whom she said she disliked even more than the Tartars, or the, well, Assyrians.

"England!" she cried, "England! The country where for every poet, there are ninety-nine *sales petits bourgeois*, some of suspect extraction! England dares ape France! I have in that hamper there an English novel of high repute in which a lady is given a perfume—an expensive perfume!—called '*Ombre Chevalier*,' which is really nothing but a fish—a delicious fish, true, but hardly suitable for scenting one's handkerchief with. On the very next page, a soi-disant philosopher mentions '*une acte gratuite*' as if all acts were feminine, and a soi-disant Parisian hotel-keeper in the story says '*je me regrette*' for '*je regrette*'!"

"*D'accord*," interjected Van, "but what about such atrocious bloomers in French translations from the English as for example—"

Unfortunately, or maybe fortunately, at that very moment Ada emitted a Russian exclamation of utmost annoyance as a steel-gray convertible glided into the glade. No sooner had it stopped than it was surrounded by the same group of townsmen, who now seemed to have multiplied in strange consequence of having shed coats and waistcoats. Thrusting his way through their circle, with every sign of wrath and contempt, young Percy de Prey, frilled-shirted and white-trousered, strode up to Marina's deckchair. He was invited to join the party despite Ada's trying to stop her silly mother with an admonishing stare and a private small shake of the head.

"I dared not hope . . . Oh, I accept with great pleasure," answered Percy, whereupon—very much whereupon—the seemingly forgetful but in reality calculating bland bandit marched back to his car (near which a last wonderstruck admirer lingered) to fetch a bouquet of longstemmed roses stored in the boot.

"What a shame that I should loathe roses," said Ada, accepting them gingerly.

The muscat wine was uncorked, Ada's and Ida's healths drunk. "The conversation became general," as Monparnasse liked to write.

Count Percy de Prey turned to Ivan Demianovich Veen:

"I'm told you like abnormal positions?"

The half-question was half-mockingly put. Van looked through his raised lunel at the honeyed sun.

"Meaning what?" he enquired.

"Well—that walking-on-your-hands trick. One of your aunt's servants is the sister of one of our servants and two pretty gossips form a dangerous team" (laughing). "The legend has it that you do it all day long, in every corner, congratulations!" (bowing).

Van replied: "The legend makes too much of my specialty. Actually, I practice it for a few minutes every other night, don't I, Ada?" (looking around for her). "May I give you, Count, some more of the mouse-and-cat—a poor pun, but mine."

"Vahn dear," said Marina, who was listening with delight to the handsome young men's vivacious and carefree prattle, "tell him about your success in London. *Zhe tampri* (please)!"

"Yes," said Van, "it all started as a rag, you know, up at Chose, but then—"

"Van!" called Ada shrilly. "I want to say something to you, Van, come here."

Dorn (flipping through a literary review, to Trigorin): "Here, a couple of months ago, a certain article was printed . . . a Letter from America, and I wanted to ask you, incidentally" (taking Trigorin by the waist and leading him to the front of the stage), "because I'm very much interested in that question . . ."

Ada stood with her back against the trunk of a tree, like a beautiful spy who has just rejected the blindfold.

"I wanted to ask you, incidentally, Van" (continuing in a whisper, with an angry flick of the wrist)—"stop playing the perfect idiot host; he came drunk as a welt, can't you see?"

The execution was interrupted by the arrival of Uncle Dan. He had a remarkably reckless way of driving, as happens so often, goodness knows why, in the case of many dour, dreary men. Weaving rapidly between the pines, he brought the little

red runabout to an abrupt stop in front of Ada and presented
her with the perfect gift, a big box of mints, white, pink and,
oh boy, green! He had also an aerogram for her, he said,
winking.

Ada tore it open—and saw it was not for her from dismal
Kalugano, as she had feared, but for her mother from Los
Angeles, a much gayer place. Marina's face gradually assumed
an expression of quite indecent youthful beatitude as she
scanned the message. Triumphantly, she showed it to Lariv-
ère-Monparnasse, who read it twice and tilted her head with
a smile of indulgent disapproval. Positively stamping her feet
with joy:

"Pedro is coming again," cried (gurgled, rippled) Marina
to her calm daughter.

"And, I suppose, he'll stay till the end of the summer,"
remarked Ada—and sat down with Greg and Lucette, for a
game of Snap, on a laprobe spread over the little ants and dry
pine needles.

"Oh no, *da net zhe*, only for a fortnight" (girlishly giggling). "After that we shall go to Houssaie, *Gollivud-tozh*"
(Marina was really in great form)—"yes, we shall all go, the
author, and the children, and Van—if he wishes."

"I wish but I can't," said Percy (sample of *his* humor).

In the meantime, Uncle Dan, very dapper in cherry-striped
blazer and variety-comic straw hat, feeling considerably intrigued by the presence of the adjacent picnickers, walked over
to them with his glass of Hero wine in one hand and a caviar
canapé in the other.

"The Accursed Children," said Marina in answer to something Percy wanted to know.

Percy, you were to die very soon—and not from that pellet
in your fat leg, on the turf of a Crimean ravine, but a couple
of minutes later when you opened your eyes and felt relieved
and secure in the shelter of the macchie; you were to die very
soon, Percy; but that July day in Ladore County, lolling under
the pines, royally drunk after some earlier festivity, with lust
in your heart and a sticky glass in your strong blond-haired
hand, listening to a literary bore, chatting with an aging actress and ogling her sullen daughter, you reveled in the spicy
situation, old sport, chin-chin, and no wonder. Burly, hand-

some, indolent and ferocious, a crack Rugger player, a cracker of country girls, you combined the charm of the off-duty athlete with the engaging drawl of a fashionable ass. I think what I hated most about your handsome moon face was that baby complexion, the smooth-skinned jaws of the easy shaver. *I* had begun to bleed every time, and was going to do so for seven decades.

"In a birdhouse fixed to that pine trunk," said Marina to her young admirer, "there was once a 'telephone.' How I'd welcome its presence right now! Ah, here he is, *enfin!*"

Her husband, minus the glass and the canapé, strolled back bringing wonderful news. They were an "exquisitely polite group." He had recognized at least a dozen Italian words. It was, he understood, a collation of shepherds. They thought, he thought, he was a shepherd too. A canvas from Cardinal Carlo de Medici's collection, author unknown, may have been at the base of that copy. Excitedly, overexcitedly, the little man said he insisted the servants take viands and wine to his excellent new friends; he got busy himself, seizing an empty bottle and a hamper that contained knitting equipment, an English novel by Quigley and a roll of toilet paper. Marina explained, however, that professional obligations demanded she call up California without delay; and, forgetting his project, he readily consented to drive her home.

Mists have long since hidden the links and loops of consecutive events, but—approximately while that departure took place, or soon after—Van found himself standing on the brink of the brook (which had reflected two pair of superposed eyes earlier in the afternoon) and chucking pebbles with Percy and Greg at the remnants of an old, rusty, indecipherable signboard on the other side.

"*Okh, nado* (I must) *passati!*" exclaimed Percy in the Slavic slang he affected, blowing out his cheeks and fumbling frantically at his fly. In all his life, said stolid Greg to Van, he had never seen such an ugly engine, surgically circumcised, terrifically oversized and high-colored, with such a phenomenal *coeur de boeuf*; nor had either of the fascinated, fastidious boys ever witnessed the like of its sustained, strongly arched, practically everlasting stream. "Phoeh!" uttered the young man with relief, and repacked.

How did the scuffle start? Did all three cross the brook stepping on slimy stones? Did Percy push Greg? Did Van jog Percy? Was there something—a stick? Twisted out of a fist? A wrist gripped and freed?

"Oho," said Percy, "you are playful, my lad!"

Greg, one bag of his plus-fours soaked, watched them helplessly—he was fond of both—as they grappled on the brink of the brook.

Percy was three years older, and a score of kilograms heavier than Van, but the latter had handled even burlier brutes with ease. Almost at once the Count's bursting face was trapped in the crook of Van's arm. The grunting Count toured the turf in a hunched-up stagger. He freed one scarlet ear, was retrapped, was tripped and collapsed under Van, who instantly put him "on his omoplates," *na lopatki*, as King Wing used to say in his carpet jargon. Percy lay panting like a dying gladiator, both shoulder blades pressed to the ground by his tormentor, whose thumbs now started to manipulate horribly that heaving thorax. Percy with a sudden bellow of pain intimated he had had enough. Van requested a more articulate expression of surrender, and got it. Greg, fearing Van had not caught the muttered plea for mercy, repeated it in the third person interpretative. Van released the unfortunate Count, whereupon he sat up, spitting, palpating his throat, rearranging the rumpled shirt around his husky torso and asking Greg in a husky voice to find a missing cufflink.

Van washed his hands in a lower shelf-pool of the brook and recognized, with amused embarrassment, the transparent, tubular thing, not unlike a sea-squirt, that had got caught in its downstream course in a fringe of forget-me-nots, good name, too.

He had started to walk back to the picnic glade when a mountain fell upon him from behind. With one violent heave he swung his attacker over his head. Percy crashed and lay supine for a moment or two. Van, his crab claws on the ready, contemplated him, hoping for a pretext to inflict a certain special device of exotic torture that he had not yet had the opportunity to use in a real fight.

"You've broken my shoulder," grumbled Percy, half-rising

and rubbing his thick arm. "A little more self-control, young devil."

"Stand up!" said Van. "Come on, stand up! Would you like more of the same or shall we join the ladies? The ladies? All right. But, if you please, walk in front of me now."

As he and his captive drew near the glade Van cursed himself for feeling rattled by that unexpected additional round; he was secretly out of breath, his every nerve twanged, he caught himself limping and correcting the limp—while Percy de Prey, in his magically immaculate white trousers and casually ruffled shirt, marched, buoyantly exercising his arms and shoulders, and seemed quite serene and in fact rather cheerful.

Presently Greg overtook them, bringing the cufflink—a little triumph of meticulous detection; and with a trite "Attaboy!" Percy closed his silk cuff, thus completing his insolent restoration.

Their dutiful companion, still running, got first to the site of the finished feast; he saw Ada, facing him with two stipple-stemmed red boletes in one hand and three in the other; and, mistaking her look of surprise at the sound of his thudding hooves for one of concern, good Sir Greg hastened to cry out from afar: "He's all right! He's all right, Miss Veen"—blind compassion preventing the young knight from realizing that she could not possibly have known yet what a clash had occurred between the beau and the beast.

"Indeed I am," said the former, taking from her a couple of her toadstools, the girl's favorite delicacy, and stroking their smooth caps. "And why shouldn't I be? Your cousin has treated Greg and your humble servant to a most bracing exhibition of Oriental Skrotomoff or whatever the name may be."

He called for wine—but the remaining bottles had been given to the mysterious pastors whose patronage the adjacent clearing had already lost: they might have dispatched and buried one of their comrades, if the stiff collar and reptilian tie left hanging from a locust branch were his. Gone also was the bouquet of roses which Ada had ordered to be put back into the boot of the Count's car—better than waste them on her, let him give them, she said, to Blanche's lovely sister.

And now Mlle Larivière clapped her hands to rouse from their siesta, Kim, the driver of her gig, and Trofim, the children's fair-bearded coachman. Ada reclenched her boletes and all Percy could find for his *Handkuss* was a cold fist.

"Jolly nice to have seen you, old boy," he said, tapping Van lightly on the shoulder, a forbidden gesture in their milieu. "Hope to play with you again soon. I wonder," he added in a lower voice, "if you shoot as straight as you wrestle."

Van followed him to the convertible.

"Van, Van come here, Greg wants to say good-bye," cried Ada, but he did not turn.

"Is that a challenge, *me faites-vous un duel?*" inquired Van.

Percy, at the wheel, smiled, slit his eyes, bent toward the dashboard, smiled again, but said nothing. Click-click went the motor, then broke into thunder and Percy drew on his gloves.

"*Quand tu voudras, mon gars,*" said Van, slapping the fender and using the terrible second person singular of duelists in old France.

The car leapt forward and disappeared.

Van returned to the picnic ground, his heart stupidly thumping; he waved in passing to Greg who was talking to Ada a little way off on the road.

"Really, I assure you," Greg was saying to her, "your cousin is not to blame. Percy started it—and was defeated in a clean match of Korotom wrestling, as used in Teristan and Sorokat—my father, I'm sure, could tell you all about it."

"You're a dear," answered Ada, "but I don't think your brain works too well."

"It never does in your presence," remarked Greg, and mounted his black silent steed, hating it, and himself, and the two bullies.

He adjusted his goggles and glided away. Mlle Larivière, in her turn, got into her gig and was borne off through the speckled vista of the forest ride.

Lucette ran up to Van and, almost kneeling, cosily embraced her big cousin around the hips, and clung to him for a moment. "Come along," said Van, lifting her, "don't forget your jersey, you can't go naked."

Ada strolled up. "My hero," she said, hardly looking at

him, with that inscrutable air she had that let one guess whether she expressed sarcasm or ecstasy, or a parody of one or the other.

Lucette, swinging her mushroom basket, chanted:

"He screwed off a nipple,
    He left him a cripple . . ."

"Lucy Veen, stop that!" shouted Ada at the imp; and Van with a show of great indignation, shook the little wrist he held, while twinkling drolly at Ada on his other side.

Thus, a carefree-looking young trio, they moved toward the waiting victoria. Slapping his thighs in dismay, the coachman stood berating a tousled footboy who had appeared from under a bush. He had concealed himself there to enjoy in peace a tattered copy of *Tattersalia* with pictures of tremendous, fabulously elongated race horses, and had been left behind by the charabanc which had carried away the dirty dishes and the drowsy servants.

He climbed onto the box, beside Trofim, who directed a vibrating "tpprr" at the backing bays, while Lucette considered with darkening green eyes the occupation of her habitual perch.

"You'll have to take her on your half-brotherly knee," said Ada in a neutral aparte.

"But won't *La maudite rivière* object," he said absently, trying to catch by its tail the sensation of fate's rerun.

"Larivière can go and" (and Ada's sweet pale lips repeated Gavronski's crude crack) . . . "That goes for Lucette too," she added.

"*Vos 'vyragences' sont assez lestes,*" remarked Van. "Are you very mad at me?"

"Oh Van, I'm not! In fact, I'm delighted you won. But I'm sixteen today. Sixteen! Older than grandmother at the time of her first divorce. It's my last picnic, I guess. Childhood is scrapped. I love you. You love me. Greg loves me. Everybody loves me. I'm glutted with love. Hurry up or she'll pull that cock off—Lucette, leave him alone at once!"

Finally the carriage started on its pleasant homeward journey.

"Ouch!" grunted Van as he received the rounded load—

explaining wrily that he had hit his right patella against a rock.

"Of course, if one goes in for horseplay . . ." murmured Ada—and opened, at its emerald ribbon, the small brown, gold-tooled book (a great success with the passing sun flecks) that she had been already reading during the ride to the picnic.

"I do fancy a little horseplay," said Van. "It has left me with quite a tingle, for more reasons than one."

"I saw you—horseplaying," said Lucette, turning her head.

"Sh-sh," uttered Van.

"I mean you and him."

"We are not interested in your impressions, girl. And don't look back all the time. You know you get carriage-sick when the road—"

"Coincidence: '*Jean qui tâchait de lui tourner la tête . . .*,'" surfaced Ada briefly.

"—when the road 'runs out of you,' as your sister once said when she was your age."

"True," mused Lucette tunefully.

She had been prevailed upon to clothe her honey-brown body. Her white jersey had filched a lot from its recent background—pine needles, a bit of moss, a cake crumb, a baby caterpillar. Her remarkably well-filled green shorts were stained with burnberry purple. Her ember-bright hair flew into his face and smelt of a past summer. Family smell; yes, coincidence: a set of coincidences slightly displaced; the artistry of asymmetry. She sat in his lap, heavily, dreamily, full of *foie gras* and peach punch, with the backs of her brown iridescent bare arms almost touching his face—touching it when he glanced down, right and left, to check if the mushrooms had been taken. They had. The little footboy was reading and picking his nose—judging by the movements of his elbow. Lucette's compact bottom and cool thighs seemed to sink deeper and deeper in the quicksand of the dream-like, dream-rephrased, legend-distorted past. Ada, sitting next to him, turning her smaller pages quicker than the boy on the box, was, of course, enchanting, obsessive, eternal and lovelier, more somberly ardent than four summers ago—but it was that other picnic which he now relived and it was Ada's soft

haunches which he now held as if she were present in duplicate, in two different color prints.

Through strands of coppery silk he looked aslant at Ada,
who puckered her lips at him in the semblance of a transmitted kiss (pardoning him at last for his part in that brawl!) and
presently went back to her vellum-bound little volume,
Ombres et couleurs, an 1820 edition of Chateaubriand's short
stories with hand-painted vignettes and the flat mummy of a
pressed anemone. The gouts and glooms of the woodland
passed across her book, her face and Lucette's right arm, on
which he could not help kissing a mosquito bite in pure tribute to the duplication. Poor Lucette stole a languorous look
at him and looked away again—at the red neck of the coachman—of that other coachman who for several months had
haunted her dreams.

We do not care to follow the thoughts troubling Ada,
whose attention to her book was far shallower than might
seem; we will not, nay, cannot follow them with any success,
for thoughts are much more faintly remembered than shadows
or colors, or the throbs of young lust, or a green snake in a
dark paradise. Therefore we find ourselves more comfortably
sitting within Van while his Ada sits within Lucette, and both
sit within Van (and all three in me, adds Ada).

He remembered with a pang of pleasure the indulgent skirt
Ada had been wearing then, so swoony-baloony as the Chose
young things said, and he regretted (smiling) that Lucette had
those chaste shorts on today, and Ada, husked-corn (laughing) trousers. In the fatal course of the most painful ailments,
sometimes (nodding gravely), sometimes there occur sweet
mornings of perfect repose—and that not owing to some
blessed pill or potion (indicating the bedside clutter) or at
least without our knowing that the loving hand of despair
slipped us the drug.

Van closed his eyes in order better to concentrate on the
golden flood of swelling joy. Many, oh many, many years later
he recollected with wonder (how could one have endured
such rapture?) that moment of total happiness, the complete
eclipse of the piercing and preying ache, the logic of intoxication, the circular argument to the effect that the most eccentric girl cannot help being faithful if she loves one as one

loves her. He watched Ada's bracelet flash in rhythm with the swaying of the victoria and her full lips, parted slightly in profile, show in the sun the red pollen of a remnant of salve drying in the transversal thumbnail lines of their texture. He opened his eyes: the bracelet was indeed flashing but her lips had lost all trace of rouge, and the certainty that in another moment he would touch their hot pale pulp threatened to touch off a private crisis under the solemn load of another child. But the little proxy's neck, glistening with sweat, was pathetic, her trustful immobility, sobering, and after all no furtive friction could compete with what awaited him in Ada's bower. A twinge in his kneecap also came to the rescue, and honest Van chided himself for having attempted to use a little pauper instead of the princess in the fairy tale—"whose precious flesh must not blush with the impression of a chastising hand," says Pierrot in Peterson's version.

With the fading of that fugitive flame his mood changed. Something should be said, a command should be given, the matter was serious or might become serious. They were now about to enter Gamlet, the little Russian village, from which a birch-lined road led quickly to Ardis. A small procession of kerchiefed peasant nymphs, unwashed, no doubt, but adorably pretty with naked shiny shoulders and high-divided plump breasts tuliped up by their corsets, walked past through a coppice, singing an old ditty in their touching English:

> *Thorns and nettles*
> *For silly girls:*
> *Ah, torn the petals,*
> *Ah, spilled the pearls!*

"You have a little pencil in your back pocket," said Van to Lucette. "May I borrow it, I want to write down that song."

"If you don't tickle me there," said the child.

Van reached for Ada's book and wrote on the fly leaf, as she watched him with odd wary eyes:

> I don't wish to see him again.
> It's serious.
> Tell M. not to receive him or I leave.
> No answer required.

She read it, and slowly, silently erased the lines with the top of the pencil which she passed back to Van, who replaced it where it had been.

"You're awfully fidgety," Lucette observed without turning. "Next time," she added, "I won't have him dislodge me."

They now swept up to the porch, and Trofim had to cuff the tiny blue-coated reader in order to have him lay his book aside and jump down to hand Ada out of the carriage.

40

Van was lying in his netted nest under the liriodendrons, reading Antiterrenus on Rattner. His knee had troubled him all night; now, after lunch, it seemed a bit better. Ada had gone on horseback to Ladore, where he hoped she would forget to buy the messy turpentine oil Marina had told her to bring him.

His valet advanced toward him across the lawn, followed by a messenger, a slender youth clad in black leather from neck to ankle, chestnut curls escaping from under a vizored cap. The strange child glanced around with an amateur thespian's exaggeration of attitude, and handed a letter, marked "confidential," to Van.

> *Dear Veen,*
>
> *In a couple of days I must leave for a spell of military service abroad. If you desire to see me before I go I shall be glad to entertain you (and any other gentleman you might wish to bring along) at dawn tomorrow where the Maidenhair road crosses Tourbière Lane. If not, I beg you to confirm in a brief note that you bear me no grudge, just as no grudge is cherished in regard to you, sir, by your obedient servant*
>
> Percy de Prey

No, Van did not desire to see the Count. He said so to the pretty messenger, who stood with one hand on the hip and

one knee turned out like an extra, waiting for the signal to
join the gambaders in the country dance after Calabro's aria.

"*Un moment,*" added Van. "I would be interested to
know—this could be decided in a jiffy behind that tree—what
you are, stable boy or kennel girl?"

The messenger did not reply and was led away by the
chuckling Bout. A little squeal suggestive of an improper
pinch came from behind the laurels screening their exit.

It was hard to decide whether that clumsy and pretentious
missive had been dictated by the fear that one's sailing off to
fight for one's country might be construed as running away
from more private engagements, or whether its conciliatory
gist had been demanded from Percy by somebody—perhaps
a woman (for instance his mother, born Praskovia Lanskoy);
anyway, Van's honor remained unaffected. He limped to the
nearest garbage can and, having burnt the letter with its
crested blue envelope, dismissed the incident from his mind,
merely noting that now, at least, Ada would cease to be pes-
tered by the fellow's attentions.

She returned late in the afternoon—without the embrocation, thank goodness. He was still lolling in his low-slung
hammock, looking rather forlorn and sulky, but having
glanced around (with more natural grace than the brown-
locked messenger had achieved), she raised her veil, kneeled
down by him and soothed him.

When lightning struck two days later (an old image that is
meant to intimate a flash-back to an old barn), Van became
aware that it brought together, in livid confrontation, two
secret witnesses; they had been hanging back in his mind since
the first day of his fateful return to Ardis: One had been murmuring with averted gaze that Percy de Prey was, and would
always be, only a dance partner, a frivolous follower; the other
had kept insinuating, with spectral insistence, that some nameless trouble was threatening the very sanity of Van's pale,
faithless mistress.

On the morning of the day preceding the most miserable
one in his life, he found he could bend his leg without wincing, but he made the mistake of joining Ada and Lucette in
an impromptu lunch on a long-neglected croquet lawn and
walked home with difficulty. A swim in the pool and a soak

in the sun helped, however, and the pain had practically gone when in the mellow heat of the long afternoon Ada returned from one of her long "brambles" as she called her botanical rambles, succinctly and somewhat sadly, for the florula had ceased to yield much beyond the familiar favorites. Marina, in a luxurious peignoir, with a large oval mirror hinged before her, sat at a white toilet table that had been carried out onto the lawn where she was having her hair dressed by senile but still wonderworking Monsieur Violette of Lyon and Ladore, an unusual outdoor activity which she explained and excused by the fact of her grandmother's having also liked *qu'on la coiffe au grand air* so as to forestall the zephyrs (as a duelist steadies his hand by walking about with a poker).

"That's our best performer," she said, indicating Van to Violette who mistook him for Pedro and bowed with *un air entendu*.

Van had been looking forward to a little walk of convalescence with Ada before dressing for dinner, but she said, as she drooped on a garden chair, that she was exhausted and filthy and had to wash her face and feet, and prepare for the ordeal of helping her mother entertain the movie people who were expected later in the evening.

"I've seen him in *Sexico*," murmured Monsieur Violette to Marina, whose ears he had shut with both hands as he moved the reflection of her head in the glass this way and that.

"No, it's getting late," muttered Ada, "and, moreover, I promised Lucette—"

He insisted in a fierce whisper—fully knowing, however, how useless it was to attempt to make her change her mind, particularly in amorous matters; but unaccountably and marvelously her dazed look melted into one of gentle glee, as if in sudden perception of new-found release. Thus a child may stare into space, with a dawning smile, upon realizing that the bad dream is over, or that a door has been left unlocked, and that one can paddle with impunity in thawed sky. Ada rid her shoulder of the collecting satchel and, under Violette's benevolent gaze following them over Marina's mirrored head, they strolled away and sought the comparative seclusion of the park alley where she had once demonstrated to him her sun-and-shade games. He held her, and kissed her, and kissed her again as if she had returned from a long and perilous journey. The sweetness of her smile was something quite unexpected and special. It was not the sly demon smile of remembered or promised ardor, but the exquisite human glow of happiness and helplessness. All their passionate pump-joy exertions, from Burning Barn to Burnberry Brook, were nothing in comparison to this *zaychik*, this "sun blick" of the smiling spirit. Her black jumper and black skirt with apron pockets lost its "in-mourning-for-a-lost flower" meaning that Marina had fancifully attached to her dress ("*nemedlenno pereodet'sya*, change immediately!" she had yelped into the green-shimmering looking-glass); instead, it had acquired the charm of a Lyaskan, old-fashioned schoolgirl uniform. They stood brow to brow, brown to white, black to black, he supporting her elbows, she playing her limp light fingers over his collarbone, and how he "ladored," he said, the dark aroma of her hair blending with crushed lily stalks, Turkish cigarettes and the lassitude that comes from "lass." "No, no, don't," she said, I must wash, quick-quick, Ada must wash; but for yet another immortal moment they stood embraced in the hushed avenue, enjoying, as they had never enjoyed before, the "happy-forever" feeling at the end of never-ending fairy tales.

That's a beautiful passage, Van. I shall cry all night (late interpolation).

As a last sunbeam struck Ada, her mouth and chin shone drenched with his poor futile kisses. She shook her head saying they must really part, and she kissed his hands as she did only in moments of supreme tenderness, and then quickly turned away, and they really parted.

One common orchid, a Lady's Slipper, was all that wilted in the satchel which she had left on a garden table and now dragged upstairs. Marina and the mirror had gone. He peeled off his training togs and took one last dip in the pool over which the butler stood, looking meditatively into the false-blue water with his hands behind his back.

"I wonder," he said, "if I haven't just seen a tadpole."

The novelistic theme of written communications has now really got into its stride. When Van went up to his room he noticed, with a shock of grim premonition, a slip of paper sticking out of the heart pocket of his dinner jacket. Penciled in a large hand, with the contour of every letter deliberately whiffled and rippled, was the anonymous injunction: "One must not berne you." Only a French-speaking person would use that word for "dupe." Among the servants, fifteen at least were of French extraction—descendants of immigrants who had settled in America after England had annexed their beautiful and unfortunate country in 1815. To interview them all—torture the males, rape the females—would be, of course, absurd and degrading. With a puerile wrench he broke his best black butterfly on the wheel of his exasperation. The pain from the fang bite was now reaching his heart. He found another tie, finished dressing and went to look for Ada.

He found both girls and their governess in one of the "nursery parlors," a delightful sitting room with a balcony on which Mlle Larivière was sitting at a charmingly ornamented Pembroke table and reading with mixed feelings and furious annotations the third shooting script of *Les Enfants Maudits*. At a larger round table in the middle of the inner room, Lucette under Ada's direction was trying to learn to draw flowers; several botanical atlases, large and small, were lying about. Everything appeared as it always used to be, the little nymphs and goats on the painted ceiling, the mellow light of the day ripening into evening, the remote dreamy rhythm of Blanche's "linen-folding" voice humming "Malbrough" (. . . *ne sait quand reviendra, ne sait quand reviendra*) and the two lovely heads, bronze-black and copper-red, inclined over the table. Van realized that he must simmer down before consulting Ada—or indeed before telling her he wished to consult her. She looked gay and elegant; she was wearing his diamonds for the first time; she had put on a new evening dress with jet gleams, and—also for the first time—transparent silk stockings.

He sat down on a little sofa, took at random one of the open volumes and stared in disgust at a group of brilliantly pictured gross orchids whose popularity with bees depended, said the text, "on various attractive odors ranging from the smell of dead workers to that of a tomcat." Dead soldiers might smell even better.

In the meantime obstinate Lucette kept insisting that the easiest way to draw a flower was to place a sheet of transparent

paper over the picture (in the present case a red-bearded po-
gonia, with indecent details of structure, a plant peculiar to
the Ladoga bogs) and trace the outline of the thing in colored
inks. Patient Ada wanted her to copy not mechanically but
"from eye to hand and from hand to eye," and to use for
model a live specimen of another orchid that had a brown
wrinkled pouch and purple sepals; but after a while she gave
in cheerfully and set aside the crystal vaselet holding the
Lady's Slipper she had picked. Casually, lightly, she went on to
explain how the organs of orchids work—but all Lucette
wanted to know, after her whimsical fashion, was: could a boy
bee impregnate a girl flower *through* something, through his
gaiters or woolies or whatever he wore?

"You know," said Ada in a comic nasal voice, turning to
Van, "you know, that child has the dirtiest mind imaginable
and now she is going to be mad at me for saying this and sob
on the Larivière bosom, and complain she has been pollinated
by sitting on your knee."

"But I can't speak to Belle about dirty things," said Lucette
quite gently and reasonably.

"What's the matter with you, Van?" inquired sharp-eyed
Ada.

"Why do you ask?" inquired Van in his turn.

"Your ears wiggle and you clear your throat."

"Are you through with those horrible flowers?"

"Yes. I'm now going to wash my hands. We'll meet downstairs. Your tie is all crooked."

"All right, all right," said Van.

> "*Mon page, mon beau page,*
> *—Mironton-mironton-mirontaine—*
> *Mon page, mon beau page . . .*"

Downstairs, Jones was already taking down the dinner gong
from its hook in the hall.

"Well, what's the matter?" she asked when they met a minute later on the drawing-room terrace.

"I found this in my jacket," said Van.

Rubbing her big front teeth with a nervous forefinger, Ada
read and reread the note.

"How do you know it's meant for you?" she asked, giving him back the bit of copybook paper.

"Well, I'm telling you," he yelled.

"*Tishe* (quiet!)!" said Ada.

"I'm telling you I found it *here*," (pointing at his heart).

"Destroy and forget," said Ada.

"Your obedient servant," replied Van.

41

Pedro had not yet returned from California. Hay fever and dark glasses did not improve G. A. Vronsky's appearance. Adorno, the star of *Hate*, brought his new wife, who turned out to have been one of the old (and most beloved) wives of another guest, a considerably more important comedian, who after supper bribed Bouteillan to simulate the arrival of a message necessitating his immediate departure. Grigoriy Akimovich went with him (having come with him in the same rented limousine), leaving Marina, Ada, Adorno and his ironically sniffing Marianne at a card table. They played *biryuch*, a variety of whist, till a Ladore taxi could be obtained, which was well after 1:00 A.M.

In the meantime Van changed back to shorts, cloaked himself in the tartan plaid and retired to his bosquet, where the bergamask lamps had not been lit at all that night which had not proved as festive as Marina had expected. He climbed into his hammock and drowsily started reviewing such French-speaking domestics as could have slipped him that ominous but according to Ada meaningless note. The first, obvious, choice was hysterical and fantastic Blanche—had there not been her timidity, her fear of being "fired" (he recalled a dreadful scene when she groveled, pleading for mercy, at the feet of Larivière, who accused her of "stealing" a bauble that eventually turned up in one of Larivière's own shoes). The ruddy face of Bouteillan and his son's grin next appeared in the focus of Van's fancy; but presently he fell asleep, and saw himself on a mountain smothered in snow, with people, trees, and a cow carried down by an avalanche.

Something roused him from that state of evil torpor. At first he thought it was the chill of the dying night, then recognized the slight creak (that had been a scream in his confused nightmare), and raising his head saw a dim light in between the shrubs where the door of the toolroom was being pushed ajar from the inside. Ada had never once come there without their prudently planning every step of their infrequent nocturnal trysts. He scrambled out of his hammock and padded toward the lighted doorway. Before him stood the pale wavering figure of Blanche. She presented an odd sight: bare armed, in her petticoat, one stocking gartered, the other down to her ankle; no slippers; armpits glistening with sweat; she was loosening her hair in a wretched simulacrum of seduction.

"*C'est ma dernière nuit au château*," she said softly, and rephrased it in her quaint English, elegiac and stilted, as spoken only in obsolete novels. " 'Tis my last night with thee."

"Your last night? With me? What do you mean?" He considered her with the eerie uneasiness one feels when listening to the utterances of delirium or intoxication.

But despite her demented look, Blanche was perfectly lucid. She had made up her mind a couple of days ago to leave Ardis Hall. She had just slipped her demission, with a footnote on the young lady's conduct, under the door of Madame. She would go in a few hours. She loved him, he was her "folly and fever," she wished to spend a few secret moments with him.

He entered the toolroom and slowly closed the door. The slowness had its uncomfortable cause. She had placed her lantern on the rung of a ladder and was already gathering up and lifting her skimpy skirt. Compassion, courtesy and some assistance on her part might have helped him to work up the urge which she took for granted and whose total absence he carefully concealed under his tartan cloak; but quite aside from the fear of infection (Bout had hinted at some of the poor girl's troubles), a graver matter engrossed him. He diverted her bold hand and sat down on the bench beside her.

Was it she who had placed that note in his jacket?

It was. She had been unable to face departure if he was to

remain fooled, deceived, betrayed. She added, in naive brackets, that she had been sure he always desired her, they could
talk afterwards. *Je suis à toi, c'est bientôt l'aube,* your dream
has come true.

"*Parlez pour vous,*" answered Van. "I am in no mood for
love-making. And I will strangle you, I assure you, if you do
not tell me the whole story in every detail, at once."

She nodded, fear and adoration in her veiled eyes. When
and how had it started? Last August, she said. *Votre demoiselle*
picking flowers, he squiring her through the tall grass, a flute
in his hand. Who he? What flute? *Mais le musicien allemand,
Monsieur Rack.* The eager informer had her own swain lying
upon her on the other side of the hedge. How anybody could
do it with *l'immonde Monsieur Rack,* who once forgot his
waistcoat in a haystack, was beyond the informer's compre-
hension. Perhaps because he made songs for her, a very pretty
one was once played at a big public ball at the Ladore Casino,
it went . . . Never mind how it went, go on with the story.
Monsieur Rack, one starry night, in a boat on the river, was
heard by the informer and two gallants in the willow bushes,
recounting the melancholy tale of his childhood, of his years
of hunger and music and loneliness, and his sweetheart wept
and threw her head back and he fed on her bare throat, *il la
mangeait de baisers dégoûtants.* He must have had her not
more than a dozen times, he was not as strong as another
gentleman—oh, cut it out, said Van—and in winter the young
lady learnt he was married, and hated his cruel wife, and in
April when he began to give piano lessons to Lucette the affair
was resumed, but then—

"That will do!" he cried and, beating his brow with his fist,
stumbled out into the sunlight.

It was a quarter to six on the wristwatch hanging from the
net of the hammock. His feet were stone cold. He groped for
his loafers and walked aimlessly for some time among the trees
of the coppice where thrushes were singing so richly, with
such sonorous force, such fluty fioriture that one could not
endure the agony of consciousness, the filth of life, the loss,
the loss, the loss. Gradually, however, he regained a semblance
of self-control by the magic method of not allowing the image
of Ada to come anywhere near his awareness of himself. This

created a vacuum into which rushed a multitude of trivial reflections. A pantomime of rational thought.

He took a tepid shower in the poolside shed, doing everything with comic deliberation, very slowly and cautiously, lest
he break the new, unknown, brittle Van born a moment ago.
He watched his thoughts revolve, dance, strut, clown a little.
He found it delightful to imagine, for instance, that a cake of
soap must be solid ambrosia to the ants swarming over it, and
what a shock to be drowned in the midst of that orgy. The
code, he reflected, did not allow to challenge a person who
was not born a gentleman but exceptions might be made for
artists, pianists, flutists, and if a coward refused, you could
make his gums bleed with repeated slaps or, still better, thrash
him with a strong cane—must not forget to choose one in
the vestibule closet before leaving forever, forever. Great fun!
He relished as something quite special the kind of one-legged
jig a naked fellow performs when focusing on the shorts he
tries to get into. He sauntered through a side gallery. He ascended the grand staircase. The house was empty, and cool,
and smelled of carnations. Good morning, and good-bye, little bedroom. Van shaved, Van pared his toe-nails, Van dressed
with exquisite care: gray socks, silk shirt, gray tie, dark-gray
suit newly pressed—shoes, ah yes, shoes, mustn't forget shoes,
and without bothering to sort out the rest of his belongings,
crammed a score of twenty-dollar gold coins into a chamois
purse, distributed handkerchief, checkbook, passport, what
else? nothing else, over his rigid person and pinned a note to
the pillow asking to have his things packed and forwarded to
his father's address. Son killed by avalanche, no hat found,
contraceptives donated to Old Guides' Home. After the passage of about eight decades all this sounds very amusing and
silly—but at the time he was a dead man going through the
motions of an imagined dreamer. He bent down with a grunt,
cursing his knee, to fix his skis, in the driving snow, on the
brink of the slope, but the skis had vanished, the bindings
were shoelaces, and the slope, a staircase.

He walked down to the mews and told a young groom,
who was almost as drowsy as he, that he wished to go to the
railway station in a few minutes. The groom looked perplexed,
and Van swore at him.

Wristwatch! He returned to the hammock where it was strapped to the netting. On his way back to the stables, around the house, he happened to look up and saw a black-haired girl of sixteen or so, in yellow slacks and a black bolero, standing on a third-floor balcony and signaling to him. She signaled telegraphically, with expansive linear gestures, indicating the cloudless sky (what a cloudless sky!), the jacaranda summit in bloom (blue! bloom!) and her own bare foot raised high and placed on the parapet (have only to put on my sandals!). Van, to his horror and shame, saw Van wait for her to come down.

She walked swiftly toward him across the iridescently glistening lawn. "Van," she said, "I must tell you my dream before I forget. You and I were high up in the Alps— Why on earth are you wearing townclothes?"

"Well, I'll tell you," drawled dreamy Van. "I'll tell you why. From a humble but reliable sauce, I mean source, excuse my accent, I have just learned *qu'on vous culbute* behind every hedge. Where can I find your tumbler?"

"Nowhere," she answered quite calmly, ignoring or not even perceiving his rudeness, for she had always known that disaster would come today or tomorrow, a question of time or rather timing on the part of fate.

"But he exists, he exists," muttered Van, looking down at a rainbow web on the turf.

"I suppose so," said the haughty child, "however, he left yesterday for some Greek or Turkish port. Moreover, he was going to do everything to get killed, if that information helps. Now listen, listen! Those walks in the woods meant nothing. Wait, Van! I was weak only twice when you had hurt him so hideously, or perhaps three times in all. Please! I can't explain in one gush, but eventually you will understand. Not everybody is as happy as we are. He's a poor, lost, clumsy boy. We are all doomed, but some are more doomed than others. He is nothing to me. I shall never see him again. He is nothing, I swear. He adores me to the point of insanity."

"I think," said Van, "we've got hold of the wrong lover. I was asking about Herr Rack, who has such delectable gums and also adores you to the point of insanity."

He turned, as they say, on his heel, and walked toward the house.

He could swear he did not look back, could not—by any optical chance, or in any prism—have seen her physically as he walked away; and yet, with dreadful distinction, he retained forever a composite picture of her standing where he left her. The picture—which penetrated him, through an eye in the back of his head, through his vitreous spinal canal, and could never be lived down, never—consisted of a selection and blend of such random images and expressions of hers that had affected him with a pang of intolerable remorse at various moments in the past. Tiffs between them had been very rare, very brief, but there had been enough of them to make up the enduring mosaic. There was the time she stood with her back against a tree trunk, facing a traitor's doom; the time he had refused to show her some silly Chose snapshots of punt girls and had torn them up in fury and she had looked away knitting her brows and slitting her eyes at an invisible view in the window. Or that time she had hesitated, blinking, shaping a soundless word, suspecting him of a sudden revolt against her odd prudishness of speech, when he challenged her brusquely to find a rhyme to "patio" and she was not quite sure if he had in mind a certain foul word and if so what was its correct pronunciation. And perhaps, worst of all, that time when she stood fiddling with a bunch of wild flowers, a gentle half-smile hanging back quite neutrally in her eyes, her lips pursed, her head making imprecise little movements as if punctuating with self-directed nods secret decisions and silent clauses in some sort of contract with herself, with him, with unknown parties hereinafter called Comfortless, Inutile, Unjust—while he indulged in a brutal outburst triggered by her suggesting—quite sweetly and casually (as she might suggest walking a little way on the edge of a bog to see if a certain orchid was out)—that they visit the late Krolik's grave in a churchyard by which they were passing—and he had suddenly started to shout ("You know I abhor churchyards, I despise, I denounce death, dead bodies are burlesque, I refuse to stare at a stone under which a roly-poly old Pole is rotting, let him feed his maggots in peace, the entomologies of death leave me cold, I detest, I despise—"); he went on ranting that way for a couple of minutes and then literally fell at her feet, kissing her feet, imploring her pardon, and for a little while longer she kept gazing at him pensively.

Those were the fragments of the tesselation, and there were others, even more trivial; but in coming together the harmless parts made a lethal entity, and the girl in yellow slacks and black jacket, standing with her hands behind her back, slightly rocking her shoulders, leaning her back now closer now less closely against the tree trunk, and tossing her hair—a definite picture that he knew he had never seen in reality—remained within him more real than any actual memory.

Marina, in kimono and curlers, stood surrounded by servants before the porch and was asking questions that nobody seemed to answer.

Van said:

"I'm not eloping with your maid, Marina. It's an optical illusion. Her reasons for leaving you do not concern me. There's a bit of business I had been putting off like a fool but now must attend to before going to Paris."

"Ada is causing me a lot of worry," said Marina with a downcast frown and a Russian wobble of the cheeks. "Please come back as soon as you can. You have such a good influence upon her. *Au revoir.* I'm very cross with everybody."

Holding up her robe she ascended the porch steps. The tame silver dragon on her back had an ant-eater's tongue according to her eldest daughter, a scientist. What did poor mother know about P's and R's? Next to nothing.

Van shook hands with the distressed old butler, thanked Bout for a silver-knobbed cane and a pair of gloves, nodded to the other servants and walked toward the carriage and pair. Blanche, standing by in a long gray skirt and straw hat, with her cheap valise painted mahogany red and secured with a crisscrossing cord, looked exactly like a young lady setting out to teach school in a Wild West movie. She offered to sit on the box next to the Russian coachman but he ushered her into the *calèche.*

They passed undulating fields of wheat speckled with the confetti of poppies and bluets. She talked all the way about the young chatelaine and her two recent lovers in melodious low tones as if in a trance, as if *en rapport* with a dead min-

strel's spirit. Only the other day from behind that row of thick
firs, look there, to your right (but he did not look—sitting
silent, both hands on the knob of his cane), she and her sister
Madelon, with a bottle of wine between them, watched Monsieur le Comte courting the young lady on the moss, crushing
her like a grunting bear as he also had crushed—many
times!—Madelon who said she, Blanche, should warn him,
Van, because she was a wee bit jealous but she also said—for
she had a good heart—better put it off until "Malbrook" *s'en
va t'en guerre*, otherwise they would fight; he had been shooting a pistol at a scarecrow all morning and that's why she
waited so long, and it was in Madelon's hand, not in hers.
She rambled on and on until they reached Tourbière; two
rows of cottages and a small black church with stained-glass
windows. Van let her out. The youngest of the three sisters,
a beautiful chestnut-curled little maiden with lewd eyes and
bobbing breasts (where had he seen her before?—recently, but
where?) carried Blanche's valise and birdcage into a poor shack
smothered in climbing roses, but for the rest, dismal beyond
words. He kissed Cendrillon's shy hand and resumed his seat
in the carriage, clearing his throat and plucking at his trousers
before crossing his legs. Vain Van Veen.

"The express does not stop at Torfyanka, does it, Trofim?"

"I'll take you five versts across the bog," said Trofim, "the
nearest is Volosyanka."

His vulgar Russian word for Maidenhair; a whistle stop;
train probably crowded.

Maidenhair. Idiot! Percy boy might have been buried by
now! Maidenhair. Thus named because of the huge spreading
Chinese tree at the end of the platform. Once, vaguely, confused with the Venus'-hair fern. She walked to the end of the
platform in Tolstoy's novel. First exponent of the inner
monologue, later exploited by the French and the Irish. *N'est
vert, n'est vert, n'est vert. L'arbre aux quarante écus d'or*, at
least in the fall. Never, never shall I hear again her "botanical"
voice fall at *biloba*, "sorry, my Latin is showing." *Ginkgo*,
gingko, ink, inkog. Known also as Salisbury's adiantofolia,
Ada's infolio, poor *Salisburia*: sunk; poor Stream of Consciousness, *marée noire* by now. Who wants Ardis Hall!

"*Barin, a barin,*" said Trofim, turning his blond-bearded face to his passenger.

"*Da?*"

"*Dazhe skvoz' kozhaniy fartuk ne stal-bï ya trogat' etu frant-suzskuyu devku.*"

Bárin: master. *Dázhe skvoz' kózhaniy fártuk*: even through a leathern apron. *Ne stal-bï ya trógat'*: I would not think of touching. *Étu*: this (that). *Frantsúzskuyu*: French (adj., accus.). *Dévku*: wench. *Úzhas, otcháyanie*: horror, despair. *Zhálost'*: pity. *Kóncheno, zagázheno, rastérzano*: finished, fouled, torn to shreds.

42

Aqua used to say that only a very cruel or very stupid person, or innocent infants, could be happy on Demonia, our splendid planet. Van felt that for him to survive on this terrible Antiterra, in the multicolored and evil world into which he was born, he had to destroy, or at least to maim for life, two men. He had to find them immediately; delay itself might impair his power of survival. The rapture of their destruction would not mend his heart, but would certainly rinse his brain. The two men were in two different spots and neither spot represented an exact location, a definite street number, an identifiable billet. He hoped to punish them in an honorable way, if Fate helped. He was not prepared for the comically exaggerated zeal Fate was to display in leading him on and then muscling in to become an over-cooperative agent.

First, he decided to go to Kalugano to settle accounts with Herr Rack. Out of sheer misery he fell asleep in a corner of a compartment, full of alien legs and voices, in the crack express tearing north at a hundred miles per hour. He dozed till noon and got off at Ladoga, where after an incalculably long wait he took another, even more jerky and crowded train. As he was pushing his unsteady way through one corridor after another, cursing under his breath the window-gazers who did

not draw in their bottoms to let him pass, and hopelessly seeking a comfortable nook in one of the first-class cars consisting
of four-seat compartments, he saw Cordula and her mother
facing each other on the window side. The two other places
were occupied by a stout, elderly gentleman in an old-
fashioned brown wig with a middle parting, and a bespectacled
boy in a sailor suit sitting next to Cordula, who was in the
act of offering him one half of her chocolate bar. Van entered,
moved by a sudden very bright thought, but Cordula's
mother did not recognize him at once, and the flurry of rein-
troductions combined with a lurch of the train caused Van to
step on the prunella-shod foot of the elderly passenger, who
uttered a sharp cry and said, indistinctly but not impolitely:
"Spare my gout (or "take care" or "look out"), young man!"

"I do not like being addressed as 'young man,' " Van told
the invalid in a completely uncalled-for, brutal burst of voice.

"Has he hurt you, Grandpa?" inquired the little boy.

"He has," said Grandpa, "but I did not mean to offend
anybody by my cry of anguish."

"Even anguish should be civil," continued Van (while the
better Van in him tugged at his sleeve, aghast and ashamed).

"Cordula," said the old actress (with the same apropos with
which she once picked up and fondled a fireman's cat that had
strayed into *Fast Colors* in the middle of her best speech),
"why don't you go with this angry young demon to the tea-
car? I think I'll take my thirty-nine winks now."

"What's wrong?" asked Cordula as they settled down in
the very roomy and rococo "crumpeter," as Kalugano College
students used to call it in the 'Eighties and 'Nineties.

"Everything," replied Van, "but what makes you ask?"

"Well, we know Dr. Platonov slightly, and there was absolutely no reason for you to be so abominably rude to the dear
old man."

"I apologize," said Van. "Let us order the traditional tea."

"Another queer thing," said Cordula, "is that you actually
noticed me today. Two months ago you snubbed me."

"You had changed. You had grown lovely and languorous.
You are even lovelier now. Cordula is no longer a virgin! Tell
me—do you happen to have Percy de Prey's address? I mean
we all know he's invading Tartary—but where could a letter

reach him? I don't care to ask your snoopy aunt to forward anything."

"I daresay the Frasers have it, I'll find out. But where is *Van* going? Where shall I find Van?"

"At home—5 Park Lane, in a day or two. Just now I'm going to Kalugano."

"That's a gruesome place. Girl?"

"Man. Do you know Kalugano? Dentist? Best hotel? Concert hall? My cousin's music teacher?"

She shook her short curls. No—she went there very seldom. Twice to a concert, in a pine forest. She had not been aware that Ada took music lessons. How was Ada?

"Lucette," he said, "Lucette takes or took piano lessons. Okay. Let's dismiss Kalugano. These crumpets are very poor relatives of the Chose ones. You're right, *j'ai des ennuis*. But you can make me forget them. Tell me something to distract me, though you distract me as it is, *un petit topinambour* as the Teuton said in the story. Tell me about your affairs of the heart."

She was not a bright little girl. But she was a loquacious and really quite exciting little girl. He started to caress her under the table, but she gently removed his hand, whispering "womenses," as whimsically as another girl had done in some other dream. He cleared his throat loudly and ordered half-a-bottle of cognac, having the waiter open it in his presence as Demon advised. She talked on and on, and he lost the thread of her discourse, or rather it got enmeshed in the rapid landscape, which his gaze followed over her shoulder, with a sudden ravine recording what Jack said when his wife 'phoned, or a lone tree in a clover field impersonating abandoned John, or a romantic stream running down a cliff and reflecting her brief bright affair with Marquis Quizz Quisana.

A pine forest fizzled out and factory chimneys replaced it. The train clattered past a roundhouse, and slowed down, groaning. A hideous station darkened the day.

"Good Lord," cried Van, "that's my stop."

He put money on the table, kissed Cordula's willing lips and made for the exit. Upon reaching the vestibule he glanced back at her with a wave of the glove he held—and crashed into somebody who had stooped to pick up a bag: "*On n'est pas goujat à ce point,*" observed the latter: a burly military man with a reddish mustache and a staff captain's insignia.

Van brushed past him, and when both had come down on the platform, glove-slapped him smartly across the face.

The captain picked up his cap and lunged at the white-faced, black-haired young fop. Simultaneously Van felt somebody embrace him from behind in well-meant but unfair restraint. Not bothering to turn his head he abolished the invisible busybody with a light "piston blow" delivered by the left elbow, while he sent the captain staggering back into his own luggage with one crack of the right hand. By now several free-show amateurs had gathered around them; so, breaking their circle, Van took his man by the arm and marched him into the waiting room. A comically gloomy porter with a copiously bleeding nose came in after them carrying the captain's three bags, one of them under his arm. Cubistic labels of remote and fabulous places color-blotted the newer of the valises. Visiting cards were exchanged. "Demon's son?" grunted Captain Tapper, of Wild Violet Lodge, Kalugano. "Correct," said Van. "I'll put up, I guess, at the Majestic; if not, a note will be left for your second or seconds. You'll have to get me one, I can't very well ask the concierge to do it."

While speaking thus, Van chose a twenty dollar piece from a palmful of gold, and gave it with a grin to the damaged old porter. "Yellow cotton," Van added: "Up each nostril. Sorry, chum."

With his hands in his trouser pockets, he crossed the square to the hotel, causing a motor car to swerve stridently on the damp asphalt. He left it standing transom-wise in regard to its ordained course, and clawed his way through the revolving door of the hotel, feeling if not happier, at least more buoyant, than he had within the last twelve hours.

The Majestic, a huge old pile, all grime outside, all leather inside, engulfed him. He asked for a room with a bath, was told all were booked by a convention of contractors, tipped the desk clerk in the invincible Veen manner, and got a passable suite of three rooms with a mahogany paneled bathtub, an ancient rocking chair, a mechanical piano and a purple canopy over a double bed. After washing his hands, he immediately went down to inquire about Rack's whereabouts. The

Racks had no telephone; they probably rented a room in the suburbs; the concierge looked up at the clock and called some sort of address bureau or lost person department. It proved closed till next morning. He suggested Van ask at a music store on Main Street.

On the way there he acquired his second walking stick: the Ardis Hall silver-knobbed one he had left behind in the Maidenhair station café. This was a rude, stout article with a convenient grip and an alpenstockish point capable of gouging out translucent bulging eyes. In an adjacent store he got a suitcase, and in the next, shirts, shorts, socks, slacks, pajamas, handkerchiefs, a lounging robe, a pullover and a pair of saffian bedroom slippers fetally folded in a leathern envelope. His purchases were put into the suitcase and sent at once to the hotel. He was about to enter the music shop when he remembered with a start that he had not left any message for Tapper's seconds, so he retraced his steps.

He found them sitting in the lounge and requested them to settle matters rapidly—he had more important business than that: "*Ne grubit' sekundantam*" (never be rude to seconds), said Demon's voice in his mind. Arwin Birdfoot, a lieutenant in the Guards, was blond and flabby, with moist pink lips and a foot-long cigarette holder. Johnny Rafin, Esq., was small, dark and dapper and wore blue suede shoes with a dreadful tan suit. Birdfoot soon disappeared, leaving Van to work out details with Johnny, who, though loyally eager to assist Van, could not conceal that his heart belonged to Van's adversary.

The Captain was a first-rate shot, Johnny said, and member of the Do-Re-La country club. Bloodthirsty brutishness did not come with his Britishness, but his military and academic standing demanded he defend his honor. He was an expert on maps, horses, horticulture. He was a wealthy landlord. The merest adumbration of an apology on Baron Veen's part would clinch the matter with a token of gracious finality.

"If," said Van, "the good Captain expects *that*, he can go and stick his pistol up his gracious anality."

"That is not a nice way of speaking," said Johnny, wincing. "My friend would not approve of it. We must remember he is a very refined person."

Was Johnny Van's second, or the Captain's?

"I'm yours," said Johnny with a languid look.

Did he or the refined Captain know a German-born pianist, Philip Rack, married, with three babies (probably)?

"I'm afraid," said Johnny, with a note of disdain, "that I don't know many people with babies in Kalugano."

Was there a good whorehouse in the vicinity?

With increasing disdain Johnny answered he was a confirmed bachelor.

"Well, all right," said Van. "I have now to go out again before the shops close. Shall I acquire a brace of dueling pistols or will the Captain lend me an army 'bruger'?"

"We can supply the weapons," said Johnny.

When Van arrived in front of the music shop, he found it locked. He stared for a moment at the harps and the guitars and the flowers in silver vases on consoles receding in the dusk of looking-glasses, and recalled the schoolgirl whom he had longed for so keenly half a dozen years ago—Rose? Roza? Was that her name? Would he have been happier with her than with his pale fatal sister?

He walked for a while along Main Street—one of a million Main Streets—and then, with a surge of healthy hunger, entered a passably attractive restaurant. He ordered a beefsteak with roast potatoes, apple pie and claret. At the far end of the room, on one of the red stools of the burning bar, a graceful harlot in black—tight bodice, wide skirt, long black gloves, black-velvet picture hat—was sucking a golden drink through a straw. In the mirror behind the bar, amid colored glints, he caught a blurred glimpse of her russety blond beauty; he thought he might sample her later on, but when he glanced again she had gone.

He ate, drank, schemed.

He looked forward to the encounter with keen exhilaration. Nothing more invigorating could have been imagined. Shooting it out with that incidental clown furnished unhoped-for relief, particularly since Rack would no doubt accept a plain thrashing in lieu of combat. Designing and re-designing various contingencies pertaining to that little duel might be compared to those helpful hobbies which polio patients, lunatics and convicts are taught by generous institutions, by enlight-

ened administrators, by ingenious psychiatrists—such as book-
binding, or putting blue beads into the orbits of dolls made
by other criminals, cripples and madmen.

At first he toyed with the idea of killing his adversary: quan-
titively, it would afford him the greatest sense of release;
qualitatively, it suggested all sorts of moral and legal complications. Inflicting a wound seemed an inept half-measure. He
decided to do something artistic and tricky, such as shooting
the pistol out of the fellow's hand, or parting for him his thick
brushy hair in the middle.

On his way back to the gloomy Majestic he acquired various
trifles: three round cakes of soap in an elongated box, shaving
cream in its cold resilient tube, ten safety-razor blades, a large
sponge, a smaller soaping sponge of rubber, hair lotion, a
comb, Skinner's Balsam, a toothbrush in a plastic container,
toothpaste, scissors, a fountain pen, a pocket diary—what
else?—yes, a small alarm clock—whose comforting presence,
however, did not prevent him from telling the concierge to
have him called at five A.M.

It was only nine P.M. in late summer; he would not have
been surprised if told it was midnight in October. He had had
an unbelievably long day. The mind could hardly grasp the
fact that this very morning, at dawn, a fey character out of
some Dormilona novel for servant maids had spoken to him,
half-naked and shivering, in the toolroom of Ardis Hall. He
wondered if the other girl still stood, arrow straight, adored
and abhorred, heartless and heartbroken, against the trunk of
a murmuring tree. He wondered if in view of tomorrow's
partie de plaisir he should not prepare for her a when-you-
receive-this note, flippant, cruel, as sharp as an icicle. No.
Better write to Demon.

Dear Dad,

in consequence of a trivial altercation with a Captain Tapper, of Wild Violet Lodge, whom I happened
to step upon in the corridor of a train, I had a pistol
duel this morning in the woods near Kalugano and am
now no more. Though the manner of my end can be
regarded as a kind of easy suicide, the encounter and the
ineffable Captain are in no way connected with the Sor-

rows of Young Veen. In 1884, during my first summer at Ardis, I seduced your daughter, who was then twelve. Our torrid affair lasted till my return to Riverlane; it was resumed last June, four years later. That happiness has been the greatest event in my life, and I have no regrets. Yesterday, though, I discovered she had been unfaithful to me, so we parted. Tapper, I think, may be the chap who was thrown out of one of your gaming clubs for attempting oral intercourse with the washroom attendant, a toothless old cripple, veteran of the first Crimean War. Lots of flowers, please!

Your loving son, Van

He carefully reread his letter—and carefully tore it up. The note he finally placed in his coat pocket was much briefer.

Dad,

I had a trivial quarrel with a stranger whose face I slapped and who killed me in a duel near Kalugano. Sorry!

Van

Van was roused by the night porter who put a cup of coffee with a local "eggbun" on his bedside table, and expertly palmed the expected *chervonetz*. He resembled somewhat Bouteillan as the latter had been ten years ago and as he had appeared in a dream, which Van now retrostructed as far as it would go: in it Demon's former valet explained to Van that the "dor" in the name of an adored river equaled the corruption of hydro in "dorophone." Van often had word dreams.

He shaved, disposed of two blood-stained safety blades by leaving them in a massive bronze ashtray, had a structurally perfect stool, took a quick bath, briskly dressed, left his bag with the concierge, paid his bill and at six punctually squeezed himself next to blue-chinned and malodorous Johnny into the latter's Paradox, a cheap "semi-racer." For two or three miles they skirted the dismal bank of the lake—coal piles, shacks, boathouses, a long strip of black pebbly mud and, in the distance, over the curving bank of autumnally misted water, the tawny fumes of tremendous factories.

"Where are we now, Johnny dear?" asked Van as they swung out of the lake's orbit and sped along a suburban avenue with clapboard cottages among laundry-linked pines.

"Dorofey Road," cried the driver above the din of the motor. "It abuts at the forest."

It abutted. Van felt a faint twinge in his knee where he had hit it against a stone when attacked from behind a week ago, in another wood. At the moment his foot touched the pine-needle strewn earth of the forest road, a transparent white butterfly floated past, and with utter certainty Van knew that he had only a few minutes to live.

He turned to his second and said:

"This stamped letter, in this handsome Majestic Hotel envelope, is addressed, as you see, to my father. I am transferring it to the back pocket of my pants. Please post it at once if the Captain, who I see has arrived in a rather funerary-looking limousine, accidentally slaughters me."

They found a convenient clearing, and the principals, pistol in hand, faced each other at a distance of some thirty paces, in the kind of single combat described by most Russian novelists and by practically all Russian novelists of gentle birth. As Arwin clapped his hands, informally signaling the permission to fire at will, Van noticed a speckled movement on his right: two little spectators—a fat girl and a boy in a sailorsuit, wearing glasses, with a basket of mushrooms between them. It was not the chocolate-muncher in Cordula's compartment, but a boy very much like him, and as this flashed through Van's mind he felt the jolt of the bullet ripping off, or so it felt, the entire left side of his torso. He swayed, but regained his balance, and with nice dignity discharged his pistol in the sun-hazy air.

His heart beat steadily, his spit was clear, his lungs felt intact, but a fire of pain raged somewhere in his left armpit. Blood oozed through his clothes and trickled down his trouserleg. He sat down, slowly, cautiously, and leaned on his right arm. He dreaded losing consciousness, but, maybe, did faint briefly, because next moment he became aware that Johnny had relieved him of the letter and was in the act of pocketing it.

"Tear it up, you idiot," said Van with an involuntary groan.

The Captain strolled up and muttered rather gloomily: "I bet you are in no condition to continue, are you?"

"I bet you can't wait—" began Van: he intended to say: "you can't wait to have me slap you again," but happened to laugh on "wait" and the muscles of mirth reacted so excruciatingly that he stopped in mid-sentence and bowed his sweating brow.

Meanwhile, the limousine was being transformed into an ambulance by Arwin. Newspapers were dismembered to protect the upholstery, and the fussy Captain added to them what looked like a potato bag or something rotting in a locker, and then after rummaging again in the car trunk and muttering about the "bloody mess" (quite a literal statement) decided to sacrifice the ancient and filthy macintosh on which a decrepit dear dog had once died on the way to the veterinary.

For half a minute Van was sure that he still lay in the car, whereas actually he was in the general ward of Lakeview (Lakeview!) Hospital, between two series of variously bandaged, snoring, raving and moaning men. When he understood this, his first reaction was to demand indignantly that he be transferred to the best private *palata* in the place and that his suitcase and alpenstock be fetched from the Majestic. His next request was that he be told how seriously he was hurt and how long he was expected to remain incapacitated. His third action was to resume what constituted the sole reason for his having to visit Kalugano (visit Kalugano!). His new quarters, where heartbroken kings had tossed in transit, proved to be a replica in white of his hotel apartment—white furniture, white carpet, white sparver. Inset, so to speak, was Tatiana, a remarkably pretty and proud young nurse, with black hair and diaphanous skin (some of her attitudes and gestures, and that harmony between neck and eyes which is the special, scarcely yet investigated secret of feminine grace fantastically and agonizingly reminded him of Ada, and he sought escape from that image in a powerful response to the charms of Tatiana, a torturing angel in her own right. Enforced immobility forbade the chase and grab of common cartoons. He begged her to massage his legs but she tested him with one glance of her grave, dark eyes—and delegated the task to Dorofey, a beefy-handed male nurse, strong enough to lift him bodily out of bed, with the sick child clasping the massive nape. When Van managed once to twiddle her breasts, she warned him she would complain if he ever repeated what she dubbed more aptly than she thought "that soft dangle." An exhibition of his state with a humble appeal for a healing caress resulted in her drily remarking that distinguished gentlemen in public parks got quite lengthy prison terms for that sort of thing. However, much later, she wrote him a charming and melancholy letter in red ink on pink paper; but other emotions and events had intervened, and he never met her again). His suitcase promptly arrived from the hotel; the stick, however, could not be located (it must be climbing nowadays Wellington Mountain, or perhaps, helping a lady to go "brambling" in Oregon); so the hospital supplied him with the Third Cane, a rather nice, knotty, cherry-dark thing with a crook and a solid black-rubber heel. Dr. Fitzbishop congratulated him on having escaped with a superficial muscle wound, the bullet having lightly grooved or, if he might say so, grazed the greater *serratus*. Doc Fitz commented on Van's wonderful recuperational power which was already in evidence, and promised to have him out of disinfectants and bandages in ten days or so if for the first three he remained as motionless as a felled tree-trunk. Did Van like music? Sportsmen usually did, didn't they? Would he care to have a Sonorola by his bed? No, he disliked music, but did the doctor, being a concert-goer, know perhaps where a musician called Rack could be found? "Ward Five," answered the doctor promptly. Van misunderstood this as the title of some piece of music and repeated his question. Would he find Rack's address at Harper's music shop? Well, they used to rent a cottage way down Dorofey Road, near the forest, but now some other people had moved in. Ward Five was where hopeless cases were kept. The poor guy had always had a bad liver and a very indifferent heart, but on top of that a poison had seeped into his system; the local "lab" could not identify it and they were now waiting for a report, on those curiously frog-green faeces, from the Luga people. If Rack had administered it to himself by his own hand, he kept "mum"; it was more likely the work of his wife who dabbled in Hindu-Andean voodoo stuff and had just had a complicated miscarriage in the maternity ward. Yes, triplets—how did he guess? Anyway, if Van was so eager to visit his old pal it would have to be as soon as he could be rolled to Ward Five in a wheelchair by Dorofey, so he'd better apply a bit of voodoo, ha-ha, on his own flesh and blood.

That day came soon enough. After a long journey down corridors where pretty little things tripped by, shaking thermometers, and first an ascent and then a descent in two different lifts, the second of which was very capacious with a metal-handled black lid propped against its wall and bits of holly or laurel here and there on the soap-smelling floor, Dorofey, like Onegin's coachman, said *priehali* ("we have arrived") and gently propelled Van, past two screened beds, toward a third one near the window. There he left Van, while he seated himself at a small table in the door corner and leisurely unfolded the Russian-language newspaper *Golos* (*Logos*).

"I am Van Veen—in case you are no longer lucid enough to recognize somebody you have seen only twice. Hospital records put your age at thirty; I thought you were younger, but even so that is a very early age for a person to die— whatever he be *tvoyu mat'*—half-baked genius or full-fledged scoundrel, or both. As you may guess by the plain but thoughtful trappings of this quiet room, you are an incurable case in one lingo, a rotting rat in another. No oxygen gadget can help you to eschew the 'agony of agony'—Professor Lamort's felicitous pleonasm. The physical torments you will be, or indeed are, experiencing, must be prodigious, but are nothing in comparison to those of a probable hereafter. The mind of man, by nature a monist, cannot accept *two* nothings; he knows there has been *one* nothing, his biological inexistence in the infinite past, for his memory is utterly blank, and *that* nothingness, being, as it were, past, is not too hard to endure. But a second nothingness—which perhaps might not be so hard to bear either—is logically unacceptable. When speaking of space we can imagine a live speck in the limitless oneness of space; but there is no analogy in such a concept with our brief life in time, because however brief (a thirty-year span is really obscenely brief!), our awareness of being is not a dot in eternity, but a slit, a fissure, a chasm running along the entire breadth of metaphysical time, bisecting it and shining—no matter how narrowly—between the back panel and fore panel. Therefore, Mr. Rack, we can speak of past time, and in a vaguer, but familiar sense, of future time, but we simply cannot expect a *second* nothing, a second void, a second blank. Oblivion is a one-night performance; we have been to it once, there will be no repeat. We must face therefore the possibility of some prolonged form of disorganized consciousness and this brings me to my main point, Mr. Rack. Eternal Rack, infinite 'Rackness' may not be much but one thing is certain: the only consciousness that persists in the hereafter is the consciousness of pain. The little Rack of today is the infinite rack of tomorrow—*ich bin ein unverbesserlicher Witzbold*. We can imagine—I think we should imagine—tiny clusters of particles still retaining Rack's personality, gathering here and there in the here-and-there-after, clinging to each other, somehow, somewhere, a web of Rack's toothaches here, a bundle of Rack's nightmares there—rather like tiny groups of obscure refugees from some obliterated country huddling together for a little smelly warmth, for dingy charities or shared recollections of nameless tortures in Tartar camps. For an old man one special little torture must be to wait in a long long queue before a remote urinal. Well, Herr Rack, I submit that the surviving cells of aging Rackness will form such lines of torment, never, never reaching the coveted filth hole in the panic and pain of infinite night. You may answer, of course, if you are versed in contemporary novelistics, and if you fancy the jargon of English writers, that a 'lower-middle-class' piano tuner who falls in love with a fast 'upper-class' girl, thereby destroying his own family, is not committing a crime deserving the castigation which a chance intruder—"

With a not unfamiliar gesture, Van tore up his prepared speech and said:

"Mr. Rack, open your eyes. I'm Van Veen. A visitor."

The hollow-cheeked, long-jawed face, wax-pale, with a fattish nose and a small round chin, remained expressionless for a moment; but the beautiful, amber, liquid, eloquent eyes with pathetically long lashes had opened. Then a faint smile glimmered about his mouth parts, and he stretched one hand, without raising his head from the oil-cloth-covered pillow (why oil-cloth?).

Van, from his chair, extended the end of his cane, which the weak hand took, and palpated politely, thinking it was a well-meant offer of support. "No, I am not yet able to walk a few steps," Rack said quite distinctly, with the German accent which would probably constitute his most durable group of ghost cells.

Van drew in his useless weapon. Controlling himself, he thumped it against the footboard of his wheelchair. Dorofey glanced up from his paper, then went back to the article that engrossed him—"A Clever Piggy (from the memoirs of an animal trainer)," or else "The Crimean War: Tartar Guerillas Help Chinese Troops." A diminutive nurse simultaneously stepped out from behind the farther screen and disappeared again.

Will he ask me to transmit a message? Shall I refuse? Shall I consent—and not transmit it?

"Have they all gone to Hollywood already? Please, tell me, Baron von Wien."

"I don't know," answered Van. "They probably have. I really—"

"Because I sent my last flute melody, and a letter for *all* the family, and no answer has come. I must vomit now. I ring myself."

The diminutive nurse on tremendously high white heels pulled forward the screen of Rack's bed, separating him from the melancholy, lightly wounded, stitched-up, clean-shaven young dandy; who was rolled out and away by efficient Dorofey.

Upon returning to his cool bright room, with the rain and the sun mingling in the half-open window, Van walked on rather ephemeral feet to the looking-glass, smiled to himself in welcome, and without Dorofey's assistance went back to bed. Lovely Tatiana glided in, and asked if he wanted some tea.

"My darling," he said, "I want *you*. Look at this tower of strength!"

"If you knew," she said, over her shoulder, "how many prurient patients have insulted me—exactly that way."

He wrote Cordula a short letter, saying he had met with a little accident, was in the suite for fallen princes in Lakeview

Hospital, Kalugano, and would be at her feet on Tuesday. He also wrote an even shorter letter to Marina, in French, thanking her for a lovely summer. This, on second thought, he decided to send from Manhattan to the Pisang Palace Hotel in Los Angeles. A third letter he addressed to Bernard Rattner, his closest friend at Chose, the great Rattner's nephew. "Your uncle has most honest standards," he wrote, in part, "but I am going to demolish him soon."

On Monday around noon he was allowed to sit in a deck-chair, on the lawn, which he had avidly gazed at for some days from his window. Dr. Fitzbishop had said, rubbing his hands, that the Luga laboratory said it was the not always lethal "*arethusoides*" but it had no practical importance now, because the unfortunate music teacher, and composer, was not expected to spend another night on Demonia, and would be on Terra, ha-ha, in time for evensong. Doc Fitz was what Russians call a *poshlyak* ("pretentious vulgarian") and in some obscure counterfashion Van was relieved not to be able to gloat over the wretched Rack's martyrdom.

A large pine tree cast its shadow upon him and his book. He had borrowed it from a shelf holding a medley of medical manuals, tattered mystery tales, the *Rivière de Diamants* collection of Monparnasse stories, and this odd volume of the *Journal of Modern Science* with a difficult essay by Ripley, "The Structure of Space." He had been wrestling with its phoney formulas and diagrams for several days now and saw he would not be able to assimilate it completely before his release from Lakeview Hospital on the morrow.

A hot sunfleck reached him, and tossing the red volume aside, he got up from his chair. With the return of health the image of Ada kept rising within him like a bitter and brilliant wave, ready to swallow him. His bandages had been removed; nothing but a special vest-like affair of flannel enveloped his torso, and though it was tight and thick it did not protect him any longer from the poisoned point of Ardis. Arrowhead Manor. *Le Château de la Flèche*, Flesh Hall.

He strolled on the shade-streaked lawn feeling much too warm in his black pajamas and dark-red dressing gown. A brick wall separated his part of the garden from the street and a little way off an open gateway allowed an asphalt drive to curve toward the main entrance of the long hospital building. He was on the point of returning to his deckchair when a smart, pale-gray four-door sedan glided in and stopped before him. The door flew open, before the chauffeur, an elderly man in tunic and breeches, had time to hand out Cordula, who now ran like a ballerina toward Van. He hugged her in a frenzy of welcome, kissing her rosy hot face and kneading her soft catlike body through her black silk dress: what a delicious surprise!

She had come all the way from Manhattan, at a hundred kilometers an hour, fearing he might have already left, though he said it would be tomorrow.

"Idea!" he cried. "Take me back with you, right away. Yes, just as I am!"

"Okay," she said, "come and stay at my flat, there's a beautiful guest room for you."

She was a good sport—little Cordula de Prey. Next moment he was sitting beside her in the car, which was backing gateward. Two nurses came running and gesturing toward them, and the chauffeur asked in French if the Countess wished him to stop.

"*Non, non, non!*" cried Van in high glee and they sped away.

Panting, Cordula said:

"My mother rang me up from Malorukino" (their country estate at Malbrook, Mayne): "the local papers said you had fought a duel. You look a tower of health, I'm so glad. I knew something nasty must have happened because little Russel, Dr. Platonov's grandson—remember?—saw you from his side of the train beating up an officer on the station platform. But, first of all, Van, *net, pozhaluysta, on nas vidit* (no, please, he sees us), I have some very bad news for you. Young Fraser, who has just been flown back from Yalta, saw Percy killed on the second day of the invasion, less than a week after they had left Goodson airport. He will tell you the whole story himself, it accumulates more and more dreadful details with every telling, Fraser does not seem to have shined in the confusion, that's why, I suppose, he keeps straightening things out."

(Bill Fraser, the son of Judge Fraser, of Wellington, wit-

nessed Lieutenant de Prey's end from a blessed ditch overgrown with cornel and medlar, but, of course, could do
nothing to help the leader of his platoon and this for a number
of reasons which he conscientiously listed in his report but
which it would be much too tedious and embarrassing to
itemize here. Percy had been shot in the thigh during a skir-
mish with Khazar guerillas in a ravine near Chew-Foot-Calais,
as the American troops pronounced "Chufutkale," the name
of a fortified rock. He had immediately assured himself, with
the odd relief of the doomed, that he had got away with a
flesh wound. Loss of blood caused him to faint, as we fainted,
too, as soon as he started to crawl or rather squirm toward
the shelter of the oak scrub and spiny bushes, where another
casualty was resting comfortably. When a couple of minutes
later, Percy—still Count Percy de Prey—regained consciousness he was no longer alone on his rough bed of gravel and
grass. A smiling old Tartar, incongruously but somehow as-
suagingly wearing American blue-jeans with his *beshmet*, was
squatting by his side. "*Bedniy, bedniy*" (you poor, poor fellow), muttered the good soul, shaking his shaven head and
clucking: "*Bol'no* (it hurts)?" Percy answered in his equally
primitive Russian that he did not feel too badly wounded:
"*Karasho, karasho ne bol'no* (good, good)," said the kindly
old man and, picking up the automatic pistol which Percy had
dropped, he examined it with naive pleasure and then shot
him in the temple. (One wonders, one always wonders, what
had been the executed individual's brief, rapid series of impressions, as preserved somewhere, somehow, in some vast
library of microfilmed last thoughts, between two moments:
between, in the present case, our friend's becoming aware of
those nice, quasi-Red Indian little wrinkles beaming at him
out of a serene sky not much different from Ladore's, and
then feeling the mouth of steel violently push through tender
skin and exploding bone. One supposes it might have been a
kind of suite for flute, a series of "movements" such as, say:
I'm alive—who's that?—civilian—sympathy—thirsty—daughter with pitcher—that's my damned gun—don't . . . *et cetera*
or rather no *cetera* . . . while Broken-Arm Bill prayed his Roman deity in a frenzy of fear for the Tartar to finish his job

and go. But, of course, an invaluable detail in that strip of thought would have been—perhaps, next to the pitcher peri— a glint, a shadow, a stab of Ardis.)

"How strange, how strange," murmured Van when Cordula had finished her much less elaborate version of the report Van later got from Bill Fraser.

What a strange coincidence! Either Ada's lethal shafts were at work, or he, Van, had somehow managed to dispatch her two wretched lovers in a duel with a dummy.

Strange, too, that he felt nothing special, except, perhaps, a kind of neutral wonder, as he listened to little Cordula. A one-track man in matters of soft passion, strange Van, strange Demon's son, was at the moment much more anxious to enjoy Cordula as soon as humanly and humanely possible, as soon as satanically and viatically feasible, than to keep deploring the fate of a fellow he hardly knew; and although Cordula's blue eyes flashed with tears once or twice, he knew perfectly well that she had never seen much of her second cousin and, in point of fact, had rather disliked him.

Cordula told Edmond: "*Arrêtez près de* what's-it-called, yes, Albion, *le* store *pour messieurs*, in Luga"; and as peeved Van remonstrated: "You can't go back to civilization in pajamas," she said firmly. "I shall buy you some clothes, while Edmond has a mug of coffee."

She bought him a pair of trousers, and a raincoat. He had been waiting impatiently in the parked car and now under the pretext of changing into his new clothes asked her to drive him to some secluded spot, while Edmond, wherever he was, had another mug.

As soon as they reached a suitable area he transferred Cordula to his lap and had her very comfortably, with such howls of enjoyment that she felt touched and flattered.

"Reckless Cordula," observed reckless Cordula cheerfully; "this will probably mean another abortion—*encore un petit enfantôme*, as my poor aunt's maid used to wail every time it happened to her. Did I say anything wrong?"

"Nothing wrong," said Van, kissing her tenderly; and they drove back to the diner.

43

Van spent a medicinal month in Cordula's Manhattan flat on Alexis Avenue. She dutifully visited her mother at their Malbrook castle two or three times a week, unescorted by Van either there or to the numerous social "flits" she attended in town, being a frivolous fun-loving little thing; but some parties she canceled, and resolutely avoided seeing her latest lover (the fashionable psychotechnician Dr. F. S. Fraser, a cousin of the late P. de P.'s fortunate fellow soldier). Several times Van talked on the dorophone with his father (who pursued an extensive study of Mexican spas and spices) and did several errands for him in town. He often took Cordula to French restaurants, English movies, and Varangian tragedies, all of which was most satisfying, for she relished every morsel, every sip, every jest, every sob, and he found ravishing the velvety rose of her cheeks and the azure-pure iris of her festively painted eyes to which indigo-black thick lashes, lengthening and upcurving at the outer canthus, added what fashion called the "harlequin slant."

One Sunday, while Cordula was still lolling in her perfumed bath (a lovely, oddly unfamiliar sight, which he delighted in twice a day), Van, "in the nude" (as his new sweetheart drolly genteelized "naked"), attempted for the first time after a month's abstinence to walk on his hands. He felt strong, and fit, and blithely turned over to the "first position" in the middle of the sun-drenched terrace. Next moment he was sprawling on his back. He tried again and lost his balance at once. He had the terrifying, albeit illusionary, feeling that his left arm was now shorter than his right, and Van wondered wrily if he ever would be able to dance on his hands again. King Wing had warned him that two or three months without practice might result in an irretrievable loss of the rare art. On the same day (the two nasty little incidents thus remained linked up in his mind forever) Van happened to answer the 'phone— a deep hollow voice which he thought was a man's wanted Cordula, but the caller turned out to be an old schoolmate, and Cordula feigned limpid delight, while making big eyes at Van over the receiver, and invented a number of unconvincing engagements.

"It's a gruesome girl!" she cried after the melodious adieux.
"Her name is Vanda Broom, and I learned only recently what
I never suspected at school—she's a regular *tribadka*—poor
Grace Erminin tells me Vanda used to make constant passes
at her and at—at another girl. There's her picture here," continued Cordula with a quick change of tone, producing a
daintily bound and prettily printed graduation album of
Spring, 1887, which Van had seen at Ardis, but in which he
had not noticed the somber beetle-browed unhappy face of
that particular girl, and now it did not matter any more, and
Cordula quickly popped the book back into a drawer; but he
remembered very well that among the various more or less
coy contributions it contained a clever pastiche by Ada Veen
mimicking Tolstoy's paragraph rhythm and chapter closings;
he saw clearly in mind her prim photo under which she had
added one of her characteristic jingles:

> In the old manor, I've parodied
> Every veranda and room,
> And jacarandas at Arrowhead
> In supernatural bloom.

It did not matter, it did not matter. Destroy and forget!
But a butterfly in the Park, an orchid in a shop window, would
revive everything with a dazzling inward shock of despair.

His main industry consisted of research at the great granite-
pillared Public Library, that admirable and formidable palace
a few blocks from Cordula's cosy flat. One is irresistibly
tempted to compare the strange longings and nauseous
qualms that enter into the complicated ecstasies accompanying the making of a young writer's first book with childbear-
ing. Van had only reached the bridal stage; then, to develop
the metaphor, would come the sleeping car of messy deflo-
ration; then the first balcony of honeymoon breakfasts, with
the first wasp. In no sense could Cordula be compared to a
writer's muse but the evening stroll back to her apartment was
pleasantly saturated with the afterglow and afterthought of the
accomplished task and the expectation of her caresses; he especially looked forward to those nights when they had an elaborate repast sent up from "Monaco," a good restaurant in the
entresol of the tall building crowned by her penthouse and its

spacious terrace. The sweet banality of their little ménage sustained him much more securely than the company of his constantly agitated and fiery father did at their rare meetings in town or was to do during a fortnight in Paris before the next term at Chose. Except gossip—gossamer gossip—Cordula had no conversation and that also helped. She had instinctively realized very soon that she should never mention Ada or Ardis. He, on his part, accepted the evident fact that she did not really love him. Her small, clear, soft, well-padded and rounded body was delicious to stroke, and her frank amazement at the variety and vigor of his love-making anointed what still remained of poor Van's crude virile pride. She would doze off between two kisses. When he could not sleep, as now often happened, he retired to the sitting room and sat there annotating his authors or else he would walk up and down the open terrace, under a haze of stars, in severely restricted meditation, till the first tramcar jangled and screeched in the dawning abyss of the city.

When in early September Van Veen left Manhattan for Lute, he was pregnant.

Part Two

I

AT the Goodson Airport, in one of the gilt-framed mirrors of its old-fashioned waiting room, Van glimpsed the silk hat of his father who sat awaiting him in an armchair of imitation marblewood, behind a newspaper that said in reversed characters: "Crimea Capitulates." At the same moment a rain-coated man with a pleasant, somewhat porcine, pink face accosted Van. He represented a famous international agency, known as the VPL, which handled Very Private Letters. After a first flash of surprise, Van reflected that Ada Veen, a recent mistress of his, could not have chosen a smarter (in all senses of the word) way of conveying to him a message whose fantastically priced, and prized, process of transmission insured an absoluteness of secrecy which neither torture nor mesmerism had been able to break down in the evil days of 1859. It was rumored that even Gamaliel on his (no longer frequent, alas) trips to Paris, and King Victor during his still fairly regular visits to Cuba or Hecuba, and, of course, robust Lord Goal, Viceroy of France, when enjoying his randonnies all over Canady, preferred the phenomenally discreet, and in fact rather creepy, infallibility of the VPL organization to such official facilities as sexually starved potentates have at their disposal for deceiving their wives. The present messenger called himself James Jones, a formula whose complete lack of connotation made an ideal pseudonym despite its happening to be his real name. A flurry and flapping had started in the mirror but Van declined to act hastily. In order to gain time (for, on being shown Ada's crest on a separate card, he felt he had to decide whether or not to accept her letter), he closely examined the badge resembling an ace of hearts which J.J. displayed with pardonable pride. He requested Van to open the letter, satisfy himself of its authenticity, and sign the card that then went back into some secret pit or pouch within the young detective's attire or anatomy. Cries of welcome and impatience from Van's father (wearing for the flight to France a scarlet-silk-lined black cape) finally caused Van to interrupt his colloquy with James and pocket the letter (which he read a few minutes later in the lavatory before boarding the airliner).

"Stocks," said Demon, "are on the zoom. Our territorial triumphs, et cetera. An American governor, my friend Bessborodko, is to be installed in Bessarabia, and a British one, Armborough, will rule Armenia. I saw you enlaced with your little Countess near the parking lot. If you marry her I will disinherit you. They're quite a notch below our set."

"In a couple of years," said Van, "I'll slide into my own little millions" (meaning the fortune Aqua had left him). "But you needn't worry, sir, we have interrupted our affair for the time being—till the next time I return to live in her *girlinière*" (Canady slang).

Demon, flaunting his flair, desired to be told if Van or his *poule* had got into trouble with the police (nodding toward Jim or John who having some other delivery to make sat glancing through Crime Copulate Bessarmenia).

"*Poule*," replied Van with the evasive taciturnity of the Roman rabbi shielding Barabbas.

"Why gray?" asked Demon, alluding to Van's overcoat. "Why that military cut? It's too late to enlist."

"I couldn't—my draft board would turn me down anyway."

"How's the wound?"

"*Komsi-komsa*. It now appears that the Kalugano surgeon messed up his job. The rip seam has grown red and raw, without any reason, and there's a lump in my armpit. I'm in for another spell of surgery—this time in London, where butchers carve so much better. Where's the *mestechko* here? Oh, I see it. Cute (a gentian painted on one door, a lady fern on the other: have to go to the herbarium)."

He did not answer her letter, and a fortnight later John James, now got up as a German tourist, all pseudo-tweed checks, handed Van a second message, in the Louvre right in front of Bosch's *Bâteau Ivre*, the one with a jester drinking in the riggings (poor old Dan thought it had something to do with Brant's satirical poem!). There would be no answer—

though answers were included, with the return ticket, in the price, as the honest messenger pointed out.

It was snowing, yet James in a fit of abstract rakishness stood fanning himself with a third letter at the front door of Van's *cottage orné* on Ranta River, near Chose, and Van asked him to stop bringing him messages.

In the course of the next two years two more letters were handed to him, both in London, and both in the hall of the Albania Palace Hotel, by another VPL agent, an elderly gent in a bowler, whose matter-of-fact, undertakerish aspect might irritate Mr. Van Veen less, thought modest and sensitive Jim, than that of a romanesque private detective. A sixth came by natural means to Park Lane. The lot (minus the last, which dealt exclusively with Ada's stage & screen ventures) is given below. Ada ignored dates, but they can be approximately determined.

[Los Angeles, early September, 1888]

You must pardon me for using such a posh (and also *poshlïy*) means of having a letter reach you, but I'm unable to find any safer service.

When I said I could not speak and would write, I meant I could not utter the proper words at short notice. I implore you. I felt that I could not produce them and arrange them orally in the necessary order. I implore you. I felt that one wrong or misplaced word would be fatal, you would simply turn away, as you did, and walk off again, and again, and again. I implore you for breath [sic! Ed.] of understanding. But now I think that I should have taken the risk of speaking, of stammering, for I see now that it is just as dreadfully hard to put my heart and honor in script—even more so because in speaking one can use a stutter as a shutter, and plead a chance slurring of words, like a bleeding hare with one side of its mouth shot off, or twist back, and improve; but against a background of snow, even the blue snow of this notepaper, the blunders are red and final. I implore you.

One thing should be established once for all, indefeasibly. I loved, love, and shall love only you. I implore you and love you with everlasting pain and passion, my darling. *Tï tut stoyal* (you stayed here), in this *karavansaray*, you in the middle of everything, always, when I must have been seven or eight, didn't you?

[Los Angeles, mid-September, 1888]

This is a second howl *iz ada* (out of Hades). Strangely, I learned on the same day, from three different sources, of your duel in K.; of P's death; and of your recuperating at his cousin's (congs, as she and I used to say). I rang her up, but she said that you had left for Paris and that R. had also died—not through your intervention, as I had thought for a moment, but through that of his wife. Neither he nor P. was technically my lover, but both are on Terra now, so it does not matter.

[Los Angeles, 1889]

We are still at the candy-pink and pisang-green albergo where you once stayed with your father. He is awfully nice to me, by the way. I enjoy going places with him. He and I have gamed at Nevada, my rhyme-name town, but you are also there, as well as the legendary river of Old Rus. *Da.* Oh, write me, one tiny note, I'm trying so hard to please you! Want some more (desperate) little topics? Marina's new director of artistic conscience defines Infinity as the farthest point from the camera which is still in fair focus. She has been cast as the deaf nun Varvara (who, in some ways, is the most interesting of Chekhov's Four Sisters). She sticks to Stan's principle of having lore and rôle overflow into everyday life, insists on keeping it up at the hotel restaurant, drinks tea *v prikusku* ("biting sugar between sips"), and feigns to misunderstand every question in Varvara's quaint way of feigning stupidity—a double imbroglio, which annoys strangers but which somehow makes me feel I'm her daughter much more distinctly than in the Ardis era. She's a great hit here, on the whole. They gave her (not quite gratis, I'm afraid) a special bungalow, labeled Marina Durmanova, in Universal City. As for me, I'm only an incidental waitress in a fourth-rate Western, hip-swinging between table-slapping drunks, but I rather enjoy the *Houssaie* atmosphere, the dutiful art, the winding hill roads, the reconstructions of streets, and the obligatory square, and a mauve shop sign on an ornate wooden façade,

and around noon all the extras in period togs queuing before
a glass booth, but I have nobody to call.

Speaking of calls, I saw a truly marvelous ornithological film
the other night with Demon. I had never grasped the fact that
the paleotropical sunbirds (look them up!) are "mimotypes"
of the New World hummingbirds, and all my thoughts, oh,
my darling, are mimotypes of yours. I know, I know! I even
know that you stopped reading at "grasped"—as in the old
days.

[California? 1890]

I love only you, I'm happy only in dreams of you, you are
my joy and my world, this is as certain and real as being aware
of one's being alive, but . . . oh, I don't accuse you!—but,
Van, you *are* responsible (or Fate through you is responsible,
ce qui revient au même) for having let loose something mad
in me when we were only children, a physical hankering, an
insatiable itch. The fire you rubbed left its brand on the most
vulnerable, most vicious and tender point of my body. Now
I have to pay for your rasping the red rash too strongly, too
soon, as charred wood has to pay for burning. When I remain
without your caresses, I lose all control of my nerves, nothing
exists any more than the ecstasy of friction, the abiding effect
of your sting, of your delicious poison. I do not accuse you,
but this is why I crave and cannot resist the impact of alien
flesh; this is why our joint past radiates ripples of boundless
betrayals. All this you are free to diagnose as a case of advanced erotomania, but there is more to it, because there exists a simple cure for all my *maux* and *throes* and that is an
extract of scarlet aril, the flesh of yew, just only yew. *Je réalise*,
as your sweet Cinderella de Torf (now Madame Trofim Fartukov) used to say, that I'm being coy and obscene. But it all
leads up to an important, important suggestion! Van, *je suis
sur la verge* (Blanche again) of a revolting amorous adventure.
I could be instantly saved by you. Take the fastest flying machine you can rent straight to El Paso, your Ada will be waiting for you there, waving like mad, and we'll continue, by the
New World Express, in a suite I'll obtain, to the burning tip
of Patagonia, Captain Grant's Horn, a Villa in Verna, my

jewel, my agony. Send me an aerogram with one Russian word—the end of my name and wit.

[Arizona, summer, 1890]

Mere pity, a Russian girl's *zhalost'*, drew me to R. (whom musical critics have now "discovered"). He knew he would die young and was always, in fact, mostly corpse, never once, I swear, rising to the occasion, even when I showed openly my compassionate non-resistance because I, alas, was brimming with Van-less vitality, and had even considered buying the services of some rude, the ruder the better, young muzhik. As to P., I could explain my submitting to his kisses (first tender and plain, later growing fiercely expert, and finally tasting of me when he returned to my mouth—a vicious circle set spinning in early Thargelion, 1888) by saying that if I stopped seeing him he would divulge my affair with my cousin to my mother. He did say he could produce witnesses, such as the sister of your Blanche, and a stable boy who, I suspect, was impersonated by the youngest of the three demoiselles de Tourbe, witches all—but enough. Van, I could make much of those threats in explaining my conduct to you. I would not mention, naturally, that they were made in a bantering tone, hardly befitting a genuine blackmailer. Nor would I mention that even if he had proceeded to recruit anonymous messengers and informers, it might have ended in his wrecking his own reputation as soon as his motives and actions were exposed, as they were bound to be in the long ruin [sic! "run" in her blue stocking. Ed.]. I would conceal, in a word, that I knew the coarse banter was meant only to drill-jar your poor brittle Ada—because, despite the coarseness, he had a keen sense of honor, odd though it may seem to you and me. No. I would concentrate entirely on the effect of the threat upon one ready to submit to any infamy rather than face the shadow of disclosure, for (and this, of course, neither he nor his informers could know), shocking as an affair between first cousins might have seemed to a law-abiding family, I refused to imagine (as you and I have always done) how Marina and Demon would have reacted in "our" case. By the jolts and skids of my syntax you will see that I cannot logically explain my behavior. I do not deny that I experienced a strange weakness during the perilous assignations I granted him, as if his brutal desire kept fascinating not only my inquisitive senses but also my reluctant intellect. I can swear, however, solemn Ada can swear that in the course of our "sylvan trysts" I successfully evaded if not pollution, at least possession before and after your return to Ardis—except for one messy occasion when he half-took me by force—the over-eager dead man.

I'm writing from Marina Ranch—not very far from the little gulch in which Aqua died and into which I myself feel like creeping some day. For the time being, I'm returning for a while to the Pisang Hotel.

I salute the good auditor.

When Van retrieved in 1940 this thin batch of five letters, each in its VPL pink silk-paper case, from the safe in his Swiss bank where they had been preserved for exactly one half of a century, he was baffled by their small number. The expansion of the past, the luxuriant growth of memory had magnified that number to at least fifty. He recalled that he had also used as a cache the desk in his Park Lane studio, but he knew he had kept there only the innocent sixth letter (Dreams of Drama) of 1891, which had perished, together with her coded notes (of 1884–88) when the irreplaceable little palazzo burnt down in 1919. Rumor attributed the bright deed to the city fathers (three bearded elders and a blue-eyed young Mayor with a fabulous amount of front teeth), who could no longer endure their craving for the space that the solid dwarf occupied between two alabaster colossi; but instead of selling them the blackened area as expected, Van gleefully erected there his famous Lucinda Villa, a miniature museum just two stories high, with a still growing collection of microphotographed paintings from all public and private galleries in the world (not excluding Tartary) on one floor and a honeycomb of projection cells on the other: a most appetizing little memorial of Parian marble, administered by a considerable staff, guarded by three heavily armed stalwarts, and open to the public only on Mondays for a token fee of one gold dollar regardless of age or condition.

No doubt the singular multiplication of those letters in retrospect could be explained by each of them casting an excruciating shadow, similar to that of a lunar volcano, over several months of his life, and tapering to a point only when the no less pangful precognition of the next message began to dawn. But many years later, when working on his *Texture of Time*, Van found in that phenomenon additional proof of real time's being connected with the interval between events, not with their "passage," not with their blending, not with their shading the gap wherein the pure and impenetrable texture of time transpires.

He told himself he would be firm and suffer in silence. Self-esteem was satisfied: the dying duelist dies a happier man than his live foe ever will be. We must not blame Van, however, for failing to persevere in his resolution, for it is not hard to understand why a seventh letter (transmitted to him by Ada's and his half-sister, at Kingston, in 1892) could make him succumb. Because he knew it was the last in the series. Because it had come from the blood-red *érable* arbors of Ardis. Because a sacramental four-year period equaled that of their first separation. Because Lucette turned out to be, against all reason and will, the impeccable paranymph.

2

Ada's letters breathed, writhed, lived; Van's *Letters from Terra*, "a philosophical novel," showed no sign of life whatsoever.

(I disagree, it's a nice, nice little book! Ada's note.)

He had written it involuntarily, so to speak, not caring a dry fig for literary fame. Neither did pseudonymity tickle him in reverse—as it did when he danced on his hands. Though "Van Veen's vanity" often cropped up in the drawing-room prattle among fan-wafting ladies, this time his long blue pride feathers remained folded. What, then, moved him to contrive a romance around a subject that had been worried to extinction in all kinds of "Star Rats," and "Space Aces"? We—whoever "we" are—might define the compulsion as a pleasurable urge to express through verbal imagery a compendium of certain inexplicably correlated vagaries observed by him in mental patients, on and off, since his first year at Chose. Van had a passion for the insane as some have for arachnids or orchids.

There were good reasons to disregard the technological details involved in delineating intercommunication between Terra the Fair and our terrible Antiterra. His knowledge of physics, mechanicalism and that sort of stuff had remained limited to the scratch of a prep-school blackboard. He consoled himself with the thought that no censor in America or Great Britain would pass the slightest reference to "magnetic" gewgaws. Quietly, he borrowed what his greatest forerunners (Counterstone, for example) had imagined in the way of a manned capsule's propulsion, including the clever idea of an initial speed of a few thousand miles per hour increasing, under the influence of a Counterstonian type of intermediate environment between sibling galaxies, to several trillions of light-years per second, before dwindling harmlessly to a parachute's indolent descent. Elaborating anew, in irrational fabrications, all that Cyraniana and "physics fiction" would have been not only a bore but an absurdity, for nobody knew how far Terra, or other innumerable planets with cottages and cows, might be situated in outer or inner space: "inner," because why not assume their microcosmic presence in the golden globules ascending quick-quick in this flute of Moët or in the corpuscles of my, Van Veen's—

(or my, Ada Veen's)

—bloodstream, or in the pus of a Mr. Nekto's ripe boil newly lanced in Nektor or Neckton. Moreover, although reference works existed on library shelves in available, and redundant, profusion, no direct access could be obtained to the banned, or burned, books of the three cosmologists, Xertigny, Yates and Zotov (pen names), who had recklessly started the whole business half a century earlier, causing, and endorsing, panic, demency and execrable *romanchiks*. All three scientists had vanished now: X had committed suicide; Y had been kidnapped by a laundryman and transported to Tartary; and Z, a ruddy, white-whiskered old sport, was driving his Yakima jailers crazy by means of incomprehensible crepitations, cease-

less invention of invisible inks, chameleonizations, nerve signals, spirals of outgoing light and feats of ventriloquism that
imitated pistol shots and sirens.

Poor Van! In his struggle to keep the writer of the letters
from Terra strictly separate from the image of Ada, he gilt and
carmined Theresa until she became a paragon of banality. This
Theresa maddened with her messages a scientist on our easily
maddened planet; his anagram-looking name, Sig Leymanski,
had been partly derived by Van from that of Aqua's last doctor. When Leymanski's obsession turned into love, and one's
sympathy got focused on his enchanting, melancholy, betrayed wife (née Antilia Glems), our author found himself
confronted with the distressful task of now stamping out in
Antilia, a born brunette, all traces of Ada, thus reducing yet
another character to a dummy with bleached hair.

After beaming to Sig a dozen communications from her
planet, Theresa flies over to him, and he, in his laboratory,
has to place her on a slide under a powerful microscope in
order to make out the tiny, though otherwise perfect, shape
of his minikin sweetheart, a graceful microorganism extending
transparent appendages toward his huge humid eye. Alas, the
testibulus (test tube—never to be confused with *testiculus*, orchid), with Theresa swimming inside like a micromermaid, is
"accidentally" thrown away by Professor Leyman's (he had
trimmed his name by that time) assistant, Flora, initially an
ivory-pale, dark-haired funest beauty, whom the author transformed just in time into a third bromidic dummy with a dun
bun.

(Antilia later regained her husband, and Flora was weeded
out. Ada's addendum.)

On Terra, Theresa had been a Roving Reporter for an
American magazine, thus giving Van the opportunity to describe the sibling planet's political aspect. This aspect gave him
the least trouble, presenting as it did a mosaic of painstakingly
collated notes from his own reports on the "transcendental
delirium" of his patients. Its acoustics were poor, proper
names often came out garbled, a chaotic calendar messed up
the order of events but, on the whole, the colored dots did
form a geomantic picture of sorts. As earlier experimentators
had conjectured, our annals lagged by about half a century

behind Terra's along the bridges of time, but overtook some of its underwater currents. At the moment of our sorry story, the king of Terra's England, yet another George (there had been, apparently, at least half-a-dozen bearing that name before him) ruled, or had just ceased to rule, over an empire that was somewhat patchier (with alien blanks and blots between the British Islands and South Africa) than the solidly conglomerated one on our Antiterra. Western Europe presented a particularly glaring gap: ever since the eighteenth century, when a virtually bloodless revolution had dethroned the Capetians and repelled all invaders, Terra's France flourished under a couple of emperors and a series of bourgeois presidents, of whom the present one, Doumercy, seemed considerably more lovable than Milord Goal, Governor of Lute! Eastward, instead of Khan Sosso and his ruthless Sovietnamur Khanate, a super Russia, dominating the Volga region and similar watersheds, was governed by a Sovereign Society of Solicitous Republics (or so it came through) which had superseded the Tsars, conquerors of Tartary and Trst. Last but not least, Athaulf the Future, a fair-haired giant in a natty uniform, the secret flame of many a British nobleman, honorary captain of the French police, and benevolent ally of Rus and Rome, was said to be in the act of transforming a gingerbread Germany into a great country of speedways, immaculate soldiers, brass bands and modernized barracks for misfits and their young.

No doubt much of that information, gleaned by our terrapists (as Van's colleagues were dubbed), came in a botched form; but the strain of sweet happiness could be always distinguished as an all-pervading note. Now the purpose of the novel was to suggest that Terra cheated, that all was not paradise there, that perhaps in some ways human minds and human flesh underwent on that sibling planet worse torments than on our much maligned Demonia. In her first letters, before leaving Terra, Theresa had nothing but praise for its rulers—especially Russian and German rulers. In her later messages from space she confessed that she had exaggerated the bliss; had been, in fact, the instrument of "cosmic propaganda"—a brave thing to admit, as agents on Terra might have yanked her back or destroyed her in flight had they man-

aged to intercept her undissembling ondulas, now mostly going one way, our way, don't ask Van by what method or
principle. Unfortunately, not only mechanicalism, but also
moralism, could hardly be said to constitute something in
which he excelled, and what we have rendered here in a few
leisurely phrases took him two hundred pages to develop and
adorn. We must remember that he was only twenty; that his
young proud soul was in a state of grievous disarray; that he
had read too much and invented too little; and that the brilliant mirages which had risen before him when he felt the first
pangs of book-birth on Cordula's terrace were now fading
under the action of prudence, as did those wonders which
medieval explores back from Cathay were afraid to reveal to
the Venetian priest or the Flemish philistine.

He devoted a couple of months at Chose to copying in a
clean hand his scarecrow scribblings and then heavily recor-
recting the result, so that his final copy looked like a first draft
when he took it to an obscure agency in Bedford to have it
secretly typed in triplicate. This he disfigured again during his
voyage back to America on board the *Queen Guinevere*. And
in Manhattan the galleys had to be reset twice, owing not only
to the number of new alterations but also to the eccentricity
of Van's proofreading marks.

Letters from Terra, by Voltemand, came out in 1891 on
Van's twenty-first birthday, under the imprint of two bo-
gus houses, "Abencerage" in Manhattan, and "Zegris" in
London.

(Had I happened to see a copy I would have recognized
Chateaubriand's *lapochka* and hence your little paw, *at once*.)

His new lawyer, Mr. Gromwell, whose really beautiful floral
name suited somehow his innocent eyes and fair beard, was a
nephew of the great Grombchevski, who for the last thirty
years or so had managed some of Demon's affairs with good
care and acumen. Gromwell nursed Van's personal fortune no
less tenderly; but he had little experience in the intricacies of
book-publishing matters, and Van was an absolute ignoramus
there, not knowing, for example, that "review copies" were
supposed to go to the editors of various periodicals or that
advertisements should be purchased and not be expected to
appear by spontaneous generation in full-page adulthood be-

tween similar blurbs boosting *The Possessed* by Miss Love and
The Puffer by Mr. Dukes.

For a fat little fee, Gwen, one of Mr. Gromwell's employees,
was delegated not only to entertain Van, but also to supply
Manhattan bookstores with one-half of the printed copies,
whilst an old lover of hers in England was engaged to place
the rest in the bookshops of London. The notion that anybody kind enough to sell his book should not keep the ten
dollars or so that every copy had cost to manufacture seemed
unfair and illogical to Van. Therefore he felt sorry for all the
trouble that underpaid, tired, bare-armed, brunette-pale shop-
girls had no doubt taken in trying to tempt dour homosexuals
with his stuff ("Here's a rather fancy novel about a girl called
Terra"), when he learned from a careful study of a statement
of sales, which his stooges sent him in February, 1892, that in
twelve months only six copies had been sold—two in England
and four in America. Statistically speaking, no reviews could
have been expected, given the unorthodox circumstances in
which poor Terra's correspondence had been handled. Curiously enough, as many as two did appear. One, by the First
Clown in *Elsinore*, a distinguished London weekly, popped up
in a survey entitled, with a British journalist's fondness for this
kind of phoney wordplay, "*Terre à terre*, 1891," and dealt with
the year's "Space Romances," which by that time had begun
to fine off. He sniffed Voltemand's contribution as the choic-
est of the lot, calling it (alas, with unerring flair) "a sumptu-
ously fripped up, trite, tedious and obscure fable, with a few
absolutely marvelous metaphors marring the otherwise total
ineptitude of the tale."

The only other compliment was paid to poor Voltemand in
a little Manhattan magazine (*The Village Eyebrow*) by the poet
Max Mispel (another botanical name—"medlar" in English),
member of the German Department at Goluba University.
Herr Mispel, who liked to air his authors, discerned in *Letters
from Terra* the influence of Osberg (Spanish writer of pretentious fairy tales and mystico-allegoric anecdotes, highly esteemed by short-shift thesialists) as well as that of an obscene
ancient Arab, expounder of anagrammatic dreams, Ben Sirine,
thus transliterated by Captain de Roux, according to Burton
in his adaptation of Nefzawi's treatise on the best method of

mating with obese or hunchbacked females (*The Perfumed Garden*, Panther edition, p. 187, a copy given to ninety-three-year-old Baron Van Veen by his ribald physician Professor Lagosse). His critique ended as follows: "If Mr. Voltemand (or Voltimand or Mandalatov) is a psychiatrist, as I think he might be, then I pity his patients, while admiring his talent."

Upon being cornered, Gwen, a fat little *fille de joie* (by inclination if not by profession), squealed on one of her new admirers, confessing she had begged him to write that article because she could not bear to see Van's "crooked little smile" at finding his beautifully bound and boxed book so badly neglected. She also swore that Max not only did not know who Voltemand really was, but had not read Van's novel. Van toyed with the idea of challenging Mr. Medlar (who, he hoped, would choose swords) to a duel at dawn in a secluded corner of the Park whose central green he could see from the penthouse terrace where he fenced with a French coach twice a week, the only exercise, save riding, that he still indulged in; but to his surprise—and relief (for he was a little ashamed to defend his "novelette" and only wished to forget it, just as another, unrelated, Veen might have denounced—if allowed a longer life—his pubescent dream of ideal bordels) Max Mushmula (Russian for "medlar") answered Van's tentative cartel with the warmhearted promise of sending him his next article, "The Weed Exiles the Flower" (Melville & Marvell).

A sense of otiose emptiness was all Van derived from those contacts with Literature. Even while writing his book, he had become painfully aware how little he knew his own planet while attempting to piece together another one from jagged bits filched from deranged brains. He decided that after completing his medical studies at Kingston (which he found more congenial than good old Chose) he would undertake long travels in South America, Africa, India. As a boy of fifteen (Eric Veen's age of florescence) he had studied with a poet's passion the timetables of three great American transcontinental trains that one day he would take—not alone (now alone). From Manhattan, via Mephisto, El Paso, Meksikansk and the Panama Chunnel, the dark-red New World Express reached Brazilia and Witch (or Viedma, founded by a Russian admiral).

There it split into two parts, the eastern one continuing to Grant's Horn, and the western returning north through Valparaiso and Bogota. On alternate days the fabulous journey began in Yukonsk, a two-way section going to the Atlantic seaboard, while another, via California and Central America, roared into Uruguay. The dark-blue African Express began in London and reached the Cape by three different routes, through Nigero, Rodosia or Ephiopia. Finally, the brown Orient Express joined London to Ceylon and Sydney, via Turkey and several Chunnels. It is not clear, when you are falling asleep, why all continents except you begin with an A.

Those three admirable trains included at least two carriages in which a fastidious traveler could rent a bedroom with bath and water closet, and a drawing room with a piano or a harp. The length of the journey varied according to Van's predormient mood, when at Eric's age he imagined the landscapes unfolding all along his comfortable, too comfortable, fauteuil. Through rain forests and mountain canyons and other fascinating places (oh, name them! Can't—falling asleep), the room moved as slowly as fifteen miles per hour but across desertorum or agricultural drearies it attained seventy, ninety-seven, night-nine, one hund, red dog—

3

In the spring of 1869, David van Veen, a wealthy architect of Flemish extraction (in no way related to the Veens of our rambling romance), escaped uninjured when the motorcar he was driving from Cannes to Calais blew a front tire on a frost-glazed road and tore into a parked furniture van; his daughter sitting beside him was instantly killed by a suitcase sailing into her from behind and breaking her neck. In his London studio her husband, an unbalanced, unsuccessful painter (ten years older than his father-in-law whom he envied and despised) shot himself upon receiving the news by cablegram from a village in Normandy called, dreadfully, Deuil.

The momentum of disaster lost none of its speed, for neither did Eric, a boy of fifteen, despite all the care and adoration which his grandfather surrounded him with, escape a
freakish fate: a fate strangely similar to his mother's.

After being removed from Note to a small private school in
Vaud Canton and then spending a consumptive summer in
the Maritime Alps, he was sent to Ex-en-Valais, whose crystal
air was supposed at the time to strengthen young lungs; instead of which its worst hurricane hurled a roof tile at him,
fatally fracturing his skull. Among the boy's belongings David
van Veen found a number of poems and the draft of an essay
entitled "Villa Venus: an Organized Dream."

To put it bluntly, the boy had sought to solace his first
sexual torments by imagining and detailing a project (derived
from reading too many erotic works found in a furnished
house his grandfather had bought near Vence from Count
Tolstoy, a Russian or Pole): namely, a chain of palatial brothels that his inheritance would allow him to establish all over
"both hemispheres of our callipygian globe." The little chap
saw it as a kind of fashionable club, with branches, or, in his
poetical phrase, "Floramors," in the vicinity of cities and spas.
Membership was to be restricted to noblemen, "handsome
and healthy," with an age limit of fifty (which must be praised
as very broadminded on the poor kid's part), paying a yearly
fee of 3650 guineas not counting the cost of bouquets, jewels
and other gallant donations. Resident female physicians,
good-looking and young ("of the American secretarial or
dentist-assistant type"), would be there to check the intimate
physical condition of "the caresser and the caressed" (another
felicitous formula) as well as their own if "the need arose."
One clause in the Rules of the Club seemed to indicate that
Eric, though frenziedly heterosexual, had enjoyed some
tender *ersatz* fumblings with schoolmates at Note (a notorious
preparatory school in that respect): at least two of the maximum number of fifty inmates in the major floramors might
be pretty boys, wearing frontlets and short smocks, not older
than fourteen if fair, and not more than twelve if dark. However, in order to exclude a regular flow of "inveterate pederasts," boy love could be dabbled in by the jaded guest only

between two sequences of three girls each, all possessed in the course of the same week—a somewhat comical, but not unshrewd, stipulation.

The candidates for every floramor were to be selected by a Committee of Club Members who would take into consideration the annual accumulation of impressions and desiderata, jotted down by the guests in a special Shell Pink Book. "Beauty and tenderness, grace and docility" composed the main qualities required of the girls, aged from fifteen to twenty-five in the case of "slender Nordic dolls," and from ten to twenty in that of "opulent Southern charmers." They would gambol and loll in "boudoirs and conservatories," invariably naked and ready for love; not so their attendants, attractively dressed handmaids of more or less exotic extraction, "unavailable to the fancy of members except by special permission from the Board." My favorite clause (for I own a photostat of that poor boy's calligraph) is that any girl in her floramor could be Lady-in-Chief by acclamation during her menstrual period. (This of course did not work, and the committee compromised by having a good-looking female homosexual head the staff and adding a bouncer whom Eric had overlooked.)

Eccentricity is the greatest grief's greatest remedy. The boy's grandfather set at once to render in brick and stone, concrete and marble, flesh and fun, Eric's fantasy. He resolved to be the first sampler of the first houri he would hire for his last house, and to live until then in laborious abstinence.

It must have been a moving and magnificent sight—that of the old but still vigorous Dutchman with his rugged reptilian face and white hair, designing with the assistance of Leftist decorators the thousand and one memorial floramors he resolved to erect all over the world—perhaps even in brutal Tartary, which he thought was ruled by "Americanized Jews," but then "Art redeemed Politics"—profoundly original concepts that we must condone in a lovable old crank. He began with rural England and coastal America, and was engaged in a Robert Adam–like composition (cruelly referred to by local wags as the Madam-I'm-Adam House), not far from Newport, Rodos Island, in a somewhat senile style, with marble columns dredged from classical seas and still encrusted with

Etruscan oyster shells—when he died from a stroke while helping to prop up a propylon. It was only his hundredth house!

His nephew and heir, an honest but astoundingly stuffy clothier in Ruinen (somewhere near Zwolle, I'm told), with a large family and a small trade, was not cheated out of the millions of guldens, about the apparent squandering of which he had been consulting mental specialists during the last ten years or so. All the hundred floramors opened simultaneously on September 20, 1875 (and by a delicious coincidence the old Russian word for September, "*ryuen'*," which might have spelled "ruin," also echoed the name of the ecstatic Neverlander's hometown). By the beginning of the new century the Venus revenues were pouring in (their final gush, it is true). A tattling tabloid reported, around 1890, that out of gratitude and curiosity "Velvet" Veen traveled once—and only once—to the nearest floramor with his entire family—and it is also said that Guillaume de Monparnasse indignantly rejected an offer from Hollywood to base a screenplay on that dignified and hilarious excursion. Mere rumors, no doubt.

Eric's grandfather's range was wide—from dodo to dada, from Low Gothic to Hoch Modern. In his parodies of paradise he even permitted himself, just a few times, to express the rectilinear chaos of Cubism (with "abstract" cast in "concrete") by imitating—in the sense described so well in Vulner's paperback *History of English Architecture* given me by good Dr. Lagosse—such ultra-utilitarian boxes of brick as the *maisons closes* of El Freud in Lubetkin, Austria, or the great-necessity houses of Dudok in Friesland.

But on the whole it was the idyllic and the romantic that he favored. English gentlemen of parts found many pleasures in Letchworth Lodge, an honest country house plastered up to its bulleyes, or Itchenor Chat with its battered chimney breasts and hipped gables. None could help admiring David van Veen's knack of making his brand-new Regency mansion look like a renovated farmhouse or of producing a converted convent on a small offshore island with such miraculous effect that one could not distinguish the arabesque from the arbutus, ardor from art, the sore from the rose. We shall always remember Little Lemantry near Rantchester or the Pseudo-

therm in the lovely cul-de-sac south of the viaduct of fabulous
Palermontovia. We appreciated greatly his blending local banality (that château girdled with chestnuts, that castello
guarded by cypresses) with interior ornaments that pandered
to all the orgies reflected in the ceiling mirrors of little Eric's
erogenetics. Most effective, in a functional sense, was the protection the architect distilled, as it were, from the ambitus of
his houses. Whether nestling in woodland dells or surrounded
by a many-acred park, or overlooking terraced groves and gardens, access to Venus began by a private road and continued
through a labyrinth of hedges and walls with inconspicuous
doors to which only the guests and the guards had keys. Cunningly distributed spotlights followed the wandering of the
masked and caped grandees through dark mazes of coppices;
for one of the stipulations imagined by Eric was that "every
establishment should open only at nightfall and close at sunrise." A system of bells that Eric may have thought up all by
himself (it was really as old as the *bautta* and the *vyshibala*)
prevented visitors from running into each other on the prem-
ises, so that no matter how many noblemen were waiting or
wenching in any part of the floramor, each felt he was the
only cock in the coop, because the bouncer, a silent and courteous person resembling a Manhattan shopwalker, did not
count, of course: you sometimes saw him when a hitch occurred in connection with your credentials or credit but he
was seldom obliged to apply vulgar force or call in an assistant.

According to Eric's plan, Councils of Elderly Noblemen
were responsible for mustering the girls. Delicately fashioned
phalanges, good teeth, a flawless epiderm, undyed hair, impeccable buttocks and breasts, and the unfeigned vim of avid
venery were the absolute prerequisites demanded by the Elders as they had been by Eric. Intactas were tolerated only if
very young. On the other hand, no woman who had ever
borne a child (even in her own childhood) could be accepted,
no matter how free she was of mammilary blemishes.

Their social rank had been left unspecified but the Com-
mittees were inclined, initially and theoretically, to recruit girls
of more or less gentle birth. Daughters of artists were preferred, on the whole, to those of artisans. Quite an unexpected
number turned out to be the children of peeved peers in cold

castles or of ruined baronesses in shabby hotels. In a list of about two thousand females working in all the floramors on January 1, 1890 (the greatest year in the annals of Villa Venus), I counted as many as twenty-two directly connected with the royal families of Europe, but at least one-quarter of all the girls belonged to plebeian groups. Owing to some nice *vstryaska* (shake-up) in the genetic kaleidoscope, or mere poker luck, or no reason at all, the daughters of peasants and peddlers and plumbers were not seldom more stylish than their middle-middle-class or upper-upper-class companions, a curious point that will please my non-gentle readers no less than the fact that the servant-girls "below" the Oriental charmers (who assisted in various rituals of silver basins, embroidered towels and dead-end smiles the client and his clickies) not seldom descended from emblazoned princely heights.

Demon's father (and very soon Demon himself), and Lord Erminin, and a Mr. Ritcov, and Count Peter de Prey, and Mire de Mire, Esq., and Baron Azzuroscudo were all members of the first Venus Club Council; but it was bashful, obese, big-nosed Mr. Ritcov's visits that really thrilled the girls and filled the vicinity with detectives who dutifully impersonated hedge-cutters, grooms, horses, tall milkmaids, new statues, old drunks and so forth, while His Majesty dallied, in a special chair built for his weight and whims, with this or that sweet subject of the realm, white, black or brown.

Because the particular floramor that I visited for the first time on becoming a member of the Villa Venus Club (not long before my second summer with my Ada in the arbors of Ardis) is today, after many vicissitudes, the charming country house of a Chose don whom I respect, and his charming family (a charming wife and a triplet of charming twelve-year-old daughters, Ala, Lolá and Lalage—especially Lalage), I cannot name it—though my dearest reader insists I *have* mentioned it somewhere before.

I had frequented bordels since my sixteenth year, but although some of the better ones, especially in France and Ireland, rated a triple red symbol in Nugg's guidebook, nothing about them pre-announced the luxury and mollitude of my first Villa Venus. It was the difference between a den and an Eden.

Three Egyptian squaws, dutifully keeping in profile (long ebony eye, lovely snub, braided black mane, honey-hued faro frock, thin amber arms, Negro bangles, doughnut earring of gold bisected by a pleat of the mane, Red Indian hairband, ornamental bib), lovingly borrowed by Eric Veen from a reproduction of a Theban fresco (no doubt pretty banal in 1420 B.C.), printed in Germany (*Künstlerpostkarte* Nr. 6034, says cynical Dr. Lagosse), prepared me by means of what parched Eric called "exquisite manipulations of certain nerves whose position and power are known only to a few ancient sexologists," accompanied by the no less exquisite application of certain ointments, not too specifically mentioned in the pornolore of Eric's Orientalia, for receiving a scared little virgin, the descendant of an Irish king, as Eric was told in his last dream in Ex, Switzerland, by a master of funerary rather than fornicatory ceremonies.

Those preparations proceeded in such sustained, unendurably delicious rhythms that Eric dying in his sleep and Van throbbing with foul life on a rococo couch (three miles south of Bedford) could not imagine how those three young ladies, now suddenly divested of their clothes (a well-known oneirotic device), could manage to draw out a prelude that kept one so long on the very lip of its resolution. I lay supine and felt twice the size I had ever been (senescent nonsense, says science!) when finally six gentle hands attempted to ease *la gosse*, trembling Adada, upon the terrible tool. Silly pity—a sentiment I rarely experience—caused my desire to droop, and I had her carried away to a feast of peach tarts and cream. The Egypsies looked disconcerted, but very soon perked up. I summoned all the twenty hirens of the house (including the sweet-lipped, glossy-chinned darling) into my resurrected presence. After considerable examination, after much flattering of haunches and necks, I chose a golden Gretchen, a pale Andalusian, and a black belle from New Orleans. The handmaids pounced upon them like pards and, having empasmed them with not unlesbian zest, turned the three rather melancholy graces over to me. The towel given me to wipe off the sweat that filmed my face and stung my eyes could have been cleaner. I raised my voice, I had the reluctant accursed casement wrenched wide open. A lorry had got stuck in the mud of a forbidden and unfinished road, and its groans and exertions dissipated the bizarre gloom. Only one of the girls stung me right in the soul, but I went through all three of them grimly and leisurely, "changing mounts in midstream" (Eric's advice) before ending every time in the grip of the ardent Ardillusian, who said as we parted, after one last spasm (although non-erotic chitchat was against the rules), that her father had constructed the swimming pool on the estate of Demon Veen's cousin.

It was now all over. The lorry had gone or had drowned, and Eric was a skeleton in the most expensive corner of the Ex cemetery ("But then, all cemeteries are ex," remarked a jovial 'protestant' priest), between an anonymous alpinist and my stillborn double.

Cherry, the only lad in our next (American) floramor, a little Salopian of eleven or twelve, looked so amusing with his copper curls, dreamy eyes and elfin cheekbones that two exceptionally sportive courtesans, entertaining Van, prevailed upon him one night to try the boy. Their joint efforts failed, however, to arouse the pretty catamite, who had been exhausted by too many recent engagements. His girlish crupper proved sadly defaced by the varicolored imprints of bestial clawings and flesh-twistings; but worst of all, the little fellow could not disguise a state of acute indigestion, marked by unappetizing dysenteric symptoms that coated his lover's shaft with mustard and blood, the result, no doubt, of eating too many green apples. Eventually, he had to be destroyed or given away.

Generally speaking, the adjunction of boys had to be discontinued. A famous French floramor was never the same after the Earl of Langburn discovered his kidnapped son, a green-eyed frail faunlet, being examined by a veterinary whom the Earl shot dead by mistake.

In 1905 a glancing blow was dealt Villa Venus from another quarter. The personage we have called Ritcov or Vrotic had been induced by the ailings of age to withdraw his patronage. However, one night he suddenly arrived, looking again as ruddy as the proverbial fiddle; but after the entire staff of his favorite floramor near Bath had worked in vain on him till an ironic Hesperus rose in a milkman's humdrum sky, the

wretched sovereign of one-half of the globe called for the
Shell Pink Book, wrote in it a line that Seneca had once composed:

subsidunt montes et juga celsa ruunt,

—and departed, weeping. About the same time a respectable
Lesbian who conducted a Villa Venus at Souvenir, the beautiful Missouri spa, throttled with her own hands (she had been
a Russian weightlifter) two of her most beautiful and valuable
charges. It was all rather sad.

When the deterioration of the club set in, it proceeded with
amazing rapidity along several unconnected lines. Girls of
flawless pedigree turned out to be wanted by the police as the
"molls" of bandits with grotesque jaws, or to have been criminals themselves. Corrupt physicians passed faded blondes who
had had half a dozen children, some of them being already
prepared to enter remote floramors themselves. Cosmeticians
of genius restored forty-year-old matrons to look and smell
like schoolgirls at their first prom. Highborn gentlemen, magistrates of radiant integrity, mild-mannered scholars, proved
to be such violent copulators that some of their younger victims had to be hospitalized and removed to ordinary lupanars.
The anonymous protectors of courtesans bought medical in-
spectors, and the Rajah of Cachou (an impostor) was infected
with a venereal disease by a (genuine) great-grandniece of
Empress Josephine. Simultaneously, economic disasters (beyond the financial or philosophical ken of invulnerable Van
and Demon but affecting many persons of their set) began to
restrict the esthetic assets of Villa Venus. Disgusting pimps
with obsequious grins disclosing gaps in their tawny teeth
popped out of rosebushes with illustrated pamphlets, and
there were fires and earthquakes, and quite suddenly, out of
the hundred original palazzos, only a dozen remained, and
even those soon sank to the level of stagnant stews, and by
1910 all the dead of the English cemetery at Ex had to be
transferred to a common grave.

Van never regretted his last visit to one last Villa Venus. A
cauliflowered candle was messily burning in its tin cup on the
window ledge next to the guitar-shaped paper-wrapped bunch
of long roses for which nobody had troubled to find, or could

have found, a vase. On a bed, some way off, lay a pregnant
woman, smoking, looking up at the smoke mingling its volutes with the shadows on the ceiling, one knee raised, one
hand dreamily scratching her brown groin. Far beyond her, a
door standing ajar gave on what appeared to be a moonlit
gallery but was really an abandoned, half-demolished, vast reception room with a broken outer wall, zigzag fissures in the
floor, and the black ghost of a gaping grand piano, emitting,
as if all by itself, spooky glissando twangs in the middle of the
night. Through a great rip in the marbleized brick and plaster,
the naked sea, not seen but heard as a panting space separated
from time, dully boomed, dully withdrew its platter of pebbles, and, with the crumbling sounds, indolent gusts of warm
wind reached the unwalled rooms, disturbing the volutes of
shadow above the woman, and a bit of dirty fluff that had
drifted down onto her pale belly, and even the reflection of
the candle in a cracked pane of the bluish casement. Beneath
it, on a rump-tickling coarse couch, Van reclined, pouting
pensively, pensively caressing the pretty head on his chest,
flooded by the black hair of a much younger sister or cousin
of the wretched florinda on the tumbled bed. The child's eyes
were closed, and whenever he kissed their moist convex lids
the rhythmic motion of her blind breasts changed or stopped
altogether, and was presently resumed.

He was thirsty, but the champagne he had brought, with
the softly rustling roses, remained sealed and he had not the
heart to remove the silky dear head from his breast so as to
begin working on the explosive bottle. He had fondled and
fouled her many times in the course of the last ten days, but
was not sure if her name was really Adora, as everybody maintained—she, and the other girl, and a third one (a maidservant, Princess Kachurin), who seemed to have been born in
the faded bathing suit she never changed and would die in,
no doubt, before reaching majority or the first really cold winter on the beach mattress which she was moaning on now in
her drugged daze. And if the child really was called Adora,
then what was she?—not Rumanian, not Dalmatian, not Si-
cilian, not Irish, though an echo of brogue could be discerned
in her broken but not too foreign English. Was she eleven or
fourteen, almost fifteen perhaps? Was it really her birthday—

this twenty-first of July, nineteen-four or eight or even several
years later, on a rocky Mediterranean peninsula?

A very distant church clock, never audible except at night,
clanged twice and added a quarter.

"*Smorchiama la secandela*," mumbled the bawd on the bed
in the local dialect that Van understood better than Italian.
The child in his arms stirred and he pulled his opera cloak
over her. In the grease-reeking darkness a faint pattern of
moonlight established itself on the stone floor, near his forever
discarded half-mask lying there and his pump-shod foot. It
was not Ardis, it was not the library, it was not even a human
room, but merely the squalid recess where the bouncer had
slept before going back to his Rugby-coaching job at a public
school somewhere in England. The grand piano in the otherwise bare hall seemed to be playing all by itself but actually
was being rippled by rats in quest of the succulent refuse
placed there by the maid who fancied a bit of music when her
cancered womb roused her before dawn with its first familiar
stab. The ruinous Villa no longer bore any resemblance to
Eric's "organized dream," but the soft little creature in Van's
desperate grasp was Ada.

4

What are dreams? A random sequence of scenes, trivial or
tragic, viatic or static, fantastic or familiar, featuring more or
less plausible events patched up with grotesque details, and
recasting dead people in new settings.

In reviewing the more or less memorable dreams I have had
during the last nine decades I can classify them by subject
matter into several categories among which two surpass the
others in generic distinctiveness. There are the professional
dreams and there are the erotic ones. In my twenties the first
kind occurred about as frequently as the second, and both had
their introductory counterparts, insomnias conditioned either
by the overflow of ten hours of vocational work or by the

memory of Ardis that a thorn in my day had maddeningly revived. After work I battled against the might of the mind-set: the stream of composition, the force of the phrase demanding to be formed could not be stopped for hours of darkness and discomfort, and when some result had been achieved, the current still hummed on and on behind the wall, even if I locked up my brain by an act of self-hypnosis (plain will, or pill, could no longer help) within some other image or meditation—but not Ardis, not Ada, for that would mean drowning in a cataract of worse wakefulness, with rage and regret, desire and despair sweeping me into an abyss where sheer physical extenuation stunned me at last with sleep.

In the professional dreams that especially obsessed me when I worked on my earliest fiction, and pleaded abjectly with a very frail muse ("kneeling and wringing my hands" like the dusty-trousered Marmlad before his Marmlady in Dickens), I might see for example that I was correcting galley proofs but that somehow (the great "somehow" of dreams!) the book had already come out, had come out literally, being proffered to me by a human hand from the wastepaper basket in its perfect, and dreadfully imperfect, stage—with a typo on every page, such as the snide "bitterly" instead of "butterfly" and the meaningless "nuclear" instead of "unclear." Or I would be hurrying to a reading I had to give—would feel exasperated by the sight of the traffic and people blocking my way, and then realize with sudden relief that all I had to do was to strike out the phrase "crowded street" in my manuscript. What I might designate as "skyscape" (not "skyscrape," as two-thirds of the class will probably take it down) dreams belongs to a subdivision of my vocational visions, or perhaps may represent a preface to them, for it was in my early pubescence that hardly a night would pass without some old or recent wake-time impression's establishing a soft deep link with my still-muted genius (for we are "van," rhyming with and indeed signifying "one" in Marina's double-you-less deep-voweled Russian pronunciation). The presence, or promise, of art in that kind of dream would come in the image of an overcast sky with a manifold lining of cloud, a motionless but hopeful white, a hopeless but gliding gray, showing artistic signs of clearing, and presently the glow of a pale sun grew through the leaner layer only to be recowled by the scud, for I was not yet ready.

Allied to the professional and vocational dreams are "dim-doom" visions: fatidic-sign nightmares, thalamic calamities, menacing riddles. Not infrequently the menace is well concealed, and the innocent incident will turn out to possess, if jotted down and looked up later, the kind of precognitive flavor that Dunne has explained by the action of "reverse memory"; but for the moment I am not going to enlarge upon the uncanny element particular to dreams—beyond observing that some law of logic should fix the number of coincidences, in a given domain, after which they cease to be coincidences, and form, instead, the living organism of a new truth ("Tell me," says Osberg's little gitana to the Moors, El Motela and Ramera, "what is the precise minimum of hairs on a body that allows one to call it 'hairy'?").

Between the dim-doom and the poignantly sensual I would place "melts" of erotic tenderness and heart-rending enchantment, chance *frôlements* of anonymous girls at vague parties, half-smiles of appeal or submission—forerunners or echoes of the agonizing dreams of regret when series of receding Adas faded away in silent reproach; and tears, even hotter than those I would shed in waking life, shook and scalded poor Van, and were remembered at odd moments for days and weeks.

Van's sexual dreams are embarrassing to describe in a family chronicle that the very young may perhaps read after a very old man's death. Two samples, more or less euphemistically worded, should suffice. In an intricate arrangement of thematic recollections and automatic phantasmata, Aqua impersonating Marina or Marina made-up to look like Aqua, arrives to inform Van, joyfully, that Ada has just been delivered of a girl-child whom he is about to know carnally on a hard garden bench while under a nearby pine, his father, or his dress-coated mother, is trying to make a transatlantic call for an ambulance to be sent from Vence at once. Another dream, recurring in its basic, unmentionable form, since 1888 and well into this century, contained an essentially triple and, in a way, tribadic, idea. Bad Ada and lewd Lucette had found a ripe, very ripe ear of Indian corn. Ada held it at both ends as if it were a mouth organ and now it *was* an organ, and she moved her parted lips along it, varnishing its shaft, and while she was making it trill and moan, Lucette's mouth engulfed its extremity. The two sisters' avid lovely young faces were now close together, doleful and wistful in their slow, almost languid play, their tongues meeting in flicks of fire and curling back again, their tumbled hair, red-bronze and black-bronze, delightfully commingling and their sleek hindquarters lifted high as they slaked their thirst in the pool of his blood.

I have some notes here on the general character of dreams. One puzzling feature is the multitude of perfect strangers with clear features, but never seen again, accompanying, meeting, welcoming me, pestering me with long tedious tales about other strangers—all this in localities familiar to me and in the midst of people, deceased or living, whom I knew well; or the curious tricks of an agent of Chronos—a very exact clock-time awareness, with all the pangs (possibly full-bladder pangs in disguise) of not getting somewhere in time, and with that clock hand before me, numerically meaningful, mechanically plausible, but combined—and that is the curious part—with an extremely hazy, hardly existing passing-of-time feeling (this theme I will also reserve for a later chapter). All dreams are affected by the experiences and impressions of the present as well as by memories of childhood; all reflect, in images or sensations, a draft, a light, a rich meal or a grave internal disorder. Perhaps the most typical trait of practically all dreams, unimportant or portentous—and this despite the presence, in stretches or patches, of fairly logical (within special limits) cogitation and awareness (often absurd) of dream-past events—should be understood by my students as a dismal weakening of the intellectual faculties of the dreamer, who is not really shocked to run into a long-dead friend. At his best the dreamer wears semi-opaque blinkers; at his worst he's an imbecile. The class (1891, 1892, 1893, 1894, et cetera) will carefully note (rustle of bluebooks) that, owing to their very nature, to that mental mediocrity and bumble, dreams cannot yield any semblance of morality or symbol or allegory or Greek myth, unless, naturally, the dreamer is a Greek or a mythicist. Metamorphoses in dreams are as common as metaphors in poetry. A writer who likens, say, the fact of imagination's weakening less rapidly than memory, to the lead of a pencil getting used up more slowly than its erasing end, is comparing two real, concrete, existing things. Do you want me to repeat that? (cries of "yes! yes!") Well, the pencil I'm holding is still conveniently long though it has served me a lot, but its rubber cap is practically erased by the very action it has been performing too many times. My imagination is still strong and serviceable but my memory is getting shorter and shorter. I compare that real experience to the condition of this real commonplace object. Neither is a symbol of the other. Similarly, when a teashop humorist says that a little conical titbit with a comical cherry on top resembles this or that (titters in the audience) he is turning a pink cake into a pink breast (tempestuous laughter) in a fraise-like frill or frilled phrase (silence). Both objects are real, they are not interchangeable, not tokens of something else, say, of Walter Raleigh's decapitated trunk still topped by the image of his wetnurse (one lone chuckle). Now the mistake—the lewd, ludicrous and vulgar mistake of the Signy-Mondieu analysts consists in their regarding a real object, a pompon, say, or a pumpkin (actually seen in a dream by the patient) as a significant abstraction of the real object, as a bumpkin's bonbon or one-half of the bust if you see what I mean (scattered giggles). There can be no emblem or parable in a village idiot's hallucinations or in last night's dream of any of us in this hall. In those random visions nothing—underscore "nothing" (grating sound of horizontal strokes)—can be construed as allowing itself to be deciphered by a witch doctor who can then cure a madman or give comfort to a killer by laying the blame on a too fond, too fiendish or too indifferent parent—secret festerings that the foster quack feigns to heal by expensive confession fests (laughter and applause).

5

Van spent the fall term of 1892 at Kingston University, Mayne, where there was a first-rate madhouse, as well as a famous

Department of Terrapy, and where he now went back to one
of his old projects, which turned on the Idea of Dimension
& Dementia ("You will 'sturb,' Van, with an alliteration on
your lips," jested old Rattner, resident pessimist of genius, for
whom life was only a "disturbance" in the rattnerterological
order of things—from "*nertoros*," not "*terra*").

Van Veen [as also, in his small way, the editor of *Ada*] liked
to change his abode at the end of a section or chapter or even
paragraph, and he had almost finished a difficult bit dealing
with the divorce between time and the contents of time (such
as action on matter, in space, and the nature of space itself)
and was contemplating moving to Manhattan (that kind of
switch being a reflection of mental rubrication rather than a
concession to some farcical "influence of environment" en-
dorsed by Marx *père*, the popular author of "historical" plays),
when he received an unexpected dorophone call which for a
moment affected violently his entire pulmonary and systemic
circulation.

Nobody, not even his father, knew that Van had recently
bought Cordula's penthouse apartment between Manhattan's
Library and Park. Besides its being the perfect place to work
in, with that terrace of scholarly seclusion suspended in a celestial void, and that noisy but convenient city lapping below
at the base of his mind's invulnerable rock, it was, in fashionable parlance, a "bachelor's folly" where he could secretly entertain any girl or girls he pleased. (One of them dubbed it
"your wing *à terre*"). But he was still in his rather dingy
Chose-like rooms at Kingston when he consented to Lucette's
visiting him on that bright November afternoon.

He had not seen her since 1888. In the fall of 1891 she had
sent him from California a rambling, indecent, crazy, almost
savage declaration of love in a ten-page letter, which shall not
be discussed in this memoir [See, however, a little farther.
Ed.]. At present, she was studying the History of Art ("the
second-rater's last refuge," she said) in nearby Queenston
College for Glamorous and *Glupovatïh* ("dumb") Girls.
When she rang him up and pleaded for an interview (in a new,
darker voice, agonizingly resembling Ada's), she intimated
that she was bringing him an important message. He suspected it would be yet another installment of her unrequited

passion, but he also felt that her visit would touch off infernal fires.

As he awaited her, walking the whole length of his brown-carpeted suite and back again, now contemplating the emblazed trees, that defied the season, through the northeast casement at the end of the passage, then returning to the sitting room which gave on sun-bordered Greencloth Court, he kept fighting Ardis and its orchards and orchids, bracing himself for the ordeal, wondering if he should not cancel her visit, or have his man convey his apologies for the suddenness of an unavoidable departure, but knowing all the time he would go through with it. With Lucette herself, he was only obliquely concerned: she inhabited this or that dapple of drifting sunlight, but could not be wholly dismissed with the rest of sun-flecked Ardis. He recalled, in passing, the sweetness in his lap, her round little bottom, her prasine eyes as she turned toward him and the receding road. Casually he wondered whether she had become fat and freckled, or had joined the graceful Zemski group of nymphs. He had left the parlor door that opened on the landing slightly ajar, but somehow missed the sound of her high heels on the stairs (or did not distinguish them from his heartbeats) while he was in the middle of his twentieth trudge "back to the ardors and arbors! Eros *qui prend son essor*! Arts that our marblery harbors: Eros, the rose and the sore." I am ill at these numbers, but e'en rhymery is easier "than confuting the past in mute prose." Who wrote that? Voltimand or Voltemand? Or the Burning Swine? A pest on his anapest! "All our old loves are corpses or wives." All our sorrows are virgins or whores.

A black bear with bright russet locks (the sun had reached its first parlor window) stood awaiting him. Yes—the Z gene had won. She was slim and strange. Her green eyes had grown. At sixteen she looked considerably more dissolute than her sister had seemed at that fatal age. She wore black furs and no hat.

"My joy (*moya radost'*)," said Lucette—just like that; he had expected more formality: all in all he had hardly known her before—except as an embered embryo.

Eyes swimming, coral nostrils distended, red mouth perilously disclosing her tongue and teeth in a preparatory half-

open skew (tame animal signaling by that slant the semblance
of a soft bite), she advanced in the daze of a commencing
trance, of an unfolding caress—the aurora, who knows (*she*
knew), of a new life for both.

"Cheekbone," Van warned the young lady.

"You prefer *skeletiki* (little skeletons)," she murmured, as
Van applied light lips (which had suddenly become even drier
than usual) to his half-sister's hot hard pommette. He could
not help inhaling briefly her Degrasse, smart, though decidedly "paphish," perfume and, through it, the flame of her
Little Larousse as he and the other said when they chose to
emprison her in bath water. Yes, very nervous and fragrant.
Indian summer too sultry for furs. The cross (*krest*) of the
best-groomed redhead (*rousse*). Its four burning ends. Because
one can't stroke (as he did now) the upper copper without
imagining at once the lower fox cub and the paired embers.

"This is where he lives," she said, looking around, turning
around, as he helped her with wonder and sorrow out of her
soft, deep, dark coat, side-thinking (he liked furs): sea bear
(*kotik*)? No, desman (*vihuhol'*). Assistant Van admired her elegant slenderness, the gray tailor-made suit, the smoky fichu
and as it wafted away, her long white neck. Take your jacket
off, he said or thought he said (standing with extended hands,
in his charcoal suit, spontaneous combustion, in his bleak parlor, in the bleak house anglophilically named Voltemand Hall
at Kingston University, fall term 1892, around four P.M.).

"I think I'll take off my jacket," she said with the usual
flitting frown of feminine fuss that fits the "thought."
"You've got central heating; we girls have tiny fireplaces."

She threw it off, revealing a sleeveless frilly white blouse.
She raised her arms to pass her fingers through her bright
curls, and he saw the expected bright hollows.

Van said, "All three casements *pourtant* are open and can
open wider; but they can do it only westward and that green
yard down below is the evening sun's praying rug, which
makes this room even warmer. Terrible for a window not to
be able to turn its paralyzed embrasure and see what's on the
other side of the house."

Once a Veen, always a Veen.

She unclicked her black-silk handbag, fished out a hand-

kerchief and, leaving the gaping bag on the edge of the sideboard, went to the farthest window and stood there, her
fragile shoulders shaking unbearably.

Van noticed a long, blue, violet-sealed envelope protruding
from the bag.

"Lucette, don't cry. That's too easy."

She walked back, dabbing her nose, curbing her childishly
humid sniffs, still hoping for the decisive embrace.

"Here's some brandy," he said. "Sit down. Where's the rest
of the family?"

She returned the balled handkerchief of many an old romance to her bag, which, however, remained unclosed.
Chows, too, have blue tongues.

"Mamma dwells in her private Samsara. Dad has had another stroke. Sis is revisiting Ardis."

"Sis! *Cesse*, Lucette! We don't want any baby serpents
around."

"This baby serpent does not quite know what tone to take
with Dr. V. V. Sector. You have not changed one bit, my pale
darling, except that you look like a ghost in need of a shave
without your summer *Glanz*."

And summer *Mädel*. He noticed that the letter, in its long
blue envelope, lay now on the mahogany sideboard. He stood
in the middle of the parlor, rubbing his forehead, not daring,
not daring, because it was Ada's notepaper.

"Like some tea?"

She shook her head. "I can't stay long. Besides, you said
something about a busy day over the phone. One can't help
being dreadfully busy after four absolutely blank years" (he
would start sobbing too if she did not stop).

"Yes. I don't know. I have an appointment around six."

Two ideas were locked up in a slow dance, a mechanical
menuet, with bows and curtseys: one was "We-have-so-much-
to-say"; the other was "We have absolutely nothing to say."
But that sort of thing can change in one instant.

"Yes, I have to see Rattner at six-thirty," murmured Van,
consulting a calendar he did not see.

"Rattner on Terra!" ejaculated Lucette. "Van is reading
Rattner on Terra. Pet must never, never disturb him and me
when we are reading Rattner!"

"I implore, my dear, no impersonations. Let us not transform a pleasant reunion into mutual torture."

What was she doing at Queenston? She had told him before. Of course. Tough course? No. Oh. From time to time both kept glancing askance at the letter to see if it was behaving itself—not dangling its legs, not picking its nose.

Return it sealed?

"Tell Rattner," she said, gulping down her third brandy as simply as if it were technicolored water. "Tell him" (the liquor was loosening her pretty viper tongue)—

(Viper? Lucette? My dead dear darling?)

—"Tell him that when in the old days you and Ada—"

The name yawned like a black doorway, then the door banged.

"—left me for him, and then came back, I knew every time that you *vsyo sdelali* (had appeased your lust, had allayed your fire)."

"One remembers those little things much too clearly, Lucette. Please, stop."

"One remembers, Van, those little things much more clearly than the big fatal ones. As for example the clothes you wore at any given moment, at a generously given moment, with the sun on the chairs and the floor. I was practically naked, of course, being a neutral pure little child. But she wore a boy's shirt and a short skirt, and all you had on were those wrinkled, soiled shorts, shorter because wrinkled, and they smelled as they always did after you'd been on Terra with Ada, with Rattner on Ada, with Ada on Antiterra in Ardis Forest—oh, they positively stank, you know, your little shorts, of lavendered Ada, and her catfood, and your caked algarroba!"

Should that letter, now next to the brandy, listen to all this? Was it from Ada after all (there was no address)? Because it was Lucette's mad, shocking letter of love that was doing the talking.

"Van, it will make you smile" [thus in the MS. Ed.].

"Van," said Lucette, "it will make you smile" (it did not: that prediction is seldom fulfilled), "but if you posed the famous Van Question, I would answer in the affirmative."

What he had asked little Cordula. In that bookshop behind

the revolving paperbacks' stand, *The Gitanilla, Our Laddies, Clichy Clichés, Six Pricks, The Bible Unabridged, Mertvago Forever, The Gitanilla . . .* He was known in the *beau monde* for asking that question the very first time he met a young lady.

"Oh, to be sure, it was not easy! In parked automobiles and at rowdy parties, thrusts had to be parried, advances fought off! And only last winter, on the Italian Riviera, there was a youngster of fourteen or fifteen, an awfully precocious but terribly shy and neurotic young violinist, who reminded Marina of her brother . . . Well, for almost three months, every blessed afternoon, I had him touch me, and I reciprocated, and after that I could sleep at last without pills, but otherwise I haven't once kissed male epithelia in all my love—I mean, life. Look, I can swear I never have, by—by William Shakespeare" (extending dramatically one hand toward a shelf with a set of thick red books).

"Hold it!" cried Van. "That's the *Collected Works of Falknermann*, dumped by my predecessor."

"Pah!" uttered Lucette.

"And, please, don't use that expletive."

"Forgive me—oh, I know, oh, I shan't."

"Of course, you know. All the same, you are very sweet. I'm glad you came."

"I'm glad, too," she said. "But Van! Don't you dare think I 'relanced' you to reiterate that I'm madly and miserably in love with you and that you can do anything you want with me. If I didn't simply press the button and slip that note into the burning slit and cataract away, it was because I *had* to see you, because there is something else you must know, even if it makes you detest and despise Ada and me. *Otvratitel'no trudno* (it is disgustingly hard) to explain, especially for a virgin—well, technically, a virgin, a *kokotische* virgin, half *poule*, half *puella*. I realize the privacy of the subject, mysterious matters that one should not discuss even with a vaginal brother—mysterious, not merely in their moral and mystical aspect—"

Uterine—but close enough. It certainly came from Lucette's sister. He knew that shade and that shape. "That shade of blue, that shape of you" (corny song on the Sonorola). Blue in the face from pleading RSVP.

"—but also in a direct physical sense. Because, darling Van, in that direct physical sense I know as much about our Ada as you."

"Fire away," said Van, wearily.

"She never wrote you about it?"

Negative Throat Sound.

"Something we used to call Pressing the Spring?"

"We?"

"She and I."

N.T.S.

"Do you remember Grandmother's scrutoir between the globe and the gueridon? In the library?"

"I don't even know what a scrutoir is; and I do not visualize the gueridon."

"But you remember the globe?"

Dusty Tartary with Cinderella's finger rubbing the place where the invader would fall.

"Yes, I do; and a kind of stand with golden dragons painted all over it."

"That's what I meant by 'gueridon.' It was really a Chinese stand japanned in red lacquer, and the scrutoir stood in between."

"China or Japan? Make up your mind. And I still don't know how your inscrutable looks. I mean, looked in 1884 or 1888."

Scrutoir. Almost as bad as the other with her Blemolopias and Molospermas.

"Van, Vanichka, we are straying from the main point. The point is that the writing desk or if you like, secretaire—"

"I hate both, but it stood at the opposite end of the black divan."

Now mentioned for the first time—though both had been tacitly using it as an orientator or as a right hand painted on a transparent signboard that a philosopher's orbitless eye, a peeled hard-boiled egg cruising free, but sensing which of its ends is proximal to an imaginary nose, sees hanging in infinite space; whereupon, with Germanic grace, the free eye sails around the glass sign and sees a left hand shining through—*that*'s the solution! (Bernard said six-thirty but I may be a little late.) The mental in Van always rimmed the sensuous: unforgettable, roughish, villous, Villaviciosa velour.

"Van, you are deliberately sidetracking the issue—"

"One can't do that with an issue."

"—because at the other end, at the *heel* end of the Vaniada divan—remember?—there was only the closet in which you two locked me up at least ten times."

"*Nu uzh i desyat'* (exaggeration). Once—and *never* more. It had a keyless hole as big as Kant's eye. Kant was famous for his cucumicolor iris."

"Well, that secretaire," continued Lucette, considering her left shoe, her very chic patent-leather Glass shoe, as she crossed her lovely legs, "that secretaire enclosed a folded card table and a top-secret drawer. And you thought, I think, it was crammed with our grandmother's love letters, written when she was twelve or thirteen. And our Ada knew, oh, she knew, the drawer was there but she had forgotten how to release the orgasm or whatever it is called in card tables and bureaus."

Whatever it is called.

"She and I challenged you to find the secret *chuvstvilishche* (sensorium) and make it work. It was the summer Belle sprained her backside, and we were left to our own devices, which had long lost the *particule* in your case and Ada's, but were touchingly pure in mine. You groped around, and felt, and felt for the little organ, which turned out to be a yielding roundlet in the rosewood under the felt you felt—I mean, under the felt you were feeling: it was a felted thumb spring, and Ada laughed as the drawer shot out."

"And it was empty," said Van.

"Not quite. It contained a minuscule red pawn that high" (showing its barleycorn-size with her finger—above what? Above Van's wrist). "I kept it for luck; I must still have it somewhere. Anyway, the entire incident pre-emblematized, to quote my Professor of Ornament, the depravation of your poor Lucette at fourteen in Arizona. Belle had returned to Canady, because Vronsky had defigured *The Doomed Children*; her successor had eloped with Demon; *papa* was in the East, *maman* hardly ever came home before dawn, the maids joined their lovers at star-rise, and I hated to sleep alone in the corner room assigned to me, even if I did not put out the pink night-light of porcelain with the transparency picture of

a lost lamb, because I was afraid of the cougars and snakes"
[quite possibly, this is not remembered speech but an extract
from her letter or letters. Ed.], "whose cries and rattlings Ada
imitated admirably, and, I think, designedly, in the desert's
darkness under my first-floor window. Well [here, it would
seem, taped speech is re-turned-on], to make a short story
sort of longish—"

Old Countess de Prey's phrase in praise of a lame mare in
her stables in 1884, thence passed on to her son, who passed
it on to his girl who passed it on to her half-sister. Thus instantly reconstructed by Van sitting with tented hands in a
red-plush chair.

"—I took my pillow to Ada's bedroom where a similar
night-light transparency thing showed a blond-bearded faddist
in a toweling robe embracing the found lamb. The night was
oven-hot and we were stark naked except for a bit of sticking
plaster where a doctor had stroked and pricked my arm, and
she was a dream of white and black beauty, *pour cogner une
fraise*, touched with fraise in four places, a symmetrical queen
of hearts."

Next moment they grappled and had such delicious fun that
they knew they would be doing it always together, for hygienic purposes, when boyless and boiling.

"She taught me practices I had never imagined," confessed
Lucette in rerun wonder. "We interweaved like serpents and
sobbed like pumas. We were Mongolian tumblers, mono-
grams, anagrams, adalucindas. She kissed my *krestik* while I
kissed hers, our heads clamped in such odd combinations that
Brigitte, a little chambermaid who blundered in with her candle, thought for a moment, though naughty herself, that we
were giving birth simultaneously to baby girls, your Ada
bringing out *une rousse*, and no one's Lucette, *une brune*.
Fancy that."

"Side-splitting," said Van.

"Oh, it went on practically every night at Marina Ranch,
and often during siestas; otherwise, in between those *vanouissements* (her expression), or when she and I had the flow,
which, believe it or not—"

"I can believe anything," said Van.

"—took place at coincident dates, we were just ordinary

sisters, exchanging routine nothings, having little in common, she collecting cactuses or running through her lines for the next audition in Sterva, and I reading a lot, or copying beautiful erotic pictures from an album of Forbidden Masterpieces that we found, *apropos,* in a box of *korsetov i khrestomatiy* (corsets and chrestomathies) which Belle had left behind, and I can assure you, they were far more realistic than the scroll-painting by Mong Mong, very active in 888, a millennium before Ada said it illustrated Oriental calisthenics when I found it by chance in the corner of one of my ambuscades. So the day passed, and then the star rose, and tremendous moths walked on all sixes up the window panes, and we tangled until we fell asleep. And that's when I learnt—" concluded Lucette, closing her eyes and making Van squirm by reproducing with diabolical accuracy Ada's demure little whimper of ultimate bliss.

At this point, as in a well-constructed play larded with comic relief, the brass campophone buzzed and not only did the radiators start to cluck but the uncapped soda water fizzed in sympathy.

Van (crossly): "I don't understand the first word . . . What's that? *L'adorée?* Wait a second" (to Lucette). "Please, stay where you are." (Lucette whispers a French child-word with two "p"s.). "Okay" (pointing toward the corridor). "Sorry, Polly. Well, is it *l'adorée?* No? Give me the context. Ah—*la durée. La durée* is not . . . sin on what? Synonymous with duration. Aha. Sorry again, I must stopper that orgiastic soda. Hold the line." (Yells down the 'cory door,' as they called the long second-floor passage at Ardis.) "Lucette, *let* it run over, who cares!"

He poured himself another glass of brandy and for a ridiculous moment could not remember what the hell he had been—yes, the polliphone.

It had died, but buzzed as soon as he recradled the receiver, and Lucette knocked discreetly at the same time.

"*La durée* . . . For goodness sake, come in without knocking . . . No, Polly, knocking does not concern you—it's my little cousin. All right. *La durée* is not synonymous with duration, being saturated—yes, as in Saturday—with that particular philosopher's thought. What's wrong now? You don't know if it's *dorée* or *durée*? D, U, R. I thought you knew French. Oh, I see. So long.

"My typist, a trivial but always available blonde, could not make out *durée* in my quite legible hand because, she says, she knows French, but not scientific French."

"Actually," observed Lucette, wiping the long envelope which a drop of soda had stained, "Bergson is only for very young people or very unhappy people, such as this available *rousse*."

"Spotting Bergson," said the assistant lecher, "rates a B minus *dans ton petit cas*, hardly more. Or shall I reward you with a kiss on your *krestik*—whatever that is?"

Wincing and rearranging his legs, our young Vandemonian cursed under his breath the condition in which the image of the four embers of a vixen's cross had now solidly put him. One of the synonyms of "condition" is "state," and the adjective "human" may be construed as "manly" (since L'Humanité means "Mankind"!), and that's how, my dears, Lowden recently translated the title of the *malheureux* Pompier's cheap novel *La Condition Humaine*, wherein, incidentally, the term "Vandemonian" is hilariously glossed as "*Koulak tasmanien d'origine hollandaise*." Kick her out before it is too late.

"If you are serious," said Lucette, passing her tongue over her lips and slitting her darkening eyes, "then, my darling, you can do it right now. But if you are making fun of me, then you're an abominably cruel Vandemonian."

"Come, come, Lucette, it means 'little cross' in Russian, that's all, what else? Is it some amulet? You mentioned just now a little red stud or pawn. Is it something you wear, or used to wear, on a chainlet round your neck? a small acorn of coral, the *glandulella* of vestals in ancient Rome? What's the matter, my dear?"

Still watching him narrowly, "I'll take a chance," she said. "I'll explain it, though it's just one of our sister's 'tender-turret' words and I thought you were familiar with her vocabulary."

"Oh, I know," cried Van (quivering with evil sarcasm, boiling with mysterious rage, taking it out on the redhaired scapegoatling, naive Lucette, whose only crime was to be suffused with the phantasmata of the other's innumerable lips). "Of course, I remember now. A foul taint in the singular can be a sacred mark in the plural. You are referring of course to the stigmata between the eyebrows of pure sickly young nuns whom priests had over-anointed there and elsewhere with cross-like strokes of the myrrherabol brush."

"No, it's much simpler," said patient Lucette. "Let's go back to the library where you found that little thing still erect in its drawer—"

"Z for Zemski. As I had hoped, you do resemble Dolly, still in her pretty pantelets, holding a Flemish pink in the library portrait above her inscrutable."

"No, no," said Lucette, "that indifferent oil presided over your studies and romps at the other end, next to the closet, above a glazed bookcase."

When will this torture end? I can't very well open the letter in front of her and read it aloud for the benefit of the audience. I have not art to reckon my groans.

"One day, in the library, kneeling on a yellow cushion placed on a Chippendale chair before an oval table on lion claws—"

[The epithetic tone strongly suggests that this speech has an epistolary source. Ed.]

"—I got stuck with six *Buchstaben* in the last round of a Flavita game. Mind you, I was eight and had not studied anatomy, but was doing my poor little best to keep up with two *Wunderkinder*. You examined and fingered my groove and quickly redistributed the haphazard sequence which made, say, LIKROT or ROTIKL and Ada flooded us both with her raven silks as she looked over our heads, and when you had completed the rearrangement, you and she came simultaneously, *si je puis le mettre comme ça* (Canady French), came falling on the black carpet in a paroxysm of incomprehensible merriment; so finally I quietly composed ROTIK ("little mouth") and was left with my own cheap initial. I hope I've thoroughly got you mixed up, Van, because *la plus laide fille du monde peut donner beaucoup plus qu'elle n'a*, and now let us say adieu, yours ever."

"Whilst the machine is to him," murmured Van.

"Hamlet," said the assistant lecturer's brightest student.

"Okay, okay," replied her and his tormentor, "but, you know, a medically minded *English* Scrabbler, having two more letters to cope with, could make, for example, STIRCOIL, a well-known sweat-gland stimulant, or CITROILS, which grooms use for rubbing fillies."

"Please stop, Vandemonian," she moaned. "Read her letter and bring me my coat."

But he continued, his features working:

"I'm amazed! I never imagined that a hand-reared scion of Scandinavian kings, Russian grand princes and Irish barons could use the language of the proverbial gutter. Yes, you're right, you behave as a cocotte, Lucette."

In sad meditation Lucette said: "As a rejected cocotte, Van."

"O *moya dushen'ka* (my dear darling)," cried Van, struck by his own coarseness and cruelty. "Please, forgive me! I'm a sick man. I've been suffering for these last four years from consanguineocanceroformia—a mysterious disease described by Coniglietto. Don't put your little cold hand on my paw— that could only hasten your end and mine. On with your story."

"Well, after teaching me simple exercises for one hand that I could practice alone, cruel Ada abandoned me. True, we never really stopped doing it together every now and then— in the ranchito of some acquaintances after a party, in a white saloon she was teaching me to drive, in the sleeping car tearing across the prairie, at sad, sad Ardis where I spent one night with her before coming to Queenston. Oh, I love her hands, Van, because they have the same *rodinka* (small birthmark), because the fingers are so long, because, in fact, they are Van's in a reducing mirror, in tender diminutive, *v laskatel'noy forme*" (the talk—as so often happened at emotional moments in the Veen-Zemski branch of that strange family, the noblest in Estotiland, the grandest on Antiterra—was speckled with Russian, an effect not too consistently reproduced in this chapter—the readers are restless tonight).

"She abandoned me," continued Lucette, tchucking on one side of the mouth and smoothing up and down with an abstract palm her flesh-pale stocking. "Yes, she started a rather sad little affair with Johnny, a young star from Fuerteventura, *c'est dans la famille*, her exact *odnoletok* (coeval), practically her twin in appearance, born the same year, the same day, the same instant—"

That was a mistake on silly Lucette's part.

"Ah, that cannot be," interrupted morose Van and after rocking this side and that with clenched hands and furrowed brow (how one would like to apply a boiling-water-soaked *Wattebausch*, as poor Rack used to call her limp arpeggiation, to that ripe pimple on his right temple), "that simply cannot be. No damned twin can do that. Not even those seen by Brigitte, a cute little number I imagine, with that candle flame flirting with her exposed nipples. The usual difference in age between twins"—he went on in a madman's voice so well controlled that it sounded overpedantic—"is seldom less than a quarter of an hour, the time a working womb needs to rest and relax with a woman's magazine, before resuming its rather unappetizing contractions. In very rare cases, when the matrix just goes on pegging away automatically, the doctor can take advantage of that and ease out the second brat who then can be considered to be, say, three minutes younger, which in dynastic happy events—doubly happy events—with all Egypt agog—may be, and has been, even more important than in a marathon finish. But the creatures, no matter how numerous, never come out *à la queue-leu-leu*. 'Simultaneous twins' is a contradiction in terms."

"*Nu uzh ne znayu* (well, I don't know)," muttered Lucette (echoing faithfully her mother's dreary intonation in that phrase, which seemingly implied an admission of error and ignorance, but tended somehow—owing to a hardly perceptible nod of condescension rather than consent—to dull and dilute the truth of her interlocutor's corrective retort).

"I only meant," she continued, "that he was a handsome Hispano-Irish boy, dark and pale, and people mistook them for twins. I did not say they were really twins. Or 'driblets.'"

Driblets? Driplets? Now who pronounced it that way? Who? Who? A dripping ewes-dropper in a dream? Did the orphans live? But we must listen to Lucette.

"After a year or so she found out that an old pederast kept him and she dismissed him, and he shot himself on a beach at high tide but surfers and surgeons saved him, and now his brain is damaged; he will never be able to speak."

"One can always fall back on mutes," said Van gloomily. "He could act the speechless eunuch in 'Stambul, my bulbul' or the stable boy disguised as a kennel girl who brings a letter."

"Van, I'm boring you?"

"Oh, nonsense, it's a gripping and palpitating little case history."

Because that was really not bad: bringing down three in as many years—besides winging a fourth. Jolly good shot—Adiana! Wonder whom she'll bag next.

"You must not press me for the details of our sweet torrid and horrid nights together, before and between that poor guy and the next intruder. If my skin were a canvas and her lips a brush, not an inch of me would have remained unpainted and vice versa. Are you horrified, Van? Do you loathe us?"

"On the contrary," replied Van, bringing off a passable imitation of bawdy mirth. "Had I not been a heterosexual male, I would have been a Lesbian."

His trite reaction to her set piece, to her desperate cunning, caused Lucette to give up, to dry up, as it were, before a black pit with people dismally coughing here and there in the invisible and eternal audience. He glanced for the hundredth time at the blue envelope, its near long edge not quite parallel to that of the glossy mahogany, its left upper corner half hidden behind the tray with the brandy and soda, its right lower corner pointing at Van's favorite novel *The Slat Sign* that lay on the sideboard.

"I want to see you again soon," said Van, biting his thumb, brooding, cursing the pause, yearning for the contents of the blue envelope. "You must come and stay with me at a flat I now have on Alex Avenue. I have furnished the guest room with *bergères* and *torchères* and rocking chairs; it looks like your mother's boudoir."

Lucette curtseyed with the wicks of her sad mouth, *à l'Américaine*.

"Will you come for a few days? I promise to behave properly. All right?"

"My notion of propriety may not be the same as yours. And what about Cordula de Prey? She won't mind?"

"The apartment is mine," said Van, "and besides, Cordula is now Mrs. Ivan G. Tobak. They are making follies in Florence. Here's her last postcard. Portrait of Vladimir Christian of Denmark, who, she claims, is the dead spit of her Ivan Giovanovich. Have a look."

"Who cares for Sustermans," observed Lucette, with something of her uterine sister's knight move of specious response, or a Latin footballer's *rovesciata*.

No, it's an elm. Half a millennium ago.

"His ancestor," Van pattered on, "was the famous or *fameux* Russian admiral who had an *épée* duel with Jean Nicot and after whom the Tobago Islands, or the Tobakoff Islands, are named, I forget which, it was so long ago, half a millennium."

"I mentioned her only because an old sweetheart is easily annoyed by the wrong conclusions she jumps at like a cat not quite making a fence and then running off without trying again, and stopping to look back."

"Who told you about that lewd cordelude—I mean, interlude?"

"Your father, *mon cher*—we saw a lot of him in the West. Ada supposed, at first, that Tapper was an invented name—that you fought your duel with another person—but that was before anybody heard of the other person's death in Kalugano. Demon said you should have simply cudgeled him."

"I could not," said Van, "the rat was rotting away in a hospital bed."

"I meant the real Tapper," cried Lucette (who was making a complete mess of her visit), "not my poor, betrayed, poisoned, innocent teacher of music, whom not even Ada, unless she fibs, could cure of his impotence."

"Driblets," said Van.

"Not necessarily *his*," said Lucette. "His wife's lover played the triple viol. Look, I'll borrow a book" (scanning on the nearest bookshelf *The Gitanilla*, *Clichy Clichés*, *Mertvago Forever*, *The Ugly New Englander*) "and curl up, *komondi*, in the next room for a few minutes, while you—Oh, I adore *The Slat Sign*."

"There's no hurry," said Van.

Pause (about fifteen minutes to go to the end of the act).

"At the age of ten," said Lucette to say something, "I was at the Vieux-Rose Stopchin stage, but our (using, that day, that year, the unexpected, thronal, authorial, jocular, technically loose, forbidden, possessive plural in speaking of her to him) sister had read at that age, in three languages, many more books than I did at twelve. However! After an appalling illness in California, I recouped myself: the Pioneers vanquished the Pyogenes. I'm not showing off but do you happen to know a great favorite of mine: Herodas?"

"Oh yes," answered Van negligently. "A ribald contemporary of Justinus, the Roman scholar. Yes, great stuff. Blinding blend of subtility and brilliant coarseness. You read it, dear, in the literal French translation with the Greek *en regard*—didn't you?—but a friend of mine here showed me a scrap of new-found text, which you could not have seen, about two children, a brother and sister, who did it so often that they finally died in each other's limbs, and could not be separated—it just stretched and stretched, and snapped back in place every time the perplexed parents let go. It is all very obscene, and very tragic, and terribly funny."

"No, I don't know that passage," said Lucette. "But Van, why are you—"

"Hay fever, hay fever!" cried Van, searching five pockets at once for a handkerchief. Her stare of compassion and the fruitless search caused such a swell of grief that he preferred to stomp out of the room, snatching the letter, dropping it, picking it up, and retreating to the farthest room (redolent of her Degrasse) to read it in one gulp.

"*O dear Van, this is the last attempt I am making. You may call it a document in madness or the herb of repentance, but I wish to come and live with you, wherever you are, for ever and ever. If you scorn the maid at your window I will aerogram my immediate acceptance of a proposal of marriage that has been made to your poor Ada a month ago in Valentine State. He is an Arizonian Russian, decent and gentle, not overbright and not fashionable. The only thing we have in common is a keen interest in many military-looking desert plants, especially various species of agave, hosts of the larvae of the most noble animals*

*in America, the Giant Skippers (Krolik, you see, is burrowing
again). He owns horses, and Cubistic pictures, and 'oil wells'
(whatever they are—our father in hell who has some too, does
not tell me, getting away with off-color allusions as is his wont).
I have told my patient Valentinian that I shall give him a definite answer after consulting the only man I have ever loved or
shall love. Try to ring me up tonight. Something is very wrong
with the Ladore line, but I am assured that the trouble will be
grappled with and eliminated before rivertide.* Tvoya, tvoya,
tvoya (*thine*). *A.*"

Van took a clean handkerchief from a tidy pile in a drawer,
an action he analogized at once by plucking a leaf from a
writing pad. It is wonderful how helpful such repetitive
rhythms on the part of coincidental (white, rectangular) objects can be at such chaotic moments. He wrote a short aerogram and returned to the parlor. There he found Lucette
putting on her fur coat, and five uncouth scholars, whom his
idiot valet had ushered in, standing in a silent circle around
the bland graceful modeling of the coming winter's fashions.
Bernard Rattner, a heavily bespectacled black-haired, red-
cheeked thick-set young man greeted Van with affable relief.

"Good Log!" exclaimed Van, "I had understood we were
to meet at your uncle's place."

With a quick gesture he centrifuged them to waiting-room
chairs, and despite his pretty cousin's protests ("It's a twenty
minute's walk; don't accompany me") campophoned for his
car. Then he clattered, in Lucette's wake, down the cataract
of the narrow staircase, *katrakatra* (*quatre à quatre*). Please,
children, not *katrakatra* (Marina).

"I also know," said Lucette as if continuing their recent
exchange, "who *he* is."

She pointed to the inscription "Voltemand Hall" on the
brow of the building from which they now emerged.

Van gave her a quick glance—but she simply meant the
courtier in *Hamlet.*

They passed through a dark archway, and as they came out
into the colored air of a delicate sunset, he stopped her and
gave her the note he had written. It told Ada to charter a
plane and be at his Manhattan flat any time tomorrow morning. He would leave Kingston around midnight by car. He

still hoped the Ladore dorophone would be in working order before his departure. *Le château que baignait le Dorophone.* Anyway, he assumed the aerogram would reach her in a couple of hours. Lucette said "uhn-uhn," it would first fly to Mont-Dore—sorry, Ladore—and if marked "urgent" would arrive at sunrise by dazzled messenger, galloping east on the post-master's fleabitten nag, because on Sundays you could not use motorcycles, old local law, *l'ivresse de la vitesse, conceptions dominicales;* but even so, she would have ample time to pack, find the box of Dutch crayons Lucette wanted her to bring *if* she came, and be in time for breakfast in Cordula's recent bedroom. Neither half-sibling was at her or his best that day.

"By the way," he said, "let's fix the date of your visit. Her letter changes my schedule. Let's have dinner at Ursus next weekend. I'll get in touch with you."

"I knew it was hopeless," she said, looking away. "I did my best. I imitated all her *shtuchki* (little stunts). I'm a better actress than she but that's not enough, I know. Go back now, they are getting dreadfully drunk on your cognac."

He thrust his hands into the warm vulvas of her mole-soft sleeves and held her for a moment on the inside by her thin bare elbows, looking down with meditative desire at her painted lips.

"*Un baiser, un seul!*" she pleaded.

"You promise not to open your mouth? not to melt? not to flutter and flick?"

"I won't, I swear!"

He hesitated. "No," said Van, "it is a mad temptation but I must not succumb. I could not live through another disaster, another sister, even one-half of a sister."

"*Takoe otchayanie* (such despair)!" moaned Lucette, wrapping herself closely in the coat she had opened instinctively to receive him.

"Might it console you to know that I expect only torture from her return? That I regard you as a bird of paradise?"

She shook her head.

"That my admiration for you is painfully strong?"

"I want Van," she cried, "and not intangible admiration—"

"Intangible? You goose. You may gauge it, you may brush

it once very lightly, with the knuckles of your gloved hand.
I said knuckles. I said once. That will do. I can't kiss you.
Not even your burning face. Good-bye, pet. Tell Edmond to
take a nap after he returns. I shall need him at two in the
morning."

6

The matter of that important discussion was a comparison of
notes regarding a problem that Van was to try to resolve in
another way many years later. Several cases of acrophobia had
been closely examined at the Kingston Clinic to determine if
they were combined with any traces or aspects of time-terror.
Tests had yielded completely negative results, but what
seemed particularly curious was that the only available case of
acute chronophobia differed by its very nature—metaphysical
flavor, psychological stamp and so forth—from that of space-
fear. True, one patient maddened by the touch of time's texture presented too small a sample to compete with a great
group of garrulous acrophobes, and readers who have been
accusing Van of rashness and folly (in young Rattner's polite
terminology) will have a higher opinion of him when they
learn that our young investigator did his best not to let Mr.
T.T. (the chronophobe) be cured too hastily of his rare and
important sickness. Van had satisfied himself that it had nothing to do with clocks or calendars, or any measurements or
contents of time, while he suspected and hoped (as only a
discoverer, pure and passionate, and profoundly inhuman, can
hope) that the dread of heights would be found by his colleagues to depend mainly on the misestimation of distances
and that Mr. Arshin, their best acrophobe, who could not step
down from a footstool, could be made to step down into
space from the top of a tower if persuaded by some optical
trick that the fire net spread fifty yards below was a mat one
inch beneath him.

Van had cold cuts brought up for them, and a gallon of
Gallows Ale—but his mind was elsewhere, and he did not

shine in the discussion which forever remained in his mind as
a grisaille of inconclusive tedium.

They left around midnight; their clatter and chatter still
came from the stairs when he began ringing up Ardis Hall—
vainly, vainly. He kept it up intermittently till daybreak, gave
up, had a structurally perfect stool (its cruciform symmetry
reminding him of the morning before his duel) and, without
bothering to put on a tie (all his favorite ones were awaiting
him in his new apartment), drove to Manhattan, taking the
wheel when he found that Edmond had needed forty-five
minutes instead of half an hour to cover one fourth of the
way.

All he had wanted to say to Ada over the dumb dorophone
amounted to three words in English, contractable to two in
Russian, to one and a half in Italian; but Ada was to maintain
that his frantic attempts to reach her at Ardis had only resulted
in such a violent rhapsody of "eagre" that finally the basement
boiler gave up and there was no hot water—no water at all,
in fact—when she got out of bed, so she pulled on her
warmest coat, and had Bouteillan (discreetly rejoicing old
Bouteillan!) carry her valises down and drive her to the airport.

In the meantime Van had arrived at Alexis Avenue, had lain
in bed for an hour, then shaved and showered, and almost
torn off with the brutality of his pounce the handle of the
door leading to the terrace as there came the sound of a celestial motor.

Despite an athletic strength of will, ironization of excessive
emotion, and contempt for weepy weaklings, Van was aware
of his being apt to suffer uncurbable blubbering fits (rising at
times to an epileptic-like pitch, with sudden howls that shook
his body, and inexhaustible fluids that stuffed his nose) ever
since his break with Ada had led to agonies, which his self-
pride and self-concentration had never foreseen in the hedon-
istic past. A small monoplane (chartered, if one judged by its
nacreous wings and illegal but abortive attempts to settle on
the central green oval of the Park, after which it melted in the
morning mist to seek a perch elsewhere) wrenched a first sob
from Van as he stood in his short "terry" on the roof terrace
(now embellished by shrubs of blue spiraea in invincible

bloom). He stood in the chill sun until he felt his skin under
the robe turn to an armadillo's pelvic plates. Cursing and
shaking both fists at breast level, he returned into the warmth
of his flat and drank a bottle of champagne, and then rang for
Rose, the sportive Negro maid whom he shared in more ways
than one with the famous, recently decorated cryptogram-
matist, Mr. Dean, a perfect gentleman, dwelling on the floor
below. With jumbled feelings, with unpardonable lust, Van
watched her pretty behind roll and tighten under its lacy bow
as she made the bed, while her lower lover could be heard
through the radiator pipes humming to himself happily (he
had decoded again a Tartar dorogram telling the Chinese
where we planned to land next time!). Rose soon finished
putting the room in order, and flirted off, and the Pandean
hum had hardly had time to be replaced (rather artlessly for
a person of Dean's profession) by a crescendo of international
creaks that a child could decipher, when the hallway bell din-
gled, and next moment whiter-faced, redder-mouthed, four-
year-older Ada stood before a convulsed, already sobbing,
ever-adolescent Van, her flowing hair blending with dark furs
that were even richer than her sister's.

He had prepared one of those phrases that sound right in
dreams but lame in lucid life: "I saw you circling above me
on libellula wings"; he broke down on " . . . ula," and fell
at her feet—at her bare insteps in glossy black Glass slippers—
precisely in the same attitude, the same heap of hopeless tenderness, self-immolation, denunciation of demoniac life, in
which he would drop in backthought, in the innermost bower
of his brain every time he remembered her impossible semi-
smile as she adjusted her shoulder blades to the trunk of the
final tree. An invisible stagehand now slipped a seat under her,
and she wept, and stroked his black curls as he went through
his fit of grief, gratitude and regret. It might have persisted
much longer had not another, physical frenzy, that had been
stirring his blood since the previous day, offered a blessed
distraction.

As if she had just escaped from a burning palace and a
perishing kingdom, she wore over her rumpled nightdress a
deep-brown, hoar-glossed coat of sea-otter fur, the famous
kamchatstkiy bobr of ancient Estotian traders, also known as

"lutromarina" on the Lyaska coast: "my natural fur," as Marina used to say pleasantly of her own cape, inherited from a Zemski granddam, when, at the dispersal of a winter ball, some lady wearing vison or coypu or a lowly *manteau de castor* (beaver, *nemetskiy bobr*) would comment with a rapturous moan on the *bobrovaya shuba*. "*Staren'kaya* (old little thing)," Marina used to add in fond deprecation (the usual counterpart of the Bostonian lady's coy "thank you" ventriloquizing her banal mink or nutria in response to polite praise—which did not prevent her from denouncing afterwards the "swank" of that "stuck-up actress," who, actually, was the least ostentatious of souls). Ada's *bobrï* (princely plural of *bobr*) were a gift from Demon, who as we know, had lately seen in the Western states considerably more of her than he had in Eastern Estotiland when she was a child. The bizarre enthusiast had developed the same *tendresse* for her as he had always had for Van. Its new expression in regard to Ada looked sufficiently fervid to make watchful fools suspect that old Demon "slept with his niece" (actually, he was getting more and more occupied with Spanish girls who were getting more and more youthful every year until by the end of the century, when he was sixty, with hair dyed a midnight blue, his flame had become a difficult nymphet of ten). So little did the world realize the real state of affairs that even Cordula Tobak, born de Prey, and Grace Wellington, born Erminin, spoke of Demon Veen, with his fashionable goatee and frilled shirtfront, as "Van's successor."

Neither sibling ever could reconstruct (and all this, including the sea-otter, must not be regarded as a narrator's evasion—we have done, in our time, much more difficult things) what they said, how they kissed, how they mastered their tears, how he swept her couch-ward, gallantly proud to manifest his immediate reaction to her being as scantily gowned (under her hot furs) as she had been when carrying her candle through that magic picture window.

After feasting fiercely on her throat and nipples he was about to proceed to the next stage of demented impatience, but she stopped him, explaining that she must first of all take her morning bath (this, indeed, was a new Ada) and that, moreover, she expected her luggage would be brought up any

moment now by the louts of the "Monaco" lounge (she had
taken the wrong entrance—yet Van had bribed Cordula's devoted janitor to practically carry Ada upstairs). "Quick,
quick," said Ada, "*da, da,* Ada'll be out of the foam in two
secs!" But mad, obstinate Van shed his terry and followed her
into the bathroom, where she strained across the low tub to
turn on both taps and then bent over to insert the bronze
chained plug; it got sucked in by itself, however, while he
steadied her lovely lyre and next moment was at the suede-
soft root, was gripped, was deep between the familiar, incomparable, crimson-lined lips. She caught at the twin cock
crosses, thus involuntarily increasing the sympathetic volume
of the water's noise, and Van emitted a long groan of deliv-
erance, and now their four eyes were looking again into the
azure brook of Pinedale, and Lucette pushed the door open
with a perfunctory knuckle knock and stopped, mesmerized
by the sight of Van's hairy rear and the dreadful scar all along
his left side.

Ada's hands stopped the water. Luggage was being bumped
down all over the flat.

"I'm not looking," said Lucette idiotically, "I only dropped
in for my box."

"Please, tip them, pet," said Van, a compulsive tipper—
"And pass me that towel," added Ada, but the ancilla was
picking up coins she had spilled in her haste, and Ada now
saw in her turn Van's scarlet ladder of sutures—"Oh my poor
darling," she cried, and out of sheer compassion allowed him
the repeat performance which Lucette's entrance had threatened to interrupt.

"I'm not sure I did bring her damned Cranach crayons,"
said Ada a moment later, making a frightened frog face. He
watched her with a sense of perfect pine-fragrant bliss, as she
squeezed out spurts of gem-like liquid from a tube of Penn-
silvestris lotion into the bath water.

Lucette had gone (leaving a curt note with her room number at the Winster Hotel for Young Ladies) when our two
lovers, now weak-legged and decently robed, sat down to a
beautiful breakfast (Ardis' crisp bacon! Ardis' translucent
honey!) brought up in the lift by Valerio, a ginger-haired elderly Roman, always ill-shaven and gloomy, but a dear old boy

(he it was who, having procured neat Rose last June, was being paid to keep her strictly for Veen and Dean).

What laughs, what tears, what sticky kisses, what a tumult
of multitudinous plans! And what safety, what freedom of
love! Two unrelated gypsy courtesans, a wild girl in a gaudy
lolita, poppy-mouthed and black-downed, picked up in a café
between Grasse and Nice, and another, a part-time model
(you have seen her fondling a virile lipstick in Fellata ads),
aptly nicknamed Swallowtail by the patrons of a Norfolk
Broads floramor, had both given our hero exactly the same
reason, unmentionable in a family chronicle, for considering
him absolutely sterile despite his prowesses. Amused by the
Hecatean diagnose, Van underwent certain tests, and although pooh-poohing the symptom as coincidental, all the
doctors agreed that Van Veen might be a doughty and durable
lover but could never hope for an offspring. How merrily little
Ada clapped her hands!

Would she like to stay in this apartment till Spring Term
(he thought in terms of Terms now) and then accompany him
to Kingston, or would she prefer to go abroad for a couple
of months—anywhere, Patagonia, Angola, Gululu in the New
Zealand mountains? Stay in this apartment? So, she liked it?
Except some of Cordula's stuff which should be ejected—as,
for example, that conspicuous Brown Hill Alma Mater of Al-
mehs left open on poor Vanda's portrait. She had been shot
dead by the girlfriend of a girlfriend on a starry night, in Ra-
gusa of all places. It was, Van said, sad. Little Lucette no
doubt had told him about a later escapade? Punning in an
Ophelian frenzy on the feminine glans? Raving about the delectations of clitorism? "*N'exagérons pas, tu sais*," said Ada,
patting the air down with both palms. "Lucette affirmed," he
said, "that she (Ada) imitated mountain lions."

He was omniscient. Better say, omni-incest.

"That's right," said the other total-recaller.

And, by the way, Grace—yes, Grace—was Vanda's real
favorite, *pas petite moi* and my little crest. She (Ada) had,
hadn't she, a way of always smoothing out the folds of the
past—making the flutist practically impotent (except with his
wife) and allowing the gentleman farmer only one embrace,
with a premature *eyakulyatsiya*, one of those hideous Russian

loan-words? Yes, wasn't it hideous, but she'd love to play Scrabble again when they'd settled down for good. But where, how? Wouldn't Mr. and Mrs. Ivan Veen do quite nicely anywhere? What about the "single" in each passport? They'd go to the nearest Consulate and with roars of indignation and/or a fabulous bribe have it corrected to married, for ever and ever.

"I'm a good, good girl. Here are her special pencils. It was very considerate and altogether charming of you to invite her next weekend. I think she's even more madly in love with you than with me, the poor pet. Demon got them in Strassburg. After all she's a demi-vierge now" ("I hear you and Dad—" began Van, but the introduction of a new subject was swamped) "and we shan't be afraid of her witnessing our *ébats*" (pronouncing on purpose, with triumphant hooliganism, for which my prose, too, is praised, the first vowel *à la Russe*).

"You do the puma," he said, "but she does—to perfection!—my favorite *viola sordina*. She's a wonderful imitatrix, by the way, and if you are even better—"

"We'll speak about my talents and tricks some other time," said Ada. "It's a painful subject. Now let's look at these snapshots."

7

During her dreary stay at Ardis, a considerably changed and enlarged Kim Beauharnais called upon her. He carried under his arm an album bound in orange-brown cloth, a dirty hue she had hated all her life. In the last two or three years she had not seen him, the light-footed, lean lad with the sallow complexion had become a dusky colossus, vaguely resembling a janizary in some exotic opera, stomping in to announce an invasion or an execution. Uncle Dan, who just then was being wheeled out by his handsome and haughty nurse into the garden where coppery and blood-red leaves were falling, clamored to be given the big book, but Kim said "Perhaps later," and joined Ada in the reception corner of the hall.

He had brought her a present, a collection of photographs
he had taken in the good old days. He had been hoping the
good old days would resume their course, but since he understood that *mossio votre cossin* (he spoke a thick Creole
thinking that its use in solemn circumstances would be more
proper than his everyday Ladore English) was not expected to
revisit the castle soon—and thus help bring the album up to
date—the best procedure *pour tous les cernés* ("the shadowed
ones," the "encircled" rather than "concerned") might be
for her to keep (or destroy and forget, so as not to hurt anybody) the illustrated document now in her pretty hands.
Wincing angrily at the *jolies*, Ada opened the album at one of
its maroon markers meaningly inserted here and there,
glanced once, reclicked the clasp, handed the grinning blackmailer a thousand-dollar note that she happened to have in
her bag, summoned Bouteillan and told him to throw Kim
out. The mud-colored scrapbook remained on a chair, under
her Spanish shawl. With a shuffling kick the old retainer expelled a swamp-tulip leaf swept in by the draft and closed the
front door again.

"*Mademoiselle n'aurait jamais dû recevoir ce gredin,*" he
grumbled on his way back through the hall.

"That's just what I was on the point of observing," said
Van when Ada had finished relating the nasty incident. "Were
the photos pretty filthy?"

"Ach!" exhaled Ada.

"That money might have furthered a worthier cause—
Home for Blind Colts or Aging Ashettes."

"Odd, your saying that."

"Why?"

"Never mind. Anyway, the beastly thing is now safe. I *had*
to pay for it, lest he show poor Marina pictures of Van se-
ducing his little cousin Ada—which would have been bad
enough; actually, as a hawk of genius, he may have suspected
the whole truth."

"So you really think that because you bought his album for
a paltry thousand all evidence has been disposed of and everything is in order?"

"Why, yes. Do you think the sum was too mean? I might
send him more. I know where to reach him. He lectures, if

you please, on the Art of Shooting Life at the School of Photography in Kalugano."

"Good place for shooting," said Van. "So you are quite sure you own the 'beastly thing'?"

"Of course, I do. It's with me, at the bottom of that trunk; I'll show it to you in a moment."

"Tell me, my love, what was your so-called I.Q. when we first met?"

"Two hundred and something. A sensational figure."

"Well, by now it has shrunk rather badly. Peeking Kim has kept all the negatives plus lots of pictures he will paste or post later."

"Would you say it has dropped to Cordula's level?"

"Lower. Now let's look at those snapshots—before settling his monthly salary."

The first item in the evil series had projected one of Van's initial impressions of Ardis Manor at an angle that differed from that of his own recollection. Its area lay between the shadow of a calèche darkening the gravel and the white step of a pillared porch shining in the sun. Marina, one arm still in the sleeve of the dust coat which a footman (Price) was helping her to remove, stood brandishing her free arm in a theatrical gesture of welcome (entirely at variance with the grimace of helpless beatitude twisting her face), while Ada in a black hockey blazer—belonging really to Vanda—spilled her hair over her bare knees as she flexed them and flipped Dack with her flowers to check his nervous barks.

Then came several preparatory views of the immediate grounds: the colutea circle, an avenue, the grotto's black O, and the hill, and the big chain around the trunk of the rare oak, *Quercus ruslan* Chât., and a number of other spots meant to be picturesque by the compiler of the illustrated pamphlet but looking a little shabby owing to inexperienced photography.

It improved gradually.

Another girl (Blanche!) stooping and squatting exactly like Ada (and indeed not unlike her in features) over Van's valise opened on the floor, and "eating with her eyes" the silhouette of Ivory Revery in a perfume advertisement. Then the cross and the shade of boughs above the grave of

Marina's dear housekeeper, Anna Pimenovna Nepraslinov (1797–1883).

Let's skip nature shots—of skunklike squirrels, of a striped fish in a bubble tank, of a canary in its pretty prison.

A photograph of an oval painting, considerably diminished, portrayed Princess Sophia Zemski as she was at twenty, in 1775, with her two children (Marina's grandfather born in 1772, and Demon's grandmother, born in 1773).

"I don't seem to remember it," said Van, "where did it hang?"

"In Marina's boudoir. And do you know who this bum in the frock coat is?"

"Looks to me like a poor print cut out of a magazine. Who's he?"

"Sumerechnikov! He took sumerographs of Uncle Vanya years ago."

"The Twilight before the Lumières. Hey, and here's Alonso, the swimming-pool expert. I met his sweet sad daughter at a Cyprian party—she felt and smelt and melted like you. The strong charm of coincidence."

"I'm not interested. Now comes a little boy."

"*Zdraste*, Ivan Dementievich," said Van, greeting his fourteen-year-old self, shirtless, in shorts, aiming a conical missile at the marble fore-image of a Crimean girl doomed to offer an everlasting draught of marble water to a dying marine from her bullet-chipped jar.

Skip Lucette skipping rope.

Ah, the famous first finch.

"No, that's a *kitayskaya punochka* (Chinese Wall Bunting). It has settled on the threshold of a basement door. The door is ajar. There are garden tools and croquet mallets inside. You remember how many exotic, alpine and polar, animals mixed with ordinary ones in our region."

Lunchtime. Ada bending low over the dripping peach improperly peeled that she is devouring (shot from the garden through the french window).

Drama and comedy. Blanche struggling with two amorous *tsigans* in the Baguenaudier Bower. Uncle Dan calmly reading a newspaper in his little red motorcar, hopelessly stuck in black mud on the Ladore road.

Two huge common Peacock moths, still connected. Grooms and gardeners brought Ada that species every blessed year; which, in a way, reminds us of you, sweet Marco d'Andrea, or you, red-haired Domenico Benci, or you, dark and broody Giovanni del Brina (who thought they were bats) or the one I dare not mention (because it is Lucette's scholarly contribution—so easily botched after the scholar's death) who likewise might have picked up, at the foot of an orchard wall, not overhung with not-yet-imported wisteria (her half-sister's addition), on a May morning in 1542, near Florence, a pair of the Pear Peacock *in copula*, the male with the feathery antennae, the female with the plain threads, to depict them faithfully (among wretched, unvisualized insects) on one side of a fenestral niche in the so-called "Elements Room" of the Palazzo Vecchio.

Sunrise at Ardis. Congs: naked Van still cocooned in his hammock under the "lidderons" as they called in Ladore the liriodendrons, not exactly a *lit d'édredon*, though worth an auroral pun and certainly conducive to the physical expression of a young dreamer's fancy undisguised by the network.

"Congratulations," repeated Van in male language. "The first indecent postcard. Bewhorny, no doubt, has a blown-up copy in his private stock."

Ada examined the pattern of the hammock through a magnifying glass (used by Van for deciphering certain details of his lunatics' drawings).

"I'm afraid there's more to come," she remarked with a catch in her voice; and taking advantage of their looking at the album in bed (which we now think lacked taste) odd Ada used the reading loupe on live Van, something she had done many times as a scientifically curious and artistically depraved child in that year of grace, here depicted.

"I'll find a *mouche* (patch) to conceal it," she said, returning to the leering caruncula in the unreticent reticulation. "By the way, you have quite a collection of black masks in your dresser."

"For masked balls (*bals-masqués*)," murmured Van.

A comparison piece: Ada's very-much-exposed white thighs (her birthday skirt had got entangled with twigs and leaves) straddling a black limb of the tree of Eden. Thereafter: several shots of the 1884 picnic, such as Ada and Grace dancing a Lyaskan fling and reversed Van nibbling at pine starworts (conjectural identification).

"That's finished," said Van, "a precious sinistral sinew has stopped functioning. I can still fence and deliver a fine punch but hand-walking is out. You shall not sniffle, Ada. Ada is not going to sniffle and wail. King Wing says that the great Vekchelo turned back into an ordinary *chelovek* at the age I'm now, so everything is perfectly normal. Ah, drunken Ben Wright trying to rape Blanche in the mews—she has quite a big part in this farrago."

"He's doing nothing of the sort. You see quite well they are dancing. It's like the Beast and the Belle at the ball where Cinderella loses her garter and the Prince his beautiful codpiece of glass. You can also make out Mr. Ward and Mrs. French in a bruegelish *kimbo* (peasant prance) at the farther end of the hall. All those rural rapes in our parts have been grossly exaggerated. *D'ailleurs*, it was Mr. Ben Wright's last petard at Ardis."

Ada on the balcony (photographed by our acrobatic *voyeur* from the roof edge) drawing one of her favorite flowers, a Ladore satyrion, silky-haired, fleshy, erect. Van thought he recalled that particular sunny evening, the excitement, the softness, and some casual words she had muttered (in connection with an inane botanical comment of his): "*my* flower opens only at dusk." The one she was moistly mauving.

A formal photograph, on a separate page: Adochka, pretty and impure in her flimsy, and Vanichka in gray-flannel suit, with slant-striped school tie, facing the *kimera* (chimera, camera) side by side, at attention, he with the shadow of a forced grin, she, expressionless. Both recalled the time (between the first tiny cross and a whole graveyard of kisses) and the occasion: it was ordered by Marina, who had it framed and set up in her bedroom next to a picture of her brother at twelve or fourteen clad in a *bayronka* (open shirt) and cupping a guinea pig in his gowpen (hollowed hands); the three looked like siblings, with the dead boy providing a vivisectional alibi.

Another photograph was taken in the same circumstances but for some reason had been rejected by capricious Marina: at a tripod table, Ada sat reading, her half-clenched hand covering the lower part of the page. A very rare, radiant, seemingly uncalled-for smile shone on her practically Moorish lips. Her hair flowed partly across her collarbone and partly down her back. Van stood inclining his head above her and looked, unseeing, at the opened book. In full, deliberate consciousness, at the moment of the hooded click, he bunched the recent past with the imminent future and thought to himself that this would remain an objective perception of the real present and that he must remember the flavor, the flash, the flesh of the present (as he, indeed, remembered it half a dozen years later—and now, in the second half of the next century).

But what about the rare radiance on those adored lips? Bright derision can easily grade, through a cline of glee, into a look of rapture:

"Do you know, Van, *what* book lay there—next to Marina's hand mirror and a pair of tweezers? I'll tell you. One of the most tawdry and *réjouissants* novels that ever 'made' the front page of the Manhattan *Times'* Book Review. I'm sure your Cordula still had it in her cosy corner where you sat temple to temple after you jilted me."

"Cat," said Van.

"Oh, much worse. Old Beckstein's *Tabby* was a masterpiece in comparison to this—this *Love under the Lindens* by one Eelmann transported into English by Thomas Gladstone, who seems to belong to a firm of Packers & Porters, because on the page which Adochka, *adova dochka* (Hell's daughter), happens to be relishing here, 'automobile' is rendered as 'wagon.' And to think, to think, that little Lucette had to study Eelmann, and three terrible Toms in her Literature course at Los!"

"You remember that trash but I remember our nonstop three-hour kiss Under the Larches immediately afterwards."

"See next illustration," said Ada grimly.

"The scoundrel!" cried Van; "He must have been creeping after us on his belly with his entire apparatus. I will have to destroy him."

"No more destruction, Van. Only love."

"But look, girl, here I'm glutting your tongue, and there I'm glued to your epiglottis, and—"

"Intermission," begged Ada, "quick-quick."

"I'm ready to oblige till I'm ninety," said Van (the vulgarity of the peep show was catchy), "ninety times a month, roughly."

"Make it even more roughly, oh much more, say a hundred and fifty, that would mean, that would mean—"

But, in the sudden storm, calculations went to the canicular devils.

"Well," said Van, when the mind took over again, "let's go back to our defaced childhood. I'm anxious"—(picking up the album from the bedside rug)—"to get rid of this burden. Ah, a new character, the inscription says: Dr. Krolik."

"Wait a sec. It may be the best Vanishing Van but it's terribly messy all the same. Okay. Yes, that's my poor nature teacher."

Knickerbockered, panama-hatted, lusting for his *babochka* (Russian for "lepidopteron"). A passion, a sickness. What could Diana know about *that* chase?

"How curious—in the state Kim mounted him here, he looks much less furry and fat than I imagined. In fact, darling, he's a big, strong, handsome old March Hare! Explain!"

"There's nothing to explain. I asked Kim one day to help me carry some boxes there and back, and here's the visual proof. Besides, that's not *my* Krolik but his brother, Karol, or Karapars, Krolik. A doctor of philosophy, born in Turkey."

"I love the way your eyes narrow when you tell a lie. The remote mirage in Effrontery Minor."

"I'm not lying!"—(with lovely dignity): "He *is* a doctor of philosophy."

"Van *ist auch* one," murmured Van, sounding the last word as "*wann.*"

"Our fondest dream," she continued, "Krolik's and my fondest dream, was to describe and depict the early stages, from ova to pupa, of all the known Fritillaries, Greater and Lesser, beginning with those of the New World. I would have been responsible for building an argynninarium (a pestproof breeding house, with temperature patterns, and other refinements—such as background night smells and night-animal calls to create a natural atmosphere in certain difficult cases)—a caterpillar needs exquisite care! There are hundreds of species and good subspecies in both hemispheres but, I repeat,

we'd begin with America. Live egg-laying females and live
food plants, such as violets of numerous kinds, airmailed from
everywhere, starting, for the heck of it, with arctic habitats—
Lyaska, Le Bras d'Or, Victor Island. The magnanery would
be also a violarium, full of fascinating flourishing plants, from
the *endiconensis* race of the Northern Marsh Violet to the minute but magnificent *Viola kroliki* recently described by Professor Hall from Goodson Bay. I would contribute colored
figures of all the instars, and line drawings of the perfect insect's genitalia and other structures. It would be a wonderful
work."

"A work of love," said Van, and turned the page.

"Unfortunately, my dear collaborator died intestate, and all
his collections, including my own little part, were surrendered
by a regular warren of collateral Kroliks to agents in Germany
and dealers in Tartary. Disgraceful, unjust, and so sad!"

"We'll find you another director of science. Now what do
we have here?"

Three footmen, Price, Norris, and Ward dressed up as grotesque firemen. Young Bout devotedly kissing the veined instep of a pretty bare foot raised and placed on a balustrade.
Nocturnal outdoor shot of two small white ghosts pressing
their noses from the inside to the library window.

Artistically *éventail*-ed all on one page were seven *fotochki*
(diminutive stills) taken within as many minutes—from a fairly
distant lurk—in a setting of tall grass, wild flowers, and over-
hanging foliage. Its shade, and the folly of peduncles, delicately camouflaged the basic details, suggesting little more
than a tussle between two incompletely clad children.

In the central miniature, Ada's only limb in sight was her
thin arm holding aloft, in a static snatch, like a banner, her
discarded dress above the daisy-starred grass. The magnifier
(now retrieved from under the bed sheet) clearly showed, top-
ping the daisies in an upper picture, the type of tight-capped
toadstool called in Scots law (ever since witching was banned)
"the Lord of Erection." Another interesting plant, Marvel's
Melon, imitating the backside of an occupied lad, could be
made out on the floral horizon of a third photo. In the next
three stills *la force des choses* ("the fever of intercourse") had
sufficiently disturbed the lush herbage to allow one to distin-

guish the details of a tangled composition consisting of clumsy Romany clips and illegal nelsons. Finally, in the last picture, the lower one in the fanlike sequence, Ada was represented by her two hands rearranging her hair while her Adam stood over her, a frond or inflorescence veiling his thigh with the deliberate casualness of an Old Master's device to keep Eden chaste.

In an equally casual tone of voice Van said: "Darling, you smoke too much, my belly is covered with your ashes. I suppose Bouteillan knows Professor Beauharnais's exact address in the Athens of Graphic Arts."

"You shall not slaughter him," said Ada. "He is subnormal, he is, perhaps, blackmailerish, but in his sordidity there is an *istoshniy ston* ("visceral moan") of crippled art. Furthermore, this page is the only really naughty one. And let's not forget that a copperhead of eight was also ambushed in the brush."

"Art my *foute*. This is the hearse of *ars*, a toilet roll of the Carte du Tendre! I'm sorry you showed it to me. That ape has vulgarized our own mind-pictures. I will either horsewhip his eyes out or redeem our childhood by making a book of it: *Ardis*, a family chronicle."

"Oh do!" said Ada (skipping another abominable glimpse —apparently, through a hole in the boards of the attic). "Look, here's our little Caliph Island!"

"I don't want to look any more. I suspect you find that filth titillating. Some nuts get a kick from motor-bikini comics."

"Please, Van, do glance! These are our willows, remember?"

> " 'The castle bathed by the Adour:
>   The guidebooks recommend that tour.' "

"It happens to be the only one in color. The willows look sort of greenish because the twigs are greenish, but actually they are leafless here, it's early spring, and you can see our red boat *Souvenance* through the rushes. And here's the last one: Kim's apotheosis of Ardis."

The entire staff stood in several rows on the steps of the pillared porch behind the Bank President Baroness Veen and the Vice President Ida Larivière. Those two were flanked by the two prettiest typists, Blanche de la Tourberie (ethereal, tearstained, entirely adorable) and a black girl who had been hired, a few days before Van's departure, to help French, who towered rather sullenly above her in the second row, the focal point of which was Bouteillan, still wearing the *costume sport* he had on when driving off with Van (*that* picture had been muffed or omitted). On the butler's right side stood three footmen; on his left, Bout (who had valeted Van), the fat, flour-pale cook (Blanche's father) and, next to French, a terribly tweedy gentleman with sightseeing strappings athwart one shoulder: actually (according to Ada), a tourist, who, having come all the way from England to see Bryant's Castle, had bicycled up the wrong road and was, in the picture, under the impression of accidentally being conjoined to a group of fellow tourists who were visiting some other old manor quite worth inspecting too. The back rows consisted of less distinguished menservants and scullions, as well as of gardeners, stableboys, coachmen, shadows of columns, maids of maids, aids, laundresses, dresses, recesses—getting less and less distinct as in those bank ads where limited little employees dimly dimidiated by more fortunate shoulders, but still asserting themselves, still smile in the process of humble dissolve.

"Isn't that wheezy Jones in the second row? I always liked the old fellow."

"No," answered Ada, "that's Price. Jones came four years later. He is now a prominent policeman in Lower Ladore. Well, that's all."

Nonchalantly, Van went back to the willows and said:

"Every shot in the book has been snapped in 1884, except this one. I never rowed you down Ladore River in early spring. Nice to note you have not lost your wonderful ability to blush."

"It's *his* error. He must have thrown in a *fotochka* taken later, maybe in 1888. We can rip it out if you like."

"Sweetheart," said Van, "the whole of 1888 has been ripped out. One need not be a sleuth in a mystery story to see that at least as many pages have been removed as retained. *I* don't mind—I mean *I* have no desire to see the *Knabenkräuter* and other pendants of your friends botanizing with you; but 1888 has been withheld and he'll turn up with it when the first grand is spent."

"I destroyed 1888 myself," admitted proud Ada; "but I swear, I solemnly swear, that the man behind Blanche, in the *perron* picture, was, and has always remained, a complete stranger."

"Good for him," said Van. "Really it has no importance. It's our entire past that has been spoofed and condemned. On second thoughts, I will not write that Family Chronicle. By the way, where is my poor little Blanche now?"

"Oh, she's all right. She's still around. You know, she came back—after you abducted her. She married our Russian coachman, the one who replaced Bengal Ben, as the servants called him."

"Oh she did? That's delicious. Madame Trofim Fartukov. I would never have thought it."

"They have a blind child," said Ada.

"Love is blind," said Van.

"She tells me you made a pass at her on the first morning of your first arrival."

"Not documented by Kim," said Van. "Will their child *remain* blind? I mean, did you get them a really first-rate physician?"

"Oh yes, hopelessly blind. But speaking of love and its myths, do you realize—because I never did before talking to her a couple of years ago—that the people around our affair had very good eyes indeed? Forget Kim, he's only the necessary clown—but do you realize that a veritable legend was growing around you and me while we played and made love?"

She had never realized, she said again and again (as if intent to reclaim the past from the matter-of-fact triviality of the album), that their first summer in the orchards and orchidariums of Ardis had become a sacred secret and creed, throughout the countryside. Romantically inclined handmaids, whose reading consisted of *Gwen de Vere* and *Klara Mertvago*, adored Van, adored Ada, adored Ardis's ardors in arbors. Their swains, plucking ballads on their seven-stringed Russian lyres under the racemosa in bloom or in old rose gardens (while the windows went out one by one in the castle), added

freshly composed lines—naive, lackey-daisical, but heartfelt—
to cyclic folk songs. Eccentric police officers grew enamored
with the glamour of incest. Gardeners paraphrased iridescent
Persian poems about irrigation and the Four Arrows of Love.
Nightwatchmen fought insomnia and the fire of the clap with
the weapons of *Vaniada's Adventures*. Herdsmen, spared by
thunderbolts on remote hillsides, used their huge "moaning
horns" as ear trumpets to catch the lilts of Ladore. Virgin
châtelaines in marble-floored manors fondled their lone flames
fanned by Van's romance. And another century would pass,
and the painted word would be retouched by the still richer
brush of time.

"All of which," said Van, "only means that our situation is
desperate."

8

Knowing how fond his sisters were of Russian fare and Russian
floor shows, Van took them Saturday night to "Ursus," the
best Franco-Estotian restaurant in Manhattan Major. Both
young ladies wore the very short and open evening gowns that
Vass "miraged" that season—in the phrase of that season:
Ada, a gauzy black, Lucette, a lustrous cantharid green. Their
mouths "echoed" in tone (but not tint) each other's lipstick;
their eyes were made up in a "surprised bird-of-paradise" style
that was as fashionable in Los as in Lute. Mixed metaphors
and double-talk became all three Veens, the children of
Venus.

The *uha*, the shashlik, the *Ai* were facile and familiar successes; but the old songs had a peculiar poignancy owing to
the participation of a Lyaskan contralto and a Banff bass, renowned performers of Russian "romances," with a touch of
heartwringing *tsiganshchina* vibrating through Grigoriev and
Glinka. And there was Flora, a slender, hardly nubile, half-
naked music-hall dancer of uncertain origin (Rumanian? Romany? Ramseyan?) whose ravishing services Van had availed
himself of several times in the fall of that year. As a "man of

the world," Van glanced with bland (perhaps too bland) unconcern at her talented charms, but they certainly added a
secret bonus to the state of erotic excitement tingling in him
from the moment that his two beauties had been unfurred
and placed in the colored blaze of the feast before him; and
that thrill was somehow augmented by his awareness (carefully
profiled, diaphanely blinkered) of the furtive, jealous, intuitive
suspicion with which Ada *and* Lucette watched, unsmilingly,
his facial reactions to the demure look of professional recognition on the part of the passing and repassing *blyadushka*
(cute whorelet), as our young misses referred to (*very* expensive and altogether delightful) Flora with ill-feigned indifference. Presently, the long sobs of the violins began to affect
and almost choke Van and Ada: a juvenile conditioning of
romantic appeal, which at one moment forced tearful Ada to
go and "powder her nose" while Van stood up with a spas-
modic sob, which he cursed but could not control. He went
back to whatever he was eating, and cruelly stroked Lucette's
apricot-bloomed forearm, and she said in Russian "I'm drunk,
and all that, but I adore (*obozhayu*), I adore, I adore, I adore
more than life you, you (*tebya, tebya*), I ache for you unbearably (*ya toskuyu po tebe nevinosimo*), and, please, don't let me
swill (*hlestat'*) champagne any more, not only because I will
jump into Goodson River if I can't hope to have you, and not
only because of the physical red thing—your heart was almost
ripped out, my poor *dushen'ka* ('darling,' more than 'darling'), it looked to me at least eight inches long—"

"Seven and a half," murmured modest Van, whose hearing
the music impaired.

"—but because you are Van, all Van, and nothing but Van,
skin and scar, the only truth of our only life, of *my* accursed
life, Van, Van, Van."

Here Van stood up again, as Ada, black fan in elegant motion, came back followed by a thousand eyes, while the opening bars of a *romance* (on Fet's glorious *Siyala noch'*) started
to run over the keys (and the bass coughed *à la russe* into his
fist before starting).

A radiant night, a moon-filled garden. Beams
Lay at our feet. The drawing room, unlit;

Wide open, the grand piano; and our hearts
Throbbed to your song, as throbbed the strings in it . . .

Then Banoffsky launched into Glinka's great amphibrachs (Mihail Ivanovich had been a summer guest at Ardis when their uncle was still alive—a green bench existed where the composer was said to have sat under the pseudoacacias especially often, mopping his ample brow):

Subside, agitation of passion!

Then other singers took over with sadder and sadder ballads—"The tender kisses are forgotten," and "The time was early in the spring, the grass was barely sprouting," and "Many songs have I heard in the land of my birth: Some in sorrow were sung, some in gladness," and the spuriously populist

There's a crag on the Ross, overgrown with wild moss
On all sides, from the lowest to highest . . .

and a series of viatic plaints such as the more modestly anapestic:

In a monotone tinkles the yoke-bell,
And the roadway is dusting a bit . . .

And that obscurely corrupted soldier dit of singular genius

Nadezhda, I shall then be back
When the true batch outboys the riot . . .

and Turgenev's only memorable lyrical poem beginning

Morning so nebulous, morning gray-dawning,
Reaped fields so sorrowful under snow coverings

and naturally the celebrated pseudo-gipsy guitar piece by Apollon Grigoriev (another friend of Uncle Ivan's)

O you, at least, do talk to me,
My seven-stringed companion,
Such yearning ache invades my soul,
Such moonlight fills the canyon!

"I declare we are satiated with moonlight and strawberry

soufflé—the latter, I fear, has not quite 'risen' to the occasion," remarked Ada in her archest, Austen-maidenish manner. "Let's all go to bed. You have seen our huge bed, pet? Look, our cavalier is yawning 'fit to declansh his masher'" (vulgar Ladore cant).

"How (ascension of Mt. Yawn) true," uttered Van, ceasing to palpate the velvet cheek of his Cupidon peach, which he had bruised but not sampled.

The captain, the *vinocherpiy*, the shashlikman, and a crew of waiters had been utterly entranced by the amount of *zernistaya ikra* and *Ai* consumed by the vaporous-looking Veens and were now keeping a multiple eye on the tray that had flown back to Van with a load of gold change and bank notes.

"Why," asked Lucette, kissing Ada's cheek as they both rose (making swimming gestures behind their backs in search of the furs locked up in the vault or somewhere), "why did the first song, *Uzh gasli v komnatah ogni*, and the 'redolent roses,' upset you more than your favorite Fet and the other, about the bugler's sharp elbow?"

"Van, too, was upset," replied Ada cryptically and grazed with freshly rouged lips tipsy Lucette's fanciest freckle.

Detachedly, merely tactually, as if he had met those two slow-moving, hip-swaying graces only that night, Van, while steering them through a doorway (to meet the sinchilla mantillas that were being rushed toward them by numerous, new, eager, unfairly, inexplicably impecunious, humans), placed one palm, the left, on Ada's long bare back and the other on Lucette's spine, quite as naked and long (had she meant the lad or the ladder? Lapse of the lisping lips?). Detachedly, he sifted and tasted this sensation, then that. His girl's ensellure was hot ivory; Lucette's was downy and damp. He too had had just about his "last straw" of champagne, namely four out of half a dozen bottles minus a rizzom (as we said at old Chose) and now, as he followed their bluish furs, he inhaled like a fool his right hand before gloving it.

"I say, Veen," whinnied a voice near him (there were lots of lechers around), "you don't rally need two, d'you?"

Van veered, ready to cuff the gross speaker—but it was only Flora, a frightful tease and admirable mimic. He tried to give her a banknote, but she fled, bracelets and breast stars flashing a fond farewell.

As soon as Edmund (not Edmond, who for security reasons—he knew Ada—had been sent back to Kingston) brought them home, Ada puffed out her cheeks, making big eyes, and headed for Van's bathroom. Hers had been turned over to the tottering guest. Van, at a geographical point a shade nearer to the elder girl, stood and used in a sustained stream the amenities of a little *vessie* (Canady form of W.C.) next to his dressing room. He removed his dinner jacket and tie, undid the collar of his silk shirt and paused in virile hesitation: Ada, beyond their bedroom and sitting room, was running her bath; to its gush a guitar rhythm, recently heard, kept adapting itself aquatically (the rare moments when he remembered her and her quite rational speech at her last sanatorium in Agavia).

He licked his lips, cleared his throat and, deciding to kill two finches with one fircone, walked to the other, southern, extremity of the flat through a boudery and manger hall (we always tend to talk Canady when *haut*). In the guest bedroom, Lucette stood with her back to him, in the process of slipping on her pale green nightdress over her head. Her narrow haunches were bare, and our wretched rake could not help being moved by the ideal symmetry of the exquisite twin dimples that only very perfect young bodies have above the buttocks in the sacral belt of beauty. Oh, they were even more perfect than Ada's! Fortunately, she turned around, smoothing her tumbled red curls while her hem dropped to knee level.

"My dear," said Van, "do help me. She told me about her Valentian *estanciero* but now the name escapes me and I hate bothering her."

"Only she never told you," said loyal Lucette, "so nothing could escape. Nope. I can't do that to your sweetheart and mine, because we know you could hit that keyhole with a pistol."

"Please, little vixen! I'll reward you with a very special kiss."

"Oh, Van," she said over a deep sigh. "You promise you won't tell her I told you?"

"I promise. No, no, no," he went on, assuming a Russian accent, as she, with the abandon of mindless love, was about to press her abdomen to his. "*Nikak-s net:* no lips, no philtrum, no nosetip, no swimming eye. Little vixen's axilla, just that—unless"—(drawing back in mock uncertainty)—"you *shave* there?"

"I stink worse when I do," confided simple Lucette and obediently bared one shoulder.

"Arm up! Point at Paradise! Terra! Venus!" commanded Van, and for a few synchronized heartbeats, fitted his working mouth to the hot, humid, perilous hollow.

She sat down with a bump on a chair, pressing one hand to her brow.

"Turn off the footlights," said Van. "I want the name of that fellow."

"Vinelander," she answered.

He heard Ada Vinelander's voice calling for her Glass bed slippers (which, as in Cordulenka's princessdom too, he found hard to distinguish from dance footwear), and a minute later, without the least interruption in the established tension, Van found himself, in a drunken dream, making violent love to Rose—no, to Ada, but in the rosacean fashion, on a kind of lowboy. She complained he hurt her "like a Tiger Turk." He went to bed and was about to doze off for good when she left his side. Where was she going? Pet wanted to see the album.

"I'll be back in a rubby," she said (tribadic schoolgirl slang), "so keep awake. From now on by the way, it's going to be *Chère-amie-fait-morata*"—(play on the generic and specific names of the famous fly)—"until further notice."

"But no sapphic *vorschmacks*," mumbled Van into his pillow.

"Oh, Van," she said, turning to shake her head, one hand on the opal doorknob at the end of an endless room. "We've been through that so many times! You admit yourself that I am only a pale wild girl with gipsy hair in a deathless ballad, in a nulliverse, in Rattner's 'menald world' where the only principle is random variation. You cannot demand," she continued—somewhere between the cheeks of his pillow (for Ada

had long vanished with her blood-brown book)—"you cannot demand pudicity on the part of a delphinet! You know
that I really love only males and, alas, only one man."

There was always something colorfully impressionistic, but
also infantile, about Ada's allusions to her affairs of the flesh,
reminding one of baffle painting, or little glass labyrinths with
two peas, or the Ardis throwing-trap—you remember?—
which tossed up clay pigeons and pine cones to be shot at, or
cockamaroo (Russian "*biks*"), played with a toy cue on the
billiard cloth of an oblong board with holes and hoops, bells
and pins among which the ping-pong-sized eburnean ball zig-
zagged with bix-pix concussions.

Tropes are the dreams of speech. Through the boxwood
maze and bagatelle arches of Ardis, Van passed into sleep.
When he reopened his eyes it was nine A.M. She lay curved
away from him, with nothing beyond the opened parenthesis,
its contents not yet ready to be enclosed, and the beloved,
beautiful, treacherous, blue-black-bronze hair smelt of Ardis,
but also of Lucette's "Oh-de-grâce."

Had she cabled him? Canceled or Postponed? Mrs. Viner
—no, Vingolfer, no, Vinelander—first Russki to taste the
labruska grape.

"*Mne snitsa saPERnik SHCHASTLEEVOY!*" (Mihail Ivanovich arcating the sand with his cane, humped on his bench
under the creamy racemes).

"I dream of a fortunate rival!"

In the meantime it's Dr. Hangover for me, and his strongest
Kaffeina pill.

Ada being at twenty a long morning sleeper, his usual practice, ever since their new life together had started, was to
shower before she awoke and, while shaving, ring from the
bathroom for their breakfast to be brought by Valerio, who
would roll in the laid table out of the lift into the sitting room
next to their bedroom. But on this particular Sunday, not
knowing what Lucette might like (he remembered her old
craving for cocoa) and being anxious to have an engagement
with Ada before the day began, even if it meant intruding
upon her warm sleep, Van sped up his ablutions, robustly
dried himself, powdered his groin, and without bothering to
put anything on re-entered the bedroom in full pride, only to

find a tousled and sulky Lucette, still in her willow green nightie, sitting on the far edge of the concubital bed, while fat-nippled Ada, already wearing, for ritual and fatidic reasons, his river of diamonds, was inhaling her first smoke of the day and trying to make her little sister decide whether she would like to try the Monaco's pancakes with Potomac syrup, or, perhaps, their incomparable amber-and-ruby bacon. Upon seeing Van, who without a flinch in his imposing deportment proceeded to place a rightful knee on the near side of the tremendous bed (Mississippi Rose had once brought there, for progressive visual-education purposes, her two small toffee-brown sisters, and a doll almost their size but white), Lucette shrugged her shoulders and made as if to leave, but Ada's avid hand restrained her.

"Pop in, pet (it all started with the little one letting wee winds go free at table, *circa* 1882). And you, Garden God, ring up room service—three coffees, half a dozen soft-boiled eggs, lots of buttered toast, loads of—"

"Oh no!" interrupted Van. "Two coffees, four eggs, *et cetera*. I refuse to let the staff know that I have two girls in my bed, one (*teste* Flora) is enough for my little needs."

"*Little* needs!" snorted Lucette. "Let me go, Ada. *I* need a bath, and *he* needs you."

"Pet stays right here," cried audacious Ada, and with one graceful swoop plucked her sister's nightdress off. Involuntarily Lucette bent her head and frail spine; then she lay back on the outer half of Ada's pillow in a martyr's pudibund swoon, her locks spreading their orange blaze against the black velvet of the padded headboard.

"Uncross your arms, silly," ordered Ada and kicked off the top sheet that partly covered six legs. Simultaneously, without turning her head, she slapped furtive Van away from her rear, and with her other hand made magic passes over the small but very pretty breasts, gemmed with sweat, and along the flat palpitating belly of a seasand nymph, down to the firebird seen by Van once, fully fledged now, and as fascinating in its own way as his favorite's blue raven. Enchantress! Acrasia!

What we have now is not so much a Casanovanic situation (that double-wencher had a definitely monochromatic pencil—in keeping with the memoirs of his dingy era) as a much

earlier canvas, of the Venetian (*sensu largo*) school, reproduced (in "Forbidden Masterpieces") expertly enough to
stand the scrutiny of a bordel's *vue d'oiseau*.

Thus seen from above, as if reflected in the ciel mirror that
Eric had naively thought up in his Cyprian dreams (actually
all is shadow up there, for the blinds are still drawn, shutting
out the gray morning), we have the large island of the bed
illumined from our left (Lucette's right) by a lamp burning
with a murmuring incandescence on the west-side bedtable.
The top sheet and quilt are tumbled at the footboardless south
of the island where the newly landed eye starts on its northern
trip, up the younger Miss Veen's pried-open legs. A dewdrop
on russet moss eventually finds a stylistic response in the aquamarine tear on her flaming cheekbone. Another trip from
the port to the interior reveals the central girl's long white
left thigh; we visit souvenir stalls: Ada's red-lacquered talons,
which lead a man's reasonably recalcitrant, pardonably yielding wrist out of the dim east to the bright russet west, and
the sparkle of her diamond necklace, which, for the nonce, is
not much more valuable than the aquamarines on the other
(west) side of Novelty Novel lane. The scarred male nude on
the island's east coast is half-shaded, and, on the whole, less
interesting, though considerably more aroused than is good
for him or a certain type of tourist. The recently repapered
wall immediately west of the now louder-murmuring (*et pour
cause*) dorocene lamp is ornamented in the central girl's honor
with Peruvian "honeysuckle" being visited (not only for its
nectar, I'm afraid, but for the animalcules stuck in it) by marvelous Loddigesia Hummingbirds, while the bedtable on that
side bears a lowly box of matches, a *karavanchik* of cigarettes,
a Monaco ashtray, a copy of Voltemand's poor thriller, and a
Lurid Oncidium Orchid in an amethystine vaselet. The companion piece on Van's side supports a similar superstrong but
unlit lamp, a dorophone, a box of Wipex, a reading loupe, the
returned Ardis album, and a separatum "Soft music as cause
of brain tumors," by Dr. Anbury (young Rattner's waggish
pen-name). Sounds have colors, colors have smells. The fire
of Lucette's amber runs through the night of Ada's odor and
ardor, and stops at the threshold of Van's lavender goat. Ten

eager, evil, loving, long fingers belonging to two different young demons caress their helpless bed pet. Ada's loose black hair accidentally tickles the local curio she holds in her left fist, magnanimously demonstrating her acquisition. Unsigned and unframed.

That about summed it up (for the magical gewgaw liquefied all at once, and Lucette, snatching up her nightdress, escaped to her room). It was only the sort of shop where the jeweler's fingertips have a tender way of enhancing the preciousness of a trinket by something akin to a rubbing of hindwings on the part of a settled lycaenid or to the frottage of a conjurer's thumb dissolving a coin; but just in such a shop the anonymous picture attributed to Grillo or Obieto, caprice or purpose, *ober-* or *unterart*, is found by the ferreting artist.

"She's terribly nervous, the poor kid," remarked Ada stretching across Van toward the Wipex. "You can order that breakfast now—unless . . . Oh, what a good sight! Orchids. I've never seen a man make such a speedy recovery."

"Hundreds of whores and scores of cuties more experienced than the future Mrs. Vinelander have told me that."

"I may not be as bright as I used to be," sadly said Ada, "but I know somebody who is not simply a cat, but a polecat, and that's Cordula Tobacco alias Madame Perwitsky. I read in this morning's paper that in France ninety percent of cats die of cancer. I don't know what the situation is in Poland."

After a while he adored [*sic!* Ed.] the pancakes. No Lucette, however, turned up, and when Ada, still wearing her diamonds (in sign of at least one more *caro* Van and a Camel before her morning bath) looked into the guest room, she found the white valise and blue furs gone. A note scrawled in Arlen Eyelid Green was pinned to the pillow.

Would go mad if remained one more night shall ski at Verma with other poor woolly worms for three weeks or so miserable

Pour Elle

Van walked over to a monastic lectern that he had acquired for writing in the vertical position of vertebrate thought and wrote what follows:

Poor L.

We are sorry you left so soon. We are even sorrier to have inveigled our Esmeralda and mermaid in a naughty prank. That sort of game will never be played again with you, darling firebird. We apollo [apologize]. Remembrance, embers and membranes of beauty make artists and morons lose all self-control. Pilots of tremendous airships and even coarse, smelly coachmen are known to have been driven insane by a pair of green eyes and a copper curl. We wished to admire and amuse you, BOP (bird of paradise). We went too far. I, Van, went too far. We regret that shameful, though basically innocent scene. These are times of emotional stress and reconditioning. Destroy and forget.

> *Tenderly yours   A & V.*
> *(in alphabetic order).*

"I call this pompous, puritanical rot," said Ada upon scanning Van's letter. "Why *should* we apollo for her having experienced a delicious *spazmochka?* I love her and would never allow you to harm her. It's curious—you know, something in the tone of your note makes me really jealous for the first time in my fire [thus in the manuscript, for 'life.' Ed.] Van, Van, somewhere, some day, after a sunbath or dance, you will sleep with her, Van!"

"Unless you run out of love potions. Do you allow me to send her these lines?"

"I do, but I want to add a few words."

Her P.S. read:

The above declaration is Van's composition which I sign reluctantly. It is pompous and puritanical. I adore you, mon petit, *and would never allow him to hurt you, no matter how gently or madly. When you're sick of Queen, why not fly over to Holland or Italy?*

> *A.*

"Now let's go out for a breath of crisp air," suggested Van. "I'll order Pardus and Peg to be saddled."

"Last night two men recognized me," she said. "Two separate Californians, but they didn't dare bow—with that silk-tuxedoed *bretteur* of mine glaring around. One was Anskar, the producer, and the other, with a cocotte, Paul Whinnier, one of your father's London pals. I sort of hoped we'd go back to bed."

"We shall now go for a ride in the park," said Van firmly, and rang, first of all, for a Sunday messenger to take the letter to Lucette's hotel—or to the Verma resort, if she had already left.

"I suppose you know what you're doing?" observed Ada.

"Yes," he answered.

"You are breaking her heart," said Ada.

"Ada girl, adored girl," cried Van, "I'm a radiant void. I'm convalescing after a long and dreadful illness. You cried over my unseemly scar, but now life is going to be nothing but love and laughter, and corn in cans. I cannot brood over broken hearts, mine is too recently mended. You shall wear a blue veil, and I the false mustache that makes me look like Pierre Legrand, my fencing master."

"*Au fond*," said Ada, "first cousins have a perfect right to ride together. And even dance or skate, if they want. After all, first cousins are almost brother and sister. It's a blue, icy, breathless day."

She was soon ready, and they kissed tenderly in their hallway, between lift and stairs, before separating for a few minutes.

"Tower," she murmured in reply to his questioning glance, just as she used to do on those honeyed mornings in the past, when checking up on happiness: "And you?"

"A regular ziggurat."

9

After some exploration, they tracked down a rerun of *The Young and the Doomed* (1890) to a tiny theater that specialized in Painted Westerns (as those deserts of nonart used to be called). Thus had Mlle Larivière's *Enfants Maudits* (1887) finally degenerated! She had had two adolescents, in a French castle, poison their widowed mother who had seduced a young neighbor, the lover of one of her twins. The author had made many concessions to the freedom of the times, and the foul fancy of scriptwriters; but both she and the leading lady disavowed the final result of multiple tamperings with the plot that had now become the story of a murder in Arizona, the victim being a widower about to marry an alcoholic prostitute, whom Marina, quite sensibly, refused to impersonate. But poor little Ada had clung to her bit part, a two-minute scene in a *traktir* (roadside tavern). During the rehearsals she felt she was doing not badly as a serpentine barmaid—until the director blamed her for moving like an angular "backfish." She had not deigned to see the final product and was not overeager to have Van see it now, but he reminded her that the same director, G. A. Vronsky, had told her she was always pretty enough to serve one day as a stand-in for Lenore Colline, who at twenty had been as attractively *gauche* as she, raising and tensing forward her shoulders in the same way, when crossing a room. Having sat through a preliminary P.W. short, they finally got to *The Young and the Doomed* only to discover that the barmaid scene of the barroom sequence had been cut out—except for a perfectly distinct shadow of Ada's elbow, as Van kindly maintained.

Next day, in their little drawing room, with its black divan, yellow cushions, and draftproof bay whose new window seemed to magnify the slow steady straight-falling snowflakes (coincidentally stylized on the cover of the current issue of *The Beau & the Butterfly* which lay on the window ledge), Ada discussed her "dramatic career." The whole matter secretly nauseated Van (so that, by contrast, her Natural History passion acquired a nostalgic splendor). For him the written word existed only in its abstract purity, in its unrepeatable appeal to an equally ideal mind. It belonged solely to its creator and could not be spoken or enacted by a mime (as Ada insisted) without letting the deadly stab of another's mind destroy the artist in the very lair of his art. A written play was intrinsically superior to the best performance of it, even if directed by the author himself. Otherwise, Van agreed with Ada that the talking screen was certainly preferable to the live theater for the simple reason that with the former a director could

attain, and maintain, his own standards of perfection throughout an unlimited number of performances.

Neither of them could imagine the partings that her professional existence "on location" might necessitate, and neither could imagine their traveling together to Argus-eyed
destinations and living together in Hollywood, U.S.A., or Ivy-
dell, England, or the sugar-white Cohnritz Hotel in Cairo.
To tell the truth they did not imagine any other life at all
beyond their present *tableau vivant* in the lovely dove-blue
Manhattan sky.

At fourteen, Ada had firmly believed she would shoot to
stardom and there, with a grand bang, break into prismatic
tears of triumph. She studied at special schools. Unsuccessful
but gifted actresses, as well as Stan Slavsky (no relation, and
not a stage name), gave her private lessons of drama, despair,
hope. Her debut was a quiet little disaster; her subsequent
appearances were sincerely applauded only by close friends.

"One's first love," she told Van, "is one's first standing
ovation, and *that* is what makes great artists—so Stan and his
girl friend, who played Miss Spangle Triangle in *Flying Rings*,
assured me. Actual recognition may come only with the last
wreath."

"Bosh!" said Van.

"Precisely—he too was hooted by hack hoods in much
older Amsterdams, and look how three hundred years later
every Poppy Group pup copies him! I still think I have talent,
but then maybe I'm confusing the right *podhod* (approach)
with talent, which does not give a dry fig for rules deduced
from past art."

"Well, at least you know that," said Van; "and you've dwelt
at length upon it in one of your letters."

"I seem to have always felt, for example, that acting should
be focused not on 'characters,' not on 'types' of something
or other, not on the *fokus-pokus* of a social theme, but exclusively on the subjective and unique poetry of the author, because playwrights, as the greatest among them has shown, are
closer to poets than to novelists. In 'real' life we are creatures
of chance in an absolute void—unless we be artists ourselves,
naturally; but in a good play I feel authored, I feel passed by

the board of censors, I feel secure, with only a breathing blackness before me (instead of our Fourth-Wall Time), I feel cuddled in the embrace of puzzled Will (he thought I was you) or in that of the much more normal Anton Pavlovich, who was always passionately fond of long dark hair."

"That you also wrote to me once."

The beginning of Ada's limelife in 1891 happened to coincide with the end of her mother's twenty-five-year-long career. What is more, both appeared in Chekhov's *Four Sisters*. Ada played Irina on the modest stage of the Yakima Academy of Drama in a somewhat abridged version which, for example, kept only the references to Sister Varvara, the garrulous *originalka* ("odd female"—as Marsha calls her) but eliminated her actual scenes, so that the title of the play might have been *The Three Sisters*, as indeed it appeared in the wittier of the local notices. It was the (somewhat expanded) part of the nun that Marina acted in an elaborate film version of the play; and the picture and she received a goodly amount of undeserved praise.

"Ever since I planned to go on the stage," said Ada (we are using her notes), "I was haunted by Marina's mediocrity, *au dire de la critique*, which either ignored her or lumped her in the common grave with other 'adequate sustainers'; or, if the role had sufficient magnitude, the gamut went from 'wooden' to 'sensitive' (the highest compliment her accomplishments had ever received). And here she was, at the most delicate moment of *my* career, multiplying and sending out to friends and foes such exasperating comments as 'Durmanova is superb as the neurotic nun, having transferred an essentially static and episodical part into *et cetera, et cetera, et cetera.*'

"Of course, the cinema has no language problems," continued Ada (while Van swallowed, rather than stifled, a yawn). "Marina and three of the men did not need the excellent dubbing which the other members of the cast, who lacked the lingo, were provided with; but our wretched Yakima production could rely on only two Russians, Stan's protégé Altshuler in the role of Baron Nikolay Lvovich Tuzenbach-Krone-Altschauer, and myself as Irina, *la pauvre et noble enfant*, who is a telegraph operator in one act, a town-council employee in another, and a schoolteacher in the end. All the rest had a

macedoine of accents—English, French, Italian—by the way
what's the Italian for 'window'?"

"*Finestra, sestra,*" said Van, mimicking a mad prompter.

"Irina (sobbing): 'Where, where has it all gone? Oh, dear,
oh, dear! All is forgotten, forgotten, muddled up in my
head—I don't remember the Italian for "ceiling" or, say,
"window." ' "

"No, 'window' comes first in that speech," said Van, "because she looks around, and then up; in the natural movement
of thought."

"Yes, of course: still wrestling with 'window,' she looks up
and is confronted by the equally enigmatic 'ceiling.' In fact,
I'm sure I played it your psychological way, but what does it
matter, what did it matter?—the performance was perfectly
odious, my baron kept fluffing every other line—but Marina,
Marina was *marvelous* in her world of shadows! 'Ten years
and one have gone by-abye since I left Moscow' "—(Ada,
now playing Varvara, copied the nun's "singsongy devotional
tone" (*pevuchiy ton bogomolki*, as indicated by Chehov and as
rendered so irritatingly well by Marina). " 'Nowadays, Old
Basmannaya Street, where you (turning to Irina) were born a
score of yearkins (*godkov*) ago, is Busman Road, lined on both
sides with workshops and garages (Irina tries to control her
tears). Why, then, should you want to go back, Arinushka?
(Irina sobs in reply).' Naturally, as would every fine player,
mother improvised quite a bit, bless her soul. And moreover
her voice—in young tuneful Russian!—is substituted for Lenore's corny brogue."

Van had seen the picture and had liked it. An Irish girl, the
infinitely graceful and melancholy Lenore Colline—

> Oh! qui me rendra ma colline
> Et le grand chêne and my colleen!

—harrowingly resembled Ada Ardis as photographed with her
mother in *Belladonna*, a movie magazine which Greg Erminin
had sent him, thinking it would delight him to see aunt and
cousin, together, on a California patio just before the film was
released. Varvara, the late General Sergey Prozorov's eldest
daughter, comes in Act One from her remote nunnery, Tsitsikar Convent, to Perm (also called Permwail), in the back-

woods of Akimsk Bay, North Canady, to have tea with Olga,
Marsha, and Irina on the latter's name day. Much to the nun's
dismay, her three sisters dream only of one thing—leaving
cool, damp, mosquito-infested but otherwise nice and peaceful "Permanent," as Irina mockingly dubs it, for high life in
remote and sinful Moscow, Id., the former capital of Estotiland. In the first edition of his play, which never quite manages
to heave the soft sigh of a masterpiece, Tchechoff (as he
spelled his name when living that year at the execrable Pension
Russe, 9, rue Gounod, Nice) crammed into the two pages of
a ludicrous expository scene all the information he wished to
get rid of, great lumps of recollections and calendar dates—
an impossible burden to place on the fragile shoulders of three
unhappy Estotiwomen. Later he redistributed that information through a considerably longer scene in which the arrival
of the *monashka* Varvara provides all the speeches needed to
satisfy the restless curiosity of the audience. This was a neat
stroke of stagecraft, but unfortunately (as so often occurs in
the case of characters brought in for disingenuous purposes)
the nun stayed on, and not until the third, penultimate, act
was the author able to bundle her off, back to her convent.

"I assume," said Van (knowing his girl), "that you did not
want any tips from Marina for your Irina?"

"It would have only resulted in a row. I always resented
her suggestions because they were made in a sarcastic, insult-
ing manner. I've heard mother birds going into neurotic paroxysms of fury and mockery when their poor little tailless ones
(*bezkhvostïe bednyachki*) were slow in learning to fly. I've had
enough of that. By the way, here's the program of *my* flop."

Van glanced through the list of players and D.P.'s and noticed two amusing details: the role of Fedotik, an artillery officer (whose comedy organ consists of a constantly clicking
camera), had been assigned to a "Kim (short for Yakim) Es-
kimossoff" and somebody called "John Starling" had been
cast as Skvortsov (a *sekundant* in the rather amateurish duel
of the last act) whose name comes from *skvorets*, starling.
When he communicated the latter observation to Ada, she
blushed as was her Old World wont.

"Yes," she said, "he was quite a lovely lad and I sort of
flirted with him, but the strain and the split were too much

for him—he had been, since pubescence, the *puerulus* of a fat ballet master, Dangleleaf, and he finally committed suicide. You see ('the blush now replaced by a *matovaya* pallor') I'm not hiding one stain of what rhymes with Perm."

"I see. And Yakim—"

"Oh, he was nothing."

"No, I mean, Yakim, at least, did not, as *his* rhymesake did, take a picture of your brother embracing his girl. Played by Dawn de Laire."

"I'm not sure. I seem to recall that our director did not mind some comic relief."

"Dawn *en robe rose et verte*, at the end of Act One."

"I think there was a click in the wings and some healthy mirth in the house. All poor Starling had to do in the play was to hollo off stage from a rowboat on the Kama River to give the signal for my fiancé to come to the dueling ground."

But let us shift to the didactic metaphorism of Chehov's friend, Count Tolstoy.

We all know those old wardrobes in old hotels in the Old World subalpine zone. At first one opens them with the utmost care, very slowly, in the vain hope of hushing the excruciating creak, the growing groan that the door emits midway. Before long one discovers, however, that if it is opened or closed with celerity, in one resolute sweep, the hellish hinge is taken by surprise, and triumphant silence achieved. Van and Ada, for all the exquisite and powerful bliss that engulfed and repleted them (and we do not mean here the rose sore of Eros alone), knew that certain memories had to be left closed, lest they wrench every nerve of the soul with their monstrous moan. But if the operation is performed swiftly, if indelible evils are mentioned between two quick quips, there is a chance that the anesthetic of life itself may allay unforgettable agony in the process of swinging its door.

Now and then she poked fun at his sexual peccadilloes, though generally she tended to ignore them as if demanding, by tacit implication, a similar kind of leniency in regard to her frailty. He was more inquisitive than she but hardly managed to learn more from her lips than he had from her letters. To her past admirers Ada attributed all the features and faults we have already been informed of, incompetence of performance, inanity and nonentity, and to her own self nothing beyond easy feminine compassion and such considerations of hygiene and sanity as hurt Van more than would a defiant avowal of passionate betrayal. Ada had made up her mind to transcend his and her sensual sins: the adjective being a near synonym of "senseless" and "soulless"; therefore not represented in the ineffable hereafter that both our young people mutely and shyly believed in. Van endeavored to follow the same line of logic but could not forget the shame and the agony even while reaching heights of happiness he had not known at his brightest hour before his darkest one in the past.

10

They took a great many precautions—all absolutely useless, for nothing can change the end (written and filed away) of the present chapter. Only Lucette and the agency that forwarded letters to him and to Ada knew Van's address. Through an amiable lady in waiting at Demon's bank, Van made sure that his father would not turn up in Manhattan before March 30. They never came out or went in together, arranging a meeting place at the Library or in an emporium whence to start the day's excursions—and it so happened that the only time they broke that rule (she having got stuck in the lift for a few panicky moments and he having blithely trotted downstairs from their common summit), they issued right into the visual field of old Mrs. Arfour who happened to be passing by their front door with her tiny tan-and-gray long-silked Yorkshire terrier. The simultaneous association was immediate and complete: she had known both families for years and was now interested to learn from chattering (rather than chatting) Ada that Van had happened to be in town just when she, Ada, had happened to return from the West; that Marina was fine; that Demon was in Mexico or Oxmice; and that Lenore Colline had a similar adorable pet with a similar adorable parting along the middle of the back. That same day (February 3, 1893) Van rebribed the already gorged janitor to have him answer all questions which any visitor, and especially a dentist's widow with a caterpillar dog, might ask about any Veens, with a brief assertion of utter ignorance. The only personage they had not reckoned with was the old scoundrel usually portrayed as a skeleton or an angel.

Van's father had just left one Santiago to view the results of an earthquake in another, when Ladore Hospital cabled that Dan was dying. He set off at once for Manhattan, eyes blazing, wings whistling. He had not many interests in life.

At the airport of the moonlit white town we call Tent, and Tobakov's sailors, who built it, called Palatka, in northern Florida, where owing to engine trouble he had to change planes, Demon made a long-distance call and received a full account of Dan's death from the inordinately circumstantial Dr. Nikulin (grandson of the great rodentiologist Kunikulinov—we can't get rid of the lettuce). Daniel Veen's life had been a mixture of the ready-made and the grotesque; but his death had shown an artistic streak because of its reflecting (as his cousin, not his doctor, instantly perceived) the man's latterly conceived passion for the paintings, and faked paintings, associated with the name of Hieronymus Bosch.

Next day, February 5, around nine A.M., Manhattan (winter) time, on the way to Dan's lawyer, Demon noted—just as he was about to cross Alexis Avenue—an ancient but insignificant acquaintance, Mrs. Arfour, advancing toward him, with her toy terrier, along his side of the street. Unhesitatingly, Demon stepped off the curb, and having no hat to raise (hats were not worn with raincloaks and besides he had just taken a very exotic and potent pill to face the day's ordeal on top of a sleepless journey), contented himself—quite properly—with a wave of his slim umbrella; recalled with a paint dab of delight one of the gargle girls of her late husband; and smoothly passed in front of a slow-clopping horse-drawn vegetable cart, well out of the way of Mrs. R4. But precisely in regard to such a contingency, Fate had prepared an alternate continuation. As Demon rushed (or, in terms of the pill, sauntered) by the Monaco, where he had often lunched, it occurred to him that his son (whom he had been unable to "contact") might still be living with dull little Cordula de Prey in the penthouse apartment of that fine building. He had never been up there—or had he? For a business consultation with Van? On a sun-hazed terrace? And a clouded drink? (He had, that's right, but Cordula was not dull and had not been present.)

With the simple and, combinationally speaking, neat, thought that, after all, there was but one sky (white, with minute, multicolored optical sparks), Demon hastened to enter the lobby and catch the lift which a ginger-haired waiter had just entered, with breakfast for two on a wiggle-wheel table and the Manhattan *Times* among the shining, ever so slightly scratched, silver cupolas. Was his son still living up there, automatically asked Demon, placing a piece of nobler metal among the domes. *Si*, conceded the grinning imbecile, he had lived there with his lady all winter.

"Then we are fellow travelers," said Demon inhaling not without gourmand anticipation the smell of Monaco's coffee, exaggerated by the shadows of tropical weeds waving in the breeze of his brain.

On that memorable morning, Van, after ordering breakfast, had climbed out of his bath and donned a strawberry-red terry-cloth robe when he thought he heard Valerio's voice from the adjacent parlor. Thither he padded, humming tunelessly, looking forward to another day of increasing happiness (with yet another uncomfortable little edge smoothed away, another raw kink in the past so refashioned as to fit into the new pattern of radiance).

Demon, clothed entirely in black, black-spatted, black-scarved, his monocle on a broader black ribbon than usual, was sitting at the breakfast table, a cup of coffee in one hand, and a conveniently folded financial section of the *Times* in the other.

He gave a slight start and put down his cup rather jerkily on noting the coincidence of color with a persistent detail in an illumined lower left-hand corner of a certain picture reproduced in the copiously illustrated catalogue of his immediate mind.

All Van could think of saying was "I am not alone" (*je ne suis pas seul*), but Demon was brimming too richly with the bad news he had brought to heed the hint of the fool who should have simply walked on into the next room and come back one moment later (locking the door behind him—

locking out years and years of lost life), instead of which he remained standing near his father's chair.

According to Bess (which is "fiend" in Russian), Dan's buxom but otherwise disgusting nurse, whom he preferred to all others and had taken to Ardis because she managed to extract orally a few last drops of "play-zero" (as the old whore called it) out of his poor body, he had been complaining for some time, even before Ada's sudden departure, that a devil combining the characteristics of a frog and a rodent desired to straddle him and ride him to the torture house of eternity. To Dr. Nikulin Dan described his rider as black, pale-bellied, with a black dorsal buckler shining like a dung beetle's back and with a knife in his raised forelimb. On a very cold morning in late January Dan had somehow escaped, through a basement maze and a toolroom, into the brown shrubbery of Ardis; he was naked except for a red bath towel which trailed from his rump like a kind of caparison, and, despite the rough going, had crawled on all fours, like a crippled steed under an invisible rider, deep into the wooded landscape. On the other hand, had he attempted to warn her she might have made her big Ada yawn and uttered something irrevocably cozy at the moment he opened the thick protective door.

"I beg you, sir," said Van, "go down, and I'll join you in the bar as soon as I'm dressed. I'm in a delicate situation."

"Come, come," retorted Demon, dropping and replacing his monocle. "Cordula won't mind."

"It's another, much more impressionable girl"—(yet another awful fumble!). "Damn Cordula! Cordula is now Mrs. Tobak."

"Oh, of course!" cried Demon. "How stupid of me! I remember Ada's fiancé telling me—he and young Tobak worked for a while in the same Phoenix bank. Of *course*. Splendid broad-shouldered, blue-eyed, blond chap. Backbay Tobakovich!"

"I don't care," said clenched Van, "if he looks like a crippled, crucified, albino toad. Please, Dad, I really must—"

"Funny your saying that. I've dropped in only to tell you poor cousin Dan has died an odd Boschean death. He thought a fantastic rodent sort of rode him out of the house. They found him too late, he expired in Nikulin's clinic, raving about that detail of the picture. I'm having the deuce of a time rounding up the family. The picture is now preserved in the Vienna Academy of Art."

"Father, I'm sorry—but I'm trying to tell you—"

"If I could write," mused Demon, "I would describe, in too many words no doubt, how passionately, how incandescently, how incestuously—*c'est le mot*—art and science meet in an insect, in a thrush, in a thistle of that ducal bosquet. Ada is marrying an outdoor man, but her mind is a closed museum, and she, and dear Lucette, once drew my attention, by a creepy coincidence, to certain details of that other triptych, that tremendous garden of tongue-in-cheek delights, circa 1500, and, namely, to the butterflies in it—a Meadow Brown, female, in the center of the right panel, and a Tortoiseshell in the middle panel, placed there as if settled on a flower—mark the 'as if,' for here we have an example of exact knowledge on the part of those two admirable little girls, because they say that actually the *wrong* side of the bug is shown, it should have been the underside, if seen, as it is, in profile, but Bosch evidently found a wing or two in the corner cobweb of his casement and showed the prettier upper surface in depicting his incorrectly folded insect. I mean I don't give a hoot for the esoteric meaning, for the myth behind the moth, for the masterpiece-baiter who makes Bosch express some bosh of his time, I'm allergic to allegory and am quite sure he was just enjoying himself by crossbreeding casual fancies just for the fun of the contour and color, and what we have to study, as I was telling your cousins, is the joy of the eye, the feel and the taste of the woman-sized strawberry that you embrace *with* him, or the exquisite surprise of an unusual orifice—but you are not following me, you want me to go, so that you may interrupt her beauty sleep, lucky beast! *A propos*, I have not been able to alert Lucette, who is somewhere in Italy, but I've managed to trace Marina to Tsitsikar—flirting there with the Bishop of Belokonsk—she will arrive in the late afternoon, wearing, no doubt, *pleureuses*, very becoming, and we shall then travel *à trois* to Ladore, because I don't think—"

Was he perhaps under the influence of some bright Chilean

drug? That torrent was simply unstoppable, a crazy spectrum, a talking palette—

"—no really, I don't think we should bother Ada in her Agavia. He is—I mean, Vinelander is—the scion, s,c,i,o,n, of one of those great Varangians who had conquered the Copper Tartars or Red Mongols—or whoever they were—who had conquered some earlier Bronze Riders—before *we* introduced our Russian roulette and Irish loo at a lucky moment in the history of Western casinos."

"I am extremely, I am hideously sorry," said Van, "what with Uncle Dan's death and your state of excitement, sir, but my girl friend's coffee is getting cold, and I can't very well stumble into our bedroom with all that infernal paraphernalia."

"I'm leaving, I'm leaving. After all we haven't seen each other—since when, August? At any rate, I hope she's prettier than the Cordula you had here before, volatile boy!"

Volatina, perhaps? Or dragonara? He definitely smelled of ether. Please, please, please, go.

"My gloves! Cloak! Thank you. Can I use your W.C.? No? All right. I'll find one elsewhere. Come over as soon as you can, and we'll meet Marina at the airport around four and then whizz to the wake, and—"

And here Ada entered. Not naked—oh no; in a pink peignoir so as not to shock Valerio—comfortably combing her hair, sweet and sleepy. She made the mistake of crying out "*Bozhe moy!*" and darting back into the dusk of the bedroom. All was lost in that one chink of a second.

"Or better—come at once, both of you, because I'll cancel my appointment and go home right now." He spoke, or thought he spoke, with the self-control and the clarity of enunciation which so frightened and mesmerized blunderers, blusterers, a voluble broker, a guilty schoolboy. Especially so now—when everything had gone to the hell curs, *k chertyam sobach'im*, of Jeroen Anthniszoon van Äken and the *molti aspetti affascinanti* of his *enigmatica arte*, as Dan explained with a last sigh to Dr. Nikulin and to nurse Bellabestia ("Bess") to whom he bequeathed a trunkful of museum catalogues and his second-best catheter.

II

The dragon drug had worn off: its aftereffects are not pleasant, combining as they do physical fatigue with a certain starkness of thought as if all color were drained from the mind. Now clad in a gray dressing gown, Demon lay on a gray couch in his third-floor study. His son stood at the window with his back to the silence. In a damask-padded room on the second floor, immediately below the study, waited Ada, who had arrived with Van a couple of minutes ago. In the skyscraper across the lane a window was open exactly opposite the study and an aproned man stood there setting up an easel and cocking his head in search of the right angle.

The first thing Demon said was:

"I insist that you face me when I'm speaking to you."

Van realized that the fateful conversation must have already started in his father's brain, for the admonishment had the ring of a self-interruption, and with a slight bow he took a seat.

"However, before I advise you of those two facts, I would like to know how long this—how long this has been . . ." ('going on,' one presumes, or something equally banal, but then all ends are banal—hangings, the Nuremberg Old Maid's iron sting, shooting oneself, last words in the brand-new Ladore hospital, mistaking a drop of thirty thousand feet for the airplane's washroom, being poisoned by one's wife, expecting a bit of Crimean hospitality, congratulating Mr. and Mrs. Vinelander—)

"It will be nine years soon," replied Van. "I seduced her in the summer of eighteen eighty-four. Except for a single occasion, we did not make love again until the summer of eighteen eighty-eight. After a long separation we spent one winter together. All in all, I suppose I have had her about a thousand times. She is my whole life."

A longish pause not unlike a fellow actor's dry-up, came in response to his well-rehearsed speech.

Finally, Demon: "The second fact may horrify you even more than the first. I know it caused me much deeper worry—moral of course, not monetary—than Ada's case—of which eventually her mother informed Cousin Dan, so that, in a sense—"

Pause, with an underground trickle.

"Some other time I'll tell you about the Black Miller; not now; too trivial."

(Dr. Lapiner's wife, born Countess Alp, not only left him, in 1871, to live with Norbert von Miller, amateur poet, Russian translator at the Italian Consulate in Geneva, and professional smuggler of neonegrine—found only in the Valais—but had imparted to her lover the melodramatic details of the subterfuge which the kindhearted physician had considered would prove a boon to one lady and a blessing to the other. Versatile Norbert spoke English with an extravagant accent, hugely admired wealthy people and, when name-dropping, always qualified such a person as "enawmously rich" with awed amorous gusto, throwing himself back in his chair and spreading tensely curved arms to enfold an invisible fortune. He had a round head as bare as a knee, a corpse's button nose, and very white, very limp, very damp hands adorned with rutilant gems. His mistress soon left him. Dr. Lapiner died in 1872. About the same time, the Baron married an innkeeper's innocent daughter and began to blackmail Demon Veen; this went on for almost twenty years, when aging Miller was shot dead by an Italian policeman on a little-known border trail, which had seemed to get steeper and muddier every year. Out of sheer kindness, or habit, Demon bade his lawyer continue to send Miller's widow—who mistook it naively for insurance money—the trimestrial sum which had been swelling with each pregnancy of the robust Swissess. Demon used to say that he would publish one day "Black Miller's" quatrains which adorned his letters with the jingle of verselets on calendarial leaves:

> My spouse is thicker, I am leaner.
> Again it comes, a new bambino.
> You must be good like I am good.
> Her stove is big and wants more wood.

We may add, to complete this useful parenthesis, that in early February, 1893, not long after the poet's death, two other less successful blackmailers were waiting in the wings: Kim who would have bothered Ada again had he not been carried out of his cottage with one eye hanging on a red thread and the other drowned in its blood; and the son of one of the former employees of the famous clandestine-message agency after it had been closed by the U.S. Government in 1928, when the past had ceased to matter, and nothing but the straw of a prison cell could reward the optimism of second-generation rogues.)

The most protracted of the several pauses having run its dark course, Demon's voice emerged to say, with a vigor that it had lacked before:

"Van, you receive the news I impart with incomprehensible calmness. I do not recall any instance, in factual or fictional life, of a father's having to tell his son that particular kind of thing in these particular circumstances. But you play with a pencil and seem as unruffled as if we were discussing your gaming debts or the demands of a wench knocked up in a ditch."

Tell him about the herbarium in the attic? About the indiscretions of (anonymous) servants? About a forged wedding date? About everything that two bright children had so gaily gleaned? I will. He did.

"She was twelve," Van added, "and I was a male primatal of fourteen and a half, and we just did not care. And it's too late to care now."

"Too late?" shouted his father, sitting up on his couch.

"Please, Dad, do not lose your temper," said Van. "Nature, as I informed you once, has been kind to me. We can afford to be careless in every sense of the word."

"I'm not concerned with semantics—or semination. One thing, and only one, matters. It is *not* too late to stop that ignoble affair—"

"No shouting and no philistine epithets," interrupted Van.

"All right," said Demon. "I take back the adjective, and I ask you instead: Is it too late to prevent your affair with your sister from wrecking her life?"

Van knew this was coming. He knew, he said, this was coming. "Ignoble" had been taken care of; would his accuser define "wrecking"?

The conversation now took a neutral turn that was far more terrible than its introductory admission of faults for which our young lovers had long pardoned their parents. How did Van imagine his sister's pursuing a scenic career? Would he admit it would be wrecked if they persisted in their relationship? Did he envisage a life of concealment in luxurious exile? Was he ready to deprive her of normal interests and a normal marriage? Children? Normal amusements?

"Don't forget 'normal adultery,' " remarked Van.

"How much better that would be!" said grim Demon, sitting on the edge of the couch with both elbows propped on his knees, and nursing his head in his hands: "The awfulness of the situation is an abyss that grows deeper the more I think of it. You force me to bring up the tritest terms such as 'family,' 'honor,' 'set,' 'law.' . . . All right, I have bribed many officials in my wild life but neither you nor I can bribe a whole culture, a whole country. And the emotional impact of learning that for almost ten years you and that charming child have been deceiving their parents—"

Here Van expected his father to take the "it-would-kill-your-mother" line, but Demon was wise enough to keep clear of it. Nothing could "kill" Marina. If any rumors of incest did come her way, concern with her "inner peace" would help her to ignore them—or at least romanticize them out of reality's reach. Both men knew all that. Her image appeared for a moment and accomplished a facile fade-out.

Demon spoke on: "I cannot disinherit you: Aqua left you enough 'ridge' and real estate to annul the conventional punishment. And I cannot denounce you to the authorities without involving my daughter, whom I mean to protect at all cost. But I can do the next proper thing, I can curse you, I can make this our last, our last—"

Van, whose finger had been gliding endlessly to and fro along the mute but soothingly smooth edge of the mahogany desk, now heard with horror the sob that shook Demon's entire frame, and then saw a deluge of tears flowing down those hollow tanned cheeks. In an amateur parody, at Van's birthday party fifteen years ago, his father had made himself up as Boris Godunov and shed strange, frightening, jet-black tears before rolling down the steps of a burlesque throne in death's total surrender to gravity. Did those dark streaks, in the present show, come from his blackening his orbits, eyelashes, eyelids, eyebrows? The funest gamester . . . the pale fatal girl, in another well-known melodrama. . . . In this one. Van gave him a clean handkerchief to replace the soiled rag. His own marble calm did not surprise Van. The ridicule of a good cry with Father adequately clogged the usual ducts of emotion.

Demon regained his composure (if not his young looks) and said:

"I believe in you and your common sense. You must not allow an old debaucher to disown an only son. If you love her, you wish her to be happy, and she will not be as happy as she could be once you gave her up. You may go. Tell her to come here on your way down."

Down. My first is a vehicle that twists dead daisies around its spokes; my second is Oldmanhattan slang for "money"; and my whole makes a hole.

As he traversed the second-floor landing, he saw, through the archway of two rooms, Ada in her black dress standing, with her back to him, at the oval window in the boudoir. He told a footman to convey her father's message to her and passed almost at a run through the familiar echoes of the stone-flagged vestibule.

My second is also the meeting place of two steep slopes. Right-hand lower drawer of my practically unused new desk—which is quite as big as Dad's, with Sig's compliments.

He judged it would take him as much time to find a taxi at this hour of the day as to walk, with his ordinary swift swing, the ten blocks to Alex Avenue. He was coatless, tieless, hatless; a strong sharp wind dimmed his sight with salty frost and played Medusaean havoc with his black locks. Upon letting himself in for the last time into his idiotically cheerful apartment, he forthwith sat down at that really magnificent desk and wrote the following note:

Do what he tells you. His logic sounds preposterous, prepsupposing [*sic*] a vague kind of "Victorian" era, as they have on Terra according to 'my mad' [?], but in a paroxysm of [illegible] I suddenly realized he was right.

Yes, right, here and there, not neither here, nor there, as most things are. You see, girl, how it is and must be. In the last window we shared we both saw a man painting [us?] but your second-floor level of vision probably prevented your seeing that he wore what looked like a butcher's apron, badly smeared. Good-bye, girl.

Van sealed the letter, found his Thunderbolt pistol in the place he had visualized, introduced one cartridge into the magazine, and translated it into its chamber. Then, standing before a closet mirror, he put the automatic to his head, at the point of the pterion, and pressed the comfortably concaved trigger. Nothing happened—or perhaps everything happened, and his destiny simply forked at that instant, as it probably does sometimes at night, especially in a strange bed, at stages of great happiness or great desolation, when we happen to die in our sleep, but continue our normal existence, with no perceptible break in the faked serialization, on the following, neatly prepared morning, with a spurious past discreetly but firmly attached behind. Anyway, what he held in his right hand was no longer a pistol but a pocket comb which he passed through his hair at the temples. It was to gray by the time that Ada, then in her thirties, said, when they spoke of their voluntary separation:

"I would have killed myself too, had I found Rose wailing over your corpse. *'Secondes pensées sont les bonnes,'* as your other, white, *bonne* used to say in her pretty patois. As to the apron, you are quite right. And what *you* did not make out was that the artist had about finished a large picture of your meek little palazzo standing between its two giant guards. Perhaps for the cover of a magazine, which rejected that picture. But, you know, there's one thing I regret," she added: "Your use of an alpenstock to release a brute's fury—not yours, not my Van's. I should never have told you about the Ladore policeman. You should never have taken him into your confidence, never connived with him to burn those files —and most of Kalugano's pine forest. *Eto unizitel'no* (it is humiliating)."

"Amends have been made," replied fat Van with a fat man's chuckle. "I'm keeping Kim safe and snug in a nice Home for

Disabled Professional People, where he gets from me loads of nicely brailled books on new processes in chromophotography."

There are other possible forkings and continuations that occur to the dream-mind, but these will do.

Part Three

I

He traveled, he studied, he taught.

He contemplated the pyramids of Ladorah (visited mainly because of its name) under a full moon that silvered the sands inlaid with pointed black shadows. He went shooting with the British Governor of Armenia, and his niece, on Lake Van. From a hotel balcony in Sidra his attention was drawn by the manager to the wake of an orange sunset that turned the ripples of a lavender sea into goldfish scales and was well worth the price of enduring the quaintness of the small striped rooms he shared with his secretary, young Lady Scramble. On another terrace, overlooking another fabled bay, Eberthella Brown, the local Shah's pet dancer (a naive little thing who thought "baptism of desire" meant something sexual), spilled her morning coffee upon noticing a six-inch-long caterpillar, with fox-furred segments, *qui rampait*, was tramping, along the balustrade and curled up in a swoon when picked up by Van—who for hours, after removing the beautiful animal to a bush, kept gloomily plucking itchy bright hairs out of his fingertips with the girl's tweezers.

He learned to appreciate the singular little thrill of following dark byways in strange towns, knowing well that he would discover nothing, save filth, and ennui, and discarded "merrycans" with "Billy" labels, and the jungle jingles of exported jazz coming from syphilitic cafés. He often felt that the famed cities, the museums, the ancient torture house and the suspended garden, were but places on the map of his own madness.

He liked composing his works (*Illegible Signatures*, 1895; *Clairvoyeurism*, 1903; *Furnished Space*, 1913; *The Texture of Time*, begun 1922), in mountain refuges, and in the drawing rooms of great expresses, and on the sundecks of white ships, and on the stone tables of Latin public parks. He would uncurl out of an indefinitely lengthy trance, and note with won-

der that the ship was going the other way or that the order
of his left-hand fingers was reversed, now beginning, clockwise, with his thumb as on his right hand, or that the marble
Mercury that had been looking over his shoulder had been
transformed into an attentive arborvitae. He would realize all
at once that three, seven, thirteen years, in one cycle of separation, and then four, eight, sixteen, in yet another, had
elapsed since he had last embraced, held, bewept Ada.

Numbers and rows and series—the nightmare and maledic-
tion harrowing pure thought and pure time—seemed bent on
mechanizing his mind. Three elements, fire, water, and air,
destroyed, in that sequence, Marina, Lucette, and Demon.
Terra waited.

For seven years, after she had dismissed her life with her
husband, a successfully achieved corpse, as irrelevant, and retired to her still dazzling, still magically well-staffed Côte
d'Azur villa (the one Demon had once given her), Van's
mother had been suffering from various "obscure" illnesses,
which everybody thought she made up, or talentedly simulated, and which she contended could be, and partly were,
cured by willpower. Van visited her less often than dutiful
Lucette, whom he glimpsed there on two or three occasions;
and once, in 1899, he saw, as he entered the arbutus-and-laurel
garden of Villa Armina, a bearded old priest of the Greek
persuasion, clad in neutral black, leaving on a motor bicycle
for his Nice parish near the tennis courts. Marina spoke to
Van about religion, and Terra, and the Theater, but never
about Ada, and just as he did not suspect she knew everything
about the horror and ardor of Ardis, none suspected *what* pain
in her bleeding bowels she was trying to allay by incantations,
and "self-focusing" or its opposite device, "self-dissolving."
She confessed with an enigmatic and rather smug smile that
much as she liked the rhythmic blue puffs of incense, and the
dyakon's rich growl on the ambon, and the oily-brown ikon
coped in protective filigree to receive the worshipper's kiss,
her soul remained irrevocably consecrated, *naperekor* (in spite
of) Dasha Vinelander, to the ultimate wisdom of Hinduism.

Early in 1900, a few days before he saw Marina, for the last
time, at the clinic in Nice (where he learned for the *first* time
the name of her illness), Van had a "verbal" nightmare,

caused, maybe, by the musky smell in the Miramas (Bouches Rouges-du-Rhône) Villa Venus. Two formless fat transparent creatures were engaged in some discussion, one repeating "I can't!" (meaning "can't die"—a difficult procedure to carry out voluntarily, without the help of the dagger, the ball, or the bowl), and the other affirming "You can, sir!" She died a fortnight later, and her body was burnt, according to her instructions.

Van, a lucid soul, considered himself less brave morally than physically. He was always (meaning well into the nineteen-sixties) to recollect with reluctance, as if wishing to suppress in his mind a petty, timorous, and stupid deed (for, actually, who knows, the later antlers might have been set right then, with green lamps greening green growths before the hotel where the Vinelanders stayed), his reacting from Kingston to Lucette's cable from Nice ("Mother died this morning the funeral dash cremation dash is to be held after tomorrow at sundown") with the request to advise him ("please advise") who else would be there, and upon getting her prompt reply that Demon had already arrived with Andrey and Ada, his cabling back: "*Désolé de ne pouvoir être avec vous.*"

He had roamed in Kingston's Cascadilla Park, in the active sweet-swarming spring dusk, so much more seraphic than that flurry of cables. The last time he had seen mummy-wizened Marina and told her he must return to America (though actually there was no hurry—only the smell in her hospital room that no breeze could dislodge), she had asked, with her new, tender, myopic, because inward, expression: "Can't you wait till I'm gone?"; and his reply had been "I'll be back on the twenty-fifth. I have to deliver an address on the Psychology of Suicide"; and she had said, stressing, now that everything was *tripitaka* (safely packed), the exact kinship: "Do tell them about your silly aunt Aqua," whereupon he had nodded, with a smirk, instead of answering: "Yes, mother." Hunched up in a last band of low sun, on the bench where he had recently fondled and fouled a favorite, lanky, awkward, black girl student, Van tortured himself with thoughts of insufficient filial affection—a long story of unconcern, amused scorn, physical repulsion, and habitual dismissal. He looked around, making wild amends, willing her spirit to give him an unequivocal,

and indeed all-deciding, sign of continued being behind the
veil of time, beyond the flesh of space. But no response came,
not a petal fell on his bench, not a gnat touched his hand. He
wondered what really kept him alive on terrible Antiterra, with
Terra a myth and all art a game, when nothing mattered any
more since the day he slapped Valerio's warm bristly cheek;
and whence, from what deep well of hope, did he still scoop
up a shivering star, when everything had an edge of agony
and despair, when another man was in every bedroom with
Ada.

2

On a bleak morning between the spring and summer of 1901,
in Paris, as Van, black-hatted, one hand playing with the warm
loose change in his topcoat pocket and the other, fawn-
gloved, upswinging a furled English umbrella, strode past a
particularly unattractive sidewalk café among the many lining
the Avenue Guillaume Pitt, a chubby bald man in a rumpled
brown suit with a watch-chained waistcoat stood up and
hailed him.

Van considered for a moment those red round cheeks, that
black goatee.

"*Ne uznayosh'* (You don't recognize me)?"

"Greg! Grigoriy Akimovich!" cried Van tearing off his
glove.

"I grew a regular *vollbart* last summer. You'd never have
known me then. Beer? Wonder what you do to look so boyish,
Van."

"Diet of champagne, not beer," said Professor Veen, putting on his spectacles and signaling to a waiter with the crook
of his 'umber.' "Hardly stops one adding weight, but keeps
the scrotum crisp."

"I'm also very fat, yes?"

"What about Grace, I can't imagine *her* getting fat?"

"Once twins, always twins. My wife is pretty portly, too."

"*Tak ti zhenat* (so you are married)? Didn't know it. How
long?"

"About two years."

"To whom?"

"Maude Sween."

"The daughter of the poet?"

"No, no, her mother is a Brougham."

Might have replied "Ada Veen," had Mr. Vinelander not been a quicker suitor. I think I met a Broom somewhere. Drop the subject. Probably a dreary union: hefty, high-handed wife, he more of a bore than ever.

"I last saw you thirteen years ago, riding a black pony—no, a black Silentium. *Bozhe moy!*"

"Yes—*Bozhe moy*, you can well say that. Those lovely, lovely agonies in lovely Ardis! Oh, I was *absolyutno bezumno* (madly) in love with your cousin!"

"You mean Miss Veen? I did not know it. How long—"

"Neither did she. I was terribly—"

"How long are you staying—"

"—terribly shy, because, of course, I realized that I could not compete with her numerous boy friends."

Numerous? Two? Three? Is it possible he never heard about the main one? All the rose hedges knew, all the maids knew, in all three manors. The noble reticence of our bedmakers.

"How long will you be staying in Lute? No, Greg, *I* ordered it. You pay for the next bottle. Tell me—"

"So odd to recall! It was frenzy, it was fantasy, it was reality in the *x* degree. I'd have consented to be beheaded by a Tartar, I declare, if in exchange I could have kissed her instep. You were her cousin, almost a brother, you can't understand that obsession. Ah, those picnics! And Percy de Prey who boasted to me about her, and drove me crazy with envy and pity, and Dr. Krolik, who, they said, also loved her, and Phil Rack, a composer of genius—dead, dead, all dead!"

"I really know very little about music but it was a great pleasure to make your chum howl. I have an appointment in a few minutes, alas. *Za tvoyo zdorovie, Grigoriy Akimovich.*"

"Arkadievich," said Greg, who had let it pass once but now mechanically corrected Van.

"*Ach* yes! Stupid slip of the slovenly tongue. How *is* Arkadiy Grigorievich?"

"He died. He died just before your aunt. I thought the

papers paid a very handsome tribute to her talent. And where is Adelaida Danilovna? Did she marry Christopher Vinelander or his brother?"

"In California or Arizona. Andrey's the name, I gather. Perhaps I'm mistaken. In fact, I never knew my cousin very well: I visited Ardis only twice, after all, for a few weeks each time, years ago."

"Somebody told me she's a movie actress."

"I've no idea, I've never seen her on the screen."

"Oh, that would be terrible, I declare—to switch on the dorotelly, and suddenly see her. Like a drowning man seeing his whole past, and the trees, and the flowers, and the wreathed dachshund. She must have been terribly affected by her mother's terrible death."

Likes the word "terrible," I declare. A terrible suit of clothes, a terrible tumor. Why must I stand it? Revolting—and yet fascinating in a weird way: my babbling shadow, my burlesque double.

Van was about to leave when a smartly uniformed chauffeur came up to inform "my lord" that his lady was parked at the corner of rue Saïgon and was summoning him to appear.

"Aha," said Van. "I see you are using your British title. Your father preferred to pass for a Chekhovian colonel."

"Maude is Anglo-Scottish and, well, likes it that way. Thinks a title gets one better service abroad. By the way, somebody told me—yes, Tobak!—that Lucette is at the Alphonse Four. I haven't asked you about your father? He's in good health?" (Van bowed.) "And how is the *guvernantka belletristka*?"

"Her last novel is called *L'ami Luc*. She just got the Lebon Academy Prize for her copious rubbish."

They parted laughing.

A moment later, as happens so often in farces and foreign cities, Van ran into another friend. With a surge of delight he saw Cordula in a tight scarlet skirt bending with baby words of comfort over two unhappy poodlets attached to the waiting-post of a sausage shop. Van stroked her with his finger-tips, and as she straightened up indignantly and turned around (indignation instantly replaced by gay recognition), he quoted

the stale but appropriate lines he had known since the days
his schoolmates annoyed him with them:

> The Veens speak only to Tobaks
> But Tobaks speak only to dogs.

The passage of years had but polished her prettiness and
though many fashions had come and gone since 1889, he happened upon her at a season when hairdos and skirtlines had
reverted briefly (another much more elegant lady was already
ahead of her) to the style of a dozen years ago, abolishing the
interruption of remembered approval and pleasure. She
plunged into a torrent of polite questions—but he had a
more important matter to settle at once—while the flame still
flickered.

"Let's not squander," he said, "the tumescence of retrieved
time on the gush of small talk. I'm bursting with energy, if
that's what you want to know. Now look; it may sound silly
and insolent but I have an urgent request. Will you cooperate
with me in cornuting your husband? It's a must!"

"Really, Van!" exclaimed angry Cordula. "You go a bit far.
I'm a happy wife. My Tobachok adores me. We'd have ten
children by now if I'd not been careful with him and others."

"You'll be glad to learn that this other has been found utterly sterile."

"Well, I'm anything but. I guess I'd cause a mule to foal
by just looking on. Moreover, I'm lunching today with the
Goals."

"*C'est bizarre*, an exciting little girl like you who can be so
tender with poodles and yet turns down a poor paunchy stiff
old Veen."

"The Veens are much too gay as dogs go."

"Since you collect adages," persisted Van, "let me quote
an Arabian one. Paradise is only one assbaa south of a pretty
girl's sash. *Eh bien?*"

"You are impossible. Where and when?"

"Where? In that drab little hotel across the street. When?
Right now. I've never seen you on a hobbyhorse yet, because
that's what *tout confort* promises—and not much else."

"I must be home not later than eleven-thirty, it's almost eleven now."

"It will take five minutes. Please!"

Astraddle, she resembled a child braving her first merry-go-round. She made a rectangular *moue* as she used that vulgar contraption. Sad, sullen streetwalkers do it with expressionless faces, lips tightly closed. She rode it twice. Their brisk nub and its repetition lasted fifteen minutes in all, not five. Very pleased with himself, Van walked with her for a stretch through the brown and green Bois de Belleau in the direction of her *osobnyachyok* (small mansion).

"That reminds me," he said, "I no longer use our Alexis apartment. I've had some poor people live there these last seven or eight years—the family of a police officer who used to be a footman at Uncle Dan's place in the country. My policeman is dead now and his widow and three boys have gone back to Ladore. I want to relinquish that flat. Would you like to accept it as a belated wedding present from an admirer? Good. We shall do it again some day. Tomorrow I have to be in London and on the third my favorite liner, *Admiral Tobakoff*, will take me to Manhattan. *Au revoir*. Tell him to look out for low lintels. Antlers can be very sensitive when new. Greg Erminin tells me that Lucette is at the Alphonse Four?"

"That's right. And where's the other?"

"I think we'll part here. It's twenty minutes to twelve. You'd better toddle along."

"*Au revoir.* You're a very bad boy and I'm a very bad girl. But it was fun—even though you've been speaking to me not as you would to a lady friend but as you probably do to little whores. Wait. Here's a top secret address where you can always"—(fumbling in her handbag)—"reach me"—(finding a card with her husband's crest and scribbling a postal cryptograph)—"at Malbrook, Mayne, where I spend every August."

She looked around, rose on her toes like a ballerina, and kissed him on the mouth. Sweet Cordula!

3

The Bourbonian-chinned, dark, sleek-haired, ageless concierge, dubbed by Van in his blazer days "Alphonse Cinq,"
believed he had just seen Mlle Veen in the Récamier room
where Vivian Vale's golden veils were on show. With a flick
of coattail and a swing-gate click, Alphonse dashed out of his
lodge and went to see. Van's eye over his umbrella crook traveled around a carousel of Sapsucker paperbacks (with that
wee striped woodpecker on every spine): *The Gitanilla, Salzman, Salzman, Salzman, Invitation to a Climax, Squirt, The
Go-go Gang, The Threshold of Pain, The Chimes of Chose, The
Gitanilla*—here a Wall Street, very "patrician" colleague of
Demon's, old Kithar K. L. Sween, who wrote verse, and the
still older real-estate magnate Milton Eliot, went by without
recognizing grateful Van, despite his being betrayed by several
mirrors.

The concierge returned shaking his head. Out of the goodness of his heart Van gave him a Goal guinea and said he'd
call again at one-thirty. He walked through the lobby (where
the author of *Agonic Lines* and Mr. Eliot, *affalés*, with a great
amount of jacket over their shoulders, *dans des fauteuils*, were
comparing cigars) and, leaving the hotel by a side exit, crossed
the rue des Jeunes Martyres for a drink at Ovenman's.

Upon entering, he stopped for a moment to surrender his
coat; but he kept his black fedora and stick-slim umbrella as
he had seen his father do in that sort of bawdy, albeit smart,
place which decent women did not frequent—at least, unescorted. He headed for the bar, and as he was in the act of
wiping the lenses of his black-framed spectacles, made out,
through the optical mist (Space's recent revenge!), the girl
whose silhouette he recalled having seen now and then (much
more distinctly!) ever since his pubescence, passing alone,
drinking alone, always alone, like Blok's *Incognita*. It was a
queer feeling—as of something replayed by mistake, part of a
sentence misplaced on the proof sheet, a scene run prematurely, a repeated blemish, a wrong turn of time. He hastened
to reequip his ears with the thick black bows of his glasses
and went up to her in silence. For a minute he stood behind
her, sideways to remembrance and reader (as she, too, was in

regard to us and the bar), the crook of his silk-swathed cane
lifted in profile almost up to his mouth. There she was, against
the aureate backcloth of a sakarama screen next to the bar,
toward which she was sliding, still upright, about to be seated,
having already placed one white-gloved hand on the counter.
She wore a high-necked, long-sleeved romantic black dress
with an ample skirt, fitted bodice and ruffy collar, from the
black soft corolla of which her long neck gracefully rose. With
a rake's morose gaze we follow the pure proud line of that
throat, of that tilted chin. The glossy red lips are parted, avid
and fey, offering a side gleam of large upper teeth. We know,
we love that high cheekbone (with an atom of powder puff
sticking to the hot pink skin), and the forward upsweep of
black lashes and the painted feline eye—all this in profile, we
softly repeat. From under the wavy wide brim of her floppy
hat of black faille, with a great black bow surmounting it, a
spiral of intentionally disarranged, expertly curled bright copper descends her flaming cheek, and the light of the bar's
"gem bulbs" plays on her *bouffant* front hair, which, as seen
laterally, convexes from beneath the extravagant brim of the
picture hat right down to her long thin eyebrow. Her Irish
profile sweetened by a touch of Russian softness, which adds
a look of mysterious expectancy and wistful surprise to her
beauty, must be seen, I hope, by the friends and admirers of
my memories, as a natural masterpiece incomparably finer and
younger than the portrait of the similarly postured lousy jade
with her Parisian *gueule de guenon* on the vile poster painted
by that wreck of an artist for Ovenman.

"Hullo there, Ed," said Van to the barman, and she turned
at the sound of his dear rasping voice.

"I didn't expect you to wear glasses. You almost got *le
paquet*, which I was preparing for the man supposedly 'gog-
gling' my hat. Darling Van! *Dushka moy!*"

"Your hat," he said, "is positively lautréamontesque—I
mean, lautrecaquesque—no, I can't form the adjective."

Ed Barton served Lucette what she called a Chambéryzette.

"Gin and bitter for me."

"I'm so happy and sad," she murmured in Russian. "*Moyo
grustnoe schastie!* How long will you be in old Lute?"

Van answered he was leaving next day for England, and

then on June 3 (this was May 31) would be taking the *Admiral Tobakoff* back to the States. She would sail with him, she cried, it was a marvelous idea, she didn't mind whither to drift, really, West, East, Toulouse, Los Teques. He pointed out that it was far too late to obtain a cabin (on that not very grand ship so much shorter than *Queen Guinevere*), and changed the subject.

"The last time I saw you," said Van, "was two years ago, at a railway station. You had just left Villa Armina and I had just arrived. You wore a flowery dress which got mixed with the flowers you carried because you moved so fast—jumping out of a green calèche and up into the Ausonian Express that had brought me to Nice."

"*Très expressioniste.* I did not see you or I would have stopped to tell you what I had just learned. Imagine, mother knew everything—your garrulous dad told her everything about Ada and you!"

"But not about you and her."

Lucette asked him not to mention that sickening, maddening girl. She was furious with Ada and jealous by proxy. Her Andrey, or rather his sister on his behalf, he was too stupid even for that, collected progressive philistine Art, bootblack blotches and excremental smears on canvas, imitations of an imbecile's doodles, primitive idols, aboriginal masks, *objets trouvés*, or rather *troués*, the polished log with its polished hole à la Heinrich Heideland. His bride found the ranch yard adorned with a sculpture, if that's the right word, by old Heinrich himself and his four hefty assistants, a huge hideous lump of bourgeois mahogany ten feet high, entitled "Maternity," the mother (in reverse) of all the plaster gnomes and pig-iron toadstools planted by former Vinelanders in front of their dachas in Lyaska.

The barman stood wiping a glass in endless slow motion as he listened to Lucette's denunciation with the limp smile of utter enchantment.

"And yet (*odnako*)," said Van in Russian, "you enjoyed your stay there, in 1896, so Marina told me."

"I did not (*nichego podobnago*)! I left Agavia minus my luggage in the middle of the night, with sobbing Brigitte. I've never seen such a household. Ada had turned into a dumb *brune.* The table talk was limited to the three C's—cactuses, cattle, and cooking, with Dorothy adding her comments on cubist mysticism. He's one of those Russians who *shlyopayut* (slap) to the toilet barefoot, shave in their underwear, wear garters, consider hitching up one's pants indecent, but when fishing out coins hold their right trouser pocket with the left hand or vice versa, which is not only indecent but vulgar. Demon is, perhaps, disappointed they don't have children, but really he 'engripped' the man after the first flush of father-in-law-hood. Dorothy is a prissy and pious monster who comes to stay for months, orders the meals, and has a private collection of keys to the servants' rooms—which our dumb brunette should have known—and other little keys to open people's hearts—she has tried, by the way, to make a practicing Orthodox not only of every American Negro she can catch, but of our sufficiently *pravoslavnaya* mother—though she only succeeded in making the Trimurti stocks go up. One beautiful, nostalgic night—"

"*Po-russki*," said Van, noticing that an English couple had ordered drinks and settled down to some quiet auditing.

"*Kak-to noch'yu* (one night), when Andrey was away having his tonsils removed or something, dear watchful Dorochka went to investigate a suspicious noise in my maid's room and found poor Brigitte fallen asleep in the rocker and Ada and me *tryahnuvshih starinoy* (reshaking old times) on the bed. That's when I told Dora I would not stand her attitude, and immediately left for Monarch Bay."

"Some people are certainly odd," said Van. "If you've finished that sticky stuff let's go back to your hotel and get some lunch."

She wanted fish, he stuck to cold cuts and salad.

"You know whom I ran into this morning? Good old Greg Erminin. It was he who told me you were around. His wife *est un peu snob*, what?"

"Everybody is *un peu snob*," said Lucette. "Your Cordula, who is also around, cannot forgive Shura Tobak, the violinist, for being her husband's neighbor in the telephone book. Immediately after lunch, we'll go to my room, a numb twenty-five, my age. I have a fabulous Japanese divan and lots of orchids just supplied by one of my beaux. Ach, *Bozhe moy*—

it has just occurred to me—I shall have to look into this—
maybe they are meant for Brigitte, who is marrying after tomorrow, at three-thirty, a head waiter at the Alphonse Trois,
in Auteuil. Anyway they are greenish, with orange and purple
blotches, some kind of delicate *Oncidium*, 'cypress frogs,' one
of those silly commercial names. I'll stretch out upon the divan like a martyr, remember?"

"Are you still half-a-martyr—I mean half-a-virgin?" inquired Van.

"A quarter," answered Lucette. "Oh, try me, Van! My divan is black with yellow cushions."

"You can sit for a minute in my lap."

"No—unless we undress and you ganch me."

"My dear, as I've often reminded you, you belong to a
princely family but you talk like the loosest Lucinda imaginable. Is it a fad in your set, Lucette?"

"I have no set, I'm a loner. Once in a while, I go out with
two diplomats, a Greek and an Englishman, who are allowed
to paw me and play with each other. A corny society painter
is working on my portrait and he and his wife caress me when
I'm in the mood. Your friend Dick Cheshire sends me presents and racing tips. It's a dull life, Van.

"I enjoy—oh, loads of things," she continued in a melancholy, musing tone of voice, as she poked with a fork at her
blue trout which, to judge by its contorted shape and bulging
eyes, had boiled alive, convulsed by awful agonies. "I love
Flemish and Dutch oils, flowers, food, Flaubert, Shakespeare,
shopping, sheeing, swimming, the kisses of beauties and
beasts—but somehow all of it, this sauce and all the riches of
Holland, form only a kind of *tonen'kiy-tonen'kiy* (thin little)
layer, under which there is absolutely nothing, except, of
course, your image, and that only adds depth and a trout's
agonies to the emptiness. I'm like Dolores—when she says
she's 'only a picture painted on air.' "

"Never could finish that novel—much too pretentious."

"Pretentious but true. It's exactly my sense of existing—a
fragment, a wisp of color. Come and travel with me to some
distant place, where there are frescoes and fountains, why
can't we travel to some distant place with ancient fountains?
By ship? By sleeping car?"

"It's safer and faster by plane," said Van. "And for Log's sake, speak Russian."

Mr. Sween, lunching with a young fellow who sported a bullfighter's sideburns and other charms, bowed gravely in the direction of their table; then a naval officer in the azure uniform of the Gulfstream Guards passed by in the wake of a dark, ivory-pale lady and said: "Hullo Lucette, hullo, Van."

"Hullo, Alph," said Van, whilst Lucette acknowledged the greeting with an absent smile: over her propped-up entwined hands she was following with mocking eyes the receding lady. Van cleared his throat as he gloomily glanced at his half-sister.

"Must be at least thirty-five," murmured Lucette, "yet still hopes to become his queen."

(His father, Alphonse the First of Portugal, a puppet potentate manipulated by Uncle Victor, had recently abdicated upon Gamaliel's suggestion in favor of a republican regime, but Lucette spoke of fragile beauty, not fickle politics.)

"That was Lenore Colline. What's the matter, Van?"

"Cats don't stare at stars, it's not done. The resemblance is much less close than it used to be—though, of course, I've not kept up with counterpart changes. *A propos*, how's the career been progressing?"

"If you mean Ada's career, I hope it's also a flop, the same as her marriage. So my getting you will be all Demon gains. I don't go often to movies, and I refused to speak to Dora and her when we met at the funeral and haven't the remotest idea of what her stage or screen exploits may have been lately."

"Did that woman tell her brother about your innocent frolics?"

"Of course not! She *drozhit* (trembles) over his bliss. But I'm sure it was she who forced Ada to write me that I 'must never try again to wreck a successful marriage'—and this I forgive Daryushka, a born blackmailer, but not Adochka. I don't care for your cabochon. I mean it's all right on your dear hairy hand, but Papa wore one like that on his hateful pink paw. He belonged to the silent-explorer type. Once he took me to a girls' hockey match and I had to warn him I'd yell for help if he didn't call off the search."

"*Das auch noch*," sighed Van, and pocketed the heavy dark-

sapphire ring. He would have put it into the ashtray had it
not been Marina's last present.

"Look, Van," she said (finishing her fourth flute). "Why
not risk it? Everything is quite simple. You marry me. You get
my Ardis. We live there, you write there. I keep melting into
the background, never bothering you. We invite Ada—alone,
of course—to stay for a while on *her* estate, for I had always
expected mother to leave Ardis to her. While she's there, I go
to Aspen or Gstaad, or Schittau, and you live with her in solid
crystal with snow falling as if forever all around *pendant que
je* shee in Aspenis. Then I come back like a shot, but she can
stay on, she's welcome, I'll hang around in case you two want
me. And then she goes back to her husband for a couple of
dreary months, see?"

"Yes, magnificent plan," said Van. "The only trouble is:
she will never come. It's now three o'clock, I have to see a
man who is to renovate Villa Armina which *I* inherited and
which will house one of my harems. Slapping a person's wrist
that way is not your prettiest mannerism on the Irish side. I
shall now escort you to your apartment. You are plainly in
need of some rest."

"I have an important, important telephone call to make,
but I don't want you to listen," said Lucette searching for the
key in her little black handbag.

They entered the hall of her suite. There, firmly resolved to
leave in a moment, he removed his glasses and pressed his
mouth to her mouth, and she tasted exactly as Ada at Ardis,
in the early afternoon, sweet saliva, salty epithelium, cherries,
coffee. Had he not sported so well and so recently, he might
not have withstood the temptation, the impardonable thrill.
She plucked at his sleeve as he started to back out of the
hallway.

"Let us kiss again, let us kiss again!" Lucette kept repeating,
childishly, lispingly, barely moving her parted lips, in a fussy
incoherent daze, doing her best to prevent him from thinking
it over, from saying no.

He said that would do.

"Oh but why? Oh please!"

He brushed away her cold trembling fingers.

"Why, Van? Why, why, why?"

"You know perfectly well why. I love her, not you, and I simply refuse to complicate matters by entering into yet another incestuous relationship."

"That's rich," said Lucette, "you've gone far enough with me on several occasions, even when I was a kid; your refusing to go further is a mere quibble on your part; and besides, besides you've been unfaithful to her with a thousand girls, you dirty cheat!"

"You shan't talk to me in that tone," said Van, meanly turning her poor words into a pretext for marching away.

"I apollo, I love you," she whispered frantically, trying to *cry* after him in a *whisper* because the corridor was all door and ears, but he walked on, waving both arms in the air without looking back, quite forgivingly, though, and was gone.

4

A teasy problem demanded Dr. Veen's presence in England.

Old Paar of Chose had written him that the "Clinic" would like him to study a singular case of chromesthesia, but that given certain aspects of the case (such as a faint possibility of trickery) Van should come and decide for himself whether he thought it worth the trouble to fly the patient to Kingston for further observation. One Spencer Muldoon, born eyeless, aged forty, single, friendless, and the third blind character in this chronicle, had been known to hallucinate during fits of violent paranoia, calling out the names of such shapes and substances as he had learned to identify by touch, or thought he recognized through the awfulness of stories about them (falling trees, extinct saurians) and which now pressed on him from all sides, alternating with periods of stupor, followed invariably by a return to his normal self, when for a week or two he would finger his blind books or listen, in red-lidded bliss, to records of music, bird songs, and Irish poetry.

His ability to break space into ranks and files of "strong" and "weak" things in what seemed a wallpaper pattern remained a mystery until one evening, when a research student

(R.S.—he wished to remain that way), who intended to trace certain graphs having to do with the metabasis of another patient, happened to leave within Muldoon's reach one of those elongated boxes of new, unsharpened, colored-chalk pencils whose mere evocation (Dixon Pink Anadel!) makes one's memory speak in the language of rainbows, the tints of their painted and polished woods being graded spectrally in their neat tin container. Poor Muldoon's childhood could not come to him with anything like *such* iridian recall, but when his groping fingers opened the box and palpated the pencils, a certain expression of sensual relish appeared on his parchment-pale face. Upon observing that the blind man's eyebrows went up slightly at red, higher at orange, still higher at the shrill scream of yellow and then stepped down through the rest of the prismatic spectrum, R.S. casually told him that the woods were dyed differently—"red," "orange," "yellow," et cetera, and quite as casually Muldoon rejoined that they also felt different one from another.

In the course of several tests conducted by R.S. and his colleagues, Muldoon explained that by stroking the pencils in turn he perceived a gamut of "stingles," special sensations somehow allied to the tingling aftereffects of one's skin contact with stinging nettles (he had been raised in the country somewhere between Ormagh and Armagh, and had often tumbled, in his adventurous boyhood, the poor thick-booted soul, into ditches and even ravines), and spoke eerily of the "strong" green stingle of a piece of blotting paper or the wet weak pink stingle of nurse Langford's perspiring nose, these colors being checked by himself against those applied by the researchers to the initial pencils. In result of the tests, one was forced to assume that the man's fingertips could convey to his brain "a tactile transcription of the prismatic specter" as Paar put it in his detailed report to Van.

When the latter arrived, Muldoon had not quite come out of a state of stupor more protracted than any preceding one. Van, hoping to examine him on the morrow, spent a delightful day conferring with a bunch of eager psychologists and was interested to spot among the nurses the familiar squint of Elsie Langford, a gaunt girl with a feverish flush and protruding teeth, who had been obscurely involved in a "poltergeist" affair at another medical institution. He had dinner with old Paar in his rooms at Chose and told him he would like to have the poor fellow transferred to Kingston, *with* Miss Langford, as soon as he was fit to travel. The poor fellow died that night in his sleep, leaving the entire incident suspended in midair within a nimbus of bright irrelevancy.

Van, in whom the pink-blooming chestnuts of Chose always induced an amorous mood, decided to squander the sudden bounty of time before his voyage to America on a twenty-four-hour course of treatment at the most fashionable and efficient of all the Venus Villas in Europe; but during the longish trip in the ancient, plushy, faintly perfumed (musk? Turkish tobacco?) limousine which he usually got from the Albania, his London hotel, for travels in England, other restless feelings joined, without dispelling it, his sullen lust. Rocking along softly, his slippered foot on a footrest, his arm in an armloop, he recalled his first railway journey to Ardis and tried—what he sometimes advised a patient doing in order to exercise the "muscles of consciousness"—namely putting oneself back not merely into the frame of mind that had preceded a radical change in one's life, but into a state of complete ignorance regarding that change. He knew it could not be done, that not the achievement, but the obstinate attempt was possible, because he would not have remembered the preface to Ada had not life turned the next page, causing now its radiant text to flash through all the tenses of the mind. He wondered if he would remember the present commonplace trip. An English late spring with literary associations lingered in the evening air. The built-in "canoreo" (an old-fashioned musical gadget which a joint Anglo-American Commission had only recently unbanned) transmitted a heart-wounding Italian song. What was he? Who was he? Why was he? He thought of his slackness, clumsiness, dereliction of spirit. He thought of his loneliness, of its passions and dangers. He saw through the glass partition the fat, healthy, reliable folds of his driver's neck. Idle images queued by—Edmund, Edmond, simple Cordula, fantastically intricate Lucette, and, by further mechanical association, a depraved little girl called Lisette, in Cannes, with breasts like lovely abscesses, whose frail favors were handled by a smelly big brother in an old bathing machine.

He turned off the canoreo and helped himself to the brandy stored behind a sliding panel, drinking from the bottle, because all three glasses were filthy. He felt surrounded by crashing great trees, and the monstrous beasts of unachieved, perhaps unachievable tasks. One such task was Ada whom he knew he would never give up; to her he would surrender the remnants of his self at the first trumpet blast of destiny. Another was his philosophic work, so oddly impeded by its own virtue—by that originality of literary style which constitutes the only real honesty of a writer. He had to do it his own way, but the cognac was frightful, and the history of thought bristled with clichés, and it was that history he had to surmount.

He knew he was not quite a savant, but completely an artist. Paradoxically and unnecessarily it had been in his "academic career," in his nonchalant and arrogant lectures, in his conduct of seminars, in his published reports on sick minds, that, starting as something of a prodigy before he was twenty, he had gained by the age of thirty-one "honors" and a "position" that many unbelievably laborious men do not reach at fifty. In his sadder moments, as now, he attributed at least part of his "success" to his rank, to his wealth, to the numerous donations, which (in a kind of extension of his overtipping the haggard beggars who cleaned rooms, manned lifts, smiled in hotel corridors) he kept showering upon worthwhile institutions and students. Maybe Van Veen did not err too widely in his wry conjecture; for on our Antiterra (and on Terra as well, according to his own writings) a powerfully plodding Administration prefers, unless moved by the sudden erection of a new building or the thunder of torrential funds, the safe drabness of an academic mediocrity to the suspect sparkle of a V.V.

Nightingales sang, when he arrived at his fabulous and ignoble destination. As usual, he experienced a surge of brutal elation as the car entered the oak avenue between two rows of phallephoric statues presenting arms. A welcome habitué of fifteen years' standing, he had not bothered to "telephone" (the new official term). A searchlight lashed him: Alas, he had come on a "gala" night!

Members usually had their chauffeurs park in a special enclosure near the guardhouse, where there was a pleasant canteen for servants, with nonalcoholic drinks and a few inexpensive and homely whores. But that night several huge police cars occupied the garage boxes and overflowed into an adjacent arbor. Telling Kingsley to wait a moment under the oaks, Van donned his *bautta* and went to investigate. His favorite walled walk soon took him to one of the spacious lawns velveting the approach to the manor. The grounds were lividly illuminated and as populous as Park Avenue—an association that came very readily, since the disguises of the astute sleuths belonged to a type which reminded Van of his native land. Some of those men he even knew by sight—they used to patrol his father's club in Manhattan whenever good Gamaliel (not reelected after his fourth term) happened to dine there in his informal gagality. They mimed what they were accustomed to mime—grapefruit vendors, black hawkers of bananas and banjoes, obsolete, or at least untimely, "copying clerks" who hurried in circles to unlikely offices, and peripatetic Russian newspaper readers slowing down to a trance stop and then strolling again behind their wide open *Estotskiya Vesti.* Van remembered that Mr. Alexander Screepatch, the new president of the United Americas, a plethoric Russian, had flown over to see King Victor; and he correctly concluded that both were now sunk in mollitude. The comic side of the detectives' display (befitting, perhaps, their dated notion of an American sidewalk, but hardly suiting a weirdly illumined maze of English hedges) tempered his disappointment as he shuddered squeamishly at the thought of sharing the frolics of historical personages or contenting himself with the brave-faced girlies they had started to use and rejected.

Here a bedsheeted statue attempted to challenge Van from its marble pedestal but slipped and landed on its back in the bracken. Ignoring the sprawling god, Van returned to the still-throbbing jolls-joyce. Purple-jowled Kingsley, an old tried friend, offered to drive him to another house, ninety miles north; but Van declined upon principle and was taken back to the Albania.

5

At five P.M., June 3, his ship had sailed from Le Havre-de-Grâce; on the evening of the same day Van embarked at Old Hantsport. He had spent most of the afternoon playing court tennis with Delaurier, the famous Negro coach, and felt very dull and drowsy as he watched the low sun's ardency break into green-golden eye-spots a few sea-serpent yards to starboard, on the far-side slope of the bow wave. Presently he decided to turn in, walked down to the A deck, devoured some of the still-life fruit prepared for him in his sitting room, attempted to read in bed the proofs of an essay he was contributing to a festschrift on the occasion of Professor Counterstone's eightieth birthday, gave it up, and fell asleep. A tempest went into convulsions around midnight, but despite the lunging and creaking (*Tobakoff* was an embittered old vessel) Van managed to sleep soundly, the only reaction on the part of his dormant mind being the dream image of an aquatic peacock, slowly sinking before somersaulting like a diving grebe, near the shore of the lake bearing his name in the ancient kingdom of Arrowroot. Upon reviewing that bright dream he traced its source to his recent visit to Armenia where he had gone fowling with Armborough and that gentleman's extremely compliant and accomplished niece. He wanted to make a note of it—and was amused to find that all three pencils had not only left his bed table but had neatly aligned themselves head to tail along the bottom of the outer door of the adjacent room, having covered quite a stretch of blue carpeting in the course of their stopped escape.

The steward brought him a "Continental" breakfast, the ship's newspaper, and the list of first-class passengers. Under "Tourism in Italy," the little newspaper informed him that a Domodossola farmer had unearthed the bones and trappings of one of Hannibal's elephants, and that two American psychiatrists (names not given) had died an odd death in the Bocaletto range: the older fellow from heart failure and his boy friend by suicide. After pondering the Admiral's morbid interest in Italian mountains, Van clipped the item and picked up the passenger list (pleasingly surmounted by the same crest that adorned Cordula's notepaper) in order to see if there was anybody to be avoided during the next days. The list yielded the Robinson couple, Robert and Rachel, old bores of the family (Bob had retired after directing for many years one of Uncle Dan's offices). His gaze, traveling on, tripped over Dr. Ivan Veen and pulled up at the next name. What constricted his heart? Why did he pass his tongue over his thick lips? Empty formulas befitting the solemn novelists of former days who thought they could explain everything.

The level of the water slanted and swayed in his bath imitating the slow seesaw of the bright-blue, white-flecked sea in the porthole of his bedroom. He rang up Miss Lucinda Veen, whose suite was on the Main Deck amidships exactly above his, but she was absent. Wearing a white polo-neck sweater and tinted glasses, he went to look for her. She was not on the Games Deck from where he looked down at some other redhead, in a canvas chair on the Sun Deck: the girl sat writing a letter at passionate speed and he thought that if ever he switched from ponderous factitude to light fiction he would have a jealous husband use binoculars to decipher from where he stood that outpour of illicit affection.

She was not on the Promenade Deck where blanket-swathed old people were reading the number-one best seller *Salzman* and awaiting with borborygmic forebubbles the eleven o'clock bouillon. He betook himself to the Grill, where he reserved a table for two. He walked over to the bar and warmly greeted bald fat Toby who had served on the *Queen Guinevere* in 1889, and 1890, and 1891, when she was still unmarried and he a resentful fool. They could have eloped to Lopadusa as Mr. and Mrs. Dairs or Sardi!

He espied their half-sister on the forecastle deck, looking perilously pretty in a low-cut, brightly flowered, wind-worried frock, talking to the bronzed but greatly aged Robinsons. She turned toward him, brushing back the flying hair from her face with a mixture of triumph and embarrassment in her expression, and presently they took leave of Rachel and Robert who beamed after them, waving similarly raised hands to her, to him, to life, to death, to the happy old days when Demon paid all the gambling debts of their son, just before he was killed in a head-on car collision.

She dispatched the *pozharskiya kotletï* with gratitude: he was not scolding her for popping up as some sort of transcendental (rather than transatlantic) stowaway; and in her eagerness to see him she had botched her breakfast after having gone dinnerless on the eve. She who enjoyed the hollows and hills of the sea, when taking part in nautical sports, or the ups and oops, when flying, had been ignominiously sick aboard this, her first liner; but the Robinsons had given her a marvelous medicine, she had slept ten hours, in Van's arms all the time, and now hoped that both he and she were tolerably awake except for the fuzzy edge left by the drug.

Quite kindly he asked where she thought she was going.

To Ardis, with him—came the prompt reply—for ever and ever. Robinson's grandfather had died in Araby at the age of one hundred and thirty-one, so Van had still a whole century before him, she would build for him, in the park, several pavilions to house his successive harems, they would gradually turn, one after the other, into homes for aged ladies, and then into mausoleums. There hung, she said, a steeplechase picture of "Pale Fire with Tom Cox Up" above dear Cordula's and Tobak's bed, in the suite "wangled in one minute flat" from them, and she wondered how it affected the Tobaks' love life during sea voyages. Van interrupted Lucette's nervous patter by asking her if her bath taps bore the same inscriptions as his: Hot Domestic, Cold Salt. Yes, she cried, Old Salt, Old Salzman, Ardent Chambermaid, Comatose Captain!

They met again in the afternoon.

To most of the *Tobakoff*'s first-class passengers the afternoon of June 4, 1901, in the Atlantic, on the meridian of Iceland and the latitude of Ardis, seemed little conducive to open-air frolics: the fervor of its cobalt sky kept being cut by glacial gusts, and the wash of an old-fashioned swimming pool rhythmically flushed the green tiles, but Lucette was a hardy girl used to bracing winds no less than to the detestable sun. Spring in Fialta and a torrid May on Minataor, the famous artificial island, had given a nectarine hue to her limbs, which looked lacquered with it when wet, but re-evolved their natural bloom as the breeze dried her skin. With glowing cheekbones and that glint of copper showing from under her tight rubber cap on nape and forehead, she evoked the Helmeted Angel of the Yukonsk Ikon whose magic effect was said to

change anemic blond maidens into *konskiya deti*, freckled red-
haired lads, children of the Sun Horse.

She returned after a brief swim to the sun terrace where
Van lay and said:

"You can't imagine"—("I can imagine anything," he insisted)—"you *can* imagine, okay, what oceans of lotions and
streams of creams I am compelled to use—in the privacy of
my balconies or in desolate sea caves—before I can exhibit
myself to the elements. I always teeter on the tender border
between sunburn and suntan—or between lobster and *Obst* as
writes Herb, my beloved painter—I'm reading his diary published by his last duchess, it's in three mixed languages and
lovely, I'll lend it to you. You see, darling, I'd consider myself
a pied cheat if the small parts I conceal in public were not of
the same color as those on show."

"You looked to me kind of sandy all over when you were
inspected in 1892," said Van.

"I'm a brand-new girl now," she whispered. "A happy new
girl. Alone with you on an abandoned ship, with ten days at
least till my next flow. I sent you a silly note to Kingston, just
in case you didn't turn up."

They were now reclining on a poolside mat face to face, in
symmetrical attitudes, he leaning his head on his right hand,
she propped on her left elbow. The strap of her green breast-
cups had slipped down her slender arm, disclosing drops and
streaks of water at the base of one nipple. An abyss of a few
inches separated the jersey he wore from her bare midriff, the
black wool of his trunks from her soaked green pubic mask.
The sun glazed her hipbone; a shadowed dip led to the five-
year-old trace of an appendectomy. Her half-veiled gaze dwelt
upon him with heavy, opaque greed, and she was right, they
were really quite alone, he had possessed Marion Armborough
behind her uncle's back in much more complex circumstances,
what with the motorboat jumping like a flying fish and his
host keeping a shotgun near the steering wheel. Joylessly, he
felt the stout snake of desire weightily unwind; grimly, he regretted not having exhausted the fiend in Villa Venus. He
accepted the touch of her blind hand working its way up his
thigh and cursed nature for having planted a gnarled tree
bursting with vile sap within a man's crotch. Suddenly Lucette

drew away, exhaling a genteel "*merde.*" Eden was full of people.

Two half-naked children in shrill glee came running toward the pool. A Negro nurse brandished their diminutive bras in angry pursuit. Out of the water a bald head emerged by spontaneous generation and snorted. The swimming coach appeared from the dressing room. Simultaneously, a tall splendid creature with trim ankles and repulsively fleshy thighs stalked past the Veens, all but treading on Lucette's emerald-studded cigarette case. Except for a golden ribbon and a bleached mane, her long, ripply, beige back was bare all the way down to the tops of her slowly and lusciously rolling buttocks, which divulged, in alternate motion, their nether bulges from under the lamé loincloth. Just before disappearing behind a rounded white corner, the Titianesque Titaness half-turned her brown face and greeted Van with a loud "hullo!"

Lucette wanted to know: *kto siya pava?* (who's that stately dame?)

"I thought she addressed *you*," answered Van. "I did not distinguish her face and do not remember that bottom."

"She gave you a big jungle smile," said Lucette, readjusting her green helmet, with touchingly graceful movements of her raised wings, and touchingly flashing the russet feathering of her armpits.

"Come with me, hm?" she suggested, rising from the mat.

He shook his head, looking up at her: "You rise," he said, "like Aurora."

"His first compliment," observed Lucette with a little cock of her head as if speaking to an invisible confidant.

He put on his tinted glasses and watched her stand on the diving board, her ribs framing the hollow of her intake as she prepared to ardis into the amber. He wondered, in a mental footnote that might come handy some day, if sunglasses or any other varieties of vision, which certainly twist our concept of "space," do not also influence our style of speech. The two well-formed lassies, the nurse, the prurient merman, the natatorium master, all looked on with Van.

"Second compliment ready," he said as she returned to his side. "You're a divine diver. *I* go in with a messy plop."

"But you swim faster," she complained, slipping off her

shoulder straps and turning into a prone position; "*Mezhdu prochim* (by the way), is it true that a sailor in Tobakoff's day was not taught to swim so he wouldn't die a nervous wreck if the ship went down?"

"A common sailor, perhaps," said Van. "When *michman* Tobakoff himself got shipwrecked off Gavaille, he swam around comfortably for hours, frightening away sharks with snatches of old songs and that sort of thing, until a fishing boat rescued him—one of those miracles that require a minimum of cooperation from all concerned, I imagine."

Demon, she said, had told her, last year at the funeral, that he was buying an island in the Gavailles ("incorrigible dreamer," drawled Van). He had "wept like a fountain" in Nice, but had cried with even more abandon in Valentina, at an earlier ceremony, which poor Marina did not attend either. The wedding—in the Greek-faith style, if you please—looked like a badly faked episode in an old movie, the priest was gaga and the *dyakon* drunk, and—perhaps, fortunately—Ada's thick white veil was as impervious to light as a widow's weeds. Van said he would not listen to that.

"Oh, you must," she rejoined, "*hotya bï potomu* (if only because) one of her *shafer*'s (bachelors who take turns holding the wedding crown over the bride's head) looked momentarily, in impassive profile and impertinent attitude (he kept raising the heavy metallic *venets* too high, too athletically high as if trying on purpose to keep it as far as possible from her head), exactly like you, like a pale, ill-shaven twin, delegated by you from wherever you were."

At a place nicely called Agony, in Terra del Fuego. He felt an uncanny tingle as he recalled that when he received there the invitation to the wedding (airmailed by the groom's sinister sister) he was haunted for several nights by dream after dream, growing fainter each time (much as her movie he was to pursue from flick-house to flick-house at a later stage of his life) of his holding that crown over her.

"Your father," added Lucette, "paid a man from *Belladonna* to take pictures—but of course, real fame begins only when one's name appears in that cine-magazine's crossword puzzle. We all know it will never happen, never! Do you hate me now?"

"I don't," he said, passing his hand over her sun-hot back and rubbing her coccyx to make pussy purr. "Alas, I don't! I love you with a brother's love and maybe still more tenderly. Would you like me to order drinks?"

"I'd like you to go on and on," she muttered, her nose buried in the rubber pillow.

"There's that waiter coming. What shall we have—Honoloolers?"

"You'll have them with Miss Condor" (nasalizing the first syllable) "when I go to dress. For the moment I want only tea. Mustn't mix drugs and drinks. Have to take the famous Robinson pill sometime tonight. Sometime tonight."

"Two teas, please."

"And lots of sandwiches, George. Foie gras, ham, anything."

"It's very bad manners," remarked Van, "to invent a name for a poor chap who can't answer: 'Yes, Mademoiselle Condor.' Best Franco-English pun I've ever heard, incidentally."

"But his name *is* George. He was awfully kind to me yesterday when I threw up in the middle of the tearoom."

"For the sweet all is sweet," murmured Van.

"And so were the old Robinsons," she rambled on. "Not much chance, is there, they might turn up here? They've been sort of padding after me, rather pathetically, ever since we happened to have lunch at the same table on the boat-train, and I realized who they were but was sure they would not recognize the little fat girl seen in eighteen eighty-five or -six, but they are hypnotically talkative—at first we thought you were French, this salmon is really delicious, what's your home town?—and I'm a weak fool, and one thing led to another. Young people are less misled by the passage of time than the established old who have not much changed lately and are not used to the long-unseen young changing."

"That's very clever, darling," said Van "—except that time itself is motionless and changeless."

"Yes, it's always *I* in your lap and the receding road. Roads move?"

"Roads move."

After tea Lucette remembered an appointment with the hair-dresser and left in a hurry. Van peeled off his jersey and stayed on for a while, brooding, fingering the little green-gemmed case with five Rosepetal cigarettes, trying to enjoy the heat of the platinum sun in its aura of "film-color" but only managing to fan, with every shiver and heave of the ship, the fire of evil temptation.

A moment later, as if having spied on his solitude the *pava* (peahen) reappeared—this time with an apology.

Polite Van, scrambling up to his feet and browing his spectacles, started to apologize in his turn (for misleading her innocently) but his little speech petered out in stupefaction as he looked at her face and saw in it a gross and grotesque caricature of unforgettable features. That mulatto skin, that silver-blond hair, those fat purple lips, reinacted in coarse negative *her* ivory, *her* raven, *her* pale pout.

"I was told," she explained, "that a great friend of mine, Vivian Vale, the cootooriay—voozavay *entendue?*—had shaved his beard, in which case he'd look rather like you, right?"

"Logically, no, ma'am," replied Van.

She hesitated for the flirt of a second, licking her lips, not knowing whether he was being rude or ready—and here Lucette returned for her Rosepetals.

"See you aprey," said Miss Condor.

Lucette's gaze escorted to a good-riddance exit the indolent motion of those gluteal lobes and folds.

"You deceived me, Van. It is, it *is* one of your gruesome girls!"

"I swear," said Van, "that she's a perfect stranger. I wouldn't deceive you."

"You deceived me many, many times when I was a little girl. If you're doing it now *tu sais que j'en vais mourir.*"

"You promised me a harem," Van gently rebuked her.

"Not today, not today! Today is sacred."

The cheek he intended to kiss was replaced by her quick mad mouth.

"Come and see my cabin," she pleaded as he pushed her away with the very spring, as it were, of his animal reaction to the fire of her lips and tongue. "I simply must show you their pillows and piano. There's Cordula's smell in all the drawers. I beseech you!"

"Run along now," said Van. "You've no right to excite me

like that. I'll hire Miss Condor to chaperone me if you do not
behave yourself. We dine at seven-fifteen."

In his bedroom he found a somewhat belated invitation to
the Captain's table for dinner. It was addressed to Dr. and
Mrs. Ivan Veen. He had been on the ship once before, in
between the *Queens*, and remembered Captain Cowley as a
bore and an ignoramus.

He called the steward and bade him carry the note back,
with the penciled scrawl: "no such couple." He lay in his bath
for twenty minutes. He attempted to focus on something else
besides a hysterical virgin's body. He discovered an insidious
omission in his galleys where an entire line was wanting, with
the vitiated paragraph looking, however, quite plausible—to
an automatic reader—since the truncated end of one sentence,
and the lower-case beginning of the other, now adjacent, fitted to form a syntactically correct passage, the insipidity of
which he might never have noticed in the present folly of his
flesh, had he not recollected (a recollection confirmed by his
typescript) that at this point should have come a rather apt,
all things considered, quotation: *Insiste, anime meus, et ad-
tende fortiter* (courage, my soul and press on strongly).

"Sure you'd not prefer the restaurant?" he inquired when
Lucette, looking even more naked in her short evening frock
than she had in her "bickny," joined him at the door of the
grill. "It's crowded and gay down there, with a masturbating
jazzband. No?"

Tenderly she shook her jeweled head.

They had huge succulent "grugru shrimps" (the yellow larvae of a palm weevil) and roast bearlet *à la Tobakoff*. Only
half-a-dozen tables were occupied, and except for a nasty
engine vibration, which they had not noticed at lunch, everything was subdued, soft, and cozy. He took advantage of her
odd demure silence to tell her in detail about the late pencil-
palpating Mr. Muldoon and also about a Kingston case of
glossolalia involving a Yukonsk woman who spoke several
Slavic-like dialects which existed, maybe, on Terra, but certainly not in Estotiland. Alas, another case (with a quibble on
cas) engaged his attention subverbally.

She asked questions with pretty co-ed looks of doelike devotion, but it did not require much scientific training on a

professor's part to perceive that her charming embarrassment and the low notes furring her voice were as much contrived as her afternoon effervescence had been. Actually she thrashed in the throes of an emotional disarray which only the heroic self-control of an American aristocrat could master. Long ago she had made up her mind that by forcing the man whom she absurdly but irrevocably loved to have intercourse with her, even once, she would, somehow, with the help of some prodigious act of nature, transform a brief tactile event into an eternal spiritual tie; but she also knew that if it did not happen on the first night of their voyage, their relationship would slip back into the exhausting, hopeless, hopelessly familiar pattern of banter and counterbanter, with the erotic edge taken for granted, but kept as raw as ever. He understood her condition or at least believed, in despair, that he *had* understood it, retrospectively, by the time no remedy except Dr. Henry's oil of Atlantic prose could be found in the medicine chest of the past with its banging door and toppling toothbrush.

As he gloomily looked at her thin bare shoulders, so mobile and tensile that one wondered if she could not cross them in front of her like stylized angel wings, he reflected abjectly that he would have to endure, if conforming to his innermost code of honor, five such days of ruttish ache—not only because she was lovely and special but because he could never go without girl pleasure for more than forty-eight hours. He feared precisely that which she wanted to happen: that once he had tasted her wound and its grip, she would keep him insatiably captive for weeks, maybe months, maybe more, but that a harsh separation would inevitably come, with a new hope and the old despair never able to strike a balance. But worst of all, while aware, and ashamed, of lusting after a sick child, he felt, in an obscure twist of ancient emotions, his lust sharpened by the shame.

They had sweet, thick Turkish coffee and surreptitiously he looked at his wrist watch to check—what? How long the torture of self-denial could still be endured? How soon were certain events coming such as a ballroom dance competition? Her age? (Lucinda Veen was only five hours old if one reversed the human "time current.")

She was such a pathetic darling that, as they proceeded to

leave the grill, he could not help, for sensuality is the best breeding broth of fatal error, caressing her glossy young shoulder so as to fit for an instant, the happiest in her life, its ideal convexity bilboquet-wise within the hollow of his palm. Then she walked before him as conscious of his gaze as if she were winning a prize for "poise." He could describe her dress only as struthious (if there existed copper-curled ostriches), accentuating as it did the swing of her stance, the length of her legs in ninon stockings. Objectively speaking, her chic was keener than that of her "vaginal" sister. As they crossed landings where velvet ropes were being hastily stretched by Russian sailors (who glanced with sympathy at the handsome pair speaking their incomparable tongue) or walked this or that deck, Lucette made him think of some acrobatic creature immune to the rough seas. He saw with gentlemanly displeasure that her tilted chin and black wings, and free stride, attracted not only blue innocent eyes but the bold stare of lewd fellow passengers. He loudly exclaimed that he would slap the next jackanapes, and involuntarily walked backward with ridiculous truculent gestures into a folded deck chair (he also running the reel of time backward, in a minor way), which caused her to emit a yelp of laughter. Feeling now much happier, enjoying his gallant champagne-temper, she steered Van away from the mirage of her admirers, back to the lift.

They examined without much interest the objects of pleasure in a display window. Lucette sneered at a gold-threaded swimsuit. The presence of a riding crop and a pickax puzzled Van. Half a dozen glossy-jacketed copies of *Salzman* were impressively heaped between a picture of the handsome, thoughtful, now totally forgotten, author and a Mingo-Bingo vase of immortelles.

He clutched at a red rope and they entered the lounge.

"Whom did she look like?" asked Lucette. "*En laid et en lard?*"

"I don't know," he lied. "Whom?"

"Skip it," she said. "You're mine tonight. Mine, mine, mine!"

She was quoting Kipling—the same phrase that Ada used to address to Dack. He cast around for a straw of Procrustean procrastination.

"Please," said Lucette, "I'm tired of walking around, I'm frail, I'm feverish, I hate storms, let's all go to bed!"

"Hey, look!" he cried, pointing to a poster. "They're showing something called *Don Juan's Last Fling*. It's prerelease and for adults only. Topical *Tobakoff!*"

"It's going to be an unmethylated bore," said Lucy (Houssaie School, 1890) but he had already pushed aside the entrance drapery.

They came in at the beginning of an introductory picture, featuring a cruise to Greenland, with heavy seas in gaudy technicolor. It was a rather irrelevant trip since their *Tobakoff* did not contemplate calling at Godhavn; moreover, the cinema theater was swaying in counterrhythm to the cobalt-and-emerald swell on the screen. No wonder the place was *emptovato*, as Lucette observed, and she went on to say that the Robinsons had saved her life by giving her on the eve a tubeful of Quietus Pills.

"Want one? One a day keeps 'no shah' away. Pun. You can chew it, it's sweet."

"Jolly good name. No, thank you, my sweet. Besides you have only five left."

"Don't worry, I have it all planned out. There may be less than five days."

"More in fact, but no matter. Our measurements of time are meaningless; the most accurate clock is a joke; you'll read all about it someday, you just wait."

"Perhaps, not. I mean, perhaps I shan't have the patience. I mean, his charwoman could never finish reading Leonardo's palm. I may fall asleep before I get through your next book."

"An art-class legend," said Van.

"That's the final iceberg, I know by the music. Let's go, Van! Or you want to see Hoole as Hooan?"

She brushed his cheek with her lips in the dark, she took his hand, she kissed his knuckles, and he suddenly thought: after all, why not? Tonight? Tonight.

He enjoyed her impatience, the fool permitted himself to be stirred by it, the cretin whispered, prolonging the free, new, apricot fire of anticipation:

"If you're a good girl we'll have drinks in my sitting room at midnight."

The main picture had now started. The three leading parts—cadaverous Don Juan, paunchy Leporello on his donkey, and not too irresistible, obviously forty-year-old, Donna Anna—were played by solid stars, whose images passed by in "semi-stills," or as some say "translucencies," in a brief introduction. Contrary to expectations, the picture turned out to be quite good.

On the way to the remote castle where the difficult lady, widowed by his sword, has finally promised him a long night of love in her chaste and chilly chamber, the aging libertine nurses his potency by spurning the advances of a succession of robust belles. A *gitana* predicts to the gloomy cavalier that before reaching the castle he will have succumbed to the wiles of her sister, Dolores, a dancing girl (lifted from Osberg's novella, as was to be proved in the ensuing lawsuit). She also predicted something to Van, for even before Dolores came out of the circus tent to water Juan's horse, Van knew who she would be.

In the magic rays of the camera, in the controlled delirium of ballerina grace, ten years of her life had glanced off and she was again that slip of a girl *qui n'en porte pas* (as he had jested once to annoy her governess by a fictitious Frenchman's mistranslation): a remembered triviality that intruded upon the chill of his present emotion with the jarring stupidity of an innocent stranger's asking an absorbed voyeur for directions in a labyrinth of mean lanes.

Lucette recognized Ada three or four seconds later, but then clutched his wrist:

"Oh, how awful! It was bound to happen. That's she! Let's go, please, let's go. You must not see her *debasing* herself. She's terribly made up, every gesture is childish and wrong—"

"Just another minute," said Van.

Terrible? Wrong? She was absolutely perfect, and strange, and poignantly familiar. By some stroke of art, by some enchantment of chance, the few brief scenes she was given formed a perfect compendium of her 1884 and 1888 and 1892 looks.

The *gitanilla* bends her head over the live table of Leporello's servile back to trace on a scrap of parchment a rough map of the way to the castle. Her neck shows white through her long black hair separated by the motion of her shoulder. It is no longer another man's Dolores, but a little girl twisting an aquarelle brush in the paint of Van's blood, and Donna Anna's castle is now a bog flower.

The Don rides past three windmills, whirling black against an ominous sunset, and saves her from the miller who accuses her of stealing a fistful of flour and tears her thin dress. Wheezy but still game, Juan carries her across a brook (her bare toe acrobatically tickling his face) and sets her down, top up, on the turf of an olive grove. Now they stand facing each other. She fingers voluptuously the jeweled pommel of his sword, she rubs her firm girl belly against his embroidered tights, and all at once the grimace of a premature spasm writhes across the poor Don's expressive face. He angrily disentangles himself and staggers back to his steed.

Van, however, did not understand until much later (when he saw—*had* to see; and then see again and again—the entire film, with its melancholy and grotesque ending in Donna Anna's castle) that what seemed an incidental embrace constituted the Stone Cuckold's revenge. In fact, being upset beyond measure, he decided to go even before the olive-grove sequence dissolved. Just then three old ladies with stony faces showed their disapproval of the picture by rising from beyond Lucette (who was slim enough to remain seated) and brushing past Van (who stood up) in three jerky shuffles. Simultaneously he noticed two people, the long-lost Robinsons, who apparently had been separated from Lucette by those three women, and were now moving over to her. Beaming and melting in smiles of benevolence and self-effacement, they sidled up and plumped down next to Lucette, who turned to them with her last, last, last free gift of staunch courtesy that was stronger than failure and death. They were craning already across her, with radiant wrinkles and twittery fingers toward Van when he pounced upon their intrusion to murmur a humorous bad-sailor excuse and leave the cinema hall to its dark lurching.

In a series of sixty-year-old actions which now I can grind into extinction only by working on a succession of words until the rhythm is right, I, Van, retired to my bathroom, shut the door (it swung open at once, but then closed of its own accord) and using a temporary expedient less far-fetched than that hit upon by Father Sergius (who chops off the wrong member in Count Tolstoy's famous anecdote), vigorously got rid of the prurient pressure as he had done the last time seventeen years ago. And how sad, how significant that the picture projected upon the screen of his paroxysm, while the unlockable door swung open again with the movement of a deaf man cupping his ear, was not the recent and pertinent image of Lucette, but the indelible vision of a bent bare neck and a divided flow of black hair and a purple-tipped paint brush.

Then, for the sake of safety, he repeated the disgusting but necessary act.

He saw the situation dispassionately now and felt he was doing right by going to bed and switching off the "ectric" light (a surrogate creeping back into international use). The blue ghost of the room gradually established itself as his eyes got used to the darkness. He prided himself on his willpower. He welcomed the dull pain in his drained root. He welcomed the thought which suddenly seemed so absolutely true, and new, and as lividly real as the slowly widening gap of the sitting room's doorway, namely, that on the morrow (which was at least, and at best, seventy years away) he would explain to Lucette, as a philosopher and another girl's brother, that he knew how agonizing and how absurd it was to put all one's spiritual fortune on one physical fancy and that his plight closely resembled hers, but that he managed, after all, to live, to work, and not pine away because he refused to wreck her life with a brief affair and because Ada was still a child. At that point the surface of logic began to be affected by a ripple of sleep, but he sprang back into full consciousness at the sound of the telephone. The thing seemed to squat for each renewed burst of ringing and at first he decided to let it ring itself out. Then his nerves surrendered to the insisting signal, and he snatched up the receiver.

No doubt he was morally right in using the first pretext at hand to keep her away from his bed; but he also knew, as a

gentleman and an artist, that the lump of words he brought
up was trite and cruel, and it was only because she could not
accept him as being either, that she believed him:

"*Mozhno pridti teper'* (can I come now)?" asked Lucette.

"*Ya ne odin* (I'm not alone)," answered Van.

A small pause followed; then she hung up.

After he had stolen away, she had remained trapped between the cozy Robinsons (Rachel, dangling a big handbag,
had squeezed by immediately to the place Van had vacated,
and Bob had moved one seat up). Because of a sort of *pudeur*
she did not inform them that the actress (obscurely and fleetingly billed as "Theresa Zegris" in the "going-up" lift-list at
the end of the picture) who had managed to obtain the small
but not unimportant part of the fatal gipsy was none other
than the pallid schoolgirl they might have seen in Ladore.
They invited Lucette to a Coke with them—proselytical tee-
totalists—in their cabin, which was small and stuffy and badly
insulated, one could hear every word and whine of two children being put to bed by a silent seasick nurse, so late, so
late—no, not children, but probably very young, very much
disappointed honeymooners.

"We understand," said Robert Robinson going for another
supply to his portable fridge, "we understand perfectly that
Dr. Veen is deeply immersed in his Inter Resting Work—personally, I sometimes regret having retired—but do you think,
Lucy, *prosit!*, that he might accept to have dinner tomorrow
with you and us and maybe Another Couple, whom he'll certainly enjoy meeting? Shall Mrs. Robinson send him a formal
invitation? Would you sign it, too?"

"I don't know, I'm very tired," she said, "and the rock and
roll are getting worse. I guess I'll go up to my hutch and take
your Quietus. Yes, by all means, let's have dinner, all of us. I
really needed that lovely cold drink."

Having cradled the nacred receiver she changed into black
slacks and a lemon shirt (planned for tomorrow morning);
looked in vain for a bit of plain notepaper without caravelle
or crest; ripped out the flyleaf of Herb's Journal, and tried to
think up something amusing, harmless, and scintillating to say
in a suicide note. But she had planned everything except that
note, so she tore her blank life in two and disposed of the

pieces in the W.C.; she poured herself a glass of dead water from a moored decanter, gulped down one by one four green pills, and, sucking the fifth, walked to the lift which took her one click up from her three-room suite straight to the red-carpeted promenade-deck bar. There, two sluglike young men were in the act of sliding off their red toadstools, and the older one said to the other as they turned to leave: "You may fool his lordship, my dear, but not me, oh, no."

She drank a "Cossack pony" of Klass vodka—hateful, vulgar, but potent stuff; had another; and was hardly able to down a third because her head had started to swim like hell. Swim like hell from sharks, Tobakovich!

She had no purse with her. She almost fell from her convex ridiculous seat as she fumbled in her shirt pocket for a stray bank note.

"Beddydee," said Toby the barman with a fatherly smile, which she mistook for a leer. "Bedtime, miss," he repeated and patted her ungloved hand.

Lucette recoiled and forced herself to retort distinctly and haughtily:

"Mr. Veen, my cousin, will pay you tomorrow and bash your false teeth in."

Six, seven—no, more than that, about ten steps up. *Dix marches.* Legs and arms. *Dimanche. Déjeuner sur l'herbe. Tout le monde pue. Ma belle-mère avale son râtelier. Sa petite chienne,* after too much exercise, gulps twice and quietly vomits, a pink pudding onto the picnic *nappe. Après quoi* she waddles off. These steps are something.

While dragging herself up she had to hang onto the rail. Her twisted progress was that of a cripple. Once on the open deck she felt the solid impact of the black night, and the mobility of the accidental home she was about to leave.

Although Lucette had never died before—no, *dived* before, Violet—from such a height, in such a disorder of shadows and snaking reflections, she went with hardly a splash through the wave that humped to welcome her. That perfect end was spoiled by her instinctively surfacing in an immediate sweep—instead of surrendering under water to her drugged lassitude as she had planned to do on her last night ashore if it ever did come to this. The silly girl had not rehearsed the technique of suicide as, say, free-fall parachutists do every day in the element of another chapter. Owing to the tumultuous swell and her not being sure which way to peer through the spray and the darkness and her own tentaclinging hair—t,a,c,l—she could not make out the lights of the liner, an easily imagined many-eyed bulk mightily receding in heartless triumph. Now I've lost my next note.

Got it.

The sky was also heartless and dark, and her body, her head, and particularly those damned thirsty trousers, felt clogged with Oceanus Nox, n,o,x. At every slap and splash of cold wild salt, she heaved with anise-flavored nausea and there was an increasing number, okay, or numbness, in her neck and arms. As she began losing track of herself, she thought it proper to inform a series of receding Lucettes—telling them to pass it on and on in a trick-crystal regression—that what death amounted to was only a more complete assortment of the infinite fractions of solitude.

She did not see her whole life flash before her as we all were afraid she might have done; the red rubber of a favorite doll remained safely decomposed among the myosotes of an unanalyzable brook; but she did see a few odds and ends as she swam like a dilettante Tobakoff in a circle of brief panic and merciful torpor. She saw a pair of new vair-furred bedroom slippers, which Brigitte had forgotten to pack; she saw Van wiping his mouth before answering, and then, still withholding the answer, throwing his napkin on the table as they both got up; and she saw a girl with long black hair quickly bend in passing to clap her hands over a dackel in a half-torn wreath.

A brilliantly illumined motorboat was launched from the not-too-distant ship with Van and the swimming coach and the oilskin-hooded Toby among the would-be saviors; but by that time a lot of sea had rolled by and Lucette was too tired to wait. Then the night was filled with the rattle of an old but still strong helicopter. Its diligent beam could spot only the dark head of Van, who, having been propelled out of the boat when it shied from its own sudden shadow, kept bobbing and bawling the drowned girl's name in the black, foam-veined, complicated waters.

6

Father:

enclosed is a self-explanatory letter which, please, read and, if unobjectionable in your opinion, forward to Mrs. Vinelander, whose address I don't know. For your own edification—although it hardly matters at this stage—Lucette never was my mistress, as an obscene ass, whom I cannot trace, implies in the "write-up" of the tragedy.

I'm told you'll be back East next month. Have your current secretary ring me up at Kingston, if you care to see me.

Ada:

I wish to correct and amplify the accounts of her death published here even before I arrived. We were not *"traveling together." We embarked at two different ports and I did not know that she was aboard. Our relationship remained what it had always been. I spent the next day (June 4) entirely with her, except for a couple of hours before dinner. We basked in the sun. She enjoyed the brisk breeze and the bright brine of the pool. She was doing her best to appear carefree but I saw how wrong things were. The romantic attachment she had formed, the infatuation she cultivated, could not be severed by logic. On top of that, somebody she could not compete with entered the picture. The Robinsons, Robert and Rachel, who, I know, planned to write to you through my father, were the penultimate people to talk to her that night. The last was a bartender. He was worried by her behavior, followed her up to the open deck and witnessed but could not stop her jump.*

I suppose it is inevitable that after such a loss one should treasure its every detail, every string that snapped, every fringe that frayed, in the immediate precession. I had sat with her through the greater part of a movie, Castles in Spain *(or some title like that), and its liberal villain was being directed to the last of them, when I decided to abandon her to the auspices of the Robinsons, who had joined us in the ship's theater. I went to bed—and was called* around 1 A.M. *mariTime,* a few moments after she had jumped overboard. Attempts to rescue her were made on a reasonable scale, but, finally, the awful decision to resume the voyage, after an hour of confusion and hope, had to be taken by the Captain. Had I found him bribable, we would still be circling today the fatal spot.

As a psychologist, I know the unsoundness of speculations as to whether Ophelia would not have drowned herself after all, without the help of a treacherous sliver, even if she had married her Voltemand. Impersonally I believe she would have died in her bed, gray and serene, had V. loved her; but since he did not really love the wretched little virgin, and since no amount of carnal tenderness could or can pass for true love, and since, above all, the fatal Andalusian wench who had come, I repeat, into the picture, was unforgettable, I am bound to arrive, dear Ada and dear Andrey, at the conclusion that whatever the miserable man could have thought up, she would have po-konchila s soboy *("put an end to herself")* all the same. In other more deeply moral worlds than this pellet of muck, there might exist restraints, principles, transcendental consolations, and even a certain pride in making happy someone one does not really love; but on this planet Lucettes are doomed.

Some poor little things belonging to her—a cigarette case, a tulle evening frock, a book dog's-eared at a French picnic—have had to be destroyed, because they stared at me. I remain your obedient servant.

Son:

I have followed your instructions, anent that letter, to the letter. Your epistolary style is so involute that I should suspect the presence of a code, had I not known you belonged to the Decadent School of writing, in company of naughty old Leo and consumptive Anton. I do not give a damn whether you slept or not with Lucette; but I know from Dorothy Vinelander that the child had been in love with you. The film you saw was, no doubt, Don Juan's Last Fling *in which Ada, indeed, impersonates (very beautifully) a Spanish girl. A jinx has been cast on our poor*

*girl's career. Howard Hool argued after the release that
he had been made to play an impossible cross between two
Dons; that initially Yuzlik (the director) had meant to
base his "fantasy" on Cervantes's crude romance; that
some scraps of the basic script stuck like dirty wool to the
final theme; and that if you followed closely the sound track
you could hear a fellow reveler in the tavern scene address
Hool twice as "Quicks." Hool managed to buy up and
destroy a number of copies while others have been locked
up by the lawyer of the writer Osberg, who claims the* gitanilla *sequence was stolen from one of his own concoctions.
In result it is impossible to purchase a reel of the picture
which will vanish like the proverbial smoke once it has fizzled out on provincial screens. Come and have dinner with
me on July 10. Evening dress.*

Cher ami,

Nous fûmes, mon mari et moi, profondément boule-
versés par l'effroyable nouvelle. C'est à moi—et je m'en
souviendrai toujours!—que presqu'à la veille de sa mort
cette pauvre fille s'est adressée pour arranger les choses
sur le *Tobakoff* qui est toujours bondé, et que désormais
je ne prendrai plus, par un peu de superstition et beaucoup de sympathie pour la douce, la tendre Lucette.
J'étais si heureuse de faire mon possible, car quelqu'un
m'avait dit que vous aussi y seriez; d'ailleurs, elle m'en
a parlé elle-même: elle semblait tellement joyeuse de
passer quelques jours sur le "pont des gaillards" avec
son cher cousin! La psychologie du suicide est un mys-
tère que nul savant ne peut expliquer.

Je n'ai jamais versé tant de larmes, la plume m'en
tombe des doigts. Nous revenons à Malbrook vers la mi-
août. Bien à vous,

                              Cordula de Prey-Tobak

Van:

*Andrey and I were deeply moved by the additional data
you provide in your dear (i.e., insufficiently stamped!) letter. We had already received, through Mr. Grombchevski,
a note from the Robinsons, who cannot forgive themselves,*

poor well-meaning friends, for giving her that seasickness medicine, an overdose of which, topped by liquor, must have impaired her capacity to survive—if she changed her mind in the cold dark water. I cannot express, dear Van, how unhappy I am, the more so as we never learned in the arbors of Ardis that such unhappiness could exist.

My only love:

This letter will never be posted. It will lie in a steel box buried under a cypress in the garden of Villa Armina, and when it turns up by chance half a millennium hence, nobody will know who wrote it and for whom it was meant. It would not have been written at all if your last line, your cry of unhappiness, were not my *cry of triumph. The burden of that excitement must be . . . [The rest of the sentence was found to be obliterated by a rusty stain when the box was dug up in 1928. The letter continues as follows]: . . . back in the States, I started upon a singular quest. In Manhattan, in Kingston, in Ladore, in dozens of other towns, I kept pursuing the picture which I had not [badly discolored] on the boat, from cinema to cinema, every time discovering a new item of glorious torture, a new convulsion of beauty in your performance. That [illegible] is a complete refutation of odious Kim's odious stills. Artistically, and ardisiacally, the best moment is one of the last—when you follow barefoot the Don who walks down a marble gallery to his doom, to the scaffold of Dona Anna's black-curtained bed, around which you flutter, my Zegris butterfly, straightening a comically drooping candle, whispering delightful but futile instructions into the frowning lady's ear, and then peering over that mauresque screen and suddenly dissolving in such natural laughter, helpless and lovely, that one wonders if* any *art could do without that erotic gasp of schoolgirl mirth. And to think, Spanish orange-tip, that all in all your magic gambol lasted but eleven minutes of stopwatch time in patches of two- or three-minute scenes!*

Alas, there came a night, in a dismal district of workshops and bleary shebeens, when for the very last time, and only halfway, because at the seduction scene the film black-

winked and shriveled, I managed to catch [*the entire end of the letter is damaged*].

7

He greeted the dawn of a placid and prosperous century (more than half of which Ada and I have now seen) with the beginning of his second philosophic fable, a "denunciation of space" (never to be completed, but forming, in rear vision, a preface to his Texture of Time). Part of that treatise, a rather mannered affair, but nasty and sound, appeared in the first issue (January, 1904) of a now famous American monthly, *The Artisan*, and a comment on the excerpt is preserved in one of the tragically formal letters (all destroyed save this one) that his sister sent him by public post now and then. Somehow, after the interchange occasioned by Lucette's death such non-clandestine correspondence had been established with the tacit sanction of Demon:

> And o'er the summits of the Tacit
> He, banned from Paradise, flew on:
> Beneath him, like a brilliant's facet,
> Mount Peck with snows eternal shone.

It would seem indeed that continued ignorance of each other's existence might have looked more suspicious than the following sort of note:

Agavia Ranch
February 5, 1905

I have just read Reflections in Sidra, *by Ivan Veen, and I regard it as a grand piece, dear Professor. The "lost shafts of destiny" and other poetical touches reminded me of the two or three times you had tea and muffins at our place in the country about twenty years ago. I was, you remember (presumptuous phrase!),* a petite fille modèle *practicing archery near a vase and a parapet and you were a shy schoolboy (with whom, as my mother guessed, I may have been a wee bit in love!), who dutifully picked up the arrows I lost in the lost shrubbery of the lost castle of*

*poor Lucette's and happy, happy Adette's childhood, now a
"Home for Blind Blacks"—both my mother and L., I'm
sure, would have backed Dasha's advice to turn it over to
her Sect. Dasha, my sister-in-law (you must meet her soon,
yes, yes, yes, she's dreamy and lovely, and lots more intel-
ligent than I), who showed me your piece, asks me to add
she hopes to "renew" your acquaintance—maybe in Switzerland, at the Bellevue in Mont Roux, in October. I think
you once met pretty Miss "Kim" Blackrent, well, that's
exactly dear Dasha's type. She is very good at perceiving
and pursuing originality and all kinds of studies which I
can't even name! She finished Chose (where she read History—our Lucette used to call it* "Sale Histoire," *so sad
and funny!). For her you're* le beau ténébreux, *because
once upon a time, once upon libellula wings, not long before my marriage, she attended—I mean at that time, I'm
stuck in my "turnstyle"—one of your public lectures on
dreams, after which she went up to you with her latest little
nightmare all typed out and neatly clipped together, and
you scowled darkly and refused to take it. Well, she's been
after Uncle Dementiy to have him admonish* le beau ténébreux *to come to Mont Roux Bellevue Hotel, in October,
around the seventeenth, I guess, and he only laughs and
says it's up to Dashenka and me to arrange matters.*

*So "congs" again, dear Ivan! You are, we both think,
a marvelous, inimitable artist who should also "only
laugh," if cretinic critics, especially lower-upper-middle-
class Englishmen, accuse his* turnstyle *of being "coy" and
"arch," much as an American farmer finds the parson
"peculiar" because he knows Greek.*

P.S.

Dushevno klanyayus' (*"am souledly bowing" an incorrect and vulgar construction evoking the image of a "bowing soul"*) nashemu zaochno dorogomu professoru (*"to
our 'unsight-unseen' dear professor"*), o kotorom mnogo
slïshal (*about whom have heard much*) ot dobrago De-
mentiya Dedalovicha i sestritsï (*from good Demon and
my sister*).

S uvazheniem (*with respect*),
Andrey Vaynlender

Furnished Space, *l'espace meublé* (known to us only as furnished and full even if its contents be "absence of substance"—which seats the mind, too), is mostly watery so far as this globe is concerned. In that form it destroyed Lucette. Another variety, more or less atmospheric, but no less gravitational and loathsome, destroyed Demon.

Idly, one March morning, 1905, on the terrace of Villa Armina, where he sat on a rug, surrounded by four or five lazy nudes, like a sultan, Van opened an American daily paper published in Nice. In the fourth or fifth worst airplane disaster of the young century, a gigantic flying machine had inexplicably disintegrated at fifteen thousand feet above the Pacific between Lisiansky and Laysanov Islands in the Gavaille region. A list of "leading figures" dead in the explosion comprised the advertising manager of a department store, the acting foreman in the sheet-metal division of a facsimile corporation, a recording firm executive, the senior partner of a law firm, an architect with heavy aviation background (a first misprint here, impossible to straighten out), the vice president of an insurance corporation, another vice president, this time of a board of adjustment whatever that might be—

"I'm hongree," said a *maussade* Lebanese beauty of fifteen sultry summers.

"Use bell," said Van, continuing in a state of odd fascination to go through the compilation of labeled lives:

—the president of a wholesale liquor-distributing firm, the manager of a turbine equipment company, a pencil manufacturer, two professors of philosophy, two newspaper reporters (with nothing more to report), the assistant controller of a wholesome liquor distribution bank (misprinted and misplaced), the assistant controller of a trust company, a president, the secretary of a printing agency—

The names of those big shots, as well as those of some eighty other men, women, and silent children who perished in blue air, were being withheld until all relatives had been reached; but the tabulatory preview of commonplace abstractions had been thought to be too imposing not to be given at once as an appetizer; and only on the following morning did Van learn that a bank president lost in the closing garble was his father.

"The lost shafts of every man's destiny remain scattered all around him," etc. (*Reflections in Sidra*).

The last occasion on which Van had seen his father was at their house, in the spring of 1904. Other people had been present: old Eliot, the real-estate man, two lawyers (Grombchevski and Gromwell), Dr. Aix, the art expert, Rosalind Knight, Demon's new secretary, and solemn Kithar Sween, a banker who at sixty-five had become an *avant-garde* author; in the course of one miraculous year he had produced *The Waistline*, a satire in free verse on Anglo-American feeding habits, and *Cardinal Grishkin*, an overtly subtle yarn extolling the Roman faith. The poem was but the twinkle in an owl's eye; as to the novel it had already been pronounced "seminal" by celebrated young critics (Norman Girsh, Louis Deer, many others) who lauded it in reverential voices pitched so high that an ordinary human ear could not make much of that treble volubility; it seemed, however, all very exciting, and after a great bang of obituary essays in 1910 ("Kithar Sween: the man and the writer," "Sween as poet and person," "Kithar Kirman Lavehr Sween: a tentative biography") both the satire and the romance were to be forgotten as thoroughly as that acting foreman's control of background adjustment—or Demon's edict.

The table talk dealt mainly with business matters. Demon had recently bought a small, perfectly round Pacific island, with a pink house on a green bluff and a sand beach like a frill (as seen from the air), and now wished to sell the precious little palazzo in East Manhattan that Van did not want. Mr. Sween, a greedy practitioner with flashy rings on fat fingers, said he might buy it if some of the pictures were thrown in. The deal did not come off.

Van pursued his studies in private until his election (at thirty-five!) to the Rattner Chair of Philosophy in the University of Kingston. The Council's choice had been a consequence of disaster and desperation; the two other candidates, solid scholars much older and altogether better than he, esteemed even in Tartary where they often traveled, starry-eyed, hand-in-hand, had mysteriously vanished (perhaps dying under false names in the never-explained accident above the smiling ocean) at the "eleventh hour," for the Chair was to be dismantled if it remained vacant for a legally limited length of time, so as to give another, less-coveted but perfectly good seat the chance to be brought in from the back parlor. Van neither needed nor appreciated the thing, but accepted it in a spirit of good-natured perversity or perverse gratitude, or simply in memory of his father who had been somehow involved in the whole affair. He did not take his task too seriously, reducing to a strict minimum, ten or so per year, the lectures he delivered in a nasal drone mainly produced by a new and hard to get "voice recorder" concealed in his waistcoat pocket, among anti-infection Venus pills, while he moved his lips silently and thought of the lamplit page of his sprawling script left unfinished in his study. He spent in Kingston a score of dull years (variegated by trips abroad), an obscure figure around which no legends collected in the university or the city. Unbeloved by his austere colleagues, unknown in local pubs, unregretted by male students, he retired in 1922, after which he resided in Europe.

8

arriving mont roux bellevue sunday
dinnertime adoration sorrow rainbows

Van got this bold cable with his breakfast on Saturday, October 10, 1905, at the Manhattan Palace in Geneva, and that same day moved to Mont Roux at the opposite end of the lake. He put up there at his usual hotel, Les Trois Cygnes. Its small, frail, but almost mythically ancient concierge had died during Van's stay four years earlier, and instead of wizened Julien's discreet smile of mysterious complicity that used to shine like a lamp through parchment, the round rosy face of a recent bellboy, who now wore a frockcoat, greeted fat old Van.

"Lucien," said Dr. Veen, peering over his spectacles, "I may have—as your predecessor would know—all kinds of queer visitors, magicians, masked ladies, madmen—*que sais-je?* and I expect miracles of secrecy from all three mute swans. Here's a prefatory bonus."

"*Merci infiniment*," said the concierge, and, as usual, Van felt infinitely touched by the courteous hyperbole provoking no dearth of philosophical thought.

He engaged two spacious rooms, 509 and 510: an Old World salon with golden-green furniture, and a charming bed chamber joined to a square bathroom, evidently converted from an ordinary room (around 1875, when the hotel was renovated and splendified). With thrilling anticipation, he read the octagonal cardboard sign on its dainty red string: Do not disturb. *Prière de ne pas déranger.* Hang this notice on the doorhandle outside. Inform Telephone Exchange. *Avisez en particulier la téléphoniste* (no emphasis, no limpid-voiced girl in the English version).

He ordered an orgy of orchids from the *rez-de-chaussée* flower shop, and one ham sandwich from Room Service. He survived a long night (with Alpine Choughs heckling a cloudless dawn) in a bed hardly two-thirds the size of the tremendous one at their unforgettable flat twelve years ago. He breakfasted on the balcony—and ignored a reconnoitering gull. He allowed himself an opulent siesta after a late lunch; took a second bath to drown time; and with stops at every other bench on the promenade spent a couple of hours strolling over to the new Bellevue Palace, just half a mile southeast.

One red boat marred the blue mirror (in Casanova's days there would have been hundreds!). The grebes were there for the winter but the coots had not yet returned.

Ardis, Manhattan, Mont Roux, our little rousse is dead. Vrubel's wonderful picture of Father, those demented diamonds staring at me, painted *into* me.

Mount Russet, the forested hill behind the town, lived up to its name and autumnal reputation, with a warm glow of curly chestnut trees; and on the opposite shore of Leman, Leman meaning Lover, loomed the crest of Sex Noir, Black Rock.

He felt hot and uncomfortable in silk shirt and gray flannels—one of his older suits that he had chosen because it happened to make him look slimmer; but he should have omitted its tightish waistcoat. Nervous as a boy at his first rendezvous! He wondered what better to hope for—that her presence should be diluted at once by that of other people or that she should manage to be alone, for the first minutes, at least? Did his glasses and short black mustache really make him look younger, as polite whores affirmed?

When he reached at long last the whitewashed and blue-shaded Bellevue (patronized by wealthy Estotilanders, Rhein-landers, and Vinelanders, but not placed in the same superclass as the old, tawny and gilt, huge, sprawling, lovable Trois Cygnes), Van saw with dismay that his watch still lagged far behind 7:00 P.M., the earliest dinner hour in local hotels. So he recrossed the lane and had a double kirsch, with a lump of sugar, in a pub. A dead and dry hummingbird moth lay on the window ledge of the lavatory. Thank goodness, symbols did not exist either in dreams or in the life in between.

He pushed through the revolving door of the Bellevue, tripped over a gaudy suitcase, and made his entrée at a ridic-ulous run. The concierge snapped at the unfortunate green-aproned *cameriere*, who had left the bag there. Yes, they were expecting him in the lounge. A German tourist caught up with him, to apologize, effusively, and not without humor, for the offending object, which, he said, was his.

"If so," remarked Van, "you should not allow spas to slap their stickers on your private appendages."

His reply was inept, and the whole episode had a faint par-amnesic tang—and next instant Van was shot dead from be-hind (such things happen, some tourists are very unbalanced) and stepped into his next phase of existence.

He stopped on the threshold of the main lounge, but hardly had he begun to scan the distribution of its scattered hu-man contents, when an abrupt flurry occurred in a distant group. Ada, spurning decorum, was hurrying toward him. Her solitary and precipitate advance consumed in reverse all the years of their separation as she changed from a dark-glittering stranger with the high hair-do in fashion to the pale-armed girl in black who had always belonged to him. At that partic-ular twist of time they happened to be the only people con-spicuously erect and active in the huge room, and heads turned and eyes peered when the two met in the middle of it as on a stage; but what should have been, in culmination of her headlong motion, of the ecstasy in her eyes and fiery jew-els, a great explosion of voluble love, was marked by incon-

gruous silence; he raised to his unbending lips and kissed her
cygneous hand, and then they stood still, staring at each other,
he playing with coins in his trouser pockets under his
"humped" jacket, she fingering her necklace, each reflecting,
as it were, the uncertain light to which all that radiance of
mutual welcome had catastrophically decreased. She was more
Ada than ever, but a dash of new elegancy had been added to
her shy, wild charm. Her still blacker hair was drawn back and
up into a glossy chignon, and the Lucette line of her exposed
neck, slender and straight, came as a heartrending surprise.
He was trying to form a succint sentence (to warn her about
the device he planned for securing a rendezvous), but she
interrupted his throat clearing with a muttered injunction:
Shrit' usï! (that mustache must go) and turned away to lead
him to the far corner from which she had taken so many years
to reach him.

The first person whom she introduced him to, at that island
of fauteuils and androids, now getting up from around a low
table with a copper ashbowl for hub, was the promised *belle-
soeur*, a short plumpish lady in governess gray, very oval-faced,
with bobbed auburn hair, a sallowish complexion, smoke-blue
unsmiling eyes, and a fleshy little excrescence, resembling a
ripe maize kernel, at the side of one nostril, added to its hy-
percritical curve by an afterthought of nature as not seldom
happens when a Russian's face is mass-produced. The next
outstretched hand belonged to a handsome, tall, remarkably
substantial and cordial nobleman who could be none other
than the Prince Gremin of the preposterous libretto, and
whose strong honest clasp made Van crave for a disinfecting
fluid to wash off contact with any of her husband's public
parts. But as Ada, beaming again, made fluttery introductions
with an invisible wand, the person Van had grossly mistaken
for Andrey Vinelander was transformed into Yuzlik, the gifted
director of the ill-fated Don Juan picture. "Vasco de Gama,
I presume," Yuzlik murmured. Beside him, ignored by him,
unknown by name to Ada, and now long dead of dreary anonymous ailments, stood in servile attitudes the two agents of
Lemorio, the flamboyant comedian (a bearded boor of excep-
tional, and now also forgotten, genius, whom Yuzlik passionately wanted for his next picture). Lemorio had stood him up

twice before, in Rome and San Remo, each time sending him for "preliminary contact" those two seedy, incompetent, virtually insane, people with whom by now Yuzlik had nothing more to discuss, having exhausted everything, topical gossip, Lemorio's sex life, Hoole's hooliganism, as well as the hobbies of his, Yuzlik's, three sons and those of their, the agents', adopted child, a lovely Eurasian lad, who had recently been slain in a night-club fracas—which closed *that* subject. Ada had welcomed Yuzlik's unexpected reality in the lounge of the Bellevue not only as a counterpoise to the embarrassment and the deceit, but also because she hoped to sidle into *What Daisy Knew*; however, besides having no spells left in the turmoil of her spirit for business blandishments, she soon understood that if Lemorio were finally engaged, he would want her part for one of his mistresses.

Finally Van reached Ada's husband.

Van had murdered good Andrey Andreevich Vinelander so often, so thoroughly, at all the dark crossroads of the mind, that now the poor chap, dressed in a hideous, funereal, double-breasted suit, with those dough-soft features slapped together anyhow, and those sad-hound baggy eyes, and the dotted lines of sweat on his brow, presented all the depressing features of an unnecessary resurrection. Through a not-too-odd oversight (or rather "undersight") Ada omitted to introduce the two men. Her husband enunciated his name, patronymic, and surname with the didactic intonations of a Russian educational-film narrator. "*Obnimemsya, dorogoy*" (let us embrace, old boy), he added in a more vibrant voice but with his mournful expression unchanged (oddly remindful of that of Kosygin, the mayor of Yukonsk, receiving a girl scout's bouquet or inspecting the damage caused by an earthquake). His breath carried the odor of what Van recognized with astonishment as a strong tranquilizer on a neocodein base, prescribed in the case of psychopathic pseudobronchitis. As Andrey's crumpled forlorn face came closer, one could distinguish various wartlets and lumps, none of them, however, placed in the one-sided jaunty position of his kid sister's naric codicil. He kept his dun-colored hair as short as a soldier's by means of his own clippers. He had the *korrektniy*, and neat appearance of the one-bath-per-week Estotian *hobereau*.

We all flocked to the dining room. Van brushed against the past as he shot an arm out to forestall a door-opening waiter, and the past (still fingering *his* necklace) recompensed him with a sidelong "Dolores" glance.

Chance looked after the seating arrangement.

Lemorio's agents, an elderly couple, unwed but having lived as man and man for a sufficiently long period to warrant a silver-screen anniversary, remained unsplit at table between Yuzlik, who never once spoke to them, and Van, who was being tortured by Dorothy. As to Andrey (who made a thready "sign of the cross" over his un-unbuttonable abdomen before necking in his napkin), he found himself seated between sister and wife. He demanded the "cart de van" (affording the real Van mild amusement), but, being a hard-liquor man, cast only a stunned look at the "Swiss White" page of the wine list before "passing the buck" to Ada who promptly ordered champagne. He was to inform her early next morning that her "*Kuzen proizvodit* (produces) *udivitel'no simpatichnoe vpechatlenie* (a remarkably sympathetic, in the sense of 'fetching,' impression)." The dear fellow's verbal apparatus consisted almost exclusively of remarkably sympathetic Russian commonplaces of language, but—not liking to speak of himself—he spoke little, especially since his sister's sonorous soliloquy (lapping at Van's rock) mesmerized and childishly engrossed him. Dorothy preambled her long-delayed report on her pet nightmare with a humble complaint ("Of course, I know that for your patients to have bad dreams is a *zhidovskaya prerogativa*"), but her reluctant analyst's attention every time it returned to her from his plate fixed itself so insistently on the Greek cross of almost ecclesiastical size shining on her otherwise unremarkable chest that she thought fit to interrupt her narrative (which had to do with the eruption of a dream volcano) to say: "I gather from your writings that you are a terrible cynic. Oh, I quite agree with Simone Traser that a dash of cynicism adorns a real man; yet I'd like to warn you that I object to anti-Orthodox jokes in case you intend making one."

By now Van had more than enough of his mad, but not interestingly mad, convive. He just managed to steady his glass, which a gesture he made to attract Ada's attention had almost knocked down, and said, without further ado, in what Ada termed afterwards a mordant, ominous and altogether inadmissible tone:

"Tomorrow morning, *je veux vous accaparer, ma chère.* As my lawyer, or yours, or both, have, perhaps, informed you, Lucette's accounts in several Swiss banks—" and he trotted out a prepared version of a state of affairs invented *in toto.* "I suggest," he added, "that if you have no other engage-ments"—(sending a questioning glance that avoided the Vinelanders by leaping across and around the three cinemat-ists, all of whom nodded in idiotic approval)—"you and I go to see Maître Jorat, or Raton, name escapes me, my adviser, *enfin,* in Luzon, half an hour's drive from here—who has given me certain papers which I have at my hotel and which I must have you sigh—I mean sign with a sigh—the matter is tedious. All right? All right."

"But, Ada," clarioned Dora, "you forget that tomorrow morning we wanted to visit the Institute of Floral Harmony in the Château Piron!"

"You'll do it after tomorrow, or Tuesday, or Tuesday week," said Van. "I'd gladly drive all three of you to that fascinating *lieu de méditation* but my fast little Unseretti seats only one passenger, and that business of untraceable deposits is terribly urgent, I think."

Yuzlik was dying to say something. Van yielded to the well-meaning automaton.

"I'm delighted and honored to dine with Vasco de Gama," said Yuzlik holding up his glass in front of his handsome facial apparatus.

The same garbling—and this gave Van a clue to Yuzlik's source of recondite information—occurred in *The Chimes of Chose* (a memoir by a former chum of Van's, now Lord Chose, which had climbed, and still clung to, the "best seller" trel-lis—mainly because of several indecent but very funny refer-ences to the Villa Venus in Ranton Brooks). While he munched the marrow of an adequate answer, with a mouthful of *sharlott* (not the charlatan "*charlotte russe*" served in most restaurants, but the hot toasty crust, with apple filling, of the authentic castle pie made by Takomin, the hotel's head cook, who hailed from California's Rose Bay), two urges were cleaving Van asunder: one to insult Yuzlik for having placed his hand on Ada's when asking her to pass him the butter two or three courses ago (he was incomparably more jealous of that liquid-eyed male than of Andrey and remembered with a shiver of pride and hate how on New Year's Eve, 1892, he had lashed out at a relative of his, foppish Van Zemski, who had permitted himself a similar caress when visiting their restaurant table, and whose jaw he had broken later, under some pretext or other, at the young prince's club); and the other—to tell Yuzlik how much he had admired *Don Juan's Last Fling*. Not being able, for obvious reasons, to satisfy urge number one he dismissed number two as secretly smacking of a poltroon's politeness and contented himself with replying, after swallowing his amber-soaked mash:

"Jack Chose's book is certainly most entertaining—especially that bit about apples and diarrhea, and the excerpts from the Venus Shell Album"—(Yuzlik's eyes darted aside in specious recollection, whereupon he bowed in effusive tribute to a common memory)—"but the rascal should have neither divulged my name nor botched my thespionym."

During that dismal dinner (enlivened only by the *sharlott* and five bottles of Moët, out of which Van consumed more than three), he avoided looking at that part of Ada which is called "the face"—a vivid, divine, mysteriously shocking part, which, in that essential form, is rarely met with among human beings (pasty and warty masks do not count). Ada, on the other hand, could not help her dark eyes from turning to him every other moment, as if, with each glance, she regained her balance; but when the company went back to the lounge and finished their coffee there, difficulties of focalization began to beset Van, whose *points de repère* disastrously decreased after the three cinematists had left.

ANDREY: *Adochka, dushka* (darling), *razskazhi zhe pro rancho, pro skot* (tell about the ranch, the cattle), *emu zhe lyubopïtno* (it cannot fail to interest him).

ADA (*as if coming out of a trance*): *O chyom tï* (you were saying something)?

ANDREY: *Ya govoryu, razskazhi emu pro tvoyo zhit'yo*

bit'yo (I was saying, tell him about your daily life, your habitual existence). *Avos' zaglyanet k nam* (maybe he'd look us up).

ADA: *Ostav', chto tam interesnago* (forget it, what's so interesting about it)?

DASHA (*turning to Ivan*): Don't listen to her. *Massa interesnago* (heaps of interesting stuff). *Delo brata ogromnoe, volnuyushchee delo, trebuyushchee ne men'she truda, chem uchyonaya dissertatsiya* (his business is a big thing, quite as demanding as a scholar's). *Nashi sel'skohozyaystvennïya mashinï i ih teni* (our agricultural machines and their shadows)—*eto tselaya kollektsiya predmetov modernoy skul'pturï i zhivopisi* (is a veritable collection of modern art) which I suspect you adore as I do.

IVAN (*to Andrey*): I know nothing about farming but thanks all the same.

(*A pause.*)

IVAN (*not quite knowing what to add*): Yes, I would certainly like to see your machinery some day. Those things always remind me of long-necked prehistoric monsters, sort of grazing here and there, you know, or just brooding over the sorrows of extinction—but perhaps I'm thinking of excavators—

DOROTHY: Andrey's machinery is anything but prehistoric! (*laughs cheerlessly*).

ANDREY: *Slovom, milosti prosim* (anyway, you are most welcome). *Budete zharit' verhom s kuzinoy* (you'll have a rollicking time riding on horseback with your cousin).

(*Pause.*)

IVAN (*to Ada*): Half-past nine tomorrow morning won't be too early for you? I'm at the Trois Cygnes. I'll come to fetch you in my tiny car—not on horseback (smiles like a corpse at Andrey).

DASHA: *Dovol'no skuchno* (rather a pity) that Ada's visit to lovely Lake Leman need be spoiled by sessions with lawyers and bankers. I'm sure you can satisfy most of those needs by having her come a few times *chez vous* and not to Luzon or Geneva.

The madhouse babble reverted to Lucette's bank accounts, Ivan Dementievich explained that she had been mislaying one checkbook after another, and nobody knew exactly in how many different banks she had dumped considerable amounts of money. Presently, Andrey who now looked like the livid Yukonsk mayor after opening the Catkin Week Fair or fighting a Forest Fire with a new type of extinguisher, grunted out of his chair, excused himself for going to bed so early, and shook hands with Van as if they were parting forever (which, indeed, they were). Van remained with the two ladies in the cold and deserted lounge where a thrifty subtraction of faraday-light had imperceptibly taken place.

"How did you like my brother?" asked Dorothy. "*On red-chayshiy chelovek* (he's a most rare human being). I can't tell you how profoundly affected he was by the terrible death of your father, and, of course, by Lucette's bizarre end. Even he, the kindest of men, could not help disapproving of her Parisian *sans-gêne*, but he greatly admired her looks—as I think you also did—no, no, do not negate it!—because, as I always said, her prettiness seemed to complement Ada's, the two halves forming together something like perfect beauty, in the Platonic sense" (that cheerless smile again). "Ada is certainly a 'perfect beauty,' a real *muirninochka*—even when she winces like that—but she is beautiful only in our little human terms, within the quotes of our social esthetics—right, Professor?— in the way a meal or a marriage or a little French tramp can be called perfect."

"Drop her a curtsey," gloomily remarked Van to Ada.

"Oh, my Adochka knows how devoted I am to her"— (opening her palm in the wake of Ada's retreating hand). "I've shared all her troubles. How many *podzharih* (tight-crotched) cowboys we've had to fire because they *delali ey glazki* (ogled her)! And how many bereavements we've gone through since the new century started! Her mother and my mother; the Archbishop of Ivankover and Dr. Swissair of Lumbago (where mother and I reverently visited him in 1888);

three distinguished uncles (whom, fortunately, I hardly knew); and your father, who, I've always maintained, resembled a Russian aristocrat much more than he did an Irish Baron. Incidentally, in her deathbed delirium—you don't mind, Ada, if I divulge to him *ces potins de famille?*—our splendid Marina was obsessed by two delusions, which mutually excluded each other—that you were married to Ada and that you and she were brother and sister, and the clash between those two ideas caused her intense mental anguish. How does your school of psychiatry explain that kind of conflict?"

"I don't attend school any longer," said Van, stifling a yawn; "and, furthermore, in my works, I try not to 'explain' anything, I merely describe."

"Still, you cannot deny that certain insights—"

It went on and on like that for more than an hour and Van's clenched jaws began to ache. Finally, Ada got up, and Dorothy followed suit but continued to speak standing:

"Tomorrow dear Aunt Beloskunski-Belokonski is coming to dinner, a delightful old spinster, who lives in a villa above Valvey. *Terriblement grande dame et tout ça. Elle aime taquiner* Andryusha *en disant qu'un simple cultivateur comme lui n'aurait pas dû épouser la fille d'une actrice et d'un marchand de tableaux.* Would you care to join us—Jean?"

Jean replied: "Alas, no, dear Daria Andrevna: *Je dois 'surveiller les kilos.'* Besides, I have a business dinner tomorrow."

"At least"—(smiling)—"you could call me Dasha."

"I do it for Andrey," explained Ada, "actually the grand' dame in question is a vulgar old skunk."

"Ada!" uttered Dasha with a look of gentle reproof.

Before the two ladies proceeded toward the lift, Ada glanced at Van—and he—no fool in amorous strategy—refrained to comment on her "forgetting" her tiny black silk handbag on the seat of her chair. He did not accompany them beyond the passage leading liftward and, clutching the token, awaited her planned return behind a pillar of hotel-hall mongrel design, knowing that in a moment she would say to her accursed companion (by now revising, no doubt, her views on the "*beau ténébreux*") as the lift's eye turned red under a quick thumb: "*Akh, sumochku zabila* (forgot my bag)!"—and instantly flitting back, like Vere's Ninon, she would be in his arms.

Their open mouths met in tender fury, and then he pounced upon her new, young, divine, Japanese neck which he had been coveting like a veritable Jupiter Olorinus throughout the evening.

"We'll vroom straight to my place as soon as you wake up, don't bother to bathe, jump into your lenclose—" and, with the burning sap brimming, he again devoured her, until (Dorothy must have reached the sky!) she danced three fingers on his wet lips—and escaped.

"Wipe your neck!" he called after her in a rapid whisper (who, and where in this tale, in this life, had also attempted a *whispered cry*?)

That night, in a post-Moët dream, he sat on the talc of a tropical beach full of sun-baskers, and one moment was rubbing the red, irritated shaft of a writhing boy, and the next was looking through dark glasses at the symmetrical shading on either side of a shining spine with fainter shading between the ribs belonging to Lucette or Ada sitting on a towel at some distance from him. Presently, she turned and lay prone, and she, too, wore sunglasses, and neither he nor she could perceive the exact direction of each other's gaze through the black amber, yet he knew by the dimple of a faint smile that she was looking at his (it had been *his* all the time) raw scarlet. Somebody said, wheeling a table nearby: "It's one of the Vane sisters," and he awoke murmuring with professional appreciation the oneiric word-play combining his name and surname, and plucked out the wax plugs, and, in a marvelous act of rehabilitation and link-up, the breakfast table clanked from the corridor across the threshold of the adjacent room, and, already munching and honey-crumbed, Ada entered his bedchamber. It was only a quarter to eight!

"Smart girl!" said Van; "but first of all I must go to the *petit endroit* (W.C.)."

That meeting, and the nine that followed, constituted the highest ridge of their twenty-one-year-old love: its complicated, dangerous, ineffably radiant coming of age. The somewhat Italianate style of the apartment, its elaborate wall lamps with ornaments of pale caramel glass, its white knobbles that produced indiscriminately light or maids, the slat-stayed, veiled, heavily curtained windows which made the morning as difficult to disrobe as a crinolined prude, the convex sliding doors of the huge white "Nuremberg Virgin"-like closet in the hallway of their suite, and even the tinted engraving by Randon of a rather stark three-mast ship on the zigzag green waves of Marseilles Harbor—in a word, the alberghian atmosphere of those new trysts added a novelistic touch (Aleksey and Anna may have asterisked here!) which Ada welcomed as a frame, as a form, something supporting and guarding life, otherwise unprovidenced on Desdemonia, where artists are the only gods. When after three or four hours of frenetic love Van and Mrs. Vinelander would abandon their sumptuous retreat for the blue haze of an extraordinary October which kept dreamy and warm throughout the duration of adultery, they had the feeling of still being under the protection of those painted Priapi that the Romans once used to set up in the arbors of Rufomonticulus.

"I shall walk you home—we have just returned from a conference with the Luzon bankers and I'm walking you back to your hotel from mine"—this was the *phrase consacrée* that Van invariably uttered to inform the fates of the situation. One little precaution they took from the start was to strictly avoid equivocal exposure on their lakeside balcony which was visible to every yellow or mauve flowerhead on the platbands of the promenade.

They used a back exit to leave the hotel.

A boxwood-lined path, presided over by a nostalgic-looking sempervirent sequoia (which American visitors mistook for a "Lebanese cedar"—if they remarked it at all) took them to the absurdly misnamed rue du Mûrier, where a princely paulownia ("mulberry tree!" snorted Ada), standing in state on its incongruous terrace above a public W.C., was shedding generously its heart-shaped dark green leaves, but retained enough foliage to cast arabesques of shadow onto the south side of its trunk. A ginkgo (of a much more luminous greenish gold than its neighbor, a dingily yellowing local birch) marked the corner of a cobbled lane leading down to the quay. They followed southward the famous Fillietaz Promenade which went along the Swiss side of the lake from Valvey to the Château de Byron (or "She Yawns Castle"). The fashionable season had ended, and wintering birds, as well as a number of knickerbockered Central Europeans, had replaced the English families as well as the Russian noblemen from Nipissing and Nipigon.

"My upper-lip space feels indecently naked." (He had shaved his mustache off with howls of pain in her presence.) "And I cannot keep sucking in my belly all the time."

"Oh, I like you better with that nice overweight—there's more of you. It's the maternal gene, I suppose, because Demon grew leaner and leaner. He looked positively Quixotic when I saw him at Mother's funeral. It was all very strange. He wore blue mourning. D'Onsky's son, a person with only one arm, threw his remaining one around Demon and both wept *comme des fontaines*. Then a robed person who looked like an extra in a technicolor incarnation of Vishnu made an incomprehensible sermon. Then she went up in smoke. He said to me, sobbing: '*I* will not cheat the poor grubs!' Practically a couple of hours after he broke that promise we had sudden visitors at the ranch—an incredibly graceful moppet of eight, black-veiled, and a kind of duenna, also in black, with two bodyguards. The hag demanded certain fantastic sums—which Demon, she said, had not had time to pay, for 'popping the hymen'—whereupon I had one of our strongest boys throw out *vsyu* (the entire) *kompaniyu*."

"Extraordinary," said Van, "they had been growing younger and younger—I mean the girls, not the strong silent boys. His old Rosalind had a ten-year-old niece, a primed chickabiddy. Soon he would have been poaching them from the hatching chamber."

"You never loved your father," said Ada sadly.

"Oh, I did and do—tenderly, reverently, understandingly, because, after all, that minor poetry of the flesh is something not unfamiliar to me. But as far as we are concerned, I mean you and I, he was buried on the same day as our uncle Dan."

"I know, I know. It's pitiful! And what use was it? Perhaps I oughtn't to tell you, but his visits to Agavia kept getting rarer and shorter every year. Yes, it was pitiful to hear him and Andrey talking. I mean, Andrey *n'a pas le verbe facile*, though he greatly appreciated—without quite understanding it—Demon's wild flow of fancy and fantastic fact, and would often exclaim, with his Russian 'tssk-tssk' and a shake of the head—complimentary and all that—'what a *balagur* (wag) you are!'—And then, one day, Demon warned me that he would not come any more if he heard again poor Andrey's poor joke (*Nu i balagur-zhe vï, Dementiy Labirintovich*) or what Dorothy, *l'impayable* ('priceless for impudence and absurdity') Dorothy, thought of my camping out in the mountains with only Mayo, a cowhand, to protect me from lions."

"Could one hear more about that?" asked Van.

"Well, nobody did. All this happened at a time when I was not on speaking terms with my husband and sister-in-law, and so could not control the situation. Anyhow, Demon did not come even when he was only two hundred miles away and simply mailed instead, from some gaming house, your lovely, lovely letter about Lucette and my picture."

"One would also like to know some details of the actual coverture—frequence of intercourse, pet names for secret warts, favorite smells—"

"*Platok momental'no* (handkerchief quick)! Your right nostril is full of damp jade," said Ada, and then pointed to a lawnside circular sign, rimmed with red, saying: *Chiens interdits* and depicting an impossible black mongrel with a white ribbon around its neck: Why, she wondered, should the Swiss magistrates forbid one to cross highland terriers with poodles?

The last butterflies of 1905, indolent Peacocks and Red Admirables, one Queen of Spain and one Clouded Yellow, were making the most of the modest blossoms. A tram on their left passed close to the promenade, where they rested and cautiously kissed when the whine of wheels had subsided. The rails hit by the sun acquired a beautiful cobalt sheen—the reflection of noon in terms of bright metal.

"Let's have cheese and white wine under that pergola," suggested Van. "The Vinelanders will lunch *à deux* today."

Some kind of musical gadget played jungle jingles; the open bags of a Tirolese couple stood unpleasantly near—and Van bribed the waiter to carry their table out, onto the boards of an unused pier. Ada admired the waterfowl population: Tufted Ducks, black with contrasty white flanks making them look like shoppers (this and the other comparisons are all

Ada's) carrying away an elongated flat carton (new tie? gloves?) under each arm, while the black tuft recalled Van's head when he was fourteen and wet, having just taken a dip in the brook. Coots (which *had* returned after all), swimming with an odd pumping movement of the neck, the way horses walk. Small grebes and big ones, with crests, holding their heads erect, with something heraldic in their demeanor. They had, she said, wonderful nuptial rituals, closely facing each other—so (putting up her index fingers bracketwise)—rather like two bookends and no books between, and, shaking their heads in turn, with flashes of copper.

"I asked you about Andrey's rituals."

"Ach, Andrey is so excited to see all those European birds! He's a great sportsman and knows our Western game remarkably well. We have in the West a very cute little grebe with a black ribbon around its fat white bill. Andrey calls it *pestroklyuvaya chomga*. And that big *chomga* there is *hohlushka*, he says. If you scowl like that once again, when I say something innocent and on the whole rather entertaining, I'm going to kiss you on the tip of the nose, in front of everybody."

Just a tiny mite artificial, not in her best Veen. But she recovered instantly:

"Oh, look at those sea gulls playing chicken."

Several *rieuses*, a few of which were still wearing their tight black summer bonnets, had settled on the vermilion railing along the lakeside, with their tails to the path, and watched which of them would stay staunchly perched at the approach of the next passerby. The majority flapped waterward as Ada and Van neared; one twitched its tail feathers and made a movement analogous to "bending one's knees" but saw it through and remained on the railing.

"I think we noticed that species only once in Arizona—at a place called Saltsink—a kind of man-made lake. Our common ones have quite different wing tips."

A Crested Grebe, afloat some way off, slowly, very slowly started to sink, then abruptly executed a jumping fish plunge, showing its glossy white underside, and vanished.

"Why on earth," asked Van, "didn't you let her know, in one way or another, that you were not angry with her? Your phoney letter made her most unhappy!"

"Pah!" uttered Ada. "She put me in a most embarrassing situation. I can quite understand her being mad at Dorothy (who meant well, poor stupid thing—stupid enough to warn me against possible 'infections' such as 'labial lesbianitis.' *Labial lesbianitis!*) but that was no reason for Lucette to look up Andrey in town and tell him she was great friends with the man I had loved before my marriage. He didn't dare annoy me with his revived curiosity, but he complained to Dorothy of Lucette's *neopravdannaya zhestokost'* (unjustified cruelty)."

"Ada, Ada," groaned Van, "I want you to get rid of that husband of yours, *and* his sister, right *now!*"

"Give me a fortnight," she said, "I have to go back to the ranch. I can't bear the thought of her poking among my things."

At first everything seemed to proceed according to the instructions of some friendly genius.

Much to Van's amusement (the tasteless display of which his mistress neither condoned nor condemned), Andrey was laid up with a cold for most of the week. Dorothy, a born nurser, considerably surpassed Ada (who, never being ill herself, could not stand the sight of an ailing stranger) in readiness of sickbed attendance, such as reading to the sweating and suffocating patient old issues of the *Golos Feniksa*; but on Friday the hotel doctor bundled him off to the nearby American Hospital, where even his sister was not allowed to visit him "because of the constant necessity of routine tests"—or rather because the poor fellow wished to confront disaster in manly solitude.

During the next days, Dorothy used her leisure to spy upon Ada. The woman was sure of three things: that Ada had a lover in Switzerland; that Van was her brother; and that he was arranging for his irresistible sister secret trysts with the person she had loved before her marriage. The delightful phenomenon of all three terms being true, but making nonsense when hashed, provided Van with another source of amusement.

The Three Swans overwinged a bastion. Anyone who called, flesh or voice, was told by the concierge or his acolytes that Van was out, that Madame André Vinelander was unknown, and that all they could do was to take a message. His car,

parked in a secluded bosquet, could not betray his presence.
In the forenoon he regularly used the service lift that communicated directly with the backyard. Lucien, something of a
wit, soon learned to recognize Dorothy's contralto: "*La voix
cuivrée a téléphoné*," "*La Trompette n'était pas contente ce
matin*," et cetera. Then the friendly Fates took a day off.

Andrey had had a first copious hemorrhage while on a business trip to Phoenix sometime in August. A stubborn, independent, not overbright optimist, he had ascribed it to a
nosebleed having gone the wrong way and concealed it from
everybody so as to avoid "stupid talks." He had had for years
a two-pack smoker's fruity cough, but when a few days after
that first "postnasal blood drip" he spat a scarlet gob into his
washbasin, he resolved to cut down on cigarettes and limit
himself to *tsigarki* (cigarillos). The next *contretemps* occurred
in Ada's presence, just before they left for Europe; he managed to dispose of his bloodstained handkerchief before she
saw it, but she remembered him saying "*Vot te na*" (well,
that's odd) in a bothered voice. Believing with most other
Estotians that the best doctors were to be found in Central
Europe, he told himself he would see a Zurich specialist whose
name he got from a member of his "lodge" (meeting place
of brotherly moneymakers), if he again coughed up blood.
The American hospital in Valvey, next to the Russian church
built by Vladimir Chevalier, his granduncle, proved to be
good enough for diagnosing advanced tuberculosis of the left
lung.

On Wednesday, October 22, in the early afternoon, Dorothy, "frantically" trying to "locate" Ada (who after her usual
visit to the Three Swans was spending a couple of profitable
hours at Paphia's "Hair and Beauty" Salon) left a message for
Van, who got it only late at night when he returned from a
trip to Sorcière, in the Valais, about one hundred miles east,
where he bought a villa for himself *et ma cousine*, and had
supper with the former owner, a banker's widow, amiable
Mme Scarlet and her blond, pimply but pretty, daughter Eveline, both of whom seemed erotically moved by the rapidity
of the deal.

He was still calm and confident; after carefully studying
Dorothy's hysterical report, he still believed that nothing threat-

ened their destiny; that at best Andrey would die right now, sparing Ada the bother of a divorce; and that at worst the man would be packed off to a mountain sanatorium in a novel to linger there through a few last pages of epilogical mopping up far away from the reality of *their* united lives. Friday morning, at nine o'clock—as bespoken on the eve—he drove over to the Bellevue, with the pleasant plan of motoring to Sorcière to show her the house.

At night a thunderstorm had rather patly broken the back of the miraculous summer. Even more patly the sudden onset of her flow had curtailed yesterday's caresses. It was raining when he slammed the door of his car, hitched up his velveteen slacks, and, stepping across puddles, passed between an ambulance and a large black Yak, waiting one behind the other before the hotel. All the wings of the Yak were spread open, two bellboys had started to pile in luggage under the chauffeur's supervision, and various parts of the old hackney car were responding with discreet creaks to the grunts of the loaders.

He suddenly became aware of the rain's reptile cold on his balding head and was about to enter the glass revolvo, when it produced Ada, somewhat in the manner of those carvedwood barometers whose doors yield either a male puppet or a female one. Her attire—that mackintosh over a high-necked dress, the fichu on her upswept hair, the crocodile bag slung across her shoulder—formed a faintly old-fashioned and even provincial ensemble. "On her there was no face," as Russians say to describe an expression of utter dejection.

She led him around the hotel to an ugly rotunda, out of the miserable drizzle, and there she attempted to embrace him but he evaded her lips. She was leaving in a few minutes. Heroic, helpless Andrey had been brought back to the hotel in an ambulance. Dorothy had managed to obtain three seats on the Geneva-Phoenix plane. The two cars were taking him, her and the heroic sister straight to the helpless airport.

She asked for a handkerchief, and he pulled out a blue one from his windjacket pocket, but her tears had started to roll and she shaded her eyes, while he stood before her with outstretched hand.

"Part of the act?" he inquired coldly.

She shook her head, took the handkerchief with a childish "*merci*," blew her nose and gasped, and swallowed, and spoke, and next moment all, all was lost.

She could not tell her husband while he was ill. Van would have to wait until Andrey was sufficiently well to bear the news and that might take some time. Of course, she would have to do everything to have him completely cured, there was a wonder-maker in Arizona—

"Sort of patching up a bloke before hanging him," said Van.

"And to think," cried Ada with a kind of square shake of stiff hands as if dropping a lid or a tray, "to think that he dutifully concealed everything! Oh, of course, I can't leave him now!"

"Yes, the old story—the flute player whose impotence has to be treated, the reckless ensign who may never return from a distant war!"

"*Ne ricane pas!*" exclaimed Ada. "The poor, poor little man! How dare you sneer?"

As had been peculiar to his nature even in the days of his youth, Van was apt to relieve a passion of anger and disappointment by means of bombastic and arcane utterances which hurt like a jagged fingernail caught in satin, the lining of Hell.

"Castle True, Castle Bright!" he now cried, "Helen of Troy, Ada of Ardis! You have betrayed the Tree and the Moth!"

"*Perestagne* (stop, *cesse*)!"

"Ardis the First, Ardis the Second, Tanned Man in a Hat, and now Mount Russet—"

"*Perestagne!*" repeated Ada (like a fool dealing with an epileptic).

"*Oh! Qui me rendra mon Hélène—*"

"Ach, *perestagne!*"

"—*et le phalène.*"

"*Je t'emplie* ('*prie*' and '*supplie*'), stop, Van. *Tu sais que j'en vais mourir.*"

"But, but, but"—(slapping every time his forehead)—"to be on the very brink of, of, of—and then have that idiot turn Keats!"

"*Bozhe moy*, I must be going. Say something to me, my darling, my only one, something that might help!"

There was a narrow chasm of silence broken only by the rain drumming on the eaves.

"Stay with me, girl," said Van, forgetting everything—pride, rage, the convention of everyday pity.

For an instant she seemed to waver—or at least to consider wavering; but a resonant voice reached them from the drive and there stood Dorothy, gray-caped and mannish-hatted, energetically beckoning with her unfurled umbrella.

"I can't, I can't, I'll write you," murmured my poor love in tears.

Van kissed her leaf-cold hand and, letting the Bellevue worry about his car, letting all Swans worry about his effects and Mme Scarlet worry about Eveline's skin trouble, he walked some ten kilometers along soggy roads to Rennaz and thence flew to Nice, Biskra, the Cape, Nairobi, the Basset range—

> *And oe'r the summits of the Basset—*

Would she write? Oh, she did! Oh, every old thing turned out superfine! Fancy raced fact in never-ending rivalry and girl giggles. Andrey lived only a few months longer, *po pal'tzam* (finger counting) one, two, three, four—say, five. Andrey was doing fine by the spring of nineteen six or seven, with a comfortably collapsed lung and a straw-colored beard (nothing like facial vegetation to keep a patient busy). Life forked and re-forked. Yes, she told him. He insulted Van on the mauve-painted porch of a Douglas hotel where Van was awaiting his Ada in a final version of *Les Enfants Maudits*. Monsieur de Tobak (an earlier cuckold) and Lord Erminin (a second-time second) witnessed the duel in the company of a few tall yuccas and short cactuses. Vinelander wore a cutaway (he would); Van, a white suit. Neither man wished to take any chances, and both fired simultaneously. Both fell. Mr. Cutaway's bullet struck the outsole of Van's left shoe (white, black-heeled), tripping him and causing a slight *fourmillement* (excited ants) in his foot—that was all. Van got his adversary plunk in the underbelly—a serious wound from which he recovered in due time, if at all (here the forking swims in the mist). Actually it was all much duller.

So she did write as she had promised? Oh, yes, yes! In seventeen years he received from her around a hundred brief notes, each containing around one hundred words, making around thirty printed pages of insignificant stuff—mainly about her husband's health and the local fauna. After helping her to nurse Andrey at Agavia Ranch through a couple of acrimonious years (she begrudged Ada every poor little hour devoted to collecting, mounting, and rearing!), and then taking exception to Ada's choosing the famous and excellent Grotonovich Clinic (for her husband's endless periods of treatment) instead of Princess Alashin's select sanatorium, Dorothy Vinelander retired to a subarctic monastery town (Ilemna, now Novostabia) where eventually she married a Mr. Brod or Bred, tender and passionate, dark and handsome, who traveled in eucharistials and other sacramental objects throughout the Severnïya Territorii and who subsequently was to direct, and still may be directing half a century later, archeological reconstructions at Goreloe (the "Lyaskan Herculanum"); what treasures he dug up in matrimony is another question.

Steadily but very slowly Andrey's condition kept deteriorating. During his last two or three years of idle existence on various articulated couches, whose every plane could be altered in hundreds of ways, he lost the power of speech, though still able to nod or shake his head, frown in concentration, or faintly smile when inhaling the smell of food (the origin, indeed, of our first beatitudes). He died one spring night, alone in a hospital room, and that same summer (1922) his widow donated her collections to a National Park museum and traveled by air to Switzerland for an "exploratory interview" with fifty-two-year-old Van Veen.

Part Four

Here a heckler asked, with the arrogant air of one wanting to see a gentleman's driving license, how did the "Prof" reconcile his refusal to grant the future the status of Time with the fact that it, the future, could hardly be considered nonexistent, since "it possessed at least one future, I mean, feature, involving such an important idea as that of absolute necessity."

Throw him out. Who said *I* shall die?

Refuting the determinist's statement more elegantly: unconsciousness, far from awaiting us, with flyback and noose, somewhere ahead, envelops both the Past and the Present from all conceivable sides, being a character not of Time itself but of organic decline natural to all things whether conscious of Time or not. That I know others die is irrelevant to the case. I also know that you, and, probably, I, were born, but that does not *prove* we went through the chronal phase called the Past: my Present, my brief span of consciousness, tells me I did, not the silent thunder of the infinite unconsciousness proper to my birth fifty-two years and 195 days ago. My first recollection goes back to mid-July, 1870, i.e., my seventh month of life (with most people, of course, retentive consciousness starts somewhat later, at three or four years of age) when, one morning, in our Riviera villa, a chunk of green plaster ornament, dislodged from the ceiling by an earthquake, crashed into my cradle. The 195 days preceding that event being indistinguishable from infinite unconsciousness, are not to be included in perceptual time, so that, insofar as my mind and my pride of mind are concerned, I am today (mid-July, 1922) quite exactly fifty-two, *et trêve de mon style plafond peint.*

In the same sense of individual, perceptual time, I can put my Past in reverse gear, enjoy this moment of recollection as much as I did the horn of abundance whose stucco pineapple just missed my head, and postulate that next moment a cosmic or corporeal cataclysm might—not kill me, but plunge me into a permanent state of stupor, of a type sensationally new to science, thus depriving natural dissolution of any logical or

chronal sense. Furthermore, this reasoning takes care of the
much less interesting (albeit important, important) Universal
Time ("we had a thumping time chopping heads") also
known as Objective Time (really, woven most coarsely of private times), the history, in a word, of humanity and humor,
and that kind of thing. Nothing prevents mankind as such
from having no future at all—if for example our genus evolves
by imperceptible (this is the ramp of my argument) degrees a
novo-sapiens species or another subgenus altogether, which
will enjoy other varieties of being and dreaming, beyond
man's notion of Time. Man, in that sense, will never die, because there may never be a taxonomical point in his evolutionary progress that could be determined as the last stage of
man in the cline turning him into Neohomo, or some horrible, throbbing slime. I think our friend will not bother us any
further.

My purpose in writing my *Texture of Time*, a difficult, delectable and blessed work, a work which I am about to place
on the dawning desk of the still-absent reader, is to purify my
own notion of Time. I wish to examine the essence of Time,
not its lapse, for I do not believe that its essence can be reduced to its lapse. I wish to caress Time.

One can be a lover of Space and its possibilities: take, for
example, speed, the smoothness and sword-swish of speed; the
aquiline glory of ruling velocity; the joy cry of the curve; and
one can be an amateur of Time, an epicure of duration. I
delight sensually in Time, in its stuff and spread, in the fall of
its folds, in the very impalpability of its grayish gauze, in the
coolness of its continuum. I wish to do something about it;
to indulge in a simulacrum of possession. I am aware that all
who have tried to reach the charmed castle have got lost in
obscurity or have bogged down in Space. I am also aware that
Time is a fluid medium for the culture of metaphors.

Why is it so difficult—so degradingly difficult—to bring the
notion of Time into mental focus and keep it there for inspection? What an effort, what fumbling, what irritating fatigue! It is like rummaging with one hand in the glove
compartment for the road map—fishing out Montenegro, the
Dolomites, paper money, a telegram—everything except the
stretch of chaotic country between Ardez and Something-

soprano, in the dark, in the rain, while trying to take advantage of a red light in the coal black, with the wipers functioning metronomically, chronometrically: the blind finger of space poking and tearing the texture of time. And Aurelius Augustinus, too, he, too, in his tussles with the same theme, fifteen hundred years ago, experienced this oddly physical torment of the shallowing mind, the *shchekotiki* (tickles) of approximation, the evasions of cerebral exhaustion—but he, at least, could replenish his brain with God-dispensed energy (have a footnote here about how delightful it is to watch him pressing on and interspersing his cogitations, between sands and stars, with vigorous little fits of prayer).

Lost again. Where was I? Where am I? Mud road. Stopped car. Time is rhythm: the insect rhythm of a warm humid night, brain ripple, breathing, the drum in my temple—these are our faithful timekeepers; and reason corrects the feverish beat. A patient of mine could make out the rhythm of flashes succeeding one another every three milliseconds (0.003!). On.

What nudged, what comforted me, a few minutes ago at the stop of a thought? Yes. Maybe the only thing that hints at a sense of Time is rhythm; not the recurrent beats of the rhythm but the gap between two such beats, the gray gap between black beats: the Tender Interval. The regular throb itself merely brings back the miserable idea of measurement, but in between, something like true Time lurks. How can I extract it from its soft hollow? The rhythm should be neither too slow nor too fast. One beat per minute is already far beyond my sense of succession and five oscillations per second make a hopeless blur. The ample rhythm causes Time to dissolve, the rapid one crowds it out. Give me, say, three seconds, then I can do both: perceive the rhythm and probe the interval. A hollow, did I say? A dim pit? But that is only Space, the comedy villain, returning by the back door with the pendulum he peddles, while I grope for the meaning of Time. What I endeavor to grasp is precisely the Time that Space helps me to measure, and no wonder I fail to grasp Time, since knowledge-gaining itself "takes time."

If my eye tells me something about Space, my ear tells me something about Time. But while Space can be contemplated, naively, perhaps, yet directly, I can listen to Time only be-

tween stresses, for a brief concave moment warily and wor-
riedly, with the growing realization that I am listening not to
Time itself but to the blood current coursing through my
brain, and thence through the veins of the neck heartward,
back to the seat of private throes which have no relation to
Time.

The direction of Time, the ardis of Time, one-way Time,
here is something that looks useful to me one moment, but
dwindles the next to the level of an illusion obscurely related
to the mysteries of growth and gravitation. The irreversibility
of Time (which is not heading anywhere in the first place) is
a very parochial affair: had our organs and orgitrons not been
asymmetrical, our view of Time might have been amphithe-
atric and altogether grand, like ragged night and jagged
mountains around a small, twinkling, satisfied hamlet. We are
told that if a creature loses its teeth and becomes a bird, the
best the latter can do when needing teeth again is to evolve
a serrated beak, never the real dentition it once possessed. The
scene is Eocene and the actors are fossils. It is an amusing
instance of the way nature cheats but it reveals as little relation
to essential Time, straight or round, as the fact of my writing
from left to right does to the course of my thought.

And speaking of evolution, can we imagine the origin and
stepping stones and rejected mutations of Time? Has there
ever been a "primitive" form of Time in which, say, the Past
was not yet clearly differentiated from the Present, so that past
shadows and shapes showed through the still soft, long, larval
"now"? Or did that evolution only refer to timekeeping, from
sandglass to atomic clock and from that to portable pulsar?
And *what* time did it take for Old Time to become Newton's?
Ponder the Egg, as the French cock said to his hens.

Pure Time, Perceptual Time, Tangible Time, Time free of
content, context, and running commentary—this is *my* time
and theme. All the rest is numerical symbol or some aspect of
Space. The texture of Space is not that of Time, and the pie-
bald four-dimensional sport bred by relativists is a quadruped
with one leg replaced by the ghost of a leg. My time is also
Motionless Time (we shall presently dispose of "flowing"
time, water-clock time, water-closet time).

The Time I am concerned with is only the Time stopped

by me and closely attended to by my tense-willed mind. Thus it would be idle and evil to drag in "passing" time. Of course, I shave longer when my thought "tries on" words; of course, I am not aware of the lag until I look at my watch; of course, at fifty years of age, one year seems to pass faster because it is a smaller fraction of my increased stock of existence and also because I am less often bored than I was in childhood between dull game and duller book. But that "quickening" depends precisely upon one's not being attentive to Time.

It is a queer enterprise—this attempt to determine the nature of something consisting of phantomic phases. Yet I trust that my reader, who by now is frowning over these lines (but ignoring, at least, his breakfast), will agree with me that there is nothing more splendid than lone thought; and lone thought must plod on, or—to use a less ancient analogy—drive on, say, in a sensitive, admirably balanced Greek car that shows its sweet temper and road-holding assurance at every turn of the alpine highway.

Two fallacies should be dealt with before we go any further. The first is the confusion of temporal elements with spatial ones. Space, the impostor, has been already denounced in these notes (which are now being set down during half a day's break in a crucial journey); his trial will take place at a later stage of our investigation. The second dismissal is that of an immemorial habit of speech. We regard Time as a kind of stream, having little to do with an actual mountain torrent showing white against a black cliff or a dull-colored great river in a windy valley, but running invariably through our chronographical landscapes. We are so used to that mythical spectacle, so keen upon liquefying every lap of life, that we end up by being unable to speak of Time without speaking of physical motion. Actually, of course, the sense of its motion is derived from many natural, or at least familiar, sources—the body's innate awareness of its own bloodstream, the ancient vertigo caused by rising stars, and, of course, our methods of measurement, such as the creeping shadow line of a gnomon, the trickle of an hourglass, the trot of a second hand—and here we are back in Space. Note the frames, the receptacles. The idea that Time "flows" as naturally as an apple thuds down on a garden table implies that it flows in and through something else and if we take that "something" to be Space then we have only a metaphor flowing along a yardstick.

But beware, *anime meus*, of the marcel wave of fashionable art; avoid the Proustian bed and the assassin pun (itself a suicide—as those who know their Verlaine will note).

We are now ready to tackle Space. We reject without qualms the artificial concept of space-tainted, space-parasited time, the space-time of relativist literature. Anyone, if he likes, may maintain that Space is the outside of Time, or the body of Time, or that Space is suffused with Time and vice versa, or that in some peculiar way Space is merely the waste product of Time, even its corpse, or that in the long, infinitely long, run Time *is* Space; that sort of gossip may be pleasing, especially when we are young; but no one shall make me believe that the movement of matter (say, a pointer) across a carved-out area of Space (say, a dial) is by nature identical with the "passing" of time. Movement of matter merely spans an extension of some other palpable matter, against which it is measured, but tells us nothing about the actual structure of impalpable Time. Similarly, a graduated tape, even of infinite length, is not Space itself, nor can the most exact odometer represent the road which I see as a black mirror of rain under turning wheels, hear as a sticky rustle, smell as a damp July night in the Alps, and feel as a smooth basis. We, poor Spatians, are better adapted, in our three-dimensional Lacrimaval, to Extension rather than to Duration: our body is capable of greater stretching than volitional recall can boast of. I cannot memorize (though I sought only yesterday to resolve it into mnemonic elements) the number of my new car but I feel the asphalt under my front tires as if they were parts of my body. Yet Space itself (like Time) is nothing I can comprehend: a place where motion occurs. A plasm in which matter—concentrations of Space plasm—is organized and enclosed. We can measure the globules of matter and the distances between them, but Space plasm itself is incomputable.

We measure Time (a second hand trots, or a minute hand jerks, from one painted mark to another) in terms of Space (without knowing the nature of either), but the spanning of Space does not always require Time—or at least does not require more time than the "now" point of the specious present contains in its hollow. The perceptual possession of a unit of space is practically instantaneous when, for example, an expert driver's eye takes in a highway symbol—the black mouth and neat archivolt within a red triangle (a blend of color and shape recognized in "no time," when properly seen, as meaning a road tunnel) or something of less immediate importance such as the delightful Venus sign ♀, which might be misunderstood as permitting whorelets to thumb rides, but actually tells the worshipper or the sightseer that a church is reflected in the local river. I suggest adding a pilcrow for persons who read while driving.

Space is related to our senses of sight, touch, and muscular effort; Time is vaguely connected with hearing (still, a deaf man would perceive the "passage" of time incomparably better than a blind limbless man would the idea of "passage"). "Space is a swarming in the eyes, and Time a singing in the ears," says John Shade, a modern poet, as quoted by an invented philosopher ("Martin Gardiner") in *The Ambidextrous Universe*, page 165. Space flutters to the ground, but Time remains between thinker and thumb, when Monsieur Bergson uses his scissors. Space introduces its eggs into the nests of Time: a "before" here, an "after" there—and a speckled clutch of Minkowski's "world-points." A stretch of Space is organically easier to measure mentally than a "stretch" of Time. The notion of Space must have been formed before that of Time (Guyau in Whitrow). The indistinguishable inane (Locke) of infinite space is mentally distinguishable (and indeed could not be imagined otherwise) from the ovoid "void" of Time. Space thrives on surds, Time is irreducible to blackboard roots and birdies. The same section of Space may seem more extensive to a fly than to S. Alexander, but a moment to him is *not* "hours to a fly," because if that were true flies would know better than wait to get swapped. I cannot imagine Space without Time, but I can very well imagine Time without Space. "Space-Time"—that hideous hybrid whose very hyphen looks phoney. One can be a hater of Space, and a lover of Time.

There are people who can fold a road map. Not this writer.

At this point, I suspect, I should say something about my attitude to "Relativity." It is not sympathetic. What many cos-

mogonists tend to accept as an objective truth is really the
flaw inherent in mathematics which parades as truth. The
body of the astonished person moving in Space is shortened
in the direction of motion and shrinks catastrophically as the
velocity nears the speed beyond which, by the fiat of a fishy
formula, no speed can be. That is his bad luck, not mine—
but I sweep away the business of his clock's slowing down.
Time, which requires the utmost purity of consciousness to
be properly apprehended, is the most rational element of life,
and my reason feels insulted by those flights of Technology
Fiction. One especially grotesque inference, drawn (I think by
Engelwein) from Relativity Theory—and destroying it, if
drawn correctly—is that the galactonaut and his domestic animals, after touring the speed spas of Space, would return
younger than if they had stayed at home all the time. Imagine
them filing out of their airark—rather like those "Lions," ju-
venilified by romp suits, exuding from one of those huge chartered buses that stop, horribly blinking, in front of a man's
impatient sedan just where the highway wizens to squeeze
through the narrows of a mountain village.

Perceived events can be regarded as simultaneous when they
belong to the same span of attention; in the same way (insidious simile, unremovable obstacle!) as one can visually possess
a unit of space—say, a vermilion ring with a frontal view of a
toy car within its white kernel, forbidding the lane into which,
however, I turned with a furious *coup de volant*. I know relativists, hampered by their "light signals" and "traveling
clocks," try to demolish the idea of simultaneity on a cosmic
scale, but let us imagine a gigantic hand with its thumb on
one star and its minimus on another—will it not be touching
both at the same time—or are tactile coincidences even more
misleading than visual ones? I think I had better back out of
this passage.

Such a drought affected Hippo in the most productive
months of Augustine's bishopric that clepsydras had to be replaced by sandglasses. He defined the Past as what is no longer
and the future as what is not yet (actually the future is a fan-
tasm belonging to another category of thought essentially different from that of the Past which, at least, was here a moment

ago—where did I put it? Pocket? But the search itself is already "past").

The Past is changeless, intangible, and "never-to-be-revisited"—terms that do not fit this or that section of Space which I see, for instance, as a white villa and its whiter (newer) garage with seven cypresses of unequal height, tall Sunday and short Monday, watching over the private road that loops past scrub oak and briar down to the public one connecting Sorcière with the highway to Mont Roux (still one hundred miles apart).

I shall now proceed to consider the Past as an accumulation of sensa, not as the dissolution of Time implied by immemorial metaphors picturing transition. The "passage of time" is merely a figment of the mind with no objective counterpart, but with easy spatial analogies. It is seen only in rear view, shapes and shades, arollas and larches silently tumbling away: the perpetual disaster of receding time, *éboulements*, landslides, mountain roads where rocks are always falling and men always working.

We build models of the past and then use them spatiologically to reify and measure Time. Let us take a familiar example. Zembre, a quaint old town on the Minder River, near Sorcière, in the Valais, was being lost by degrees among new buildings. By the beginning of this century it had acquired a definitely modern look, and the preservation people decided to act. Today, after years of subtle reconstruction, a replica of the old Zembre, with its castle, its church, and its mill extrapolated onto the other side of the Minder, stands opposite the modernized town and separated from it by the length of a bridge. Now, if we replace the spatial view (as seen from a helicopter) by the chronal one (as seen by a retrospector), and the material model of old Zembre by the mental model of it in the Past (say, around 1822), the modern town and the model of the old turn out to be something else than two points in the same place at different times (in spatial perspective they *are* at the same time in different places). The space in which the modern town coagulates is immediately real, while that of its retrospective image (as seen apart from material restoration) shimmers in an imaginary space and we cannot use any bridge to walk from the one to the other. In other words (as one puts it when both writer and reader flounder at last in hopeless confusion of thought), by making a model of the old town in one's mind (and on the Minder) all we do is to spatialize it (or actually drag it out of its own element onto the shore of Space). Thus the term "one century" does *not* correspond in any sense to the hundred feet of steel bridge between modern and model towns, and *that* is what we wished to prove and have now proven.

The Past, then, is a constant accumulation of images. It can be easily contemplated and listened to, tested and tasted at random, so that it ceases to mean the orderly alternation of linked events that it does in the large theoretical sense. It is now a generous chaos out of which the genius of total recall, summoned on this summer morning in 1922, can pick anything he pleases: diamonds scattered all over the parquet in 1888; a russet black-hatted beauty at a Parisian bar in 1901; a humid red rose among artificial ones in 1883; the pensive half-smile of a young English governess, in 1880, neatly reclosing her charge's prepuce after the bedtime treat; a little girl, in 1884, licking the breakfast honey off the badly bitten nails of her spread fingers; the same, at thirty-three, confessing, rather late in the day, that she did not like flowers in vases; the awful pain striking him in the side while two children with a basket of mushrooms looked on in the merrily burning pine forest; and the startled quonk of a Belgian car, which he had over-taken and passed yesterday on a blind bend of the alpine high-way. Such images tell us nothing about the texture of time into which they are woven—except, perhaps, in one matter which happens to be hard to settle. Does the coloration of a recollected object (or anything else about its visual effect) dif-fer from date to date? Could I tell by its tint if it comes earlier or later, lower or higher, in the stratigraphy of my past? Is there any mental uranium whose dream-delta decay might be used to measure the age of a recollection? The main difficulty, I hasten to explain, consists in the experimenter not being able to use the *same* object at different times (say, the Dutch stove with its little blue sailing boats in the nursery of Ardis Manor in 1884 and 1888) because of the two or more impressions borrowing from one another and forming a compound image in the mind; but if different objects are to be chosen (say, the faces of two memorable coachmen: Ben Wright, 1884, and Trofim Fartukov, 1888), it is impossible, insofar as my own research goes, to avoid the intrusion not only of different characteristics but of different emotional circumstances, that do not allow the two objects to be considered essentially equal before, so to speak, their being exposed to the action of Time. I am not sure that such objects cannot be discovered. In my professional work, in the laboratories of psychology, I have devised myself many a subtle test (one of which, the method of determining female virginity without physical examination, today bears my name). Therefore we can assume that the experiment *can* be performed—and how tantalizing, then, the discovery of certain exact levels of decreasing saturation or deepening brilliance—so exact that the "something" which I vaguely perceive in the image of a remembered but unidentifiable person, and which assigns it "somehow" to my early boyhood rather than to my adolescence, can be labeled if not with a name, at least with a definite date, e.g., January 1, 1908 (eureka, the "e.g." worked—*he* was my father's former house tutor, who brought me *Alice in the Camera Obscura* for my eighth birthday).

Our perception of the Past is not marked by the link of succession to as strong a degree as is the perception of the Present and of the instants immediately preceding its point of reality. I usually shave every morning and am accustomed to change the blade in my safety razor after every second shave; now and then I happen to skip a day, have to scrape off the next a tremendous growth of loud bristle, whose obstinate presence my fingers check again and again between strokes, and in such cases I use a blade only once. Now, when I visualize a recent series of shaves, I ignore the element of succession: all I want to know is whether the blade left in my silver plough has done its work once or twice; if it was once, the order of the two bristle-growing days in my mind has no importance—in fact, I tend to hear and feel the second, grittier, morning first, and *then* to throw in the shaveless day, in consequence of which my beard grows in reverse, so to speak.

If now, with some poor scraps of teased-out knowledge relating to the colored contents of the Past, we shift our view

and regard it simply as a coherent reconstruction of elapsed
events, some of which are retained by the ordinary mind less
clearly, if at all, than the others, we can indulge in an easier
game with the light and shade of its avenues. Memory-images
include after-images of sound, regurgitated, as it were, by the
ear which recorded them a moment ago while the mind was
engaged in avoiding hitting schoolchildren, so that actually
we can replay the message of the church clock after we have
left Turtsen and its hushed but still-echoing steeple behind.
Reviewing those last steps of the immediate Past involves less
physical time than was needed for the clock's mechanism to
exhaust its strokes, and it is this mysterious "less" which is a
special characteristic of the still-fresh Past into which the Present slipped during that instant inspection of shadow sounds.
The "less" indicates that the Past is in no need of clocks and
the succession of its events is not clock time, but something
more in keeping with the authentic rhythm of Time. We have
suggested earlier that the dim intervals between the dark beats
have the *feel* of the texture of Time. The same, more vaguely,
applies to the impressions received from perceiving the gaps
of unremembered or "neutral" time between vivid events. I
happen to remember in terms of color (grayish blue, purple,
reddish gray) my three farewell lectures—public lectures—on
Mr. Bergson's Time at a great university a few months ago. I
recall less clearly, and indeed am able to suppress in my mind
completely, the six-day intervals between blue and purple and
between purple and gray. But I visualize with perfect clarity
the circumstances attending the actual lectures. I was a little
late for the first (dealing with the Past) and observed with a
not-unpleasant thrill, as if arriving at my own funeral, the brilliantly lighted windows of Counterstone Hall and the small
figure of a Japanese student who, being also late, overtook me
at a wild scurry, and disappeared in the doorway long before
I reached its semicircular steps. At the second lecture—the
one on the Present—during the five seconds of silence and
"inward attention" which I requested from the audience in
order to provide an illustration for the point I, or rather the
speaking jewel in my waistcoat pocket, was about to make
regarding the true perception of time, the behemoth snores
of a white-bearded sleeper filled the house—which, of course,

collapsed. At the third and last lecture, on the Future ("Sham Time"), after working perfectly for a few minutes, my secretly recorded voice underwent an obscure mechanical disaster, and I preferred simulating a heart attack and being carried out into the night forever (insofar as lecturing was concerned) to trying to decipher and sort out the batch of crumpled notes in pale pencil which poor speakers are obsessed with in familiar dreams (attributed by Dr. Froid of Signy-Mondieu-Mondieu to the dreamer's having read in infancy his adulterous parents' love letters). I give these ludicrous but salient details to show that the events to be selected for the test should be not only gaudy and graduated (three lectures in three weeks), but related to each other by their main feature (a lecturer's misadventures). The two intervals of five days each are seen by me as twin dimples, each brimming with a kind of smooth, grayish mist, and a faint suggestion of shed confetti (which, maybe, might leap into color if I allowed some casual memory to form in between the diagnostic limits). Because of its situation among dead things, that dim continuum cannot be as sensually groped for, tasted, harkened to, as Veen's Hollow between rhythmic beats; but it shares with it one remarkable indicium: the immobility of perceptual Time. Synesthesia, to which I am inordinately prone, proves to be of great help in this type of task—a task now approaching its crucial stage, the flowering of the Present.

Now blows the wind of the Present at the top of the Past— at the top of the passes I have been proud to reach in my life, the Umbrail, the Fluela, the Furka, of my clearest consciousness! The moment changes at the point of perception only because I myself am in a constant state of trivial metamorphosis. To give myself time to time Time I must move my mind in the direction opposite to that in which I am moving, as one does when one is driving past a long row of poplars and wishes to isolate and stop one of them, thus making the green blur reveal and offer, yes, offer, its every leaf. Cretin behind me.

This act of attention is what I called last year the "Deliberate Present" to distinguish it from its more general form termed (by Clay in 1882) the "Specious Present." The conscious construction of one, and the familiar current of the other give us three or four seconds of what can be felt as nowness. This nowness is the only reality we know; it follows the colored nothingness of the no-longer and precedes the absolute nothingness of the future. Thus, in a quite literal sense, we may say that conscious human life lasts always only one moment, for at any moment of deliberate attention to our own flow of consciousness we cannot know if that moment will be followed by another. As I shall later explain, I do not believe that "anticipation" ("looking forward to a promotion or fearing a social blunder" as one unfortunate thinker puts it) plays any significant part in the formation of the specious present, nor do I believe that the future is transformed into a third panel of Time, even if we do anticipate something or other—a turn of the familiar road or the picturesque rise of two steep hills, one with a castle, the other with a church, for the more lucid the forevision the less prophetic it is apt to be. Had that rascal behind me decided to risk it just now he would have collided head-on with the truck that came from beyond the bend, and I and the view might have been eclipsed in the multiple smash.

Our modest Present is, then, the time span that one is directly and actually aware of, with the lingering freshness of the Past still perceived as part of the nowness. In regard to everyday life and the habitual comfort of the body (reasonably healthy, reasonably strong, breathing the green breeze, relishing the after-taste of the most exquisite food in the world—a boiled egg), it does not matter that we can never enjoy the *true* Present, which is an instant of zero duration, represented by a rich smudge, as the dimensionless point of geometry is by a sizable dot in printer's ink on palpable paper. The normal motorist, according to psychologists and policemen, can perceive, visually, a unit of time as short in extension as one tenth of a second (I had a patient, a former gambler, who could identify a playing card in a five-times-faster flash!). It would be interesting to measure the instant we need to become aware of disappointed or fulfilled expectation. Smells can be very sudden, and in most people the ear and sense of touch work quicker than the eye. Those two hitch-hikers really smelled—the male one revoltingly.

Since the Present is but an imaginary point without an

awareness of the immediate past, it is necessary to define that awareness. Not for the first time will Space intrude if I say that what we are aware of as "Present" is the constant building up of the Past, its smoothly and relentlessly rising level. How meager! How magic!

Here they are, the two rocky ruin-crowned hills that I have retained for seventeen years in my mind with decalcomaniac romantic vividness—though not quite exactly, I confess; memory likes the *otsebyatina* ("what one contributes oneself"); but the slight discrepancy is now corrected and the act of artistic correction enhances the pang of the Present. The sharpest feeling of nowness, in visual terms, is the deliberate possession of a segment of Space collected by the eye. This is Time's only contact with Space, but it has a far-reaching reverberation. To be eternal the Present must depend on the conscious spanning of an infinite expansure. Then, and only then, is the Present equatable with Timeless Space. I have been wounded in my duel with the Impostor.

And now I drive into Mont Roux, under garlands of heart-rending welcome. Today is Monday, July 14, 1922, five-thirteen P.M. by my wrist watch, eleven fifty-two by my car's built-in clock, four-ten by all the timepieces in town. The author is in a confused state of exhilaration, exhaustion, expectancy and panic. He has been climbing with two Austrian guides and a temporarily adopted daughter in the incomparable Balkan mountains. He spent most of May in Dalmatia, and June in the Dolomites, and got letters in both places from Ada telling him of her husband's death (April 23, in Arizona). He started working his way west in a dark-blue Argus, dearer to him than sapphires and morphos because she happened to have ordered an exactly similar one to be ready for her in Geneva. He collected three additional villas, two on the Adriatic and one at Ardez in the Northern Grisons. Late on Sunday, July 13, in nearby Alvena, the concierge of the Alraun Palace handed him a cable that had waited for him since Friday

ARRIVING MONT ROUX TROIS CYGNES MONDAY DINNERTIME I WANT YOU TO WIRE ME FRANKLY IF THE DATE AND THE WHOLE TRALALA ARE INCONVENIENT.

He transmitted by the new "instantogram," flashed to the
Geneva airport, a message ending in the last word of her 1905
cable; and despite the threats of a torrential night set out by
car for the Vaud. Traveling too fast and too wildly, he somehow missed the Oberhalbstein road at the Sylvaplana fork (150
kilometers south of Alvena); wriggled back north, via Chi-
avenna and Splügen, to reach in apocalyptic circumstances
Highway 19 (an unnecessary trip of 100 kilometers); veered by
mistake east to Chur; performed an unprintable U-turn, and
covered in a couple of hours the 175-kilometer stretch westward to Brig. The pale flush of dawn in his rear-vision mirror
had long since turned to passionately bright daylight when he
looped south, by the new Pfynwald road, to Sorcière, where
seventeen years ago he had bought a house (now Villa Jolana).
The three or four servants he had left there to look after it
had taken advantage of his lengthy absence to fade away; so,
with the enthusiastic help of two hitch-hikers stranded in the
vicinity—a disgusting youth from Hilden and his long-haired,
slatternly, languorous Hilda—he had to break into his own
house. His accomplices were mistaken if they expected to find
loot and liquor there. After throwing them out he vainly
courted sleep on a sheetless bed and finally betook himself to
the bird-mad garden, where his two friends were copulating
in the empty swimming pool and had to be shooed off again.
It was now around noon. He worked for a couple of hours
on his *Texture of Time*, begun in the Dolomites at the Lammermoor (not the best of his recent hotels). The utilitarian
impulse behind the task was to keep him from brooding on
the ordeal of happiness awaiting him 150 kilometers west; it
did not prevent a healthy longing for a hot breakfast from
making him interrupt his scribbling to seek out a roadside inn
on his way to Mont Roux.

The Three Swans where he had reserved rooms 508-509-510
had undergone certain changes since 1905. A portly, plum-
nosed Lucien did not recognize him at once—and then
remarked that Monsieur was certainly not "deperishing"—
although actually Van had almost reverted to his weight of
seventeen years earlier, having shed several kilos in the Balkans
rock-climbing with crazy little Acrazia (now dumped in a fashionable boarding school near Florence). No, Madame Vinn

Landère had not called. Yes, the hall had been renovated. Swiss-German Louis Wicht now managed the hotel instead of his late father-in-law Luigi Fantini. In the lounge, as seen through its entrance, the huge memorable oil—three ample-haunched Ledas swapping lacustrine impressions—had been replaced by a neoprimitive masterpiece showing three yellow eggs and a pair of plumber's gloves on what looked like wet bathroom tiling. As Van stepped into the "elevator" followed by a black-coated receptionist, it acknowledged his footfall with a hollow clank and then, upon moving, feverishly began transmitting a fragmentary report on some competition—possibly a tricycle race. Van could not help feeling sorry that this blind functional box (even smaller than the slop-pail lift he had formerly used at the back) now substituted for the luxurious affair of yore—an ascentive hall of mirrors—whose famous operator (white whiskers, eight languages) had become a button.

In the hallway of 509, Van recognized the *Bruslot à la sonde* picture next to the pregnant-looking white closet (under whose round sliding doors the corner of the carpet, now gone, would invariably catch). In the salon itself, only a lady's bureau and the balcony view were familiar. Everything else—the semi-transparent shredded-wheat ornaments, the glass flowerheads, the silk-covered armchairs—had been superseded by *Hoch-modern* fixtures.

He showered and changed, and finished the flask of brandy in his dressing case, and called the Geneva airport and was told that the last plane from America had just arrived. He went for a stroll—and saw that the famous "mûrier," that spread its great limbs over a humble lavatory on a raised terrace at the top of a cobbled lane, was now in sumptuous purple-blue bloom. He had a beer at the café opposite the railway station, and then, automatically, entered the flower shop next door. He must be gaga to have forgotten what she said the last time about her strange anthophobia (somehow stemming from that debauche *à trois* thirty years ago). Roses she never liked anyway. He stared and was easily outstared by small Carols from Belgium, long-stemmed Pink Sensations, vermilion Superstars. There were also zinnias, and chrysanthemums, and potted aphelandras, and two graceful fringetails in an inset aquarium. Not wishing to disappoint the courteous old florist, he bought seventeen odorless Baccara roses, asked for the directory, opened it at Ad-Au, Mont Roux, lit upon "Addor, Yolande, Mlle secrét., rue des Délices, 6," and with American presence of mind had his bouquet sent there.

People were already hurrying home from work. Mademoiselle Addor, in a sweat-stained frock, was climbing the stairs. The streets had been considerably quieter in the sourdine Past. The old Morris pillar, upon which the present Queen of Portugal figured once as an actress, no longer stood at the corner of Chemin de Mustrux (old corruption of the town's name). Must Trucks roar through Must Rux?

The chambermaid had drawn the curtains. He wrenched them all open as if resolved to prolong to its utmost limit the torture of that day. The ironwork balcony jutted out far enough to catch the slanting rays. He recalled his last glimpse of the lake on that dismal day in October, 1905, after parting with Ada. Fuligula ducks were falling and rising upon the rainpocked swell in concentrated enjoyment of doubled water; along the lake walk scrolls of froth curled over the ridges of advancing gray waves and every now and then a welter heaved sufficiently high to splash over the parapet. But now, on this radiant summer evening, no waves foamed, no birds swam; only a few seagulls could be seen, fluttering white over their black reflections. The wide lovely lake lay in dreamy serenity, fretted with green undulations, ruffed with blue, patched with glades of lucid smoothness between the ackers; and, in the lower right corner of the picture, as if the artist had wished to include a very special example of light, the dazzling wake of the westering sun pulsated through a lakeside lombardy poplar that seemed both liquefied and on fire.

A distant idiot leaning backward on waterskis behind a speedboat started to rip the canvas; fortunately, he collapsed before doing much harm, and at the same instant the drawing-room telephone rang.

Now it so happened that she had never—never, at least, in adult life—spoken to him by phone; hence the phone had preserved the very essence, the bright vibration, of her vocal cords, the little "leap" in her larynx, the laugh clinging to the contour of the phrase, as if afraid in girlish glee to slip off the

quick words it rode. It was the timbre of their past, as if the
past had put through that call, a miraculous connection ("Ardis, one eight eight six"—*comment? Non, non, pas huitante-
huit—huitante-six*). Goldenly, youthfully, it bubbled with all
the melodious characteristics he knew—or better say recollected, at once, in the sequence they came: that *entrain*, that
whelming of quasi-erotic pleasure, that assurance and animation—and, what was especially delightful, the fact that she was
utterly and innocently unaware of the modulations entrancing
him.

There had been trouble with her luggage. There still was.
Her two maids, who were supposed to have flown over the
day before on a Laputa (freight airplane) with her trunks, had
got stranded somewhere. All she had was a little valise. The
concierge was in the act of making some calls for her. Would
Van come down? She was *neveroyatno golodnaya* (incredibly
hungry).

That telephone voice, by resurrecting the past and linking
it up with the present, with the darkening slate-blue mountains beyond the lake, with the spangles of the sun wake dancing through the poplar, formed the centerpiece in his deepest
perception of tangible time, the glittering "now" that was the
only reality of Time's texture. After the glory of the summit
there came the difficult descent.

Ada had warned him in a recent letter that she had
"changed considerably, in contour as well as in color." She
wore a corset which stressed the unfamiliar stateliness of her
body enveloped in a black-velvet gown of a flowing cut both
eccentric and monastic, as their mother used to favor. She had
had her hair bobbed page-boy-fashion and dyed a brilliant
bronze. Her neck and hands were as delicately pale as ever
but showed unfamiliar fibers and raised veins. She made lavish
use of cosmetics to camouflage the lines at the outer corners
of her fat carmined lips and dark-shadowed eyes whose
opaque iris now seemed less mysterious than myopic owing
to the nervous flutter of her painted lashes. He noted that her
smile revealed a gold-capped upper premolar; he had a similar
one on the other side of his mouth. The metallic sheen of her
fringe distressed him less than that velvet gown, full-skirted,
square-shouldered, of well-below-the-calf length, with hip-

padding which was supposed both to diminish the waist and disguise by amplification the outline of the now buxom pelvis. Nothing remained of her gangling grace, and the new mellowness, and the velvet stuff, had an irritatingly dignified air of obstacle and defense. He loved her much too tenderly, much too irrevocably, to be unduly depressed by sexual misgivings; but his senses certainly remained stirless—so stirless in fact, that he did not feel at all anxious (as she and he raised their flashing champagne glasses in parody of the crested-grebe ritual) to involve his masculine pride in a half-hearted embrace immediately after dinner. If he was expected to do so, that was too bad; if he was not, that was even worse. At their earlier reunions the constraint, subsisting as a dull ache after the keen agonies of Fate's surgery, used to be soon drowned in sexual desire, leaving life to pick up by and by. Now they were on their own.

The utilitarian trivialities of their table talk—or, rather, of his gloomy monologue—seemed to him positively degrading. He explained at length—fighting her attentive silence, sloshing across the puddles of pauses, abhorring himself—that he had a long and hard journey; that he slept badly; that he was working on an investigation of the nature of Time, a theme that meant struggling with the octopus of one's own brain. She looked at her wrist watch.

"What I'm telling you," he said harshly, "has nothing to do with timepieces." The waiter brought them their coffee. She smiled, and he realized that her smile was prompted by a conversation at the next table, at which a newcomer, a stout sad Englishman, had begun a discussion of the menu with the maître d'hôtel.

"I'll start," said the Englishman, "with the bananas."

"That's not bananas, sir. That's *ananas*, pineapple juice."

"Oh, I see. Well, give me some clear soup."

Young Van smiled back at young Ada. Oddly, that little exchange at the next table acted as a kind of delicious release.

"When I was a kid," said Van, "and stayed for the first—or rather, second—time in Switzerland, I thought that 'Verglas' on roadway signs stood for some magical town, always around the corner, at the bottom of every snowy slope, never seen, but biding its time. I got your cable in the Engadine where there are *real* magical places, such as Alraun or Alruna —which means a tiny Arabian demon in a German wizard's mirror. By the way, we have the old apartment upstairs with an additional bedroom, number five-zero-eight."

"Oh dear. I'm afraid you must cancel poor 508. If I stayed for the night, 510 would do for both of us, but I've got bad news for you. I can't stay. I must go back to Geneva directly after dinner to retrieve my things and maids, whom the authorities have apparently put in a Home for Stray Females because they could not pay the absolutely medieval new *droits de douane*—isn't Switzerland in Washington State, sort of, *après tout*? Look, don't scowl"—(patting his brown blotched hand on which their shared birthmark had got lost among the freckles of age, like a babe in autumn woods, *on peut les suivre en reconnaissant* only Mascodagama's disfigured thumb and the beautiful almond-shaped nails)—"I promise to get in touch with you in a day or two, and then we'll go on a cruise to Greece with the Baynards—they have a yacht and three adorable daughters who still swim in the tan, okay?"

"I don't know what I loathe more," he replied, "yachts or Baynards; but can I help you in Geneva?"

He could not. Baynard had married his Cordula, after a sensational divorce—Scotch veterinaries had had to saw off her husband's antlers (last call for that joke).

Ada's Argus had not yet been delivered. The gloomy black gloss of the hackney Yak and the old-fashioned leggings of its driver reminded him of her departure in 1905.

He saw her off—and ascended, like a Cartesian glassman, like spectral Time standing at attention, back to his desolate fifth floor. Had they lived together these seventeen wretched years, they would have been spared the shock and the humiliation; their aging would have been a gradual adjustment, as imperceptible as Time itself.

His Work-in-Progress, a sheaf of notes tangling with his pajamas, came to the rescue as it had done at Sorcière. Van swallowed a favodorm tablet and, while waiting for it to relieve him of himself, a matter of forty minutes or so, sat down at a lady's bureau to his "lucubratiuncula."

Does the ravage and outrage of age deplored by poets tell the naturalist of Time anything about Time's essence? Very

little. Only a novelist's fancy could be caught by this small
oval box, once containing Duvet de Ninon (a face powder,
with a bird of paradise on the lid), which has been forgotten
in a not-quite-closed drawer of the bureau's arc of triumph—
not, however, triumph over Time. The blue-green-orange
thing looked as if he were meant to be deceived into thinking
it had been waiting there seventeen years for the bemused,
smiling finder's dream-slow hand: a shabby trick of feigned
restitution, a planted coincidence—and a bad blunder, since
it had been Lucette, now a mermaid in the groves of Atlantis
(and not Ada, now a stranger somewhere near Morges in a
black limousine) who had favored that powder. Throw it away
lest it mislead a weaker philosopher; what I am concerned with
is the delicate texture of Time, void of all embroidered events.

Let us recapitulate.

Physiologically the sense of Time is a sense of continuous
becoming, and if "becoming" has a voice, the latter might
be, not unnaturally, a steady vibration; but for Log's sake, let
us not confuse Time with Tinnitus, and the seashell hum of
duration with the throb of our blood. Philosophically, on the
other hand, Time is but memory in the making. In every individual life there goes on from cradle to deathbed the gradual
shaping and strengthening of that *backbone of consciousness*,
which is the Time of the strong. "To be" means to know one
"has been." "Not to be" implies the only "new" kind of
(sham) time: the future. I dismiss it. Life, love, libraries, have
no future.

Time is anything but the popular triptych: a no-longer existing Past, the durationless point of the Present, and a "not-
yet" that may never come. No. There are only two panels.
The Past (ever-existing in my mind) and the Present (to which
my mind gives duration and, therefore, reality). If we make a
third compartment of fulfilled expectation, the foreseen, the
foreordained, the faculty of prevision, perfect forecast, we are
still applying our mind to the Present.

If the Past is perceived as a storage of Time, and if the
Present is the process of that perception, the future, on the
other hand, is not an item of Time, has nothing to do with
Time and with the dim gauze of its physical texture. The future is but a quack at the court of Chronos. Thinkers, social

thinkers, feel the Present as pointing beyond itself toward a not yet realized "future"—but that is topical utopia, progressive politics. Technological Sophists argue that by taking advantage of the Laws of Light, by using new telescopes revealing ordinary print at cosmic distances through the eyes of our nostalgic agents on another planet, we can actually see our own past (Goodson discovering the Goodson and that sort of thing) including documentary evidence of our not knowing what lay in store for us (and our knowing *now*), and that consequently the Future did exist yesterday and by inference does exist today. This may be good physics but is execrable logic, and the Tortoise of the Past will never overtake the Achilles of the future, no matter how we parse distances on our cloudy blackboards.

What we do at best (at worst we perform trivial tricks) when postulating the future, is to expand enormously the specious present causing it to permeate any amount of time with all manner of information, anticipation and precognition. At best, the "future" is the idea of a hypothetical present based on our experience of succession, on our faith in logic and habit. Actually, of course, our hopes can no more bring it into existence than our regrets change the Past. The latter has at least the taste, the tinge, the tang, of our individual being. But the future remains aloof from our fancies and feelings. At every moment it is an infinity of branching possibilities. A determinate scheme would abolish the very notion of time (here the pill floated its first cloudlet). The unknown, the not yet experienced and the unexpected, all the glorious "x" intersections, are the inherent parts of human life. The determinate scheme by stripping the sunrise of its surprise would erase all sunrays—

The pill had really started to work. He finished changing into his pajamas, a series of fumbles, mostly unfinished, which he had begun an hour ago, and fumbled into bed. He dreamed that he was speaking in the lecturing hall of a transatlantic liner and that a bum resembling the hitch-hiker from Hilden was asking sneeringly how did the lecturer explain that in our dreams we know we shall awake, is not that analogous to the certainty of death and if so, the future—

At daybreak he sat up with an abrupt moan, and trembling:

if he did not act *now*, he would lose her forever! He decided
to drive at once to the Manhattan in Geneva.

Van welcomed the renewal of polished structures after a
week of black fudge fouling the bowl slope so high that no
amount of flushing could dislodge it. Something to do with
olive oil and the Italian type water closets. He shaved, bathed,
rapidly dressed. Was it too early to order breakfast? Should he
ring up her hotel before starting? Should he rent a plane? Or
might it, perhaps, be simpler—

The door-folds of his drawing room balcony stood wide
open. Banks of mist still crossed the blue of the mountains
beyond the lake, but here and there a peak was tipped with
ocher under the cloudless turquoise of the sky. Four tremendous trucks thundered by one after another. He went up to
the rail of the balcony and wondered if he had ever satisfied
the familiar whim by going platch—had he? had he? You could
never know, really. One floor below, and somewhat adjacently,
stood Ada engrossed in the view.

He saw her bronze bob, her white neck and arms, the pale
flowers on her flimsy peignoir, her bare legs, her high-heeled
silver slippers. Pensively, youngly, voluptuously, she was
scratching her thigh at the rise of the right buttock: Ladore's
pink signature on vellum at mosquito dusk. Would she look
up? All her flowers turned up to him, beaming, and she made
the royal-grant gesture of lifting and offering him the mountains, the mist and the lake with three swans.

He left the balcony and ran down a short spiral staircase to
the fourth floor. In the pit of his stomach there sat the suspicion that it might not be room 410, as he conjectured, but
412 or even 414. What would happen if she had not understood, was not on the lookout? She had, she was.

When, "a little later," Van, kneeling and clearing his throat,
was kissing her dear cold hands, gratefully, gratefully, in full
defiance of death, with bad fate routed and her dreamy afterglow bending over him, she asked:

"Did you really think I had gone?"

"*Obmanshchitsa* (deceiver), *obmanshchitsa*," Van kept repeating with the fervor and gloat of blissful satiety.

"I told him to turn," she said, "somewhere near Morzhey

("morses" or "walruses," a Russian pun on "Morges"—
maybe a mermaid's message). And *you* slept, you could sleep!"

"I worked," he replied, "my first draft is done."

She confessed that on coming back in the middle of the
night she had taken to her room from the hotel bookcase (the
night porter, an avid reader, had the key) the British Encyclopedia volume, here it was, with this article on Space-Time:
" 'Space' (it says here, rather suggestively) 'denotes the property, you are my property, in virtue of which, you are my
virtue, rigid bodies can occupy different positions.' Nice?
Nice."

"Don't laugh, my Ada, at our philosophic prose," remonstrated her lover. "All that matters just now is that I have
given new life to Time by cutting off Siamese Space and the
false future. My aim was to compose a kind of novella in the
form of a treatise on the Texture of Time, an investigation of
its veily substance, with illustrative metaphors gradually increasing, very gradually building up a logical love story, going
from past to present, blossoming as a concrete story, and just
as gradually reversing analogies and disintegrating again into
bland abstraction."

"I wonder," said Ada, "I wonder if the attempt to discover
those things is worth the stained glass. We can know the time,
we can know a time. We can never know Time. Our senses
are simply not meant to perceive it. It is like—"

Part Five

I

I, Van Veen, salute you, life, Ada Veen, Dr. Lagosse, Stepan Nootkin, Violet Knox, Ronald Oranger. Today is my ninety-seventh birthday, and I hear from my wonderful new Every-rest chair a spade scrape and footsteps creak in the snow-sparkling garden, and my old Russian valet, who is deafer than he thinks, pull out and push in nose-ringed drawers in the dressing room. This Part Five is not meant as an epilogue; it is the true introduction of my ninety-seven percent true, and three percent likely, *Ada or Ardor, a family chronicle.*

Of all their many houses, in Europe and in the Tropics, the château recently built at Ex, in the Swiss Alps, with its pillared front and crenelated turrets, became their favorite, especially in midwinter, when the famous glittering air, *le cristal d'Ex,* "matches the highest forms of human thought—pure mathematics & decipherment" (unpublished ad).

At least twice a year our happy couple indulged in fairly long travels. Ada did not breed or collect butterflies any more, but throughout her healthy and active old age loved to film them in their natural surroundings, at the bottom of her garden or the end of the world, flapping and flitting, settling on flowers or filth, gliding over grass or granite, fighting or mating. Van accompanied her on picture-shooting journeys to Brazil, the Congo, New Guinea, but secretly preferred a long drink under a tent to a long wait under a tree for some rarity to come down to the bait and be taken in color. One would need another book to describe Ada's adventures in Adaland. The films—and the crucified actors (Identification Mounts)—can be seen by arrangement at the Lucinda Museum, 5, Park Lane, Manhattan.

2

He had lived up to the ancestral motto: "As healthy a Veen as father has been." At fifty he could look back at the narrowing recession of only one hospital corridor (with a pair of white-shod trim feet tripping away), along which he had ever been wheeled. He now noticed, however, that furtive, furcating cracks kept appearing in his physical well-being, as if inevitable decomposition were sending out to him, across static gray time, its first emissaries. A stuffed nose caused a stifling dream, and, at the door of the slightest cold, intercostal neuralgia waited with its blunt spear. The more spacious his bedside table grew the more cluttered it became with such absolute necessities of the night as nose drops, eucalyptic pastilles, wax earplugs, gastric tablets, sleeping pills, mineral water, zinc ointment, a spare cap for its tube lest the original escape under the bed, and a large handkerchief to wipe the sweat accumulating between right jaw and right clavicle, neither being accustomed to his new fleshiness and insistence on sleeping on one side only, so as not to hear his heart: he had made the mistake one night in 1920 of calculating the maximal number of its remaining beats (allowing for another half-century), and now the preposterous hurry of the countdown irritated him and increased the rate at which he could hear himself dying. During his solitary and quite superfluous peregrinations, he had developed a morbid sensitivity to night noises in luxury hotels (the gogophony of a truck rated three distressibles; the Saturday-night gawky cries exchanged by young apprentices in the empty street, thirty; a radiator-relayed snore from downstairs, three hundred); but, though indispensable at times of total despair, earplugs had the disadvantage (especially after too much wine) of magnifying the throbbing in his temples, the weird squeaks in his inexplored nasal cavity, and the atrocious creak of his neck vertebras. To an echo of that creak, transmitted vascularly to the brain before the system of sleep took over, he put down the eerie detonation that took place somewhere in his head at the instant that his senses played false to his consciousness. Antacid mints and the like proved sometimes insufficient to relieve the kind of good old-fashioned heartburn, which invariably afflicted him after certain rich sauces; but on the other hand, he looked forward with juvenile zest to the delightful effect of a spoonful of sodium bicarbonate dissolved in water that was sure to release three or four belches as big as the speech balloons in the "funnies" of his boyhood.

Before he met (at eighty) tactful and tender, ribald and learned, Dr. Lagosse who thenceforth resided and traveled with him and Ada, he had detested physicians. Notwithstanding his own medical training, he could not shake off a sneaky, credulous feeling, befitting a yokel, that the doctor who pumped up a sphygmomanometer or listened in to his wheeze already knew (but still kept secret) what fatal illness had been diagnosed with the certainty of death itself. He wryly remembered his late brother-in-law, when he caught himself concealing from Ada that his bladder troubled him on and off or that he had had another spell of dizziness after paring his toenails (a task he performed himself, being unable to endure any human hand to touch his bare feet).

As if doing his best to avail himself of his body, soon to be removed like a plate wherefrom one collects the last sweet crumbs, he now prized such small indulgences as squeezing out the vermicule of a blackhead, or obtaining with the long nail of his little finger the gem of an itch from the depths of his left ear (the right one was less interesting), or permitting himself what Bouteillan used to brand as *le plaisir anglais*— holding one's breath, and making one's own water, smooth and secret, while lying chin-deep in one's bath.

On the other hand, the pains of life affected him more acutely than in the past. He groaned, on the tympanic rack, when a saxophone blared, or when a subhuman young moron let loose the thunder of an infernal motorcycle. The obstructive behavior of stupid, inimical things—the wrong pocket, the ruptured shoestring, the idle hanger toppling with a shrug and a hingle-tingle in the darkness of a wardrobe—made him utter the Oedipean oath of his Russian ancestry.

He had stopped aging at about sixty-five but by sixty-five he had changed in muscle and bone more sharply than people who had never gone in for such a variety of athletic pursuits as he had enjoyed in his prime. Squash and tennis gave way to ping-pong; then, one day, a favorite paddle, still warm from his grip, was forgotten in the playroom of a club, and the club was never revisited. During his sixth decade some punching-bag exercise had done duty for the wrestling and pugilistics of his earlier years. Gravitational surprises now made skiing grotesque. He could still click foils at sixty, but a few minutes of practice blinded him with sweat; so fencing soon shared the fate of the table tennis. He could never overcome his snobbish prejudice against golf; it was too late to begin, anyway. At seventy, he tried jogging before breakfast in a secluded lane, but the clacking and bouncing of his breasts reminded him too dreadfully that he was thirty kilograms heavier than in his youth. At ninety, he still danced on his hands—in a recurrent dream.

Normally, one or two sleeping pills helped him to hold at bay the monster of insomnia for three or four hours in one blessed blur, but sometimes, particularly after he had completed a mental task, a night of excruciating restlessness would grade into morning migraine. No pill could cope with that torment. There he sprawled, curled up, uncurled, turned off and turned on the bedside light (a gurgling new surrogate—real lammer having been forbidden again by 1930), and physical despair pervaded his unresolvable being. Steady and strong struck his pulse; supper had been adequately digested; his daily ration of one bottle of burgundy had not been exceeded—and yet that wretched restlessness continued to make of him an outcast in his own home: Ada was fast asleep, or comfortably reading, a couple of doors away; the various domestics in their more remote quarters had long passed over to the inimical multitude of local sleepers that seemed to blanket the surrounding hills with the blackness of their repose; he alone was denied the unconsciousness he so fiercely scorned and so assiduously courted.

3

During the years of their last separation, his libertinism had remained essentially as implacable as before; but sometimes the score of love-making would drop to once in four days, and sometimes he would realize with a shock that a whole week had passed in unruffled chastity. The series of exquisite harlots might still alternate with runs of amateur charmers at chance resorts and might still be broken by a month of inventive love in the company of some frivolous women of fashion (there was one red-haired English virgin, Lucy Manfristan, seduced June 4, 1911, in the walled garden of her Norman manor and carried away to Fialta, on the Adriatic, whom he recalled with a special little shiver of lust); but those false romances only fatigued him; the indifferently plumbed *palazzina* would soon be given away, the badly sunburnt girl sent back—and he would need something really nasty and tainted to revive his manhood.

Upon starting in 1922 a new life with Ada, Van firmly resolved to be true to her. Save for a few discreet, and achingly draining, surrenders to what Dr. Lena Wien has so aptly termed "onanistic voyeurism," he somehow managed to stick to his resolution. The ordeal was morally rewarding, physically preposterous. As pediatricians are often cursed with impossible families, so our psychologist presented a not uncommon case of subdivided personality. His love for Ada was a condition of being, a steady hum of happiness unlike anything he had met with professionally in the lives of the singular and the insane. He would have promptly plunged into boiling pitch to save her just as he would have sprung to save his honor at the drop of a glove. Their life together responded antiphonally to their first summer in 1884. She never refused to help him achieve the more and more precious, because less and less frequent, gratification of a fully shared sunset. He saw reflected in her everything that his fastidious and fierce spirit sought in life. An overwhelming tenderness impelled him to kneel suddenly at her feet in dramatic, yet utterly sincere attitudes, puzzling to anyone who might enter with a vacuum cleaner. And on the same day his other compartments and subcompartments would be teeming with longings and regrets, and plans of rape and riot. The most hazardous moment was when he and she moved to another villa, with a new staff and new neighbors, and his senses would be exposed in icy, fantastic detail, to the gipsy girl poaching peaches or the laundry woman's bold daughter.

In vain he told himself that those vile hankerings did not differ, in their intrinsic insignificance, from the anal pruritis which one tries to relieve by a sudden fit of scratching. Yet he knew that by daring to satisfy the corresponding desire for a young wench he risked wrecking his life with Ada. How horribly and gratuitously it might hurt her, he foreglimpsed one day in 1926 or '27 when he caught the look of proud despair she cast on nothing in particular before walking away to the car that was to take her on a trip in which, at the last moment, he had declined to join her. He had declined—and had simulated the grimace and the limp of podagra—because he had just realized, what she, too, had realized—that the beautiful native girl smoking on the back porch would offer her mangoes to Master as soon as Master's housekeeper had left for the Film Festival in Sindbad. The chauffeur had already opened the car door, when, with a great bellow, Van overtook Ada and they rode off together, tearful, voluble, joking about his foolishness.

"It's funny," said Ada, "what black, broken teeth they have hereabouts, those *blyadushki*."

("Ursus," Lucette in glistening green, "Subside, agitation of passion," Flora's bracelets and breasts, the whelk of Time.)

He discovered that a touch of subtle sport could be derived from constantly fighting temptation while constantly dreaming of somehow, sometime, somewhere, yielding to it. He also discovered that whatever fire danced in those lures, he could not spend one day without Ada; that the solitude he needed to sin properly did not represent a matter of a few seconds behind an evergreen bush, but a comfortable night in an impregnable fortress; and that, finally, the temptations, real or conjured up before sleep, were diminishing in frequency. By the age of seventy-five fortnightly intimacies with cooperative Ada, mostly *Blitzpartien*, sufficed for perfect contentment. The successive secretaries he engaged got plainer and plainer (culminating in a coconut-haired female with a horse mouth who wrote love notes to Ada); and by the time Violet Knox broke the lackluster series Van Veen was eighty-seven and completely impotent.

4

Violet Knox [now Mrs. Ronald Oranger. Ed.], born in 1940, came to live with us in 1957. She was (and still is—ten years later) an enchanting English blonde with doll eyes, a velvet carnation and a tweed-cupped little rump [. . . . .]; but such designs, alas, could no longer flesh my fancy. She has been responsible for typing out this memoir—the solace of what are, no doubt, my last ten years of existence. A good daughter, an even better sister, and half-sister, she had supported for ten years her mother's children from two marriages, besides laying aside [something]. I paid her [generously] per month, well realizing the need to ensure unembarrassed silence on the part of a puzzled and dutiful maiden. Ada called her "*Fialochka*" and allowed herself the luxury of admiring "little Violet" 's cameo neck, pink nostrils, and fair pony-tail. Sometimes, at dinner, lingering over the liqueurs, my Ada would consider my typist (a great lover of Koo-Ahn-Trow) with a dreamy gaze, and then, quick-quick, peck at her flushed cheek. The situation might have been considerably more complicated had it arisen twenty years earlier.

I do not know why I should have devoted so much attention to the hoary hairs and sagging apparatus of the venerable Veen. Rakes never reform. They burn, sputter a few last green sparks, and go out. Far greater importance must be attached by the self-researcher and his faithful companion to the un-believable intellectual surge, to the creative explosion, that oc-curred in the brain of this strange, friendless, rather repulsive nonagenarian (cries of "no, no!" in lectorial, sororial, editorial brackets).

More fiercely than ever he execrated all sham art, from the crude banalities of junk sculpture to the italicized passages meant by a pretentious novelist to convey his fellow hero's cloudbursts of thought. He had even less patience than before with the "Sig" (Signy-M.D.-M.D.) school of psychiatry. Its founder's epoch-making confession ("In my student days I became a de*flower*er because I failed to pass my botany ex-amination") he prefixed, as an epigraph, to one of his last papers (1959) entitled *The Farce of Group Therapy in Sexual Maladjustment*, the most damaging and satisfying blast of its kind (the Union of Marital Counselors and Catharticians at first wanted to sue but then preferred to detumefy).

Violet knocks at the library door and lets in plump, short, bow-tied Mr. Oranger, who stops on the threshold, clicks his heels, and (as the heavy hermit turns with an awkward sweep of frieze robe) darts forward almost at a trot not so much to stop with a masterful slap the avalanche of loose sheets which the great man's elbow has sent sliding down the lectern-slope, as to express the eagerness of his admiration.

Ada, who amused herself by translating (for the Oranger editions *en regard*) Griboyedov into French and English, Baudelaire into English and Russian, and John Shade into Russian and French, often read to Van, in a deep medium-esque voice, the published versions made by other workers in that field of semiconsciousness. The verse translations in English were especially liable to distend Van's face in a grotesque grin which made him look, when he was not wearing his dental plates, exactly like a Greek comedial mask. He could not tell who disgusted him more: the well-meaning mediocrity, whose attempts at fidelity were thwarted by lack of artistic insight as well as by hilarious errors of textual interpretation, or the professional poet who embellished with his own inventions the dead and helpless author (whiskers here, private parts there)—a method that nicely camouflaged the paraphrast's ignorance of the From language by having the bloomers of inept scholarship blend with the whims of flowery imitation.

As Ada, Mr. Oranger (a born catalyzer), and Van were discussing those matters one afternoon in 1957 (Van's and Ada's book *Information and Form* had just come out), it suddenly occurred to our old polemicist that all his published works—even the extremely abstruse and specialized *Suicide and Sanity* (1912), *Compitalia* (1921), and *When an Alienist Cannot Sleep* (1932), to cite only a few—were not epistemic tasks set to himself by a savant, but buoyant and bellicose exercises in literary style. He was asked why, then, did he not let himself go, why did he not choose a big playground for a match between Inspiration and Design; and with one thing leading to another it was resolved that he would write his memoirs—to be published posthumously.

He was a very slow writer. It took him six years to write

the first draft and dictate it to Miss Knox, after which he revised the typescript, rewrote it entirely in long hand (1963–
1965) and redictated the entire thing to indefatigable Violet,
whose pretty fingers tapped out a final copy in 1967. E, p, i—
why "*y*," my dear?

5

Ada, who resented the insufficiency of her brother's fame, felt
soothed and elated by the success of *The Texture of Time*
(1924). That work, she said, always reminded her, in some
odd, delicate way, of the sun-and-shade games she used to
play as a child in the secluded avenues of Ardis Park. She
said she had been somehow responsible for the metamorphoses of the lovely larvae that had woven the silk of "Veen's
Time" (as the concept was now termed in one breath, one
breeze, with "Bergson's Duration," or "Whitehead's Bright
Fringe"). But a considerably earlier and weaker work, the
poor little *Letters from Terra*, of which only half a dozen copies existed—two in Villa Armina and the rest in the stacks of
university libraries—was even closer to her heart because of
its nonliterary associations with their 1892–93 sojourn in Manhattan. Sixty-year-old Van crustily and contemptuously dismissed her meek suggestion to the effect that it should be
republished, together with the Sidra reflections and a very
amusing anti-Signy pamphlet on Time in Dreams. Seventy-
year-old Van regretted his disdain when Victor Vitry, a brilliant French director, based a completely unauthorized picture
on *Letters from Terra* written by "Voltemand" half a century
before.

Vitry dated Theresa's visit to Antiterra as taking place in
1940, but 1940 by the Terranean calendar, and about 1890 by
ours. The conceit allowed certain pleasing dips into the modes
and manners of our past (did you remember that horses wore
hats—yes, *hats*—when heat waves swept Manhattan?) and
gave the impression—which physics-fiction literature had

much exploited—of the capsulist traveling backward in terms of time. Philosophers asked nasty questions, but were ignored by the wishing-to-be-gulled moviegoers.

In contrast to the cloudless course of Demonian history in the twentieth century, with the Anglo-American coalition managing one hemisphere, and Tartary, behind her Golden Veil, mysteriously ruling the other, a succession of wars and revolutions were shown shaking loose the jigsaw puzzle of Terrestrial autonomies. In an impressive historical survey of Terra rigged up by Vitry—certainly the greatest cinematic genius ever to direct a picture of such scope or use such a vast number of extras (some said more than a million, others, half a million men and as many mirrors)—kingdoms fell and dictatordoms rose, and republics half-sat, half-lay in various attitudes of discomfort. The conception was controversial, the execution flawless. Look at all those tiny soldiers scuttling along very fast across the trench-scarred wilderness, with explosions of mud and things going *pouf-pouf* in silent French now here, now there!

In 1905, Norway with a mighty heave and a long dorsal ripple unfastened herself from Sweden, her unwieldy co-giantess, while in a similar act of separation the French parliament, with parenthetical outbursts of *vive émotion*, voted a divorce between State and Church. Then, in 1911, Norwegian troops led by Amundsen reached the South Pole and simultaneously the Italians stormed into Turkey. In 1914 Germany invaded Belgium and the Americans tore up Panama. In 1918 they and the French defeated Germany while she was busily defeating Russia (who had defeated her own Tartars some time earlier). In Norway there was Siegrid Mitchel, in America Margaret Undset, and in France, Sidonie Colette. In 1926 Abd-el-Krim surrendered, after yet another photogenic war, and the Golden Horde again subjugated Rus. In 1933, Athaulf Hindler (also known as Mittler—from "to mittle," mutilate) came to power in Germany, and a conflict on an even more spectacular scale than the 1914–1918 war was under way, when Vitry ran out of old documentaries and Theresa, played by his wife, left Terra in a cosmic capsule after having covered the Olympic Games held in Berlin (the Norwegians took most of the

prizes, but the Americans won the fencing event, an outstand-
ing achievement, and beat the Germans in the final football
match by three goals to one).

Van and Ada saw the film nine times, in seven different
languages, and eventually acquired a copy for home use. They
found the historical background absurdly farfetched and considered starting legal proceedings against Vitry—not for having stolen the L.F.T. idea, but for having distorted Terrestrial
politics as obtained by Van with such diligence and skill from
extrasensorial sources and manic dreams. But fifty years had
elapsed, and the novella had not been copyrighted; in fact,
Van could not even prove that "Voltemand" was he. Reporters, however, ferreted out his authorship, and in a mag-
nanimous gesture, he allowed it to be publicized.

Three circumstances contributed to the picture's excep-
tional success. One factor was, of course, that organized religion, disapproving of Terra's appeal to sensation-avid sects,
attempted to have the thing banned. A second attraction came
from a little scene that canny Vitry had not cut out: in a flashback to a revolution in former France, an unfortunate extra,
who played one of the under-executioners, got accidentally
decapitated while pulling the comedian Steller, who played a
reluctant king, into a guillotinable position. Finally, the third,
and even more human reason, was that the lovely leading lady,
Norwegian-born Gedda Vitry, after titillating the spectators
with her skimpy skirts and sexy rags in the existential sequences, came out of her capsule on Antiterra stark naked,
though, of course, in miniature, a millimeter of maddening
femininity dancing in "the charmed circle of the microscope"
like some lewd elf, and revealing, in certain attitudes, I'll be
damned, a pinpoint glint of pubic floss, gold-powdered!

L.F.T. tiny dolls, L.F.T. breloques of coral and ivory, appeared in souvenir shops, from Agony, Patagonia, to Wrin-
kleballs, Le Bras d'Or. L.F.T. clubs sprouted. L.F.T. girlies
minced with mini-menus out of roadside snackettes shaped
like spaceships. From the tremendous correspondence that
piled up on Van's desk during a few years of world fame, one
gathered that thousands of more or less unbalanced people
believed (so striking was the visual impact of the Vitry-Veen
film) in the secret Government-concealed identity of Terra

and Antiterra. Demonian reality dwindled to a casual illusion. Actually, we had passed through all that. Politicians, dubbed Old Felt and Uncle Joe in forgotten comics, had really existed. Tropical countries meant, not only Wild Nature Reserves but famine, and death, and ignorance, and shamans, and agents from distant Atomsk. Our world *was*, in fact, mid-twentieth-century. Terra convalesced after enduring the rack and the stake, the bullies and beasts that Germany inevitably generates when fulfilling her dreams of glory. Russian peasants and poets had not been transported to Estotiland, and the Barren Grounds, ages ago—they were dying, at this very moment, in the slave camps of Tartary. Even the governor of France was not Charlie Chose, the suave nephew of Lord Goal, but a bad-tempered French general.

6

Nirvana, Nevada, Vaniada. By the way, should I not add, my Ada, that only at the very last interview with poor dummy-mummy, soon after my premature—I mean, premonitory—nightmare about "You can, Sir," she employed *mon petit nom*, Vanya, Vanyusha—never had before, and it sounded so odd, so tend . . . (voice trailing off, radiators tinkling).

"Dummy-mum"—(laughing). "Angels, too, have brooms —to sweep one's soul clear of horrible images. My black nurse was Swiss-laced with white whimsies."

Sudden ice hurtling down the rain pipe: brokenhearted stalactite.

Recorded and replayed in their joint memory was their early preoccupation with the strange idea of death. There is one exchange that it would be nice to enact against the green moving backdrop of one of our Ardis sets. The talk about "double guarantee" in eternity. Start just before that.

"I know there's a Van in Nirvana. I'll be with him in the depths *moego ada*, of my Hades," said Ada.

"True, true" (bird-effects here, and acquiescing branches, and what you used to call "golden gouts").

"As lovers *and* siblings," she cried, "we have a double chance of being together in eternity, in terrarity. Four pairs of eyes in paradise!"

"Neat, neat," said Van.

Something of the sort. One great difficulty. The strange mirage-shimmer standing in for death should not appear too soon in the chronicle and yet it should permeate the first amorous scenes. Hard but not insurmountable (I can do anything, I can tango and tap-dance on my fantastic hands). By the way, who dies first?

Ada. Van. Ada. Vaniada. Nobody. Each hoped to go first, so as to concede, by implication, a longer life to the other, and each wished to go last, in order to spare the other the anguish, or worries, of widowhood. One solution would be for you to marry Violet.

"Thank you. *J'ai tâté de deux tribades dans ma vie, ça suffit.* Dear Emile says '*terme qu'on évite d'employer.*' How right he is!"

"If not Violet, then a local Gauguin girl. Or Yolande Kickshaw."

Why? Good question. Anyway, Violet must not be given this part to type. I'm afraid we're going to wound a lot of people (openwork American lilt)! Oh come, art cannot hurt. I can, and how!

Actually the question of mortal precedence has now hardly any importance. I mean, the hero and heroine should get so close to each other by the time the horror begins, so *organically* close, that they overlap, intergrade, interache, and even if Vaniada's end is described in the epilogue we, writers and readers, should be unable to make out (myopic, myopic) who exactly survives, Dava or Vada, Anda or Vanda.

I had a schoolmate called Vanda. And *I* knew a girl called Adora, little thing in my last floramor. What makes me see that bit as the purest *sanglot* in the book? What is the worst part of dying?

For you realize there are three facets to it (roughly corresponding to the popular tripartition of Time). There is, first, the wrench of relinquishing forever all one's memories—that's a commonplace, but what courage man must have had to go through that commonplace again and again and not give up the rigmarole of accumulating again and again the riches of consciousness that will be snatched away! Then we have the second facet—the hideous physical pain—for obvious reasons let us not dwell upon that. And finally, there is the featureless pseudo-future, blank and black, an everlasting nonlastingness, the crowning paradox of our boxed brain's eschatologies!

"Yes," said Ada (aged eleven and a great hair-tosser), "yes—but take a paralytic who forgets the entire past gradually, stroke by stroke, who dies in his sleep like a good boy, and who has believed all his life that the soul is immortal—isn't that desirable, isn't that a quite comfortable arrangement?"

"Cold comfort," said Van (aged fourteen and dying of other desires). "You lose your immortality when you lose your memory. And if you land then on Terra Caelestis, with your pillow and chamberpot, you are made to room not with Shakespeare or even Longfellow, but with guitarists and cretins."

She insisted that if there were no future, then one had the right of making up a future, and in that case one's very own future did exist, insofar as one existed oneself. Eighty years quickly passed—a matter of changing a slide in a magic lantern. They had spent most of the morning reworking their translation of a passage (lines 569–572) in John Shade's famous poem:

> . . . Soveti mï dayom
> Kak bït' vdovtsu: on poteryal dvuh zhyon;
> On ih vstrechaet—lyubyashchih, lyubimïh,
> Revnuyushchih ego drug k druzhke . . .

> (. . . *We give advice*
> *To widower. He has been married twice:*
> *He meets his wives; both loved, both loving, both*
> *Jealous of one another . . .*)

Van pointed out that here was the rub—one is free to imagine any type of hereafter, of course: the generalized paradise promised by Oriental prophets and poets, or an individual combination; but the work of fancy is handicapped—to a quite hopeless extent—by a logical ban: you cannot bring your friends along—or your enemies for that matter—to the party. The transposition of all our remembered relationships into an Elysian life inevitably turns it into a second-rate continuation of our marvelous mortality. Only a Chinaman or a retarded child can imagine being met, in that Next-Installment World, to the accompaniment of all sorts of tail-wagging and groveling of welcome, by the mosquito executed eighty years ago upon one's bare leg, which has been amputated since then and now, in the wake of the gesticulating mosquito, comes back, stomp, stomp, stomp, here I am, stick me on.

She did not laugh; she repeated to herself the verses that had given them such trouble. The Signy brain-shrinkers would gleefully claim that the reason the three "boths" had been skipped in the Russian version was not at all, oh, not at all, because cramming three cumbersome amphibrachs into the pentameter would have necessitated adding at least one more verse for carrying the luggage:

"Oh, Van, oh Van, we did not love her enough. *That's* whom you should have married, the one sitting feet up, in ballerina black, on the stone balustrade, and then everything would have been all right—I would have stayed with you both in Ardis Hall, and instead of that happiness, handed out gratis, instead of all that we *teased* her to death!"

Was it time for the morphine? No, not yet. Time-and-pain had not been mentioned in the *Texture*. Pity, since an element of pure time enters into pain, into the thick, steady, solid duration of I-can't-bear-it pain; nothing gray-gauzy about it, solid as a black bole, I can't, oh, call Lagosse.

Van found him reading in the serene garden. The doctor followed Ada into the house. The Veens had believed for a whole summer of misery (or made each other believe) that it was a touch of neuralgia.

Touch? A giant, with an effort-contorted face, clamping and twisting an engine of agony. Rather humiliating that physical pain makes one supremely indifferent to such moral issues as Lucette's fate, and rather amusing, if that is the right word, to constate that one bothers about problems of style even at those atrocious moments. The Swiss doctor, who had been told everything (and had even turned out to have known at medical school a nephew of Dr. Lapiner) displayed an intense interest in the almost completed but only partly corrected book and drolly said it was not a person or persons but *le bouquin* which he wanted to see *guéri de tous ces accrocs* before it was too late. It was. What everybody thought would be Violet's supreme achievement, ideally clean, produced on special Atticus paper in a special cursive type (the glorified version of Van's hand), with the master copy bound in purple calf for Van's ninety-seventh birthday, had been immediately blotted out by a regular inferno of alterations in red ink and blue pencil. One can even surmise that if our time-racked, flat-lying couple ever intended to die they would die, as it were, *into* the finished book, into Eden or Hades, into the prose of the book or the poetry of its blurb.

Their recently built castle in Ex was inset in a crystal winter. In the latest *Who's Who* the list of his main papers included by some bizarre mistake the title of a work he had never written, though planned to write many pains: *Unconsciousness and the Unconscious.* There was no pain to do it now—and it was high pain for *Ada* to be completed. "*Quel livre, mon Dieu, mon Dieu,*" Dr. [Professor. Ed.] Lagosse exclaimed, weighing the master copy which the flat pale parents of the future Babes, in the brown-leaf Woods, a little book in the Ardis Hall nursery, could no longer prop up in the mysterious first picture: two people in one bed.

Ardis Hall—the Ardors and Arbors of Ardis—this is the leitmotiv rippling through *Ada*, an ample and delightful chronicle, whose principal part is staged in a dream-bright America—for are not our childhood memories comparable to Vineland-borne caravelles, indolently encircled by the white birds of dreams? The protagonist, a scion of one of our most illustrious and opulent families, is Dr. Van Veen, son of Baron "Demon" Veen, that memorable Manhattan and Reno figure. The end of an extraordinary epoch coincides with Van's no less extraordinary boyhood. Nothing in world literature, save maybe Count Tolstoy's reminiscences, can vie in pure joyousness and Arcadian innocence with the "Ardis" part of the book. On the fabulous country estate of his art-collecting uncle, Daniel Veen, an ardent childhood romance develops in a series of fascinating scenes between Van and pretty Ada, a truly unusual *gamine*, daughter of Marina, Daniel's stage-struck wife. That the relationship is not simply dangerous *cousinage*, but possesses an aspect prohibited by law, is hinted in the very first pages.

In spite of the many intricacies of plot and psychology, the story proceeds at a spanking pace. Before we can pause to take breath and quietly survey the new surroundings into which the writer's magic carpet has, as it were, spilled us, another attractive girl, Lucette Veen, Marina's younger daughter, has also been swept off her feet by Van, the irresistible rake. Her tragic destiny constitutes one of the highlights of this delightful book.

The rest of Van's story turns frankly and colorfully upon his long love-affair with Ada. It is interrupted by her marriage to an Arizonian cattle-breeder whose fabulous ancestor discovered our country. After her husband's death our lovers are reunited. They spend their old age traveling together and dwelling in the various villas, one lovelier than another, that Van has erected all over the Western Hemisphere.

Not the least adornment of the chronicle is the delicacy of pictorial detail: a latticed gallery; a painted ceiling; a pretty plaything stranded among the forget-me-nots of a brook; butterflies and butterfly orchids in the margin of the romance; a misty view descried from marble steps; a doe at gaze in the ancestral park; and much, much more.

Notes to Ada

BY VIVIAN DARKBLOOM

p. 7 All happy families etc.: mistranslations of Russian classics are ridiculed here. The opening sentence of Tolstoy's novel is turned inside out and Anna Arkadievna's patronymic given an absurd masculine ending, while an incorrect feminine one is added to her surname. "Mount Tabor" and "Pontius" allude to the transfigurations (Mr. G. Steiner's term, I believe) and betrayals to which great texts are subjected by pretentious and ignorant versionists.

p. 7 Severnïya Territorii: Northern Territories. Here and elsewhere transliteration is based on the old Russian orthography.

p. 7 granoblastically: in a tesselar (mosaic) jumble.

p. 7 Tofana: allusion to "aqua tofana" (see any good dictionary).

p. 7 sur-royally: fully antlered, with terminal prongs.

p. 8 Durak: "fool" in Russian.

p. 8 Lake Kitezh: allusion to the legendary town of Kitezh which shines at the bottom of a lake in a Russian fairy tale.

p. 9 Mr. Eliot: we shall meet him again, on pages 367 and 404, in company of the author of "The Waistline" and "Agonic Lines."

p. 9 Counter-Fogg: Phileas Fogg, Jules Verne's globetrotter, traveled from West to East.

p. 9 Goodnight Kids: their names are borrowed, with distortions, from a comic strip for French-speaking children.

p. 10 Dr. Lapiner: for some obscure but not unattractive reason, most of the physicians in the book turn out to bear names connected with rabbits. The French "*lapin*" in Lapiner is matched by the Russian "*Krolik*," the name of Ada's beloved lepidopterist (p. 11, *et passim*) and the Russian "*zayats*" (hare) sounds like "Seitz" (the German gynecologist on page 183); there is a Latin "*cuniculus*" in "*Nikulin*" ("grandson of the great rodentiologist Kunikulinov," p. 347), and a Greek "*lagos*" in "Lagosse" (the doctor who attends Van in his old age). Note also Coniglietto, the Italian cancer-of-the-blood specialist, p. 303.

p. 11 *mizernoe*: Franco-Russian form of "miserable" in the sense of "paltry."

469

p. 11   *c'est bien le cas de le dire*: and no mistake.

p. 11   *lieu de naissance*: birthplace.

p. 11   *pour ainsi dire*: so to say.

p. 11   Jane Austen: allusion to rapid narrative information imparted through dialogue, in *Mansfield Park*.

p. 11   "Bear-Foot," not "bare foot": both children are naked.

p. 11   Stabian flower girl: allusion to the celebrated mural painting (the so-called "Spring") from Stabiae in the National Museum of Naples: a maiden scattering blossoms.

p. 14   Raspberries; ribbon: allusions to ludicrous blunders in Lowell's versions of Mandelshtam's poems (in the *N.Y. Review* 23 December 1965).

p. 14   Belokonsk: the Russian twin of "Whitehorse" (city in N.W. Canada).

p. 15   *en connaissance de cause*: knowing what it was all about (Fr.).

p. 16   Aardvark: apparently, a university town in New England.

p. 16   Gamaliel: a much more fortunate statesman than our W. G. Harding.

p. 17   interesting condition: family way.

p. 18   Lolita, Texas: this town exists, or, rather, existed, for it has been renamed, I believe, after the appearance of the notorious novel.

p. 18   *penyuar*: Russ., peignoir.

p. 18   *beau milieu*: right in the middle.

p. 18   Faragod: apparently, the god of electricity.

p. 19   Braques: allusion to a bric-à-brac painter.

p. 22   *entendons-nous*: let's have it clear (Fr.).

p. 22   *Yukonets*: inhabitant of Yukon (Russ.).

p. 23   lammer: amber (Fr: l'ambre), allusion to electricity.

p. 24   my lad, my pretty, etc.: paraphrase of a verse in Housman.

p. 24   ballatetta: fragmentation and distortion of a passage in a "little ballad" by the Italian poet Guido Cavalcanti (1255–1300). The relevant lines are: "you frightened and weak little voice that comes weeping from my woeful heart, go with my soul and that ditty, telling of a destroyed mind."

p. 25   Nuss: German for "nut."

p. 26   *Khristosik*: little Christ (Russ.).

p. 26   *rukuliruyushchiy*: Russ., from Fr. *roucoulant*, cooing.

p. 27   horsepittle: "hospital," borrowed from a passage in Dickens' *Bleak House*. Poor Jo's pun, not a poor Joycean one.

p. 28   *aujourd'hui, heute*: to-day (Fr., Germ.).

p. 29   *Princess Lointaine*: Distant Princess, title of a French play.

p. 30   *pour attraper le client*: to fool the customer.

p. 33   *Je parie*, etc.: I bet you do not recognize me, Sir.

p. 33   *tour du jardin*: a stroll in the garden.

p. 34   Lady Amherst: confused in the child's mind with the learned lady after whom a popular pheasant is named.

p. 35   with a slight smile: a pet formula of Tolstoy's denoting cool superiority, if not smugness, in a character's manner of speech.

p. 36   *pollice verso*: Lat., thumbs down.

p. 38   Sumerechnikov: the name is derived from "*sumerki*" ("dusk" in Russian).

p. 41   lovely Spanish poem: really *two* poems—Jorge Guillén's *Descanso en jardin* and his *El otono: isla*).

p. 43   *Monsieur a quinze ans*, etc.: You are fifteen, Sir, I believe, and I am nineteen, I know. . . . You Sir, have known town girls no doubt; as to me, I'm a virgin, or almost one. Moreover . . .

p. 43   *rien qu'une petite fois*: just once.

p. 44   *mais va donc jouer avec lui*: come on, go and play with him.

p. 44   *se morfondre*: mope.

p. 44   *au fond*: actually.

p. 44   *Je l'ignore*: I don't know.

p. 44   *cache-cache*: hide-and-seek.

p. 45   *infusion de tilleul*: lime tea.

p. 47   *Les amours du Dr. Mertvago*: play on "Zhivago" ("*zhiv*" means in Russian "alive" and "*mertv*" dead).

p. 47   *grand chêne*: big oak.

p. 48   *quelle idée*: the idea!

p. 49   *Les malheurs de Swann*: cross between *Les Malheurs de Sophie* by Mme de Ségur (née Countess Rostopchin) and Proust's *Un Amour de Swann*.

p. 53   *monologue intérieur*: the so-called "stream-of-consciousness" device, used by Leo Tolstoy (in describing, for instance, Anna's last impressions whilst her carriage rolls through the streets of Moscow).

p. 55   Mr. Fowlie: see Wallace Fowlie, Rimbaud (1946).

p. 55   *soi-disant*: would-be.

p. 55   *les robes vertes*, etc.: the green and washed-out frocks of the little girls.

p. 56   *angel moy*: Russ., "my angel."

p. 56   *en vain*, etc.: In vain, one gains in play
The Oka river and Palm Bay . . .

p. 57   *bambin angélique*: angelic little lad.

p. 58   *groote*: Dutch, "great."

p. 59   *un machin* etc.: a thing as long as this that almost wounded the child in the buttock.

p. 60 pensive reeds: Pascal's metaphor of man, *un roseau pensant.*

p. 61 horsecart: an old anagram. It leads here to a skit on Freudian dream charades ("symbols in an orchal orchestra"), p. 62.

p. 61 *buvard*: blotting pad.

p. 61 *Kamargsky*: La Camargue, a marshy region in S. France combined with *Komar*, "mosquito," in Russian and *moustique* in French.

p. 62 *sa petite collation du matin*: light breakfast.

p. 63 *tartine au miel*: bread-and-butter with honey.

p. 64 Osberg: another good-natured anagram, scrambling the name of a writer with whom the author of *Lolita* has been rather comically compared. Incidentally, that title's pronunciation has nothing to do with English or Russian (*pace* an anonymous owl in a recent issue of the *TLS*).

p. 64 *mais ne te* etc.: now don't fidget like that when you put on your skirt! A well-bred little girl . . .

p. 65 *très en beauté*: looking very pretty.

p. 65 *calèche*: victoria.

p. 66 *pecheneg*: a savage.

p. 67 *grande fille*: girl who has reached puberty.

p. 69 *La Rivière de Diamants*: Maupassant and his "*La Parure*" (p. 73) did not exist on Antiterra.

p. 69 *copie* etc.: copying in their garret.

p. 69 *à grand eau*: swilling the floors.

p. 70 *désinvolture*: uninhibitedness.

p. 70 *vibgyor*: violet-indigo-blue-green-yellow-orange-red.

p. 71 *sans façons*: unceremoniously.

p. 72 *strapontin*: folding seat in front.

p. 73 *décharné*: emaciated.

p. 73 *cabane*: hut.

p. 73 *allons donc*: oh, come.

p. 73 *pointe assassine*: the point (of a story or poem) that murders artistic merit.

p. 73 *quitte à tout dire* etc.: even telling it all to the widow if need be.

p. 73 *il pue*: he stinks.

p. 74 *Atala*: a short novel by Chateaubriand.

p. 75 *un juif*: a Jew.

p. 76 *et pourtant*: and yet.

p. 76 *ce beau jardin* etc.: This beautiful garden blooms in May, but in Winter never, never, never, never, never is green etc.

p. 78 *chort!*: Russ., "devil."

p. 83 *mileyshiy*: Russ., "dearest."

p. 83 *partie* etc.: exterior fleshy part that frames the mouth . . .

the two edges of a simple wound . . . it is the member that licks.

p. 84 *pascaltrezza*: in this pun, which combines Pascal with *scaltrezza* (Ital., "sharp wit") and *treza* (a Provençal word for "tressed stalks"), the French "*pas*" negates the "*pensant*" of the "*roseau*" in his famous phrase "man is a thinking reed."

p. 86 Katya: the ingénue in Turgenev's "Fathers and Children."

p. 86 a *trouvaille*: a felicitous find.

p. 86 Ada, who liked crossing orchids: she crosses here two French authors, Baudelaire and Chateaubriand.

p. 86 *mon enfant*, etc.: my child, my sister, think of the thickness of the big oak at Tagne, think of the mountain, think of the tenderness—

p. 87 *recueilli*: concentrated, rapt.

p. 87 canteen: a reference to the "scrumpets" (crumpets) provided by school canteens.

p. 90 *puisqu'on* etc.: since we broach this subject.

p. 91 *hument*: inhale.

p. 92 *tout le reste*: all the rest.

p. 92 *zdravstvuyte* etc.: Russ., lo and behold: the apotheosis.

p. 92 Mlle Stopchin: a representative of Mme de Ségur, née Rostopchin, author of *Les Malheurs de Sophie* (nomenclatorially occupied on Antiterra by *Les Malheurs de Swann*).

p. 92 *au feu!*: fire!

p. 92 *flambait*: was in flames.

p. 93 Ashette: "Cendrillon" in the French original.

p. 93 *en croupe*: riding pillion.

p. 95 *à reculons*: backwards.

p. 97 The Nile is settled: a famous telegram sent by an African explorer.

p. 97 *parlez pour vous*: speak for yourself.

p. 98 *trempée*: soaked.

p. 101 *je l'ai vu* etc.: "I saw it in one of the wastepaper-baskets of the library."

p. 101 *aussitôt après*: immediately after.

p. 102 *ménagez* etc.: go easy on your Americanisms.

p. 103 *leur chute* etc.: their fall is slow . . . one can follow them with one's eyes, recognizing—

p. 103 Lowden: a portmanteau name combining two contemporary bards.

p. 103 *baguenaudier*: French name of bladder senna.

p. 104 Floeberg: Flaubert's style is mimicked in this pseudo quotation.

p. 105   *pour ne pas* etc.: so as not to put any ideas in her head.

p. 105   *en lecture*: "out."

p. 106   *cher, trop cher René*: dear, too dear (his sister's words in Cha-
            teaubriand's *René*).

p. 106   *Chiron*: doctor among centaurs: an allusion to Updike's best
            novel.

p. 107   London weekly: a reference to Alan Brien's *New Statesman*
            column.

p. 107   *Höhensonne*: ultra-violet lamp.

p. 107   *bobo*: little hurt.

p. 107   *démission* etc.: tearful notice.

p. 107   *les deux enfants* etc.: "therefore the two children could make
            love without any fear."

p. 108   *fait divers*: news item.

p. 109   *blin*: Russ., pancake.

p. 110   *qui le sait*: who knows.

p. 111   Heinrich Müller: author of *Poxus*, etc.

p. 112   *Ma soeur te souvient-il encore*: first line of the third sextet of
            Chateaubriand's *Romance à Hélène* ("Combien j'ai douce
            souvenance") composed to an Auvergne tune that he heard
            during a trip to Mont Dore in 1805 and later inserted in his
            novella *Le Dernier Abencerage*. The final (fifth) sextet begins
            with "*Oh! qui me rendra mon Hélène. Et ma montagne et le
            grand chêne*"—one of the leitmotivs of the present novel.

p. 112   *sestra moya* etc.: my sister, do you remember the mountain,
            and the tall oak, and the Ladore?

p. 112   *oh! qui me rendra* etc.: oh who will give me back my Aline,
            and the big oak, and my hill?

p. 112   Lucile: the name of Chateaubriand's actual sister.

p. 112   la Dore etc.: the Dore and the agile swallow.

p. 113   *vendange*: vine-harvest.

p. 115   Rockette: corresponds to Maupassant's *La Petite Rocque*.

p. 115   *chaleur du lit*: bed warmth.

p. 116   *horosho*: Russ., all right.

p. 118   *mironton* etc.: burden of a popular song.

p. 119   Lettrocalamity: a play on Ital. *elettrocalamita*, electromagnet.

p. 122   Bagrov's grandson: allusion to *Childhood Years of Bagrov's
            Grandson* by the minor writer Sergey Aksakov (A.D. 1791–
            1859).

p. 123   *hobereaux*: country squires.

p. 123   *biryul'ki proshlago*: Russ., the Past's baubles.

p. 125   *traktir*: Russ., pub.

p. 125   (avoir le) *vin triste*: to be melancholy in one's cups.

p. 125   *au cou rouge* etc.: with the ruddy and stout neck of a widower still full of sap.

p. 125   *gloutonnerie*: gourmandise.

p. 125   *tant pis*: too bad.

p. 126   *je rêve* etc.: I must be dreaming. It cannot be that anyone should spread butter on top of all that indigestible and vile British dough.

p. 126   *et ce n'est que* etc.: and it is only the first slice.

p. 126   *lait caillé*: curds and whey.

p. 126   *shlafrok*: Russ., from Germ. *Schlafrock*, dressing gown.

p. 127   *tous les* etc.: all the tires are new.

p. 127   *tel un*: thus a wild lily entrusting the wilderness.

p. 127   *non* etc.: no, Sir, I simply am very fond of you, Sir, and of your young lady.

p. 128   *qu'y puis-je?* what can I do about it?

p. 128   Stumbling on melons . . . arrogant fennels: allusions to passages in Marvell's "Garden" and Rimbaud's "Mémoire."

p. 131   *d'accord*: Okay.

p. 134   *la bonne surprise*: what a good surprise.

p. 135   *amour propre, sale amour*: pun borrowed from Tolstoy's "*Resurrection*."

p. 136   *quelque petite* etc.: some little laundress.

p. 136   Toulouse: Toulouse-Lautrec.

p. 137   *dura*: Russ., fool (fem.).

p. 137   *The Headless Horseman*: Mayn Reid's title is ascribed here to Pushkin, author of *The Bronze Horseman*.

p. 138   Lermontov: author of *The Demon*.

p. 138   Tolstoy etc.: Tolstoy's hero, Haji Murad (a Caucasian chieftain), is blended here with General Murat, Napoleon's brother-in-law, and with the French revolutionary leader Marat assassinated in his bath by Charlotte Corday.

p. 139   Lute: from "Lutèce," ancient name of Paris.

p. 140   *constatait* etc.: noted with pleasure.

p. 141   Shivering aurora, laborious old Chose: a touch of Baudelaire.

p. 143   *golubyanka*: Russ., small blue butterfly.

p. 143   *petit bleu*: Parisian slang for pneumatic post (an express message on blue paper).

p. 143   *cousin*: mosquito.

p. 144   *mademoiselle* etc.: the young lady has a pretty bad pneumonia, I regret to say, Sir.

p. 144   Granial Maza: a perfume named after Mt. Kazbek's "*gran' almaza*" (diamond's facet) of Lermontov's *The Demon*.

p. 147   *inquiétante*: disturbing.

p. 149   yellow-blue Vass: the phrase is consonant with *ya lyublyu vas* ("I love you" in Russian).

p. 152   *mais, ma pauvre amie* etc.: but, my poor friend, it was imitation jewelry.

p. 152   *nichego ne podelaesh'*: Russ., nothing to be done.

p. 153   *elle le mangeait* etc.: she devoured him with her eyes.

p. 153   *petits vers* etc.: fugitive poetry and silkworms.

p. 155   Uncle Van: allusion to a line in Chekhov's play *Uncle Vanya*: We shall see the sky swarming with diamonds.

p. 158   *Les Enfants Maudits*: the accursed children.

p. 159   *du sollst* etc.: Germ., you must not listen.

p. 159   *on ne parle pas* etc.: one does not speak like that in front of a dog.

p. 160   *que voulez-vous dire*: what do you mean.

p. 162   Forestday: Rack's pronunciation of "Thursday."

p. 162   *furchtbar*: Germ., dreadful.

p. 163   Ero: thus the h-dropping policeman in Wells' *Invisible Man* defined the latter's treacherous friend.

p. 165   *mais qu'est-ce* etc.: but what did your cousin do to you.

p. 167   *petit-beurre*: a tea biscuit.

p. 172   *unschicklich*: Germ., improper (understood as "not chic" by Ada).

p. 174   *ogon'*: Russ., fire.

p. 175   Microgalaxies: known on Terra as *Les Enfants du Capitaine Grant*, by Jules Verne.

p. 175   *ailleurs*: elsewhere.

p. 176   *alfavit*: Russ., alphabet.

p. 177   *particule*: "*de*" or "*d'*."

p. 177   Pat Rishin: a play on "patrician." One may recall Podgoretz (Russ. "underhill") applying that epithet to a popular critic, a would-be expert in Russian as spoken in Minsk and elsewhere. Minsk and Chess also figure in Chapter Six of *Speak, Memory* (p. 133, N.Y. ed. 1966).

p. 179   Gerschizhevsky: a Slavist's name gets mixed here with that of Chizhevki, another Slavist.

p. 180   *Je ne peux* etc.: I can do nothing, but nothing.

p. 180   *Buchstaben*: Germ., letters of the alphabet.

p. 180   *c'est tout simple*: it's quite simple.

p. 181   *pas facile*: not easy.

p. 181   Cendrillon: Cinderella.

p. 181   *mon petit . . . que dis-je*: darling . . . in fact.

p. 183   *elle est folle* etc.: she is insane and evil.

p. 183   Beer Tower: pun on "Tourbière."

p. 184 *chayku*: Russ., tea (diminutive).

p. 184 Ivanilich: a pouf plays a marvelous part in Tolstoy's *The Death of Ivan Ilyich*, where it sighs deeply under a friend of the widow's.

p. 184 *cousinage*: cousinhood is a dangerous neighborhood.

p. 184 *on s'embrassait*: kissing went on in every corner.

p. 184 *erunda*: Russ., nonsense.

p. 184 *hier und da*: Germ., here and there.

p. 185 *raffolait* etc.: was crazy about one of his mares.

p. 186 *tout est bien*: everything is all right.

p. 187 *tant mieux*: so much the better.

p. 187 Tuzenbakh: Van recites the last words of the unfortunate Baron in Chekhov's *Three Sisters* who does not know what to say but feels urged to say something to Irina before going to fight his fatal duel.

p. 187 *kontretain*: Russian mispronunciation of *contretemps*.

p. 189 *kameristochka*: Russ., young chambermaid.

p. 190 *en effet*: indeed.

p. 190 *petit nègre*: little Negro in the flowering field.

p. 190 *ce sera* etc.: it will be a dinner for four.

p. 190 Wagging his left forefinger: that gene did not miss his daughter (see p. 180, where the name of the cream is also prefigured).

p. 191 Lyovka: derogative or folksy diminutive of Lyov (Leo).

p. 193 *antranou* etc.: Russian mispronunciation of Fr. *entre nous soit dit*, between you and me.

p. 193 *filius aqua*: "son of water," bad pun on *filum aquae*, the middle way, "the thread of the stream."

p. 194 *une petite juive* etc.: a very aristocratic little Jewess.

p. 195 *ça va*: it goes.

p. 195 *seins durs*: mispronunciation of *sans dire* "without saying."

p. 195 *passe encore*: may still pass muster.

p. 196 *Lorsque* etc.: When her fiancé had gone to war, the unfortunate and noble maiden closed her piano, sold her elephant.

p. 196 By chance preserved: The verses are by chance preserved

I have them, here they are:

(*Eugene Onegin*, Six: XXI: 1–2)

p. 197 *Klubsessel*: Germ., easy chair.

p. 198 *devant les gens*: in front of the servants.

p. 198 Fanny Price: the heroine of Jane Austen's *Mansfield Park*.

p. 198 *grib*: Russ., mushroom.

p. 199 *vodochki*: Russ., pl. of *vodochka*, diminutive of *vodka*.

p. 200 *zakusochniy* etc.: Russ., table with hors-d'oeuvres.

p. 200 *petits soupers*: intimate suppers.

p. 200 Persty: Evidently Pushkin's *vinograd*:

> as elongated and transparent
> as are the fingers of a girl.
> (*devï molodoy, jeune fille*)

p. 200 *ciel-étoilé*: starry sky.

p. 203 *ne pikhtite*: Russ., do not wheeze.

p. 205 *vous me comblez*: you overwhelm me with kindness.

p. 205 *pravda*: Russ., it's true.

p. 205 *gelinotte*: hazel-hen.

p. 205 *le feu* etc.: the so delicate fire of virginity

> that on her brow . . .

p. 205 *po razschyotu po moemu*: an allusion to Famusov (in Gri-boedov's *Gore ot uma*), calculating the pregnancy of a lady friend.

p. 205 *protestuyu*: Russ., I protest.

p. 205 *seriozno*: Russ., seriously.

p. 205 *quoi que ce soit*: whatever it might be.

p. 206 *en accuse* etc.: . . . brings out its beauty.

p. 206 certicle: anagram of "electric."

p. 206 *Tetrastes* etc.: Latin name of the imaginary "Peterson's Grouse" from Wind River Range, Wyo.

p. 207 Great good man: a phrase that Winston Churchill, the British politician, enthusiastically applied to Stalin.

p. 208 *voulu*: intentional.

p. 209 *echt* etc.: Germ., a genuine German.

p. 209 *Kegelkugel*: Germ., skittle-ball.

p. 209 *partir* etc.: to go away is to die a little, and to die is to go away a little too much.

p. 210 tangelo: a cross between the tangerine and the pomelo (grapefruit).

p. 211 *fal'shivo*: Russ., false.

p. 212 *rozï . . . beryozï*: Russ., roses . . . birches.

p. 212 *ou comme ça?*: or like that?

p. 216 *sale* etc.: dirty little Philistine.

p. 216 *d'accord*: Okay.

p. 217 *zhe* etc.: Russ., distortion of *je t'en prie*.

p. 217 Trigorin etc.: a reference to a scene in *The Seagull*.

p. 218 Houssaie: French, a "holly wood." *Gollivud-tozh* means in Russian "known also as Hollywood."

p. 219 *enfin*: at last.

p. 219 *passati*: pseudo-Russian pun on "pass water."

p. 219 *coeur de boeuf*: bull's heart (in shape).

p. 222 *quand tu voudras* etc.: any time, my lad.

p. 223   *la maudite* etc.: the confounded (governess).

p. 223   *vos* etc.: Franco-Russ., your expressions are rather free.

p. 224   *qui tâchait* etc.: who was trying to turn her head.

p. 225   *ombres* etc.: shadows and colors.

p. 229   *qu'on la coiffe* etc.: to have her hair done in the open.

p. 229   *un air entendu*: a knowing look.

p. 231   *ne sait quand* etc.: knows not when he'll come back.

p. 232   *mon beau page*: my pretty page.

p. 234   *c'est ma dernière*: this is my last night in the manor.

p. 235   *je suis* etc.: I'm yours, it's soon dawn.

p. 235   *parlez pour vous*: speak for yourself.

p. 235   *immonde*: unspeakable.

p. 235   *il la mangeait* etc.: he devoured her with disgusting kisses.

p. 237   *qu'on vous culbute*: that they tumble you.

p. 240   *marée noire*: black tide.

p. 243   *j'ai des ennuis*: I have worries.

p. 243   *topinambour*: tuber of the girasole; pun on "pun" ("*calembour*").

p. 243   *on n'est pas* etc.: what scurvy behavior.

p. 244   Tapper: "Wild Violet," as well as "Birdfoot" (p. 245), reflects the "pansy" character of Van's adversary and of the two seconds.

p. 245   Rafin, Esq.: pun on "Rafinesque," after whom a violet is named.

p. 245   Do-Re-La: "Ladore" musically jumbled.

p. 247   *partie* etc.: picnic.

p. 250   *palata*: Russ., ward.

p. 252   *tvoyu mat'*: Russ., "Thy mother": the end of a popular Russian oath.

p. 253   *Ich bin* etc.: Germ., I'm an incorrigible joker.

p. 255   uncle: "my uncle has most honest principles."
                 (*Eug. Onegin*, One: I:1)

p. 258   *encore un* etc.: one more "baby ghost" (pun).

p. 261   the last paragraph of Part One imitates, in significant brevity of intonation (as if spoken by an outside voice), a famous Tolstoyan ending, with Van in the role of Kitty Lyovin.

p. 263   *poule*: tart.

p. 263   *komsi* etc.: *comme-ci comme-ça* in Russ., mispronunciation: so-so.

p. 263   *mestechko*: Russ., little place.

p. 263   *bateau ivre*: "sottish ship," title of Rimbaud's poem here used instead of "ship of fools."

p. 264   *poshliy*: Russ., vulgar.

p. 265   *da*: Russ., yes.

p. 266 *ce qui* etc.: which amounts to the same thing.

p. 266 *maux*: aches.

p. 266 aril: coating of certain seeds.

p. 266 Grant etc.: Jules Verne in *Captain Grant's Children* has "*agonie*" (in a discovered message) turn out to be part of "Patagonie."

p. 270 Cyraniana: allusion to Cyrano de Bergerac's *Histoire comique des Etats de la Lune*.

p. 270 *Nekto*: Russ., quidam.

p. 270 *romanchik*: Russ., novelette.

p. 271 Sig Leymanski: anagram of the name of a waggish British novelist keenly interested in physics fiction.

p. 273 Abencerage, Zegris: Families of Granada Moors (their feud inspired Chateaubriand).

p. 275 *fille de joie*: whore.

p. 279 *maison close*: brothel.

p. 280 *vyshibala*: Russ., bouncer.

p. 282 *Künstlerpostkarte*: Germ., art picture postcards.

p. 282 *la gosse*: the little girl.

p. 284 *subsidunt* etc.: mountains subside and heights deteriorate.

p. 286 *smorchiama*: let us snuff out the candle.

p. 287 Marmlad in Dickens: or rather Marmeladov in Dostoevsky, whom Dickens (in translation) greatly influenced.

p. 288 *frôlements*: light touchings.

p. 291 *sturb*: pun on Germ., *sterben*, to die.

p. 292 *qui prend* etc.: that takes wing.

p. 292 all our old etc.: Swinburne.

p. 293 Larousse: pun: *rousse*, "redhair" in French.

p. 293 *pourtant*: yet.

p. 294 *cesse*: cease.

p. 294 *Glanz*: Germ., luster.

p. 294 *Mädel*: Germ., girl.

p. 295 *vsyo sdelali*: Russ., had done everything.

p. 296 relanced: from Fr. *relancer*, to go after.

p. 299 *cogner* etc.: pun ("to coin a phrase").

p. 299 *fraise*: strawberry red.

p. 299 *krestik*: Anglo-Russian, little crest.

p. 299 *vanouissements*: "Swooning in Van's arms."

p. 302 I have not art etc.: Hamlet.

p. 302 *si je puis* etc.: if I may put it that way.

p. 302 *la plus laide* etc.: the ugliest girl in the world can give much more than she has.

p. 304 *Wattebausch*: Germ., piece of cottonwool.

p. 304 *à la queue* etc.: in Indian file.

p. 306 making follies: Fr. *faire des folies*, living it up.

p. 306 *komondi*: Russian French: *comme on dit*, as they say.

p. 307 *Vieux-Rose* etc.: Ségur-Rostopchin's books in the *Bibliothèque Rose* edition.

p. 309 *l'ivresse* etc.: the intoxication of speed, conceptions on Sundays.

p. 309 *un baiser* etc.: one single kiss.

p. 313 *shuba*: Russ., fur coat.

p. 316 *ébats*: frolics.

p. 317 *mossio* etc.: *monsieur* your cousin.

p. 317 *jolies*: pretty.

p. 317 *n'aurait* etc.: should never have received that scoundrel.

p. 317 Ashettes: Cinderellas.

p. 319 Sumerechnikov: His name comes from Russ., *sumerki*, twilight; see also p. 38.

p. 319 *zdraste*: abbrev. form of *zdravstvuyte*, the ordinary Russian greeting.

p. 320 *lit* etc.: pun on "eider-down bed."

p. 321 *d'ailleurs*: anyhow.

p. 321 *pétard*: Mr. Ben Wright, a poet in his own right, is associated throughout with *pets* (farts).

p. 321 *bayronka*: from Bayron, Russ., Byron.

p. 322 *réjouissants*: hilarious.

p. 322 Beckstein: transposed syllables.

p. 322 *Love under the Lindens*: O'Neill, Thomas Mann, and his translator tangle in this paragraph.

p. 323 vanishing etc.: allusion to "vanishing cream."

p. 323 *auch*: Germ., also.

p. 324 *éventail*: fan.

p. 324 *fotochki*: Russ., little photos.

p. 325 *foute*: French swear word made to sound "foot."

p. 325 *ars*: Lat., art.

p. 325 *Carte du Tendre*: "Map of Tender Love," sentimental allegory of the seventeenth century.

p. 326 *Knabenkräuter*: Germ., orchids (and testicles).

p. 327 *perron*: porch.

p. 328 *romances, tsiganshchina*: Russ., pseudo-Tsigan ballads.

p. 331 *vinocherpiy*: Russ., the "wine-pourer."

p. 331 *zernistaya ikra*: "large-grained" caviar (Russ.).

p. 331 *uzh gasli* etc.: Russ., the lights were already going out in the rooms.

p. 333 *Nikak-s net*: Russ., certainly not.

p. 333 famous fly: see p. 109, *Serromyia*.

p. 333 *Vorschmacks*: Germ., hors-d'oeuvres.

p. 336   *et pour cause*: and no wonder.

p. 336   *karavanchik*: small caravan of camels (Russ.).

p. 337   *oberart* etc.: Germ, superspecies; subspecies.

p. 338   *spazmochka*: Russ., little spasm.

p. 338   *bretteur*: duelling bravo.

p. 339   *au fond*: actually.

p. 341   *fokus-pokus*: Russ., bogus magic.

p. 342   *au dire* etc.: according to the reviewers.

p. 343   *finestra, sestra*: Ital., window; Russ., sister.

p. 343   *Arinushka*: Russ., folksy diminutive of "Irina."

p. 343   *oh qui me rendra* etc.: Oh, who'll give me back
                                my hill and the big oak.

p. 344   *sekundant*: Russ., second.

p. 345   *puerulus*: Lat., little lad.

p. 345   *matovaya*: Russ., dull-toned.

p. 345   *en robe* etc.: in a pink and green dress.

p. 347   R 4: "rook four," a chess indication of position (pun on the
         woman's name).

p. 350   *c'est le mot*: that's the right word.

p. 350   *pleureuses*: widow's weeds.

p. 351   *Bozhe moy*: Russ., good Heavens.

p. 355   ridge: money.

p. 357   *secondes pensées* etc.: second thoughts are the good ones.

p. 357   *bonne*: housemaid.

p. 360   *dyakon*: deacon.

p. 361   *désolé* etc.: distressed at being unable to be with you.

p. 362   So you are married, etc.: see *Eugene Onegin*, Eight: XVIII:
         1–4.

p. 363   *za tvoyo* etc.: Russ., your health.

p. 364   *guvernantka* etc.: Russ., governess-novelist.

p. 366   *moue*: little grimace.

p. 367   *affalés* etc.: sprawling in their armchairs.

p. 368   *bouffant*: puffed up.

p. 368   *gueule* etc.: simian facial angle.

p. 368   *grustnoe* etc.: Russ., she addresses him as "my sad bliss."

p. 369   *troués*: with a hole or holes.

p. 370   engripped: from *prendre en grippe*, to conceive a dislike.

p. 370   *pravoslavnaya*: Russ., Greek-Orthodox.

p. 372   *das auch noch*: Germ., and that too.

p. 373   *pendant que je* etc.: while I am skiing.

p. 378   *Vesti*: Russ., News.

p. 382   *Obst*: Germ., fruit.

p. 385   I love you with a brother's love etc.: see *Eugene Onegin*,
         Four: XVI: 3–4.

p. 382 cootooriay etc.: mispronunciation of "*couturier*," dress-maker, "*vous avez entendu*," you've heard (about him).

p. 386 *tu sais* etc.: you know it will kill me.

p. 387 *Insiste* etc.: quotation from St. Augustine.

p. 388 Henry: Henry James's style is suggested by the italicized "*had*."

p. 389 *en laid et en lard*: in an ugly and fleshy version.

p. 390 *emptovato*: Anglo-Russian, rather empty.

p. 391 *slip*: Fr., panties.

p. 394 *pudeur*: modesty, delicacy.

p. 394 *prosit*: Germ., your health.

p. 395 *Dimanche* etc.: Sunday. Lunch on the grass. Everybody stinks. My mother-in-law swallows her dentures. Her little bitch, etc. After which, etc. (see p. 382, a painter's diary Lucette has been reading).

p. 396 Nox: Lat., at night.

p. 399 *Cher ami*, etc.: Dear friend, my husband and I were deeply upset by the frightful news. It was to me—and this I'll always remember—that practically on the eve of her death the poor girl addressed herself to arrange things on the *Tobakoff*, which is always crowded and which from now on I'll never take again, slightly out of superstition and very much out of sympathy for gentle, tender Lucette. I had been so happy to do all I could, as somebody had told me that you would be there too. Actually, she said so herself; she seemed so joyful to spend a few days on the upper deck with her dear cousin! The psychology of suicide is a mystery that no scientist can explain. I have never shed so many tears, it almost makes me drop my pen. We return to Malbrook around mid-August. Yours ever.

p. 401 And o'er the summits of the Tacit etc.: parody of four lines in Lermontov's *The Demon* (see also p. 115).

p. 402 *le beau ténébreux*: wrapt in Byronic gloom.

p. 405 *que sais-je*: what do I know.

p. 406 *Merci* etc.: My infinite thanks.

p. 407 *cameriere*: Ital., hotel manservant who carries the luggage upstairs, vacuum-cleans the rooms, etc.

p. 408 *libretto*: that of the opera *Eugene Onegin*, a travesty of Push-kin's poem.

p. 409 *korrektniy*: Russ., correct.

p. 409 *hobereau*: country squire.

p. 410 cart de van: Amer., mispronunciation of *carte des vins*.

p. 410 *zhidovskaya*: Russ. (vulg.), Jewish.

p. 411 *je veux* etc.: I want to get hold of you, my dear.

p. 411   *enfin*: in short.

p. 411   Luzon: Amer., mispronunciation of "Lausanne."

p. 411   *lieu*: place.

p. 413   (a pause): This and the whole conversation parody Chekhov's mannerisms.

p. 414   *muirninochka*: Hiberno-Russian caressive term.

p. 415   *potins de famille*: family gossip.

p. 415   *terriblement* etc.: terribly grand and all that, she likes to tease him by saying that a simple farmer like him should not have married the daughter of an actress and an art dealer.

p. 415   *je dois* etc.: I must watch my weight.

p. 416   *Olorinus*: from Lat. *olor*, swan (Leda's lover).

p. 416   *lenclose*: distorted "clothes" (influenced by "Ninon de Lenclos"), the courtesan in Vere de Vere's novel mentioned above.

p. 417   Aleksey etc.: Vronski and his mistress.

p. 417   *phrase* etc.: stock phrase.

p. 418   She Yawns: Chillon's.

p. 418   D'Onsky: see p. 15.

P. 418   *comme* etc.: shedding floods of tears.

p. 418   *N'a pas le verbe* etc.: lacks the gift of the gab.

p. 419   *chiens* etc.: dogs not allowed.

p. 420   *rieuses*: black-headed gulls.

p. 421   *Golos* etc.: Russ., *The Phoenix Voice*, Russian-language newspaper in Arizona.

p. 422   *la voix* etc.: the brassy voice telephoned . . . the trumpet did not sound pleased this morning.

p. 422   *contretemps*: mishap.

p. 424   *phalène*: moth (see also p. 112).

p. 424   *tu sais* etc: you know it will kill me.

p. 425   *Bozhe moy*: Russ., oh, my God.

p. 427   *et trève* etc.: and enough of that painted-ceiling style of mine.

p. 430   ardis: arrow.

p. 430   ponder: pun on Fr. *pondre*, to lay an egg (allusion to the problem of what came first, egg or hen).

p. 432   *anime* etc.: Lat., soul.

p. 432   assassin pun: a pun on *pointe assassine* (from a poem by Verlaine).

p. 432   Lacrimaval: Italo-Swiss. Pseudo-place-name, "vale of tears."

p. 434   *coup de volant*: one twist of the steering wheel.

p. 436   dream-delta: allusion to the disintegration of an imaginary element.

p. 440   unfortunate thinker: Samuel Alexander, English philosopher.

p. 442   Villa Jolana: named in honor of a butterfly, belonging to the subgenus *Jolana*, which breeds in the Pfynwald (see also p. 104).

p. 443   Vinn Landère: French distortion of "Vinelander."

p. 443   *à la sonde*: in soundings (for the same ship see p. 417).

p. 445   *Comment* etc.: what's that? no, no, not 88, but 86.

p. 447   *droits* etc.: custom-house dues.

p. 447   *après tout*: after all.

p. 447   *on peut* etc.: see p. 196.

p. 447   lucubratiuncula: bit of writing in the lamplight.

p. 448   *duvet*: fluff.

p. 450   simpler: simpler to take off from the balcony.

p. 451   mermaid: allusion to Lucette.

p. 452   Stepan Nootkin: Van's valet.

p. 457   *blyadushki*: little whores (echo of p. 328).

p. 457   *Blitzpartien*: Germ., quickies (quick chess games).

p. 459   *Compitalia*: Lat., crossroads.

p. 460   E, p, i: referring to "epistemic" (see above).

p. 464   *j'ai tâté* etc.: I have known two Lesbians in my life, that's enough.

p. 464   *terme* etc.: term one avoids using.

p. 467   *le bouquin . . . guéri*, etc.: the book . . . cured of all its snags.

p. 467   *quel livre* etc.: what a book, good God.

p. 467   *gamine*: lassie.

TRANSPARENT THINGS

To Véra

I

HERE'S the person I want. Hullo, person! Doesn't hear me. Perhaps if the future existed, concretely and individually, as something that could be discerned by a better brain, the past would not be so seductive: its demands would be balanced by those of the future. Persons might then straddle the middle stretch of the seesaw when considering this or that object. It might be fun.

But the future has no such reality (as the pictured past and the perceived present possess); the future is but a figure of speech, a specter of thought.

Hullo, person! What's the matter, don't pull me. I'm *not* bothering him. Oh, all right. Hullo, person . . . (last time, in a very small voice).

When *we* concentrate on a material object, whatever its situation, the very act of attention may lead to our involuntarily sinking into the history of that object. Novices must learn to skim over matter if they want matter to stay at the exact level of the moment. Transparent things, through which the past shines!

Man-made objects, or natural ones, inert in themselves but much used by careless life (you are thinking, and quite rightly so, of a hillside stone over which a multitude of small animals have scurried in the course of incalculable seasons) are particularly difficult to keep in surface focus: novices fall through the surface, humming happily to themselves, and are soon reveling with childish abandon in the story of this stone, of that heath. I shall explain. A thin veneer of immediate reality is spread over natural and artificial matter, and whoever wishes to remain in the now, with the now, on the now, should please not break its tension film. Otherwise the inexperienced miracle-worker will find himself no longer walking on water but descending upright among staring fish. More in a moment.

2

As the person, Hugh Person (corrupted "Peterson" and pronounced "Parson" by some) extricated his angular bulk from
the taxi that had brought him to this shoddy mountain resort
from Trux, and while his head was still lowered in an opening
meant for emerging dwarfs, his eyes went up—not to acknowledge the helpful gesture sketched by the driver who had
opened the door for him but to check the aspect of the Ascot
Hotel (Ascot!) against an eight-year-old recollection, one fifth
of his life, engrained by grief. A dreadful building of gray
stone and brown wood, it sported cherry-red shutters (not all
of them shut) which by some mnemoptical trick he remembered as apple green. The steps of the porch were flanked with
electrified carriage lamps on a pair of iron posts. Down those
steps an aproned valet came tripping to take the two bags,
and (under one arm) the shoebox, all of which the driver had
alertly removed from the yawning boot. Person pays alert
driver.

The unrecognizable hall was no doubt as squalid as it had
always been.

At the desk, while signing his name and relinquishing his
passport, he asked in French, English, German, and English
again if old Kronig, the director whose fat face and false jo-
viality he so clearly recalled, was still around.

The receptionist (blond bun, pretty neck) said no, Monsieur Kronig had left to become manager, imagine, of the Fantastic in Blur (or so it sounded). A grassgreen skyblue postcard
depicting reclining clients was produced in illustration or
proof. The caption was in three languages and only the
German part was idiomatic. The English one read: Lying
Lawn—and, as if on purpose, a fraudulent perspective had
enlarged the lawn to monstrous proportions.

"He died last year," added the girl (who *en face* did not
resemble Armande one bit), abolishing whatever interest a
photochrome of the Majestic in Chur might have presented.

"So there is nobody who might remember me?"

"I regret," she said with his late wife's habitual intonation.

She also regretted that since he could not tell her *which*
room on the third floor he had occupied she, in turn, could

not give it to him, especially as the floor was full. Clasping his brow Person said it was in the middle three-hundreds and faced east, the sun welcomed him on his bedside rug, though the room had practically no view. He wanted it very badly, but the law required that records be destroyed when a director, even a former director, did what Kronig had done (suicide being a form of account fakery, one supposed). Her assistant, a handsome young fellow in black, with pustules on chin and throat, took Person up to a fourth-floor room and all the way kept staring with a telly viewer's absorption at the blank bluish wall gliding down, while, on the other hand, the no less rapt mirror in the lift reflected, for a few lucid instants, the gentleman from Massachusetts, who had a long, lean, doleful face with a slightly undershot jaw and a pair of symmetrical folds framing his mouth in what would have been a rugged, horsey, mountain-climbing arrangement had not his melancholy stoop belied every inch of his fantastic majesty.

The window faced east all right but there certainly was a view: namely, a tremendous crater full of excavating machines (silent on Saturday afternoon and all Sunday).

The apple-green-aproned valet brought the two valises and the cardboard box with "Fit" on its wrapper; after which Person remained alone. He knew the hotel to be antiquated but this was overdoing it. The *belle chambre au quatriéme*, although too large for one guest (but too cramped for a group), lacked every kind of comfort. He remembered that the lower room where he, a big man of thirty-two, had cried more often and more bitterly than he ever had in his sad childhood, had been ugly too but at least had not been so sprawling and cluttered as his new abode. Its bed was a nightmare. Its "bathroom" contained a bidet (ample enough to accommodate a circus elephant, sitting) but no bath. The toilet seat refused to stay up. The tap expostulated, letting forth a strong squirt of rusty water before settling down to produce the meek normal stuff—which you do not appreciate sufficiently, which is a flowing mystery, and, yes, yes, which deserves monuments to be erected to it, cool shrines! Upon leaving that ignoble lavatory, Hugh gently closed the door after him but like a stupid pet it whined and immediately followed him into the room. Let us now illustrate our difficulties.

3

In his search for a commode to store his belongings Hugh Person, a tidy man, noticed that the middle drawer of an old desk relegated to a dark corner of the room, and supporting there a bulbless and shadeless lamp resembling the carcass of a broken umbrella, had not been reinserted properly by the lodger or servant (actually neither) who had been the last to check if it was empty (nobody had). My good Hugh tried to woggle it in; at first it refused to budge; then, in response to the antagony of a chance tug (which could not help profiting from the cumulative energy of several jogs) it shot out and spilled a pencil. This he briefly considered before putting it back.

It was not a hexagonal beauty of Virginia juniper or African cedar, with the maker's name imprinted in silver foil, but a very plain, round, technically faceless old pencil of cheap pine, dyed a dingy lilac. It had been mislaid ten years ago by a carpenter who had not finished examining, let alone fixing, the old desk, having gone away for a tool that he never found. Now comes the act of attention.

In his shop, and long before that at the village school, the pencil has been worn down to two-thirds of its original length. The bare wood of its tapered end has darkened to plumbeous plum, thus merging in tint with the blunt tip of graphite whose blind gloss alone distinguishes it from the wood. A knife and a brass sharpener have thoroughly worked upon it and if it were necessary we could trace the complicated fate of the shavings, each mauve on one side and tan on the other when fresh, but now reduced to atoms of dust whose wide, wide dispersal is panic catching its breath but one should be above it, one gets used to it fairly soon (there are worse terrors). On the whole, it whittled sweetly, being of an old-fashioned make. Going back a number of seasons (not as far, though, as Shakespeare's birth year when pencil lead was discovered) and then picking up the thing's story again in the "now" direction, we see graphite, ground very fine, being mixed with moist clay by young girls and old men. This mass, this pressed caviar, is placed in a metal cylinder which has a blue eye, a sapphire with a hole drilled in it, and through this the caviar is forced. It issues in one continuous appetizing rodlet (watch for our little friend!), which looks as if it retained the shape of an earthworm's digestive tract (but watch, watch, do not be deflected!). It is now being cut into the lengths required for these particular pencils (we glimpse the cutter, old Elias Borrowdale, and are about to mouse up his forearm on a side trip of inspection but we stop, stop and recoil, in our haste to identify the individual segment). See it baked, see it boiled in fat (here a shot of the fleecy fat-giver being butchered, a shot of the butcher, a shot of the shepherd, a shot of the shepherd's father, a Mexican) and fitted into the wood.

Now let us not lose our precious bit of lead while we prepare the wood. Here's the tree! *This* particular pine! It is cut down. Only the trunk is used, stripped of its bark. We hear the whine of a newly invented power saw, we see logs being dried and planed. Here's the board that will yield the integument of the pencil in the shallow drawer (still not closed). We recognize its presence in the log as we recognized the log in the tree and the tree in the forest and the forest in the world that Jack built. We recognize that presence by something that is perfectly clear to us but nameless, and as impossible to describe as a smile to somebody who has never seen smiling eyes.

Thus the entire little drama, from crystallized carbon and felled pine to this humble implement, to this transparent thing, unfolds in a twinkle. Alas, the solid pencil itself as fingered briefly by Hugh Person still somehow eludes us! But *he* won't, oh no.

4

This was his fourth visit to Switzerland. The first one had been eighteen years before when he had stayed for a few days at Trux with his father. Ten years later, at thirty-two, he had revisited that old lakeside town and had successfully courted a sentimental thrill, half wonder and half remorse, by going

to see their hotel. A steep lane and a flight of old stairs led to
it from lake level where the local train had brought him to a
featureless station. He had retained the hotel's name, Loc-
quet, because it resembled the maiden name of his mother, a
French Canadian, whom Person Senior was to survive by less
than a year. He also remembered that it was drab and cheap,
and abjectly stood next to another, much better hotel,
through the *rez-de-chaussée* windows of which you could make
out the phantoms of pale tables and underwater waiters. Both
hotels had gone now, and in their stead there rose the Banque
Bleue, a steely edifice, all polished surfaces, plate glass, and
potted plants.

He had slept in a kind of halfhearted alcove, separated by
an archway and a clothes tree from his father's bed. Night is
always a giant but this one was especially terrible. Hugh had
always had his own room at home, he hated this common
grave of sleep, he grimly hoped that the promise of separate
bedchambers would be kept at subsequent stops of their Swiss
tour shimmering ahead in a painted mist. His father, a man
of sixty, shorter than Hugh and also pudgier, had aged un-
appetizingly during his recent widowhood; his things let off a
characteristic foresmell, faint but unmistakable, and he
grunted and sighed in his sleep, dreaming of large unwieldy
blocks of blackness, which had to be sorted out and removed
from one's path or over which one had to clamber in agonizing attitudes of debility and despair. We cannot find in the
annals of European tours, recommended by the family doctors
of retired old parties to allay lone grief, even one trip which
achieved that purpose.

Person Senior had always had clumsy hands but of late the
way he fumbled for things in the bathwater of space, groping
for the transparent soap of evasive matter, or vainly endeavored to tie or untie such parts of manufactured articles as had
to be fastened or unfastened, was growing positively comic.
Hugh had inherited some of that clumsiness; its present exaggeration annoyed him as a repetitious parody. On the morning of the widower's last day in so-called Switzerland (i.e., very
shortly before the event that for him would cause everything
to become "so-called") the old duffer wrestled with the Venetian blind in order to examine the weather, just managed

to catch a glimpse of wet pavement before the blind rede-
scended in a rattling avalanche, and decided to take his umbrella. It was badly folded, and he began to improve its
condition. At first Hugh watched in disgusted silence, nostrils
flaring and twitching. The scorn was unmerited since lots of
things exist, from live cells to dead stars, that undergo now
and then accidental little mishaps at the not always able or
careful hands of anonymous shapers. The black laps flipped
over untidily and had to be redone, and by the time the eye
of the ribbon was ready for use (a tiny tangible circle between
finger and thumb), its button had disappeared among the
folds and furrows of space. After watching for a while these
inept gropings, Hugh wrenched the umbrella out of his father's hands so abruptly that the old man kept kneading the air
for another moment before responding with a gentle apologetic smile to the sudden discourtesy. Still not saying a word,
Hugh fiercely folded and buttoned up the umbrella—which,
to tell the truth, hardly acquired a better shape than his father
would have finally given it.

What were their plans for the day? They would have breakfast in the same place where they had dined on the eve, and
would then do some shopping and a lot of sightseeing. A local
miracle of nature, the Tara cataract, was painted on the water-
closet door in the passage, as well as reproduced in a huge
photograph on the wall of the vestibule. Dr. Person stopped
at the desk to inquire with his habitual fussiness if there was
any mail for him (not that he expected any). After a short
search a telegram for a Mrs. Parson turned up, but nothing
for him (save the muffled shock of an incomplete coincidence). A rolled-up measuring tape happened to be lying near
his elbow, and he started to wind it around his thick waist,
losing the end several times and explaining the while to the
somber concierge that he intended to purchase in town a pair
of summer trousers and wished to go about it lucidly. That
rigmarole was so hateful to Hugh that he started to move
toward the exit even before the gray tape had been rewound
again.

5

After breakfast they found a suitable-looking shop. *Confections. Notre vente triomphale de soldes.* Our windfall triumphantly sold, translated his father, and was corrected by Hugh with tired contempt. A basket with folded shirts stood on an iron tripod outside the window, unprotected from the rain that had now increased. There came a roll of thunder. Let's pop in here, nervously said Dr. Person, whose fear of electric storms was yet another source of irritation to his son.

That morning, Irma, a weary and worried shopgirl, happened to be alone in charge of the shabby garment store into which Hugh reluctantly followed his father. Her two co-workers, a married couple, had just been hospitalized after a fire in their little apartment, the boss was away on business, and more people were dropping in than habitually would on a Thursday. At present she was in the act of helping three elderly women (part of a busload from London) to make up their minds and at the same time directing another person, a German blonde in black, to a place for passport pictures. Each old woman in turn spread the same flower-patterned dress against her bosom, and Dr. Person eagerly translated their cockney cackle into bad French. The girl in mourning came back for a parcel she had forgotten. More dresses were spread-eagled, more price tags squinted at. Yet another customer entered with two little girls. In between Dr. Person asked for a pair of slacks. He was given a few pairs to try on in an adjacent cubicle; and Hugh slipped out of the shop.

He strolled aimlessly, keeping in the shelter of various architectural projections, for it was in vain that the daily paper of that rainy town kept clamoring for arcades to be built in its shopping district. Hugh examined the items in a souvenir store. He found rather fetching the green figurine of a female skier made of a substance he could not identify through the show glass (it was "alabasterette," imitation aragonite, carved and colored in the Grumbel jail by a homosexual convict, rugged Armand Rave, who had strangled his boyfriend's incestuous sister). And what about that comb in a real-leather etui, what about, what about it—oh, it would get fouled up in no time and it would take an hour of work to remove the grime from between its tight teeth by using one of the smaller blades of that penknife there, bristling in a display of insolent innards. Cute wrist watch, with picture of doggy adorning its face, for only twenty-two francs. Or should one buy (for one's college roommate) that wooden plate with a central white cross surrounded by all twenty-two cantons? Hugh, too, was twenty-two and had always been harrowed by coincident symbols.

A dingdong bell and a blinking red light at the grade crossing announced an impending event: inexorably the slow barrier came down.

Its brown curtain was only half drawn, disclosing the elegant legs, clad in transparent black, of a female seated inside. We are in a terrific hurry to recapture that moment! The curtain of a sidewalk booth with a kind of piano stool, for the short or tall, and a slot machine enabling one to take one's own snapshot for passport or sport. Hugh eyed the legs and then the sign on the booth. The masculine ending and the absence of an acute accent flawed the unintentional pun:

$$3 \; P^{\text{hotos}}_{\text{oses}}$$

As he, still a virgin, imagined those daring attitudes a double event happened: the thunder of a nonstop train crashed by, and magnesium lightning flashed from the booth. The blonde in black, far from being electrocuted, came out closing her handbag. Whatever funeral she had wished to commemorate with the image of fair beauty craped for the occasion, it had nothing to do with a third simultaneous event next door.

One should follow her, it would be a good lesson—follow her instead of going to gape at a waterfall: good lesson for the old man. With an oath and a sigh Hugh retraced his steps, which was once a trim metaphor, and went back to the shop. Irma told neighbors later that she had been sure the gentleman had left with his son for at first she could not make out what the latter was saying despite his fluent French. When she did, she laughed at her stupidity, swiftly led Hugh to the fitting room and, still laughing heartily, drew the green, not brown, curtain open with what became in retrospect a dramatic gesture. Spatial disarrangement and dislocation have

always their droll side, and few things are funnier than three
pairs of trousers tangling in a frozen dance on the floor—
brown slacks, blue jeans, old pants of gray flannel. Awkward
Person Senior had been struggling to push a shod foot
through the zigzag of a narrow trouser leg when he felt a
roaring redness fill his head. He died before reaching the floor,
as if falling from some great height, and now lay on his back,
one arm outstretched, umbrella and hat out of reach in the
tall looking glass.

6

This Henry Emery Person, our Person's father, might be described as a well-meaning, earnest, dear little man, or as a
wretched fraud, depending on the angle of light and the position of the observer. A lot of handwringing goes about in
the dark of remorse, in the dungeon of the irreparable. A
schoolboy, be he as strong as the Boston strangler—show
your hands, Hugh—cannot cope with all his fellows when all
keep making cruel remarks about his father. After two or three
clumsy fights with the most detestable among them, he had
adopted a smarter and meaner attitude of taciturn semiac-
quiescence which horrified him when he remembered those
times; but by a curious twist of conscience the awareness of
his own horror comforted him as proving he was not altogether a monster. He now had to do something about a number of recollected unkindnesses of which he had been guilty
up to that very day; they were to be as painfully disposed of
as had been the dentures and glasses which the authorities left
with him in a paper bag. The only kinsman he could turn up,
an uncle in Scranton, advised him over the ocean to have the
body cremated abroad rather than shipped home; actually, the
less recommended course proved to be the easier one in many
respects, and mainly because it allowed Hugh to get rid of
the dreadful object practically at once.

Everybody was very helpful. One would like in particular to
express one's gratitude to Harold Hall, the American consul

in Switzerland, who was instrumental in extending all possible assistance to our poor friend.

Of the two thrills young Hugh experienced, one was general, the other specific. The general sense of liberation came first, as a great breeze, ecstatic and clean, blowing away a lot of life's rot. Specifically, he was delighted to discover three thousand dollars in his father's battered, but plump, wallet. Like many a young man of dark genius who feels in a wad of bills all the tangible thickness of immediate delights, he had no practical sense, no ambition to make more money, and no qualms about his future means of subsistence (these proved negligible when it transpired that the cash had been more than a tenth of the actual inheritance). That same day he moved to much finer lodgings in Geneva, had *homard à l'américaine* for dinner, and went to find his first whore in a lane right behind his hotel.

For optical and animal reasons sexual love is less transparent than many other much more complicated things. One knows, however, that in his home town Hugh had courted a thirty-eight-year-old mother and her sixteen-year-old daughter but had been impotent with the first and not audacious enough with the second. We have here a banal case of protracted erotic itch, of lone practice for its habitual satisfaction, and of memorable dreams. The girl he accosted was stumpy but had a lovely, pale, vulgar face with Italian eyes. She took him to one of the better beds in a hideous old roominghouse—to the precise "number," in fact, where ninety-one, ninety-two, nearly ninety-three years ago a Russian novelist had sojourned on his way to Italy. The bed—a different one, with brass knobs—was made, unmade, covered with a frock coat, made again; upon it stood a half-open green-checkered grip, and the frock coat was thrown over the shoulders of the night-shirted, bare-necked, dark-tousled traveler whom we catch in the act of deciding what to take out of the valise (which he will send by mail coach ahead) and transfer to the knapsack (which he will carry himself across the mountains to the Italian frontier). He expects his friend Kandidatov, the painter, to join him here any moment for the outing, one of those light-hearted hikes that romantics would undertake even during a drizzly spell in August; it rained even more in those uncom-

fortable times; his boots are still wet from a ten-mile ramble
to the nearest casino. They stand outside the door in the attitude of expulsion, and he has wrapped his feet in several
layers of German-language newspaper, a language which incidentally he finds easier to read than French. The main problem now is whether to confide to his knapsack or mail in his
grip his manuscripts: rough drafts of letters, an unfinished
short story in a Russian copybook bound in black cloth, parts
of a philosophical essay in a blue cahier acquired in Geneva,
and the loose sheets of a rudimentary novel under the provisional title of *Faust in Moscow*. As he sits at that deal table,
the very same upon which our Person's whore has plunked
her voluminous handbag, there shows through that bag, as it
were, the first page of the *Faust* affair with energetic erasures
and untidy insertions in purple, black, reptile-green ink. The
sight of his handwriting fascinates him; the chaos on the page
is to him order, the blots are pictures, the marginal jottings
are wings. Instead of sorting his papers, he uncorks his portable ink and moves nearer to the table, pen in hand. But at
that minute there comes a joyful banging on the door. The
door flies open and closes again.

Hugh Person followed his chance girl down the long steep
stairs, and to her favorite street corner where they parted for
many years. He had hoped that the girl would keep him till
morn—and thus spare him a night at the hotel, with his dead
father present in every dark corner of solitude; but when she
saw him inclined to stay she misconstrued his plans, brutally
said it would take much too long to get such a poor performer
back into shape, and ushered him out. It was not a ghost,
however, that prevented him from falling asleep, but the stuff-
iness. He opened wide both casements; they gave on a parking
place four floors below; the thin meniscus overhead was too
wan to illumine the roofs of the houses descending toward
the invisible lake; the light of a garage picked out the steps of
desolate stairs leading into a chaos of shadows; it was all very
dismal and very distant, and our acrophobic Person felt the
pull of gravity inviting him to join the night and his father.
He had walked in his sleep many times as a naked boy but
familiar surroundings had guarded him, till finally the strange
disease had abated. Tonight, on the highest floor of a strange

hotel, he lacked all protection. He closed the windows and sat in an armchair till dawn.

7

In the nights of his youth when Hugh had suffered attacks of somnambulism, he would walk out of his room hugging a pillow, and wander downstairs. He remembered awakening in odd spots, on the steps leading to the cellar or in a hall closet among galoshes and storm coats, and while not overly frightened by those barefoot trips, the boy did not care "to behave like a ghost" and begged to be locked up in his bedroom. This did not work either, as he would scramble out of the window onto the sloping roof of a gallery leading to the schoolhouse dormitories. The first time he did it the chill of the slates against his soles roused him, and he traveled back to his dark nest avoiding chairs and things rather by ear than otherwise. An old and silly doctor advised his parents to cover the floor near his bed with wet towels and place basins with water at strategic points, and the only result was that having circumvented all obstacles in his magic sleep, he found himself shivering at the foot of a chimney with the school cat for companion. Soon after that sally the spectral fits became rarer; they practically stopped in his late adolescence. As a penultimate echo came the strange case of the struggle with a bedside table. This was when Hugh attended college and lodged with a fellow student, Jack Moore (no relation), in two rooms of the newly built Snyder Hall. Jack was awakened in the middle of the night, after a weary day of cramming, by a burst of crashing sounds coming from the bed-sitting room. He went to investigate. Hugh, in his sleep, had imagined that his bedside table, a little three-legged affair (borrowed from under the hallway telephone), was executing a furious war dance all by itself, as he had seen a similar article do at a séance when asked if the visiting spirit (Napoleon) missed the springtime sunsets of St. Helena. Jack Moore found Hugh energetically leaning from his couch and with both arms embracing and crushing the inoffensive object, in a ludicrous effort to stop its inexistent motion. Books, an ashtray, an alarm clock, a box of cough drops, had all been shaken off, and the tormented wood was emitting snaps and crackles in the idiot's grasp. Jack Moore pried the two apart. Hugh silently turned over and went to sleep.

8

During the ten years that were to elapse between Hugh Person's first and second visits to Switzerland he earned his living in the various dull ways that fall to the lot of brilliant young people who lack any special gift or ambition and get accustomed to applying only a small part of their wits to humdrum or charlatan tasks. What they do with the other, much greater, portion, how and where their real fancies and feelings are housed, is not exactly a mystery—there are no mysteries now—but would entail explications and revelations too sad, too frightful, to face. Only experts, for experts, should probe a mind's misery.

He could multiply eight-digit numbers in his head, and lost that capacity in the course of a few gray diminishing nights during hospitalization with a virus infection at twenty-five. He had published a poem in a college magazine, a long rambling piece that began rather auspiciously:

> Blest are suspension dots . . . The sun was setting
> a heavenly example to the lake . . .

He was the author of a letter to the London *Times* which was reproduced a few years later in the anthology *To the Editor: Sir*, and a passage of which read:

> Anacreon died at eighty-five choked by "wine's skeleton" (as another Ionian put it), and a gypsy predicted to the chessplayer Alyokhin that he would be killed in Spain by a dead bull.

For seven years after graduating from the university he had

been the secretary and anonymous associate of a notorious fraud, the late symbolist Atman, and was wholly responsible for such footnotes as:

> The cromlech (associated with mleko, milch, milk) is obviously a symbol of the Great Mother, just as the menhir ("mein Herr") is as obviously masculine.

He had been in the stationery business for another spell and a fountain pen he had promoted bore his name: The Person Pen. But that remained his greatest achievement.

As a sulky person of twenty-nine he joined a great publishing firm, where he worked in various capacities—research assistant, scout, associate editor, copy editor, proofreader, flatterer of our authors. A sullen slave, he was placed at the disposal of Mrs. Flankard, an exuberant and pretentious lady with a florid face and octopus eyes whose enormous romance *The Stag* had been accepted for publication on condition that it be drastically revised, ruthlessly cut, and partly rewritten. The rewritten bits, consisting of a few pages here and there, were supposed to bridge the black bleeding gaps of generously deleted matter between the retained chapters. That job had been performed by one of Hugh's colleagues, a pretty ponytail who had since left the firm. As a novelist she possessed even less talent than Mrs. Flankard, and Hugh was now cursed with the task of healing not only the wounds she had inflicted but the warts she had left intact. He had tea several times with Mrs. Flankard in her charming suburban house decorated almost exclusively with her late husband's oils, early spring in the parlor, summertime in the dining room, all the glory of New England in the library, and winter in the bedchamber. Hugh did not linger in that particular room, for he had the uncanny feeling that Mrs. Flankard was planning to be raped beneath Mr. Flankard's mauve snowflakes. Like many overripe and still handsome lady artists, she seemed to be quite unaware that a big bust, a wrinkled neck, and the smell of stale femininity on an eau de cologne base might repel a nervous male. He uttered a grunt of relief when "our" book finally got published.

On the strength of *The Stag*'s commercial success he found himself assigned a more glamorous task. "Mister R.", as he was called in the office (he had a long German name, in two installments, with a nobiliary particle between castle and crag), wrote English considerably better than he spoke it. On contact with paper it acquired a shapeliness, a richness, an ostensible dash, that caused some of the less demanding reviewers in his adopted country to call him a master stylist.

Mr. R. was a touchy, unpleasant, and rude correspondent. Hugh's dealings with him across the ocean—Mr. R. lived mostly in Switzerland or France—lacked the hearty glow of the Flankard ordeal; but Mr. R., though perhaps not a master of the very first rank, was at least a true artist who fought on his own ground with his own weapons for the right to use an unorthodox punctuation corresponding to singular thought. A paperback edition of one of his earlier works was painlessly steered into production by our accommodating Person; but then began a long wait for the new novel which R. had promised to deliver before the end of that spring. Spring passed without any result—and Hugh flew over to Switzerland for a personal interview with the sluggish author. This was the second of his four European trips.

9

He made Armande's acquaintance in a Swiss railway carriage one dazzling afternoon between Thur and Versex on the eve of his meeting with Mr. R. He had boarded a slow train by mistake; she had chosen one that would stop at the small station from which a bus line went up to Witt, where her mother owned a chalet. Armande and Hugh had simultaneously settled in two window seats facing each other on the lake side of the coach. An American family occupied the corresponding four-seat side across the aisle. Hugh unfolded the *Journal de Genève.*

Oh, she was pretty and would have been exquisitely so had her lips been fuller. She had dark eyes, fair hair, a honey-hued skin. Twin dimples of the crescentic type came down her tanned cheeks on the sides of her mournful mouth. She wore a black suit over a frilly blouse. A book lay in her lap under her black-gloved hands. He thought he recognized that flame-and-soot paperback. The mechanism of their first acquaintance was ideally banal.

They exchanged a glance of urbane disapproval as the three American kids began pulling sweaters and pants out of a suitcase in savage search for something stupidly left behind (a heap of comics—by now taken care of, with the used towels, by a brisk hotel maid). One of the two adults, catching Armande's cold eye, responded with a look of good-natured helplessness. The conductor came for the tickets.

Hugh, tilting his head slightly, satisfied himself that he had been right: it was indeed the paperback edition of *Figures in a Golden Window*.

"One of ours," said Hugh with an indicative nod.

She considered the book in her lap as if seeking in it some explanation of his remark. Her skirt was very short.

"I mean," he said, "I work for that particular publisher. For the American publisher of the hard-cover edition. Do you like it?"

She answered in fluent but artificial English that she detested surrealistic novels of the poetic sort. She demanded hard realistic stuff reflecting our age. She liked books about Violence and Oriental Wisdom. Did it get better farther on?

"Well, there's a rather dramatic scene in a Riviera villa, when the little girl, the narrator's daughter——"

"June."

"Yes. June sets her new dollhouse on fire and the whole villa burns down; but there's not much violence, I'm afraid; it is all rather symbolic, in the grand manner, and, well, curiously tender at the same time, as the blurb says, or at least said, in our first edition. That cover is by the famous Paul Plam."

She would finish it, of course, no matter how boring, because every task in life should be brought to an end like completing that road above Witt, where they had a house, a chalet de luxe, but had to trudge up to the Drakonita cableway until that new road had been finished. *The Burning Window* or whatever it was called had been given her only the day before, on her twenty-third birthday, by the author's stepdaughter whom he probably——

"Julia."

Yes. Julia and she had both taught in the winter at a school for foreign young ladies in the Tessin. Julia's stepfather had just divorced her mother whom he had treated in an abominable fashion. What had they taught? Oh, posture, rhythmics—things like that.

Hugh and the new, irresistible person had by now switched to French, which he spoke at least as well as she did English. Asked to guess her nationality he suggested Danish or Dutch. No, her father's family came from Belgium, he was an architect who got killed last summer while supervising the demolition of a famous hotel in a defunct spa; and her mother was born in Russia, in a very noble milieu, but of course completely ruined by the revolution. Did he like his job? Would he mind pulling that dark blind down a little? The low sun's funeral. Was that a proverb, she queried? No, he had just made it up.

In a diary he kept in fits and starts Hugh wrote that night in Versex:

"Spoke to a girl on the train. Adorable brown naked legs and golden sandals. A schoolboy's insane desire and a romantic tumult never felt previously. Armande Chamar. *La particule aurait juré avec la dernière syllabe de mon prénom.* I believe Byron uses 'chamar,' meaning 'peacock fan,' in a very noble Oriental milieu. Charmingly sophisticated, yet marvelously naive. Chalet above Witt built by father. If you find yourself in those *parages.* Wished to know if I liked my job. My job! I replied: 'Ask me what I *can* do, not what I *do,* lovely girl, lovely wake of the sun through semitransparent black fabric. I can commit to memory a whole page of the directory in three minutes flat but am incapable of remembering my own telephone number. I can compose patches of poetry as strange and new as you are, or as anything a person may write three hundred years hence, but I have never published one scrap of verse except some juvenile nonsense at college. I have evolved on the playing courts of my father's school a devastating return of service—a cut clinging drive—

but am out of breath after one game. Using ink and aquarelle I can paint a lakescape of unsurpassed translucence with all the mountains of paradise reflected therein, but am unable to draw a boat or a bridge or the silhouette of human panic in the blazing windows of a villa by Plam. I have taught French in American schools but have never been able to get rid of my mother's Canadian accent, though I hear it clearly when I whisper French words. *Ouvre ta robe, Déjanire* that I may mount *sur mon bûcher*. I can levitate one inch high and keep it up for ten seconds, but cannot climb an apple tree. I possess a doctor's degree in philosophy, but have no German. I have fallen in love with you but shall do nothing about it. In short I am an all-round genius.' By a coincidence worthy of that other genius, his stepdaughter had given her the book she was reading. Julia Moore has no doubt forgotten that I possessed her a couple of years ago. Both mother and daughter are intense travelers. They have visited Cuba and China, and suchlike dreary, primitive spots, and speak with fond criticism of the many charming and odd people they made friends with there. *Parlez-moi de son* stepfather. Is he *très fasciste*? Could not understand why I called Mrs. R.'s left-wingism a commonplace bourgeois vogue. *Mais au contraire*, she and her daughter adore radicals! Well, I said, Mr. R., *lui*, is immune to politics. My darling thought that was the trouble with him. Toffee-cream neck with a tiny gold cross and a *grain de beauté*. Slender, athletic, lethal!' "

10

He did do something about it, despite all that fond criticism of himself. He wrote her a note from the venerable Versex Palace where he was to have cocktails in a few minutes with our most valuable author whose best book you did not like. Would you permit me to call on you, say Wednesday, the fourth? Because I shall be by then at the Ascot Hotel in your Witt, where I am told there is some excellent skiing even in summer. The main object of my stay *here*, on the other hand, is to find out when the old rascal's current book will be finished. It is queer to recall how keenly only the day before yesterday I had looked forward to seeing the great man at last in the flesh.

There was even more of it than our Person had expected on the strength of recent pictures. As he peeped through a vestibule window and watched him emerge from his car, no clarion of repute, no scream of glamour reverbed through his nervous system, which was wholly occupied with the bare-thighed girl in the sun-shot train. Yet what a grand sight R. presented—his handsome chauffeur helping the obese old boy on one side, his black-bearded secretary supporting him on the other, and two *chasseurs* from the hotel going through a mimicry of tentative assistance on the porch steps. The reporter in Person noted that Mr. R. wore Wallabees of a velvety cocoa shade, a lemon shirt with a lilac neck scarf, and a rumpled gray suit that seemed to have no distinction whatever— at least, to a plain American. Hullo, Person! They sat down in the lounge near the bar.

The illusory quality of the entire event was enhanced by the appearance and speech of the two characters. That monumental man with his clayey makeup and false grin, and Mr. Tamworth of the brigand's beard, seemed to be acting out a stiffly written scene for the benefit of an invisible audience from which Person, a dummy, kept turning away as if moved with his chair by Sherlock's concealed landlady, no matter how he sat or where he looked in the course of the brief but boozy interview. It was indeed all sham and waxworks as compared to the reality of Armande, whose image was stamped on the eye of his mind and shone through the show at various levels, sometimes upside down, sometimes on the teasing marge of his field of vision, but always there, always true and thrilling. The commonplaces he and she had exchanged blazed with authenticity when placed for display against the forced guffaws in the bogus bar.

"Well, you certainly look remarkably fit," said Hugh with effusive mendacity after the drinks had been ordered.

Baron R. had coarse features, a sallow complexion, a lumpy nose with enlarged pores, shaggy bellicose eyebrows, an unerring stare, and a bulldog mouth full of bad teeth. The streak of nasty inventiveness so conspicuous in his writings also appeared in the prepared parts of his speech, as when he said, as he did now, that far from "looking fit" he felt more and more a creeping resemblance to the cinema star Reubenson who once played old gangsters in Florida-staged films; but no such actor existed.

"Anyway—how are you?" asked Hugh, pressing his disadvantage.

"To make a story quite short," replied Mr. R. (who had an exasperating way not only of trotting out hackneyed formulas in his would-be colloquial thickly accented English, but also of getting them wrong), "I had not been feeling any too healthy, you know, during the winter. My liver, you know, was holding something against me."

He took a long sip of whiskey, and, rinsing his mouth with it in a manner Person had never yet witnessed, very slowly replaced his glass on the low table. Then, *à deux* with the muzzled stuff, he swallowed it and shifted to his second English style, the grand one of his most memorable characters:

"Insomnia and her sister Nocturia harry me, of course, but otherwise I am as hale as a pane of stamps. I don't think you met Mr. Tamworth. Person, pronounced Parson; and Tamworth: like the English breed of black-blotched swine."

"No," said Hugh, "it does not come from Parson, but rather from Peterson."

"O.K., son. And how's Phil?"

They discussed briefly R.'s publisher's vigor, charm, and acumen.

"Except that he wants me to write the wrong books. He wants——" assuming a coy throaty voice as he named the titles of a competitor's novels, also published by Phil—"he wants *A Boy for Pleasure* but would settle for *The Slender Slut*, and all *I* can offer him is not *Tralala* but the first and dullest tome of my *Tralatitions.*"

"I assure you that he is waiting for the manuscript with utmost impatience. By the way——"

By the way, indeed! There ought to exist some rhetorical term for that twist of nonlogic. A unique view through a black weave ran by the way. By the way, I shall lose my mind if I do not get her.

"—by the way, I met a person yesterday who has just seen your stepdaughter——"

"Former stepdaughter," corrected Mr. R. "Quite a time no see, and I hope it remains so. Same stuff, son" (this to the barman).

"The occasion was rather remarkable. Here was this young woman, reading——"

"Excuse me," said the secretary warmly, and folding a note he had just scribbled, passed it to Hugh.

"Mr. R. resents all mention of Miss Moore and her mother."

And I don't blame him. But where was Hugh's famous tact? Giddy Hugh knew quite well the whole situation, having got it from Phil, not Julia, an impure but reticent little girl.

This part of our translucing is pretty boring, yet we must complete our report.

Mr. R. had discovered one day, with the help of a hired follower, that his wife Marion was having an affair with Christian Pines, son of the well-known cinema man who had directed the film *Golden Windows* (precariously based on the best of our author's novels). Mr. R. welcomed the situation since he was assiduously courting Julia Moore, his eighteen-year-old stepdaughter, and now had plans for the future, well worthy of a sentimental lecher whom three or four marriages had not sated yet. Very soon, however, he learned from the same sleuth, who is at present dying in a hot dirty hospital on Formosa, an island, that young Pines, a handsome frog-faced playboy, soon also to die, was the lover of both mother and daughter, whom he had serviced in Cavaliere, Cal., during two summers. Hence the separation acquired more pain and plenitude than R. had expected. In the midst of all this, our Person, in his discreet little way (though actually he was half an inch taller than big R.), had happened to nibble, too, at the corner of the crowded canvas.

II

Julia liked tall men with strong hands and sad eyes. Hugh had met her first at a party in a New York house. A couple of days later he ran into her at Phil's place and she asked if he cared to see *Cunning Stunts*, an "avant garde" hit, she had two tickets for herself and her mother, but the latter had had to leave for Washington on legal business (related to the divorce proceedings as Hugh correctly surmised): would he care to escort her? In matters of art, "avant garde" means little more than conforming to some daring philistine fashion, so, when the curtain opened, Hugh was not surprised to be regaled with the sight of a naked hermit sitting on a cracked toilet in the middle of an empty stage. Julia giggled, preparing for a delectable evening. Hugh was moved to enfold in his shy paw the childish hand that had accidentally touched his kneecap. She was wonderfully pleasing to the sexual eye with her doll's face, her slanting eyes and topaz-teared earlobes, her slight form in an orange blouse and black skirt, her slender-jointed limbs, her exotically sleek hair squarely cut on the forehead. No less pleasing was the conjecture that in his Swiss retreat, Mr. R., who had bragged to an interviewer of being blessed with a goodish amount of telepathic power, was bound to experience a twinge of jealousy at the present moment of spacetime.

Rumors had been circulating that the play might be banned after its very first night. A number of rowdy young demonstrators in protest against that contingency managed to disrupt the performance which they were actually supporting. The bursting of a few festive little bombs filled the hall with bitter smoke, a brisk fire started among unwound serpentines of pink and green toilet paper, and the theater was evacuated. Julia announced she was dying of frustration and thirst. A famous bar next to the theater proved hopelessly crowded and "in the radiance of an Edenic simplification of mores" (as R. wrote in another connection) our Person took the girl to his flat. Unwisely he wondered—after a too passionate kiss in the taxi had led him to spill a few firedrops of impatience—if he would not disappoint the expectations of Julia, who according to Phil had been debauched at thirteen by R., right at the start of her mother's disastrous marriage.

The bachelor's flat Hugh rented on East Sixty-fifth had been found for him by his firm. Now it so happened that those rooms were the same in which Julia had visited one of her best young males a couple of years before. She had the good taste to say nothing, but the image of that youth, whose death in a remote war had affected her greatly, kept coming out of the bathroom or fussing with things in the fridge, and interfering so oddly with the small business in hand that she refused to be unzipped and bedded. Naturally after a decent interval the child gave in and soon found herself assisting big Hugh in his blundersome love-making. No sooner, however, had the poking and panting run their customary course and Hugh, with a rather forlorn show of jauntiness, had gone for more drinks, than the image of bronzed and white-buttocked Jimmy Major again replaced bony reality. She noticed that the closet mirror as seen from the bed reflected exactly the same still-life arrangement, oranges in a wooden bowl, as it had in the garland-brief days of Jim, a voracious consumer of the centenarian's fruit. She was almost sorry when upon looking around she located the source of the vision in the folds of her bright things thrown over the back of a chair.

She canceled their next assignation at the last moment and soon afterwards went off to Europe. In Person's mind the affair left hardly anything more than a stain of light lipstick on tissue paper—and a romantic sense of having embraced a great writer's sweetheart. Time, however, sets to work on those ephemeral affairs, and a new flavor is added to the recollection.

We now see a torn piece of *La Stampa* and an empty wine bottle. A lot of construction work was going on.

12

A lot of construction work was going on around Witt, scarring and muddying the entire hillside upon which he was told he would find Villa Nastia. Its immediate surroundings had more or less been tidied up, forming an oasis of quiet amidst the clanging and knocking wilderness of clay and cranes. There even gleamed a boutique among the shops forming a hemicircle around a freshly planted young rowan under which some litter had already been left, such as a workman's empty bottle and an Italian newspaper. Person's power of orientation now failed him but a woman selling apples from a neighboring stall set him straight again. An overaffectionate large white dog started to frisk unpleasantly in his wake and was called back by the woman.

He walked up a steepish asphalted path which had a white wall on one side with firs and larches showing above. A grilled door in it led to some camp or school. The cries of children at play came from behind the wall and a shuttlecock sailed over it to land at his feet. He ignored it, not being the sort of man who picks up things for strangers—a glove, a rolling coin.

A little farther, an interval in the stone wall revealed a short flight of stairs and the door of a whitewashed bungalow signed Villa Nastia in French cursive. As happens so often in R.'s fiction, "nobody answered the bell." Hugh noticed several other steps lateral to the porch, descending (after all that stupid climbing!) into the pungent dampness of boxwood. These led him around the house and into its garden. A boarded, only half-completed splash pool adjoined a small lawn, in the center of which a stout middle-aged lady, with greased limbs of a painful pink, lay sunbathing in a deck chair. A copy, no doubt the same, of the *Figures* et cetera paperback, with a folded letter (which we thought wiser our Person should not recognize) acting as marker, lay on top of the one-piece swimsuit into which her main bulk had been stuffed.

Madame Charles Chamar, *née* Anastasia Petrovna Potapov (a perfectly respectable name that her late husband garbled as "Patapouf"), was the daughter of a wealthy cattle dealer who had emigrated with his family to England from Ryazan via Kharbin and Ceylon soon after the Bolshevist revolution. She had long grown accustomed to entertaining this or that young man whom capricious Armande had stood up; but the new beau was dressed like a salesman, and had something about him (your genius, Person!) that puzzled and annoyed Madame Chamar. She liked people to fit. The Swiss boy, with whom Armande was skiing at the moment on the permanent snows high above Witt, fitted. So did the Blake twins. So did the old guide's son, golden-haired Jacques, a bobsled champion. But my gangly and gloomy Hugh Person, with his awful tie, vulgarly fastened to his cheap white shirt, and impossible chestnut suit, did not belong to her accepted world. When told that Armande was enjoying herself elsewhere and might not be back for tea, he did not bother to conceal his surprise and displeasure. He stood scratching his cheek. The inside of his Tyrolean hat was dark with sweat. Had Armande got his letter?

Madame Chamar answered in the noncommittal negative—though she might have consulted the telltale book marker, but out of a mother's instinctive prudence refrained from doing so. Instead she popped the paperback into her garden bag. Automatically, Hugh mentioned that he had recently visited its author.

"He lives somewhere in Switzerland, I think?"

"Yes, at Diablonnet, near Versex."

"Diablonnet always reminds me of the Russian for 'apple trees': *yabloni*. He has a nice house?"

"Well, we met in Versex, in a hotel, not at his home. I'm told it's a very large and a very old-fashioned place. We discussed business matters. Of course the house is always full of his rather, well, frivolous guests. I shall wait for a little while and then go."

He refused to shed his jacket and relax in a lawn chair alongside Madame Chamar. Too much sun caused his head to swim, he explained. "*Alors allons dans la maison,*" she said, faithfully translating from Russian. Seeing the efforts she was making to rise, Hugh offered to help her; but Madame Chamar bade him sharply stand well away from her chair lest his proximity prove a "psychological obstruction." Her unwieldy corpulence could be moved only by means of one precise little wiggle; in order to make it she had to concentrate upon the idea of trying to fool gravity until something clicked inwardly and the right jerk happened like the miracle of a sneeze. Meantime she lay in her chair motionless, and as it were ambushed, with brave sweat glistening on her chest and above the purple arches of her pastel eyebrows.

"This is completely unnecessary," said Hugh, "I am quite happy to wait here in the shade of a tree, but shade I must have. I never thought it would be so hot in the mountains."

Abruptly, Madame Chamar's entire body gave such a start that the frame of her deck chair emitted an almost human cry. The next moment she was in a sitting position, with both feet on the ground.

"Everything is well," she declared cozily, and stood up, now robed in bright terry cloth with the suddenness of a magic metamorphosis. "Come, I want to offer you a nice cold drink and show you my albums."

The drink turned out to be a tall faceted glass of tepid tap-water with a spoonful of homemade strawberry jam clouding it a mallowish hue. The albums, four big bound volumes, were laid out on a very low, very round table in the very *moderne* living room.

"I now leave you for some minutes," said Madame Chamar, and in full view of the public ascended with ponderous energy the completely visible and audible stairs leading to a similarly overt second floor, where one could see a bed through an open door and a bidet through another. Armande used to say that this product of her late father's art was a regular showpiece attracting tourists from distant countries such as Rhodesia and Japan.

The albums were quite as candid as the house, though less depressing. The Armande series, which exclusively interested our *voyeur malgré lui*, was inaugurated by a photograph of the late Potapov, in his seventies, looking very dapper with his gray little imperial and his Chinese house jacket, making the wee myopic sign of the Russian cross over an invisible baby in its deep cot. Not only did the snapshots follow Armande through all the phases of the past and all the improvements of amateur photography, but the girl also came in various states of innocent undress. Her parents and aunts, the insatiable takers of cute pictures, believed in fact that a girl child of ten, the dream of a Lutwidgean, had the same right to total nudity as an infant. The visitor constructed a pile of albums to screen the flame of his interest from anybody overhead on the landing, and returned several times to the pictures of little Armande in her bath, pressing a proboscidate rubber toy to her shiny stomach or standing up, dimple-bottomed, to be lathered. Another revelation of impuberal softness (its middle line just distinguishable from the less vertical grass-blade next to it) was afforded by a photo of her in which she sat in the buff on the grass, combing her sun-shot hair and spreading wide, in false perspective, the lovely legs of a giantess.

He heard a toilet flush upstairs and with a guilty wince slapped the thick book shut. His retractile heart moodily withdrew, its throbs quietened; but nobody came down from those infernal heights, and he went back, rumbling, to his silly pictures.

Toward the end of the second album the photography burst into color to celebrate the vivid vestiture of her adolescent molts. She appeared in floral frocks, fancy slacks, tennis shorts, swimsuits, amidst the harsh greens and blues of the commercial spectrum. He discovered the elegant angularity of her suntanned shoulders, the long line of her haunch. He learned that at eighteen the torrent of her pale hair reached the small of her back. No matrimonial agency could have offered its clients such variations on the theme of one virgin. In the third album he found, with an enjoyable sense of homecoming, glimpses of his immediate surroundings: the lemon and black cushions of the divan at the other end of the room and the Denton mount of a bird-wing butterfly on the mantelpiece. The fourth, incomplete album began with a sparkle of her chastest images: Armande in a pink parka, Armande jewel-bright, Armande careening on skis through the sugar dust.

At last, from the upper part of the transparent house, Madame Chamar warily trudged downstairs, the jelly of a bare forearm wobbling as she clutched at the balustrade rail. She was now clad in an elaborate summer dress with flounces, as if she too, like her daughter, had been passing through several stages of change. "Don't get up, don't get up," she cried, patting the air with one hand, but Hugh insisted he'd better go. "Tell her," he added, "tell your daughter when she returns from her glacier, that I was extremely disappointed. Tell her I shall be staying a week, two weeks, three weeks here, at the grim Ascot Hotel in the pitiful village of Witt. Tell her I shall telephone if she does not. Tell her," he continued, now walking down a slippery path among cranes and power shovels immobilized in the gold of the late afternoon, "tell her that my system is poisoned by her, by her twenty sisters, her twenty dwindlings in backcast, and that I shall perish if I cannot have her."

He was still rather simple as lovers go. One might have said to fat, vulgar Madame Chamar: how dare you exhibit your child to sensitive strangers? But our Person vaguely imagined that this was a case of modern immodesty current in Madame Chamar's set. What "set," good Lord? The lady's mother had been a country veterinary's daughter, same as Hugh's mother (by the only coincidence worth noting in the whole rather sad affair). Take those pictures away, you stupid nudist!

She rang him up around midnight, waking him in the pit of an evanescent, but definitely bad, dream (after all that melted cheese and young potatoes with a bottle of green wine at the hotel's *carnotzet*). As he scrabbled up the receiver, he groped with the other hand for his reading glasses, without which, by some vagary of concomitant senses, he could not attend to the telephone properly.

"You Person?" asked her voice.

He already knew, ever since she had recited the contents of the card he had given her on the train, that she pronounced his first name as "You."

"Yes, it's me, I mean 'you,' I mean you mispronounce it most enchantingly."

"I do not mispronounce anything. Look, I never re-ceived——"

"Oh, you do! You drop your haitches like—like pearls into a blindman's cup."

"Well, the correct pronunciation is 'cap.' I win. Now listen, tomorrow I'm occupied, but what about Friday—if you can be ready *à sept heures précises*?"

He certainly could.

She invited "Percy," as she declared she would call him from now on, since he detested "Hugh," to come with her for a bit of summer skiing at Drakonita, or Darkened Heat, as he misheard it, which caused him to conjure up a dense forest protecting romantic ramblers from the blue blaze of an alpine noon. He said he had never learned to ski on a holiday at Sugarwood, Vermont, but would be happy to stroll beside her, along a footpath not only provided for him by fancy but also swept clean with a snowman's broom—one of those instant unverified visions which can fool the cleverest man.

13

Now we have to bring into focus the main street of Witt as it was on Thursday, the day after her telephone call. It teems with transparent people and processes, into which and through which we might sink with an angel's or author's delight, but we have to single out for this report only one Person. Not an extensive hiker, he limited his loafing to a tedious survey of the village. A grim stream of cars rolled and rolled, some seeking with the unwieldy wariness of reluctant machinery a place to park, others coming from, or heading for, the much more fashionable resort of Thur, twenty miles north. He passed several times by the old fountain dribbling through the geranium-lined trough of a hollowed log; he examined the post office and the bank, the church and the tourist agency, and a famous black hovel that was still allowed to survive with its cabbage patch and scarecrow crucifix between a boardinghouse and a laundry.

He drank beer in two different taverns. He lingered before a sports shop; relingered—and bought a nice gray turtleneck sweater with a tiny and very pretty American flag embroidered over the heart. "Made in Turkey," whispered its label.

He decided it was time for some more refreshments—and saw her sitting at a sidewalk café. You swerved toward her, thinking she was alone; then noticed, too late, a second handbag on the opposite chair. Simultaneously her companion came out of the tea shop and, resuming her seat, said in that lovely New York voice, with that harlot dash he would have recognized even in heaven:

"The john is a joke."

Meanwhile Hugh Person, unable to shed the mask of an affable grin, had come up and was invited to join them.

An adjacent customer, comically resembling Person's late
Aunt Melissa whom we like very much, was reading l'*Erald
Tribune*. Armande believed (in the vulgar connotation of the
word) that Julia Moore had met Percy. Julia believed she had.
So did Hugh, indeed, yes. Did his aunt's double permit him
to borrow her spare chair? He was welcome to it. She was a
dear soul, with five cats, living in a toy house, at the end of a
birch avenue, in the quietest part of——

Interrupting us with an earsplitting crash an impassive waitress, a poor woman in her own right, dropped a tray with
lemonades and cakes, and crouched, splitting into many small
quick gestures peculiar to that woman, her face impassive.

Armande informed Percy that Julia had come all the way
from Geneva to consult her about the translation of a number
of phrases with which she, Julia, who was going tomorrow to
Moscow, desired to "impress" her Russian friends. Percy,
here, worked for her stepfather.

"My *former* stepfather, thank Heavens," said Julia. "By the
way, Percy, if that's your *nom de voyage*, perhaps you may
help. As she explained, I want to dazzle some people in Moscow, who promised me the company of a famous young Russian poet. Armande has supplied me with a number of darling
words, but we got stuck at—" (taking a slip of paper from
her bag)—"'I want to know how to say: 'What a cute little
church, what a big snowdrift.' You see we do it first into
French and she thinks 'snowdrift' is *rafale de neige*, but I'm
sure it can't be *rafale* in French and *rafalovich* in Russian, or
whatever they call a snowstorm."

"The word you want," said our Person, "is *congère*, feminine gender, I learned it from my mother."

"Then it's *sugrob* in Russian," said Armande and added
dryly: "Only there won't be much snow there in August."

Julia laughed. Julia looked happy and healthy. Julia had
grown even prettier than she had been two years ago. Shall I
now see her in dreams with those new eyebrows, that new
long hair? How fast do dreams catch up with new fashions?
Will the next dream still stick to her Japanese-doll hairdo?

"Let me order something for you," said Armande to Percy,
not making, however, the offering gesture that usually goes
with that phrase.

Percy thought he would like a cup of hot chocolate. The dreadful fascination of meeting an old flame in public! Armande had nothing to fear, naturally. *She* was in a totally different class, beyond competition. Hugh recalled R.'s famous novella *Three Tenses*.

"There was something else we didn't quite settle, Armande, or did we?"

"Well, we spent two hours at it," remarked Armande, rather grumpily—not realizing, perhaps, that she had nothing to fear. The fascination was of a totally different, purely intellectual or artistic order, as brought out so well in *Three Tenses*: a fashionable man in a night-blue tuxedo is supping on a lighted veranda with three bare-shouldered beauties, Alice, Beata, and Claire, who have never seen one another before. A. is a former love, B. is his present mistress, C. is his future wife.

He regretted now not having coffee as Armande and Julia were having. The chocolate proved unpalatable. You were served a cup of hot milk. You also got, separately, a little sugar and a dainty-looking envelope of sorts. You ripped open the upper margin of the envelope. You added the beige dust it contained to the ruthlessly homogenized milk in your cup. You took a sip—and hurried to add sugar. But no sugar could improve the insipid, sad, dishonest taste.

Armande, who had been following the various phases of his astonishment and disbelief, smiled and said:

"Now you know what 'hot chocolate' has come to in Switzerland. My mother," she continued, turning to Julia (who with the revelatory *sans-gêne* of the Past Tense, though actually she prided herself on her reticence, had lunged with her little spoon toward Hugh's cup and collected a sample), "my mother actually broke into tears when she was first served this stuff, because she remembered so tenderly the chocolate of her chocolate childhood."

"Pretty beastly," agreed Julia, licking her plump pale lips, "but still I prefer it to our American fudge."

"That's because you are the most unpatriotic creature in the world," said Armande.

The charm of the Past Tense lay in its secrecy. Knowing Julia, he was quite sure she would not have told a chance friend about their affair—one sip among dozens of swallows. Thus, at this precious and brittle instant, Julia and he (*alias* Alice and the narrator) formed a pact of the past, an impalpable pact directed against reality as represented by the voluble street corner, with its swish-passing automobiles, and trees, and strangers. The B. of the trio was Busy Witt, while the main stranger—and this touched off another thrill—was his sweetheart of the morrow, Armande, and Armande was as little aware of the future (which the author, of course, knew in every detail) as she was of the past that Hugh now retasted with his brown-dusted milk. Hugh, a sentimental simpleton, and somehow not a very *good* Person (good ones are above that, he was merely a rather dear one), was sorry that no music accompanied the scene, no Rumanian fiddler dipped heartward for two monogram-entangled sakes. There was not even a mechanical rendition of "Fascination" (a waltz) by the café's loudplayer. Still there did exist a kind of supporting rhythm formed by the voices of foot passengers, the clink of crockery, the mountain wind in the venerable mass of the corner chestnut.

Presently, they started to leave. Armande reminded him of tomorrow's excursion. Julia shook hands with him and begged him to pray for her when she would be saying to that very passionate, very prominent poet *je t'aime* in Russian which sounded in English (gargling with the phrase) "yellow blue tibia." They parted. The two girls got into Julia's smart little car. Hugh Person started walking back to his hotel, but then pulled up short with a curse and went back to retrieve his parcel.

14

Friday morning. A quick Coke. A belch. A hurried shave. He put on his ordinary clothes, throwing in the turtleneck for style. Last interview with the mirror. He plucked a black hair out of a red nostril.

The first disappointment of the day awaited him on the

stroke of seven at their rendezvous (the post-office square), where he found her attended by three young athletes, Jack, Jake, and Jacques, whose copper faces he had seen grinning around her in one of the latest photographs of the fourth album. Upon noticing the sullen way his Adam's apple kept working she gaily suggested that perhaps he did not care to join them after all "because we want to walk up to the only cable car that works in summer and that's quite a climb if you're not used to it." White-toothed Jacques, half-embracing the pert maiden, remarked confidentially that *monsieur* should change into sturdier brogues, but Hugh retorted that in the States one hiked in any old pair of shoes, even sneakers. "We hoped," said Armande, "we might induce you to learn skiing: we keep all the gear up there, with the fellow who runs the place, and he's sure to find something for you. You'll be making tempo turns in five lessons. Won't you, Percy? I think you should also need a parka, it may be summer here, at two thousand feet, but you'll find polar conditions at over nine thousand." "The little one is right," said Jacques with feigned admiration, patting her on the shoulder. "It's a forty-minute saunter," said one of the twins. "Limbers you up for the slopes."

It soon transpired that Hugh would not be able to keep up with them and reach the four-thousand-foot mark to catch the gondola just north of Witt. The promised "stroll" proved to be a horrible hike, worse than anything he had experienced on school picnics in Vermont or New Hampshire. The trail consisted of very steep ups and very slippery downs, and gigantic ups again, along the side of the next mountain, and was full of old ruts, rocks, and roots. He labored, hot, wretched Hugh, behind Armande's blond bun, while she lightly followed light Jacques. The English twins made up the rear guard. Possibly, had the pace been a little more leisurely, Hugh might have managed that simple climb, but his heartless and mindless companions swung on without mercy, practically bounding up the steep bits and zestfully sliding down the declivities, which Hugh negotiated with outspread arms, in an attitude of entreaty. He refused to borrow the stick he was offered, but finally, after twenty minutes of torment, pleaded for a short breathing spell. To his dismay not Armande but

Jack and Jake stayed with him as he sat on a stone, bending his head and panting, a pearl of sweat hanging from his pointed nose. They were taciturn twins and now merely exchanged silent glances as they stood a little above him on the trail, arms akimbo. He felt their sympathy ebbing and begged them to continue on their way, he would follow shortly. When they had gone he waited a little and then limped back to the village. At one spot between two forested stretches he rested again, this time on an open bluff where a bench, eyeless but eager, faced an admirable view. As he sat there smoking, he noticed his party very high above him, blue, gray, pink, red, waving to him from a cliff. He waved back and resumed his gloomy retreat.

But Hugh Person refused to give up. Mightily shod, alpenstocked, munching gum, he again accompanied them next morning. He begged them to let him set his own pace, without waiting for him anywhere, and he would have reached the cableway had he not lost his bearings and ended up in a brambly burn at the end of a logging road. Another attempt a day or two later was more successful. He almost reached timberline—but there the weather changed, a damp fog enveloped him, and he spent a couple of hours shivering all alone in a smelly shippon, waiting for the whirling mists to uncover the sun once more.

Another time he volunteered to carry after her a pair of new skis she had just acquired—weird-looking, reptile-green things made of metal and fiberglass. Their elaborate bindings looked like first cousins of orthopedic devices meant to help a cripple to walk. He was allowed to shoulder those precious skis, which at first felt miraculously light but soon grew as heavy as great slabs of malachite, under which he staggered in Armande's wake like a clown helping to change properties in a circus arena. His load was snatched from him as soon as he sat down for a rest. He was offered a paper bag (four small oranges) in exchange but he pushed it away without looking.

Our Person was obstinate and monstrously in love. A fairy-tale element seemed to imbue with its Gothic rose water all attempts to scale the battlements of her Dragon. Next week he made it and thereafter established himself as less of a nuisance.

15

As he sat sipping rum on the sun terrace of the Café du Glacier below Drakonita Hut and rather smugly contemplated, with the exhilaration of liquor in the mountain air, the skiing area (such a magic sight after so much water and matted grass!); as he took in the glaze of the upper runs, the blue herringbones lower down, the varicolored little figures outlined by the brush of chance against the brilliant white as if by a Flemish master's hand, Hugh told himself that this might make an admirable jacket design for *Christies and Other Lassies*, a great skier's autobiography (thoroughly revised and enriched by a number of hands in the office), the typescript of which he had recently copy-edited, querying, as he now recalled, such terms as "*godilles*" and "*wedeln*" (rom ?). It was fun to peer over one's third drink at the painted little people skimming along, losing a ski here, a pole there, or victoriously veering in a spray of silver powder. Hugh Person, now shifting to kirsch, wondered if he could force himself to follow her advice ("such a nice big slouchy sporty-looking Yank and can't ski!") and identify himself with this or that chap charging straight down in a stylish crouch, or else be doomed to repeat for ever and ever the after-fall pause of a bulky novice asprawl on his back in hopeless, good-humored repose.

He never could pinpoint, with his dazzled and watery eyes, Armande's silhouette among the skiers. Once, however, he was sure he had caught her, floating and flashing, red-anoraked, bare-headed, agonizingly graceful, there, there, and now there, jumping a bump, shooting down nearer and nearer, going into a tuck—and abruptly changing into a goggled stranger.

Presently she appeared from another side of the terrace, in glossy green nylon, carrying her skis, but with her formidable boots still on. He had spent enough time studying skiwear in Swiss shops to know that shoe leather had been replaced by plastic, and laces by rigid clips. "You look like the first girl on the moon," he said, indicating her boots, and if they had not been especially close fitting she would have wiggled her toes inside as a woman does when her footwear happens to be discussed in flattering terms (smiling toes taking over the making of mouths).

"Listen," she said as she considered her Mondstein Sexy (their incredible trade name), "I'll leave my skis here, and change into walking shoes and return to Witt with you *à deux*. I've quarreled with Jacques, and he has left with his dear friends. All is finished, thank God."

Facing him in the heavenly cable car she gave a comparatively polite version of what she was to tell him a little later in disgustingly vivid detail. Jacques had demanded her presence at the onanistic sessions he held with the Blake twins at their chalet. Once already he had made Jack show her his implement but she had stamped her foot and made them behave themselves. Jacques had now presented her with an ultimatum—either she join them in their nasty games or he would cease being her lover. She was ready to be ultramodern, socially and sexually, but this was offensive, and vulgar, and as old as Greece.

The gondola would have gone on gliding forever in a blue haze sufficient for paradise had not a robust attendant stopped it before it turned to reascend for good. They got out. It was spring in the shed where the machinery performed its humble and endless duty. Armande with a prim "excuse me" absented herself for a moment. Cows stood among the dandelions outside, and radio music came from the adjacent *buvette*.

In a timid tremor of young love Hugh wondered if he might dare kiss her at some likely pause in their walk down the winding path. He would try as soon as they reached the rhododendron belt where they might stop, she to shed her parka, he to remove a pebble from his right shoe. The rhododendrons and junipers gave way to alder, and the voice of familiar despair started urging him to put off the pebble and the butterfly kiss to some later occasion. They had entered the fir forest when she stopped, looked around, and said (as casually as if she were suggesting they pick mushrooms or raspberries):

"And now one is going to make love. I know a nice mossy spot just behind those trees where we won't be disturbed, if you do it quickly."

Orange peel marked the place. He wanted to embrace her in the preliminaries required by his nervous flesh (the "quickly" was a mistake) but she withdrew with a fishlike flip of the body, and sat down on the whortleberries to take off her shoes and trousers. He was further dismayed by the ribbed fabric of thick-knit black tights that she wore under her ski pants. She consented to pull them down only just as far as necessary. Nor did she let him kiss her, or caress her thighs.

"Well, bad luck," she said finally but as she twisted against him trying to draw up her tights, he regained all at once the power to do what was expected of him.

"One will go home now," she remarked immediately afterwards in her usual neutral tone, and in silence they continued their brisk downhill walk.

At the next turn of the trail the first orchard of Witt appeared at their feet, and farther down one could see the glint of a brook, a lumberyard, mown fields, brown cottages.

"I hate Witt," said Hugh. "I hate life. I hate myself. I hate that beastly old bench." She stopped to look the way his fierce finger pointed, and he embraced her. At first she tried to evade his lips but he persisted desperately. All at once she gave in, and the minor miracle happened. A shiver of tenderness rippled her features, as a breeze does a reflection. Her eyelashes were wet, her shoulders shook in his clasp. That moment of soft agony was never to be repeated—or rather would never be granted the time to come back again after completing the cycle innate in its rhythm; yet that brief vibration in which she dissolved with the sun, the cherry trees, the forgiven landscape, set the tone for his new existence with its sense of "all-is-well" despite her worst moods, her silliest caprices, her harshest demands. That kiss, and not anything preceding it, was the real beginning of their courtship.

She disengaged herself without a word. A long file of little boys followed by a scoutmaster climbed toward them along the steep path. One of them hoisted himself on an adjacent round rock and jumped down with a cheerful squeal. "*Grüss Gott,*" said their teacher in passing by Armande and Hugh. "Hello there," responded Hugh. "He'll think you're crazy," said she.

Through a beech grove and across a river, they reached the

outskirts of Witt. A short cut down a muddy slope between half-built chalets took them to Villa Nastia. Anastasia Petrovna was in the kitchen, placing flowers in vases. "Come here, Mamma," cried Armande: "*Zheniha privela*, I've brought my fiancé."

16

Witt had a new tennis court. One day Armande challenged Hugh to a set.

Ever since childhood and its nocturnal fears, sleep had been our Person's habitual problem. The problem was twofold. He was obliged, sometimes for hours, to woo the black automaton with an automatic repetition of some active image—that was one trouble. The other referred to the quasi-insane state into which sleep put him, once it did come. He could not believe that decent people had the sort of obscene and absurd nightmares which shattered his night and continued to tingle throughout the day. Neither the incidental accounts of bad dreams reported by friends nor the case histories in Freudian dream books, with their hilarious elucidations, presented anything like the complicated vileness of his almost nightly experience.

In his adolescence he attempted to solve the first part of the problem by an ingenious method which worked better than pills (these if too mild induced too little sleep, and if strong enhanced the vividness of monstrous visions). The method he hit upon was repeating in mind with metronomic precision the successive strokes of an outdoor game. The only game he had ever played in his youth and could still play at forty was tennis. Not only did he play tolerably well, with a certain easy stylishness (caught years ago from a dashing cousin who coached the boys at the New England school of which his father had been headmaster), but he had invented a shot which neither Guy, nor Guy's brother-in-law, an even finer professional, could either make or take. It had an element of art-for-art's sake about it, since it could not deal with low, awkward balls, required an ideally balanced stance (not easy to assume in a hurry) and, by itself, never won him a match. The Person Stroke was executed with a rigid arm and blended a vigorous drive with a clinging cut that followed the ball from the moment of impact to the end of the stroke. The impact (and this was the nicest part) had to occur at the far end of the racket's netting, with the performer standing well away from the bounce of the ball and as it were reaching out for it. The bounce had to be fairly high for the head of the racket to adhere properly, without a shadow of "twist," and then to propel the "glued" ball in a stiff trajectory. If the "cling" was not enduring enough or if it started too proximally, in the middle of the racket, the result was a very ordinary, floppy, slow-curving "galosh," quite easy, of course, to return; but when controlled accurately, the stroke reverberated with a harsh crack throughout one's forearm and whizzed off in a strongly controlled, very straight skim to a point near the baseline. On hitting the ground it clung to it in a way felt to be of the same order as the adherence of the ball to the strings during the actual stroke. While retaining its direct velocity, the ball hardly rose from the ground; in fact, Person believed that, with tremendous, all-consuming practice, the shot could be made not to bounce at all but roll with lightning speed along the surface of the court. Nobody could return an un-bouncing ball, and no doubt in the near future such shots would be ruled out as illegal spoilsports. But even in its inventor's rough version it could be delightfully satisfying. The return was invariably botched in a most ludicrous fashion, because of the low-darting ball refusing to be scooped up, let alone properly hit. Guy and the other Guy were intrigued and annoyed whenever Hugh managed to bring off his "cling drive"—which unfortunately for him was not often. He recouped himself by not telling the puzzled professionals, who tried to imitate the stroke (and achieved merely a feeble spin), that the trick lay not in the cut but in the cling, and not only in the cling itself but in the place where it occurred at the head of the strings as well as in the rigidity of the reaching-out movement of the arm. Hugh treasured his stroke mentally for years, long after the chances to use it dwindled to one or two shots in a desultory game. (In fact, the last time he executed it was that day at Witt with Armande, whereupon she walked off the court and could not be coaxed back.) Its chief use had been a means of putting himself to sleep. In those pre-dormitory exercises he greatly perfected his stroke, for instance quickening its preparation (when tackling a fast serve) and learning to reproduce its mirror image backhandedly (instead of running around the ball like a fool). No sooner had he found a comfortable place for his cheek on a cool soft pillow than the familiar firm thrill would start running through his arm, and he would be slamming his way through one game after another. There were additional trimmings: explaining to a sleepy reporter, "Cut it hard and yet keep it intact"; or winning in a mist of well-being the Davis Cup brimming with the poppy.

Why did he give up that specific remedy for insomnia when he married Armande? Surely not because she criticized his pet stroke as an insult and a bore? Was it the novelty of the shared bed, and the presence of another brain humming near his, that disturbed the privacy of the somnorific—and rather sophomoric—routine? Perhaps. Anyhow he gave up trying, persuaded himself that one or two entirely sleepless nights per week constituted for him a harmless norm, and on other nights contented himself with reviewing the events of the day (an automaton in its own right), the cares and *misères* of routine life with now and then the peacock spot that prison psychiatrists called "having sex."

He had said that on top of the trouble in going to sleep, he experienced dream anguish?

Dream anguish was right! He might vie with the best lunatics in regard to the recurrence of certain nightmare themes. In some cases he could establish a first rough draft, with versions following in well-spaced succession, changing in minute detail, polishing the plot, introducing some new repulsive situation, yet every time rewriting a version of the same, otherwise inexisting, story. Let's hear the repulsive part. Well, one erotic dream in particular had kept recurring with cretinous urgency over a period of several years, before and after Armande's death. In that dream which the psychiatrist (a weirdie, son of an unknown soldier and a Gypsy mother) dismissed as "much too direct," he was offered a sleeping beauty on a great platter garnished with flowers, and a choice of tools on a cushion. These differed in length and breadth, and their number and assortment varied from dream to dream. They lay in a row, neatly aligned: a yard-long one of vulcanized rubber with a violet head, then a thick short burnished bar, then again a thinnish skewerlike affair, with rings of raw meat and translucent lard alternating, and so on—these are random samples. There was not much sense in selecting one rather than another—the coral or the bronze, or the terrible rubber—since whatever he took changed in shape and size, and could not be properly fitted to his own anatomical system, breaking off at the burning point or snapping in two between the legs or bones of the more or less disarticulated lady. He desired to stress the following point with the fullest, fiercest, anti-Freudian force. Those oneiric torments had nothing to do, either directly or in a "symbolic" sense, with anything he had experienced in conscious life. The erotic theme was just one theme among others, as *A Boy for Pleasure* remained just an extrinsic whimsy in relation to the whole fiction of the serious, too serious writer who had been satirized in a recent novel.

In another no less ominous nocturnal experience, he would find himself trying to stop or divert a trickle of grain or fine gravel from a rift in the texture of space and being hampered in every conceivable respect by cobwebby, splintery, filamentary elements, confused heaps and hollows, brittle debris, collapsing colossuses. He was finally blocked by masses of rubbish, and *that* was death. Less frightening but perhaps imperiling a person's brain to an even greater extent were the "avalanche" nightmares at the rush of awakening when their imagery turned into the movement of verbal colluvia in the valleys of Toss and Thurn, whose gray rounded rocks, *Roches étonnées*, are so termed because of their puzzled and grinning surface, marked by dark "goggles" (*écarquillages*). Dreamman is an idiot not wholly devoid of animal cunning; the fatal flaw in his mind corresponds to the splutter produced by tongue twisters: "the risks scoundrels take."

He was told what a pity he had not seen his analyst as soon as the nightmares grew worse. He replied he did not own one. Very patiently the doctor rejoined that the pronoun had been used not possessively but domestically as, for example, in advertisements: "Ask your grocer." Had Armande ever consulted an analyst? If that was a reference to Mrs. Person and not to a child or a cat, then the answer was no. As a girl she seemed to have been interested in Neobuddhism and that sort of stuff, but in America new friends urged her to get, what you call, analyzed and she said she might try it after completing her Oriental studies.

He was advised that in calling her by her first name one simply meant to induce an informal atmosphere. One always did that. Only yesterday one had put another prisoner completely at ease by saying: You'd better tell Uncle your dreams or you might burn. Did Hugh, or rather Mr. Person, have "destructive urges" in his dreams—this was something that had not been made sufficiently clear. The term itself might not be sufficiently clear. A sculptor could sublimate the destructive urge by attacking an inanimate object with chisel and hammer. Major surgery offered one of the most useful means of draining off the destructive urge: a respected though not always lucky practitioner had admitted privately how difficult he found it to stop himself from hacking out every organ in sight during an operation. Everyone had secret tensions stored up from infancy. Hugh need not be ashamed of them. In fact at puberty sexual desire arises as a substitute for the desire to kill, which one normally fulfills in one's dreams; and insomnia is merely the fear of becoming aware in sleep of one's unconscious desires for slaughter and sex. About eighty percent of all dreams enjoyed by adult males are sexual. See Clarissa Dark's findings—she investigated singlehanded some two hundred healthy jailbirds whose terms of imprisonment were shortened, of course, by the number of nights spent in the Center's dormitory. Well, one hundred seventy-eight of the men were seen to have powerful erections during the stage of sleep called HAREM ("Has A Rapid Eye Movement") marked by visions causing a lustful ophthalmic roll, a kind of internal ogling. By the way, when did Mr. Person begin to hate Mrs. Person? No answer. Was hate, maybe, part of his feeling for her from the very first moment? No answer. Did he ever buy her a turtleneck sweater? No answer. Was he annoyed when she found it too tight at the throat?

"I shall vomit," said Hugh, "if you persist in pestering me with all that odious rot."

<h1 style="text-align:center">17</h1>

We shall now discuss love.

What powerful words, what weapons, are stored up in the mountains, at suitable spots, in special caches of the granite heart, behind painted surfaces of steel made to resemble the mottling of the adjacent rocks! But when moved to express his love, in the days of brief courtship and marriage, Hugh Person did not know where to look for words that would convince her, that would touch her, that would bring bright tears to her hard dark eyes! Per contra, something he said by chance, not planning the pang and the poetry, some trivial phrase, would prompt suddenly a hysterically happy response on the part of that dry-souled, essentially unhappy woman. Conscious attempts failed. If, as happened sometimes, at the grayest of hours, without the remotest sexual intent, he interrupted his reading to walk into her room and advance toward her on his knees and elbows like an ecstatic, undescribed, unarboreal sloth, howling his adoration, cool Armande would tell him to get up and stop playing the fool. The most ardent addresses he could think up—my princess, my sweetheart, my angel, my animal, my exquisite beast—merely exasperated her. "Why," she inquired, "can't you talk to me in a natural human manner, as a gentleman talks to a lady, why must you put on such a clownish act, why can't you be serious, and plain, and believable?" But love, he said, was anything but believable, real life *was* ridiculous, yokels laughed at love. He tried to kiss the hem of her skirt or bite the crease of her trouserleg, her instep, the toe of her furious foot—and as he groveled, his unmusical voice muttering maudlin, exotic, rare, common nothings and everythings, into his own ear, as it were, the simple expression of love became a kind of degenerate avian performance executed by the male alone, with no female in sight—long neck straight, then curved, beak dipped, neck straightened again. It all made him ashamed of himself but he could not stop and she could not understand, for at such times he never came up with the right word, the right waterweed.

He loved her in spite of her unlovableness. Armande had many trying, though not necessarily rare, traits, all of which he accepted as absurd clues in a clever puzzle. She called her mother, to her face, *skotina*, "brute"—not being aware, naturally, that she would never see her again after leaving with Hugh for New York and death. She liked to give carefully planned parties, and no matter how long ago this or that gracious gathering had taken place (ten months, fifteen months, or even earlier before her marriage, at her mother's house in Brussels or Witt) every party and topic remained for ever preserved in the humming frost of her tidy mind. She visualized those parties in retrospect as stars on the veil of the undulating past, and saw her guests as the extremities of her own personality: vulnerable points that had to be treated thenceforth with nostalgic respect. If Julia or June remarked casually that they had never met art critic C. (the late Charles Chamar's cousin), whereas both Julia and June had attended the party, as registered in Armande's mind, she might get very nasty, denouncing the mistake in a disdainful drawl, and adding, with belly-dance contortions: "In that case you must have forgotten also the little sandwiches from Père Igor" (some special shop) "which you enjoyed so much." Hugh had never seen such a vile temper, such morbid *amour-propre*, so self-centered a nature. Julia, who had skied and skated with her, thought her a darling, but most women criticized her, and in telephone chats with one another mimicked her rather pathetic little tricks of attack and retort. If anybody started to say "Shortly before I broke my leg——" she would chime in with the triumphant: "And I broke both in my childhood!" For some occult reason she used an ironic and on the whole disagreeable tone of voice when addressing her husband in public.

She had strange whims. During their honeymoon in Stresa, on their last night there (his New York office was clamoring for his return), she decided that last nights were statistically the most dangerous ones in hotels without fire escapes, and their hotel looked indeed most combustible, in a massive old-fashioned way. For some reason or other, television producers consider that there is nothing more photogenic and universally fascinating than a good fire. Armande, viewing the Italian telenews, had been upset or feigned to be upset (she was fond of making herself interesting) by one such calamity on the local screen—little flames like slalom flaglets, huge ones like sudden demons, water squirting in intersecting curves like so many rococo fountains, and fearless men in glistening oilskin who directed all sorts of muddled operations in a fantasy of smoke and destruction. That night at Stresa she insisted they rehearse (he in his sleeping shorts, she in a Chudo-Yudo pajama) an acrobatic escape in the stormy murk by climbing down the overdecorated face of their hotel, from their fourth story to the second one, and thence to the roof of a gallery amidst tossing remonstrative trees. Hugh vainly reasoned with her. The spirited girl affirmed that as an expert rock-climber she knew it could be done by using footholds which various applied ornaments, generous juttings and little railed balconies here and there provided for one's careful descent. She ordered Hugh to follow her and train an electric torch on her from above. He was also supposed to keep close enough to help her if need be by holding her suspended, and thus increased in vertical length, while she probed the next step with a bare toe.

Hugh, despite forelimb strength, was a singularly inept anthropoid. He badly messed up the exploit. He got stuck on a ledge just under their balcony. His flashlight played erratically over a small part of the façade before slipping from his grasp. He called down from his perch entreating her to return. Underfoot a shutter opened abruptly. Hugh managed to scramble back onto his balcony, still roaring her name, though persuaded by now that she had perished. Eventually, however, she was located in a third-floor room where he found her wrapped up in a blanket smoking peacefully, supine on the bed of a stranger, who sat in a chair by the bed, reading a magazine.

Her sexual oddities perplexed and distressed Hugh. He put up with them during their trip. They became routine stuff when he returned with a difficult bride to his New York apartment. Armande decreed they regularly make love around tea-time, in the living room, as upon an imaginary stage, to the steady accompaniment of casual small talk, with both per-formers decently clothed, he wearing his best business suit and a polka-dotted tie, she a smart black dress closed at the throat. In concession to nature, undergarments could be parted, or even undone, but only very, very discreetly, without the least break in the elegant chitchat: impatience was pronounced un-seemly, exposure, monstrous. A newspaper or coffee-table book hid such preparations as he absolutely had to conduct, wretched Hugh, and woe to him if he winced or fumbled during the actual commerce; but far worse than the awful pull of long underwear in the chaos of his pinched crotch or the crisp contact with her armor-smooth stockings was the pre-requisite of light colloquy, about acquaintances, or politics, or zodiacal signs, or servants, and in the meantime, with visible hurry banned, the poignant work had to be brought surrep-titiously to a convulsive end in a twisted half-sitting position on an uncomfortable little divan. Hugh's mediocre potency might not have survived the ordeal had she concealed from him more completely than she thought she did the excitement derived from the contrast between the fictitious and the fac-tual—a contrast which does, after all, have claims to artistic subtlety if we recall the customs of certain Far Eastern people, virtually halfwits in many other respects. But his chief support lay in the never deceived expectancy of the dazed ecstasy that gradually idiotized her dear features, notwithstanding her ef-forts to maintain the flippant patter. In a sense he preferred the parlor setting to the even less normal decor of those rare occasions when she desired him to possess her in bed, well under the bedclothes, while she telephoned, gossiping with a female friend or hoaxing an unknown male. Our Person's ca-pacity to condone all this, to find reasonable explanations and so forth, endears him to us, but also provokes limpid mirth, alas, at times. For example, he told himself that she refused to strip because she was shy of her tiny pouting breasts and the scar of a ski accident along her thigh. Silly Person!

Was she faithful to him throughout the months of their marriage spent in frail, lax, merry America? During their first and last winter there she went a few times to ski without him,

at Aval, Quebec, or Chute, Colorado. While alone, he forbade
himself to dwell in thought on the banalities of betrayal, such
as holding hands with a chap or permitting him to kiss her
good night. Those banalities were to him quite as excruciating
to imagine as would be voluptuous intercourse. A steel door
of the spirit remained securely shut as long as she was away,
but no sooner had she arrived, her face brown and shiny, her
figure as trim as that of an air hostess, in that blue coat with
flat buttons as bright as counters of gold, than something
ghastly opened up in him and a dozen lithe athletes started
swarming around and prying her apart in all the motels of his
mind, although actually, as we know, she had enjoyed full
conjunction with only a dozen crack lovers in the course of
three trips.

Nobody, least of all her mother, could understand why Armande married a rather ordinary American with a not very
solid job, but we must end now our discussion of love.

18

In the second week of February, about one month before
death separated them, the Persons flew over to Europe for a
few days: Armande, to visit her mother dying in a Belgian
hospital (the dutiful daughter came too late), and Hugh, at
his firm's request, to look up Mr. R. and another American
writer, also residing in Switzerland.

It was raining hard when a taxi deposited him in front of
R.'s big, old, and ugly country house above Versex. He made
his way up a graveled path between streams of bubbly rain-
water running on both sides of it. He found the front door
ajar, and while tramping the mat noticed with amused surprise
Julia Moore standing with her back to him at the telephone
table in the vestibule. She now wore again the pretty pageboy
hairdo of the past and the same orange blouse. He had finished wiping his feet when she put back the receiver and
turned out to be a totally different girl.

"Sorry to have made you wait," she said, fixing on him a

pair of smiling eyes. "I'm replacing Mr. Tamworth, who is vacationing in Morocco."

Hugh Person entered the library, a comfortably furnished but decidedly old-fashioned and quite inadequately lighted room, lined with encyclopedias, dictionaries, directories, and the author's copies of the author's books in multiple editions and translations. He sat down in a club chair and drew a list of points to be discussed from his briefcase. The two main questions were: how to alter certain much too recognizable people in the typescript of *Tralatitions* and what to do with that commercially impossible title.

Presently R. came in. He had not shaved for three or four days and wore ridiculous blue overalls which he found convenient for distributing about him the tools of his profession, such as pencils, ball pens, three pairs of glasses, cards, jumbo clips, elastic bands, and—in an invisible state—the dagger which after a few words of welcome he pointed at our Person.

"I can only repeat," he said, collapsing in the armchair vacated by Hugh and motioning him to a similar one opposite, "what I said not once but often already: you can alter a cat but you cannot alter my characters. As to the title, which is a perfectly respectable synonym of the word 'metaphor,' no savage steeds will pull it from under me. My doctor advised Tamworth to lock up my cellar, which he did and concealed the key which the locksmith will not be able to duplicate before Monday and I'm too proud, you know, to buy the cheap wines they have in the village, so all I can offer you—you shake your head in advance and you're jolly right, son—is a can of apricot juice. Now allow me to talk to you about titles and libels. You know, that letter you wrote me tickled me black in the face. I have been accused of trifling with minors, but my minor characters are untouchable, if you permit me a pun."

He went on to explain that if your true artist had chosen to form a character on the basis of a living individual, any rewriting aimed at disguising that character was tantamount to destroying the living prototype as would driving, you know, a pin through a little doll of clay, and the girl next door falls dead. If the composition was artistic, if it held not only water but wine, then it was invulnerable in one sense and

horribly fragile in another. Fragile, because when a timid editor made the artist change "slender" to "plump," or
"brown" to "blond" he disfigured both the image and the
niche where it stood and the entire chapel around it; and invulnerable, because no matter how drastically you changed the
image, its prototype would remain recognizable by the shape
of the hole left in the texture of the tale. But apart from all
that, the customers whom he was accused of portraying were
much too cool to announce their presence and their resentment. In fact they would rather enjoy listening to the tattle
in literary salons with a little knowing air, as the French say.

The question of the title—*Tralatitions*—was another kettle
of fish. Readers did not realize that two types of title existed.
One type was the title found by the dumb author or the clever
publisher after the book had been written. *That* was simply a
label stuck on and tapped with the side of the fist. Most of
our worst best-sellers had that kind of title. But there was the
other kind: the title that shone through the book like a watermark, the title that was born with the book, the title to
which the author had grown so accustomed during the years
of accumulating the written pages that it had become part of
each and of all. No, Mr. R. could not give up *Tralatitions*.

Hugh made bold to remark that the tongue tended to substitute an "l" for the second of the three "t's."

"The tongue of ignorance," shouted Mr. R.

His pretty little secretary tripped in and announced that he
should not get excited or tired. The great man rose with an
effort and stood quivering and grinning, and proffering a large
hairy hand.

"Well," said Hugh, "I shall certainly tell Phil how strongly
you feel about the points he has raised. Good-bye, sir, you
will be getting a sample of the jacket design next week."

"So long and soon see," said Mr. R.

19

We are back in New York and this is their last evening together.

After serving them an excellent supper (a little on the rich side, perhaps, but not overabundant—neither was a big eater) obese Pauline, the *femme de ménage*, whom they shared with a Belgian artist in the penthouse immediately above them, washed the dishes and left at her usual hour (nine fifteen or thereabouts). Since she had the annoying propensity of sitting down for a moment to enjoy a bit of TV, Armande always waited for her to have gone before running it for her own pleasure. She now turned it on, let it live for a moment, changed channels—and killed the picture with a snort of disgust (her likes and dislikes in these matters lacked all logic, she might watch one or two programs with passionate regularity or on the contrary not touch the set for a week as if punishing that marvelous invention for a misdemeanor known only to her, and Hugh preferred to ignore her obscure feuds with actors and commentators). She opened a book, but here Phil's wife rang up to invite her on the morrow to the preview of a Lesbian drama with a Lesbian cast. Their conversation lasted twenty-five minutes, Armande using a confidential undertone, and Phyllis speaking so sonorously that Hugh, who sat at a round table correcting a batch of galleys, could have heard, had he felt so inclined, both sides of the trivial torrent. He contented himself instead with the résumé Armande gave him upon returning to the settee of gray plush near the fake fireplace. As had happened on previous occasions, around ten o'clock a most jarring succession of bumps and scrapes suddenly came from above: it was the cretin upstairs dragging a heavy piece of inscrutable sculpture (catalogued as "*Pauline anide*") from the center of his studio to the corner it occupied at night. In invariable response, Armande glared at the ceiling and remarked that in the case of a less amiable and helpful neighbor she would have complained long ago to Phil's cousin (who managed the apartment house). When placidity was restored, she started to look for the book she had had in her hand before the telephone rang. Her husband always felt a flow of special tenderness that reconciled him to the boring or brutal ugliness of what not very happy people call "life" every time that he noted in neat, efficient, clear-headed Armande the beauty and helplessness of human abstraction. He now found the object of her pathetic search (it was in the magazine rack near the telephone) and, as he restored it to her, he was allowed to touch with reverent lips her temple and a strand of blond hair. Then he went back to the galleys of *Tralatitions* and she to her book, which was a French touring guide that listed many splendid restaurants, forked and starred, but not very many "pleasant, quiet, well-situated hotels" with three or more turrets and sometimes a little red songbird on a twig.

"Here's a cute coincidence," observed Hugh. "One of his characters, in a rather bawdy passage—by the way should it be 'Savoie' or 'Savoy'?"

"What's the coincidence?"

"Oh. One of his characters is consulting a Michelin, and says: there's many a mile between Condom in Gascogne and Pussy in Savoie."

"The Savoy is a hotel," said Armande and yawned twice, first with clenched jaws, then openly. "I don't know why I'm so tired," she added, "but I know all this yawning only sidetracks sleep. I think I'll sample my new tablets tonight."

"Try imagining you're skimming on skis down a very smooth slope. I used to play tennis mentally when I was young and it often helped, especially with new, very white balls."

She remained seated, lost in thought, for another moment, then red-ribboned the place and went for a glass to the kitchen.

Hugh liked to read a set of proofs twice, once for the defects of the type and once for the virtues of the text. It worked better, he believed, if the eye check came first and the mind's pleasure next. He was now enjoying the latter and while not looking for errors, still had a chance to catch a missed booboo—his own or the printer's. He also permitted himself to query, with the utmost diffidence, in the margin of a second copy (meant for the author), certain idiosyncrasies of style and spelling, hoping the great man would understand that not genius but grammar was being questioned.

After a long consultation with Phil it had been decided not to do anything about the risks of defamation involved in the frankness with which R. described his complicated love life. He had "paid for it once in solitude and remorse, and now was ready to pay in hard cash any fool whom his story might hurt" (abridged and simplified citation from his latest letter). In a long chapter of a much more libertine nature (despite the grandiose wording) than the jock talk of the fashionable writers he criticized, R. showed a mother and daughter regaling their young lover with spectacular caresses on a mountain ledge above a scenic chasm and in other less perilous spots. Hugh did not know Mrs. R. intimately enough to assess her resemblance to the matron of the book (loppy breasts, flabby thighs, coon-bear grunts during copulation, and so forth); but the daughter in manner and movement, in breathless speech, in many other features with which he was not consciously familiar but which fitted the picture, was certainly Julia, although the author *had* made her fair-haired, and played down the Eurasian quality of her beauty. Hugh read with interest and concentration, but through the translucidity of the textual flow he still was correcting proof as some of us try to do—mending a broken letter here, indicating italics there, his eye and his spine (the true reader's main organ) collaborating rather than occluding each other. Sometimes he wondered what the phrase really meant—what exactly did "rimiform" suggest and how did a "balanic plum" look, or should he cap the 'b' and insert a 'k' after 'l'? The dictionary he used at home was less informative than the huge battered one in the office and he was now stumped by such beautiful things as "all the gold of a kew tree" and "a dappled nebris." He queried the middle word in the name of an incidental character "Adam von Librikov" because the German particle seemed to clash with the rest; or was the entire combination a sly scramble? He finally crossed out his query, but on the other hand reinstated the "Reign of Cnut" in another passage: a humbler proofreader before him had supposed that either the letters in the last word should be transposed or that it be corrected to "the Knout"—she was of Russian descent, like Armande.

Our Person, our reader, was not sure he entirely approved of R.'s luxuriant and bastard style; yet, at its best ("the gray rainbow of a fog-dogged moon"), it was diabolically evocative. He also caught himself trying to establish on the strength of fictional data at what age, in what circumstances, the writer had begun to debauch Julia: had it been in her childhood—

tickling her in her bath, kissing her wet shoulders, then one day carrying her wrapped in a big towel to his lair, as delectably described in the novel? Or did he flirt with her in her first college year, when he was paid two thousand dollars for reading to an enormous gown-and-town audience some short story of his, published and republished many times before but really wonderful stuff? How good to have *that* type of talent!

20

It was past eleven by now. He put out the lights in the living room and opened the window. The windy March night found something to finger in the room. An electric sign, DOPPLER, shifted to violet through the half-drawn curtains and illumined the deadly white papers he had left on the table.

He let his eyes get used to the obscurity in the next room, and presently stole in. Her first sleep was marked usually by a clattering snore. One could not help marveling how such a slender and dainty girl could churn up so ponderous a vibration. It had bothered Hugh at the early stage of their marriage because of the implicit threat of its going on all night. But something, some outside noise, or a jolt in her dream, or the discreet clearing of a meek husband's throat, caused her to stir, to sigh, to smack her lips, perhaps, or turn on her side, after which she slept mutely. This change of rhythm had apparently taken place while he was still working in the parlor; and now, lest the entire cycle recur, he tried to undress as quietly as possible. He later remembered pulling out very gingerly an exceptionally creaky drawer (whose voice he never noticed at other times) to get a fresh pair of the briefs which he wore in lieu of pajamas. He swore under his breath at the old wood's stupid plaint and refrained from pushing the drawer back; but the floor boards took over as soon as he started to tiptoe to his side of the double bed. Did that wake her? Yes, it did, hazily, or at least teased a hole in the hay, and she murmured something about the light. Actually all that impinged on the darkness was an angled beam from the living room, the door of which he had left ajar. He now closed it gently as he groped his way to the bed.

He lay open-eyed for a while listening to another tenacious small sound, the pinking of waterdrops on the linoleum under a defective radiator. You said you thought you were in for a sleepless night? Not exactly. He felt in fact quite sleepy and in no need of the alarmingly effective "Murphy Pill" which he resorted to now and then; but despite the drowsiness he was aware that a number of worries had crept up ready to pounce. What worries? Ordinary ones, nothing very serious or special. He lay on his back waiting for them to collect, which they did in unison with the pale blotches stealing up to take their accustomed position upon the ceiling as his eyes got used to the dark. He reflected that his wife was again feigning a feminine ailment to keep him away; that she probably cheated in many other ways; that he too betrayed her in a sense by concealing from her the one night spent with another girl, premaritally, in terms of time, but spatially in this very room; that preparing other people's books for publication was a debasing job; that no manner of permanent drudgery or temporary dissatisfaction mattered in the face of his ever growing, ever more tender, love for his wife; that he would have to consult an ophthalmologist sometime next mouth. He substituted an 'n' for the wrong letter and continued to scan the motley proof into which the blackness of closed vision was now turning. A double systole catapulted him into full consciousness again, and he promised his uncorrected self that he would limit his daily ration of cigarettes to a couple of heartbeats.

"And then you dropped off?"

"Yes. I may have still struggled to make out a vague line of print but—yes, I slept."

"Fitfully, I imagine?"

"No, on the contrary, my sleep was never deeper. You see, I had not slept for more than a few minutes the night before."

"O.K. Now I wonder if you are aware that psychologists attached to great prisons must have studied, among other things, that part of thanatology which deals with means and methods of violent death?"

Person emitted a weary negative sound.

"Well, let me put it this way: the police like to know what tool was used by the offender; the thanatologist wishes to know why and how it was used. Clear so far?"

Weary affirmative.

"Tools are, well—tools. They may, in fact, be an integral part of the worker, as, say, the carpenter's square is indeed part of the carpenter. Or the tools may be of flesh and bone like these" (taking Hugh's hands, patting each in turn, placing them on his palms for display or as if to begin some children's game).

His huge hands were returned to Hugh like two empty dishes. Next, it was explained to him that in strangling a young adult one of two methods was commonly used: the amateurish, none too efficient, frontal attack, and the more professional approach made from behind. In the first method, the eight fingers stiffly encircle the victim's neck while the two thumbs compress his or her throat; one runs, however, the risk of her or his hands seizing one's wrists or otherwise fighting off the assault. The second, much safer way, from behind, consists in pressing both thumbs hard against the back of the boy's or, preferably, girl's neck and working upon the throat with one's fingers. The first hold is dubbed among us "Pouce," the second "Fingerman." We know you attacked from the rear, but the following question arises: when you planned to throttle your wife why did you choose the Fingerman? Because you instinctively felt that its sudden and vigorous grip presented the best chance of success? Or did you have other, subjective, considerations in mind, such as thinking you'd really hate to watch her changes of facial expression during the process?

He did not plan anything. He had slept throughout the horrible automatic act, waking up only when both had landed on the floor by the bed.

He had mentioned dreaming the house was on fire?

That's right. Flames spurted all around and whatever one saw came through scarlet strips of vitreous plastic. His chance bedmate had flung the window wide open. Oh, who was she? She came from the past—a streetwalker he had picked up on his first trip abroad, some twenty years ago, a poor girl of mixed parentage, though actually American and very sweet, called Giulia Romeo, the surname means "pilgrim" in archaic Italian, but then we all are pilgrims, and all dreams are anagrams of diurnal reality. He dashed after her to stop her from jumping out. The window was large and low; it had a broad sill padded and sheeted, as was customary in that country of ice and fire. Such glaciers, such dawns! Giulia, or Julie, wore a Doppler shift over her luminous body and prostrated herself on the sill, with outspread arms still touching the wings of the window. He glanced down across her, and there, far below, in the chasm of the yard or garden, the selfsame flames moved like those tongues of red paper which a concealed ventilator causes to flicker around imitation yule logs in the festive shop-windows of snowbound childhoods. To leap, or try to lower oneself on knotted ledgelinen (the knotting was being demonstrated by a medievalish, sort of Flemish, long-necked shop-girl in a speculum at the back of his dream), seemed to him madness, and poor Hugh did all he could to restrain Juliet. Trying for the best hold, he had clutched her around the neck from behind, his square-nailed thumbs digging into her violet-lit nape, his eight fingers compressing her throat. A writhing windpipe was being shown on a screen of science cinema across the yard or street, but for the rest everything had become quite secure and comfortable: he had clamped Julia nicely and would have saved her from certain death if in her suicidal struggle to escape from the fire she had not slipped somehow over the sill and taken him with her into the void. What a fall! What a silly Julia! What luck that Mr. Romeo still gripped and twisted and cracked that crooked cricoid as X-rayed by the firemen and mountain guides in the street. How they flew! Superman carrying a young soul in his embrace!

The impact of the ground was far less brutal than he had expected. This is a bravura piece and not a patient's dream, Person. I shall have to report you. He hurt his elbow, and her night table collapsed with the lamp, a tumbler, a book; but Art be praised—she was safe, she was with him, she was lying quite still. He groped for the fallen lamp and neatly lit it in its unusual position. For a moment he wondered what his wife was doing there, prone on the floor, her fair hair spread as if she were flying. Then he stared at his bashful claws.

21

Dear Phil,

This, no doubt, is my last letter to you. I am leaving you. I am leaving you for another even greater Publisher. In that House I shall be proofread by cherubim—or misprinted by devils, depending on the department my poor soul is assigned to. So adieu, dear friend, and may your heir auction this off most profitably.

Its holographical nature is explained by the fact that I prefer it not to be read by Tom Tam or one of his boy typists. I am mortally sick after a botched operation in the only private room of a Bolognese hospital. The kind young nurse who will mail it has told me with dreadful carving gestures something I paid her for as generously as I would her favors if I still were a man. Actually the favors of death knowledge are infinitely more precious than those of love. According to my almond-eyed little spy, the great surgeon, may his own liver rot, lied to me when he declared yesterday with a deathhead's grin that the *operazione* had been *perfetta*. Well, it had been so in the sense Euler called zero the perfect number. Actually, they ripped me open, cast one horrified look at my decayed *fegato*, and without touching it sewed me up again.

I shall not bother you with the Tamworth problem. You should have seen the smug expression of the oblong fellow's bearded lips when he visited me this morning. As you know—as everybody, even Marion, knows—he gnawed his way into all my affairs, crawling into every cranny, collecting every German-accented word of mine, so that now he can boswell the dead man just as he had bossed very well the living one. I am also writing my and your lawyer about the measures I would like to be taken after my departure in order to thwart Tamworth at every turn of his labyrinthian plans.

The only child I have ever loved is the ravishing, silly, treacherous little Julia Moore. Every cent and centime I possess as well as all literary remains that can be twisted out of Tamworth's clutches must go to her, whatever the ambiguous obscurities contained in my will: Sam knows what I am hinting at and will act accordingly.

The last two parts of my Opus are in your hands. I am very sorry that Hugh Person is not there to look after its publication. When you acknowledge this letter do not say a word of having received it, but instead, in a kind of code that would tell me you bear in mind this letter, give me, as a good old gossip, some information about him—why, for example, was he jailed, for a year—or more?—if he was found to have acted in a purely epileptic trance; why was he transferred to an asylum for the criminal insane after his case was reviewed and no crime found? And why was he shuttled between prison and madhouse for the next five or six years before ending up as a privately treated patient? How can one treat dreams, unless one is a quack? Please tell me all this because Person was one of the nicest persons I knew and also because you can smuggle all kinds of secret information for this poor soul in your letter about him.

Poor soul is right, you know. My wretched liver is as heavy as a rejected manuscript; they manage to keep the hideous hyena pain at bay by means of frequent injections but somehow or other it remains always present *behind* the wall of my flesh like the muffled thunder of a permanent avalanche which obliterates there, beyond me, all the structures of my imagination, all the landmarks of my conscious self. It is comic— but I used to believe that dying persons saw the vanity of things, the futility of fame, passion, art, and so forth. I believed that treasured memories in a dying man's mind dwindled to rainbow wisps; but now I feel just the contrary: my most trivial sentiments and those of all men have acquired gigantic proportions. The entire solar system is but a reflection in the crystal of my (or your) wrist watch. The more I shrivel the bigger I grow. I suppose this is an uncommon phenomenon. Total rejection of all religions ever dreamt up by man and total composure in the face of total death! If I could explain this triple totality in one big book, that book would become no doubt a new bible and its author the founder of a new creed. Fortunately for my self-esteem that book will not be written—not merely because a dying man cannot write books but because that particular one would never express in one flash what can only be understood *immediately*.

Note added by the recipient:

Received on the day of the writer's death. File under Repos—R.

22

Person hated the sight and the feel of his feet. They were uncommonly graceless and sensitive. Even as a grown man he avoided looking at them when undressing. Hence he escaped the American mania of going barefoot at home—that throwback across childhood to plainer and thriftier times. What a jaggy chill he experienced at the mere thought of catching a toenail in the silk of a sock (silk socks were out, too)! Thus a woman shivers at the squeak of a rubbed pane. They were knobby, they were weak, they always hurt. Buying shoes equaled seeing the dentist. He now cast a long look of dislike at the article he had bought at Brig on the way to Witt. Nothing is ever wrapped up with such diabolical neatness as a shoebox. Ripping the paper off afforded him nervous relief. This pair of revoltingly heavy brown mountain boots had already once been tried on in the shop. They were certainly the right size, and quite as certainly they were not as comfortable as the salesman assured him they were. Snug, yes, but oppressively so. He pulled them on with a groan and laced them with imprecations. No matter, it must be endured. The climb he contemplated could not be accomplished in town shoes: the first and only time he had attempted to do so, he had kept losing his footing on slippery slabs of rock. These at least gripped treacherous surfaces. He also remembered the blisters inflicted by a similar pair, but made of chamois, that he had acquired eight years ago and thrown away when leaving Witt. Well, the left pinched a little less than the right—lame consolation.

He discarded his dark heavy jacket and put on an old windbreaker. As he went down the passage he encountered three steps before reaching the lift. The only purpose he could assign to them was that they warned him he was going to suffer.

But he dismissed the little ragged edge of pain, and lit a cigarette.

Typically, in the case of a second-rate hotel, its best view of the mountains was from the corridor windows at its north end. Dark, almost black rocky heights streaked with white, some of the ridges blending with the sullen overcast sky; lower down the fur of coniferous forests, still lower the lighter green of fields. Melancholy mountains! Glorified lumps of gravity!

The floor of the valley, with the townlet of Witt and various hamlets along a narrow river, consisted of dismal small meadows, with barbed-wire fences enclosing them and with a rank flowering of tall fennel for sole ornament. The river was as straight as a canal and all smothered in alder. The eye roamed wide but found no comfort in taking in the near and the far, this muddy cowtrack athwart a mowed slope or that plantation of regimented larches on the opposite rise.

The first stage of his revisitation (Person was prone to pilgrimages as had been a French ancestor of his, a Catholic poet and well-nigh a saint) consisted of a walk through Witt to a cluster of chalets on a slope above it. The townlet itself seemed even uglier and stragglier. He recognized the fountain, and the bank, and the church, and the great chestnut tree, and the café. And there was the post office, with the bench near its door waiting for letters that never came.

He crossed the bridge without stopping to listen to the vulgar noise of the stream which could tell him nothing. The slope had a fringe of firs at the top and beyond them stood additional firs—misty phantoms or replacement trees—in a grayish array under rain clouds. A new road had been built and new houses had grown, crowding out the meager landmarks he remembered or thought he remembered.

He now had to find Villa Nastia, which still retained a dead old woman's absurd Russian diminutive. She had sold it just before her last illness to a childless English couple. He would glance at the porch, as one uses a glazed envelope to slip in an image of the past.

Hugh hesitated at a street corner. Just beyond it a woman was selling vegetables from a stall. *Est-ce que vous savez, Madame*—Yes, she did, it was up that lane. As she spoke, a large, white, shivering dog crawled from behind a crate and with a shock of futile recognition Hugh remembered that eight years ago he had stopped right here and had noticed that dog, which was pretty old even then and had now braved fabulous age only to serve his blind memory.

The surroundings were unrecognizable—except for the white wall. His heart was beating as after an arduous climb. A blond little girl with a badminton racket crouched and picked up her shuttlecock from the sidewalk. Farther up he located Villa Nastia, now painted a celestial blue. All its windows were shuttered.

23

Choosing one of the marked trails leading into the mountains, Hugh recognized another detail of the past, namely the venerable inspector of benches—bird-defiled benches as old as he—that were rotting in shady nooks here and there, brown leaves below, green leaves above, by the side of a resolutely idyllic footpath ascending toward a waterfall. He remembered the inspector's pipe studded with Bohemian gems (in harmony with its owner's furuncular nose) and also the habit Armande had of exchanging ribald comments in Swiss-German with the old fellow while he was examining the rubbish under a cracked seat.

The region now offered tourists an additional number of climbs and cableways as well as a new motorcar road from Witt to the gondola station which Armande and her friends used to reach on foot. In his day Hugh had carefully studied the public map, a great Carte du Tendre or Chart of Torture, spread out on a billboard near the post office. Had he wished now to travel in comfort to the glacier slopes he could have taken the new bus which connected Witt with the Drakonita cable car. He wanted, however, to do it the old hard way and to pass through the unforgettable forest on his way up. He hoped the Drakonita gondola would be the remembered one—a small cabin with two benches facing each other. It rode up keeping some twenty yards above a strip of turfy slope

in a cutting between fir trees and alder bushes. Every thirty
seconds or so it negotiated a pylon with a sudden rattle and
shake but otherwise it glided with dignity.

Hugh's memory had bunched into one path the several
wood trails and logging roads that led to the first difficult
stage of the ascent—namely, a jumble of boulders and a jungle
of rhododendrons, through which one struck upward to reach
the cable car. No wonder he soon lost his way.

His memory, in the meantime, kept following its private
path. Again he was panting in her merciless wake. Again she
was teasing Jacques, the handsome Swiss boy with fox-red
body hair and dreamy eyes. Again she flirted with the eclectic
English twins, who called gullies Cool Wars and ridges Ah
Rates. Hugh, despite his tremendous physique, had neither
the legs nor the lungs to keep up with them even in memory.
And when the foursome had accelerated their climbing pace
and vanished with their cruel ice axes and coils of rope and
other instruments of torture (equipment exaggerated by ignorance), he rested on a rock, and, looking down, seemed to
see through the moving mists the making of the very mountains that his tormentors trod, the crystalline crust heaving up
with his heart from the bottom of an immemorial *more* (sea).
Generally, however, he would be urged not to straggle after
them even before they were out of the forest, a dismal group
of old firs, with steep muddy paths and thickets of wet willow
herb.

He now ascended through that wood, panting as painfully
as he had in the past when following Armande's golden nape
or a huge knapsack on a naked male back. As then the pressure
of the shoecap upon his right foot had soon scraped off a
round of skin at the joint of the third toe, resulting in a red
eye burning there through every threadbare thought. He finally shook the forest off and reached a rock-strewn field and
a barn that he thought he recalled, but the stream where he
had once washed his feet and the broken bridge which suddenly spanned the gap of time in his mind were nowhere to
be seen. He walked on. The day seemed a little brighter but
presently a cloud palmed the sun again. The path had reached
the pastures. He noticed a large white butterfly drop outspread on a stone. Its papery wings, blotched with black and

maculated with faded crimson, had transparent margins of an unpleasant crimped texture, which shivered slightly in the cheerless wind. Hugh disliked insects; this one looked particularly gross. Nevertheless, a mood of unusual kindliness made him surmount the impulse to crush it under a blind boot. With the vague idea that it must be tired and hungry and would appreciate being transferred to a nearby pin-cushion of little pink flowers, he stooped over the creature but with a great shuffle and rustle it evaded his handkerchief, sloppily flapped to overcome gravity, and vigorously sailed away.

He walked up to a signpost. Forty-five minutes to Lammerspitz, two hours and a half to Rimperstein. This was not the way to the glacier gondola. The distances indicated seemed as dull as delirium.

Round-browed gray rocks with patches of black moss and pale-green lichen lined the trail beyond the signpost. He looked at the clouds blurring the distant peaks or sagging like blubber between them. It was not worthwhile continuing that lone climb. Had she passed here, had her soles once imprinted their elaborate pattern in that clay? He considered the remnants of a solitary picnic, bits of eggshell broken off by the fingers of another solitary hiker who had sat here a few minutes ago, and a crumpled plastic bag into which a succession of rapid feminine hands had once conveyed with tiny tongs white apple roundlets, black prunes, nuts, raisins, the sticky mummy of a banana—all this digested by now. The grayness of rain would soon engulf everything. He felt a first kiss on his bald spot and walked back to the woods and widowhood.

Days like this give sight a rest and allow other senses to function more freely. Earth and sky were drained of all color. It was either raining or pretending to rain or not raining at all, yet still appearing to rain in a sense that only certain old Northern dialects can either express verbally or not express, but *versionize*, as it were, through the ghost of a sound produced by a drizzle in a haze of grateful rose shrubs. "Raining in Wittenberg, but not in Wittgenstein." An obscure joke in *Tralatitions*.

24

Direct interference in a person's life does not enter our scope of activity, nor, on the other, tralatitiously speaking, hand, is his destiny a chain of predeterminate links: some "future" events may be likelier than others, O.K., but all are chimeric, and every cause-and-effect sequence is always a hit-and-miss affair, even if the lunette has actually closed around your neck, and the cretinous crowd holds its breath.

Only chaos would result if some of us championed Mr. X, while another group backed Miss Julia Moore, whose interests, such as distant dictatorships, turned out to clash with those of her ailing old suitor Mr. (now Lord) X. The most we can do when steering a favorite in the best direction, in circumstances not involving injury to others, is to act as a breath of wind and to apply the lightest, the most indirect pressure such as *trying* to induce a dream that we *hope* our favorite will recall as prophetic if a likely event does actually happen. On the printed page the words "likely" and "actually" should be italicized too, at least *slightly*, to indicate a *slight* breath of wind inclining those characters (in the sense of both signs and personae). In fact, we depend on italics to an even greater degree than do, in their arch quaintness, writers of children's books.

Human life can be compared to a person dancing in a variety of forms around his own self: thus the vegetables of our first picture book encircled a boy in his dream—green cucumber, blue eggplant, red beet, Potato *père*, Potato *fils*, a girly asparagus, and, oh, many more, their spinning *ronde* going faster and faster and gradually forming a transparent ring of banded colors around a dead person or planet.

Another thing we are not supposed to do is to explain the inexplicable. Men have learned to live with a black burden, a huge aching hump: the supposition that "reality" may be only a "dream." How much more dreadful it would be if the very awareness of your being aware of reality's dreamlike nature were also a dream, a built-in hallucination! One should bear in mind, however, that there is no mirage without a vanishing point, just as there is no lake without a closed circle of reliable land.

We have shown our need for quotation marks ("reality," "dream"). Decidedly, the signs with which Hugh Person still peppers the margins of galleys have a metaphysical or zodiacal import! "Dust to dust" (the dead are good mixers, that's quite certain, at least). A patient in one of Hugh's mental hospitals, a bad man but a good philosopher, who was at that time terminally ill (hideous phrase that no quotes can cure) wrote for Hugh in the latter's Album of Asylums and Jails (a kind of diary he kept in those dreadful years):

> It is generally assumed that if man were to establish the fact of survival after death, he would also solve, or be on the way to solving, the riddle of Being. Alas, the two problems do not necessarily overlap or blend.

We shall close the subject on this bizarre note.

25

What had you expected of your pilgrimage, Person? A mere mirror rerun of hoary torments? Sympathy from an old stone? Enforced re-creation of irrecoverable trivia? A search for lost time in an utterly distinct sense from Goodgrief's dreadful "*Je me souviens, je me souviens de la maison où je suis né*" or, indeed, Proust's quest? He had never experienced here (save once at the end of his last ascent) anything but boredom and bitterness. Something else had made him revisit dreary drab Witt.

Not a belief in ghosts. Who would care to haunt half-remembered lumps of matter (he did not know that Jacques lay buried under six feet of snow in Chute, Colorado), uncertain itineraries, a club hut which some spell prevented him from reaching and whose name anyway had got hopelessly mixed with "Draconite," a stimulant no longer in production but still advertised on fences and even cliff walls. Yet something connected with spectral visitations had impelled him to come all the way from another continent. Let us make this a little clearer.

Practically all the dreams in which she had appeared to him after her death had been staged not in the settings of an American winter but in those of Swiss mountains and Italian lakes. He had not even found the spot in the woods where a gay band of little hikers had interrupted an unforgettable kiss. The desideratum was a moment of contact with her essential image in exactly remembered surroundings.

Upon returning to the Ascot Hotel he devoured an apple, pulled off his clay-smeared boots with a snarl of rejection, and, ignoring his sores and dampish socks, changed to the comfort of his town shoes. Back now to the torturing task!

Thinking that some small visual jog might make him recall the number of the room that he had occupied eight years ago, he walked the whole length of the third-floor corridor—and after getting only blank stares from one number after another, halted: the expedient had worked. He saw a very black 313 on a very white door and recalled instantly how he had told Armande (who had promised to visit him and did not wish to be announced): "Mnemonically it should be imagined as three little figures in profile, a prisoner passing by with one guard in front of him and another behind." Armande had rejoined that this was too fanciful for her, and that she would simply write it down in the little agenda she kept in her bag.

A dog yapped on the inner side of the door: the mark, he told himself, of substantial occupancy. Nevertheless, he carried away a feeling of satisfaction, the sense of having recovered an important morsel of that particular past.

Next, he proceeded downstairs and asked the fair receptionist to ring up the hotel in Stresa and find out if they could let him have for a couple of days the room where Mr. and Mrs. Hugh Person had stayed eight years ago. Its name, he said, sounded like "Beau Romeo." She repeated it in its correct form but said it might take a few minutes. He would wait in the lounge.

There were only two people there, a woman eating a snack in a far corner (the restaurant was unavailable, not yet having been cleaned after a farcical fight) and a Swiss businessman flipping through an ancient number of an American magazine (which had actually been left there by Hugh eight years ago, but this line of life nobody followed up). A table next to the

Swiss gentleman was littered with hotel pamphlets and fairly recent periodicals. His elbow rested on the *Transatlantic*. Hugh tugged at the magazine and the Swiss gentleman fairly sprang up in his chair. Apologies and counter-apologies blossomed into conversation. Monsieur Wilde's English resembled in many ways that of Armande, both in grammar and intonation. He had been shocked beyond measure by an article in Hugh's *Transatlantic* (borrowing it for a moment, wetting his thumb, finding the place and slapping the page with the back of his fingers as he returned the thing opened on the offensive article).

"One talks here of a man who murdered his spouse eight years ago and——"

The receptionist, whose desk and bust he could distinguish in miniature from where he sat, was signaling to him from afar. She burst out of her enclosure and advanced toward him:

"One does not reply," she said, "do you want me to keep trying?"

"Yes, oh yes," said Hugh, getting up, bumping into somebody (the woman who had enveloped the fat that remained of her ham in a paper napkin and was leaving the lounge). "Yes. Oh, excuse me. Yes, by all means. Do call Information or something."

Well, that murderer had been given life eight years ago (Person was given it, in an older sense, eight years ago, too, but squandered, squandered all of it in a sick dream!), and now, suddenly, he was set free, because, you see, he had been an exemplary prisoner and had even taught his cellmates such things as chess, Esperanto (he was a confirmed Esperantist), the best way to make pumpkin pie (he was also a pastry cook by trade), the signs of the zodiac, gin rummy, et cetera, et cetera. For some people, alas, a gal is nothing but a unit of acceleration used in geodesy.

It was appalling, continued the Swiss gentleman, using an expression Armande had got from Julia (now Lady X), really appalling how crime was pampered nowadays. Only today a temperamental waiter who had been accused of stealing a case of the hotel's Dôle (which Monsieur Wilde did not recommend, between parentheses) punched the maître d'hôtel in the eye, black-buttering it gravely. Did his interlocutor suppose that the hotel called the police? No, mister, they did not. *Eh bien*, on a higher (or lower) level the situation is similar. Had the bilinguist ever considered the problem of prisons?

Oh, he had. He himself had been jailed, hospitalized, jailed again, tried twice for throttling an American girl (now Lady X): "At one stage I had a monstrous cellmate—during a whole year. If I were a poet (but I'm only a proofreader) I would describe to you the celestial nature of solitary confinement, the bliss of an immaculate toilet, the liberty of thought in the ideal jail. The purpose of prisons" (smiling at Monsieur Wilde who was looking at his watch and not seeing much anyway) "is certainly not to cure a killer, nor is it only to punish him (how can one punish a man who has everything with him, within him, around him?). Their *only* purpose, a pedestrian purpose but the only logical one, is to prevent a killer from killing again. Rehabilitation? Parole? A myth, a joke. Brutes cannot be corrected. Petty thieves are not worth correcting (in their case punishment suffices). Nowadays, certain deplorable trends are current in *soi-disant* liberal circles. To put it concisely a killer who sees himself as a victim is not only a murderer but a moron."

"I think I must go," said poor stolid Wilde.

"Mental hospitals, wards, asylums, all that is also familiar to me. To live in a ward in a heap with thirty or so incoherent idiots is hell. I faked violence in order to get a solitary cell or to be locked up in the damned hospital's security wing, ineffable paradise for *this* kind of patient. My only chance to remain sane was by appearing subnormal. The way was thorny. A handsome and hefty nurse liked to hit me one forehand slap sandwiched between two backhand ones—and I returned to blessed solitude. I should add that every time my case came up, the prison psychiatrist testified that I refused to discuss what he called in his professional jargon 'conjugal sex.' I am sadly happy to say, sadly proud, too, that neither the guards (some of them humane and witty) nor the Freudian inquisitors (all of them fools or frauds) broke or otherwise changed the sad person I am."

Monsieur Wilde, taking him for a drunk or madman, had lumbered away. The pretty receptionist (flesh is flesh, the red sting is *l'aiguillon rouge*, and my love would not mind) had begun to signal again. He got up and walked to her desk. The Stresa hotel was undergoing repairs after a fire. *Mais* (pretty index erect)——

All his life, we are glad to note, our Person had experienced the curious sensation (known to three famous theologians and two minor poets) of there existing behind him—at his shoulder, as it were—a larger, incredibly wiser, calmer and stronger stranger, morally better than he. This was, in fact, his main "umbral companion" (a clownish critic had taken R. to task for that epithet) and had he been without that transparent shadow, we would not have bothered to speak about our dear Person. During the short stretch between his chair in the lounge and the girl's adorable neck, plump lips, long eyelashes, veiled charms, Person was conscious of something or somebody warning him that he should leave Witt there and then for Verona, Florence, Rome, Taormina, if Stresa was out. He did not heed his shadow, and fundamentally he may have been right. We thought that he had in him a few years of animal pleasure; we were ready to waft that girl into his bed, but after all it was for him to decide, for him to die, if he wished.

Mais! (a jot stronger than "but" or even "however") she had some good news for him. He had wanted to move to Floor Three, hadn't he? He could do so tonight. The lady with the little dog was leaving before dinner. It was a history rather amusing. It appeared that her husband looked after dogs when their masters had to absent themselves. The lady, when she voyaged herself, generally took with her a small animal, choosing from among those that were most melancholic. This morning her husband telephoned that the owner had returned earlier from his trip and was reclaiming his pet with great cries.

26

The hotel restaurant, a rather dismal place furnished in a rustic style, was far from full, but one expected two large families on the next day, and there was to be, or would have been (the folds of tenses are badly disarranged in regard to the building under examination) quite a nice little stream of Germans in the second, and cheaper, half of August. A new homely girl in a folklore costume revealing a lot of creamy bosom had replaced the younger of the two waiters, and a black patch masked the grim captain's left eye. Our Person was to be moved to room 313 right after dinner; he celebrated the coming event by drinking his sensible fill—a Bloody Ivan (vodka and tomato juice) before the pea soup, a bottle of Rhine with the pork (disguised as "veal cutlets") and a double marc with his coffee. Monsieur Wilde looked the other way as the dotty, or drugged, American passed by his table.

The room was exactly as he wanted it or had wanted it (tangled tenses again!) for her visit. The bed in its southwestern corner stood neatly caparisoned, and the maid who would or might knock in a little while to open it was not or would not be let in—if ins and outs, doors and beds still endured. On the bedside table a new package of cigarettes and a traveling clock had for neighbor a nicely wrapped box containing the green figurine of a girl skier which shone through the double kix. The little bedside rug, a glorified towel of the same pale blue as the bedspread, was still tucked under the night table, but since she refused in advance (capricious! prim!) to stay until dawn, she would not see, she would never see, the little rug doing its duty to receive the first square of sun and the first touch of Hugh's sticking-plastered toes. A bunch of bellflowers and bluebonnets (their different shades having a lovers' quarrel) had been placed, either by the assistant manager, who respected sentiment, or by Person himself, in a vase on the commode next to Person's shed tie, which was of a third shade of blue but of another material (sericanette). A mess of sprouts and mashed potatoes, colorfully mixed with pinkish meat, could be discerned, if properly focused, performing hand-over-fist evolutions in Person's entrails, and one could also make out in that landscape of serpents and caves two or three apple seeds, humble travelers from an earlier meal. His heart was tear-shaped, and undersized for such a big chap.

Returning to the correct level, we see Person's black rain-

coat on a hook and his charcoal-gray suitcoat over the back
of a chair. Under the dwarf writing desk, full of useless drawers, in the northeastern corner of the lamplit room, the bottom of the wastepaper basket, recently emptied by the valet,
retains a smudge of grease and a shred of paper napkin. The
little spitz dog is asleep on the back seat of an Amilcar being
driven by the kennelman's wife back to Trux.

Person visited the bathroom, emptied his bladder, and
thought of taking a shower, but she could come any moment
now—if she came at all! He pulled on his smart turtleneck,
and found a last antacid tablet in a remembered but not immediately located coat pocket (it is curious what difficulty
some people have in distinguishing at one glance the right
side from the left in a chaired jacket). She always said that real
men had to be impeccably dressed, yet ought not to bathe
too often. A male whiff from the *gousset* could, she said, be
most attractive in certain confrontations, and only ladies and
chambermaids should use deodorants. Never in his life had he
waited for anybody or anything with such excitement. His
brow was moist, he had the shakes, the corridor was long and
silent, the few occupants of the hotel were mostly downstairs,
in the lounge, chatting or playing cards, or just happily bal-
ancing on the soft brink of sleep. He bared the bed and rested
his head on the pillow while the heels of his shoes were still
in communication with the floor. Novices love to watch such
fascinating trifles as the shallow hollow in a pillow as seen
through a person's forehead, frontal bone, rippling brain, oc-
cipital bone, the back of the head, and its black hair. In the
beginning of our always entrancing, sometimes terrifying, new
being that kind of innocent curiosity (a child playing with
wriggly refractions in brook water, an African nun in an arctic
convent touching with delight the fragile clock of her first
dandelion) is not unusual, especially if a person and the shadows of related matter are being followed from youth to death.
Person, *this* person, was on the imagined brink of imagined
bliss when Armande's footfalls approached—striking out both
"imagined" in the proof's margin (never too wide for corrections and queries!). This is where the orgasm of art courses
through the whole spine with incomparably more force than
sexual ecstasy or metaphysical panic.

At this moment of her now indelible dawning through the limpid door of his room he felt the elation a tourist feels, when taking off and—to use a neo-Homeric metaphor—the earth slants and then regains its horizontal position, and practically in no spacetime we are thousands of feet above land, and the clouds (fleecy light clouds, very white, more or less widely separated) seem to lie on a flat sheet of glass in a celestial laboratory and, through this glass, far below it, bits of gingerbread earth show, a scarred hillside, a round indigo lake, the dark green of pine woods, the incrustations of villages. Here comes the air hostess bringing bright drinks, and she is Armande who has just accepted his offer of marriage though he warned her that she overestimated a lot of things, the pleasures of parties in New York, the importance of his job, a future inheritance, his uncle's stationery business, the mountains of Vermont—and now the airplane explodes with a roar and a retching cough.

Coughing, our Person sat up in asphyxiating darkness and groped for the light, but the click of the lamp was as ineffective as the attempt to move a paralyzed limb. Because the bed in his fourth-floor room had been in another, northern position, he now made for the door and flung it open instead of trying to escape, as he thought he could, through the window which stood ajar and banged wider as soon as a fatal draft carried in the smoke from the corridor.

The fire, fed first by oil-soaked rags planted in the basement and then helped up by lighter fluid judiciously sprayed here and there on stairs and walls, swept up rapidly through the hotel—although "fortunately," as the local paper was to put it next morning, "only a few people perished because only a few rooms happened to be occupied."

Now flames were mounting the stairs, in pairs, in trios, in redskin file, hand in hand, tongue after tongue, conversing and humming happily. It was not, though, the heat of their flicker, but the acrid dark smoke that caused Person to retreat back into the room; excuse me, said a polite flamelet holding open the door he was vainly trying to close. The window banged with such force that its panes broke into a torrent of rubies, and he realized before choking to death that a storm outside was aiding the inside fire. At last, suffocation made him try to get out by climbing out and down, but there were no ledges or balconies on that side of the roaring house. As he reached the window a long lavender-tipped flame danced up to stop him with a graceful gesture of its gloved hand. Crumbling partitions of plaster and wood allowed human cries to reach him, and one of his last wrong ideas was that those were the shouts of people anxious to help him, and not the howls of fellow men. Rings of blurred colors circled around him, reminding him briefly of a childhood picture in a frightening book about triumphant vegetables whirling faster and faster around a nightshirted boy trying desperately to awake from the iridescent dizziness of dream life. Its ultimate vision was the incandescence of a book or a box grown completely transparent and hollow. This is, I believe, *it*: not the crude anguish of physical death but the incomparable pangs of the mysterious mental maneuver needed to pass from one state of being to another.

Easy, you know, does it, son.

LOOK AT THE HARLEQUINS!

To Véra

I. Other Books by the Narrator

in russian:

Tamara   1925
Pawn Takes Queen   1927
Plenilune   1929
Camera Lucida (Slaughter in the Sun)   1931
The Red Top Hat   1934
The Dare   1950

in english:

See under Real   1939
Esmeralda and Her Parandrus   1941
Dr. Olga Repnin   1946
Exile from Mayda   1947
A Kingdom by the Sea   1962
Ardis   1970

Part One

I

I MET the first of my three or four successive wives in somewhat odd circumstances, the development of which resembled a clumsy conspiracy, with nonsensical details and a main
plotter who not only knew nothing of its real object but insisted
on making inept moves that seemed to preclude the slightest
possibility of success. Yet out of those very mistakes he unwit-
tingly wove a web, in which a set of reciprocal blunders on my
part caused me to get involved and fulfill the destiny that was
the only aim of the plot.

Some time during the Easter Term of my last Cambridge
year (1922) I happened to be consulted, "as a Russian," on
certain niceties of make-up in an English version of Gogol's
Inspector which the Glowworm Group, directed by Ivor Black,
a fine amateur actor, intended to stage. He and I had the same
tutor at Trinity, and he drove me to distraction with his tedious miming of the old man's mincing ways—a performance
he kept up throughout most of our lunch at the Pitt. The
brief business part turned out to be even less pleasant. Ivor
Black wanted Gogol's Town Mayor to wear a dressing gown
because "wasn't it merely the old rascal's nightmare and
didn't *Revizor*, its Russian title, actually come from the French
for 'dream,' *rêve*?" I said I thought it a ghastly idea.

If there were any rehearsals, they took place without me.
In fact, it occurs to me now that I do not really know if his
project ever saw the footlights.

Shortly after that, I met Ivor Black a second time—at some
party or other, in the course of which he invited me and five
other men to spend the summer at a Côte d'Azur villa he had
just inherited, he said, from an old aunt. He was very drunk
at the moment and seemed surprised when a week or so later
on the eve of his departure I reminded him of his exuberant
invitation, which, it so happened, I alone had accepted. We

both were unpopular orphans, and should, I remarked, band together.

Illness detained me in England for another month and it was only at the beginning of July that I sent Ivor Black a polite postcard advising him that I might arrive in Cannes or Nice some time next week. I am virtually sure I mentioned Saturday afternoon as the likeliest date.

Attempts to telephone from the station proved futile: the line remained busy, and I am not one to persevere in a struggle with faulty abstractions of space. But my afternoon was poisoned, and the afternoon is my favorite item of time. I had been coaxing myself into believing, at the start of my long journey, that I felt fairly fit; by now I felt terrible. The day was unseasonably dull and damp. Palm trees are all right only in mirages. For some reason, taxis, as in a bad dream, were unobtainable. Finally I boarded a small smelly bus of blue tin. Up a winding road, with as many turns as "stops by request," the contraption reached my destination in twenty minutes—about as long as it would have taken me to get there on foot from the coast by using an easy shortcut that I was to learn by heart, stone by stone, broom by brush, in the course of that magic summer. It appeared anything but magic during that dismal drive! The main reason I had agreed to come was the hope of treating in the "brilliant brine" (Bennett? Barbellion?) a nervous complaint that skirted insanity. The left side of my head was now a bowling alley of pain. On the other side an inane baby was staring at me across its mother's shoulder over the back of the seat in front of me. I sat next to a warty woman in solid black and pitted nausea against the lurches between green sea and gray rockwall. By the time we finally made it to the village of Carnavaux (mottled plane trunks, picturesque hovels, a post office, a church) all my senses had converged into one golden image; the bottle of whisky which I was bringing Ivor in my portmanteau and which I swore to sample even before he glimpsed it. The driver ignored the question I put to him, but a tortoise-like little priest with tremendous feet who was getting off before me indicated, without looking at me, a transverse avenue. The Villa Iris, he said, was at three minutes of march. As I prepared to carry my two bags up that lane toward a triangle of sudden

sunlight my presumptive host appeared on the opposite pavement. I remember—after the passing of half a century!—that
I wondered fleetingly if I had packed the right clothes. He
wore plus fours and brogues but was incongruously stockingless, and the inch of shin he showed looked painfully pink.
He was heading, or feigned to be heading, for the post office
to send me a telegram suggesting I put off my visit till August
when a job he now had in Cannice would no longer threaten
to interfere with our frolics. He hoped, furthermore, that Sebastian—whoever that was—might still be coming for the
grape season or lavender gala. Muttering thus under his
breath, he relieved me of the smaller of my bags—the one
with the toilet things, medical supplies, and an almost finished
garland of sonnets (which would eventually go to a Russian
émigré magazine in Paris). Then he also grabbed my portmanteau that I had set down in order to fill my pipe. Such
lavishness in the registration of trivialities is due, I suppose, to
their being accidentally caught in the advance light of a great
event. Ivor broke the silence to add, frowning, that he was
delighted to welcome me as a house guest, but that he should
warn me of something he ought to have told me about in
Cambridge. I might get frightfully bored by the end of a week
or so because of one melancholy fact. Miss Grunt, his former
governess, a heartless but clever person, liked to repeat that
his little sister would never break the rule of "children should
not be heard" and indeed would never hear it said to anybody. The melancholy fact was that his sister—but, perhaps,
he had better postpone the explanation of her case till we and
the bags were installed more or less.

2

"What kind of childhood did *you* have, McNab" (as Ivor insisted on calling me because I looked, he thought, like the
haggard yet handsome young actor who adopted that name
in the last years of his life or at least fame)?

Atrocious, intolerable. There should be a natural, inter-natural, law against such inhuman beginnings. Had my morbid terrors not been replaced at the age of nine or ten by more abstract and trite anxieties (problems of infinity, eternity, identity, and so forth), I would have lost my reason long before finding my rhymes. It was not a matter of dark rooms, or one-winged agonizing angels, or long corridors, or nightmare mirrors with reflections overflowing in messy pools on the floor—it was not *that* bedchamber of horrors, but simply, and far more horribly, a certain insidious and relentless connection with other states of being which were not exactly "previous" or "future," but definitely out of bounds, mortally speaking. I was to learn more, much more about those aching links only several decades later, so "let us not anticipate" as the condemned man said when rejecting the filthy old blindfold.

The delights of puberty granted me temporary relief. I was spared the morose phase of self-initiation. Blest be my first sweet love, a child in an orchard, games of exploration—and her outspread five fingers dripping with pearls of surprise. A house tutor let me share with him the ingénue in my grand-uncle's private theater. Two lewd young ladies rigged me up once in a lacy chemise and a Lorelei wig and laid me to sleep between them, "a shy little cousin," as in a ribald novella, while their husbands snored in the next room after the boar hunt. The great houses of various relatives with whom I dwelt on and off in my early teens under the pale summer skies of this or that province of old Russia offered me as many compliant handmaids and fashionable flirts as might have done closets and bowers a couple of centuries earlier. In a word, if the years of my infancy might have provided the subject for the kind of learned thesis upon which a paedopsychologist founds a lifetime of fame, my teens, on the other hand, could have yielded, and in fact did yield, quite a number of erotic passages scattered like rotting plums and brown pears throughout an aging novelist's books. Indeed, the present memoir derives much of its value from its being a *catalogue raisonné* of the roots and origins and amusing birth canals of many images in my Russian and especially English fiction.

I saw my parents infrequently. They divorced and remarried and redivorced at such a rapid rate that had the custodians of my fortune been less alert, I might have been auctioned out finally to a pair of strangers of Swedish or Scottish descent, with sad bags under hungry eyes. An extraordinary grand-aunt, Baroness Bredow, born Tolstoy, amply replaced closer blood. As a child of seven or eight, already harboring the secrets of a confirmed madman, I seemed even to her (who also was far from normal) unduly sulky and indolent; actually, of course, I kept daydreaming in a most outrageous fashion.

"Stop moping!" she would cry: "Look at the harlequins!"

"What harlequins? Where?"

"Oh, everywhere. All around you. Trees are harlequins, words are harlequins. So are situations and sums. Put two things together—jokes, images—and you get a triple harlequin. Come on! Play! Invent the world! Invent reality!"

I did. By Jove, I did. I invented my grand-aunt in honor of my first daydreams, and now, down the marble steps of memory's front porch, here she slowly comes, sideways, sideways, the poor lame lady, touching each step edge with the rubber tip of her black cane.

(When she cried out those four words, they came out in a breathless dactylic line with a swift lispy lilt, as if it were "look-aty," assonating with "lickety" and introducing tenderly, ingratiatingly those "harlequins" who arrived with festive force, the "har" richly stressed in a burst of inspired persuasion followed by a liquid fall of sequin-like syllables).

I was eighteen when the Bolshevist revolution struck—a strong and anomalous verb, I concede, used here solely for the sake of narrative rhythm. The recurrence of my childhood's disarray kept me in the Imperial Sanatorium at Tsarskoe for most of the next winter and spring. In July, 1918, I found myself recuperating in the castle of a Polish landowner, a distant relation of mine, Mstislav Charnetski (1880–1919?). One autumn evening poor Mstislav's young mistress showed me a fairy-tale path winding through a great forest where a last aurochs had been speared by a first Charnetski under John III (Sobieski). I followed that path with a knapsack on my back and—why not confess—a tremor of remorse and anxiety in my young heart. Was I right in abandoning my cousin in the blackest hour of Russia's black history? Did I know how to exist alone in strange lands? Was the diploma I had received after being examined by a special committee (presided by

Mstislav's father, a venerable and corrupt mathematician) in all the subjects of an ideal lyceum, which I had never attended bodily, sufficient for Cambridge without some infernal entrance test? I trudged all night, through a labyrinth of moonlight, imagining the rustlings of extinct animals. Dawn at last miniated my ancient map. I thought I had crossed the frontier when a bare-headed Red Army soldier with a Mongol face who was picking whortleberries near the trail challenged me: "And whither," he asked picking up his cap from a stump, "may you be rolling (*katishsya*), little apple (*yablochko*)? *Pokazyvay-ka dokumentiki* (Let me see your papers)."

I groped in my pockets, fished out what I needed, and shot him dead, as he lunged at me; then he fell on his face, as if sunstruck on the parade ground, at the feet of his king. None of the serried tree trunks looked his way, and I fled, still clutching Dagmara's lovely little revolver. Only half an hour later, when I reached at last another part of the forest in a more or less conventional republic, only then did my calves cease to quake.

After a period of loafing through unremembered German and Dutch towns, I crossed over to England. The Rembrandt, a little hotel in London, was my next address. The two or three small diamonds that I kept in a chamois pouch melted away faster than hailstones. On the gray eve of poverty, the author, then a self-exiled youth (I transcribe from an old diary), discovered an unexpected patron in the person of Count Starov, a grave old-fashioned Mason who had graced several great Embassies during a spacious span of international intercourse, and who since 1913 had resided in London. He spoke his mother tongue with pedantic precision, yet did not spurn rotund folksy expressions. He had no sense of humor whatever. His man was a young Maltese (I loathe tea but dared not call for brandy). Nikifor Nikodimovich, to use his tongue-twisterish Christian name *cum* patronymic, was rumored to have been for years on end an admirer of my beautiful and bizarre mother, whom I knew mainly from stock phrases in an anonymous memoir. A *grande passion* can be a convenient mask, but on the other hand, a gentlemanly devotion to her memory can alone explain his paying for my education in England and leaving me, after his death in 1927, a modest subsidy (the Bolshevist *coup* had ruined him as it had all our clan). I must admit, however, that I felt embarrassed by the sudden live glances of his otherwise dead eyes set in a large, pasty, dignified face, of the sort that Russian writers used to call "carefully shaven" (*tshchatel'no vybritoe*), no doubt because the ghosts of patriarchal beards had to be laid, in the presumed imagination of readers (long dead by now). I did my best to put down those interrogatory flashes to a search for some traits of the exquisite woman whom once upon a time he had handed into a *calèche*, and whom, after waiting for her to settle down and open her parasol, he would heavily join in the springy vehicle; but at the same time I could not help wondering if my old *grandee* had escaped a perversion that was current in so-called circles of high diplomacy. N.N. sat in his easy chair as in a voluminous novel, one pudgy hand on the elbow-rest griffin, the other, signet-ringed, fingering on the Turkish table beside him what looked like a silver snuffbox but contained, in fact, a small supply of bead-like cough drops or rather droplets, colored lilac, green, and, I believe, coral. I should add that some information obtained later showed me to be detestably wrong in conjecturing on his part anything but a quasi-paternal interest in me, as well as in another youth, the son of a notorious St. Petersburg courtesan who preferred an electric brougham to a *calèche*; but enough of those edible beads.

3

To return to Carnavaux, to my luggage, to Ivor Black carrying it, with a big show of travail, and muttering comedy stuff in some rudimentary role.

The sun had regained full control, when we entered a garden, separated from the road by a stone wall and a row of cypresses. Emblematic irises surrounded a green pondlet presided over by a bronze frog. From under a curly holm oak a graveled path ran between two orange trees. At one end of the lawn a eucalypt cast its striate shade across the canvas of a lounge chair. This is not the arrogance of total recall but an attempt at fond reconstruction based on old snapshots in an old bonbon box with a fleur-de-lis on its lid.

It was no use ascending the three steps of the front entrance, "hauling two tons of stones," said Ivor Black: he had forgotten the spare key, had no servants to answer bells on Saturday afternoons, and as he had explained earlier could not communicate by normal means with his sister though she had to be somewhere inside, almost certainly crying in her bedroom as she usually would whenever guests were expected, especially weekenders who might be around at all hours, well into Tuesday. So we walked round the house, skirting prickly-pear shrubs that caught at the raincoat over my arm. I suddenly heard a horrible subhuman sound and glanced at Ivor, but the cur only grinned.

It was a large, lemon-breasted, indigo-blue ara with striped white cheeks squawking intermittently on its bleak back-porch perch. Ivor had dubbed it Mata Hari partly because of its accent but chiefly by reason of its political past. His late aunt, Lady Wimberg, when already a little gaga, around Nineteen Fourteen or Fifteen, had been kind to that tragic old bird, said to have been abandoned by a shady stranger with a scarred face and a monocle. It could say *allô*, Otto, and pa-pa, a modest vocabulary, somehow suggestive of a small anxious family in a hot country far from home. Sometimes when I work too late and the spies of thought cease to relay messages, a wrong word in motion feels somehow like the dry biscuit that a parrot holds in its great slow hand.

I do not remember seeing Iris before dinner (or perhaps I glimpsed her standing at a stained window on the stairs with her back to me as I popped back from the *salle d'eau* and its hesitations to my ascetic room across the landing). Ivor had taken care to inform me that she was a deaf-mute and such a shy one, too, that even now, at twenty-one, she could not make herself learn to read male lips. That sounded odd. I had always thought that the infirmity in question confined the patient in an absolutely safe shell as limpid and strong as shatterproof glass, within which no shame or sham could exist. Brother and sister conversed in sign language using an alphabet which they had invented in childhood and which had gone through several revised editions. The present one consisted of preposterously elaborate gestures in the low relief of a pantomime that mimicked things rather than symbolized them. I barged in with some grotesque contribution of my own but Ivor asked me sternly not to play the fool, she easily got offended. The whole affair (with a sullen maid, an old Canniçoise slapping down plates in the margin of the scene) belonged to another life, to another book, to a world of vaguely incestuous games that I had not yet consciously invented.

Both were small, but exquisitely formed, young people, and the family likeness between them could not escape one though Ivor was quite plain looking, with sandy hair and freckles, and she a suntanned beauty with a black bob and eyes like clear honey. I do not recall the dress she wore at our first meeting, but I know that her thin arms were bare and stung my senses at every palm grove and medusa-infested island that she outlined in the air while her brother translated for me her patterns in idiotic asides. I had my revenge after dinner. Ivor had gone to fetch my whisky. Iris and I stood on the terrace in the saintly dusk. I was lighting my pipe while Iris nudged the balustrade with her hip and pointed out with mermaid undulations—supposed to imitate waves—the shimmer of seaside lights in a parting of the india-ink hills. At that moment the telephone rang in the drawing room behind us, and she quickly turned around—but with admirable presence of mind transformed her dash into a nonchalant shawl dance. In the meantime Ivor had already skated phoneward across the parquetry to hear what Nina Lecerf or some other neighbor wanted. We liked to recall, Iris and I, in our later intimacy that revelation scene with Ivor bringing us drinks to toast her fairy-tale recovery and she, without minding his presence, putting her light hand on my knuckles: I stood gripping the balustrade in exaggerated resentment and was not prompt enough, poor dupe, to acknowledge her apology by a Continental hand kiss.

4

A familiar symptom of my complaint, not its gravest one but the toughest to get rid of after every relapse, belongs to what Moody, the London specialist, was the first to term the "numerical nimbus" syndrome. His account of my case has been recently reprinted in his collected works. It teems with ludicrous inaccuracies. That "nimbus" means nothing. "Mr. N., a Russian nobleman" did *not* display any "signs of degeneracy." He was not "32" but 22 when he consulted that fatuous celebrity. Worst of all, Moody lumps me with a Mr. V.S. who is less of a postscriptum to the abridged description of *my* "nimbus" than an intruder whose sensations are mixed with mine throughout that learned paper. True, the symptom in question is not easy to describe, but I think I can do better than either Professor Moody or my vulgar and voluble fellow sufferer.

At its worst it went like this: An hour or so after falling asleep (generally well after midnight and with the humble assistance of a little Old Mead or Chartreuse) I would wake up (or rather "wake in") momentarily mad. The hideous pang in my brain was triggered by some hint of faint light in the line of my sight, for no matter how carefully I might have topped the well-meaning efforts of a servant by my own struggles with blinds and purblinds, there always remained some damned slit, some atom or dimmet of artificial streetlight or natural moonlight that signaled inexpressible peril when I raised my head with a gasp above the level of a choking dream. Along the dim slit brighter points traveled with dreadful meaningful intervals between them. Those dots corresponded, perhaps, to my rapid heartbeats or were connected optically with the blinking of wet eyelashes but the rationale of it is inessential; its dreadful part was my realizing in helpless panic that the event had been stupidly unforeseen, yet had been bound to happen and was the representation of a fatidic problem which had to be solved lest I perish and indeed might have been solved now if I had given it some forethought or had been less sleepy and weak-witted at this all-important moment. The problem itself was of a calculatory order: certain relations between the twinkling points had to be measured or, in my case, guessed, since my torpor prevented me from counting them properly, let alone recalling what the *safe* number should be. Error meant instant retribution—beheading by a giant or worse; the right guess, per contra, would allow me to escape into an enchanting region situated just beyond the gap I had to wriggle through in the thorny riddle, a region resembling in its idyllic abstraction those little landscapes engraved as suggestive vignettes—a brook, a *bosquet*—next to capital letters of weird, ferocious shape such as a Gothic *B* beginning a chapter in old books for easily frightened children. But how could I know in my torpor and panic that *this* was the simple solution, that the brook and the boughs and the beauty of the Beyond all began with the initial of Being?

There were nights, of course, when my reason returned at once and I rearranged the curtains and presently slept. But at other, more critical times, when I was far from well yet and would experience that nobleman's nimbus, it took me up to several hours to abolish the optical spasm which even the light of day could not overcome. My first night in any new place never fails to be hideous and is followed by a dismal day. I was racked with neuralgia, I was jumpy, and pustulous, and unshaven, and I refused to accompany the Blacks to a seaside party to which I had been, or was told I had been, also invited. In fact, those first days at Villa Iris are so badly distorted in my diary, and so blurred in my mind, that I am not sure if, perhaps, Iris and Ivor were not absent till the middle of the week. I remember, however, that they were kind enough to arrange an appointment for me with a doctor in Cannice. This presented itself as a splendid opportunity to check the incompetence of my London luminary against that of a local one.

The appointment was with Professor Junker, a double personage, consisting of husband and wife. They had been practicing as a team for thirty years now, and every Sunday, in a secluded, though consequently rather dirty, corner of the beach, the two analyzed each other. They were supposed by their patients to be particularly alert on Mondays, but I was not, having got frightfully tight in one or two pubs before reaching the mean quarter where the Junkers and other doctors lived, as I seemed to have gathered. The front entrance was all right being among the flowers and fruit of a market

place, but wait till you see the back. I was received by the
female partner, a squat old thing wearing trousers, which was
delightfully daring in 1922. That theme was continued immediately outside the casement of the W.C. (where I had to
fill an absurd vial large enough for a doctor's purpose but not
for mine) by the performance that a breeze was giving above
a street sufficiently narrow for three pairs of long drawers to
cross over on a string in as many strides or leaps. I commented
on this and on a stained-glass window in the consulting room
featuring a mauve lady exactly similar to the one on the stairs
of Villa Iris. Mrs. Junker asked me if I liked boys or girls, and
I looked around saying guardedly that I did not know what
she had to offer. She did not laugh. The consultation was not
a success. Before diagnosing neuralgia of the jaw, she wanted
me to see a dentist when sober. It was right across, she said.
I know she rang him up to arrange my visit but do not remember if I went there the same afternoon or the next. His
name was Molnar with that *n* like a grain in a cavity; I used
him some forty years later in *A Kingdom by the Sea.*

A girl whom I took to be the dentist's assistant (which,
however, she was much too holidayish in dress to be) sat
cross-legged talking on the phone in the hallway and merely
directed me to a door with the cigarette she was holding without otherwise interrupting her occupation. I found myself in
a banal and silent room. The best seats had been taken. A
large conventional oil, above a cluttered bookshelf, depicted
an alpine torrent with a fallen tree lying across it. From the
shelf a few magazines had already wandered at some earlier
consultation hour onto an oval table which supported its own
modest array of things, such as an empty flower vase and a
watch-size *casse-tête.* This was a wee circular labyrinth, with
five silvery peas inside that had to be coaxed by judicious turns
of the wrist into the center of the helix. For waiting children.

None were present. A corner armchair contained a fat fellow
with a nosegay of carnations across his lap. Two elderly ladies
were seated on a brown sofa—strangers to each other, if one
took into account the urbane interval between them. Leagues
away from them, on a cushioned stool, a cultured-looking
young man, possibly a novelist, sat holding a small memo-

randa book in which he kept penciling separate items—possibly the description of various objects his eyes roved over in between notes—the ceiling, the wallpaper, the picture, and the hairy nape of a man who stood by the window, with his hands clasped behind him, and gazed idly, beyond flapping underwear, beyond the mauve casement of the Junkers' W.C., beyond the roofs and foothills, at a distant range of mountains where, I idly thought, there still might exist that withered pine bridging the painted torrent.

Presently a door at the end of the room flew open with a laughing sound, and the dentist entered, ruddy-faced, bow-tied, in an ill-fitting suit of festive gray with a rather jaunty black armband. Handshakes and congratulations followed. I started reminding him of our appointment, but a dignified old lady in whom I recognized Madame Junker interrupted me saying it was her mistake. In the meantime Miranda, the daughter of the house whom I had seen a moment ago, inserted the long pale stems of her uncle's carnations into a tight vase on the table which by now was miraculously draped. A soubrette placed upon it, amid much applause, a great sunset-pink cake with "50" in calligraphic cream. "What a charming attention!" exclaimed the widower. Tea was served and several groups sat down, others stood, glass in hand. I heard Iris warning me in a warm whisper that it was spiced apple juice, not liquor, so with raised hands I recoiled from the tray proffered by Miranda's fiancé, the person whom I had caught using a spare moment to check certain details of the dowry. "We were not expecting you to turn up," said Iris, giving the show away, for this could not be the *partie de plaisir* to which I had been invited ("They have a lovely place on a rock"). No, I believe that much of the confused impressions listed here in connection with doctors and dentists must be classed as an oneiric experience during a drunken siesta. This is corroborated scriptorially. Glancing through my oldest notes in pocket diaries, with telephone numbers and names elbowing their way among reports on events, factual or more or less fictional, I notice that dreams and other distortions of "reality" are written down in a special left-slanted hand—at least in the earlier entries, before I gave up following accepted distinctions. A lot of the pre-Cantabrigian stuff displays that script (but the soldier really did collapse in the path of the fugitive king).

5

I know I have been called a solemn owl but I do detest practical jokes and am bored stiff ("Only humorless people use that phrase," according to Ivor) by a constant flow of facetious insults and vulgar puns ("A stiff borer is better than a limp one"—Ivor again). He was a good chap, however, and it was not really respite from his banter that made me welcome his regular week-day absences. He worked in a travel agency run by his Aunt Betty's former *homme d'affaires*, an eccentric in his own right, who had promised Ivor a bonus in the form of an Icarus phaeton if he was good.

My health and handwriting very soon reverted to normal, and I began to enjoy the South. Iris and I lounged for hours (she wearing a black swimsuit, I flannels and blazer) in the garden, which I preferred at first, before the inevitable seduction of seabathing, to the flesh of the *plage*. I translated for her several short poems by Pushkin and Lermontov, paraphrasing and touching them up for better effect. I told her in dramatic detail of my escape from my country. I mentioned great exiles of old. She listened to me like Desdemona.

"I'd love to learn Russian," she said with the polite wistfulness which goes with that confession. "My aunt was practically born in Kiev and at seventy-five still remembered a few Russian and Rumanian words, but I am a rotten linguist. How do you say 'eucalypt' in your language?"

"*Evkalipt.*"

"Oh, that would make a nice name for a man in a short story. 'F. Clipton.' Wells has a 'Mr. Snooks' that turns out to derive from 'Seven Oaks.' I adore Wells, don't you?"

I said that he was the greatest romancer and magician of our time, but that I could not stand his sociological stuff.

Nor could she. And did I remember what Stephen said in

The Passionate Friends when he left the room—the neutral room—where he had been allowed to see his mistress for the very last time?

"I can answer that. The furniture there was slip-covered, and he said, 'It's because of the flies.'"

"Yes! Isn't that marvelous! Just blurting out something so as not to cry. It makes one think of the housefly an old Master would paint on a sitter's hand to show that the person had died in the meantime."

I said I always preferred the literal meaning of a description to the symbol behind it. She nodded thoughtfully but did not seem convinced.

And who was our favorite modern poet? How about Housman?

I had seen him many times from afar and once, plain. It was in the Trinity Library. He stood holding an open book but looking at the ceiling as if trying to remember something—perhaps, the way another author had translated that line.

She said she would have been "terribly thrilled." She uttered those words thrusting forward her earnest little face and vibrating it, the face, with its sleek bangs, rapidly.

"You ought to be thrilled *now*! After all, I'm *here*, this is the summer of 1922, this is your brother's house—"

"It is not," she said, sidestepping the issue (and at the twist of her speech I felt a sudden overlap in the texture of time as if this had happened before or would happen again); "It is *my* house, Aunt Betty left it to *me* as well as some money, but Ivor is too stupid or proud to let me pay his appalling debts."

The shadow of my rebuke was more than a shadow. I actually believed even then, in my early twenties, that by mid-century I would be a famous and free author, living in a free, universally respected Russia, on the English quay of the Neva or on one of my splendid estates in the country, and writing there prose and poetry in the infinitely plastic tongue of my ancestors: among them I counted one of Tolstoy's grand-aunts and two of Pushkin's boon companions. The forefeel of fame was as heady as the old wines of nostalgia. It was remembrance in reverse, a great lakeside oak reflected so picturesquely in such clear waters that its mirrored branches looked like glorified roots. I felt this future fame in my toes, in the tips of my fingers, in the hair of my head, as one feels the shiver caused by an electric storm, by the dying beauty of a singer's dark voice just before the thunder, or by one line in *King Lear*. Why do tears blur my glasses when I invoke that phantasm of fame as it tempted and tortured me then, five decades ago? Its image was innocent, its image was genuine, its difference from what actually was to be breaks my heart like the pangs of separation.

No ambition, no honors tainted the fanciful future. The President of the Russian Academy advanced toward me to the sound of slow music with a wreath on the cushion he held—and had to retreat growling as I shook my graying head. I saw myself correcting the page proof of a new novel which was to change the destiny of Russian literary style as a matter of course—*my* course (with no self-love, no smugness, no surprise on my part)—and reworking so much of it in the margin—where inspiration finds its sweetest clover—that the whole had to be set anew. When the book made its belated appearance, as I gently aged, I might enjoy entertaining a few dear sycophantic friends in the arbor of my favorite manor of Marevo (where I had first "looked at the harlequins") with its alley of fountains and its shimmering view of a virgin bit of Volgan steppe-land. It *had* to be that way.

From my cold bed in Cambridge I surveyed a whole period of new Russian literature. I looked forward to the refreshing presence of inimical but courteous critics who would chide me in the St. Petersburg literary reviews for my pathological indifference to politics, major ideas in minor minds, and such vital problems as overpopulation in urban centers. No less amusing was it to envisage the inevitable pack of crooks and ninnies abusing the smiling marble, and ill with envy, maddened by their own mediocrity, rushing in pattering hordes to the lemming's doom but presently all running back from the opposite side of the stage, having missed not only the point of my book but also their rodential Gadara.

The poems I started composing after I met Iris were meant to deal with her actual, unique traits—the way her forehead wrinkled when she raised her eyebrows, waiting for me to see the point of her joke, or the way it developed a totally different set of soft folds as she frowned over the Tauchnitz in which she searched for the passage she wanted to share with me. My instrument, however, was still too blunt and immature; it could not express the divine detail, and *her* eyes, *her* hair became hopelessly generalized in my otherwise well-shaped strophes.

None of those descriptive and, let us be frank, banal pieces, were good enough (particularly when nakedly Englished without rhyme or treason) to be shown to Iris; and, besides, an odd shyness—which I had never felt before when courting a girl in the brisk preliminaries of my carnal youth—kept me back from submitting to Iris a tabulation of her charms. On the night of July 20, however, I composed a more oblique, more metaphysical little poem which I decided to show her at breakfast in a literal translation that took me longer to write than the original. The title, under which it appeared in an *émigré* daily in Paris (October 8, 1922, after several reminders on my part and one please-return request) was, and is, in the various anthologies and collections that were to reprint it in the course of the next fifty years, *Vlyublyonnost'*, which puts in a golden nutshell what English needs three words to express.

> *My zabyváem chto vlyublyónnost'*
> *Ne prósto povorót litsá,*
> *A pod kupávami bezdónnost',*
> *Nochnáya pánika plovtsá.*
>
> *Pokúda snítsya, snís', vlyublyónnost',*
> *No probuzhdéniem ne múch',*
> *I lúchshe nedogovoryónnost'*
> *Chem éta shchél' i étot lúch.*
>
> *Napomináyu chto vlyublyónnost'*
> *Ne yáv', chto métiny ne té,*
> *Chto mózhet-byt' potustorónnost'*
> *Priotvorílas' v temnoté.*

"Lovely," said Iris. "Sounds like an incantation. What does it mean?"

"I have it here on the back. It goes like this. We forget—or rather tend to forget—that being in love (*vlyublyonnost'*) does not depend on the facial angle of the loved one, but is a bottomless spot under the nenuphars, *a swimmer's panic in the night* (here the iambic tetrameter happens to be rendered—last line of the first stanza, *nochnáya pánika plovtsá*). Next stanza: While the dreaming is good—in the sense of 'while the going is good'—do keep appearing to us in our dreams, *vlyublyonnost'*, but do not torment us by waking us up or telling too much: reticence is better than that chink and that moonbeam. Now comes the last stanza of this philosophical love poem."

"This what?"

"Philosophical love poem. *Napomináyu*, I remind you, that *vlyublyonnost'* is not wide-awake reality, that the markings are not the same (a moon-striped ceiling, *polosatyy ot luny potolok*, is, for instance, not the same kind of reality as a ceiling by day), and that, maybe, the hereafter stands slightly ajar in the dark. *Voilà*."

"Your girl," remarked Iris, "must be having a jolly good time in your company. Ah, here comes our breadwinner. *Bonjour*, Ives. The toast is all gone, I'm afraid. We thought you'd left hours ago."

She fitted her palm for a moment to the cheek of the teapot. And it went into *Ardis*, it all went into *Ardis*, my poor dead love.

6

After fifty summers, or ten thousand hours, of sunbathing in various countries, on beaches, benches, roofs, rocks, decks, ledges, lawns, boards, and balconies, I might have been unable to recall my novitiate in sensory detail had not there been those old notes of mine which are such a solace to a pedantic memoirist throughout the account of his illnesses, marriages, and literary life. Enormous amounts of Shaker's Cold Cream were rubbed by kneeling and cooing Iris into my back as I lay prone on a rough towel in the blaze of the *plage*. Beneath my shut eyelids pressed to my forearm swam purple photomatic shapes: "Through the prose of sun blisters came the poetry of her touch—," thus in my pocket diary, but I can improve upon my young preciosity. Through the itch of my skin, and in fact seasoned by that itch to an exquisite degree of rather ridiculous enjoyment, the touch of her hand on my shoulder blades and along my spine resembled too closely a deliberate caress not to be deliberate mimicry, and I could not curb a hidden response to those nimble fingers when in a final gratuitous flutter they traveled down to my very coccyx, before fading away.

"There," said Iris with exactly the same intonation as that used, at the end of a more special kind of treatment, by one of my Cambridge sweethearts, Violet McD., an experienced and compassionate virgin.

She, Iris, had had several lovers, and as I opened my eyes and turned to her, and saw her, and the dancing diamonds in the blue-green inward of every advancing, every tumbling wave, and the wet black pebbles on the sleek forebeach with dead foam waiting for live foam—and, oh, there it comes, the crested wave line, trotting again like white circus ponies abreast—I understood, as I perceived her against that backdrop, how much adulation, how many lovers had helped form and perfect my Iris, with that impeccable complexion of hers, that absence of any uncertainty in the profile of her high cheekbone, the elegance of the hollow beneath it, the *accroche-coeur* of a sleek little flirt.

"By the way," said Iris as she changed from a kneeling to a half-recumbent position, her legs curled under her, "by the way, I have not apologized yet for my dismal remark about that poem. I now have reread your "Valley Blondies" (*vlyublyonnost'*) a hundred times, both the English for the matter and the Russian for the music. I think it's an absolutely divine piece. Do you forgive me?"

I pursed my lips to kiss the brown iridescent knee near me but her hand, as if measuring a child's fever, palmed my forehead and stopped its advance.

"We are watched," she said, "by a number of eyes which seem to look everywhere except in our direction. The two nice English schoolteachers on my right—say, twenty paces away—have already told me that your resemblance to the naked-neck photo of Rupert Brooke is *a-houri-sang*—they know a little French. If you ever try to kiss me, or my leg, again, I'll beg you to leave. I've been sufficiently hurt in my life."

A pause ensued. The iridescence came from atoms of quartz. When a girl starts to speak like a novelette, all you need is a little patience.

Had I posted the poem to that *émigré* paper? Not yet; my garland of sonnets had had to be sent first. The two people (lowering my voice) on my left were fellow expatriates, judging by certain small indices. "Yes," agreed Iris, "they practically got up to stand at attention when you started to recite that Pushkin thing about waves lying down in adoration at her feet. What other signs?"

"He kept stroking his beard very slowly from top to tip as he looked at the horizon and she smoked a cigarette with a cardboard mouthpiece."

There was also a child of ten or so cradling a large yellow beach ball in her bare arms. She seemed to be wearing nothing but a kind of frilly harness and a very short pleated skirt revealing her trim thighs. She was what in a later era amateurs were to call a "nymphet." As she caught my glance she gave me, over our sunny globe, a sweet lewd smile from under her auburn fringe.

"At eleven or twelve," said Iris, "I was as pretty as that French orphan. That's her grandmother all in black sitting on a spread Cannice-Matin with her knitting. I let smelly gentlemen fondle me. I played indecent games with Ivor—oh nothing very unusual, and anyway he now prefers dons to donnas—at least that's what he says."

She talked a little about her parents who by a fascinating coincidence had died on the same day, she at seven A.M. in New York, he at noon in London, only two years ago. They had separated soon after the war. She was American and horrible. You don't speak like that of your mother but she was really horrible. Dad was Vice President of the Samuels Cement Company when he died. He came from a respectable family and had "good connections." I asked what grudge exactly did Ivor bear to "society" and vice versa? She vaguely replied he disliked the "fox-hunting set" and the "yachting crowd." I said those were abominable clichés used only by Philistines.

In my set, in my world, in the opulent Russia of my boyhood we stood so far above any concept of "class" that we only laughed or yawned when reading about "Japanese Barons" or "New England Patricians." Yet strangely enough Ivor stopped clowning and became a normal serious individual only when he straddled his old, dappled, bald hobbyhorse and started reviling the English "upper classes"—especially their pronunciation. It was, I remonstrated, a speech superior in quality to the best Parisian French, and even to a Petersburgan's Russian; a delightfully modulated whinny, which both he and Iris were rather successfully, though no doubt unconsciously, imitating in their everyday intercourse, when not making protracted fun of a harmless foreigner's stilted or outdated English. By the way what was the nationality of the bronzed old man with the hoary chest hair who was wading out of the low surf preceded by his bedrabbled dog—I thought I knew his face.

It was, she said, Kanner, the great pianist and butterfly hunter, his face and name were on all the Morris columns. She was getting tickets for at least two of his concerts; and there, right there, where his dog was shaking itself, the P. family (exalted old name) had basked in June when the place was practically empty, and cut Ivor, though he knew young L.P. at Trinity. They'd now moved down there. Even more select. See that orange dot? That's their cabana. Foot of the Mirana Palace. I said nothing but I too knew young P. and disliked him.

Same day. Ran into him in the Mirana Men's Room. Was effusively welcomed. Would I care to meet his sister, tomorrow is what? Saturday. Suggested they stroll over tomorrow afternoon to the foot of the Victoria. Sort of cove to your right. I'm there with friends. Of course you know Ivor Black. Young P. duly turned up, with lovely, long-limbed sister. Ivor—frightfully rude. Rise, Iris, you forget we are having tea with Rapallovich and Chicherini. That sort of stuff. Idiotic feuds. Lydia P. screamed with laughter.

Upon discovering the effect of that miracle cream, at my boiled-lobster stage, I switched from a conservative *caleçon de bain* to a briefer variety (still banned at the time in stricter paradises). The delayed change resulted in a bizarre stratification of tan. I recall sneaking into Iris's room to contemplate myself in a full-length looking glass—the only one in the house—on a morning she had chosen for a visit to a beauty salon, which I called up to make sure she was there and not in the arms of a lover. Except for a Provençal boy polishing the banisters, there was nobody around, thus allowing me to indulge in one of my oldest and naughtiest pleasures: circulating stark naked all over a strange house.

The full-length portrait was not altogether a success, or rather contained an element of levity not improper to mirrors and medieval pictures of exotic beasts. My face was brown, my torso and arms caramel, a carmine equatorial belt undermargined the caramel, then came a white, more or less triangular, southward pointed space edged with the redundant carmine on both sides, and (owing to my wearing shorts all day) my legs were as brown as my face. Apically, the white of the abdomen, brought out in frightening *repoussé*, with an ugliness never noticed before, a man's portable zoo, a symmetrical mass of animal attributes, the elephant proboscis, the twin sea urchins, the baby gorilla, clinging to my underbelly with its back to the public.

A warning spasm shot through my nervous system. The fiends of my incurable ailment, "flayed consciousness," were shoving aside my harlequins. I sought first-aid distraction in the baubles of my love's lavender-scented bedroom: a Teddy bear dyed violet, a curious French novel (*Du côté de chez Swann*) that I had bought for her, a trim pile of freshly laundered linen in a Moïse basket, a color photograph of two girls in a fancy frame, obliquely inscribed as "The Lady Cressida and thy sweet Nell, Cambridge 1919"; I mistook the former for Iris herself in a golden wig and a pink make-up; a closer inspection, however, showed it to be Ivor in the part of that highly irritating girl bobbing in and out of Shakespeare's flawed farce. But, then, Mnemosyne's chromodiascope can also become a bore.

In the music room the boy was now cacophonically dusting the keys of the Bechstein as with less zest I resumed my nudist rambles. He asked me what sounded like "*Hora?*," and I demonstrated my wrist turning it this way and that to reveal only a pale ghost of watch and watch bracelet. He completely misinterpreted my gesture and turned away shaking his stupid head. It was a morning of errors and failures.

I made my way to the pantry for a glass or two of wine, the best breakfast in times of distress. In the passage I trod on a shard of crockery (we had heard the crash on the eve) and danced on one foot with a curse as I tried to examine the imaginary gash in the middle of my pale sole.

The litre of *rouge* I had visualized was there all right, but I could not find a corkscrew in any of the drawers. Between bangs the macaw could be heard crying out something crude and dreary. The postman had come and gone. The editor of *The New Aurora* (*Novaya Zarya*) was afraid (dreadful poltroons, those editors) that his "modest *émigré* venture (*nachinanie*)" could not etc.—a crumpled "etc." that flew into the garbage pail. Wineless, wrathful, with Ivor's *Times* under my arm, I slapped up the back stairs to my stuffy room. The rioting in my brain had now started.

It was then that I resolved, sobbing horribly into my pillow, to preface tomorrow's proposal of marriage with a confession that might make it unacceptable to my Iris.

7

If one looked from our garden gate down the asphalted avenue leading through leopard shade to the village some two hundred paces east, one saw the pink cube of the little post office, its green bench in front, its flag above, all this limned with the numb brightness of a color transparency, between the last two plane trees of the twin files marching on both sides of the road.

On the right (south) side of the avenue, across a marginal ditch, overhung with brambles, the intervals between the mottled trunks disclosed patches of lavender or lucerne and, farther away, the low white wall of a cemetery running parallel to our lane as those things are apt to do. On the left (north) side, through analogous intervals, one glimpsed an expanse of rising ground, a vineyard, a distant farm, pine groves, and the outline of mountains. On the penult tree trunk of that side somebody had pasted, and somebody else partly scraped off, an incoherent notice.

We walked down that avenue nearly every morning, Iris and I, on our way to the village square and—from there by lovely shortcuts—to Cannice and the sea. Now and then she liked to return on foot, being one of those small but strong lassies who can hurdle, and play hockey, and climb rocks, and then shimmy till any pale mad hour (*"do bezúmnogo blédnogo chása"*—to quote from my first direct poem to her). She usually wore her "Indian" frock, a kind of translucent wrap, over her skimpy swimsuit, and as I followed close behind, and sensed the solitude, the security, the all-permitting dream, I had trouble walking in my bestial state. Fortunately it was not the none-so-very-secure solitude that held me back but a moral decision to confess something very grave before I made love to her.

As seen from those escarpments, the sea far below spread in majestic wrinkles, and, owing to distance and height, the recurrent line of foam arrived in rather droll slow motion because we knew it was sure, as we had been sure, of its strapping pace, and now that restraint, that stateliness . . .

Suddenly there came from somewhere within the natural jumble of our surroundings a roar of unearthly ecstasy.

"Goodness," said Iris, "I do hope that's not a happy escapee from Kanner's Circus." (No relation—at least, so it seemed—to the pianist.)

We walked on, now side by side: after the first of the half-dozen times it crossed the looping main road, our path grew wider. That day as usual I argued with Iris about the English names of the few plants I could identify—rock roses and griselda in bloom, agaves (which she called "centuries"), broom and spurge, myrtle and arbutus. Speckled butterflies came and went like quick sun flecks in the occasional tunnels of foliage, and once a tremendous olive-green fellow, with a rosy flush somewhere beneath, settled on a thistlehead for an instant. I know nothing about butterflies, and indeed do not care for the fluffier night-flying ones, and would hate any of them to touch me: even the prettiest gives me a nasty shiver like some floating spider web or that bathroom pest on the Riviera, the silver louse.

On the day now in focus, memorable for a more important matter but carrying all kinds of synchronous trivia attached to it like burrs or incrustated like marine parasites, we noticed a butterfly net moving among the beflowered rocks, and presently old Kanner appeared, his panama swinging on its vest-button string, his white locks flying around his scarlet brow, and the whole of his person still radiating ecstasy, an echo of which we no doubt had heard a minute ago.

Upon Iris immediately describing to him the spectacular green thing, Kanner dismissed it as *eine* "Pandora" (at least that's what I find jotted down), a common southern *Falter* (butterfly). "*Aber* (but)," he thundered, raising his index, "when you wish to look at a real rarity, never before observed west of Nieder-Österreich, then I will show what I have just caught."

He leant his net against a rock (it fell at once, Iris picked it up reverently) and, with profuse thanks (to Psyche? Baalzebub? Iris?) that trailed away accompanimentally, produced from a compartment in his satchel a little stamp envelope and shook out of it very gently a folded butterfly onto the palm of his hand.

After one glance Iris told him it was merely a tiny, very young Cabbage White. (She had a theory that houseflies, for instance, *grow*.)

"Now look with attention," said Kanner ignoring her quaint remark and pointing with compressed tweezers at the triangular insect. "What you see is the inferior side—the under white of the left *Vorderflügel* ('fore wing') and the under yellow of the left *Hinterflügel* ('hind wing'). I will not open the wings but I think you can believe what I'm going to tell you. On the upper side, which you can't see, this species shares with its nearest allies—the Small White and Mann's White, both common here—the typical little spots of the fore wing, namely a black full stop in the male and a black *Doppelpunkt* ('colon') in the female. In those allies the punctuation is reproduced on the underside, and only in the species of which you see a folded specimen on the flat of my hand is

the wing blank beneath—a typographical caprice of Nature!
Ergo it is an Ergane."

One of the legs of the reclining butterfly twitched.

"Oh, it's alive!" cried Iris.

"No, it can't fly away—one pinch was enough," rejoined
Kanner soothingly, as he slipped the specimen back into its
pellucid hell; and presently, brandishing his arms and net in
triumphant farewells, he was continuing his climb.

"The brute!" wailed Iris. She brooded over the thousand
little creatures he had tortured, but a few days later, when
Ivor took us to the man's concert (a most poetical rendition
of Grünberg's suite *Les Châteaux*) she derived some consolation from her brother's contemptuous remark: "All that butterfly business is only a publicity stunt." Alas, as a fellow madman I knew better.

All I had to do when we reached our stretch of *plage* in
order to absorb the sun was to shed shirt, shorts, and sneakers.
Iris shrugged off her wrap and lay down, bare limbed, on the
towel next to mine. I was rehearsing in my head the speech I
had prepared. The pianist's dog was today in the company of
a handsome old lady, his fourth wife. The nymphet was being
buried in hot sand by two young oafs. The Russian lady was
reading an *émigré* newspaper. Her husband was contemplating the horizon. The two English women were bobbing in
the dazzling sea. A large French family of slightly flushed al-
binos was trying to inflate a rubber dolphin.

"I'm ready for a dip," said Iris.

She took out of the beach bag (kept for her by the Victoria
concierge) her yellow swim bonnet, and we transferred our
towels and things to the comparative quiet of an obsolete
wharf of sorts upon which she liked to dry afterwards.

Already twice in my young life a fit of *total* cramp—the
physical counterpart of lightning insanity—had all but over-
powered me in the panic and blackness of bottomless water.
I see myself as a lad of fifteen swimming at dusk across a
narrow but deep river with an athletic cousin. He is beginning
to leave me behind when a special effort I make results in a
sense of ineffable euphoria which promises miracles of propulsion, dream prizes on dream shelves—but which, at its satanic climax, is replaced by an intolerable spasm first in one

leg, then in the other, then in the ribs and both arms. I have often attempted to explain, in later years, to learned and ironical doctors, the strange, hideous, *segmental* quality of those pulsating pangs that made a huge worm of me with limbs transformed into successive coils of agony. By some fantastic fluke a third swimmer, a stranger, was right behind me and helped to pull me out of an abysmal tangle of water-lily stems.

The second time was a year later, on the West-Caucasian coast. I had been drinking with a dozen older companions at the birthday party of the district governor's son and, around midnight, a dashing young Englishman, Allan Andoverton (who was to be, around 1939, my first British publisher!) had suggested a moonlight swim. As long as I did not venture too far in the sea, the experience seemed quite enjoyable. The water was warm; the moon shone benevolently on the starched shirt of my first evening clothes spread on the shingly shore. I could hear merry voices around me; Allan, I remember, had not bothered to strip and was fooling with a champagne bottle in the dappled swell; but presently a cloud engulfed everything, a great wave lifted and rolled me, and soon I was too upset in all senses to tell whether I was heading for Yalta or Tuapse. Abject fear set loose instantly the pain I already knew, and I would have drowned there and then had not the next billow given me a boost and deposited me near my own trousers.

The shadow of those repellent and rather colorless recollections (mortal peril is colorless) remained always present in my "dips" and "splashes" (another word of hers) with Iris. She got used to my habit of staying in comfortable contact with the bed of shallows, while she executed "crawls" (if that is what those overarm strokes were called in the Nineteen-Twenties) at quite a distance away; but that morning I nearly did a very stupid thing.

I was gently floating to and fro in line with the shore and sinking a probing toe every now and then to ascertain if I could still feel the oozy bottom with its unappetizing to the touch, but on the whole friendly, vegetables, when I noticed that the seascape had changed. In the middle distance a brown motorboat manned by a young fellow in whom I recognized L.P. had described a foamy half-circle and stopped beside Iris.

She clung to the bright brim, and he spoke to her, and then made as if to drag her into his boat, but she flipped free, and he sped away, laughing.

It all must have lasted a couple of minutes, but had the rascal with his hawkish profile and white cable-stitched sweater stayed a few seconds longer or had my girl been abducted by her new beau in the thunder and spray, I would have perished; for while the scene endured, some virile instinct rather than one of self-preservation had caused me to swim toward them a few insensible yards, and now when I assumed a perpendicular position to regain my breath I found underfoot nothing but water. I turned and started swimming landward—and already felt the ominous foreglow, the strange, never yet described aura of total cramp creeping over me and forming its deadly pact with gravity. Suddenly my knee struck blessed sand, and in a mild undertow I crawled on all fours onto the beach.

8

"I have a confession to make, Iris, concerning my mental health."

"Wait a minute. Must peel this horrid thing off—as far down—as far down as it can decently go."

We were lying, I supine, she prone, on the wharf. She had torn off her cap and was struggling to shrug off the shoulder straps of her wet swimsuit, so as to expose her entire back to the sun; a secondary struggle was taking place on the near side, in the vicinity of her sable armpit, in her unsuccessful efforts not to show the white of a small breast at its tender juncture with her ribs. As soon as she had wriggled into a satisfactory state of decorum, she half-reared, holding her black bodice to her bosom, while her other hand conducted that delightful rapid monkey-scratching search a girl performs when groping for something in her bag—in this instance a mauve package of cheap Salammbôs and an expensive lighter; whereupon she again pressed her bosom to the spread towel.

Her earlobe burned red through her black liberated "Medusa," as that type of bob was called in the young twenties. The moldings of her brown back, with a patch-size beauty spot below the left shoulder blade and a long spinal hollow, which redeemed all the errors of animal evolution, distracted me painfully from the decision I had taken to preface my proposal with a special, tremendously important confession. A few aquamarines of water still glistened on the underside of her brown thighs and on her strong brown calves, and a few grains of wet gravel had stuck to her rose-brown ankles. If I have described so often in my American novels (*A Kingdom by the Sea, Ardis*) the unbearable magic of a girl's back, it is mainly because of my having loved Iris. Her compact little nates, the most agonizing, the fullest, and sweetest bloom of her puerile prettiness, were as yet unwrapped surprises under the Christmas tree.

Upon resettling in the waiting sun after this little flurry, Iris protruded her fat underlip as she exhaled smoke and presently remarked: "Your mental health is jolly good, I think. You are sometimes strange and somber, and often silly, but that's in character with *ce qu'on appelle* genius."

"What do *you* call 'genius'?"

"Well, seeing things others don't see. Or rather the invisible links between things."

"I am speaking, then, of a humble morbid condition which has nothing to do with genius. We shall start with a specific example and an authentic decor. Please close your eyes for a moment. Now visualize the avenue that goes from the post office to your villa. You see the plane trees converging in perspective and the garden gate between the last two?"

"No," said Iris, "the last one on the right is replaced by a lamppost—you can't make it out very clearly from the village square—but it is really a lamppost in a coat of ivy."

"Well, no matter. The main thing is to imagine we're looking from the village *here* toward the garden gate *there*. We must be very careful about our here's and there's in this problem. For the present 'there' is the quadrangle of green sunlight in the half-opened gate. We now start to walk up the avenue. On the second tree trunk of the right-side file we notice traces of some local proclamation—"

"It was Ivor's proclamation. He proclaimed that things had changed and Aunt Betty's protégés should stop making their weekly calls."

"Splendid. We continue to walk toward the garden gate. Intervals of landscape can be made out between the plane trees on both sides. On your right—please, close your eyes, you will see better—on your right there's a vineyard; on your left, a churchyard—you can distinguish its long, low, very low, wall—"

"You make it sound rather creepy. And I want to add something. Among the blackberries, Ivor and I discovered a crooked old tombstone with the inscription *Dors, Médor!* and only the date of death, 1889; a found dog, no doubt. It's just before the last tree on the left side."

"So now we reach the garden gate. We are about to enter— but you stop all of a sudden: you've forgotten to buy those nice new stamps for your album. We decide to go back to the post office."

"Can I open my eyes? Because I'm afraid I'm going to fall asleep."

"On the contrary: now is the moment to shut your eyes tight and concentrate. I want you to imagine yourself turning on your heel so that 'right' instantly becomes 'left,' and you instantly see the 'here' as a 'there,' with the lamppost now on your left and dead Médor now on your right, and the plane trees converging toward the post office. Can you do that?"

"Done," said Iris. "About-face executed. I now stand facing a sunny hole with a little pink house inside it and a bit of blue sky. Shall we start walking back?"

"*You* may, I can't! This is the point of the experiment. In actual, physical life I can turn as simply and swiftly as anyone. But mentally, with my eyes closed and my body immobile, I am unable to switch from one direction to the other. Some swivel cell in my brain does not work. I can cheat, of course, by setting aside the mental snapshot of one vista and leisurely selecting the opposite view for my walk back to my starting point. But if I do not cheat, some kind of atrocious obstacle, which would drive me mad if I persevered, prevents me from imagining the twist which transforms one direction into another, directly opposite. I am crushed, I am carrying the whole world on my back in the process of trying to visualize my turning around and making myself see in terms of 'right' what I saw in terms of 'left' and vice versa."

I thought she had fallen asleep, but before I could entertain the thought that she had not heard, not understood anything of what was destroying me, she moved, rearranged her shoulder straps, and sat up.

"First of all, we shall agree," she said, "to cancel all such experiments. Secondly, we shall tell ourselves that what we had been trying to do was to solve a stupid philosophical riddle—on the lines of what does 'right' and 'left' *mean* in our absence, when nobody is looking, in pure space, and what, anyway, is space; when I was a child I thought space was the inside of a nought, any nought, chalked on a slate and perhaps not quite tidy, but still a good clean zero. I don't want you to go mad or to drive me mad, because those perplexities are catching, and so we'll drop the whole business of revolving avenues altogether. I would like to seal our pact with a kiss, but we shall have to postpone that. Ivor is coming in a few minutes to take us for a spin in his new car, but perhaps you do not care to come, and so I propose we meet in the garden, for a minute or two, just before dinner, while he is taking his bath."

I asked what Bob (L.P.) had been telling her in my dream. "It was not a dream," she said. "He just wanted to know if his sister had phoned about a dance they wanted us all three to come to. If she had, nobody was at home."

We repaired for a snack and a drink to the Victoria bar, and presently Ivor joined us. He said, nonsense, he could dance and fence beautifully on the stage but was a regular bear at private affairs and would hate to have his innocent sister pawed by all the *rastaquouères* of the Côte.

"Incidentally," he added, "I don't much care for P.'s obsession with moneylenders. He practically ruined the best one in Cambridge but has nothing but conventional evil to repeat about them."

"My brother is a funny person," said Iris, turning to me as in play. "He conceals our ancestry like a dark treasure, yet will flare up publicly if someone calls someone a Shylock."

Ivor prattled on: "Old Maurice (his employer) is dining

with us tonight. Cold cuts and a *macédoine au* kitchen rum.
I'll also get some tinned asparagus at the English shop; it's
much better than the stuff they grow here. The car is not
exactly a Royce, but it rolls. Sorry Vivian is too queasy to
come. I saw Madge Titheridge this morning and she said
French reporters pronounce her family name *'Si c'est riche.'*
Nobody's laughing today."

9

Being too excited to take my usual siesta, I spent most of the
afternoon working on a love poem (and this is the last entry
in my 1922 pocket diary—exactly one month after my arrival
in Carnavaux). In those days I seemed to have had two muses:
the essential, hysterical, genuine one, who tortured me with
elusive snatches of imagery and wrung her hands over my inability to appropriate the magic and madness offered me; and
her apprentice, her palette girl and stand-in, a little logician,
who stuffed the torn gaps left by her mistress with explanatory
or meter-mending fillers which became more and more numerous the further I moved away from the initial, evanescent,
savage perfection. The treacherous music of Russian rhythms
came to my specious rescue like those demons who break the
black silence of an artist's hell with imitations of Greek poets
and prehistorical birds. Another and final deception would
come with the Fair Copy in which, for a short while, callig-
raphy, vellum paper, and India ink beautified a dead doggerel.
And to think that for almost five years I kept trying and kept
getting caught—until I fired that painted, pregnant, meek,
miserable little assistant!

I dressed and went downstairs. The french window giving
on the terrace was open. Old Maurice, Iris, and Ivor sat enjoying Martinis in the orchestra seats of a marvelous sunset.
Ivor was in the act of mimicking someone, with bizarre intonations and extravagant gestures. The marvelous sunset has
not only remained as a backdrop of a life-transforming evening, but endured, perhaps, behind the suggestion I made to

my British publishers, many years later, to bring out a coffee-
table album of auroras and sunsets, in the truest possible
shades, a collection that would also be of scientific value, since
some learned celestiologist might be hired to discuss samples
from various countries and analyze the striking and never before discussed differences between the color schemes of evening and dawn. The album came out eventually, the price was
high and the pictorial part passable; but the text was supplied
by a luckless female whose pretty prose and borrowed poetry
botched the book (Allan and Overton, London, 1949).

For a couple of moments, while idly attending to Ivor's
strident performance, I stood watching the huge sunset. Its
wash was of a classical light-orange tint with an oblique bluish-
black shark crossing it. What glorified the combination was
a series of ember-bright cloudlets riding along, tattered and
hooded, above the red sun which had assumed the shape of
a pawn or a baluster. "Look at the sabbath witches!" I was
about to cry, but then I saw Iris rise and heard her say: "That
will do, Ives. Maurice has never met the person, it's all lost
on him."

"Not at all," retorted her brother, "he will meet him in a
minute and *recognize* him (the verb was an artist's snarl), that's
the point!"

Iris left the terrace via the garden steps, and Ivor did not
continue his skit, which a swift playback that now burst on
my consciousness identified as a clever burlesque of my voice
and manner. I had the odd sensation of a piece of myself being
ripped off and tossed overboard, of my being separated from
my own self, of flying forward and at the same time turning
away. The second action prevailed, and presently, under the
holm oak, I joined Iris.

The crickets were stridulating, dusk had filled the pool, a
ray of the outside lamp glistened on two parked cars. I kissed
her lips, her neck, her necklace, her neck, her lips. Her response dispelled my ill humor; but I told her what I thought
of the idiot before she ran back to the festively lit villa.

Ivor personally brought up my supper, right to my bedside
table, with well-concealed dismay at being balked of his art's
reward and charming apologies for having offended me, and
"had I run out of pyjamas?" to which I replied that, on the

contrary, I felt rather flattered, and in fact always slept naked in summer, but preferred not to come down lest a slight headache prevent me from not living up to that splendid impersonation.

I slept fitfully, and only in the small hours glided into a deeper spell (illustrated for no reason at all with the image of my first little inamorata in the grass of an orchard) from which I was rudely roused by the spattering sounds of a motor. I slipped on a shirt and leant out of the window, sending a flock of sparrows whirring out of the jasmin, whose luxuriant growth reached up to the second floor, and saw, with a sensual start, Ivor putting a suitcase and a fishing rod into his car which stood, throbbing, practically in the garden. It was a Sunday, and I had been expecting to have him around all day, but there he was getting behind the wheel and slamming the door after him. The gardener was giving tactical directions with both arms; his pretty little boy was also there, holding a yellow and blue feather duster. And then I heard her lovely English voice bidding her brother have a good time. I had to lean out a little more to see her; she stood on a patch of cool clean turf, barefooted, barecalved, in an ample-sleeved peignoir, repeating her joyful farewell, which he could no longer hear.

I dashed to the W.C. across the landing. A few moments later, as I left my gurgling and gulping retreat, I noticed her on the other side of the staircase. She was entering my room. My polo shirt, a very short, salmon-colored affair, could not hide my salient impatience.

"I hate to see the stunned look on the face of a clock that has stopped," she said, as she stretched a slender brown arm up to the shelf where I had relegated an old egg timer lent me in lieu of a regular alarm. As her wide sleeve fell back I kissed the dark perfumed hollow I had longed to kiss since our first day in the sun.

The door key would not work, that I knew; still I tried, and was rewarded by the silly semblance of recurrent clicks that did not lock anything. Whose step, whose sick young cough came from the stairs? Yes of course that was Jacquot, the gardener's boy who rubbed and dusted things every morning. He might butt in, I said, already speaking with difficulty. To polish, for instance, that candlestick. Oh, what does it matter, she whispered, he's only a conscientious child, a poor foundling, as all our dogs and parrots are. Your tum, she said, is still as pink as your shirt. And please do not forget, darling, to clear out before it's too late.

How far, how bright, how unchanged by eternity, how disfigured by time! There were bread crumbs and even a bit of orange peel in the bed. The young cough was now muted, but I could distinctly hear creakings, controlled footfalls, the hum in an ear pressed to the door. I must have been eleven or twelve when the nephew of my grand-uncle visited the Moscow country house where I was spending that hot and hideous summer. He had brought his passionate bride with him—straight from the wedding feast. Next day at the siesta hour, in a frenzy of curiosity and fancy, I crept to a secret spot under the second-floor guest-room window where a gardener's ladder stood rooted in a jungle of jasmin. It reached only to the top of the closed first-floor shutters, and though I found a foothold above them, on an ornamental projection, I could only just grip the sill of a half-open window from which confused sounds issued. I recognized the jangle of bedsprings and the rhythmic tinkle of a fruit knife on a plate near the bed, one post of which I could make out by stretching my neck to the utmost; but what fascinated me most were the manly moans coming from the invisible part of the bed. A superhuman effort afforded me the sight of a salmon-pink shirt over the back of a chair. He, the enraptured beast, doomed to die one day as so many are, was now repeating her name with ever increasing urgency, and by the time my foot slipped he was in full cry, thus drowning the noise of my sudden descent into a crackle of twigs and a snowstorm of petals.

10

Just before Ivor returned from his fishing trip, I moved to the Victoria, where she visited me daily. That was not enough;

but in the autumn Ivor migrated to Los Angeles to join his half-brother in directing the Amenic film company (for which, thirty years later, long after Ivor's death over Dover, I was to write the script of *Pawn Takes Queen*, my most popular at the time, but far from best, novel), and we returned to our beloved villa, in the really quite nice blue Icarus, Ivor's thoughtful wedding present.

Sometime in October my benefactor, now in the last stage of majestic senility, came for his annual visit to Mentone, and, without warning, Iris and I dropped in to see him. His villa was incomparably grander than ours. He staggered to his feet to take between his wax-pale palms Iris's hand and stare at her with blue bleary eyes for at least five seconds (a little eternity, socially) in a kind of ritual silence, after which he embraced me with a slow triple cross-kiss in the awful Russian tradition.

"Your bride," he said, using, I knew, the word in the sense of *fiancée* (and speaking an English which Iris said later was exactly like mine in Ivor's unforgettable version) "is as beautiful as your wife will be!"

I quickly told him—in Russian—that the *maire* of Cannice had married us a month ago in a brisk ceremony. Nikifor Nikodimovich gave Iris another stare and finally kissed her hand, which I was glad to see she raised in the proper fashion (coached, no doubt, by Ivor who used to take every opportunity to paw his sister).

"I misunderstood the rumors," he said, "but all the same I am happy to make the acquaintance of such a charming young lady. And where, pray, in what church, will the vow be sanctified?"

"In the temple we shall build, Sir," said Iris—a trifle insolently, I thought.

Count Starov "chewed his lips," as old men are wont to do in Russian novels. Miss Vrode-Vorodin, the elderly cousin who kept house for him, made a timely entrance and led Iris to an adjacent alcove (illuminated by a resplendent portrait by Serov, 1896, of the notorious beauty, Mme. de Blagidze, in Caucasian costume) for a nice cup of tea. The Count wished to talk business with me and had only ten minutes "before his injection."

What was my wife's maiden name?

I told him. He thought it over and shook his head. What was her mother's name?

I told him that, too. Same reaction. What about the financial aspect of the marriage?

I said she had a house, a parrot, a car, and a small income—I didn't know exactly how much.

After another minute's thought, he asked me if I would like a permanent job in the White Cross? It had nothing to do with Switzerland. It was an organization that helped Russian Christians all over the world. The job would involve travel, interesting connections, promotion to important posts.

I declined so emphatically that he dropped the silver pill box he was holding and a number of innocent gum drops were spilled all over the table at his elbow. He swept them onto the carpet with a gesture of peevish dismissal.

What then was I intending to do?

I said I'd go on with my literary dreams and nightmares. We would spend most of the year in Paris. Paris was becoming the center of *émigré* culture and destitution.

How much did I think I could earn?

Well, as N.N. knew, currencies were losing their identities in the whirlpool of inflation, but Boris Morozov, a distinguished author, whose fame had preceded his exile, had given me some illuminating "examples of existence" when I met him quite recently in Cannice where he had lectured on Baratynski at the local *literaturnyy* circle. In his case, four lines of verse would pay for a *bifsteck pommes*, while a couple of essays in the *Novosti emigratsii* assured a month's rent for a cheap *chambre garnie*. There were also readings, in large auditoriums, at least twice a year, which might bring him each time the equivalent of, say, one hundred dollars.

My benefactor thought this over and said that as long as he lived I would receive a check for half that amount every first of the month, and that he would bequeath me a certain sum in his testament. He named the sum. Its paltriness took me aback. This was a foretaste of the disappointing advances publishers were to offer me after a long, promising, pencil-tapping pause.

We rented a two-room apartment in the 16th *arrondisse-*

ment, rue Despréaux, 23. The hallway connecting the rooms led, on the front side, to a bathroom and kitchenette. Being a solitary sleeper by principle and inclination, I relinquished the double bed to Iris, and slept on the couch in the parlor. The concierge's daughter came to clean up and cook. Her culinary capacities were limited, so we often broke the monotony of vegetable soups and boiled meat by eating at a Russian *restoranchik*. We were to spend seven winters in that little flat.

Owing to the foresight of my dear guardian and benefactor (1850?–1927), an old-fashioned cosmopolitan with a lot of influence in the right quarters, I had become by the time of my marriage the subject of a snug foreign country and thus was spared the indignity of a *nansenskiy pasport* (a pauper's permit, really), as well as the vulgar obsession with "documents," which provoked such evil glee among the Bolshevist rulers, who perceived some similarity between red tape and Red rule and a certain affinity between the civil plight of a hobbled expatriate and the political immobilization of a Soviet slave. I could, therefore, take my wife to any vacational resort in the world without waiting several weeks for a visa, and then being refused, perhaps, a return visa to our accidental country of residence, in this case France, because of some flaw in our precious and despicable papers. Nowadays (1970), when my British passport has been superseded by a no less potent American one, I still treasure that 1922 photo of the mysterious young man I then was, with the mysteriously smiling eyes and the striped tie and the wavy hair. I remember spring trips to Malta and Andalusia, but every summer, around the first of July, we drove to Carnavaux and stayed there for a month or two. The parrot died in 1925, the footboy vanished in 1927. Ivor visited us twice in Paris, and I think she saw him also in London where she went at least once a year to spend a few days with "friends," whom I did not know, but who sounded harmless—at least to a certain point.

I should have been happier. I had *planned* to be happier. My health continued patchy with ominous shapes showing through its flimsier edges. Faith in my work never wavered, but despite her touching intentions to participate in it, Iris remained on its outside, and the better it grew the more alien it became to her. She took desultory lessons in Russian, interrupting them regularly, for long periods, and finished by developing a dull habitual aversion to the language. I soon noticed that she had ceased trying to look attentive and bright when Russian, and Russian only, was spoken in her presence (after some primitive French had been kept up for the first minute or two of the party in polite concession to her disability).

This was, at best, annoying; at worst, heartrending; it did not, however, affect my sanity as something else threatened to do.

Jealousy, a masked giant never encountered before in the frivolous affairs of my early youth, now stood with folded arms, confronting me at every corner. Certain little sexual quirks in my sweet, docile, tender Iris, inflections of lovemaking, felicities of fondling, the easy accuracy with which she adapted her flexible frame to every pattern of passion, seemed to presuppose a wealth of experience. Before starting to suspect the present, I felt compelled to get my fill of suspecting her past. During the examinations to which I subjected her on my worst nights, she dismissed her former romances as totally insignificant, without realizing that this reticence left more to my imagination than would the most luridly overstated truth.

The three lovers (a figure I wrested from her with the fierceness of Pushkin's mad gambler and with even less luck) whom she had had in her teens remained nameless, and therefore spectral; devoid of any individual traits, and therefore identical. They performed their sketchy *pas* in the back of her lone act like the lowliest members of the *corps de ballet*, in a display of mawkish gymnastics rather than dance, and it was clear that none of them would ever become the male star of the troupe. She, the ballerina, on the other hand, was a dim diamond with all the facets of talent ready to blaze, but under the pressure of the nonsense around her had, for the moment, to limit her steps and gestures to an expression of cold coquetry, of flirtatious evasion—waiting as she was for the tremendous leap of the marble-thighed athlete in shining tights who was to erupt from the wings after a decent prelude. We thought I had been chosen for that part but we were mistaken.

Only by projecting thus on the screen of my mind those stylized images, could I allay the anguish of carnal jealousy centered on specters. Yet not seldom I chose to succumb to it. The french window of my studio in Villa Iris gave on the same red-tiled balcony as my wife's bedroom did, and could be set half-open at such an angle as to provide two different views melting into one another. It caught obliquely, through the monastic archway leading from room to room, part of her bed and of her—her hair, a shoulder—which otherwise I could not see from the old-fashioned lectern at which I wrote; but the glass also held, at arm's length as it were, the green reality of the garden with a peregrination of cypresses along its sidewall. So half in bed and half in the pale hot sky, she would recline, writing a letter that was crucified on my second-best chessboard. I knew that if I asked, the answer would be "Oh, to an old schoolmate," or "To Ivor," or "To old Miss Kupalov," and I also knew that in one way or another the letter would reach the post office at the end of the plane-tree avenue without my seeing the name on the envelope. And still I let her write as she comfortably floated in the life belt of her pillow, above the cypresses and the garden wall, while all the time I gauged—grimly, recklessly—to what depths of dark pigment the tentacled ache would go.

II

Most of those Russian lessons consisted of her taking one of my poems or essays to this or that Russian lady, Miss Kupalov or Mrs. Lapukov (neither of whom had much English) and having it paraphrased orally for her in a kind of makeshift Volapük. On my pointing out to Iris that she was losing her time at this hit-and-miss task, she cast around for some other alchemic method which might enable her to read everything I wrote. I had begun by then (1925) my first novel (*Tamara*) and she coaxed me into letting her have a copy of the first chapter, which I had just typed out. This she carried to an agency that dealt in translations into French of utilitarian texts such as applications and supplications addressed by Russian refugees to various rats in the ratholes of various *commissariats*. The person who agreed to supply her with the "literal version," which she paid for in *valuta*, kept the typescript for two months and warned her when delivering it that my "article" had presented almost insurmountable difficulties, "being written in an idiom and style utterly unfamiliar to the ordinary reader." Thus an anonymous imbecile in a shabby, cluttered, clattering office became my first critic and my first translator.

I knew nothing of that venture, until I found her one day bending her brown curls over sheets of foolscap almost perforated by the violence of the violet characters that covered it without any semblance of margin. I was, in those days, naively opposed to any kind of translation, partly because my attempts to turn two or three of my first compositions into my own English had resulted in a feeling of morbid revolt—and in maddening headaches. Iris, her cheek on her fist and her eyes rolling in languid doubt, looked up at me rather sheepishly, but with that gleam of humor that never left her in the most absurd or trying circumstances. I noticed a blunder in the first line, a boo-boo in the next, and without bothering to read any further, tore up the whole thing—which provoked no reaction, save a neutral sigh, on the part of my thwarted darling.

In compensation for being debarred from my writings, she decided to become a writer herself. Beginning with the middle Twenties and to the end of her short, squandered, uncharmed life, my Iris kept working on a detective novel in two, three, four successive versions, in which the plot, the people, the setting, everything kept changing in bewildering bursts of frantic deletions—everything except the names (none of which I remember).

Not only did she lack all literary talent, but she had not even the knack of imitating the small number of gifted authors among the prosperous but ephemeral purveyors of "crime fiction" which she consumed with the indiscriminate zest of a model prisoner. How, then, did my Iris know why this had to be altered, that rejected? What instinct of genius ordered her to destroy the whole heap of her drafts on the eve, practically on the eve, of her sudden death? All the odd girl could ever visualize, with startling lucidity, was the crimson cover of the final, ideal paperback on which the villain's hairy fist would be shown pointing a pistol-shaped cigarette lighter at the reader—who was not supposed to guess until everybody in the book had died that it was, in fact, a pistol.

Let me pick out several fatidic points, cleverly disguised at the time, within the embroidery of our seven winters.

During a lull in a magnificent concert for which we had not been able to obtain adjacent seats, I noticed Iris eagerly welcoming a melancholy-looking woman with drab hair and thin lips; I certainly had met her, somewhere, quite recently, but the very insignificance of her appearance canceled the pursuit of a vague recollection, and I never asked Iris about it. She was to become my wife's last teacher.

Every author believes, when his first book is published, that those that acclaim it are his personal friends or impersonal peers, while its revilers can only be envious rogues and non-entities. No doubt I might have had similar illusions about the way *Tamara* was reviewed in the Russian-language periodicals of Paris, Berlin, Prague, Riga, and other cities; but by that time I was already engrossed in my second novel, *Pawn Takes Queen*, and my first one had dwindled to a pinch of colored dust in my mind.

The editor of *Patria*, the *émigré* monthly in which *Pawn Takes Queen* had begun to be serialized, invited "Irida Osi-povna" and me to a literary samovar. I mention it only because this was one of the few salons that my unsociability deigned to frequent. Iris helped with the sandwiches. I smoked my pipe and observed the feeding habits of two major novelists, three minor ones, one major poet, five minor ones of both sexes, one major critic (Demian Basilevski), and nine minor ones, including the inimitable "Prostakov-Skotinin," a Russian comedy name (meaning "simpleton and brute") applied to him by his archrival Hristofor Boyarski.

The major poet, Boris Morozov, an amiable grizzly bear of a man, was asked how his reading in Berlin had gone, and he said: "*Nichevo*" (a "so-so" tinged with a "well enough") and then told a funny but not memorable story about the new President of the Union of *Émigré* Writers in Germany. The lady next to me informed me she had adored that treacherous

conversation between the Pawn and the Queen about the husband and would they really defenestrate the poor chess player?
I said they would but not in the next issue, and not for good:
he would live forever in the games he had played and in the
multiple exclamation marks of future annotators. I also
heard—my hearing is almost on a par with my sight—snatches
of general talk such as an explanatory, "She is an Englishwoman," murmured from behind a hand five chairs away by
one guest to another.

All that would have been much too trivial to record unless
meant to serve as the commonplace background, at any such
meeting of exiles, against which a certain reminder flickered
now and then, between the shoptalk and the tattle—a line of
Tyutchev or Blok, which was cited in passing, as well as an
everlasting presence, with the familiarity of devotion and as
the secret height of art, and which ornamented sad lives with
a sudden cadenza coming from some celestial elsewhere, a
glory, a sweetness, the patch of rainbow cast on the wall by a
crystal paperweight we cannot locate. That was what my Iris
was missing.

To return to the trivia: I recall regaling the company with
one of the howlers I had noticed in the "translation" of *Tamara*. The sentence *vidnelos' neskol'ko barok* ("several barges
could be seen") had become *la vue était assez baroque*. The
eminent critic Basilevski, a stocky, fair-haired old fellow in a
rumpled brown suit, shook with abdominal mirth—but then
his expression changed to one of suspicion and displeasure.
After tea he accosted me and insisted gruffly that I had made
up that example of mistranslation. I remember answering that,
if so, he, too, might well be an invention of mine.

As we strolled home, Iris complained she would never learn
to cloud a glass of tea with a spoonful of cloying raspberry
jam. I said I was ready to put up with her deliberate insularity
but implored her to cease announcing *à la ronde*: "Please,
don't mind me: I love the sound of Russian." *That* was an
insult, like telling an author his book was unreadable but
beautifully printed.

"I am going to make reparations," she gaily replied. "I've
never been able to find a proper teacher, I always believed you
were the only one—and you refused to teach me, because you

were busy, because you were tired, because it bored you, because it was bad for your nerves. I've discovered at last someone who speaks both languages, yours and mine, as two
natives in one, and can make all the edges fit. I am thinking
of Nadia Starov. In fact it's her own suggestion."

Nadezhda Gordonovna Starov was the wife of a *leytenant*
Starov (Christian name unimportant), who had served under
General Wrangel and now had some office job in the White
Cross. I had met him in London recently, as fellow pallbearer
at the funeral of the old Count, whose bastard or "adopted
nephew" (whatever that meant), he was said to be. He was a
dark-eyed, dark-complexioned man, three or four years my
senior; I thought him rather handsome in a brooding, gloomy
way. A head wound received in the civil war had left him with
a terrifying tic that caused his face to change suddenly, at var-
iable intervals, as if a paper bag were being crumpled by an
invisible hand. Nadezhda Starov, a quiet, plain woman with
an indefinable Quakerish look about her, clocked those intervals for some reason, no doubt of a medical nature, the man
himself being unconscious of his "fireworks" unless he happened to see them in a mirror. He had a macabre sense of
humor, beautiful hands, and a velvety voice.

I realized now that it was Nadezhda Gordonovna whom
Iris had been talking to in that concert hall. I cannot say exactly when the lessons began or how long that fad lasted; a
month or two months at the most. They took place either in
Mrs. Starov's lodgings or in one of the Russian tearooms both
ladies frequented. I kept a little list of telephone numbers so
that Iris might be warned that I could always make sure of
her whereabouts if, say, I felt on the brink of losing my mind
or wanted her to buy on the way home a tin of my favorite
Brown Prune tobacco. She did *not* know, on the other hand,
that I would never have dared ring her up, lest her not being
where she said she would be cause me even a few minutes of
an agony that I could not face.

Sometime around Christmas, 1929, she casually told me that
those lessons had been discontinued quite a while ago: Mrs.
Starov had left for England, and it was rumored that she
would not return to her husband. The lieutenant, it seemed,
was quite a dasher.

12

At a certain mysterious point toward the end of our last winter in Paris something in our relationship changed for the better. A wave of new warmth, new intimacy, new tenderness, swelled and swept away all the delusions of distance—tiffs, silences, suspicions, retreats into castles of *amour-propre* and the like— which had obstructed our love and of which I alone was guilty. A more amiable, merrier mate I could not have imagined. Endearments, love names (based in my case on Russian forms) reentered our customary exchanges. I broke the monastic rules of work on my novella in verse *Polnolunie* (Plenilune) by riding with her in the Bois or dutifully escorting her to fashion-show teases and exhibitions of *avant-garde* frauds. I surmounted my contempt for the "serious" cinema (depicting heartrending problems with a political twist), which she preferred to American buffoonery and the trick photography of Germanic horror films. I even gave a talk on my Cambridge days at a rather pathetic English Ladies Club, to which she belonged. And to top the treat, I told her the plot of my next novel (*Camera Lucida*).

One afternoon, in March or early April, 1930, she peeped into my room and, being admitted, handed me the duplicate of a typewritten sheet, numbered 444. It was, she said, a tentative episode in her interminable tale, which would soon display more deletions than insertions. She was stuck, she said. Diana Vane, an incidental but on the whole nice girl, sojourning in Paris, happened to meet, at a riding school, a strange Frenchman, of Corsican, or perhaps Algerian, origin, passionate, brutal, unbalanced. He mistook Diana—and kept on mistaking her despite her amused remonstrations—for his former sweetheart, also an English girl, whom he had last seen ages ago. We had here, said the author, a sort of hallucination, an obsessive fancy, which Diana, a delightful flirt with a keen sense of humor, allowed Jules to entertain during some twenty riding lessons; but then his attentions grew more realistic, and she stopped seeing him. There had been nothing between them, and yet he simply could not be dissuaded from confusing her with the girl he once had possessed or thought he had, for that girl, too, might well have been only the afterimage of a still earlier romance or remembered delirium. It was a very bizarre situation.

Now this page was supposed to be a last ominous letter written by that Frenchman in a foreigner's English to Diana. I was to read it as if it were a real letter and suggest, as an experienced writer, what might be the next development or disaster.

Beloved!

I am not capable to represent to myself that you really desire to tear up any connection with me. God sees, I love you more than life—more than two lives, your and my, together taken. Are you not ill? Or maybe you have found another? Another lover, yes? Another victim of your attraction? No, no, this thought is too horrible, too humiliating for us both.

My supplication is modest and just. Give only one more interview to me! One interview! I am prepared to meet with you it does not matter where—on the street, in some café, in the Forest of Boulogne—but I must see you, must speak with you and open to you many mysteries before I will die. Oh, this is no threat! I swear that if our interview will lead to a positive result, if, otherwise speaking, you will permit me to hope, only to hope, then, oh then, I will consent to wait a little. But you must reply to me without retardment, my cruel, stupid, adored little girl!

Your Jules

"There's one thing," I said, carefully folding the sheet and pocketing it for later study, "one thing the little girl should know. This is not a romantic Corsican writing a *crime passionnel* letter; it is a Russian blackmailer knowing just enough English to translate into it the stalest Russian locutions. What puzzles me is how did you, with your three or four words of Russian—*kak pozhivaete* and *do svidaniya*—how did you, the author, manage to think up those subtle turns, and imitate the mistakes in English that only a Russian would make? Impersonation, I know, runs in the family, but still—"

Iris replied (with that quaint *non sequitur* that I was to give to the heroine of my *Ardis* forty years later) that, yes, indeed, I was right, she must have had too many muddled lessons in

Russian and she would certainly correct that extraordinary impression by simply giving the whole letter in French—from which, she had been told, incidentally, Russian *had* borrowed a lot of clichés.

"But that's beside the point," she added. "You don't understand—the point is what should happen next—I mean, logically? What should my poor girl do about that bore, that brute? She is uncomfortable, she is perplexed, she is frightened. Should this situation end in slapstick or tragedy?"

"In the wastepaper basket," I whispered, interrupting my work to gather her small form onto my lap as I often did, the Lord be thanked, in that fatal spring of 1930.

"Give me back that scrap," she begged gently, trying to thrust her hand into the pocket of my dressing gown, but I shook my head and embraced her closer.

My latent jealousy should have been fanned up to a furnace roar by the surmise that my wife had been transcribing an authentic letter—received, say, from one of the wretched, unwashed *émigré* poeticules, with smooth glossy hair and eloquent liquid eyes, whom she used to meet in the salons of exile. But after reexamining the thing, I decided that it just might be her own composition with some of the planted faults, borrowed from the French (*supplication, sans tarder*), while others could be subliminal echoes of the Volapük she had been exposed to, during sessions with Russian teachers, through bilingual or trilingual exercises in tawdry textbooks. Thus, instead of losing myself in a jungle of evil conjectures, all I did was preserve that thin sheet with its unevenly margined lines so characteristic of her typing in the faded and cracked briefcase before me, among other mementos, other deaths.

13

On the morning of April 23, 1930, the shrill peal of the hallway telephone caught me in the act of stepping into my bathwater.

Ivor! He had just arrived in Paris from New York for an

important conference, would be busy all afternoon, was leaving tomorrow, would like to—

Here intervened naked Iris, who delicately, unhurriedly, with a radiant smile, appropriated the monologizing receiver. A minute later (her brother with all his defects was a mercifully concise phoner), she, still beaming, embraced me, and we moved to her bedroom for our last "*fairelamourir*" as she called it in her tender aberrant French.

Ivor was to fetch us at seven P.M. I had already put on my old dinner jacket; Iris stood sideways to the hallway mirror (the best and brightest in the whole flat) veering gently as she tried to catch a clear view of the back of her silky dark bob in the hand glass she held at head level.

"If you're ready," she said, "I'd like you to buy some olives. He'll be coming here after dinner, and he likes them with his 'postbrandy.'"

So I went downstairs and crossed the street and shivered (it was a raw cheerless night) and pushed open the door of the little delicatessen shop opposite, and a man behind me stopped it from closing with a strong hand. He wore a trench coat and a beret, his dark face was twitching. I recognized Lieutenant Starov.

"Ah!" he said. "A whole century we did not meet!"

The cloud of his breath gave off an odd chemical smell. I had once tried sniffing cocaine (which only made me throw up), but this was some other drug.

He removed a black glove for one of those circumstantial handshakes my compatriots think proper to use at every entry and exit, and the liberated door hit him between the shoulder blades.

"Pleasant meeting!" he went on in his curious English (not parading it as might have seemed but using it by unconscious association). "I see you are in a *smoking*. Banquet?"

I bought my olives, replying the while, in Russian, that, yes, my wife and I were dining out. Then I skipped a farewell handshake, by taking advantage of the shopgirl's turning to him for the next transaction.

"What a shame," exclaimed Iris—"I wanted the black ones, not the green!"

I told her I refused to go back for them because I did not want to run into Starov again.

"Oh, that's a detestable person," she said. "I'm sure he'll try now to come and see us, hoping for some *vaw-dutch-ka*. I'm sorry you spoke to him."

She flung the window open and leant out just as Ivor was emerging from his taxi. She blew him an exuberant kiss and shouted, with illustrative gestures, that we were coming down.

"How nice it would be," she said as we hurried downstairs, "if you'd be wearing an opera cloak. You could wrap it around both of us as the Siamese twins do in your story. Now, quick!"

She dashed into Ivor's arms, and was the next moment in the safety of the cab.

"Paon d'Or," Ivor told the driver. "Good to see you, old boy," he said to me, with a distinct American intonation (which I shyly imitated at dinner until he growled: "Very funny").

The Paon d'Or no longer exists. Although not quite tops, it was a nice clean place, much patronized by American tourists, who called it "Pander" or "Pandora" and always ordered its "putty saw-lay," and that, I guess, is what we had. I remember more clearly a glazed case hanging on the gold-figured wall next to our table: it displayed four Morpho butterflies, two huge ones similar in harsh sheen but differently shaped, and two smaller ones beneath them, the left of a sweeter blue with white stripes and the right gleaming like silvery satin. According to the headwaiter, they had been caught by a convict in South America.

"And how's my friend Mata Hari?" inquired Ivor turning to us again, his spread hand still flat on the table as he had placed it when swinging toward the "bugs" under discussion.

We told him the poor ara sickened and had to be destroyed. And what about his automobile, was she still running? She jolly well was—

"In fact," Iris continued, touching my wrist, "we've decided to set off tomorrow for Cannice. Pity you can't join us, Ives, but perhaps you might come later."

I did not want to object, though I had never heard of that decision.

Ivor said that if ever we wanted to sell Villa Iris he knew someone who would snap it up any time. Iris, he said, knew him too: David Geller, the actor. "He was (turning to me) her first beau before you blundered in. She must still have somewhere that photo of him and me in *Troilus and Cressida* ten years ago. He's Helen of Troy in it, I'm Cressida."

"Lies, lies," murmured Iris.

Ivor described his own house in Los Angeles. He proposed discussing with me after dinner a script he wished me to prepare based on Gogol's *Inspector* (we were back at the start, so to speak). Iris asked for another helping of whatever it was we were eating.

"You will die," said Ivor. "It's monstrously rich. Remember what Miss Grunt (a former governess to whom he would assign all kinds of gruesome apothegms) used to say: 'The white worms lie in wait for the glutton.' "

"That's why I want to be burned when I die," remarked Iris.

He ordered a second or third bottle of the indifferent white wine I had had the polite weakness to praise. We drank to his last film—I forget its title—which was to be shown tomorrow in London, and later in Paris, he hoped.

Ivor did not look either very well or very happy; he had developed a sizable bald spot, freckled. I had never noticed before that his eyelids were so heavy and his lashes so coarse and pale. Our neighbors, three harmless Americans, hearty, flushed, vociferous, were, perhaps, not particularly pleasant, but neither Iris nor I thought Ivor's threat "to make those Bronxonians pipe down" justified, seeing that he, too, was talking in fairly resonant tones. I rather looked forward to the end of the dinner—and to coffee at home—but Iris on the contrary seemed inclined to enjoy every morsel and drop. She wore a very open, jet-black frock and the long onyx earrings I had once given her. Her cheeks and arms, without their summer tan, had the mat whiteness that I was to distribute—perhaps too generously—among the girls of my future books. Ivor's roving eyes, while he talked, tended to appraise her bare shoulders, but by the simple trick of breaking in with some question, I managed to keep confusing the trajectory of his gaze.

At last the ordeal came to a close. Iris said she would be back in a minute; her brother suggested we "repair for a leak." I declined—not because I did not need it—I did—but because I knew by experience that a talkative neighbor and the sight of his immediate stream would inevitably afflict me with urinary impotence. As I sat smoking in the lounge of the restaurant I pondered the wisdom of suddenly transferring the established habit of work on *Camera Lucida* to other surroundings, another desk, another lighting, another pressure of outside calls and smells—and I saw my pages and notes flash past like the bright windows of an express train that did not stop at my station. I had decided to talk Iris out of her plan when brother and sister appeared from opposite sides of the stage, beaming at one another. She had less than fifteen minutes of life left.

Numbers are bleary along rue Despréaux, and the taximan missed our front porch by a couple of house lengths. He suggested reversing his cab, but impatient Iris had already alighted, and I scrambled out after her, leaving Ivor to pay the taxi. She cast a look around her; then started to walk so fast toward our house that I had trouble catching up with her. As I was about to cup her elbow, I heard Ivor's voice behind me, calling out that he had not enough change. I abandoned Iris and ran back to Ivor, and just as I reached the two palm readers, they and I heard Iris cry out something loud and brave, as if she were driving away a fierce hound. By the light of a streetlamp we glimpsed the figure of a mackintoshed man stride up to her from the opposite sidewalk and fire at such close range that he seemed to prod her with his large pistol. By now our taximan, followed by Ivor and me, had come near enough to see the killer stumble over her collapsed and curled up body. Yet he did not try to escape. Instead he knelt down, took off his beret, threw back his shoulders, and in this ghastly and ludicrous attitude lifted his pistol to his shaved head.

The story that appeared among other *faits-divers* in the Paris dailies after an investigation by the police—whom Ivor and I contrived to mislead thoroughly—amounted to what follows—I translate: a White Russian, Wladimir Blagidze, *alias* Starov, who was subject to paroxysms of insanity, ran amuck Friday night in the middle of a calm street, opened fire at random, and after killing with one pistol shot an English tourist Mrs. [name garbled], who chanced to be passing by, blew his brains out beside her. Actually he did not die there and then, but retained in his remarkably tough brainpan fragments of consciousness and somehow lingered on well into May, which was unusually hot that year. Out of some perverse dream-like curiosity, Ivor visited him at the very special hospital of the renowned Dr. Lazareff, a very round, mercilessly round, building on the top of a hill, thickly covered with horse chestnut, wild rose, and other poignant plants. The hole in Blagidze's mind had caused a complete set of recent memories to escape; but the patient remembered quite clearly (according to a Russian male nurse good at decoding the tales of the tortured) how at six years of age he was taken to a pleasure park in Italy where a miniature train consisting of three open cars, each seating six silent children, with a battery-operated green engine that emitted at realistic intervals puffs of imitation smoke, pursued a circular course through a brambly picturesque nightmare grove whose dizzy flowers nodded continuous assent to all the horrors of childhood and hell.

From somewhere in the Orkneys, Nadezhda Gordonovna and a clerical friend arrived in Paris only after her husband's burial. Moved by a false sense of duty, she attempted to see me so as to tell me "everything." I evaded all contact with her, but she managed to locate Ivor in London before he left for the States. I never asked him, and the dear funny fellow never revealed to me what that "everything" was; I refuse to believe that it could have amounted to much—and I knew enough, anyway. By nature I am not vindictive; yet I like to dwell in fancy on the image of that little green train, running on, round and round, forever.

Part Two

I

A CURIOUS form of self-preservation moves us to get rid, instantly, irrevocably, of all that belonged to the loved one we lost. Otherwise, the things she touched every day and kept in their proper context by the act of handling them start to become bloated with an awful mad life of their own. Her dresses now wear their own selves, her books leaf through their own pages. We suffocate in the tightening circle of those monsters that are misplaced and misshapen because she is not there to tend them. And even the bravest among us cannot meet the gaze of her mirror.

How to get rid of them is another problem. I could not drown them like kittens; in fact, I could not drown a kitten, let alone her brush or bag. Nor could I watch a stranger collect them, take them away, come back for more. Therefore, I simply abandoned the flat, telling the maid to dispose in any manner she chose of all those unwanted things. Unwanted! At the moment of parting they appeared quite normal and harmless; I would even say they looked taken aback.

At first I tried putting up in a third-rate hotel in the center of Paris. I would fight terror and solitude by working all day. I completed one novel, began another, wrote forty poems (all robbers and brothers under their motley skin), a dozen short stories, seven essays, three devastating reviews, one parody. The business of not losing my mind during the night was taken care of by swallowing an especially potent pill or buying a bedmate.

I remember a dangerous dawn in May (1931? or 1932?); all the birds (mostly sparrows) were singing as in Heine's month of May, with demonic monotonous force—that's why I know it must have been a wonderful May morning. I lay with my face to the wall and in a muddled ominous way considered the question should "we" not drive earlier than usual to Villa Iris. An obstacle, however, kept preventing me from under-

taking that journey: the car and the house had been sold, so
Iris had told me herself at the Protestant cemetery, because
the masters of her faith and fate interdicted cremation. I
turned in bed from the wall to the window, and Iris was lying
with her dark head to me on the window side of the bed. I
kicked off the bedclothes. She was naked, save for her black-
stockinged legs (which was strange but at the same time recalled something from a parallel world, for my mind stood
astride on two circus horses). In an erotic footnote, I reminded myself for the ten thousandth time to mention somewhere that there is nothing more seductive than a girl's back
with the profiled rise of the haunch accentuated by her lying
sidelong, one leg slightly bent. "*J'ai froid*," said the girl as I
touched her shoulder.

The Russian term for any kind of betrayal, faithlessness,
breach of trust, is the snaky, watered-silk word *izmena* which
is based on the idea of change, shift, transformation. This der-
ivation had never occurred to me in my constant thoughts
about Iris, but now it struck me as the revelation of a be-
witchment, of a nymph's turning into a whore—and this
called for an immediate and vociferous protest. One neighbor
thumped the wall, another rattled the door. The frightened
girl, snatching up her handbag and my raincoat, bolted out
of the room, and a bearded individual entered instead, farci-
cally clad in a nightshirt and wearing rubbers on his bare feet.
The crescendo of my cries, cries of rage and distress, ended
in a hysterical fit. I think some attempt was made to whisk
me off to a hospital. In any case, I had to find another home
sans tarder, a phrase I cannot hear without a spasm of anguish
by mental association with her lover's letter.

A small patch of countryside kept floating before my eyes
like some photic illusion. I let my index finger stray at random
over a map of northern France; the point of its nail stopped
at the town of Petiver or Petit Ver, a small worm or verse,
which sounded idyllic. An autobus took me to a road station
not very far from Orléans, I believe. All I remember of my
abode is its oddly slanting floor which corresponded to a slant
in the ceiling of the café under my room. I also remember a
pastel-green park to the east of the town, and an old castle.
The summer I spent there is a mere smudge of color on the

dull glass of my mind; but I did write a few poems—at least one of which, about a company of acrobats staging a show on the church square, has been reprinted a number of times in the course of forty years.

When I returned to Paris I found that my kind friend Stepan Ivanovich Stepanov, a prominent journalist of independent means (he was one of those very few lucky Russians who had happened to transfer themselves and their money abroad before the Bolshevik *coup*), had not only organized my second or third public reading (*vecher*, "evening," was the Russian term consecrated to that kind of performance) but wanted me to stay in one of the ten rooms of his spacious old-fashioned house (Avenue Koch? Roche? It abuts, or abutted, on the statue of a general whose name escapes me but surely lurks somewhere among my old notes).

Its residents were at the moment old Mr. and Mrs. Stepanov, their married daughter Baroness Borg, her eleven-year-old child (the Baron, a businessman, had been sent by his firm to England), and Grigoriy Reich (1899–1942?), a gentle, melancholy, lean, young poet, of no talent whatever, who under the pen name of Lunin contributed a weekly elegy to the *Novosti* and acted as Stepanov's secretary.

I could not avoid coming down in the evenings to join the frequent gatherings of literary and political personages in the ornate salon or in the dining room with its huge oblong table and the oil portrait *en pied* of the Stepanovs' young son who had died in 1920 while trying to save a drowning schoolmate. Nearsighted, gruffly jovial Alexander Kerenski would usually be there, brusquely raising his eyeglass to stare at a stranger or greeting an old friend with a ready quip in that rasping voice of his, most of its strength lost years ago in the roar of the Revolution. Ivan Shipogradov, eminent novelist and recent Nobel Prize winner, would also be present, radiating talent and charm, and—after a few jiggers of vodka—delighting his intimates with the kind of Russian bawdy tale that depends for its artistry on the rustic gusto and fond respect with which it treats our most private organs. A far less engaging figure was I. A. Shipogradov's old rival, a fragile little man in a sloppy suit, Vasiliy Sokolovski (oddly nicknamed "Jeremy" by I.A.), who since the dawn of the century had been devoting

volume after volume to the mystical and social history of a
Ukrainian clan that had started as a humble family of three in
the sixteenth century but by volume six (1920) had become a
whole village, replete with folklore and myth. It was good to
see old Morozov's rough-hewn clever face with its shock of
dingy hair and bright frosty eyes; and for a special reason I
closely observed podgy dour Basilevski—not because he had
just had or was about to have a row with his young mistress,
a feline beauty who wrote doggerel verse and vulgarly flirted
with me, but because I hoped he had already seen the fun I
had made of him in the last issue of a literary review in which
we both collaborated. Although his English was inadequate
for the interpretation of, say, Keats (whom he defined as "a
pre-Wildean aesthete in the beginning of the Industrial Era")
Basilevski was fond of attempting just that. In discussing recently the "not altogether displeasing preciosity" of my own
stuff, he had imprudently quoted a popular line from Keats,
rendering it as:

Vsegda nas raduet krasivaya veshchitsa

which in retranslation gives:

"A pretty bauble always gladdens us."

Our conversation, however, turned out to be much too brief
to disclose whether or not he had appreciated my amusing
lesson. He asked me what I thought of the new book he was
telling Morozov (a monolinguist) about—namely Maurois'
"impressive work on Byron," and upon my answering that I
had found it to be impressive trash, my austere critic muttered,
"I don't think you have read it," and went on educating the
serene old poet.

I would steal away long before the party broke up. The
sounds of farewells usually reached me as I glided into insomnia.

I spent most of the day working, ensconced in a deep armchair, with my implements conveniently resting before me on
a special writing board provided by my host, a great lover of
handy knickknacks. Somehow or other I had started to gain
weight since my bereavement and by now had to make two
or three lurching efforts in order to leave my overaffectionate

seat. Only one little person visited me; for her I kept my door slightly ajar. The board's proximal edge had a thoughtful incurvature to accommodate an author's abdomen, and the distal side was equipped with clamps and rubberbands to hold papers and pencils in place; I got so used to those comforts that I regretted ungratefully the absence of toilet fixtures—such as one of those hollow canes said to be used by Orientals.

Every afternoon, at the same hour, a silent push opened the door wider, and the granddaughter of the Stepanovs brought in a tray with a large glass of strong tea and a plate of ascetic zwiebacks. She advanced, eyes bent, moving carefully her white-socked, blue-sneakered feet; coming to a near stop when the tea tossed; and advancing again with the slow steps of a clockwork doll. She had flaxen hair and a freckled nose, and I chose the gingham frock with the glossy black belt for her to wear when I had her continue her mysterious progress right into the book I was writing, *The Red Top Hat*, in which she becomes graceful little Amy, the condemned man's ambiguous consoler.

Those were nice, nice interludes! One could hear the Baroness and her mother playing *à quatre mains* in the salon downstairs as they had played and replayed, no doubt, for the last fifteen years. I had a box of chocolate-coated biscuits to supplement the zwiebacks and tempt my little visitor. The writing board was put aside and replaced by her folded limbs. She spoke Russian fluently but with Parisian interjections and interrogatory sounds, and those bird notes lent something eerie to the responses I obtained, as she dangled one leg and bit her biscuit, to the ordinary questions one puts to a child; and then quite suddenly in the midst of our chat, she would wriggle out of my arms and make for the door as if somebody were summoning her, though actually the piano kept stumbling on and on in the homely course of a family happiness in which I had no part and which, in fact, I had never known.

My stay at the Stepanovs' had been supposed to last a couple of weeks; it lasted two months. At first I felt comparatively well, or at least comfortable and refreshed, but a new sleeping pill which had worked so well at its beguiling stage began refusing to cope with certain reveries which, as suggested subsequently by an incredible sequel, I should have succumbed to like a man and got done with no matter how; instead of that I took advantage of Dolly's removal to England to find a new dwelling for my miserable carcass. This was a bed-sitting-room in a shabby but quiet tenement house on the Left Bank, "at the corner of rue St. Supplice," says my pocket diary with grim imprecision. An ancient cupboard of sorts contained a primitive shower bath; but there were no other facilities. Going out two or three times a day for a meal, or a cup of coffee, or an extravagant purchase at a delicatessen, afforded me a small *distraction*. In the next block I found a cinema that specialized in old horse operas and a tiny brothel with four whores ranging in age from eighteen to thirty-eight, the youngest being also the plainest.

I was to spend many years in Paris, tied to that dismal city by the threads of a Russian writer's livelihood. Nothing then, and nothing now, in backcast, had or has for me any of the spell that enthralled my compatriots. I am not thinking of the blood spot on the darkest stone of its darkest street; that is *hors-concours* in the way of horror; I just mean that I regarded Paris, with its gray-toned days and charcoal nights, merely as the chance setting for the most authentic and faithful joys of my life: the colored phrase in my mind under the drizzle, the white page under the desk lamp awaiting me in my humble home.

2

Since 1925 I had written and published four novels; by the beginning of 1934 I was on the point of completing my fifth, *Krasnyy Tsilindr* (*The Red Top Hat*), the story of a beheading. None of those books exceeded ninety thousand words but my method of choosing and blending them could hardly be called a timesaving expedient.

A first draft, made in pencil, filled several blue *cahiers* of the kind used in schools, and upon reaching the saturation point of revision presented a chaos of smudges and scriggles. To this corresponded the disorder of the text which followed a regular sequence only for a few pages, being then interrupted by some chunky passage that belonged to a later, or earlier, part of the story. After sorting out and repaginating all this, I applied myself to the next stage: the fair copy. It was tidily written with a fountain pen in a fat and sturdy exercise book or ledger. Then an orgy of new corrections would blot out by degrees all the pleasure of specious perfection. A third phase started where legibility stopped. Poking with slow and rigid fingers at the keys of my trusty old *mashinka* ("machine"), Count Starov's wedding present, I would be able to type some three hundred words in one hour instead of the round thousand with which some popular novelist of the previous century could cram it in longhand.

In the case of *The Red Top Hat*, however, the neuralgic aches which had been spreading through my frame like an inner person of pain, all angles and claws, for the last three years, had now attained my extremities, and made the task of typing a fortunate impossibility. By economizing on my favorite nutriments, such as *foie gras* and Scotch whisky, and postponing the making of a new suit, I calculated that my modest income allowed me to hire an expert typist, to whom I would dictate my corrected manuscript during, say, thirty carefully planned afternoons. I therefore inserted a prominent wanter, with name and telephone, in the *Novosti*.

Among the three or four typists who offered their services, I chose Lyubov Serafimovna Savich, the granddaughter of a country priest and the daughter of a famous SR (Social Revolutionist) who had recently died in Meudon upon completing his biography of Alexander the First (a tedious work in two volumes entitled *The Monarch and the Mystic*, now available to American students in an indifferent translation, Harvard, 1970).

Lyuba Savich started working for me on February 1, 1934. She came as often as necessary and was willing to stay any number of hours (the record she set on an especially memorable occasion was from one to eight). Had there been a Miss Russia and had the age of prize misses been prolonged to just under thirty, beautiful Lyuba would have won the title. She was a tall woman with slim ankles, big breasts, broad shoulders, and a pair of gay blue eyes in a round rosy face. Her auburn hair must have always felt as being in a state of imminent disarray for she constantly stroked its side wave, in a graceful elbow-raised gesture, when talking to me. *Zdraste*, and once more *zdraste*, Lyubov Serafimovna—and, oh, what a delightful amalgam that was, with *lyubov* meaning "love," and Serafim ("seraph") being the Christian name of a reformed terrorist!

As a typist L.S. was magnificent. Hardly had I finished dictating one sentence, as I paced back and forth, than it had reached her furrow like a handful of grain, and with one eyebrow raised she was already looking at me, waiting for the next strewing. If a sudden alteration for the better occurred to me in mid session, I preferred not to spoil the wonderful give-and-take rhythm of our joint work by introducing painful pauses of word weighing—especially enervating and sterile when a self-conscious author is aware that the bright lady at the waiting typewriter is longing to come up with a helpful suggestion; I contented myself therefore with marking the passage in my manuscript so as later to desecrate with my scrawl her immaculate creation; but she was only glad, of course, to retype the page at her leisure.

We usually had a ten-minute break around four—or four-thirty if I could not rein in snorting Pegasus on the dot. She would retire for a minute, closing one door after another with a really unearthly gentleness, to the humble *toilettes* across the corridor, and would reappear, just as silently, with a repowdered nose and a repainted smile, and I would have ready for her a glass of *vin ordinaire* and a pink gaufrette. It was during those innocent intervals that there began a certain thematic movement on the part of fate.

Would I like to know something? (Dilatory sip and lip lick.) Well, at all my five public readings since the first on September 3, 1928, in the Salle Planiol, she had been present, she had applauded till her palms (showing palms) ached, and had made up her mind that next time she'd be smart and plucky enough to push her way through the crowd (yes, crowd—no need to smile ironically) with the firm intention of clasping my hand and pouring out her soul in a single word, which, however, she could never find—and that's why, inexorably, she would always be left standing and beaming like a fool in the middle of the vacated hall. Would I despise her for having an album with reviews of my books pasted in—Morozov's and Yablokov's lovely essays as well as the trash of such hacks as Boris Nyet, and Boyarski? Did I know it was *she* who had left that mysterious bunch of irises on the spot where the urn with my wife's ashes had been interred four years ago? Could I imagine that she could recite by heart every poem I had published in the *émigré* press of half-a-dozen countries? Or that she remembered thousands of enchanting minutiae scattered through all my novels such as the mallard's quack-quack (in *Tamara*) "which to the end of one's life would taste of Russian black bread because one had shared it with ducks in one's childhood," or the chess set (in *Pawn Takes Queen*) with a missing Knight "replaced by some sort of counter, a little orphan from another, unknown, game?"

All this was spread over several sessions and distilled very cunningly, and already by the end of February when a copy of *The Red Top Hat*, an impeccable typescript, lapped in an opulent envelope, had been delivered by hand (hers again) to the offices of *Patria* (the foremost Russian magazine in Paris), I felt enmeshed in a bothersome web.

Not only had I never experienced the faintest twinge of desire in regard to beautiful Lyuba, but the indifference of my senses was turning to positive repulsion. The softer her glances fluttered, the more ungentlemanly my reaction became. Her very refinement had a dainty edge of vulgarity that infested with the sweetness of decay her entire personality. I began to notice with growing irritation such pathetic things as her odor, a quite respectable perfume (*Adoration*, I think) precariously overlaying the natural smell of a Russian maiden's seldom bathed body: for an hour or so *Adoration* still held, but after that the underground would start to conduct more and more frequent forays, and when she raised her arms to put on her hat—but never mind, she was a well-meaning creature, and I hope she is a happy grandmother today.

I would be a cad to describe our last meeting (March 1 of the same year). Suffice it to say that in the middle of typing a rhymed Russian translation that I had made of Keats' *To Autumn* ("Season of mists and mellow fruitfulness") she broke down, and tormented me till at least eight P.M. with her confessions and tears. When at last she left, I lost another hour composing a detailed letter asking her never to come back. Incidentally, it was the first time that an unfinished leaf was left by her in my typewriter. I removed it and rediscovered it several weeks later among my papers, and then deliberately preserved it because it was Annette who completed the job, with a couple of typos and an x-ed erasure in the last lines— and something about the juxtaposition appealed to my combinational slant.

3

In this memoir my wives and my books are interlaced monogrammatically like some sort of watermark or *ex libris* design; and in writing this oblique autobiography—oblique, because dealing mainly not with pedestrian history but with the mirages of romantic and literary matters—I consistently try to dwell as lightly as inhumanly possible on the evolution of my mental illness. Yet Dementia is one of the characters in my story.

By the mid-Thirties little had changed in my health since the first half of 1922 and its awful torments. My battle with factual, respectable life still consisted of sudden delusions, sudden reshufflings—kaleidoscopic, stained-glass reshufflings!— of fragmented space. I still felt Gravity, that infernal and humiliating contribution to our perceptual world, grow into me like a monstrous toenail in stabs and wedges of intolerable pain (incomprehensible to the happy simpleton who finds nothing fantastic and agonizing in the escape of a pencil or penny *under* something—under the desk on which one will live, under the bed on which one will die). I still could not cope with the abstraction of direction in space, so that any given stretch of the world was either permanently "right-hand" or permanently "left-hand," or at best the one could be changed to the other only by a spine-dislocating effort of the will. Oh, how things and people tortured me, my dear heart, I could not tell you! In point of fact you were not yet even born.

Sometime in the mid-Thirties, in black accursed Paris, I remember visiting a distant relative of mine (a niece of the
LATH lady!). She was a sweet old stranger. She sat all day in
a straight-back armchair exposed to the continuous attacks of
three, four, more than four, deranged children, whom she was
paid (by the Destitute Russian Noblewomen's Aid Association) to watch, while their parents were working in places not
so dreadful and dreary in themselves as dreary and difficult to
reach by public conveyance. I sat on an old hassock at her
feet. Her talk flowed on and on, smooth, untroubled, reflecting the image of radiant days, serenity, wealth, goodness. Yet
all the time this or that poor little monster with a slavering
mouth and a squint would move upon her from behind a
screen or a table and rock her chair or clutch at her skirt.
When the squealing became too loud she would only wince
a little which hardly affected her reminiscent smile. She kept
a kind of fly whisk within easy reach and this she occasionally
brandished to chase away the bolder aggressors; but all the
time, all the time, she continued her purling soliloquy and I
understood that I, too, should ignore the rude turmoil and
din around her.

I submit that my life, my plight, the voice of words that
was my sole joy and the secret struggle with the wrong shape
of things, bore some resemblance to that poor lady's predicament. And mind you, those were my best days, with only a
pack of grimacing goblins to hold at bay.

The zest, the strength, the clarity of my art remained unimpaired—at least to a certain extent. I enjoyed, I persuaded
myself to enjoy, the solitude of work and that other, even
more subtle solitude, the solitude of an author facing, from
behind the bright shield of his manuscript, an amorphous audience, barely visible in its dark pit.

The jumble of spatial obstacles separating my bedside lamp
from the illumined islet of a public lectern was abolished by
the magic of thoughtful friends who helped me to get to this
or that remote hall without my having to tussle with horribly
small and thin, sticky, bus-ticket slips or to venture into the
thunderous maze of the *Métro*. As soon as I was safely plat-
formed with my typed or handwritten sheets at breastbone
level on the desk before me, I forgot all about the presence

of three hundred eavesdroppers. A decanter of watered vodka, my only lectorial whim, was also my only link with the material universe. Similar to a painter's spotlight on the brown brow of some ecstatical ecclesiastic at the moment of divine revelation, the radiance enclosing me brought out with oracular accuracy every imperfection in my text. A memoirist has noted that not only did I slow down now and then while unclipping a pencil and replacing a comma by a semicolon, but that I had been known to stop and frown over a sentence and reread it, and cross it out, and insert a correction and "remouth the whole passage with a kind of defiant complacency."

My handwriting was good in fair copies, but I felt more comfortable with a typescript before me, and I was again without an expert typist. To insert the same wanter in the same paper would have been foolhardy: what if it were to bring back Lyuba, flushed with renewed hope, and rewind that damned cycle all over again?

I rang up Stepanov, thinking he might help; he guessed he could, and after a muffled confabulation with his fussy wife, just on the brim of the membrane (all I made out was "mad people are unpredictable"), she took over. They knew a very decent girl who had worked at the Russian nursery school "Passy na Rousi" to which Dolly had gone four or five years ago. The girl's name was Anna Ivanovna Blagovo. Did I know Oksman, the owner of the Russian bookshop on rue Cuvier?

"Yes, slightly. But I want to ask you—"

"Well," she went on, interrupting me, "Annette *sekretarstvovala* for him while his regular typist was hospitalized, but she is now quite well again, and you might—"

"That's fine," I said, "but I want to ask you, Berta Abramovna, why did you accuse me of being an 'unpredictable madman'? I can assure you that I am not in the habit of raping young women—"

"*Gospod' s vami, golubchik!* (What an idea, my dear!)" exclaimed Mrs. Stepanov and proceeded to explain that she had been scolding her absentminded husband for sitting down on her new handbag when attending to the telephone.

Although I did not believe one word of her version (too quick! too glib!), I pretended to accept it and promised to look up her bookseller. A few minutes later as I was about to open the window and strip in front of it (at moments of raw widowerhood a soft black night in the spring is the most soothing *voyeuse* imaginable), Berta Stepanov telephoned to say that the oxman (what a shiver my Iris derived from Dr. Moreau's island zoo—especially from such bits as the "screaming shape," still half-bandaged, escaping out of the lab!) would be up till dawn in his shop, among nightmare-inherited ledgers. She knew, hey-hey (Russian chuckle), that I was a noctambule, so perhaps I might like to stroll over to the Boyan Bookshop *sans tarder*, without retardment, vile term. I might, indeed.

After that jarring call, I saw little to choose between the tossings of insomnia and a walk to rue Cuvier which leads to the Seine, where according to police statistics an average of forty foreigners and God knows how many unfortunate natives drown yearly between wars. I have never experienced the least urge to commit suicide, that silly waste of selfhood (a gem in any light). But I must admit that on that particular night on the fourth or fifth or fiftieth anniversary of my darling's death, I must have looked pretty suspect, in my black suit and dramatic muffler, to an average policeman of the riparian department. And it is a particularly bad sign when a hatless person sobs as he walks, being moved not by lines he might have composed himself but by something he hideously mistakes for his own and presently flinches, yet is too much of a coward to make amends:

> *Zvezdoobraznost' nebesnyh zvyozd*
> *Vidish' tol'ko skvoz' slyozy . . .*
> (Heavenly stars are seen as stellate
> only through tears.)

I am much bolder now, of course, much bolder and prouder than the ambiguous hoodlum caught progressing that night between a seemingly endless fence with its tattered posters and a row of spaced streetlamps whose light would delicately select for its heart-piercing game overhead a young emerald-bright linden leaf. I now confess that I was bothered that night, and the next and some time before, by a dream feeling that my life was the nonidentical twin, a parody, an inferior variant of another man's life, somewhere on this or another earth. A demon, I felt, was forcing me to impersonate that other man, that other writer who was and would always be incomparably greater, healthier, and crueler than your obedient servant.

4

The "Boyan" publishing firm (Morozov's and mine was the "Bronze Horseman," its main rival), with a bookshop (selling not only *émigré* editions but also tractor novels from Moscow) and a lending library, occupied a smart three-story house of the *hôtel particulier* type. In my day it stood between a garage and a cinema: forty years before (in the vista of reverse metamorphosis) the former had been a fountain and the latter a group of stone nymphs. The house had belonged to the Merlin de Malaune family and had been acquired at the turn of the century by a Russian cosmopolitan, Dmitri de Midoff who with his friend S. I. Stepanov established there the headquarters of an anti-despotic conspiracy. The latter liked to recall the sign language of old-fashioned rebellion: the half-drawn curtain and alabaster vase revealed in the drawing-room window so as to indicate to the expected guest from Russia that the way was clear. An aesthetic touch graced revolutionary intrigues in those years. Midoff died soon after World War One, and by that time the Terrorist party, to which those cozy people belonged, had lost its "stylistic appeal" as Stepanov himself put it. I do not know who later acquired the house or how it happened that Oks (Osip Lvovich Oksman, 1885?–1943?) rented it for his business.

The house was dark except for three windows: two adjacent rectangles of light in the middle of the upper-floor row, d8 and e8, Continental notation (where the letter denotes the file and the number the rank of a chess square) and another light just below at e7. Good God, had I forgotten at home the note I had scribbled for the unknown Miss Blagovo? No, it was still there in my breast pocket under the old, treasured, horribly hot and long Trinity College muffler. I hesitated between a side door on my right—marked *Magazin*—and the main entrance, with a chess coronet above the bell. Finally I chose the coronet. We were playing a *Blitz* game: my opponent moved at once, lighting the vestibule fan at d6. One could not help wondering if under the house there might not exist the five lower floors which would complete the chessboard and that somewhere, in subterranean mystery, new men might not be working out the doom of a fouler tyranny.

Oks, a tall, bony, elderly man with a Shakespearean pate, started to tell me how honored he was at getting a chance to welcome the author of *Camera*—here I thrust the note I carried into his extended palm and prepared to leave. He had dealt with hysterical artists before. None could resist his bland bookside manner.

"Yes, I know all about it," he said, retaining and patting my hand. "She'll call you; though, to tell the truth, I do not envy anybody having to use the services of that capricious, absentminded young lady. We'll go up to my study, unless you prefer—no, I don't think so," he continued, opening a double door on the left and dubiously switching on the light for a moment to reveal a chilly reading room in which a long baize-covered table, dingy chairs, and the cheap busts of Russian classics contradicted a lovely painted ceiling swarming with naked children among purple, pink, and amber clusters of grapes. On the right (another tentative light snapped) a short passage led to the shop proper where I recalled having once had a row with a pert old female who objected to my not wishing to pay for a few copies of my own novel. So we walked up the once noble stairs, which now had something seldom seen even in Viennese dream comics, namely disparate balustrades, the sinistral one an ugly new ramp-and-railing affair and the other, the original ornate set of battered, doomed, but still charming carved wood with supports in the form of magnified chess pieces.

"I am honored—" began Oks all over again, as we reached his so-called *Kabinet* (study), at e7, a room cluttered with ledgers, packed books, half-unpacked books, towers of books, heaps of newspapers, pamphlets, galleys, and slim white paperback collections of poems—tragic offals, with the cool, restrained titles then in fashion—*Prokhlada* ("coolness"), *Sderzhannost'* ("restraint").

He was one of those persons who for some reason or other are often interrupted, but whom no force in our blessed galaxy will prevent from completing their sentence, despite new interruptions, of an elemental or poetical nature, the death of his interlocutor ("I was just saying to him, doctor—"), or the entrance of a dragon. In fact it would seem that those interruptions actually help to polish the phrase and give it its final form. In the meantime the agonizing itch of its being unfinished poisons the mind. It is worse than the pimple which cannot be sprung before one gets home, and is almost as bad as a lifer's recollection of that last little rape nipped in the sweet bud by the intrusion of an accursed policeman.

"I am deeply honored," finished at last Oks, "to welcome to this historic house the author of *Camera Obscura*, your finest book in my modest opinion!"

"It ought to be modest," I said, controlling myself (opal ice in Nepal before the avalanche), "because, you idiot, the title of *my* novel is *Camera Lucida*."

"There, there," said Oks (really a very dear man and a gentleman), after a terrible pause during which all the remainders opened like fairy-tale flowers in a fancy film, "A slip of the tongue does not deserve such a harsh rebuke. *Lucida, Lucida*, by all means! *A propos*—concerning Anna Blagovo (another piece of unfinished business—or, who knows, a touching attempt to divert and pacify me with an interesting anecdote), I am not sure you know that I am Berta's first cousin. Thirty-five years ago in St. Petersburg she and I worked in the same student organization. We were preparing the assassination of the Premier. How far all that is! His daily route had to be closely established; I was one of the observers. Standing at a certain corner every day in the disguise of a vanilla-ice-cream vendor! Can you imagine that? Nothing came of our plans. They were thwarted by Azef, the great double agent."

I saw no point in prolonging my visit, but he produced a bottle of cognac, and I accepted a drink, for I was beginning to tremble again.

"Your *Camera*," he said, consulting a ledger, "has been selling not badly in my shop, not badly at all: twenty-three—

sorry, twenty-five—copies in the first half of last year, and fourteen in the second. Of course, genuine fame, not mere commercial success, depends on the behavior of a book in the Lending Department, and there all your titles are hits. Not to leave this unsubstantiated, let us go up to the stacks."

I followed my energetic host to the upper floor. The lending library spread like a gigantic spider, bulged like a monstrous tumor, oppressed the brain like the expanding world of delirium. In a bright oasis amidst the dim shelves I noticed a group of people sitting around an oval table. The colors were vivid and sharp but at the same time remote-looking as in a magic-lantern scene. A good deal of red wine and golden brandy accompanied the animated discussion. I recognized the critic Basilevski, his sycophants Hristov and Boyarski, my friend Morozov, the novelists Shipogradov and Sokolovski, the honest nonentity Suknovalov, author of the popular social satire *Geroy nashey ery* ("Hero of Our Era") and two young poets, Lazarev (collection *Serenity*) and Fartuk (collection *Silence*). Some of the heads turned toward us, and the benevolent bear Morozov even struggled to his feet, grinning—but my host said they were having a business meeting and should be left alone.

"You have glimpsed," he added, "the parturition of a new literary review, *Prime Number*s; at least they *think* they are parturiating: actually, they are boozing and gossiping. Now let me show you something."

He led me to a distant corner and triumphantly trained his flashlight on the gaps in *my* shelf of books.

"Look," he cried, "how many copies are out. All of *Princess Mary* is out, I mean *Mary*—damn it, I mean *Tamara*. I love *Tamara*, I mean your *Tamara*, not Lermontov's or Rubinstein's. Forgive me. One gets so confused among so many damned masterpieces."

I said I was not feeling well and would like to go home. He offered to accompany me. Or would I like a taxi? I did not. He kept furtively directing at me the electric torch through his incarnadined fingers to see if I was not about to faint. With soothing sounds he led me down a side staircase. The spring night, at least, felt real.

After a moment of rumination and an upward glance at the

lighted windows, Oks beckoned to the night watchman who was stroking the sad little dog of a dog-walking neighbor. I saw my thoughtful companion shake hands with the gray-cloaked old fellow, then point to the light of the revelers, then look at his watch, then tip the man, and shake hands with him in parting, as if the ten-minute walk to my lodgings were a perilous pilgrimage.

"*Bon*," he said upon rejoining me. "If you don't want a taxi, let us set out on foot. He will take care of my imprisoned visitors. There are heaps of things I want you to tell me about your work and your life. Your *confrères* say you are 'arrogant and unsocial' as Onegin describes himself to Tatiana but we can't all be Lenskis, can we? Let me take advantage of this pleasant stroll to describe my two meetings with your celebrated father. The first was at the opera in the days of the First Duma. I knew, of course, the portraits of its most prominent members. From high up in the gods I, a poor student, saw him appear in a rosy loge with his wife and two little boys, one of which must have been you. The other time was at a public discussion of current politics in the auroral period of the Revolution; he spoke immediately after Kerenski, and the contrast between our fiery friend and your father, with his English *sangfroid* and absence of gesticulation—"

"My father," I said, "died six months before I was born."

"Well, I seem to have goofed again (*opyat' oskandalilsya*)," observed Oks, after taking quite a minute to find his handkerchief, blow his nose with the grandiose deliberation of Varlamov in the role of Gogol's Town Mayor, wrap up the result, and pocket the swaddle. "Yes, I'm not lucky with you. Yet that image remains in my mind. The contrast was truly remarkable."

I was to run into Oks again, three or four times at least, in the course of the dwindling years before World War Two. He used to welcome me with a knowing twinkle as if we shared some very private and rather naughty secret. His superb library was eventually grabbed by the Germans who then lost it to the Russians, even better grabbers in that time-honored game. Osip Lvovich himself was to die when attempting an intrepid escape—when almost having escaped—barefoot, in bloodstained underwear, from the "experimental hospital" of a Nazi concentration camp.

5

My father was a gambler and a rake. His society nickname was Demon. Vrubel has portrayed him with his vampire-pale cheeks, his diamond eyes, his black hair. What remained on the palette has been used by me, Vadim, son of Vadim, for touching up the father of the passionate siblings in the best of my English romaunts, *Ardis* (1970).

The scion of a princely family devoted to a gallery of a dozen Tsars, my father resided on the idyllic outskirts of history. His politics were of the casual, reactionary sort. He had a dazzling and complicated sensual life, but his culture was patchy and commonplace. He was born in 1865, married in 1896, and died in a pistol duel with a young Frenchman on October 22, 1898, after a card-table fracas at Deauville, some resort in gray Normandy.

There might be nothing particularly upsetting about a well-meaning, essentially absurd and muddled old duffer mistaking me for some other writer. I myself have been known, in the lecture hall, to say Shelley when I meant Schiller. But that a fool's slip of the tongue or error of memory should establish a sudden connection with another world, so soon after my imagining with especial dread that I might be permanently impersonating somebody living as a real being beyond the constellation of my tears and asterisks—*that* was unendurable, *that* dared not happen!

As soon as the last sound of poor Oksman's farewells and excuses had subsided, I tore off the striped woollen snake strangling me and wrote down in cipher every detail of my meeting with him. Then I drew a thick line underneath and a caravan of question marks.

Should I ignore the coincidence and its implications? Should I, on the contrary, repattern my entire life? Should I abandon my art, choose another line of achievement, take up chess seriously, or become, say, a lepidopterist, or spend a dozen years as an obscure scholar making a Russian translation of *Paradise Lost* that would cause hacks to shy and asses to kick? But only the writing of fiction, the endless re-creation of my fluid self could keep me more or less sane. All I did finally was drop my pen name, the rather cloying and somehow misleading "V. Irisin" (of which my Iris herself used to say that it sounded as if I were a villa), and revert to my own family name.

It was with this name that I decided to sign the first installment of my new novel *The Dare* for which the *émigré* magazine *Patria* was waiting. I had finished rewriting in reptile-green ink (a placebo to enliven my task) a second or third fair copy of the opening chapter, when Annette Blagovo came to discuss hours and terms.

She came on May 2, 1934, half-an-hour late, and as persons do who have no sense of duration, laid the blame for her lateness on her innocent watch, an object for measuring motion, not time. She was a graceful blonde of twenty-six years or so, with very attractive though not exceptionally pretty features. She wore a gray tailor-made jacket over a white silk blouse that looked frilly and festive because of a kind of bow between the lapels, to one of which was pinned a bunchlet of violets. Her short smartly cut gray skirt had a nice dash about it, and all in all she was far more chic and *soignée* than an average Russian young lady.

I explained to her (in what struck her—so she told me much later—as the unpleasantly bantering tone of a cynic sizing up a possible conquest) that I proposed to dictate to her every afternoon "right into the typewriter" (*pryamo v mashinku*) heavily corrected drafts or else chunks and sausages of fair copy that I would probably revise "in the lonely hours of night," to quote A. K. Tolstoy, and have her retype next day. She did not remove her close-fitting hat, but peeled off her gloves and, pursing her bright pink freshly painted mouth, put on large tortoiseshell-rimmed glasses, and the effect somehow enhanced her looks: she desired to see my machine (her icy demureness would have turned a saint into a salacious jester), had to hurry to another appointment but just wanted to check if she could use it. She took off her green cabochon ring (which I was to find after her departure) and seemed about to tap out a quick sample but a second glance satisfied her that my typewriter was of the same make as her own.

Our first session proved pretty awful. I had learned my part with the care of a nervous actor, but did not reckon with the kind of fellow performer who misses or fluffs every other cue. She asked me not to go so fast. She put me off by fatuous remarks: "There is no such expression in Russian," or "Nobody knows that word (*vzvoden'*, a welter)—why don't you just say "big wave" if that's what you mean? When anger affected my rhythm and it took me some time to unravel the end of a sentence in its no longer familiar labyrinth of cancellations and carets, she would sit back and wait like a provocative martyr and stifle a yawn or study her fingernails. After three hours of work, I examined the result of her dainty and impudent rattle. It teemed with misspellings, typos, and ugly erasures. Very meekly I said that she seemed unaccustomed to deal with literary (i.e. non-humdrum) stuff. She answered I was mistaken, she loved literature. In fact, she said, in just the past five months she had read Galsworthy (in Russian), Dostoyevski (in French), General Pudov-Usurovski's huge historical novel *Tsar Bronshteyn* (in the original), and *L'Atlantide* (which I had not heard of but which a dictionary ascribes to Pierre Benoît, *romancier français né à Albi*, a hiatus in the Tarn). Did she know Morozov's poetry? No, she did not much care for poetry in any form; it was inconsistent with the tempo of modern life. I chided her for not having read any of my stories or novels, and she looked annoyed and perhaps a little frightened (fearing, the little goose, I might dismiss her), and presently was giving me a curiously erotic satisfaction by promising me that now she would look up *all* my books and would certainly know by heart *The Dare*.

The reader must have noticed that I speak only in a very general way about my Russian fictions of the Nineteen-Twenties and Thirties, for I assume that he is familiar with them or can easily obtain them in their English versions. At this point, however, I must say a few words about *The Dare* (*Podarok Otchizne* was its original title, which can be translated as "a gift to the fatherland"). When in 1934 I started to dictate its beginning to Annette, I knew it would be my longest novel. I did not foresee however that it would be almost as long as General Pudov's vile and fatuous "historical" romance about the way the Zion Wisers usurped St. Rus. It took me about four years in all to write its four hundred pages, many of which Annette typed at least twice. Most of it had been serialized in *émigré* magazines by May, 1939, when she and I, still childless, left for America; but in book form, the Russian original appeared only in 1950 (Turgenev Publishing House, New York), followed another decade later by an English translation, whose title neatly refers not only to the well-known device used to bewilder noddies but also to the daredevil nature of Victor, the hero and part-time narrator.

The novel begins with a nostalgic account of a Russian childhood (much happier, though not less opulent than mine). After that comes adolescence in England (not unlike my own Cambridge years); then life in *émigré* Paris, the writing of a first novel (*Memoirs of a Parrot Fancier*) and the tying of amusing knots in various literary intrigues. Inset in the middle part is a complete version of the book my Victor wrote "on a dare": this is a concise biography and critical appraisal of Fyodor Dostoyevski, whose politics my author finds hateful and whose novels he condemns as absurd with their black-bearded killers presented as mere negatives of Jesus Christ's conventional image, and weepy whores borrowed from maudlin romances of an earlier age. The next chapter deals with the rage and bewilderment of *émigré* reviewers, all of them priests of the Dostoyevskian persuasion; and in the last pages my young hero accepts a flirt's challenge and accomplishes a final gratuitous feat by walking through a perilous forest into Soviet territory and as casually strolling back.

I am giving this summary to exemplify what even the poorest reader of my *Dare* must surely retain, unless electrolysis destroys some essential cells soon after he closes the book. Now part of Annette's frail charm lay in her forgetfulness which veiled everything toward the evening of everything, like the kind of pastel haze that obliterates mountains, clouds, and even its own self as the summer day swoons. I know I have seen her many times, a copy of *Patria* in her languid lap, follow the printed lines with the pendulum swing of eyes suggestive of reading, and actually reach the "To be continued" at the end of the current installment of *The Dare*. I also know that she had typed every word of it and most of its commas. Yet the fact remains that she retained nothing—perhaps in result of her having decided once for all that my prose was not merely "difficult" but hermetic ("nastily hermetic," to repeat the compliment Basilevski paid me the moment he realized—a moment which came in due time—that his manner and mind were being ridiculed in Chapter Three by my gloriously happy Victor). I must say I forgave her readily her attitude to my work. At public readings, I admired her public smile, the "archaic" smile of Greek statues. When her rather dreadful parents asked to see my books (as a suspicious physician might ask for a sample of semen), she gave them to read by mistake another man's novel because of a silly similarity of titles. The only real shock I experienced was when I overheard her informing some idiot woman friend that my *Dare* included biographies of "Chernolyubov and Dobroshevski"! She actually started to argue when I retorted that only a lunatic would have chosen a pair of third-rate publicists to write about—spoonerizing their names in addition!

6

I have noticed, or seem to have noticed, in the course of my long life, that when about to fall in love or even when still unaware of having fallen in love, a dream would come, introducing me to a latent inamorata at morning twilight in a somewhat infantile setting, marked by exquisite aching stirrings that I knew as a boy, as a youth, as a madman, as an old dying voluptuary. The sense of recurrence ("seem to have noticed") is very possibly a built-in feeling: for instance I may have had that dream only once or twice ("in the course of my long life") and its familiarity is only the dropper that comes with the drops. The place in the dream, per contra, is not a familiar room but one remindful of the kind we children awake in after a Christmas masquerade or midsummer name day, in a great house, belonging to strangers or distant cousins. The impression is that the beds, two small beds in the present case, have been put in and placed against the opposite walls of a room that is not a bedroom at heart, a room with no furniture except those two separate beds: property masters are lazy, or economical, in one's dreams as well as in early novellas.

In one of the beds I find myself just awoken from some secondary dream of only formulary importance; and in the far bed against the right-hand wall (direction also supplied), a girl, a younger, slighter, and gayer Annette in this particular variant (summer of 1934 by daytime reckoning), is playfully, quietly talking to herself but actually, as I understand with a delicious quickening of the nether pulses, is feigning to talk, is talking for my benefit, so as to be noticed by me.

My next thought—and it intensifies the throbbings—concerns the strangeness of boy and girl being assigned to sleep in the same makeshift room: by error, no doubt, or perhaps the house was full and the distance between the two beds, across an empty floor, might have been deemed wide enough for perfect decorum in the case of children (my average age has been thirteen all my life). The cup of pleasure is brimming by now and before it spills I hasten to tiptoe across the bare parquet from my bed to hers. Her fair hair gets in the way of my kisses, but presently my lips find her cheek and neck, and her nightgown has buttons, and she says the maid has come into the room, but it is too late, I cannot restrain myself, and the maid, a beauty in her own right, looks on, laughing.

That dream I had a month or so after I met Annette, and her image in it, that early version of her voice, soft hair, tender skin, obsessed me and amazed me with delight—the delight of discovering I loved little Miss Blagovo. At the time of the dream she and I were still on formal terms, super-formal in fact, so I could not tell it to her with the necessary evocations and associations (as set down in these notes); and merely saying "I dreamt of you" would have amounted to the thud of a platitude. I did something much more courageous and honorable. Before revealing to her what she called (speaking of another couple) "serious intentions"—and before even solving the riddle of *why* really I loved her—I decided to tell her of my incurable illness.

7

She was elegant, she was languid, she was rather angelic in one sense, and dismally stupid in many others. I was lonely, and frightened, and reckless with lust—not sufficiently reckless, however, not to warn her by means of a vivid instance—half paradigm and half object lesson—of what she laid herself open to by consenting to marry me.

> *Milostivaya Gosudarynya*
>> *Anna Ivanovna!*
> [Anglice *Dear Miss Blagovo*]
>
> *Before entertaining you viva-voce of a subject of the utmost importance, I beg you to join me in the conduct of an experiment that will describe better than a learned article would one of the typical facets of my displaced mental crystal. So here goes.*
>
> *With your permission it is night now and I am in bed (decently clad, of course, and with every organ in decent repose), lying supine, and imagining an ordinary moment in an ordinary place. To further protect the purity of the experiment, let the visualized spot be an invented one. I imagine myself coming out of a bookshop and pausing on the curb before crossing the street to the little sidewalk café directly opposite. No cars are in sight. I cross. I imagine myself reaching the little café. The afternoon sun occupies one of its chairs and the half of a table, but otherwise its open-air section is empty and very inviting: nothing but brightness remains of the recent shower. And here I stop short as I recollect that I had an umbrella.*
>
> *I do not intend to bore you,* glubokouvazhaemaya (*dear*) Anna Ivanovna, *and still less do I wish to crumple this third or fourth poor sheet with the crashing sound only*

*punished paper can make; but the scene is not sufficiently
abstract and schematic, so let me retake it.*

*I, your friend and employer Vadim Vadimovich, lying
in bed on my back in ideal darkness (I got up a minute
ago to recurtain the moon that peeped between the folds of
two paragraphs), I imagine diurnal Vadim Vadimovich
crossing a street from a bookshop to a sidewalk café. I am
encased in my vertical self: not looking down but ahead,
thus only indirectly aware of the blurry front of my cor-
pulent figure, of the alternate points of my shoes, and of
the rectangular form of the parcel under my arm. I imagine myself walking the twenty paces needed to reach the
opposite sidewalk, then stopping with an unprintable curse
and deciding to go back for the umbrella I left in the shop.*

*There is an affliction still lacking a name; there is,
Anna (you must permit me to call you that, I am ten
years your senior and very ill), something dreadfully wrong
with my sense of direction, or rather my power over conceived space, because at this juncture I am unable to
execute mentally, in the dark of my bed, the simple
about-face (an act I perform without thinking in physical
reality!) which would allow me to picture instantly in my
mind the once already traversed asphalt as now being* before *me, and the vitrine of the bookshop being now within
sight and not somewhere behind.*

*Let me dwell briefly on the procedure involved; on my
inability to follow it consciously in my mind—my unwieldy
and disobedient mind! In order to make myself imagine
the pivotal process I have to force an opposite revolution of
the decor: I must try, dear friend and assistant, to swing
the entire length of the street, with the massive façades
of its houses before and behind me, from one direction to
another in the slow wrench of a half circle, which is like
trying to turn the colossal tiller of a rusty recalcitrant rudder so as to transform oneself by conscious degrees from,
say, an east-facing Vadim Vadimovich into a west-sun-
blinded one. The mere thought of that action leads the
bedded recliner to such a muddle and dizziness that one
prefers scrapping the about-face altogether, wiping, so to
speak, the slate of one's vision, and beginning the return*

journey in one's imagination as if it were an initial one, without any previous crossing of the street, and therefore without any of the intermediate horror—the horror of struggling with the steerage of space and crushing one's chest in the process!

Voilà. *Sounds rather tame, doesn't it,* en fait de démence, *and, indeed, if I stop brooding over the thing, I decrease it to an insignificant flaw—the missing pinkie of a freak born with nine fingers. Considering it closer, however, I cannot help suspecting it to be a warning symptom, a foreglimpse of the mental malady that is known to affect eventually the entire brain. Even that malady may not be as imminent and grave as the storm signals suggest; I only want you to be aware of the situation before proposing to you, Annette. Do not write, do not phone, do not mention this letter, if and when you come Friday afternoon; but,* please, *if you do, wear, in propitious sign, the Florentine hat that looks like a cluster of wild flowers. I want you to celebrate your resemblance to the fifth girl from left to right, the flower-decked blonde with the straight nose and serious gray eyes, in Botticelli's* Primavera, *an allegory of Spring, my love, my allegory.*

On Friday afternoon, for the first time in two months she came "on the dot" as my American friends would say. A wedge of pain replaced my heart, and little black monsters started to play musical chairs all over my room, as I noticed that she wore her usual recent hat, of no interest or meaning. She took it off before the mirror and suddenly invoked Our Lord with rare emphasis.

"*Ya idiotka,*" she said. "I'm an idiot. I was looking for my pretty wreath, when papa started to read to me something about an ancestor of yours who quarreled with Peter the Terrible."

"Ivan," I said.

"I didn't catch the name, but I saw I was late and pulled on (*natsepila*) this *shapochka* instead of the wreath, your wreath, the wreath you ordered."

I was helping her out of her jacket. Her words filled me with dream-free wantonness. I embraced her. My mouth sought the hot hollow between neck and clavicle. It was a brief but thorough embrace, and I boiled over, discreetly, deliciously, merely by pressing myself against her, one hand cupping her firm little behind and the other feeling the harp strings of her ribs. She was trembling all over. An ardent but silly virgin, she did not understand why my grip had relaxed with the suddenness of sleep or windlorn sails.

Had she read only the beginning and end of my letter? Well, yes, she had skipped the poetical part. In other words, she had not the slightest idea what I was driving at? She promised, she said, to reread it. She had grasped, however, that I loved her? She had, but how could she be sure that I *really* loved her? I was so strange, so, so—she couldn't express it— yes, STRANGE in every respect. She never had met anyone like me. Whom then did she meet, I inquired: trepanners? trombonists? astronomists? Well, mostly military men, if I wished to know, officers of Wrangel's army, gentlemen, interesting people, who spoke of danger and duty, of bivouacs in the steppe. Oh, but look here, I too can speak of "deserts idle, rough quarries, rocks"—No, she said, they did not *invent.* They talked of spies they had hanged, they talked of international politics, of a new film or book that explained the meaning of life. And never one unchaste joke, not one horrid risqué comparison. . . . As in my books? Examples, examples! No, she would not give examples. She would not be pinned down to whirl on the pin like a wingless fly.

Or butterfly.

We were walking, one lovely morning, on the outskirts of Bellefontaine. Something flicked and lit.

"Look at that harlequin," I murmured, pointing cautiously with my elbow.

Sunning itself against the white wall of a suburban garden was a flat, symmetrically outspread butterfly, which the artist had placed at a slight angle to the horizon of his picture. The creature was painted a smiling red with yellow intervals between black blotches; a row of blue crescents ran along the inside of the toothed wing margins. The only feature to rate a shiver of squeamishness was the glistening sweep of bronzy silks coming down on both sides of the beastie's body.

"As a former kindergarten teacher I can tell you," said helpful Annette, "that it's a most ordinary nettlefly (*krapivnitsa*). How many little hands have plucked off its wings and brought them to me for approval!"

It flicked and was gone.

8

In view of the amount of typing to be done, and of her doing it so slowly and badly, she made me promise not to bother her with what Russians call "calf cuddlings" during work. At other times all she allowed me were controlled kisses and flexible holds: our first embrace had been "brutal" she said (having caught on very soon after that in the matter of certain male secrets). She did her best to conceal the melting, the helplessness that overwhelmed her in the natural course of caresses when she would begin to palpitate in my arms before pushing me away with a puritanical frown. Once the back of her hand chanced to brush against the taut front of my trousers; she uttered a chilly "*pardon*" (Fr.), and then went into a sulk upon my saying I hoped she had not hurt herself.

I complained of the ridiculous obsolete turn our relationship was taking. She thought it over and promised that as soon as we were "officially engaged," we would enter a more modern era. I assured her I was ready to proclaim its advent any day, any moment.

She took me to see her parents with whom she shared a two-room apartment in Passy. He had been an army surgeon before the Revolution and, with his close-cropped gray head, clipped mustache, and neat imperial, bore a striking resemblance (abetted no doubt by the eager spirit that patches up worn parts of the past with new impressions of the same order) to the kindly but cold-fingered (and cold-earlobed) doctor who treated the "inflammation of the lungs" I had in the winter of 1907.

As with so many Russians *émigrés* of declining strength and lost professions, it was hard to say what exactly were Dr. Blagovo's personal resources. He seemed to spend life's overcast evening either reading his way through sets of thick magazines (1830 to 1900 or 1850 to 1910), which Annette brought him from Oksman's Lending Library, or sitting at a table and filling by means of a regularly clicking tobacco injector the semi-transparent ends of carton-tubed cigarettes of which he never consumed more than thirty per day to avoid intercadence at night. He had practically no conversation and could not retell correctly any of the countless historical anecdotes he found in the battered tomes of *Russkaya Starina* ("Russian ancientry")—which explains where Annette got her inability to remember the poems, the essays, the stories, the novels she had typed for me (my grumble is repetitious, I know, but the matter rankles—a word which comes from *dracunculus*, a "baby dragon"). He was also one of the last gentlemen I ever met who still wore a dickey and elastic-sided boots.

He asked me—and that remained his only memorable question—why I did not use in print the title which went with my thousand-year-old name. I replied that I was the kind of snob who assumes that bad readers are by nature aware of an author's origins but who hopes that good readers will be more interested in his books than in his stemma. Dr. Blagovo was a stupid old bloke, and his detachable cuffs could have been cleaner; but today, in sorrowful retrospect, I treasure his memory: he was not only the father of my poor Annette, but also the grandfather of my adored and perhaps still more unfortunate daughter.

Dr. Blagovo (1867–1940) had married at the age of forty a provincial belle in the Volgan town of Kineshma, a few miles south from one of my most romantic country estates, famous for its wild ravines, now gravel pits or places of massacre, but *then* magnificent evocations of sunken gardens. She wore elaborate make-up and spoke in simpering accents, reducing nouns and adjectives to over-affectionate forms which even the Russian language, a recognized giant of diminutives, would only condone on the wet lips of an infant or tender nurse ("Here," said Mrs. Blagovo, "is your *chaishko s molochishkom* [teeny tea with weeny milk]"). She struck me as an extraordinarily garrulous, affable, and banal lady, with a good taste in clothes (she worked in a *salon de couture*). A certain tenseness could be sensed in the atmosphere of the household.

Annette was obviously a difficult daughter. In the brief course of my visit I could not help noticing that the voice of the parent addressing her developed little notes of obsequious panic (*notki podobostrastnoy paniki*). Annette would occasionally curb with an opaque, almost ophidian, look, her mother's volubility. As I was leaving, the old girl paid me what she thought was a compliment: "You speak Russian with a Parisian *grasseyement* and your manners are those of an Englishman." Annette, behind her, uttered a low warning growl.

That same evening I wrote to her father informing him that she and I had decided to marry; and on the following afternoon, when she arrived for work, I met her in morocco slippers and silk dressing gown. It was a holiday—the Festival of Flora—I said, indicating, with a not wholly normal smile, the carnations, camomiles, anemones, asphodels, and blue cockles in blond corn, which decorated my room in our honor. Her gaze swept over the flowers, champagne, and caviar *canapés*; she snorted and turned to flee; I plucked her back into the room, locked the door and pocketed its key.

I do not mind recalling that our first tryst was a flop. It took me so long to persuade her that this was the day, and she made such a fuss about which ultimate inch of clothing could be removed and which parts of her body Venus, the Virgin, and the *maire* of our *arrondissement* allowed to be touched, that by the time I had her in a passably convenient position of surrender, I was an impotent wreck. We were lying naked, in a loose clinch. Presently her mouth opened against mine in her first free kiss. I regained my vigor. I hastened to possess her. She exclaimed I was disgustingly hurting her and with a vigorous wriggle expulsed the blooded and thrashing fish. When I tried to close her fingers around it in humble substitution, she snatched her hand away, calling me a dirty *débauché* (*gryaznyy razvratnik*). I had to demonstrate myself the messy act while she looked on in amazement and sorrow.

We did better next day, and finished the flattish champagne; I never could quite tame her, though. I remember most promising nights in Italian lakeside hotels when everything was suddenly botched by her misplaced primness. But on the other hand I am happy now that I was never so vile and inept as to ignore the exquisite contrast between her irritating prudery and those rare moments of sweet passion when her features acquired an expression of childish concentration, of solemn delight, and her little moans just reached the threshold of my undeserving consciousness.

9

By the end of the summer, and of the next chapter of *The Dare*, it became clear that Dr. Blagovo and his wife were looking forward to a regular Greek-Orthodox wedding—a taperlit gold-and-gauze ceremony, with high priest and low priest and a double choir. I do not know if Annette was astonished when I said I intended to cut out the mummery and prosaically register our union before a municipal officer in Paris, London, Calais, or on one of the Channel Islands; but she certainly did not mind astonishing her parents. Dr. Blagovo requested an interview in a stiffly worded letter ("Prince! Anna has informed us that you would prefer—"); we settled for a telephone conversation: two minutes of Dr. Blagovo (including pauses caused by his deciphering a hand that must have been the despair of apothecaries) and five of his wife, who after rambling about irrelevant matters entreated me to reconsider my decision. I refused, and was set upon by a go-between, good old Stepanov, who rather unexpectedly, given his liberal views, urged me in a telephone call from somewhere in England (where the Borgs now lived) to keep up a beautiful Christian tradition. I changed the subject and begged him to arrange a beautiful literary *soirée* for me upon his return to Paris.

In the meantime some of the gayer gods came with gifts. Three windfalls scatter-thudded around me in a simultaneous act of celebration: *The Red Topper* was bought for publication in English with a two-hundred-guinea advance; James Lodge of New York offered for *Camera Lucida* an even handsomer sum (one's sense of beauty was easily satisfied in those days); and a contract for the cinema rights to a short story was being prepared by Ivor Black's half-brother in Los Angeles. I had now to find adequate surroundings for completing *The Dare* in greater comfort than that in which I wrote its first part; and immediately after that, or concurrently with its last chapter, I would have to examine, and, no doubt, revise heavily, the English translation now being made of my *Krasnyy Tsilindr* by an unknown lady in London (who rather inauspiciously had started to suggest, before a roar of rage stopped her, that "certain passages, not quite proper or too richly or obscurely phrased, would have to be toned down, or omitted altogether, for the benefit of the sober-minded English reader"). I also expected to have to face a business trip to the United States.

For some odd psychological reason, Annette's parents, who kept track of those developments, were now urging her to go through no matter what form of marriage, civil or pagan (*grazhdanskiy ili basurmanskiy*), without delay. Once that little tricolor farce over, Annette and I paid our tribute to Russian tradition by traveling from hotel to hotel during two months, going as far as Venice and Ravenna, where I thought of Byron and translated Musset. Back in Paris, we rented a three-room apartment on the charming rue Guevara (named after an Andalusian playwright of long ago) a two-minute walk from the Bois. We usually lunched at the nearby Le Petit Diable Boiteux, a modest but excellent restaurant, and had cold cuts for dinner in our kitchenette. I had somehow expected Annette to be a versatile cook, and she did improve later, in rugged America. On rue Guevara her best achievement remained the Soft-Boiled Egg: I do not know how she did it, but she managed to prevent the fatal crack that produced an ectoplasmic swell in the dancing water when I took over.

She loved long walks in the park among the sedate beeches and the prospective-looking babes; she loved cafés, fashion shows, tennis matches, circular bike races at the Vélodrome, and especially the cinema. I soon realized that a little recreation put her in a lovemaking mood—and I was frightfully amorous and strong in our four last years in Paris, and quite unable to stand capricious denials. I drew the line, however, at an overdose of athletic sports—a metronomic tennis ball twanging to and fro or the ghastly hairy legs of hunchbacks on wheels.

The second part of the Thirties in Paris happened to be marked by a marvelous surge of the exiled arts, and it would be pretentious and foolish of me not to admit that whatever some of the more dishonest critics wrote about me, I stood at the peak of that period. In the halls where readings took place, in the back rooms of famous cafés, at private literary parties, I enjoyed pointing out to my quiet and stylish companion the various ghouls of the inferno, the crooks and the creeps, the benevolent nonentities, the groupists, the guru nuts, the pious pederasts, the lovely hysterical Lesbians, the gray-locked old realists, the talented, illiterate, intuitive new critics (Adam Atropovich was their unforgettable leader).

I noted with a sort of scholarly pleasure (like that of tracking down parallel readings) how attentive, how eager to honor her were the three or four, always black-suited, grandmasters of Russian letters (people I admired with grateful fervor, not only because their high-principled art had enchanted my prime, but also because the banishment of their books by the Bolshevists represented the greatest indictment, absolute and immortal, of Lenin's and Stalin's regime). No less *empressés* around her (perhaps in subliminal zeal to earn some of the rare praise I deigned to bestow on the pure voice of the impure) were certain younger writers whom their God had created two-faced: despicably corrupt or inane on one side of their being and shining with poignant genius on the other. In a word, her appearance in the *beau monde* of *émigré* literature echoed amusingly Chapter Eight of *Eugene Onegin* with Princess N.'s moving coolly through the fawning ballroom throng.

I might have been displeased by the tolerance she showed Basilevski (knowing none of his works and only vaguely aware of his preposterous reputation) had it not occurred to me that the theme of her sympathy was repeating, as it were, the friendly phase of my own initial relations with that *faux bonhomme*. From behind a more or less Doric column I overheard him asking my naïve gentle Annette had she any idea why I hated so fiercely Gorki (for whom he cultivated total veneration). Was it because I resented the world fame of a proletarian? Had I really read any of that wonderful writer's books? Annette had looked puzzled but all at once a charming childish smile illumined her whole face and she recalled *The Mother*, a corny Soviet film that I had criticized, she said, "because the tears rolling down the faces were too big and too slow."

"Aha! That explains a lot," proclaimed Basilevski with gloomy satisfaction.

10

I received the typed translations of *The Red Topper* (sic) and *Camera Lucida* virtually at the same time, in the autumn of 1937. They proved to be even more ignoble than I expected. Miss Haworth, an Englishwoman, had spent three happy years in Moscow where her father had been Ambassador; Mr. Kulich was an elderly Russian-born New Yorker who signed his letters Ben. Both made identical mistakes, choosing the wrong term in their identical dictionaries, and with identical recklessness never bothering to check the treacherous homonym of a familiar-looking word. They were blind to contextual shades of color and deaf to nuances of noise. Their classification of natural objects seldom descended from the class to the family; still more seldom to the genus in the strict sense. They confused the specimen with the species; Hop, Leap, and Jump wore in their minds the drab uniform of regimented synonymity; and not one page passed without a boner. What struck me as especially fascinating, in a dreadful diabolical way, was their taking for granted that a respectable author could have written this or that descriptive passage, which their ignorance and carelessness had reduced to the cries and grunts of a cretin. In all their habits of expression Ben Kulich and Miss Haworth were so close that I now think they might have been secretly married to one another and had corresponded regularly when trying to settle a tricky paragraph; or else, maybe, they used to meet midway for lexical picnics on the grassy lip of some crater in the Azores.

It took me several months to revise those atrocities and dictate my revisions to Annette. She derived her English from the four years she had spent at an American boarding school in Constantinople (1920–1924), the Blagovos' first stage of

westward expatriation. I was amazed to see how fast her vocabulary grew and improved in the performance of her new
functions and was amused by the innocent pride she took in
correctly taking down the blasts and sarcasms I directed in
letters to Allan & Overton, London, and James Lodge, New
York. In fact, her *doigté* in English (and French) was better
than in the typing of Russian texts. Minor stumbles were, of
course, bound to occur in any language. One day, in referring
to the carbon copy of a spate of corrections already posted to
my patient Allan, I discovered a trivial slip she had made, a
mere typo ("here" instead of "hero," or perhaps "that" instead of "hat," I don't even remember—but there was an "h"
somewhere, I think) which, however, gave the sentence a dismally flat, but, alas, not implausible sense (verisimilitude has
been the undoing of many a conscientious proofreader). A
telegram could eliminate the fault incontinently, but an overworked edgy author finds such events jarring—and I voiced
my annoyance with unwarranted vehemence. Annette started
looking for a telegram form in the (wrong) drawer and said,
without raising her head:

"She would have helped you so much better than I, though
I really am doing my best (*strashno starayus'*, trying terribly)."

We never referred to Iris—that was a tacit condition in the
code of our marriage—but I instantly understood that Annette meant *her* and not the inept English girl whom an
agency had sent me several weeks before and got back with
wrappage and string. For some occult reason (overwork again)
I felt the tears welling and before I could get up and leave
the room, I found myself shamelessly sobbing and hitting a
fat anonymous book with my fist. She glided into my arms,
also weeping, and that same evening we went to see René
Clair's new film, followed by supper at the Grand Velour.

During those months of correcting and partly rewriting *The
Red Topper* and the other thing, I began to experience the
pangs of a strange transformation. I did not wake up one Central European morning as a great scarab with more legs than
any beetle can have, but certain excruciating tearings of secret
tissues did take place in me. The Russian typewriter was closed
like a coffin. The end of *The Dare* had been delivered to *Patria*. Annette and I planned to go in the spring to England

(a plan never executed) and in the summer of 1939 to America (where she was to die fourteen years later). By the middle of 1938 I felt I could sit back and quietly enjoy both the private praise bestowed upon me by Andoverton and Lodge in their letters and the public accusations of aristocratic obscurity which facetious criticules in the Sunday papers directed at the style of such passages in the English versions of my two novels as had been authored by me alone. It was, however, quite a different matter "to work without net" (as Russian acrobats say), when attempting to compose a novel straight in English, for now there was no Russian safety net spread below, between me and the lighted circlet of the arena.

As was also to happen in regard to my next English books (including the present sketch), the title of my first one came to me at the moment of impregnation, long before actual birth and growth. Holding that name to the light, I distinguished the entire contents of the semitransparent capsule. The title was to be without any choice or change: *See under Real.* A preview of its eventual tribulations in the catalogues of public libraries could not have deterred me.

The idea may have been an oblique effect of the insult dealt by the two bunglers to my careful art. An English novelist, a brilliant and unique performer, was supposed to have recently died. The story of his life was being knocked together by the uninformed, coarse-minded, malevolent Hamlet Godman, an Oxonian Dane, who found in this grotesque task a Kovalevskian "outlet" for the literary flops that his proper mediocrity fully deserved. The biography was being edited, rather unfortunately for its reckless concocter, by the indignant brother of the dead novelist. As the opening chapter unfolded its first reptilian coil (with insinuations of "masturbation guilt" and the castration of toy soldiers) there commenced what was to me the delight and the magic of my book: fraternal footnotes, half-a-dozen lines per page, then more, then much more, which started to question, then refute, then demolish by ridicule the would-be biographer's doctored anecdotes and vulgar inventions. A multiplication of such notes at the bottom of the page led to an ominous increase (no doubt disturbing to clubby or convalescent readers) of astronomical symbols bespeckling the text. By the end of the biographee's college years the height of the critical apparatus had reached one third of each page. Editorial warnings of a national disaster—flooded fields and so on—accompanied a further rise of the water line. By page 200 the footnote material had crowded out three-quarters of the text and the type of the note had changed, psychologically at least (I loathe typographical frolics in books) from brevier to long primer. In the course of the last chapters the commentary not only replaced the entire text but finally swelled to boldface. "We witness here the admirable phenomenon of a bogus *biographie romancée* being gradually supplanted by the true story of a great man's life." For good measure I appended a three-page account of the great annotator's academic career: "He now teaches Modern Literature, including his brother's works, at Paragon University, Oregon."

This is the description of a novel written almost forty-five years ago and probably forgotten by the general public. I have never reread it because I reread (*je relis, perechityvayu*—I'm teasing an adorable mistress!) only the page proofs of my paperbacks; and for reasons which, I am sure, J. Lodge finds judicious, the thing is still in its hard-cover instar. But in rosy retrospect I feel it as a pleasurable event, and have completely dissociated it in my mind from the terrors and torments that attended the writing of that rather lightweight little satire.

Actually, its composition, despite the pleasure (maybe also noxious) that the iridescent bubbles in my alembics gave me after a night of inspiration, trial, and triumph (look at the harlequins, everybody look—Iris, Annette, Bel, Louise, and you, you, my ultimate and immortal one!), almost led to the dementia paralytica that I feared since youth.

In the world of athletic games there has never been, I think, a World Champion of Lawn Tennis *and* Ski; yet in two Literatures, as dissimilar as grass and snow, I have been the first to achieve that kind of feat. I do not know (being a complete non-athlete, whom the sports pages of a newspaper bore almost as much as does its kitchen section) what physical stress may be involved in serving one day a sequence of thirty-six aces at sea level and on the next soaring from a ski jump 136 meters through bright mountain air. Colossal, no doubt, and, perhaps, inconceivable. But *I* have managed to transcend the rack and the wrench of literary metamorphosis.

We think in images, not in words; all right; when, however, we compose, recall, or refashion at midnight in our brain something we wish to say in tomorrow's sermon, or have said to Dolly in a recent dream, or wish we had said to that impertinent proctor twenty years ago, the images we think in are, of course, verbal—and even audible if we happen to be lonely and old. We do not usually think in words, since most of life is mimodrama, but we certainly do imagine words when we need them, just as we imagine everything else capable of being perceived in this, or even in a still more unlikely, world. The book in my mind appeared at first, under my right cheek (I sleep on my noncardial side), as a varicolored procession with a head and a tail, winding in a general western direction through an attentive town. The children among you and all my old selves on their thresholds were being promised a stunning show. I then saw the show in full detail with every scene in its place, every trapeze in the stars. Yet it was not a masque, not a circus, but a bound book, a short novel in a tongue as far removed as Thracian or Pahlavi from the fata-morganic prose that I had willed into being in the desert of exile. An upsurge of nausea overcame me at the thought of imagining a hundred-thousand adequate words and I switched on the light and called to Annette in the adjacent bedroom to give me one of my strictly rationed tablets.

The evolution of my English, like that of birds, had had its ups and downs. A beloved Cockney nurse had looked after me from 1900 (when I was one year old) to 1903. She was followed by a succession of three English governesses (1903–1906, 1907–1909, and November, 1909, to Christmas of the same year) whom I see over the shoulder of time as representing, mythologically, Didactic Prose, Dramatic Poetry, and the Erotic Idyll. My grand-aunt, a dear person with uncommonly liberal views, gave in, however, to domestic considerations, and discharged Cherry Neaple, my last shepherdess. After an interlude of Russian and French pedagogy, two English tutors more or less succeeded each other between 1912 and 1916, rather comically overlapping in the spring of 1914 when they competed for the favors of a young village beauty who had been my girl in the first place. English fairy tales had been replaced around 1910 by the B.O.P., immediately followed by all the Tauchnitz volumes that had accumulated in the family libraries. Throughout adolescence I read, in pairs, and both with the same rich thrill, *Othello* and *Onegin*, Tyutchev and Tennyson, Browning and Blok. During my three Cambridge years (1919–1922) and thereafter, till April 23, 1930, my domestic tongue remained English, while the body of my own Russian works started to grow and was soon to disorb my household gods.

So far so good. But the phrase itself is a glib cliché; and the question confronting me in Paris, in the late Thirties, was precisely could I fight off the formula and rip up the ready-made, and switch from my glorious self-developed Russian, not to the dead leaden English of the high seas with dummies in sailor suits, but an English I alone would be responsible for, in all its new ripples and changing light?

I daresay the description of my literary troubles will be skipped by the common reader; yet for my sake, rather than his, I wish to dwell mercilessly on a situation that was bad enough before I left Europe but almost killed me during the crossing.

Russian and English had existed for years in my mind as two worlds detached from one another. (It is only today that some interspatial contact has been established: "A knowledge of Russian," writes George Oakwood in his astute essay on my *Ardis*, 1970, "will help you to relish much of the wordplay in the most English of the author's English novels; consider for instance this: 'The champ and the chimp came all the way from Omsk to Neochomsk.' What a delightful link between a real round place and 'ni-o-chyom,' the About-Nothing land of modern philosophic linguistics!") I was acutely aware of the syntactic gulf separating their sentence structures. I feared (unreasonably, as was to transpire eventually) that my allegiance to Russian grammar might interfere with an apostatical courtship. Take tenses: how different their elaborate and strict minuet in English from the free and fluid interplay between the present and the past in their Russian counterpart (which Ian Bunyan has so amusingly compared in last Sunday's NYT to "a dance of the veil performed by a plump graceful lady in a circle of cheering drunks"). The fantastic number of natural-looking nouns that the British and the Americans apply in lovely technical senses to very specific objects also distressed me. What is the exact term for the little cup in which you place the diamond you want to cut? (We call it "dop," the pupal case of a butterfly, replied my informer, an old Boston jeweler who sold me the ring for my third bride). Is there not a nice special word for a pigling? ("I am toying with 'snork,' " said Professor Noteboke, the best translator of Gogol's immortal *The Carrick*). I want the right word for the break in a boy's voice at puberty, I said to an amiable opera basso in the adjacent deck chair during my first transatlantic voyage. ("I think," he said, "it's called 'ponticello,' a small bridge, *un petit pont, mostik* . . . . Oh, you're Russian too?")

The traversal of my particular bridge ended, weeks after landing, in a charming New York apartment (it was leant to Annette and me by a generous relative of mine and faced the sunset flaming beyond Central Park). The neuralgia in my right forearm was a gray adumbration compared to the solid black headache that no pill could pierce. Annette rang up James Lodge, and he, out of the misdirected kindness of his heart, had an old little physician of Russian extraction examine me. The poor fellow drove me even crazier than I was by not only insisting on discussing my symptoms in an execrable version of the language I was trying to shed, but on translating into it various irrelevant terms used by the Viennese Quack and his apostles (*simbolizirovanie, mortidnik*). Yet his visit, I must confess, strikes me in retrospect as a most artistic coda.

Part Three

I

NEITHER *Slaughter in the Sun* (as the English translation of *Camera Lucida* got retitled while I lay helplessly hospitalized in New York) nor *The Red Topper* sold well. My ambitious, beautiful, strange *See under Real* shone for a breathless instant on the lowest rung of the bestseller list in a West Coast paper, and vanished for good. In those circumstances I could not refuse the lectureship offered me in 1940 by Quirn University on the strength of my European reputation. I was to develop a plump tenure there and expand into a Full Professor by 1950 or 1955: I can't find the exact date in my old notes.

Although I was adequately remunerated for my two weekly lectures on European Masterpieces and one Thursday seminar on Joyce's *Ulysses* (from a yearly 5000 dollars in the beginning to 15,000 in the Fifties) and had furthermore several splendidly paid stories accepted by *The Beau and the Butterfly*, the kindest magazine in the world, I was not really comfortable until my *Kingdom by the Sea* (1962) atoned for a fraction of the loss of my Russian fortune (1917) and bundled away all financial worries till the end of worrisome time. I do not usually preserve cuttings of adverse criticism and envious abuse; but I do treasure the following definition: "This is the only known case in history when a European pauper ever became his own American uncle [*amerikanskiy dyadyushka, oncle d'Amérique*]," so phrased by my faithful Zoilus, Demian Basilevski; he was one of the very few larger saurians in the *émigré* marshes who followed me in 1939 to the hospitable and altogether admirable U.S.A., where with egg-laying promptness he founded a Russian-language quarterly which he is still directing today, thirty-five years later, in his heroic dotage.

The furnished apartment we finally rented on the upper floor of a handsome house (10 Buffalo St.) was much to my liking because of an exceptionally comfortable study with a great bookcase full of works on American lore including an

encyclopedia in twenty volumes. Annette would have preferred one of the *dacha*-like structures which the Administration also showed us; but she gave in when I pointed out to
her that what looked snug and quaint in summer was bound
to be chilly and weird the rest of the year.

Annette's emotional health caused me anxiety: her graceful
neck seemed even longer and thinner. An expression of mild
melancholy lent a new, unwelcome, beauty to her Botticellian
face: its hollowed outline below the zygoma was accentuated
by her increasing habit of sucking in her cheeks when hesi-
tative or pensive. All her cold petals remained closed in our
infrequent lovemaking. Her abstraction grew perilous: stray
cats at night knew that the same erratic deity that had not
shut the kitchen window would leave ajar the door of the
fridge; her bath regularly overflowed while she telephoned,
knitting her innocent brows (what on earth did she care for
my pains, *my* welling insanity!), to find out how the first-floor
person's migraine or menopause was faring; and that vague-
ness of hers in relation to me was also responsible for her
omitting a precaution she was supposed to take, so that by
the autumn, which followed our moving into the accursed
Langley house, she informed me that the doctor she had just
consulted looked the very image of Oksman and that she was
two-months pregnant.

An angel is now waiting under my restless heels. Doomful
despair would invade my poor Annette when she tried to cope
with the intricacies of an American household. Our landlady,
who occupied the first floor, resolved her perplexities in a jiffy.
Two ravishing wiggly-bottomed Bermudian coeds, wearing
their national costume, flannel shorts and open shirts, and
practically twins in appearance, who took the celebrated "Hotel" course at Quirn, came to cook and char for her, and she
offered to share with us their services.

"She's a veritable angel," confided Annette to me in her
touchingly phony English.

I recognized in the woman the Assistant Professor of Russian whom I had met in a brick building on the campus when
the head of her remarkably dreary department, meek myopic
old Noteboke, invited me to attend an Advanced Group Class
(*My govorim po-russki. Vy govorite? Pogovorimte togda*—that

kind of awful stuff). Happily I had no connection whatever with Russian grammar at Quirn—except that my wife was eventually saved from utter boredom by being engaged to help beginners under Mrs. Langley's direction.

Ninel Ilinishna Langley, a displaced person in more senses than one, had recently left her husband, the "great" Langley, author of *A Marxist History of America*, the bible (now out of print) of a whole generation of morons. I do not know the reason of their separation (after one year of American Sex, as the woman told Annette, who relayed the information to me in a tone of idiotic condolence); but I did have the occasion of seeing and disliking Professor Langley at an official dinner on the eve of his departure for Oxford. I disliked him for his daring to question my teaching *Ulysses* my way—in a purely textual light, without organic allegories and quasi-Greek myths and that sort of tripe; his "Marxism," on the other hand, was a pleasantly comic and very mild affair (too mild, perhaps, for his wife's taste) compared to the general attitude of ignorant admiration which American intellectuals had toward Soviet Russia. I remember the sudden hush, and furtive exchange of incredulous grimaces, when at a party, given for me by the most eminent member of our English department, I described the Bolshevist state as Philistine in repose and bestial in action; internationally vying in rapacious deceit with the praying mantis; doctoring the mediocrity of its literature by first sparing a few talents left over from a previous period and then blotting them out with their own blood. One professor, a left-wing moralist and dedicated muralist (he was experimenting that year with automobile paint), stalked out of the house. He wrote me next day, however, a really magnificent, larger-than-nature letter of apology saying that he could not be really cross with the author of *Esmeralda and Her Parandrus* (1941), which despite its "motley style and baroque imagery" was a masterpiece "pinching strings of personal poignancy which he, a committed artist, never knew could vibrate in him." Reviewers of my books took the same line, chiding me formally for underestimating the "greatness" of Lenin, yet paying me compliments of a kind that could not fail to touch, in the long run, even me, a scornful and austere author, whose homework in Paris had never received its due.

Even the President of Quirn, who timorously sympathized with the fashionable Sovietizers, was really on my side: he told me when he called on us (while Ninel crept up to grow an ear on our landing) that he was proud, etc., and had found my "last (?) book very interesting" though he could not help regretting that I took every opportunity of criticizing "our Great Ally" in my classes. I answered, laughing, that this criticism was a child's caress when set alongside the public lecture on "The Tractor in Soviet Literature" that I planned to deliver at the end of the term. He laughed, too, and asked Annette what it was like to live with a genius (she only shrugged her pretty shoulders). All this was *très américain* and thawed a whole auricle in my icy heart.

But to return to good Ninel.

She had been christened Nonna at birth (1902) and renamed twenty years later Ninel (or Ninella), as petitioned by her father, a Hero of Toil and a toady. She wrote it Ninella in English but her friends called her Ninette or Nelly just as my wife's Christian name Anna (as Nonna liked to observe) turned into Annette and Netty.

Ninella Langley was a stocky, heavily built creature with a ruddy and rosy face (the two tints unevenly distributed), short hair dyed a mother-in-law ginger, brown eyes even madder than mine, very thin lips, a fat Russian nose, and three or four hairs on her chin. Before the young reader heads for Lesbos, I wish to say that as far as I could discover (and I am a peerless spy) there was nothing sexual in her ludicrous and unlimited affection for my wife. I had not yet acquired the white Desert Lynx that Annette did not live to see, so it was Ninella who took her shopping in a dilapidated jalopy while the resourceful lodger, sparing the copies of his own novels, would autograph for the grateful twins old mystery paperbacks and unreadable pamphlets from the Langley collection in the attic whose dormer looked out obligingly on the road to, and from, the Shopping Center. It was Ninella who kept her adored "Netty" well supplied with white knitting wool. It was Ninella who twice daily invited her for a cup of coffee or tea in her rooms; but the woman made a point of avoiding our flat, at least when we were at home, under the pretext that it still reeked of her husband's tobacco: I rejoined that it was my own pipe—and later, on the same day, Annette told me I really ought not to smoke so much, especially indoors; and she also upheld another absurd complaint coming from downstairs, namely, that I walked back and forth too late and too long, right over Ninella's forehead. Yes—and a third grievance: why didn't I put back the encyclopedia volumes in alphabetic order as her husband had always been careful to do, for (he said) "a misplaced book is a lost book"—quite an aphorism.

Dear Mrs. Langley was not particularly happy about her job. She owned a lakeside bungalow ("Rustic Roses") thirty miles north of Quirn, not very far from Honeywell College, where she taught summer school and with which she intended to be even more closely associated, if a "reactionary" atmosphere persisted at Quirn. Actually, her only grudge was against decrepit Mme. de Korchakov, who had accused her, in public, of having a *sdobnyy* ("mellow") Soviet accent and a provincial vocabulary—all of which could not be denied, although Annette maintained I was a heartless bourgeois to say so.

2

The infant Isabel's first four years of life are so firmly separated in my consciousness by a blank of seven years from Bel's girlhood that I seem to have had two different children, one a cheerful red-cheeked little thing, and the other her pale and morose elder sister.

I had laid in a stock of ear plugs; they proved superfluous: no crying came from the nursery to interfere with my work— *Dr. Olga Repnin*, the story of an invented Russian professor in America, which was to be published (after a bothersome spell of serialization entailing endless proofreading) by Lodge in 1946, the year Annette left me, and acclaimed as "a blend of humor and humanism" by alliteration-prone reviewers, comfortably unaware of what I was to prepare some fifteen years later for their horrified delectation.

I enjoyed watching Annette as she took color snapshots of

the baby and me in the garden. I loved perambulating a fascinated Isabel through the groves of larches and beeches along Quirn Cascade River, with every loop of light, every eyespot of shade escorted, or so it seemed, by the baby's gay approbation. I even agreed to spend most of the summer of 1945 at Rustic Roses. There, one day, as I was returning with Mrs. Langley from the nearest liquor store or newspaper stand, something she said, some intonation or gesture, released in me the passing shudder, the awful surmise, that it was not with my wife but with me that the wretched creature had been in love from the very start.

The torturous tenderness I had always felt for Annette gained new poignancy from my feelings for our little child (I "trembled" over her as Ninella put it in her coarse Russian, complaining it might be bad for the baby, even if one "subtracted the overacting"). That was the human side of our marriage. The sexual side disintegrated altogether.

For quite a time after her return from the maternity ward, echoes of her pangs in the darkest corridors of my brain and a frightening stained window at every turn—the afterimage of a wounded orifice—pursued me and deprived me of all my vigor. When everything in me healed, and my lust for her pale enchantments rekindled, its volume and violence put an end to the brave but essentially inept efforts she had been making to reestablish some sort of amorous harmony between us without departing one jot from the puritanical norm. She now had the gall—the pitiful girlish gall—to insist I see a psychiatrist (recommended by Mrs. Langley) who would help me to think "softening" thoughts at moments of excessive engorgement. I said her friend was a monster and she a goose, and we had our worst marital quarrel in years.

The creamy-thighed twins had long since returned with their bicycles to the island of their birth. Plainer young ladies came to help with the housekeeping. By the end of 1945 I had virtually ceased visiting my wife in her cold bedroom.

Sometime in mid-May, 1946, I traveled to New York—a five-hour train trip—to lunch with a publisher who was offering me better terms for a collection of stories (*Exile from Mayda*) than good Lodge. After a pleasant meal, in the sunny haze of that banal day, I walked over to the Public Library, and by a banal miracle of synchronization she came dancing down those very steps, Dolly von Borg, now twenty-four, as I trudged up toward her, a fat famous writer in his powerful forties. Except for a gleam of gray in the abundant fair mane that I had cultivated for my readings in Paris, more than a decade ago, I do not believe I could have changed sufficiently to warrant her saying, as she began doing, that she would never have recognized me had she not been so fond of the picture of meditation on the back of *See under*. I recognized her because I had never lost track of her image, readjusting it once in a while: the last time I had notched the score was when her grandmother, in response to my wife's Christmas greetings, in 1939, sent us from London a postcard-size photo of a bare-shouldered flapper with a fluffy fan and false eyelashes in some high-school play, terribly chi-chi. In the two minutes we had on those steps—she pressing with both hands a book to her breast, I at a lower level, standing with my right foot placed on the next step, her step, and slapping my knee with a glove (many a tenor's only known gesture)—in those two minutes we managed to exchange quite a lot of plain information.

She was now studying the History of the Theater at Columbia University. Parents and grandparents were tucked away in London. I had a child, right? Those shoes I wore were lovely. Students called my lectures fabulous. Was I happy?

I shook my head. When and where could I see her?

She had always had a crush on me, oh yes, ever since I used to mesmerize her in my lap, playing sweet Uncle Gasper, muffing every other line, and now all had come back and she certainly wished to do something about it.

She had a remarkable vocabulary. Summarize her. Mirages of motels in the eye of the penholder. Did she have a car?

Well, that was rather sudden (laughing). She could borrow, perhaps, his old sedan though he might not like the notion (pointing to a nondescript youth who was waiting for her on the sidewalk). He had just bought a heavenly Hummer to go places with her.

Would she mind telling me *when* we could meet, please.

She had read all my novels, at least all the English ones. Her Russian was rusty!

The hell with my novels! When?

I had to let her think. She might visit me at the end of the term. Terry Todd (now measuring the stairs with his eyes, preparing to mount) had briefly been a student of mine; he got a D minus for his first paper and quit Quirn.

I said I consigned all the D people to everlasting oblivion. Her "end of the term" might bend away into Minus Eternity. I required more precision.

She would let me know. She would call me next week. No, she would not part with her own telephone number. She told me to look at that clown (he was now coming up the steps). Paradise was a Persian word. It was simply Persian to meet again like that. She might drop in at my office for a few moments, just to chat about old times. She knew how busy—

"Oh, Terry: this is *the* writer, the man who wrote *Emerald and the Pander*."

I do not recall what I had planned to look up in the library. Whatever it was, it was not that unknown book. Aimlessly I walked up and down several halls; abjectly visited the W.C.; but simply could not, short of castrating myself, get rid of her new image in its own portable sunlight—the straight pale hair, the freckles, the banal pout, the Lilithan long eyes—though I knew she was only what one used to call a "little tramp" and, perhaps, *because* she was just that.

I gave my penultimate "Masterpieces" lecture of the spring term. I gave my ultimate one. An assistant distributed the blue books for the final examination in that course (which I had curtailed for reasons of health) and collected them while three or four hopeless hopefuls still kept scribbling madly in separate spots of the hall. I held my last Joyce seminar of the year. Little Baroness Borg had forgotten the end of the dream.

In the last days of the spring term a particularly stupid baby-sitter told me that some girl whose name she had not quite caught—Tallbird or Dalberg—had phoned that she was on her way to Quirn. It so happened that a Lily Talbot in my Masterpieces class had missed the examination. On the following day I walked over to my office for the ordeal of reading the damned heap on my desk. Quirn University Official Examination Book. All academic work is conducted on the assumption of general horror. Write on the consecutive right-

and left-hand pages. What does "consecutive" really mean, Sir? Do you want us to describe *all* the birds in the story or only one? As a rule, one-tenth of the three hundred minds preferred the spelling "Stern" to "Sterne" and "Austin" to "Austen."

The telephone on my spacious desk (it "slept two" as my ribald neighbor Professor King, an authority on Dante, used to say) rang, and this Lily Talbot started to explain, volubly, unconvincingly, in a kind of lovely, veiled, and confidential voice, why she had not taken the examination. I could not remember her face or her figure, but the subdued melody tickling my ear contained such intimations of young charm and surrender that I could not help chiding myself for overlooking her in my class. She was about to come to the point when an eager childish rap at the door diverted my attention. Dolly walked in, smiling. Smiling, she indicated with a tilt of her chin that the receiver should be cradled. Smiling, she swept the examination books off the desk and perched upon it with her bare shins in my face. What might have promised the most refined ardors turned out to be the tritest scene in this memoir. I hastened to quench a thirst that had been burning a hole in the mixed metaphor of my life ever since I had fondled a quite different Dolly thirteen years earlier. The ultimate convulsion rocked the desk lamp, and from the class just across the corridor came a burst of applause at the end of Professor King's last lecture of the season.

When I came home, I found my wife alone on the porch swinging gently if not quite straight in her favorite glider and reading the *Krasnaya Niva* ("Red Corn"), a Bolshevist magazine. Her purveyor of *literatura* was away giving some future mistranslators a final examination. Isabel had been out of doors and was now taking a nap in her room just above the porch.

In the days when the *bermudki* (as Ninella indecently called them) used to minister to my humble needs, I experienced no guilt after the operation and confronted my wife with my usual, fondly ironical smile; but on *this* occasion I felt my flesh coated with stinging slime, and my heart missed a thump, when she said, glancing up and stopping the line with her finger: "Did that girl get in touch with you at your office?"

I answered as a fictional character might "in the affirmative": "Her people," I added, "wrote you, it appears, about her coming to study in New York, but you never showed me that letter. *Tant mieux*, she's a frightful bore."

Annette looked utterly confused: "I'm speaking," she said, "or trying to speak, about a student called Lily Talbot who telephoned an hour ago to explain why she missed the exam. Who is *your* girl?"

We proceeded to disentangle the two. After some moral hesitation ("You know, we both owe a lot to her grandparents") Annette conceded we really need not entertain little strays. She seemed to recall the letter because it contained a reference to her widowed mother (now moved to a comfortable home for the old into which I had recently turned my villa at Carnavaux—despite my lawyer's well-meaning objections). Yes, yes, she had mislaid it—and would find it some day in some library book that had never been returned to an unattainable library. A strange appeasement was now flowing through my poor veins. The romance of her absentmindedness always made me laugh heartily. I laughed heartily. I kissed her on her infinitely tender-skinned temple.

"How does Dolly Borg look now?" asked Annette. "She used to be a very homely and very brash little brat. Quite repulsive, in fact."

"That's what she still is," I practically shouted, and we heard little Isabel crow: "*Ya prosnulas'*," through the yawn of the window: "I am awake." How lightly the spring cloudlets scudded! How glibly that red-breasted thrush on the lawn pulled out its unbroken worm! Ah—and there was Ninella, home at last, getting out of her car, with the string-bound corpses of *cahiers* under her study arm. "Gosh," said I to myself, in my ignoble euphoria, "there's something quite nice and cozy about old Ninel after all!" Yet only a few hours later the light of Hell had gone out, and I writhed, I wrung my four limbs, yes, in an agony of insomnia, trying to find some combination between pillow and back, sheet and shoulder, linen and leg, to help me, help me, oh, help me to reach the Eden of a rainy dawn.

3

The increasing disarray of my nerves was such that the bother of getting a driver's license could not be contemplated: hence I had to rely on Dolly's use of Todd's dirty old sedan in order to seek the conventional darkness of country lanes that were difficult to find and disappointing when found. We had three such rendezvous, near New Swivington or thereabouts, in the complicated vicinity of Casanovia of all places, and despite my muddled condition I could not help noticing that Dolly welcomed the restless wanderings, the wrong turns, the torrents of rain which attended our sordid little affair. "Just think," she said one especially boggy June night in unknown surroundings, "how much simpler things would be if somebody explained the situation to your wife, just think!"

On realizing she had gone too far with that proposed thought, Dolly changed tactics and rang me up at my office to tell me with a great show of jubilant excitement that Bridget Dolan, a medical student and a cousin of Todd's, was offering us for a small remuneration her flat in New York on Monday and Thursday afternoons when she worked as a nurse at the Holy Something Hospital. Inertia rather than Eros caused me to give it a try; I kept up the pretext of having to complete the literary research I was supposed to be conducting in the Public Library, and traveled in a crowded Pullman from one nightmare to another.

She met me in front of the house, strutting in triumph, brandishing a little key that caught a glint of sun in the hothouse mizzle. I was so very weak from the journey that I had trouble getting out of the taxi, and she helped me to the front door, chattering the while like a bright child. Fortunately the mysterious flat was on the ground floor—I could not have faced a lift's closure and spasm. A surly janitrix (reminding me in mnemonic reverse of the Cerberean bitches in the hotels of Soviet Siberia which I was to stop at a couple of decades later) insisted on my writing down my name and address in a ledger ("That's the rule," sang out Dolly, who had already picked up some intones of local delivery). I had the presence of mind to put down the dumbest address I could produce at the moment, Dumbert Dumbert, Dumberton. Dolly, humming, added unhurriedly my raincoat to those hanging in a communal hallway. If she had ever experienced the pangs of neuralgic delirium, she would not have fumbled with that key when she knew quite well that the door of what should have been an exquisitely private apartment was not even properly closed. We entered a preposterous, evidently ultra-modern living room with painted hard furniture and one lone little white rocker supporting a plush biped rat instead of a sulky child. Doors were still with me, were always with me. The one on the left, being slightly ajar, let in voices from an adjacent suite or asylum. "There's a party going on there!" I expostulated, and Dolly deftly and softly drew that door almost shut. "They're a nice friendly group," she said, "and it's really too warm in these rooms to choke every chink. Second on the right. Here we are."

Here we were. Nurse Dolan for the sake of atmosphere and professional empathy had rigged up her bedroom in hospital style: a snow-pure cot with a system of levers that would have rendered even Big Peter (in the *Red Topper*) impotent; white-washed commodes and glazed cabinets; a bedhead chart dear to humorists; and a set of rules tacked to the bathroom door.

"Now off with that jacket," cried Dolly gaily, "while I unlace those lovely shoes" (crouching nimbly, and nimbly re-crouching, at my retreating feet).

I said: "You have lost your mind, my dear, if you think I could contemplate making love in this appalling place."

"What do you want then?" she asked, angrily brushing away a strand of hair from her flushed face and uncoiling back to her natural length: "Where would you find another such dandy, hygienic, utterly—"

A visitor interrupted her: a brown, gray-cheeked old dackel carrying horizontally a rubber bone in its mouth. It entered from the parlor, placed the obscene red thing on the linoleum, and stood looking at me, at Dolly, at me again, with melancholy expectation on its raised dogface. A pretty bare-armed girl in black slipped in, grabbed the animal, kicked its toy back into the parlor, and said: "Hullo, Dolly! If you and your friend want some drinks afterwards, please join us. Bridget phoned she'd be home early. It's J.B.'s birthday."

"Righto, Carmen," replied Dolly, and turning to me con-

tinued in Russian: "I think you need that drink right away.
Oh, come along! And for God's sake leave that jacket and
waistcoat here. You are drenched with sweat."

She forced me out of the room; I went rumbling and
groaning; she gave a perfunctory pat to the creaseless cot and
followed the man of snow, the man of tallow, the dying lop-
sided man.

Most of the party had now invaded the parlor from the next
room. I cringed and tried to hide my face as I recognized
Terry Todd. He raised his glass in delicate congratulation.
What that slut had done to ensure a thwarted beau's complicity, I shall never know; but I should never have put her in
my *Krasnyy Tsilindr*; that's the way you breed live monsters—
from little ballerinas in books. Another person I had once seen
already—in a car that kept passing us somewhere in the country—a young actor with handsome Irish features, pressed
upon me what he called a Honolulu Cooler, but at the eoan
stage of an attack I am beyond alcohol, so could only taste
the pineapple part of the mixture. Amidst a circle of sycophants a bull-size old fellow in a short-sleeved shirt monogrammed "J.B." posed, one hairy arm around Dolly, for a
naughty shot that his wife snapped. Carmen removed my
sticky glass on her neat little tray with a pillbox and a ther-
mometer in the corner. Not finding a seat, I had to lean
against the wall, and the back of my head caused a cheap
abstract in a plastic frame to start swinging above me: it was
stopped by Todd who had sidled up to me and now said,
lowering his voice: "Everything is settled, Prof, to everybody's
satisfaction. I've kept in touch with Mrs. Langley, sure I have,
she and the missus are writing you. I believe they've already
left, the kid thinks you're in Heaven—now, now, what's the
matter?"

I am not a fighter. I only hurt my hand against a tall lamp
and lost both shoes in the scuffle. Terry Todd vanished—forever. The telephone was being used in one room and ringing
in the other. Dolly, retransformed by the alchemy of her blazing anger—and now untellable from the little girl who had
hurled a three-letter French word at me when I told her I
found it wiser to stop taking advantage of her grandfather's
hospitality—virtually tore my necktie in two, yelling she could

easily get me jailed for rape but preferred to see me crawling back to my consort and harem of baby-sitters (her new vocabulary, though, remained richly theatrical, even when she shrieked).

I felt trapped like a silver pea teased into the center of a toy maze. A threatening crowd, held back by J.B., the head doctor, separated me from the exit; so I retreated to Bridget's private wardette and saw, with a sense of relief (also "eoan" alas) that beyond a previously unnoticed, half-opened French window there extended to a fabulous distance an inner court, or only one comforting part of an inner court, with lightly robed patients circulating in a geometry of lawns and garden walks, or quietly sitting on benches. I staggered out, and as my white-socked feet touched the cool turf I noticed that the vagabond wench had undone the ankle strings of the long linen underpants I was wearing. Somehow, somewhere, I had shed and lost all the rest of my clothes. As I stood there, my head brimming with a blackness of pain seldom known before, I became aware of a flurry of motion beyond the court. Far, far away, nurse Dolan or Nolan (at that distance such nice distinctions no longer mattered) emerged from a wing of the hospital and came running to my assistance. Two males followed her with a stretcher. A helpful patient gathered up the blanket they had dropped.

"You know, you know . . . you should have never done that," she cried panting. "Don't move, they'll help you to get up (I had collapsed on the turf). If you'd escaped after surgery you might have died right where you are. On such a lovely day, too!"

And so I was carried by two sturdy palanquiners who stank all the way (the hind bearer solidly, the front man in rhythmic wafts) not to Bridget's bed but to a real hospital cot in a ward for three between two old men, both dying of cerebritis.

4

Rustic Roses
13. IV. 46

The step I have taken, Vadim, is not subject to discussion (ne podlezhit obsuzhdeniyu). *You must accept my departure as a* fait accompli.[1] *Had I really loved you I would not have left you; but I never loved you really, and maybe your escapade—which no doubt is not your first since our arrival in this sinister* (zloveshchuyu) *"free" country[2]—is for me a mere pretext for leaving you.*

*We have never been very happy together, you and I, during our twelve[3] years of marriage. You regarded me from the start as a cute, dutiful, but definitely disappointing little circus animal[4] which you tried to teach immoral disgusting tricks—*condemned as such *according to the faithful companion without whom I might not have survived in ghastly "Kvirn"[5] by the latest scientific stars of our fatherland. I, on the other hand, was so painfully nonplussed by your* trenne (sic)[6] de vie, *your habits, your black-locked[7] friends, your decadent novels, and—why not admit it?—your pathological revolt against Art and Progress in the Soviet Land, including the restoration of lovely old churches,[8] that I would have divorced you, had I dared upset[9] poor papa and mama who were so eager in their dignity and naïveté to have their daughter addressed—by whom, good Lord?—as "Your Serenity"* (Siyatel'stvo).

Now comes a serious demand, an absolute injunction. Never, never—at least while I am still alive—never, I repeat, shall you try to communicate with the child. I do not know—Nelly is better versed in this—what the legal situation is, but I know that in certain respects you are a gentleman and it is to the gentleman that I say and shout: Please, please, keep away! If some dreadful American illness strikes me, then remember I wish her to be brought up as a Russian Christian.[10]

I was sorry to learn about your hospitalization. This is your second, and I hope last, attack of neurasthenia[11] since the time we made the mistake of leaving Europe instead

*of waiting quietly for the Soviet Army to liberate it from
the fascists. Good-bye.*

P.S. Nelly wishes to add a few lines.

*Thank you, Netty. I shall indeed be brief. The infor-
mation imparted to us by your girlfriend's fiancé and his
mother,*[12] *a saintly woman of infinite compassion and common sense, lacked, fortunately, the element of dreadful
surprise. A roommate of Berenice Mudie (the one that stole
the cut-crystal decanter Netty gave me) had already been
spreading certain odd rumors a couple of years ago; I tried
to protect your sweet wife by not allowing that gossip to
reach her or at least by drawing her attention to it in a
very oblique, half-humorous way long after those prosti-
tutes had gone. But now let us talk* turkey.[13]

*There can be no problem, I am sure, in separating your
things from hers. She says: "Let him take the countless copies of his novels and all the tattered dictionaries"; but she
must be allowed to keep her household treasures such as my
little birthday gifts to her—the silver-plated caviar bowl
as well as the six pale-green handblown wine glasses, etc.*

*I can especially sympathize with Netty in this domestic
catastrophe because my own marriage resembled hers in
many, many ways. It began so auspiciously! I was stranded
and lost in a territory suddenly occupied by Estonian fascists, a poor little war-tossed Moscow girl,*[14] *when I first
met Professor Langley in quite romantic circumstances: I
was interpreting for him (the study of foreign languages
stands at a remarkable level in the Soviet Land); but when
I was shipped with other DP's to the U.S. and we met
again and married, all went wrong—he ignored me in
the daytime, and our nights were full of* incompatibility.[15]
*One good consequence is that I inherited, so to speak, a
lawyer, Mr. Horace Peppermill, who has consented to
grant you a consultation and help you to settle all business
details. It will be wise on your part to follow Professor
Langley's example and give your wife a monthly allowance
while placing a sizable "guarantee sum" in the bank
which can be available to her in extreme cases and, naturally, after your demise or during an overprotracted*

terminal illness. We do not have to remind you that Mrs. Blagovo should continue to receive regularly her usual check until further notice.

The Quirn house will be offered for sale immediately— it is overflowing with odious memories. Consequently, as soon as they let you out, which I hope will happen without retardment (bez zamedleniya, sans tarder), *move out of the house, please.*[16] *I am not on speaking terms with Miss Myrna Soloway—or, in reality, simply Soloveychik—of my department, but I understand she is very good at ferreting out places for rent.*

We have fine weather here after all that rain. The lake is beautiful at this time of the year! We are going to refurnish our dear little dacha. *Its only drawback in one sense (an asset in all others!) is that it stands a wee bit apart from civilization or at least from Honeywell College. The police are always on the lookout for bathers in the nude, prowlers, etc. We are seriously thinking of acquiring a big Alsatian!*[17]

COMMENTARY

1. *En français dans le texte.*
2. The first four or five lines are no doubt authentic, but then come various details which convince me that not Netty but Nelly masterminded the entire communication. Only a Soviet woman would speak like that of America.
3. At first typed "fourteen" but expertly erased and replaced by the correct "twelve," as seen clearly in the carbon copy that I found pinned, "just in case," to the blotter in my study. Netty would have been totally incapable of producing such a clean typescript— especially with the New Orthography machine used by her friend.
4. The term in the text is *durovskiy zveryok*, meaning a small animal trained by the famous Russian clown Durov, a reference less familiar to my wife than to a person of the older generation to which her friend belonged.
5. Contemptuous transliteration of "Quirn."
6. Symptomatic misspelling of *train*. Annette's French was excellent. Ninette's French (as well as her English) was a joke.
7. My wife coming as she did from an obscurant Russian milieu was

no paragon of racial tolerance; but she would never have used the vulgar anti-Semitic phraseology typical of her friend's character and upbringing.

8. The interpolation of those "lovely old churches" is a stock platitude of Soviet patriotism.

9. Actually my wife rather liked to upset her people on every possible occasion.

10. I might have done something about it had I known for sure *whose* wish it was. To spite her parents—a strange but constant policy on her part—Annette never went to church, not even at Easter. As to Mrs. Langley, devotional decorum was the motto; the woman made the sign of the cross every time American Jupiter split the black clouds.

11. "Neurasthenia" indeed!

12. A totally new character—this mother. Myth? Impersonation act? I turned to Bridget for some explanation; she said there was no such person around (the real Mrs. Todd died long ago) and advised me "to drop the subject" with the irritating curtness of one dismissing a topic as the product of another's delirium. I am ready to agree that my recollection of the scene at her apartment is tainted by the state I was in, but that "saintly mother" must remain an enigma.

13. *En Anglais dans le texte.*

14. The little Muscovite must have been around forty at the time.

15. *En Anglais dans le texte.*

16. This I did not dream of doing before my lease expired, which it did on August 1, 1946.

17. Let us refrain from a final comment.

Good-bye, Netty and Nelly. Good-bye, Annette and Ninette. Good-bye, Nonna Anna.

Part Four

I

LEARNING to drive that "Caracal" (as I fondly called my new white coupé) had its comic as well as dramatic side, but after two flunks and a few little repairs, I found myself legally and physically fit at last to spin off West on a protracted tour. There was, true, a moment of acute distress, as the first distant mountains disowned suddenly any likeness to lilac clouds, when I recalled the trips Iris and I used to make to the Riviera in our old Icarus. If she did occasionally allow me to take the wheel, it was only in a spirit of fun, for she was such a sportive girl. With what sobs I now remembered the time when I managed to hit the postman's bicycle which had been left leaning against a pink wall at the entrance of Carnavaux, and how my Iris doubled up in beautiful mirth as the thing slithered off in front of us!

I spent what remained of the summer exploring the incredibly lyrical Rocky Mountain states, getting drunk on whiffs of Oriental Russia in the sagebrush zone and on the North Russian fragrances so faithfully reproduced above timberline by certain small bogs along trickles of sky between the snowbank and the orchid. And yet—was that all? What form of mysterious pursuit caused me to get my feet wet like a child, to pant up a talus, to stare every dandelion in the face, to start at every colored mote passing just beyond my field of vision? What was the dream sensation of having come empty-handed—without what? A gun? A wand? This I dared not probe lest I wound the raw fell under my thin identity.

Skipping the academic year, in a kind of premature "sabbatical leave" that left the Trustees of Quirn University speechless, I wintered in Arizona where I tried to write *The Invisible Lath*, a book rather similar to that in the reader's hands. No doubt I was not ready for it and perhaps toiled too much over inexpressible shades of emotion; anyway I smothered it under too many layers of sense as a Russian peasant

woman, in her stuffy log house, might overlay (*zaspat'*) her
baby in heavy oblivion after making hay or being thrashed by
her drunken husband.

I pushed on to Los Angeles—and was sorry to learn that
the cinema company I had counted upon was about to fold
after Ivor Black's death. On my way back, in early spring, I
rediscovered the dear phantasmata of my childhood in the
tender green of aspen groves at high altitudes here and there,
on conifer-clothed ridges. For almost six months I roamed
again from motel to motel, several times having my car
scratched and cracked by cretinous rival drivers and finally
trading it in for a sedate Bellargus sedan of a celestial blue
that Bel was to compare with that of a Morpho.

Another odd thing: with prophetic care I took down in my
diary all my stops, all my motels (*Mes Moteaux* as Verlaine
might have said!), the Lakeviews, the Valley Views, the Mountain Views, the Plumed Serpent Court in New Mexico, the
Lolita Lodge in Texas, Lone Poplars, that if recruited might
have patrolled a whole river, and enough sunsets to keep all
the bats of the world—and one dying genius—happy. LATH,
LATH, Look At The Harlequins! Look at that strange fever
rash of viatic tabulation in which I persevered as if I knew that
those motor courts prefigured the stages of my future travels
with my darling daughter.

In late August, 1947, suntanned, and more edgy than ever,
I returned to Quirn and transferred my belongings from storage to the new dwelling (1 Larchdell Road) found for me by
efficient and cute Miss Soloway. This was a charming two-
storied gray-stone house, with a picture window and a white
grand in the long drawing-room, three virginal bedrooms upstairs and a library in the basement. It had belonged to the
late Alden Landover, the greatest American belle-lettrist of the
half-century. With the help of the beaming Trustees—and
rather taking advantage of their joy at welcoming me back to
Quirn—I resolved to buy that house. I loved its scholarly
odor, a treat seldom granted to my exquisitely sensitive
Brunn's membrane, and I also loved its picturesque isolation
amidst a tremendous unkempt garden above a larched and
golden-rodded steep slope.

To keep Quirn grateful, I also decided to reorganize com-

pletely my contribution to its fame. I scrapped my Joyce seminar which in 1945 had attracted (if that is the word) only six
students—five grim graduates and one not quite normal soph-
omore. In compensation I added a third lecture in Masterpieces (now including *Ulysses*) to my weekly quota. The chief
innovation, however, lay in my bold presentation of knowledge. During my first years at Quirn I had accumulated two
thousand pages of literary comments typed out by my assistant
(I notice I have not introduced him yet: Waldemar Exkul, a
brilliant young Balt, incomparably more learned than I; *dixi*,
Ex!). These I had the Photostat people multiply to accommodate at least three hundred students. At the end of every
week each received a batch of the forty pages that I had recited
to them, with certain addenda, in the lecture hall. The "certain addenda" were a concession to the Trustees who reasonably remarked that without this catch nobody would need to
attend my classes. The three hundred copies of the two thousand typed pages were to be signed by the readers and returned to me before the final examination. There were flaws
at first in the system (for example, only 153 incomplete sets,
many unsigned, were returned in 1948) but on the whole it
worked, or should have worked.

Another decision I took was to make myself more available
to faculty members than I had been before. The red needle
of my dial scale now quiver-stopped at a very conservative
figure, when, stark naked, arms hanging like those of a clumsy
troglodyte, I stood on the fatal platform and with the help of
my new housemaid, an enchanting black girl with an Egyptian
profile, managed to make out what lay midway in the blur
between my reading glasses and my long-distance ones: a
great triumph, which I marked by acquiring several new "costumes," as my Dr. Olga Repnin says in the novel of that
name—"I don't know (all 'o's' as in 'don' and 'anon') why
your horseband wears such not modern costumes." I visited
quite frequently the Pub, a college tavern, where I tried to
mix with white-shoed young males, but somehow ended up
by getting involved with professional barmaids. And I entered
in my pocket diary the addresses of some twenty fellow professors.

Most treasured among my new friends was a frail-looking,

sad-looking, somewhat monkey-faced man with a shock of black hair, gray-streaked at fifty-five, the enchantingly talented poet Audace whose paternal ancestor was the eloquent and ill-fated Girondist of that name ("*Bourreau, fais ton devoir envers la Liberté!*") but who did not know a word of French and spoke American with a flat Midwestern accent. Another interesting glimpse of descent was provided by Louise Adamson, the young wife of our Chairman of English: her grandmother, Sybil Lanier, had won the Women's National Golf Championship in 1896 at Philadelphia!

Gerard Adamson's literary reputation was immensely superior to that of the immensely more important, bitter, and modest Audace. Gerry was a big flabby hulk of a man who must have been nearing sixty when after a life of aesthetic asceticism he surprised his special coterie by marrying that porcelain-pretty and very fast girl. His famous essays—on Donne, on Villon, on Eliot—his philosophic poetry, his recent *Laic Litanies* and so forth meant nothing to me, but he was an appealing old drunk, whose humor and erudition could break the resistance of the most unsociable outsider. I caught myself enjoying the frequent parties at which good old Noteboke and his sister Phoneme, the delightful Kings, the Adamsons, my favorite poet, and a dozen other people did all they could to entertain and comfort me.

Louise, who had an inquisitive aunt at Honeywell, kept me informed, at tactful intervals, of Bel's well-being. One spring day in 1949 or 1950 I happened to stop at the Plaza Liquor Store in Rosedale after a business meeting with Horace Peppermill and was about to back out of the parking lot when I saw Annette bending over a baby carriage in front of a grocery store at the other end of the shopping area. Something about her inclined neck, her melancholy concentration, the ghost of a smile directed at the child in the stroller, sent such a pang of pity through my nervous system that I could not resist accosting her. She turned toward me and even before I uttered some wild words—of regret, of despair, of tenderness—there she was shaking her head, forbidding me to come near. "*Nikogda,*" she murmured, "never," and I could not bear to decipher the expression on her pale drawn face. A woman came out of the shop and thanked her for tending the little

stranger—a pale and thin infant, looking almost as ill as Annette. I hurried back to the parking lot, scolding myself for
not realizing at once that Bel must be a girl of seven or eight
by this time. Her mother's moist starry stare kept pursuing
me for several nights; I even felt too ill to attend an Easter
party at one of the friendly Quirn houses.

During this or some other period of despondency, I heard
one day the hall bell tinkle, and my Negro maid, little Nefertitty as I had dubbed her, hasten to open the front door.
Slipping out of bed I pressed my bare flesh to the cool window
ledge but was not in time to glimpse the entrant or entrants,
no matter how far I leant out into a noisy spring downpour.
A freshness of flowers, clusters and clouds of flowers, reminded me of some other time, some other casement. I made
out part of the Adamsons' glossy black car beyond the garden
gate. Both? She alone? *Solus rex?* Both, alas—to judge by the
voices reaching me from the hallway through my transparent
house. Old Gerry, who disliked unnecessary stairs and had a
morbid fear of contagion, remained in the living room. Now
his wife's steps and voice were coming up. We had kissed for
the first time a few days before, in the Notebokes' kitchen—
rummaging for ice, finding fire. I had good reason to hope
that the intermission before the obligatory scene would be
brief.

She entered, set down two bottles of port for the invalid,
and pulled off her wet sweater over her tumbled chestnut-
brown, violet-brown curls and naked clavicles. Artistically,
strictly artistically, I daresay she was the best-looking of my
three major loves. She had upward-directed thin eyebrows,
sapphire eyes registering (and that's the right word) constant
amazement at earth's paradise (the only one she would ever
know, I'm afraid), pink-flushed cheekbones, a rosebud mouth,
and a lovely concave abdomen. In less time than it took her
husband, a quick reader, to skim down two columns of print,
we had "attired" him. I put on blue slacks and a pink shirt
and followed her downstairs.

Her husband sat in a deep armchair, reading a London
weekly bought at the Shopping Center. He had not bothered
to take off his horrible black raincoat—a voluminous robe of
oilskin that conjured up the image of a stagecoach driver in a

lashing storm. He now removed however his formidable spectacles. He cleared his throat with a characteristic rumble. His
purple jowls wobbled as he tackled the ordeal of rational
speech:

GERRY   *Do you ever see this paper, Vadim* (accenting "Vadim" incorrectly on the first syllable)? *Mister* (naming a particularly lively criticule) *has demolished your Olga* (my novel
about the *professorsha*; it had come out only now in the
British edition).

VADIM   *May I give you a drink? We'll toast him and roast
him.*

GERRY   *Yet he's right, you know. It is your worst book.* Chute
complète, *says the man. Knows French, too.*

LOUISE   *No drinks. We've got to rush home. Now heave out
of that chair. Try again. Take your glasses and paper. There.*
Au revoir, *Vadim.* I'll bring you those pills *tomorrow morning after I drive* him *to school.*

How different it all was, I mused, from the refined adul-
teries in the castles of my early youth! Where was the romantic
thrill of a glance exchanged with one's new mistress in the
presence of a morose colossus—the Jealous Husband? Why
did the recollection of the recent embrace not blend any
longer as it used to do with the certainty of the next one,
forming a sudden rose in an empty flute of crystal, a sudden
rainbow on the white wallpaper? What did Emma see a fashionable woman drop into that man's silk hat? Write legibly.

2

The mad scholar in *Esmeralda and Her Parandrus* wreathes
Botticelli and Shakespeare together by having Primavera end
as Ophelia with all her flowers. The loquacious lady in *Dr.
Olga Repnin* remarks that tornadoes and floods are really sensational only in North America. On May 17, 1953, several papers printed a photograph of a family, complete with birdcage,

phonograph, and other valuable possessions, riding it out on the roof of their shack in the middle of Rosedale Lake. Other papers carried the picture of a small Ford caught in the upper branches of an intrepid tree with a man, a Mr. Byrd, whom Horace Peppermill said he knew, still in the driver's seat, stunned, bruised, but alive. A prominent personality in the Weather Bureau was accused of criminally delayed forecasts. A group of fifteen schoolchildren who had been taken to see a collection of stuffed animals donated by Mrs. Rosenthal, the benefactor's widow, to the Rosedale Museum, were safe in the sudden darkness of that sturdy building when the twister struck. But the prettiest lakeside cottage got swept away, and the drowned bodies of its two occupants were never retrieved.

Mr. Peppermill, whose natural faculties were no match for his legal acumen, warned me that if I desired to relinquish the child to her grandmother in France, certain formalities would have to be complied with. I observed quietly that Mrs. Blagovo was a half-witted cripple and that my daughter, whom her schoolteacher harbored, should be brought by that person to my house AT ONCE. He said he would fetch her himself early next week.

After weighing and reweighing every paragraph of the house, every parenthesis of its furniture, I decided to lodge her in the former bedroom of the late Landover's companion whom he called his nurse or his fiancée depending on his mood of the moment. This was a lovely chamber, east of mine, with lilac butterflies enlivening its wallpaper and a large, low, flouncy bed. I peopled its white bookshelf with Keats, Yeats, Coleridge, Blake, and four Russian poets (in the New Orthography). Although I told myself with a sigh that she would, no doubt, prefer "comics" to my dear bespangled mimes and their wands of painted lath, I felt compelled in my choice by what is termed the "ornamental instinct" among ornithologists. Moreover, knowing well how essential a pure strong light is to reading in bed, I asked Mrs. O'Leary, my new charwoman and cook (borrowed from Louise Adamson who had left with her husband for a long sojourn in England) to screw a couple of hundred-watt bulbs into a tall bedside lamp. Two dictionaries, a writing pad, a little alarm clock, and a Junior Manicure Set (suggested by Mrs. Noteboke, who had a twelve-year-old daughter) were attractively placed on a spacious and stable bedtable. All this was but a rough, naturally. The fair copy would come in due time.

Landover's nurse or fiancée could rush to his assistance either along a short passage or through the bathroom between the two bedrooms: Landover had been a large man and his long deep tub was a soaker's delight. Another, narrower bathroom followed Bel's bedroom easterly—and here I really missed my dainty Louise when racking my brain for the correct epithet between well-scrubbed and perfumed. Mrs. Noteboke could not help me: her daughter, who used the messy parental facilities, had no time for silly deodorants and loathed "foam." Wise old Mrs. O'Leary, on the other hand, held before her mind's eye Mrs. Adamson's creams and crystals in a Flemish artist's detail and made me long for her employer's speedy return by conjuring up that picture, which she then proceeded to simplify, but not vulgarize, while retaining such major items as the huge sponge, the jumbo cake of lavender soap, and a delicious toothpaste.

Walking still farther sunriseward, we reach the corner guest room (above the round dining room at the east end of the first floor); this I transformed with the help of a handyman, Mrs. O'Leary's cousin, into an efficiently furnished studio. It contained, when I finished with it, a couch with boxy pillows, an oak desk with a revolving chair, a steel cabinet, a bookcase, *Klingsor's Illustrated Encyclopedia* in twenty volumes, crayons, writing tablets, state maps, and (to cite the *School Buyer's Guide* for 1952–1953) "a globe ball that lifts out of a cradle so that every child can hold the world in his or her lap."

Was that all? No. I found for the bedroom a framed photograph of her mother, Paris, 1934, and for the studio a reproduction in color of Levitan's *Clouds above a Blue River* (the Volga, not far from my Marevo), painted around 1890.

Peppermill was to bring her on May 21, around four P.M. I had to fill somehow the abyss of the afternoon. Angelic Ex had already read and marked the entire batch of exams, but he thought I might want to see some of the works he had reluctantly failed. He had dropped in some time on the eve and had left them downstairs on the round table in the round room next to the hallway at the west end of the house. My poor hands ached and trembled so dreadfully that I could hardly leaf through those poor *cahiers*. The round window gave on the driveway. It was a warm gray day. Sir! I need a passing mark desperately. *Ulysses* was written in Zurich and Greece and therefore consists of too many foreign words. One of the characters in Tolstoy's *Death of Ivan* is the notorious actress Sarah Bernard. Stern's style is very sentimental and illiterative. A car door banged. Mr. Peppermill came with a duffel bag in the wake of a tall fair-haired girl in blue jeans carrying, and slowing down, to change from hand to hand, an unwieldy valise.

Annette's moody mouth and eyes. Graceful but plain.

Fortified by a serenacin tablet, I received my daughter and lawyer with the neutral dignity for which effusive Russians in Paris used to detest me so heartily. Peppermill accepted a drop of brandy. Bel had a glass of peach juice and a brown biscuit. I indicated to Bel—who was displaying her palms in a polite Russian allusion—the dining-room toilet, an old-fashioned touch on the architect's part. Horace Peppermill handed me a letter from Bel's teacher Miss Emily Ward. Fabulous Intelligence Quotient of 180. Menses already established. Strange, marvelous child. One does not quite know whether to curb or encourage such precocious brilliance. I accompanied Horace halfway back to his car, fighting off, successfully, the disgraceful urge to tell him how staggered I was by the bill his office had recently sent me.

"Let me now show you your *apartámenty*. You speak Russian, don't you?"

"I certainly do, but I can't write it. I also know a little French."

She and her mother (whom she mentioned as casually as if Annette were in the next room copying something for me on a soundless typewriter) had spent most of last summer at Carnavaux with *babushka*. I would like to have learned what room exactly Bel had occupied in the villa, but an oddly obtrusive, though irrelevant-looking, recollection somehow prevented me from asking: shortly before her death Iris had dreamed one night that she had given birth to a fat boy with dusky red cheeks and almond eyes and the blue shadow of mutton chops: "A horrible Omarus K."

Oh yes, said Bel, she had loved it. Especially the path down, down to the sea and the aroma of rosemary (*chudnyy zapakh rozmarina*). I was tortured and charmed by her "shadowless" *émigré* Russian, untainted, God bless Annette, by the Langley woman's fruity Sovietisms.

Did Bel recognize me? She looked me over with serious gray eyes.

"I recognize your hands and your hair."

"*On se tutoie* in Russian henceforward. All right. Let's go upstairs."

She approved of the studio: "A schoolroom in a picture book." She opened the medicine chest in her bathroom. "Empty—but I know what I'll put there." The bedroom "enchanted" her. *Ocharovatel'no!* (Annette's favorite praise word.) She criticized, though, the bedside bookshelf: "What, no Byron? No Browning? Ah, Coleridge! The little golden sea snakes. Miss Ward gave me an anthology for Russian Easter: I can recite your last duchess—I mean 'My Last Duchess.'"

I caught my breath with a moan. I kissed her. I wept. I sat, shaking, on a fragile chair that creaked in response to my hunched-up paroxysm. Bel stood looking away, looking up at a prismatic reflection on the ceiling, looking down at her luggage, which Mrs. O'Leary, a dumpy but doughty woman, had already brought up.

I apologized for my tears. Bel inquired in a socially perfect let's-change-the-subject manner if there was a television set in the house. I said we'd get one tomorrow. I would leave her now to her own devices. Dinner in half-an-hour. She had noticed, she said, that a picture she'd like to see was being shown in town. After dinner we drove to The Strand Theater.

Says a scribble in my diary: Does not much care for boiled chicken. *The Black Widow*. With Gene, Ginger, and George. Have passed the "illiterative" sentimentalist and all the rest.

3

If Bel is alive today, she is thirty-two—exactly your age at the moment of writing (February 15, 1974). The last time I saw her, in 1959, she was not quite seventeen; and between eleven and a half and seventeen and a half she has changed very slightly in the medium of memory, where blood does not course through immobile time as fast as it does in the perceptual present. Especially unaffected by linear growth is my vision of her pertaining to 1953–1955, the three years in which she was totally and uniquely mine: I see it today as a composite portrait of rapture, in which a mountain in Colorado, my translating *Tamara* into English, Bel's high school accomplishments, and an Oregon forest intergrade in patterns of transposed time and twisted space that defy chronography and charting.

One change, one gradational trend I must note, however. This was my growing awareness of her beauty. Scarcely a month after her arrival I was already at a loss to understand how she could have struck me as "plain." Another month elapsed and the elfin line of her nose and upper lip in profile came as an "expected revelation"—to use a formula I have applied to certain prosodic miracles in Blake and Blok. Because of the contrast between her pale-gray iris and very black lashes, her eyes seemed rimmed with kohl. Her hollowed cheek and long neck were pure Annette, but her fair hair, which she wore rather short, gave off a richer sheen as if the tawny strands were mixed with gold-olive ones in thick straight stripes of alternate shades. All this is easily described and this also goes for the regular striation of bright bloom along the outside of forearm and leg, which, in fact, smacks of self-plagiarism, for I had given it both to Tamara and Esmeralda, not counting several incidental lassies in my short stories (see for example page 537 of the *Exile from Mayda* collection, Goodminton, New York, 1947). The general type and bone structure of her pubescent radiance cannot be treated, however, with a crack player's brio and chalk-biting serve. I am reduced—a sad confession!—to something I have also used before, and even in this book—the well-known method of degrading one species of art by appealing to another. I am thinking of Serov's *Five-petaled Lilac*, oil, which depicts a tawny-haired girl of twelve or so sitting at a sun-flecked table and manipulating a raceme of lilac in search of that lucky token. The girl is no other than Ada Bredow, a first cousin of mine whom I flirted with disgracefully that very summer, the sun of which ocellates the garden table and her bare arms. What hack reviewers of fiction call "human interest" will now overwhelm my reader, the gentle tourist, when he visits the Hermitage Museum in Leningrad, where I have seen with my own rheumy eyes, on a visit to Sovietland a few years ago, that picture which belonged to Ada's grandmother before being handed over to the People by a dedicated purloiner. I believe that this enchanting little girl was the model of my partner in a recurrent dream of mine with a stretch of parquetry between two beds in a makeshift demonic guest room. Bel's resemblance to her—same cheekbones, same chin, same knobby wrists, same tender flower—can be only alluded to, not actually listed. But enough of this. I have been trying to do something very difficult and I will tear it up if you say I have succeeded too well, because I do not want, and never wanted, to succeed, in this dismal business of Isabel Lee— though at the same time I was intolerably happy.

When asked—at last!—had she loved her mother (for I could not get over Bel's apparent indifference to Annette's terrible death) she thought for such a long time that I decided she had forgotten my question, but finally (like a chessplayer resigning after an abyss of meditation), she shook her head. What about Nelly Langley? This she answered at once: Langley was mean and cruel and hated her, and only last year whipped her; she had welts all over (uncovering for display her right thigh, which now, at least, was impeccably white and smooth).

The education she got in Quirn's best private school for Young Ladies (you, her coeval, were there for a few weeks, in the same class, but you and she somehow missed making friends with each other) was supplemented by the two summers we spent roaming all over the Western states. What memories, what lovely smells, what mirages, near-mirages, substantiated mirages, accumulated along Highway 138— Sterling, Fort Morgan (El. 4325), Greeley, well-named Loveland—as we approached the paradise part of Colorado!

From Lupine Lodge, Estes Park, where we spent a whole month, a path margined with blue flowers led through aspen groves to what Bel drolly called The Foot of the Face. There was also the Thumb of the Face, at its southern corner. I have a large glossy photograph taken by William Garrell who was the first, I think, to reach The Thumb, in 1940 or thereabouts, showing the East Face of Longs Peak with the checkered lines of ascent superimposed in a loopy design upon it. On the back of this picture—and as immortal in its own little right as the picture's subject—a poem by Bel, neatly copied in violet ink, is dedicated to Addie Alexander, "First woman on Peak, eighty years ago." It commemorates our own modest hikes:

> *Longs' Peacock Lake:*
> *the Hut and its Old Marmot;*
> *Boulderfield and its Black Butterfly;*
> *And the intelligent trail.*

She had composed it while we were sharing a picnic lunch, somewhere between those great rocks and the beginning of The Cable, and after testing the result mentally a number of times, in frowning silence, she finally scribbled it on a paper napkin which she handed to me with my pencil.

I told her how wonderful and artistic it was—particularly the last line. She asked: what's "artistic"? I said: "Your poem, you, your way with words."

In the course of that ramble, or perhaps on a later occasion, but certainly in the same region, a sudden storm swept upon the glory of the July day. Our shirts, shorts, and loafers seemed to dwindle to nothing in the icy mist. A first hailstone hit a tin can, another my bald spot. We sought refuge in a cavity under a jutting rock. Thunderstorms to me are agony. Their evil pressure destroys me; their lightning forks through my brain and breast. Bel knew this; huddling against me (for my comfort rather than hers!), she kept giving me a quick little kiss on the temple at every bang of thunder, as if to say: That one's over, you're still safe. I now felt myself longing for those crashes never to cease; but presently they turned to half-hearted rumbles, and the sun found emeralds in a patch of wet turf. She could not stop shivering, though, and I had to thrust my hands under her skirt and rub her thin body, till it glowed, so as to ward off "pneumonia" which she said, laughing jerkily, was a "new," was a "moon," was a "new moon" and a "moan," a "new moan," thank you.

There is a hollow of dimness again in the sequence, but it must have been soon after that, in the same motor court, or in the next, on the way home, that she slipped into my room at dawn, and sat down on my bed—move your legs—in her pyjama top to read me another poem:

> *In the dark basement, I stroked*
> *the silky head of a wolf.*
> *When the light returned*
> *and all cried: "Ah!,"*
> *it turned out to be only*
> *Médor, a dead dog.*

I again praised her talent, and kissed her more warmly, perhaps, than the poem deserved; for, actually, I found it rather obscure, but did not say so, and presently she yawned and fell asleep on my bed, a practice I usually did not tolerate. Today, however, on rereading those strange lines, I see through their starry crystal the tremendous commentary I could write about them, with galaxies of reference marks and footnotes like the reflections of brightly lit bridges spanning black water. But my daughter's soul is hers, and my soul is mine, and may Hamlet Godman rot in peace.

4

As late as the start of the 1954–1955 school year, with Bel nearing her thirteenth birthday, I was still deliriously happy, still seeing nothing wrong or dangerous, or absurd or downright cretinous, in the relationship between my daughter and me. Save for a few insignificant lapses—a few hot drops of overflowing tenderness, a gasp masked by a cough and that sort of stuff—my relations with her remained essentially innocent. But whatever qualities I might have possessed as a Professor of Literature, nothing but incompetence and a reckless laxity of discipline can I see today in the rearview reflection of that sweet wild past.

Others forestalled me in perspicacity. My first critic hap-

pened to be Mrs. Noteboke, a stout dark lady in suffragettish
tweeds, who instead of keeping her Marion, a depraved and
vulgar nymphet, from snooping on a schoolmate's home life,
lectured me on the upbringing of Bel and strongly advised my
hiring an experienced, preferably German, governess to look
after her day and night. My second critic—a much more tactful and understanding one—was my secretary, Myrna Soloway, who complained that she could not keep track of the
literary magazines and clippings in my mail—because of their
being intercepted by an unscrupulous and avid little reader—
and who gently added that Quirn High School, the last refuge
of common sense in my incredible plight, was astounded by
Bel's lack of manners almost as much as by her intelligence
and familiarity with "Proust and Prévost." I spoke to Miss
Lowe, the rather pretty petite headmistress, and she mentioned "boarding facilities," which sounded like some kind of
wooden jail, and the even more dismal ("with all those rippling birdcalls and wickering trills in the woods, Miss Lowe—
in the woods"!) "summer instruction" to replace the "eccen-
tricities of an artist's ('A great artist's, Professor') household." She pointed out to the giggling and apprehensive
artist that a young daughter should be treated as a potential
component of our society and not as a fancy pet. Throughout
that talk I could not shake off the feeling of its all being a
nightmare that I had had or would have in some other existence, some other bound sequence of numbered dreams.

An atmosphere of vague distress was gathering (to speak in
verbal clichés about a cliché situation) around my metaphor-
ical head, when there occurred to me a simple and brilliant
solution of all my problems and troubles.

The tall looking glass before which many of Landover's
houris had onduled in their brief brown glory now served me
to behold the image of a lion-hued fifty-five-year-old would-
be athlete performing waist-slimming and chest-expanding exercises by means of an "Elmago" ("Combines the mechanical
know-how of the West with the magic of Mithra"). It was a
good image. An old telegram (found unopened in an issue of
Artisan, a literary review, filched by Bel from the hallway
table), was addressed to me by a Sunday paper in London,
asking me to comment on the rumors—which I had already

heard—to the effect that I was the main candidate in the abstract scramble for what our American kid brothers called "the most prestigious prize in the world." This, too, might impress the rather success-minded person I had in view. Finally, I knew that in the vacational months of 1955 a series of strokes had killed off in London poor old Gerry Adamson, a great guy, and that Louise was free. Too free in fact. An urgent letter I now wrote her, summoning her back to Quirn at once, for a serious Discussion of a matter concerning both her and me, reached her only after describing a comic circle via four fashionable spots on the Continent. I never saw the wire she said she sent me from New York on October 1.

On October 2, an abnormally warm day, the first of a weeklong series, Mrs. King telephoned in the afternoon to invite me with rather enigmatic little laughs to an "impromptu *soirée*, in a few hours, say at nine P.M. after you have tucked in your adorable daughter." I agreed to come because Mrs. King was an especially nice soul, the kindest on the campus.

I had a black headache and decided that a two-mile walk in the cool clear night would do me good. My dealings with space and spatial transitions are so diabolically complicated that I do not recall whether I really walked, or drove, or limited myself to pacing up and down the open gallery running along the front side of our second floor, or what.

The first person to whom my hostess introduced me—with a subdued fanfare of social elation—was the "English" cousin with whom Louise had been staying in Devonshire, Lady Morgain, "daughter of our former Ambassador and widow of the Oxford medievalist"—shadowy figures on a briefly lit screen. She was a rather deaf and decidedly dotty witch in her middle fifties, comically coiffured and dowdily dressed, and she and her belly advanced upon me with such energetic eagerness that I scarcely had time to sidestep the well-meant attack before getting wedged "between the books and the bottles" as poor Gerry used to say in reference to academic cocktails. I passed into a different, far more stylish world as I bent to kiss Louise's expertly swanned cool little hand. My dear old Audace welcomed me with the kind of Latin accolade that he had especially developed to mark the highest degree of spiritual kinship and mutual esteem. John King, whom I had seen on the eve in a college corridor, greeted me with raised arms as if the fifty hours elapsed since our last chat had been magically blown-up into half a century. We were only six people in a spacious parlor, not counting two painted girl-children in Tyrolean dress, whose presence, identity, and very existence have remained to this day a familiar mystery—familiar, because such zigzag cracks in the plaster are typical of the prisons or palaces into which recrudescent derangement merrily leads me whenever I have prepared to make, as I was to do now, a difficult, climactic announcement that demanded absolute clarity of concentration. So, as I just said, we were only six animal people in that room (and two little phantoms), but through the translucid unpleasant walls I could make out—without looking!—rows and tiers of dim spectators, with the sense of a sign in my brain meaning "standing room only" in the language of madness.

We were now sitting at a round clockfaced table (practically undistinguishable from the one in the Opal Room of my house, west of the albino Stein), Louise at twelve o'clock, Professor King at two, Mrs. Morgain at four, Mrs. King in green silk at eight, Audace at ten, and I at six, presumably, or a minute past, because Louise was not quite opposite, or maybe she had pushed her chair a sixty-second space closer to Audace although she had sworn to me on the *Social Register* as well as on a *Who's Who* that he had never made that pass at her somehow suggested by his magnificent little poem in the *Artisan*.

> *Speaking of, ah, yesternights,*
> *I had you, dear, within earshot*
> *of that party downstairs,*
> *on the broad bed of my host*
> *piled with the coats of your guests,*
> *old macks, mock minks,*
> *one striped scarf (mine),*
> *a former flame's furs*
> *(more rabbit than flipperling),*
> *yea, a mountain of winters,*
> *like that upon which flunkeys sprawl*
> *in the vestibule of the Opera,*

Canto One of Onegin,
where under the chandeliers
of a full house, you, dear,
should have been the dancer
flying, like fluff, in a decor
of poplars and fountains.

I started to speak in the high, clear, insolent voice (taught me by Ivor on the beach of Cannice) by which I instilled the fear of Phoebus when inaugurating a recalcitrant seminar in my first years of teaching at Quirn: "What I plan to discuss is the curious case of a close friend of mine whom I shall call—"

Mrs. Morgain set down her glass of whisky and leaned toward me confidentially: "You know I met little Iris Black in London, around 1919, I guess. Her father was a business friend of my father, the Ambassador. I was a starry-eyed American gal. She was a fantastic beauty and *most* sophisticated. I remember how thrilled I was later to learn that she had gone and married a Russian Prince!"

"Fay," cried Louise from twelve to four: "Fay! His Highness is making his throne speech."

Everyone laughed, and the two bare-thighed Tyrolean children chasing each other around the table bounced across my knees and were gone again.

"I shall call this close friend of mine, whose case we are about to examine, Mr. Twidower, a name with certain connotations, as those of you who remember the title story in my *Exile from Mayda* will note."

(Three people, the Kings and Audace, raised three hands, looking at one another in shared smugness.)

"This person, who is in the mighty middle of life, thinks of marrying a third time. He is deeply in love with a young woman. Before proposing to her, however, honesty demands that he confess he is suffering from a certain ailment. I wish they would stop jolting my chair every time they run by. 'Ailment' is perhaps too strong a term. Let's put it this way: there are certain flaws, he says, in the mechanism of his mind. The one he told me about is harmless in itself but very distressing and unusual, and may be a symptom of some imminent, more serious disorder. So here goes. When this person is lying in bed and imagining a familiar stretch of street, say, the right-hand sidewalk from the Library to, say—"

"The Liquor Store," put in King, a relentless wag.

"All right, Recht's Liquor Store. It is about three hundred yards away—"

I was again interrupted, this time by Louise (whom, in fact, I was solely addressing). She turned to Audace and informed him that she could never visualize any distance in yards unless she could divide it by the length of a bed or a balcony.

"Romantic," said Mrs. King. "Go on, Vadim."

"Three hundred paces away along the same side as the College Library. Now comes my friend's problem. He can walk in his mind there and back but he can't perform in his mind the actual about-face that transforms 'there' into 'back.' "

"Must call Rome," muttered Louise to Mrs. King, and was about to leave her seat, but I implored her to hear me out. She resigned herself, warning me however that she could not understand a word of my peroration.

"Repeat that bit about twisting around in your mind," said King. "Nobody understood."

"I did," said Audace: "We suppose the Liquor Store happens to be closed, and Mr. Twidower, who is a friend of mine too, turns on his heel to go back to the Library. In the reality of life he performs this action without a hitch or hiatus, as simply and unconsciously as we all do, even if the artist's critical eye does see—*A toi*, Vadim."

"Does see," I said, accepting the relay-race baton, "that, depending on the speed of one's revolution, palings and awnings pass counterwise around you either with the heavy lurch of a merry-go-round or (saluting Audace) in a single brisk flip like that of the end of a striped scarf (Audace smiled, acknowledging the Audacianism) that one flings over one's shoulder. But when one lies immobile in bed and rehearses or rather replays in one's mind the process of turning, in the manner described, it is not so much the pivotal swing which is hard to perceive mentally—it is its result, the reversion of vista, the transformation of direction, *that's* what one vainly strives to imagine. Instead of the liquor-store direction smoothly turning into the opposite one, as it does in the simplicity of waking life, poor Twidower is baffled—"

I had seen it coming but had hoped that I would be allowed to complete my sentence. Not at all. With the infinitely slow and silent movement of a gray tomcat, which he resembled with his bristly whiskers and arched back, King left his seat. He started to tiptoe, with a glass in each hand, toward the golden glow of a densely populated sideboard. With a dramatic slap of both hands against the edge of the table I caused Mrs. Morgain to jump (she had either dozed off or aged tremendously in the last few minutes) and stopped old King in his tracks; he silently turned like an automaton (illustrating my story) and as silently stole back to his seat with the empty Arabesque glasses.

"The mind, my friend's mind, is baffled, as I was saying, by something dreadfully strainful and irksome in the machinery of the change from one position to another, from east to west or west to east, from one damned nymphet to another— I mean I'm losing the thread of my tale, the zipper of thought has stuck, this is absurd—"

Absurd and very embarrassing. The two cold-thighed, cheesy-necked girleens were now engaged in a quarrelsome game as to who should sit on my left knee, that side of my lap where the honey was, trying to straddle Left Knee, warbling in Tyrolese and pushing each other off, and cousin Fay kept bending toward me and saying with a macabre accent: "*Elles vous aiment tant!*" Finally I pinched and twisted the nearest buttock, and with a squeal they resumed their running around, like that eternal little pleasure-park train, brushing the brambles.

I still could not disentangle my thoughts, but Audace came to my rescue.

"To conclude," he said (and an audible ouf! was emitted by cruel Louise), "our patient's trouble concerns not a certain physical act but the imagining of its performance. All he can do in his mind is omit the swiveling part altogether and shift from one visual plane to another with the neutral flash of a slide change in a magic lantern, whereupon he finds himself facing in a direction which has lost, or rather never contained, the idea of 'oppositeness.' Does anybody wish to comment?"

After the usual pause that follows such offers, John King said: "My advice to your Mr. Twitter is to dismiss that nonsense once for all. It's charming nonsense, it's colorful nonsense, but it's also harmful nonsense. Yes, Jane?"

"My father," said Mrs. King, "a professor of botany, had a rather endearing quirk: he could memorize historical dates and telephone numbers—for example our number 9743—only insofar as they contained primes. In our number he remembered two figures, the second and last, a useless combination; the other two were only black gaps, missing teeth."

"Oh, that's good," cried Audace, genuinely delighted.

I remarked it was not at all the same thing. My friend's affliction resulted in nausea, dizziness, *kegelkugel* headache.

"Well yes, I understand, but my father's quirk also had its side effects. It was not so much his inability to memorize, say, his house number in Boston, which was 68 and which he saw every day, but the fact that he could do nothing about it; that nobody, but nobody could explain *why* all he could make out at the far end of his brain was not 68 but a bottomless hole."

Our host resumed his vanishing act with more deliberation than before. Audace lidded his empty glass with his palm. Though swine-drunk, I longed for mine to be refilled, but was bypassed. The walls of the round room had grown more or less opaque again, God bless them, and the Dolomite Dollies were no longer around.

"In the days when I longed to be a ballerina," said Louise, "and was Blanc's little favorite, I always rehearsed exercises in my mind lying in bed, and had no difficulty whatever in imagining swirls and whirls. It is a matter of practice, Vadim. Why don't you just roll over in bed when you want to see yourself walking back to that Library? We must be going now, Fay, it's past midnight."

Audace glanced at his wristwatch, uttered the exclamation which Time must be sick of hearing, and thanked me for a wonderful evening. Lady Morgain's mouth mimicked the pink aperture of an elephant's trunk as it mutely formed the word "loo" to which Mrs. King, fussily swishing in green, immediately took her. I remained alone at the round table, then struggled to my feet, drained the rest of Louise's daiquiri, and joined her in the hallway.

She had never melted and shivered so nicely in my embrace as she did now.

"How many quadruped critics," she asked after a tender pause in the dark garden, "would accuse you of leg pulling if you published the description of those funny feelings. Three, ten, a herd?"

"Those are not really 'feelings' and they are not really 'funny.' I just wished you to be aware that if I go mad it will be in consequence of my games with the idea of space. 'Rolling over' would be cheating and besides would not help."

"I'll take you to an absolutely divine analyst."

"That's all you can suggest?"

"Why, yes."

"Think, Louise."

"Oh. I'm also going to marry you. Yes, of course, you idiot."

She was gone before I could reclasp her slender form. The star-dusted sky, usually a scary affair, now vaguely amused me: it belonged, with the autumn *fadeur* of barely visible flowers, to the same issue of *Woman's Own World* as Louise. I made water into a sizzle of asters and looked up at Bel's window, square c2. Lit as brightly as e1, the Opal Room. I went back there and noted with relief that kind hands had cleared and tidied the table, the round table with the opalescent rim, at which I had delivered a most successful introductory lecture. I heard Bel's voice calling me from the upper landing, and taking a palmful of salted almonds ascended the stairs.

5

Rather early next morning, a Sunday, as I stood, shawled in terry cloth, and watched four eggs rolling and bumping in their inferno, somebody entered the living room through a side door that I never bothered to lock.

Louise! Louise dressed up in hummingbird mauve for church. Louise in a sloping beam of mellow October sun. Louise leaning against the grand piano, as if about to sing and looking around with a lyrical smile.

I was the first to break our embrace.

VADIM   No, darling, no. My daughter may come down any minute. Sit down.

LOUISE   (*examining an armchair and then settling in it*) Pity. You know, I've been here many times before! In fact I was laid on that grand at eighteen. Aldy Landover was ugly, unwashed, brutal—and absolutely irresistible.

VADIM   Listen, Louise. I have always found your free, frivolous style very fetching. But you will be moving into this house very soon now, and we want a little more dignity, don't we?

LOUISE   We'll have to change that blue carpet. It makes the Stein look like an iceberg. And there should be a riot of flowers. So many big vases and not one Strelitzia! There was a whole shrub of lilac down there in my time.

VADIM   It's October, you know. Look, I hate to bring this up, but isn't your cousin waiting in the car? It would be very irregular.

LOUISE   Irregular, my foot. She won't be up before lunch. Ah, Scene Two.

(*Bel wearing only slippers and a cheap necklace of iridescent glass—a Riviera souvenir—comes down at the other end of the living room beyond the piano. She has already turned kitchenward showing the beaupage back of her head and delicate shoulder blades when she becomes aware of our presence and retraces her steps.*)

BEL   (*addressing me and casually squinting at my amazed visitor*) Ya bezumno golodnaya (*I'm madly hungry*).

VADIM   Louise dear, this is my daughter Bel. She's walking in her sleep, really, hence the, uh, non-attire.

LOUISE   Hullo, Annabel. The non-attire is very becoming.

BEL   (*correcting Louise*) Isa.

VADIM   Isabel, this is Louise Adamson, an old friend of mine, back from Rome. I hope we'll be seeing a lot of her.

BEL   How do you do (*question-markless*).

VADIM   Well, run along, Bel, and put on something. Breakfast is ready. (*To Louise*) Would you like to have breakfast too? Hard-boiled eggs? A Coke with a straw? (*Pale violin climbing stairs*)

LOUISE   Non, merci. I'm flabbergasted.

VADIM   Yes, things have been getting a little out of hand, but you'll see, she's a special child, there's no other child like her. All we need is your presence, your touch. She has inherited the habit of circulating in a state of nature from me. An Edenic gene. Curious.

LOUISE   Is this a two-people nudist colony or has Mrs. O'Leary also joined?

VADIM   (*laughing*) No, no, she's not here on Sundays. Everything is fine, I assure you. Bel is a docile angel. She—

LOUISE   (*rising to leave*) There she comes to be fed (*Bel descends the stairs in a skimpy pink robe*). Drop in around tea time. Fay is being taken by Jane King to a lacrosse game in Rosedale. (*Exits*)

BEL   Who's she? Former student of yours? Drama? Elocution?

VADIM   (*moving fast*) Bozhe moy! (*good Lord!*). The eggs! They must be as hard as jade. Come along. I'll acquaint you with the situation, as your schoolmistress says.

6

The grand was the first to go—it was carried out by a gang of staggering iceberg movers and donated by me to Bel's school, which I had reasons to pamper: I am not an easily frightened man but when I am frightened I am very much frightened, and at a second interview that I had had with the schoolmistress, my impersonation of an indignant Charles Dodgson was only saved from failure by the sensational news of my being about to marry an irreproachable socialite, the widow of our most pious philosopher. Louise, per contra, regarded the throwing out of a symbol of luxury as a personal affront and a crime: a concert piano of that kind costs, she said, as least as much as her old Hecate convertible, and she was not quite as wealthy as, no doubt, I thought she was, a statement representing that knot in Logic: the double-hitch lie which does not make one truth. I appeased her by gradually overcrowding the Music Room (if a time series be transformed into sudden space) with the modish gadgets she loved, singing furniture, miniature TV sets, stereorphics, portable orchestras, better and better video sets, remote-control instruments for turning those things on or off, and an automatic telephone dialer. For Bel's birthday she gave her a Rain Sound machine to promote sleep; and to celebrate *my* birthday she murdered a neurotic's night by getting me a thousand-dollar bedside Pantomime clock with twelve yellow radii on its black face instead of figures, which made it look blind to me or feigning blindness like some repulsive beggar in a hideous tropical town; in compensation that terrible object possessed a secret beam that projected Arabic numerals (2:00, 2:05, 2:10, 2:15, and so forth) on the ceiling of my new sleeping quarters, thus demolishing the sacred, complete, agonizingly achieved occlusion of its oval window. I said I'd buy a gun and shoot it in the mug, if she did not send it back to the fiend who sold it to her. She replaced it by "something especially made for people who like originality," namely a silver-plated umbrella stand in the shape of a giant jackboot—there was "something about rain strangely attractive to her" as her "analyst" wrote me in one of the silliest letters that man ever wrote to man. She was also fond of small expensive animals, but here I stood firm, and she never got the long-coated Chihuahua she coldly craved.

I did not expect much of Louise the Intellectual. The only time I saw her shed big tears, with interesting little howls of real grief, was when on the first Sunday of our marriage all the newspapers carried photographs of the two Albanian authors (a bald-domed old epicist and a long-haired woman compiler of children's books) who shared out between them the Prestigious Prize that she had told everybody I was sure to win that year. On the other hand she had only flipped through my novels (she was to read more attentively, though, *A Kingdom by the Sea*, which I began slowly to pull out of myself in 1957 like a long brain worm, hoping it would not break), while consuming all the "serious" bestsellers discussed by sister consumers belonging to the Literary Group in which she liked to assert herself as a writer's wife.

I also discovered that she considered herself a connoisseur of Modern Art. She blazed with anger at me when I said I doubted that the appreciation of a green stripe across a blue background had *any* connection with its definition in a glossy catalogue as "producing a virtually Oriental atmosphere of spaceless time and timeless space." She accused me of trying to wreck her entire view of the world by maintaining—in a facetious vein, she hoped—that only a Philistine misled by the solemn imbeciles paid to write about exhibitions could tolerate rags, rinds, and fouled paper rescued from a garbage can and discussed in terms "of warm splashes of color" and "good-natured irony." But perhaps most touching and terrible of all was her honestly believing that painters painted "what they felt"; that a rather rough and rumpled landscape dashed off in the Provence might be gratefully and proudly interpreted by art students if a psychiatrist explained to them that the advancing thundercloud represented the artist's clash with his father, and the rolling grainfield the early death of his mother in a shipwreck.

I could not prevent her from purchasing specimens of the pictorial art in vogue but I judiciously steered some of the more repulsive objects (such as a collection of daubs produced by "naïve" convicts) into the round dining room where they swam blurrily in the candlelight when we had guests for supper. Our routine meals generally took place in the snackbar niche between the kitchen and the housemaid's quarters. Into that niche Louise introduced her new Cappuccino Espresso Maker, while at the opposite end of the house, in the Opal Room, a heavily built, hedonically appareled bed with a padded headboard was installed for me. The adjacent bathroom had a less comfortable tub than my former one, and certain inconveniences attended my excursions, two or three nights per week, to the connubial chamber—via drawing room, creaky stairs, upper landing, second-floor corridor, and past the inscrutable chink-gleam of Bel's door; but I treasured my privacy more than I resented its drawbacks. I had the "Turkish *toupet*," as Louise called it, to forbid her to communicate with me by thumping on her floor. Eventually I had an interior telephone put in my room, to be used only in certain emergencies: I was thinking of such nervous states as the feeling of imminent collapse that I experienced sometimes in my nocturnal bouts with eschatological obsessions; and there was always the half-full box of sleeping pills that only she could have filched.

The decision to let Bel stay in her apartment, with Louise as her only neighbor, instead of refurnishing a spiral of space by allotting those two east-end rooms to Louise—"perhaps I too need a studio?"—while transferring Bel with bed and books to the Opal Room downstairs and leaving me upstairs in my former bedchamber, was taken by me firmly despite Louise's rather bitchy countersuggestions, such as removing the tools of my trade from the library in the basement and banishing Bel with all her belongings to that warm, dry, nice and quiet lair. Though I knew I would never give in, the very process of shuffling rooms and accessories in my mind made me literally ill. On top of that, I felt, perhaps wrongly, that Louise was enjoying the hideous banality of a stepmother-versus-stepdaughter situation. I did not exactly regret marrying her, I recognized her charm and functional qualities, but my adoration for Bel was the sole splendor, the sole breathtaking mountain in the drab plain of my emotional life. Being in many ways an extraordinarily stupid person, I had simply not reckoned with the tangles and tensions of what was meant to look like a model household. The moment I woke up—or at least the moment I saw that getting up was the only way to fool early-morning insomnia—I started wondering what new project Louise would invent that day with which to harass my girl. When two years later this gray old dolt and his volatile wife, after treating Bel to a tedious Swiss tour, left her in Larive, between Hex and Trex, at a "finishing" school (finishing childhood, finishing the innocence of young imagination), it was our 1955–1957 period of life *à trois* in the Quirn house, and not my earlier mistakes, that I recalled with curses and sobs.

She and her stepmother stopped speaking to each other altogether; they communicated, if need be, by signs: Louise, for instance, pointing dramatically at the ruthless clock and Bel tapping in the negative on the crystal of her loyal little wristwatch. She lost all affection for me, twisting away gently when I attempted a perfunctory caress. She adopted again the wan absent expression that had dimmed her features at her arrival from Rosedale. Camus replaced Keats. Her marks deteriorated. She no longer wrote poetry. One day as Louise and I were packing for our next trip to Europe (London, Paris, Pisa, Stresa, and—in small print—Larive) I started removing some old maps, Colorado, Oregon, from the silk "cheek" inside a valise, and the moment my secret prompter uttered that "*shcheka*" I came across a poem of hers written long before Louise's intrusion into her trustful young life. I thought it might do Louise good to read it and handed her the exercise-book page (all ragged along its torn root but still mine) on which the following lines were penciled:

> *At sixty, if I'll look back,*
> *jungles and hills will hide*
> *the notch, the source, the sand*
> *and a bird's footprints across it.*
> *I'll see nothing at all*
> *with my old eyes,*
> *yet I'll know it was there, the source.*
>
> *How come, then, that when I look back*
> *at twelve—one fifth of the stretch!—*
> *with visibility presumably better*
> *and no junk in between,*
> *I can't even imagine*
> *that patch of wet sand*
> *and the walking bird*
> *and the gleam of my source?*

"Almost Poundian in purity," remarked Louise—which annoyed me, because I thought Pound a fake.

7

Château Vignedor, Bel's charming boarding school in Switzerland, on a charming hill three hundred meters above charming Larive on the Rhône, had been recommended to Louise in the autumn of 1957 by a Swiss lady in Quirn's French Department. There were two other "finishing" schools of the same general type that might have done just as well, but Louise set her sights on Vignedor because of a chance remark made not even by her Swiss friend but by a chance girl in a chance travel agency who summed up the qualities of the school in one phrase: "Many Tunisian princesses."

It offered five main subjects (French, Psychology, Savoir-vivre, Couture, Cuisine), various sports (under the direction of Christine Dupraz, the once famous skier), and a dozen additional classes on request (which would keep the plainest girl there till she married), including Ballet and Bridge. Another *supplément*—especially suitable for orphans or unneeded children—was a summer trimester, filling up the year's last remaining segment with excursions and nature studies, to be spent by a few lucky girls at the home of the headmistress, Madame de Turm, an Alpine chalet some twelve hundred meters higher: "Its solitary light, twinkling in a black fold of the mountains, can be seen," said the prospectus in four languages, "from the Château on clear nights." There was also some kind of camp for differently handicapped local children in different years conducted by our medically inclined sports directress.

1957, 1958, 1959. Sometimes, seldom, hiding from Louise, who objected to Bel's twenty well-spaced monosyllables' costing us fifty dollars, I would call her from Quirn, but after a few such calls I received a curt note from Mme. de Turm, asking me not to upset my daughter by telephoning, and so retreated into my dark shell. Dark shell, dark years of my heart! They coincided oddly with the composition of my most vigorous, most festive, and commercially most successful novel, *A Kingdom by the Sea*. Its demands, the fun and the fancy of it, its intricate imagery, made up in a way for the absence of my beloved Bel. It was also bound to reduce, though I was hardly conscious of that, my correspondence with her (well-meant, chatty, dreadfully artificial letters which she seldom troubled to answer). Even more startling, of course, more incomprehensible to me, in groaning retrospect, is the effect my self-entertainment had on the number and length of our visits between 1957 and 1960 (when she eloped with a progressive blond-bearded young American). You were appalled to learn the other day, when we discussed the present notes, that I had seen "beloved Bel" only four times in three summers and that only two of our visits lasted as long as a couple of weeks. I must add, however, that she resolutely declined to spend her vacations at home. I ought never, of course, have dumped her in Europe. I should have elected to sweat it out in my hellish household, between a childish woman and a somber child.

The work on my novel also impinged on my marital mores, making of me a less passionate and more indulgent husband: I let Louise go on suspiciously frequent trips to out-of-town unlisted eye specialists and neglected her in the meantime for Rose Brown, our cute housemaid who took three soapshowers daily and thought frilly black panties "did something to guys."

But the greatest havoc wrought by my work was its effect on my lectures. To it I sacrificed, like Cain, the flowers of my summers, and, like Abel, the sheep of the campus. Because of it, the process of my academic discarnation reached its ultimate stage. The last vestiges of human interconnection were severed, for I not only vanished physically from the lecture hall but had my entire course taped so as to be funneled through the College Closed Circuit into the rooms of headphoned students. Rumor had it that I was ready to quit; in fact, an anonymous punster wrote in the *Quirn Quarterly*, Spring, 1959: "His Temerity is said to have asked for a raise before emeriting."

In the summer of that year my third wife and I saw Bel for the last time. Allan Garden (after whom the genus of the Cape Jasmin should have been named, so great and triumphant was the flower in his buttonhole) had just been united in wedlock to his youthful Virginia, after several years of cloudless concubinage. They were to live to the combined age of 170 in absolute bliss, yet one grim fateful chapter remained to be

constructed. I toiled over its first pages at the wrong desk, in
the wrong hotel, above the wrong lake, with a view of the
wrong *isoletta* at my left elbow. The only right thing was a
pregnant-shaped bottle of Gattinara before me. In the middle
of a mangled sentence Louise came to join me from Pisa,
where I gathered—with amused indifference—that she had
recoupled with a former lover. Playing on the strings of her
meek uneasiness I took her to Switzerland, which she detested. An early dinner with Bel was scheduled at the Larive
Grand Hotel. She arrived with that Christ-haired youth, both
purple trousered. The maître d'hôtel murmured something
over the menu to my wife, and she rode up and brought down
my oldest necktie for the young lout to put around his Adam's
apple and scrawny neck. His grandmother had been related
by marriage, so it turned out, to a third cousin of Louise's
grandfather, the not quite untarnished Boston banker. This
took care of the main course. We had coffee and kirsch in the
lounge, and Charlie Everett showed us pictures of the summer
Camp for Blind Children (who were spared the sight of its
drab locust trees and rings of ashed refuse amidst the riverside
burdocks) which he and Bella (Bella!) were supervising. He
was twenty-five years old. He had spent five years studying
Russian, and spoke it as fluently, he said, as a trained seal. A
sample justified the comparison. He was a dedicated "revolutionary," and a hopeless nincompoop, knowing nothing,
crazy about jazz, existentialism, Leninism, pacifism, and African Art. He thought snappy pamphlets and catalogues so
much more "meaningful" than fat old books. A sweet, stale,
and unhealthy smell emanated from the poor fellow.
Throughout the dinner and coffee-drinking ordeal I never
once—never once, reader!—looked up at my Bel, but as we
were about to part (forever) I did look at her, and she had
new twin lines from nostrils to wicks, and she wore granny
glasses, and a middle part, and had lost all her pubescent prettiness, remnants of which I had still glimpsed during a visit to
Larive a spring and winter ago. They had to be back at half-
past-twenty, alas—not really "alas."

"Come and see us at Quirn soon, soon, Dolly," I said, as
we all stood on the sidewalk with mountains outlined in solid

black against an aquamarine sky, and choughs jacking harshly, flying in flocks to roost, away, away.

I cannot explain the slip, but it angered Bel more than anything had ever angered her at any time.

"What is he saying?" she cried, looking in turn at Louise, at her beau, and again at Louise. "What does he mean? Why does he call me 'Dolly'? Who is she for God's sake? Why, why (turning to me), why did you say that?"

"*Obmolvka, prosti* (lapse of the tongue, sorry)," I replied, dying, trying to turn everything into a dream, a dream about that hideous last moment.

They walked briskly toward their little Klop car, he half-overtaking her, already poking the air with his car key, on her left, on her right. The aquamarine sky was now silent, darkish and empty, save for a star-shaped star about which I wrote a Russian elegy ages ago, in another world.

"What a charming, good-natured, civilized, sexy young fellow," said Louise as we stamped into the lift. "Are you in the mood tonight? Right away, Vad?"

Part Five

I

THIS penultimate part of LATH, this spirited episode in my otherwise somewhat passive existence, is horribly hard to set down, reminding me of the pensums, which the cruelest of my French governesses used to inflict upon me—some old saw to be copied *cent fois* (hiss and spittle)—in punishment for my adding my own marginal illustrations to those in her *Petit Larousse* or for exploring under the schoolroom table the legs of Lalage L., a little cousin, who shared lessons with me that unforgettable summer. I have, indeed, repeated the story of my dash to Leningrad in the late nineteen-sixties innumerable times in my mind, to packed audiences of my scribbling or dreaming selves—and yet I keep doubting both the necessity and the success of my dismal task. But you have argued the question, you are tenderly adamant, yes, and your decree is that I should relate my adventure in order to lend a semblance of significance to my daughter's futile fate.

In the summer of 1960, Christine Dupraz, who ran the summer camp for disabled children between cliff and highway, just east of Larive, informed me that Charlie Everett, one of her assistants, had eloped with my Bel after burning—in a grotesque ceremony that she visualized more clearly than I— his passport and a little American flag (bought at a souvenir stall especially for that purpose) "right in the middle of the Soviet Consul's back garden"; whereupon the new "Karl Ivanovich Vetrov" and the eighteen-year-old Isabella, a *ci-devant*'s daughter, had gone through some form of mock marriage in Berne and incontinently headed for Russia.

The same mail brought me an invitation to discuss in New York with a famous *compère* my sudden Number One position on the Bestselling Authors list, inquiries from Japanese, Greek, Turkish publishers, and a postcard from Parma with the scrawl: "Bravo for Kingdom from Louise and Victor." I never learned who Victor was, by the way.

Brushing all my engagements aside, I surrendered again—
after quite a few years of abstinence!—to the thrill of secret
investigations. Spying had been my *clystère de Tchékhov* even
before I married Iris Black whose later passion for working on
an interminable detective tale had been sparked by this or that
hint I must have dropped, like a passing bird's lustrous
feather, in relation to my experience in the vast and misty field
of the Service. In my little way I have been of some help to
my betters. The tree, a blue-flowering ash, whose cortical
wound I caught the two "diplomats," Tornikovski and Kali-
kakov, using for their correspondence, still stands, hardly
scarred, on its hilltop above San Bernardino. But for structural
economy I have omitted that entertaining strain from this
story of love and prose. Its existence, however, helped me now
to ward off—for a while, at least—the madness and anguish
of hopeless regret.

It was child's play to find Karl's relatives in the U.S.;
namely, two gaunt aunts who disliked the boy even more than
they did one another. Aunt Number One assured me he had
never left Switzerland—they were still forwarding his Third
Class mail to her in Boston. Aunt Number Two, the Philadelphia Fright, said he liked music and was vegetating in
Vienna.

I had overestimated my forces. A serious relapse hospitalized me for nearly a whole year. The complete rest ordered
by all my doctors was then botched by my having to stand by
my publisher in a long legal fight against obscenity charges
leveled at my novel by stuffy censors. I was again very ill. I
still feel the pressure of the hallucinations that beset me, as
my search for Bel got somehow mixed up with the controversy
over my novel, and I saw as clearly as one sees mountains or
ships, a great building, all windows lit, trying to advance upon
me, through this or that wall of the ward, seeking as it were
a weak spot to push through and ram my bed.

In the late Sixties I learned that Bel was now definitely married to Vetrov but that he had been sent to some remote place
of unspecified work. Then came a letter.

It was forwarded to me by an old respectable businessman
(I shall call him A.B.) with a note saying that he was "in
textiles" though by education "an engineer"; that he repre-

sented "a Soviet firm in the U.S. and vice versa"; that the letter he was enclosing came from a lady working in his Leningrad office (I shall call her Dora) and concerned my daughter "whom he did not have the honor to know but who, he believed, needed my assistance." He added that he would be flying back to Leningrad in a month's time and would be glad if I "contacted him." The letter from Dora was in Russian.

> *Much-respected Vadim Vadimovich!*
>
> *You probably receive many letters from people in our country who manage to obtain your books—not an easy enterprise! The present letter, however, is not from an admirer but simply from a friend of Isabella Vadimovna Vetrov with whom she has been sharing a room for more than a year now.*
>
> *She is ill, she has no news from her husband, and she is without a kopek.*
>
> *Please, get in touch with the bearer of this note. He is my employer, and also a distant relative, and has agreed to bring a few lines from you, Vadim Vadimovich, and a little money, if possible, but the main thing, the main thing* (glavnoe, glavnoe) *is to come in person* (lichno). *Let him know if you can come and if yes, when and where we could meet to discuss the situation. Everything in life is urgent* (speshno, *"pressing," "not to be postponed"*) *but some things are dreadfully urgent and this is one of them.*
>
> *In order to convince you that she is here, with me, telling me to write you and unable to write herself, I am appending a little clue or token that only you and she can decode: ". . . and the intelligent trail* (i umnitsa tropka)."

For a minute I sat at the breakfast table—under the compassionate stare of Brown Rose—in the attitude of a cave dweller clasping his hands around his head at the crash of rocks breaking above him (women make the same gesture when something falls in the next room). My decision was, of course, instantly taken. I perfunctorily patted Rose's young buttocks through her light skirt, and strode to the telephone.

A few hours later I was dining with A.B. in New York (and in the course of the next month was to exchange several long-distance calls with him from London). He was a superb little man, perfectly oval in shape, with a bald head and tiny feet expensively shod (the rest of his envelope looked less classy). He spoke friable English with a soft Russian accent, and native Russian with Jewish question marks. He thought that I should begin by seeing Dora. He settled for me the exact spot where she and I might meet. He warned me that in preparing to visit the weird Wonderland of the Soviet Union a traveler's first step was the very Philistine one of being assigned a *nomer* (hotel room) and that only after he had been granted one could the "visa" be tackled. Over the tawny mountain of "Bogdan's" brown-speckled, butter-soaked, caviar-accompanied *bliny* (which A.B. forbade me to pay for though I was lousy with *A Kingdom*'s money), he spoke poetically, and at some length, about his recent trip to Tel Aviv.

My next move—a visit to London—would have been altogether delightful, had I not been overwhelmed all the time by anxiety, impatience, anguished forebodings. Through several venturesome gentlemen—a former lover of Allan Andoverton's and two of my late benefactor's mysterious chums—I had retained some innocent ties with the BINT, as Soviet agents acronymize the well-known, too well-known, British intelligence service. Consequently it was possible for me to obtain a false or more-or-less false passport. Since I may want to avail myself again of those facilities, I cannot reveal here my exact alias. Suffice it to say that some teasing similarity with my real family name could make the assumed one pass, if I got caught, for a clerical error on the part of an absent-minded consul and for indifference to official papers on that of the deranged bearer. Let us suppose my real name to have been "Oblonsky" (a Tolstoyan invention); then the false one would be, for example, the mimetic "O. B. Long," an oblong blursky, so to speak. This I could expand into, say, Oberon Bernard Long, of Dublin or Dumberton, and live with it for years on five or six continents.

I had escaped from Russia at the age of not quite nineteen, leaving across my path in a perilous forest the felled body of a Red soldier. I had then dedicated half a century to berating, deriding, twisting into funny shapes, wringing out like blood-wet towels, kicking neatly in Evil's stinkiest spot, and otherwise tormenting the Soviet regime at every suitable turn of my writings. In fact, no more consistent critic of Bolshevist brutality and basic stupidity existed during all that time at the literary level to which my output belonged. I was thus well aware of two facts: that under my own name I would not be given a room at the Evropeyskaya or Astoria or any other Leningrad hotel unless I made some extraordinary amends, some abjectly exuberant recantation; and that if I talked my way to that hotel room as Mr. Long or Blong, and got interrupted, there might be no end of trouble. I decided therefore not to get interrupted.

"Shall I grow a beard to cross the frontier?" muses homesick General Gurko in Chapter Six of *Esmeralda and Her Parandrus.*

"Better than none," said Harley Q., one of my gayest advisers. "But," he added, "do it before we glue on and stamp O.B.'s picture and don't lose weight afterwards." So I grew it—during the atrocious heartracking wait for the room I could not mock up and the visa I could not forge. It was an ample Victorian affair, of a nice, rough, tawny shade threaded with silver. It reached up to my apple-red cheekbones and came down to my waistcoat, commingling on the way with my lateral yellow-gray locks. Special contact lenses not only gave another, dumbfounded, expression to my eyes, but somehow changed their very shape from squarish leonine, to round Jovian. Only upon my return did I notice that the old tailor-made trousers, on me and in my bag, displayed my real name on the inside of the waistband.

My good old British passport, which had been handled cursorily by so many courteous officers who had never opened my books (the only real identity papers of its accidental holder), remained, after a procedure, that both decency and incompetence forbid me to describe, physically the same in many respects; but certain of its other features, details of substance and items of information, were, let us say, "modified" by a new method, an alchemysterious treatment, a technique of genius, "still not understood elsewhere," as the chaps in the lab tactfully expressed people's utter unawareness of a discovery that might have saved countless fugitives and secret agents. In other words nobody, no forensic chemist not in the know, could suspect, let alone prove, that my passport was false. I do not know why I dwell on this subject with such tedious persistence. Probably, because I *otlynivayu*—"shirk" —the task of describing my visit to Leningrad; yet I can't put it off any longer.

2

After almost three months of fretting I was ready to go. I felt lacquered from head to foot, like that naked ephebe, the bright *clou* of a pagan procession, who died of dermal asphyxia in his coat of golden varnish. A few days before my actual departure there occurred what seemed a harmless shift at the time. I was to wing off on a Thursday from Paris. On Monday a melodious female voice reached me at my nostalgically lovely hotel, rue Rivoli, to tell me that something—perhaps a hushed-up crash in a Soviet veil of mist—had clogged the general schedule and that I could board an Aeroflot turboprop to Moscow either this Wednesday or the next. I chose the former, of course, for it did not affect the date of my rendezvous.

My traveling companions were a few English and French tourists and a goodish bunch of gloomy officials from Soviet trade missions. Once inside the aircraft, a certain illusion of cheap unreality enveloped me—to linger about me for the rest of my trip. It was a very warm day in June and the farcical air-conditioning system failed to outvie the whiffs of sweat and the sprayings of *Krasnaya Moskva*, an insidious perfume which imbued even the hard candy (named *Ledenets vzlyotnyy*, "take-off caramel," on the wrapper) generously distributed to us before the start of the flight. Another fairy-tale touch was the bright dapple—yellow curlicues and violet eyespots—adorning the blinds. A similarly colored waterproof bag in the seat pocket before me was ominously labeled "for waste disposal"—such as the disposal of my identity in that fairyland.

My mood and mental condition needed strong liquor rather than another round of *vzlyotnyy* or some nice reading matter;

still I accepted a publicity magazine from a stout, unsmiling, bare-armed stewardess in sky blue, and was interested to learn that (in contrast to current triumphs) Russia had not done so well in the Soccer Olympics of 1912 when the "Tsarist team" (consisting presumably of ten boyars and one bear) lost 12–0 to a German side.

I had taken a tranquilizer and hoped to sleep at least part of the way; but a first, and only, attempt at dozing off was resolutely thwarted by a still fatter stewardess, in a still stronger aura of onion sweat, asking me nastily to draw in the leg that I had stuck out too far into the aisle where she circulated with more and more publicity material. I envied darkly my windowside neighbor, an elderly Frenchman—or, anyway, scarcely a compatriot of mine—with a straggly gray-black beard and a terrible tie, who slept through the entire five-hour flight, disdaining the sardines and even the vodka which I could not resist, though I had a flask of better stuff in my hip pocket. Perhaps historians of photography could help me some day to define how, by precisely what indices, I am enabled to establish that the recollection of an anonymous unplaceable face goes back to 1930–1935, say, and not to 1945–1950. My neighbor was practically the twin of a person I had known in Paris, but who? A fellow writer? A concierge? A cobbler? The difficulty of determination grated less than the riddle of its limits as suggested by the degree of perceived "shading" and the "feel" of the image.

I got a closer but still more teasing look at him when, toward the close of our journey, my raincoat fell from the rack and landed upon him, and he grinned amiably enough as he emerged from under the sudden awakener. And I glimpsed again his fleshy profile and thick eyebrow while submitting for inspection the contents of my only valise and fighting the insane urge to question the propriety of the phrasing in the English form of the Customs Declaration: ". . . miniature graphics, slaughtered fowl, live animals and birds."

I saw him again, but not as clearly, during our transfer by bus from one airport to another through some shabby environs of Moscow—a city which I had never seen in my life and which interested me about as much as, say, Birmingham. On the plane to Leningrad, however, he was again next to me, this time on the inner side. Mixed odors of dour hostess and "Red Moscow," with a gradual prevalence of the first ingredient, as our bare-armed angels multiplied their last ministrations, accompanied us from 21:18 to 22:33. In order to draw out my neighbor before he and his riddle vanished, I asked him, in French, if he knew anything about a picturesque group that had boarded our aircraft in Moscow. He replied, with a Parisian *grasseyement*, that they were, he believed, Iranian circus people touring Europe. The men looked like harlequins in mufti, the women like birds of paradise, the children like golden medallions, and there was one dark-haired pale beauty in black bolero and yellow sharovars who reminded me of Iris or a prototype of Iris.

"I hope," I said, "we'll see them perform in Leningrad."

"Pouf!" he rejoined. "They can't compete with our Soviet circus."

I noted the automatic "our."

Both he and I were billeted in the Astoria, a hideous pile built around World War One, I think. The heavily bugged (I had been taught by Guy Gayley a way of finding that out in one gleeful twinkle) and therefore sheepish-looking room "*de luxe*," with orange curtains and an orange-draped bed in its old-world alcove, did have a private bath as stipulated, but it took me some time to cope with a convulsive torrent of clay-colored water. "Red Moscow's" last stand took place on a cake of incarnadine soap. "Meals," said a notice, "may be served in the rooms." For the heck of it I tried ordering an evening snack; nothing happened, and I spent another hungry hour in the recalcitrant restaurant. The Iron Curtain is really a lampshade: its variety here was gemmed with glass incrustations in a puzzle of petals. The *kotleta po kievski* I ordered took forty-four minutes to come from Kiev—and two seconds to be sent back as a non-cutlet, with a tiny oath (murmured in Russian) that made the waitress start and gape at me and my *Daily Worker*. The Caucasian wine was undrinkable.

A sweet little scene happened to be enacted as I hurried toward the lift, trying to recall where I had put my blessed Burpies. A flushed athletic *liftyorsha* wearing several bead necklaces was in the act of being replaced by a much older woman of the pensioned type, at whom she shouted while

stomping out of the lift: "*Ya tebe eto popomnyu, sterva!* (I'll
get even with you, dirty bitch)"—and proceeded to barge into
me and almost knock me down (I am a large, but fluff-light
old fellow). "*Shtoy-ty suyoshsya pod nogi?* (Why do you get
underfoot?)" she cried in the same insolent tone of voice
which left the night attendant quietly shaking her gray head
all the way up to my floor.

Between two nights, two parts of a serial dream, in which
I vainly tried to locate Bel's street (whose name, by a superstition current for centuries in conspiratorial circles I had preferred not to be told), while knowing perfectly well that she
lay bleeding and laughing in an alcove diagonally across the
room, a few barefooted steps from my bed, I wandered about
the city, idly trying to derive some emotional benefit from my
being born there almost three-quarters of a century ago. Either because it could never get over the presence of the bog
on which a popular bully had built it, or for some other reason
(nobody, according to Gogol, knows), St. Petersburg was no
place for children. I must have passed there insignificant parts
of a few Decembers, and no doubt an April or two; but at
least a dozen winters of my nineteen pre-Cambridge ones
were spent on Mediterranean or Black Sea coasts. As to summers, to my young summers, all of them had bloomed for me
on the great country estates of my family. Thus I realized with
silly astonishment that, except for picture postcards (views of
conventional public parks with lindens looking like oaks and
a pistachio palace instead of the remembered pinkish one, and
relentlessly gilded church domes—all of it under an Italianate
sky), I had never seen my native city in June or July. Its aspect,
therefore, evoked no thrill of recognition; it was an unfamiliar,
if not utterly foreign, town, still lingering in some other era:
an undefinable era, not exactly remote, but certainly preceding
the invention of body deodorants.

Warm weather had come to stay, and everywhere, in travel
agencies, in foyers, in waiting rooms, in general stores, in trol-
leybuses, in elevators, on escalators, in every damned corridor,
everywhere, and especially where women worked, or had
worked, invisible onion soup was cooking on invisible stoves.
I was to remain only a couple of days in Leningrad and had
not the time to get used to those infinitely sad emanations.

From travelers I knew that our ancestral mansion no longer existed, that the very lane where it had stood between two streets in the Fontanka area had been lost, like some connective tissue in the process of organic degeneration. What then succeeded in transfixing my memory? That sunset, with a triumph of bronze clouds and flamingo-pink meltings in the far-end archway of the Winter Canalet, might have been first seen in Venice. What else? The shadow of railings on granite? To be quite honest, only the dogs, the pigeons, the horses, and the very old, very meek cloakroom attendants seemed familiar to me. They, and perhaps the façade of a house on Gertsen Street. I may have gone there to some children's fête ages ago. The floral design running above the row of its upper windows caused an eerie shiver to pass through the root of wings that we all grow at such moments of dream-like recollection.

Dora was to meet me Friday morning on the Square of the Arts in front of the Russian Museum near the statue of Pushkin erected some ten years before by a committee of weathermen. An Intourist folder had yielded a tinted photograph of the spot. The meteorological associations of the monument predominated over its cultural ones. Frock-coated Pushkin, the right-side lap of his garment permanently agitated by the Nevan breeze rather than by the violence of lyrical afflatus, stands looking upward and to the left while his right hand is stretched out the other way, sidewise, to test the rain (a very natural attitude at the time lilacs bloom in the Leningrad parks). It had dwindled, when I arrived, to a warm drizzle, a mere murmur in the lindens above the long garden benches. Dora was supposed to be sitting on Pushkin's left, *id est* my right. The bench was empty and looked dampish. Three or four children, of the morose, drab, oddly old-fashioned aspect that Soviet kids have, could be seen on the other side of the pedestal, but otherwise I was loitering all alone, holding the *Humanité* in my hand instead of the *Worker* which I was supposed to signal with discreetly but had not been able to obtain that day. I was in the act of spreading the newspaper on the bench when a lady with the predicted limp came along a garden path toward me. She wore the, also expected, pastel-pink coat, had a clubfoot, and walked with the aid of a sturdy cane.

She also carried a diaphanous little umbrella which had not figured in the list of attributes. I dissolved in tears at once (though I was farced with pills). Her gentle beautiful eyes were also wet.

Had I got A.B.'s telegram? Sent two days ago to my Paris address? Hotel Moritz?

"That's garbled," I said, "and besides I left earlier. Doesn't matter. Is she much worse?"

"No, no, on the contrary. I knew you would come all the same, but something has happened. Karl turned up on Tuesday while I was in the office and took her away. He also took my new suitcase. He has no sense of ownership. He will be shot some day like a common thief. The first time he got into trouble was when he kept declaring that Lincoln and Lenin were brothers. And last time—"

Nice voluble lady, Dora. What was Bel's illness exactly?

"Splenic anemia. And last time, he told his best student in the language school that the only thing people should do was to love one another and pardon their enemies."

"An original mind. Where do you suppose—"

"Yes, but the best student was an informer, and Karlusha spent a year in a *tundrovyy* House of Rest. I don't know where he took her now. I even don't know whom to ask."

"But there must be *some* way. She must be brought back, taken out of this hole, this hell."

"That's impossible. She adores, she worships Karlusha. *C'est la vie*, as the Germans say. It's a pity A.B. is in Riga till the end of the month. You saw very little of him. Yes, it's a pity, he's a freak and a dear (*chudak i dushka*) with four nephews in Israel, which sounds, he says, as 'the dramatic persons in a pseudoclassical play.' One of them was my husband. Life gets sometimes very complicated, and the more complicated the happier it should be, one would think, but in reality 'complicated' always means for some reason *grust' i toska* (sorrow and heartache)."

"But look here, can't *I* do something? Can't I sort of hang around and make inquiries, and perhaps seek advice from the Embassy—"

"She is not English any more and was never American. It's hopeless, I tell you. We were very close, she and I, in my very

complicated life, but, imagine, Karl did not allow her to leave
at least one little word for me—and for you, of course. She
had informed him, unfortunately, that you were coming, and
this he could not bear in spite of all the sympathy he works
up for all unsympathetic people. You know, I saw your face
last year—or was it two years ago?—two years, rather—in a
Dutch or Danish magazine, and I would have recognized you
at once, anywhere."

"With the beard?"

"Oh, it does not change you one droplet. It's like wigs or
green spectacles in old comedies. As a girl I dreamt of becoming a female clown, 'Madam Byron,' or 'Trek Trek.' But tell
me, Vadim Vadimovich—I mean Gospodin Long—haven't
they found you out? Don't they intend to make much of you?
After all, you're the secret pride of Russia. Must you go now?"

I detached myself from the bench—with some scraps of
L'Humanité attempting to follow me—and said, yes, I had
better be going before the pride outstripped the prudence. I
kissed her hand whereupon she remarked that she had seen it
done only in a movie called *War and Peace*. I also begged
her, under the dripping lilacs, to accept a wad of bank notes
to be used for any purpose she wished including the price of
that suitcase for her trip to Sochi. "And he also took my whole
set of safety pins," she murmured with her all-beautifying
smile.

3

I cannot be sure it was not again my fellow traveler, the black-
hatted man, whom I saw hurrying away as I parted with Dora
and our National Poet, leaving the latter to worry forever
about all that wasted water (compare the Tsarskoselski Statue
of a rock-dwelling maiden who mourns her broken but still
brimming jar in one of his own poems); but I know I saw
Monsieur Pouf at least twice in the restaurant of the Astoria,
as well as in the corridor of the sleeping car on the night train
that I took in order to catch the earliest Moscow-Paris plane.

On that plane he was prevented from sitting next to me by the presence of an elderly American lady, with pink and violet wrinkles and rufous hair: we kept alternately chatting, dozing and drinking Bloody Marshas, *her* joke—not appreciated by our sky-blue hostess. It was delightful to observe the amazement expressed by old Miss Havemeyer (her rather incredible name) when I told her that I had spurned the Intourist's offer of a sightseeing tour of Leningrad; that I had not peeped into Lenin's room in the Smolny; had not visited one cathedral; had not eaten something called "tabaka chicken"; and that I had left that beautiful, *beautiful* city without seeing a single ballet or variety show. "I happen to be," I explained, "a triple agent and you know how it is—" "Oh!" she exclaimed, with a pulling-away movement of the torso as if to consider me from a nobler angle. "Oh! But that's vurry glamorous!"

I had to wait some time for my jet to New York, and being a little tight and rather pleased with my plucky journey (Bel, after all was not too gravely ill and not too unhappily married; Rosabel sat reading, no doubt, a magazine in the living room, checking in it the Hollywood measurements of her leg, ankle 8½ inches, calf 12½, creamy thigh 19½; and Louise was in Florence or Florida). With a hovering grin, I noticed and picked up a paperback somebody had left on a seat next to mine in the transit lounge of the Orly airport. I was the mouse of fate on that pleasant June afternoon between a shop of wines and a shop of perfumes.

I held in my hands a copy of a Formosan (!) paperback reproduced from the American edition of *A Kingdom by the Sea*. I had not seen it yet—and preferred not to inspect the pox of misprints that, no doubt, disfigured the pirated text. On the cover a publicity picture of the child actress who had played my Virginia in the recent film did better justice to pretty Lola Sloan and her lollypop than to the significance of my novel. Although slovenly worded by a hack with no inkling of the book's art, the blurb on the back of the limp little volume rendered faithfully enough the factual plot of my *Kingdom*.

Bertram, an unbalanced youth, doomed to die shortly in an asylum for the criminal insane, sells for ten dollars

his ten-year-old sister Ginny to the middle-aged bachelor
Al Garden, a wealthy poet who travels with the beautiful
child from resort to resort through America and other
countries. A state of affairs that looks at first blush—and
"blush" is the right word—like a case of irresponsible per-
version (described in brilliant detail never attempted be-
fore) develops by the grees [misprint] *into a genuine*
dialogue of tender love. Garden's feelings are reciprocated
by Ginny, the initial "victim" who at eighteen, a normal
nymph, marries him in a warmly described religious cer-
emony. All seems to end honky-donky [sic!] *in foreverlast-*
ing bliss of a sort fit to meet the sexual demands of the
most rigid, or frigid, humanitarian, had there not been
running its chaotic course, in a sheef [sheaf?] *of parallel*
lives beyond our happy couple's ken, the tragic tiny [des-
tiny?] *of Virginia Garden's inconsolable parents, Oliver*
and [?], *whom the clever author by every means in his*
power, prevents from tracking their daughter Dawn
[sic!!]. *A Book-of-the-Decade choice.*

I pocketed it upon noticing that my long-lost fellow traveler, goat-bearded and black-hatted, as I knew him, had come
up from the lavatory or the bar: Would he follow me to New
York or was it to be our last meeting? Last, last. He had given
himself away: The moment he came near, the moment his
mouth opened in the tense-lower-lip shape that discharges,
with a cheerless up-and-down shake of the head, the exclamation "*Ekh!,*" I knew not only that he was as Russian as I,
but that the ancient acquaintance whom he resembled so
strikingly was the father of a young poet, Oleg Orlov, whom
I had met in Paris, in the Nineteen-Twenties. Oleg wrote
"poems in prose" (long after Turgenev), absolutely worthless
stuff, which his father, a half-demented widower, would try
to "place," pestering with his son's worthless wares the dozen
or so periodicals of the emigration. He could be seen in the
waiting room miserably fawning on a harassed and curt secretary, or attempting to waylay an assistant editor between
office and toilet, or writing in stoic misery, at a corner of a
crowded table, a special letter pleading the cause of some horrible little poem that had been already rejected. He died in

the same Home for the Aged where Annette's mother had spent her last years. Oleg, in the meantime, had joined the small number of *littérateurs* who decided to sell the bleak liberty of expatriation for the rosy mess of Soviet pottage. His budtime had kept its promise. The best he had achieved during the last forty or fifty years was a medley of publicity pieces, commercial translations, vicious denunciations, and—in the domain of the arts—a prodigious resemblance to the physical aspect, voice, mannerisms, and obsequious impudence of his father.

"*Ekh!*" he exclaimed, "*Ekh*, Vadim Vadimovich *dorogoy* (dear), aren't you ashamed of deceiving our great warm-hearted country, our benevolent, credulous government, our overworked Intourist staff, in this nasty infantile manner! A Russian writer! Snooping! Incognito! By the way, I am Oleg Igorevich Orlov, we met in Paris when we were young."

"What do you want, *merzavetz* (you scoundrel)?" I coldly inquired as he plopped into the chair on my left.

He raised both hands in the "see-I'm-unarmed" gesture: "Nothing, nothing. Except to ruffle (*potormoshit'*) your conscience. Two courses presented themselves. We had to choose. Fyodor Mihaylovich [?] himself had to choose. Either to welcome you *po amerikanski* (the American way) with reporters, interviews, photographers, girls, garlands, and, naturally, Fyodor Mihaylovich himself [President of the Union of Writers? Head of the 'Big House'?]; or else to ignore you—and that's what we did. By the way: forged passports may be fun in detective stories, but our people are just not interested in passports. Aren't you sorry now?"

I made as if to move to another seat, but he made as if to accompany me there. So I stayed where I was, and feverishly grabbed something to read—that book in my coat pocket.

"*Et ce n'est pas tout!*" he went on. "Instead of writing for us, your compatriots, you, a Russian writer of genius, betray them by concocting, for your paymasters, *this* (pointing with a dramatically quivering index at *A Kingdom by the Sea* in my hands), this obscene novelette about little Lola or Lotte, whom some Austrian Jew or reformed pederast rapes after murdering her mother—no, excuse me—*marrying* mama first before murdering her—we like to legalize everything in the West, don't we, Vadim Vadimovich?"

Still restraining myself, though aware of the uncontrollable cloud of black fury growing within my brain, I said: "You are mistaken. You are a somber imbecile. The novel I wrote, the novel I'm holding now, is *A Kingdom by the Sea*. You are talking of some other book altogether."

"*Vraiment?* And maybe you visited Leningrad merely to chat with a lady in pink under the lilacs? Because, you know, you and your friends are phenomenally naïve. The reason Mister (it rhymed with 'Easter' in his foul serpent-mouth) Vetrov was permitted to leave a certain labor camp in Vadim—odd coincidence—so he might fetch his wife, is that he has been cured now of his mystical mania—cured by such nutcrackers, such shrinkers as are absolutely unknown in the philosophy of your Western *sharlatany*. Oh yes, precious (*dragotsennyy*) Vadim Vadimovich—"

The swing I dealt old Oleg with the back of my left fist was of quite presentable power, especially if we remember—and I remembered it as I swung—that our combined ages made 140.

There ensued a pause while I struggled back to my feet (unaccustomed momentum had somehow caused me to fall from my seat).

"*Nu, dali v mordu. Nu, tak chtozh?*" he muttered (Well, you've given me one in the mug. Well, what does it matter?). Blood blotched the handkerchief he applied to his fat muzhikian nose.

"*Nu, dali,*" he repeated and presently wandered away.

I looked at my knuckles. They were red but intact. I listened to my wristwatch. It ticked like mad.

Part Six

I

SPEAKING of philosophy, I recalled when starting to re-
adjust myself, very temporarily, to the corners and crannies
of Quirn, that somewhere in my office I kept a bundle of notes
(on the Substance of Space), prepared formerly toward an
account of my young years and nightmares (the work now
known as *Ardis*). I also needed to sort out and remove from
my office, or ruthlessly destroy, a mass of miscellanea which
had accumulated ever since I began teaching.

That afternoon—a sunny and windy September afternoon—
I had decided, with the unaccountable suddenness of genuine
inspiration, that 1969–1970 would be my last term at Quirn
University. I had, in fact, interrupted my siesta that day to
request an immediate interview with the Dean. I thought his
secretary sounded a little grumpy on the phone; true, I declined to explain anything beforehand, beyond confiding to
her, in an informal bantering manner, that the numeral "7"
always reminded me of the flag an explorer sticks in the cra-
nium of the North Pole.

After setting out on foot and reaching the seventh poplar I
realized that there might be quite a load of papers to bring
from my office, so I went back for my car, and then had difficulty in finding a place to park near the library where I intended to return a number of books which were months, if
not years, overdue. In result, I was a little late for my appointment with the Dean, a new man and not my best reader. He
consulted, rather demonstratively, the clock and muttered he
had a "conference" in a few minutes at some other place,
probably invented.

I was amused rather than surprised by the vulgar joy he did
not trouble to conceal at the news of my resignation. He
hardly heard the reasons which common courtesy impelled me
to give (frequent headaches, boredom, the efficiency of modern recording, the comfortable income my recent novel sup-

plied, and so forth). His whole manner changed—to use a cliché he deserves. He paced to and fro, positively beaming. He grasped my hand in a burst of brutal effusion. Certain fastidious blue-blooded animals prefer surrendering a limb to the predator rather than suffer ignoble contact. I left the Dean encumbered with a marble arm that he kept carrying in his prowlings like a trayed trophy, not knowing where to put it down.

So off to my office I stalked, a happy amputee, more than ever eager to clean up drawers and shelves. I began, however, by dashing off a note to the President of the University, another new man, informing him with a touch of French *malice*, rather than English "malice," that my entire set of one hundred lectures on European Masterpieces was about to be sold to a generous publisher who offered me an advance of half-a-million bucks (a salubrious exaggeration), thus making transmissions of my course no longer available to students, best regards, sorry not to have met you personally.

In the name of moral hygiene I had got rid long ago of my Bechstein desk. Its considerably smaller substitute contained note paper, scratch paper, office envelopes, photostats of my lectures, a copy of *Dr. Olga Repnin* (hardback) which I had intended for a colleague (but had spoiled by misspelling his name), and a pair of warm gloves belonging to my assistant (and successor) Exkul. Also three boxfuls of paper clips and a half-empty flask of whisky. From the shelves, I swept into the wastebasket, or onto the floor in its vicinity, heaps of circulars, separata, a displaced ecologist's paper on the ravages committed by a bird of some sort, the *Ozimaya Sovka* ("Lesser Winter-Crop Owl"?), and the tidily bound page proofs (mine always come in the guise of long, horribly slippery and unwieldy snakes) of picaresque trash, full of cricks and punts, imposed on me by proud publishers hoping for a rave from the lucky bastard. A mess of business correspondence and my tractatule on Space I stuffed into a large worn folder. Adieu, lair of learning!

Coincidence is a pimp and cardsharper in ordinary fiction but a marvelous artist in the patterns of fact recollected by a non-ordinary memoirist. Only asses and geese think that the re-collector skips this or that bit of his past because it is dull

or shoddy (that sort of episode here, for example, the interview with the Dean, and how scrupulously it is recorded!). I
was on the way to the parking lot when the bulky folder under
my arm—replacing my arm, as it were—burst its string and
spilled its contents all over the gravel and grassy border. You
were coming from the library along the same campus path,
and we crouched side by side collecting the stuff. You were
pained you said later (*zhalostno bylo*) to smell the liquor on
my breath. On the breath of that great writer.

I say "you" retroconsciously, although in the logic of life
you were not "you" yet, for we were not actually acquainted
and you were to become really "you" only when you said,
catching a slip of yellow paper that was availing itself of a
bluster to glide away with false insouciance:

<blockquote>"No, you don't."</blockquote>

Crouching, smiling, you helped me to cram everything
again into the folder and then asked me how my daughter
was—she and you had been schoolmates some fifteen years
ago, and my wife had given you a lift several times. I then
remembered your name and in a photic flash of celestial color
saw you and Bel looking like twins, silently hating each other,
both in blue coats and white hats, waiting to be driven somewhere by Louise. Bel and you would both be twenty-eight on
January 1, 1970.

A yellow butterfly settled briefly on a clover head, then
wheeled away in the wind.

"*Metamorphoza*," you said in your lovely, elegant Russian.

Would I care to have some snapshots (additional snapshots)
of Bel? Bel feeding a chipmunk? Bel at the school dance? (Oh,
I remember that dance—she had chosen for escort a sad fat
Hungarian boy whose father was assistant manager of the
Quilton Hotel—I can still hear Louise snorting!)

We met next morning in my carrel at the College Library,
and after that I continued to see you every day. I will not
suggest, LATH is not meant to suggest, that the petals and
plumes of my previous loves are dulled or coarsened when
directly contrasted with the purity of your being, the magic,
the pride, the reality of your radiance. Yet "reality" *is* the key

word here; and the gradual perception of that reality was nearly fatal to me.

Reality would be only adulterated if I now started to narrate what you know, what I know, what nobody else knows, what shall never, never be ferreted out by a matter-of-fact, father-of-muck, mucking biograffitist. And how did your affair develop, Mr. Blong? Shut up, Ham Godman! And when did you decide to leave together for Europe? Damn you, Ham!

See under Real, my first novel in English, thirty-five years ago!

One little item of subhuman interest I can disclose, however, in this interview with posterity. It is a foolish, embarrassing trifle and I never told you about it, so here goes. It was on the eve of our departure, around March 15, 1970, in a New York hotel. You were out shopping. ("I think"—you said to me just now when I tried to check that detail without telling you why—"I think I bought a beautiful blue suitcase with a zipper"—miming the word with a little movement of your dear delicate hand—"which proved to be absolutely useless.") I stood before the closet mirror of my bedroom in the north end of our pretty "suite," and proceeded to take a final decision. All right, I could not live without you; but was I worthy of you—I mean, in body and spirit? I was forty-three years older than you. The Frown of Age, two deep lines forming a capital lambda, ascended between my eyebrows. My forehead, with its three horizontal wrinkles that had not really overasserted themselves in the last three decades, remained round, ample and smooth, waiting for the summer tan that would scumble, I knew, the liver spots on my temples. All in all, a brow to be enfolded and fondled. A thorough haircut had done away with the leonine locks; what remained was of a neutral, grayish-dun tint. My large handsome glasses magnified the senile group of wart-like little excrescences under each lower eyelid. The eyes, once an irresistible hazel-green, were now oysterous. The nose, inherited from a succession of Russian boyars, German barons, and, perhaps (if Count Starov who sported some English blood was my real father), at least one Peer of the Realm, had retained its bone hump and tip rime, but had developed on the frontal flesh, within its owner's memory, an aggravating gray hairlet that grew faster and faster between yanks. My dentures did not do justice to my former attractively irregular teeth and (as I told an expensive but obtuse dentist who did not understand what I meant) "seemed to ignore my smile." A furrow sloped down from each nosewing, and a jowl pouch on each side of my chin formed in three-quarter-face the banal flexure common to old men of all races, classes, and professions. I doubted that I had been right in shaving off my glorious beard and the trim mustache that had lingered, on try, for a week or so after my return from Leningrad. Still, I passed my face, giving it a C-minus mark.

Since I had never been much of an athlete, the deterioration of my body was neither very marked, nor very interesting. I gave it a C plus, mainly for my routing tank after tank of belly fat in a war with obesity waged between intervals of retreat and rest since the middle Fifties. Apart from incipient lunacy (a problem with which I prefer to deal separately), I had been in excellent health throughout adulthood.

What about the state of my art? What could I offer to you there? You had studied, as I hope you recall, Turgenev in Oxford and Bergson in Geneva, but thanks to family ties with good old Quirn and Russian New York (where a last *émigré* periodical was still deploring, with idiotic innuendoes, my "apostasy") you had followed pretty closely, as I discovered, the procession of my Russian and English harlequins, followed by a tiger or two, scarlet-tongued, and a libellula girl on an elephant. You had also studied those obsolete photocopies— which proved that my method *avait du bon* after all—*pace* the monstrous accusations leveled at them by a pack of professors in envious colleges.

As I peered, stripped naked and traversed by opaline rays, into another, far deeper mirror, I saw the whole vista of my Russian books and was satisfied and even thrilled by what I saw: *Tamara*, my first novel (1925): a girl at sunrise in the mist of an orchard. A grandmaster betrayed in *Pawn Takes Queen*. *Plenilune*, a moonburst of verse. *Camera Lucida*, the spy's mocking eye among the meek blind. The *Red Top Hat* of decapitation in a country of total injustice. And my best in the series: young poet writes prose on a *Dare*.

That Russian batch of my books was finished and signed and thrust back into the mind that had produced them. All of them had been gradually translated into English either by myself or under my direction, with my revisions. Those final English versions as well as the reprinted originals would be now dedicated to you. That was good. That was settled. Next picture:

My English originals, headed by the fierce *See under Real* (1940), led through the changing light of *Esmeralda and Her Parandrus*, to the fun of *Dr. Olga Repnin* and the dream of *A Kingdom by the Sea*. There was also the collection of short stories *Exile from Mayda*, a distant island; and *Ardis*, the work I had resumed at the time we met—at the time, too, of a deluge of postcards (postcards!) from Louise hinting at last at a move which I wanted her to be the first to make.

If I estimated the second batch at a lower value than the first, it was owing not only to a diffidence some will call coy, others, commendable, and myself, tragic, but also because the contours of my American production looked blurry to me; and they looked that way because I knew I would always keep hoping that my *next* book—not simply the one in progress, like *Ardis*—but something I had never attempted yet, something miraculous and unique, would at last answer fully the craving, the aching thirst that a few disjunct paragraphs in *Esmeralda* and *The Kingdom* were insufficient to quench. I believed I could count on your patience.

2

I had not the slightest desire to reimburse Louise for being forced to shed me; and I hesitated to embarrass her by supplying my lawyer with the list of her betrayals. They were stupid and sordid, and went back to the days when I still was reasonably faithful to her. The "divorce dialogue," as Horace Peppermill, Junior, horribly called it, dragged on during the entire spring: You and I spent part of it in London and the rest in Taormina, and I kept putting off talks of *our* marriage (a delay you regarded with royal indifference). What really bothered me was having also to postpone the tedious statement (to be repeated for the fourth time in my life) that would have to precede any such talks. I fumed. It was a shame to leave you in the dark regarding my derangement.

Coincidence, the angel with the eyed wings mentioned before, spared me the humiliating rigmarole that I had found necessary to go through before proposing to each of my former wives. On June 15, at Gandora, in the Tessin, I received a letter from young Horace giving me excellent news: Louise had discovered (*how* does not matter) that at various periods of our marriage I had had her shadowed, in all sorts of fascinating old cities, by a private detective (Dick Cockburn, a staunch friend of mine); that the tapes of love calls and other documents were in my lawyer's hands; and that she was ready to make every possible concession to speed up matters, being anxious to marry again—this time the son of an Earl. And on the same fatidic day, at a quarter past five in the afternoon, I finished transcribing on 733 medium-sized Bristol cards (each holding about 100 words), with a fine-nibbed pen and in my smallest fair-copy hand, *Ardis*, a stylized memoir dealing with the arbored boyhood and ardent youth of a great thinker who by the end of the book tackles the itchiest of all noumenal mysteries. One of the early chapters contained an account (couched in an overtly personal, intolerably tortured tone) of my own tussles with the Specter of Space and the myth of Cardinal Points.

By 5:30 I had consumed, in a fit of private celebration, most of the caviar and all the champagne in the friendly fridge of our bungalow on the green grounds of the Gandora Palace Hotel. I found you on the veranda and told you I would like you to devote the next hour to reading attentively—

"I read everything attentively."

"—this batch of thirty cards from *Ardis*." After which I thought you might meet me somewhere on my way back from my late-afternoon stroll: always the same—to the *spartitraffico* fountain (ten minutes) and thence to the edge of a pine plantation (another ten minutes). I left you reclining in a lounge chair with the sun reproducing the amethyst lozenges of the veranda windows on the floor, and barring your bare shins and the insteps of your crossed feet (right toe twitching now and then in some obscure connection with the tempo of assimilation or a twist in the text). In a matter of minutes you would have learned (as only Iris had learned before you—the others were no eaglesses) what I wished you to be aware of when consenting to be my wife.

"Careful, please, when you cross," you said, without raising your eyes but then looking up and tenderly pursing your lips before going back to *Ardis*.

Ha! Weaving a little! Was that really I, Prince Vadim Blonsky, who in 1815 could have outdrunk Pushkin's mentor, Kaverin? In the golden light of a mere quart of the stuff all the trees in the hotel park looked like araucarias. I congratulated myself on the neatness of my stratagem though not quite knowing whether it concerned my third wife's recorded frolics or the disclosure of my infirmity through a bloke in a book. Little by little the soft spicy air did me good: my soles clung more firmly to gravel and sand, clay and stone. I became aware that I had gone out wearing morocco slippers and a torn, bleached denim trousers-and-top with, paradoxically, my passport in one nipple pocket and a wad of Swiss bank notes in the other. Local people in Gandino or Gandora, or whatever the town was called, knew the face of the author of *Un regno sul mare* or *Ein Königreich an der See* or *Un Royaume au Bord de la Mer*, so it would have been really fatuous on my part to prepare the cue and the cud for the reader in case a car was really to hit me.

Soon I was feeling so happy and bright that when I passed by the sidewalk café just before reaching the square, it seemed a good idea to stabilize the fizz still ascending in me by means of a jigger of something—and yet I demurred, and passed by, cold-eyed, knowing how sweetly, yet firmly, you disapproved of the most innocent tippling.

One of the streets projecting west beyond the traffic island traversed the Corso Orsini and immediately afterwards, as if having achieved an exhausting feat, degenerated into a soft dusty old road with traces of gramineous growth on both sides, but none of pavement.

I could say what I do not remember having been moved to say in years, namely: My happiness was complete. As I walked,

I read those cards with you, at your pace, your diaphanous index at my rough peeling temple, my wrinkled finger at your turquoise temple-vein. I caressed the facets of the Blackwing pencil you kept gently twirling, I felt against my raised knees the fifty-year-old folded chessboard, Nikifor Starov's gift (most of the noblemen were badly chipped in their baize-lined mahogany box!), propped on your skirt with its pattern of irises. My eyes moved with yours, my pencil queried with your own faint little cross in the narrow margin a solecism I could not distinguish through the tears of space. Happy tears, radiant, shamelessly happy tears!

A goggled imbecile on a motorcycle who I thought had seen me and would slow down to let me cross Corso Orsini in peace swerved so clumsily to avoid killing me that he skidded and ended up facing me some way off after an ignominious wobble. I ignored his roar of hate and continued my steady stroll westward in the changed surroundings I have already mentioned. The practically rural old road crept between modest villas, each in its nest of tall flowers and spreading trees. A rectangle of cardboard on one of the west-side wickets said "Rooms" in German; on the opposite side an old pine supported a sign "For Sale" in Italian. Again on the left, a more sophisticated houseowner offered "Lunchings." Still fairly far was the green vista of the *pineta*.

My thoughts reverted to *Ardis*. I knew that the bizarre mental flaw you were now reading about would pain you; I also knew that its display was a mere formality on my part and could not obstruct the natural flow of our common fate. A gentlemanly gesture. In fact, it might compensate for what you did not yet know, what I would have to tell you too, what I suspected you would call the not quite savory little method (*gnusnovaten'kiy sposob*) of my "getting even" with Louise. All right—but what about *Ardis*? Apart from my warped mind, did you like it or loathe it?

Composing, as I do, whole books in my mind before releasing the inner word and taking it down in pencil or pen, I find that the final text remains for a while committed to memory, as distinct and perfect as the floating imprint that a light bulb leaves on the retina. I was able therefore to rerun the actual images of those cards you read: they were projected on the screen of my fancy together with the gleam of your topaz ring and the beat of your eyelashes, and I could calculate how far you had read not simply by consulting my watch but by actually following one line after the other to the right-hand brink of each card. The lucidity of the image was correlated with the quality of the writing. You knew my work too well to be ruffled by a too robust erotic detail, or annoyed by a too recondite literary allusion. It was bliss reading *Ardis* with you that way, triumphing that way over the stretch of colored space separating my lane from your lounge chair. Was I an excellent writer? I was an excellent writer. That avenue of statues and lilacs where Ada and I drew our first circles on the dappled sand was visualized and re-created by an artist of lasting worth. The hideous suspicion that even *Ardis*, my most private book, soaked in reality, saturated with sun flecks, might be an unconscious imitation of another's unearthly art, *that* suspicion might come later; at the moment—6:18 P.M. on June 15, 1970, in the Tessin—nothing could scratch the rich humid gloss of my happiness.

I was now reaching the end of my usual preprandial walk. The *ra-ta-ta*, *ta-ta*, *tac* of a typist's finishing a last page came from a window through motionless foliage, reminding me pleasantly that I had long since eschewed the long labor of having my immaculate manuscripts typed when they could be reproduced photographically in one hum. It was now the publisher who bore the brunt of having my hand transformed directly into printed characters; and I know he disliked the procedure as a well-bred entomologist may find revolting an irregular insect's skipping some generally accepted stage of metamorphosis.

Only a few steps—twelve, eleven—remained before I would start to walk back: I felt you were thinking of this in a reversal of distant perception, just as I felt a kind of mental loosening, which told me you had finished reading those thirty cards, placed them in their proper order, tidied the stack by knocking its base slightly against the table, found the elastic lying there in the assumed shape of a heart, banded the batch, carried it to the safety of my desk, and were now preparing to meet me on my way back to Gandora Palace.

A low wall of gray stone, waist-high, paunch-thick, built in

the general shape of a transversal parapet, put an end to whatever life the road still had as a town street. A narrow passage
for pedestrians and cyclists divided the parapet in the middle,
and the width of that gap was preserved beyond it in a path
which after a flick or two slithered into a fairly dense young
pinewood. You and I had rambled there many times on gray
mornings, when lakeside or poolside lost all attraction; but
that evening, as usual, I terminated my stroll at the parapet,
and stood in perfect repose, facing the low sun, my spread
hands enjoying the smoothness of its top edge on both sides
of the passage. A tactile something, or the recent *ra-ta-tac*,
brought back and completed the image of my 733, twelve cen-
timeters by ten-and-a-half Bristol cards, which you would read
chapter by chapter whereupon a great pleasure, a parapet of
pleasure, would perfect my task: in my mind there arose, endowed with the clean-cut compactness of some great solid—
an altar! a mesa!—the image of the shiny photocopier in one
of the offices of our hotel. My trustful hands were still spread,
but my soles no longer sensed the soft soil. I wished to go
back to you, to life, to the amethyst lozenges, to the pencil
lying on the veranda table, and I could not. What used to
happen so often in thought, now had happened for keeps: I
could not turn. To make that movement would mean rolling
the world around on its axis and that was as impossible as
traveling back physically from the present moment to the previous one. Maybe I should not have panicked, should have
waited quietly for the stone of my limbs to regain some tingle
of flesh. Instead, I performed, or imagined performing, a wild
wrenching movement—and the globe did not bulge. I must
have hung in a spread-eagle position for a little while longer
before ending supine on the intangible soil.

Part Seven

I

THERE exists an old rule—so old and trite that I blush to mention it. Let me twist it into a jingle—to stylize the staleness:

> The I of the book
> Cannot die in the book.

I am speaking of serious novels, naturally. In so-called *Planchette-Fiction* the unruffled narrator, after describing his own dissolution, can continue thus: "I found myself standing on a staircase of onyx before a great gate of gold in a crowd of other bald-headed angels . . ."

Cartoon stuff, folklore rubbish, hilarious atavistic respect for precious minerals!

And yet—

And yet I feel that during three weeks of general paresis (if that is what it was) I have gained some experience; that when my night really comes I shall not be totally unprepared. Problems of identity have been, if not settled, at least set. Artistic insights have been granted. I was allowed to take my palette with me to very remote reaches of dim and dubious being.

Speed! If I could have given my definition of death to the stunned fisherman, to the mower who stopped wiping his scythe with a handful of grass, to the cyclist embracing in terror a willow sapling on one green bank and actually getting up to the top of a taller tree on the opposite side with his machine and girlfriend, to the black horses gaping at me like people with trick dentures all through my strange skimming progress, I would have cried one word: Speed! Not that those rural witnesses ever existed. My impression of prodigious, inexplicable, and to tell the truth rather silly and degrading speed (death is silly, death is degrading) would have been conveyed to a perfect void, without one fisherman tearing by, without one blade of grass bloodied by his catch, without any reference mark altogether. Imagine me, an old gentleman, a

distinguished author, gliding rapidly on my back, in the wake
of my outstretched dead feet, first through that gap in the
granite, then over a pinewood, then along misty water meadows, and then simply between marges of mist, on and on,
imagine that sight!

Madness had been lying in wait for me behind this or that
alder or boulder since infancy. I got used by degrees to feeling
the sepia stare of those watchful eyes as they moved smoothly
along the line of my passage. Yet I have known madness not
only in the guise of an evil shadow. I have seen it also as a
flash of delight so rich and shattering that the very absence of
an immediate object on which it might settle was to me a
form of escape.

For practical purposes, such as keeping body-mind and
mind-body in a state of ordinary balance, so as not to imperil
one's life or become a burden to friends or governments, I
preferred the latent variety, the awfulness of that watchful
thing that meant at best the stab of neuralgia, the distress of
insomnia, the battle with inanimate things which have never
disguised their hatred of me (the runaway button which *con-*
descends to be located, the paper clip, a thievish slave, not
content to hold a couple of humdrum letters, but managing
to catch a precious leaf from another batch), and at worst a
sudden spasm of space as when the visit to one's dentist turns
into a burlesque party. I preferred the muddle of such attacks
to the motley of madness which, after pretending to adorn
my existence with special forms of inspiration, mental ecstasy,
and so forth, would stop dancing and flitting around me and
would pounce upon me, and cripple me, and for all I know
destroy me.

2

At the start of the great seizure, I must have been totally
incapacitated, from top to toe, while my mind, the images
racing through me, the tang of thought, the genius of insomnia, remained as strong and active as ever (except for the blots

in between). By the time I had been flown to the Lecouchant Hospital in coastal France, highly recommended by Dr. Genfer, a Swiss relative of its director, I became aware of certain curious details: from the head down I was paralyzed in symmetrical patches separated by a geography of weak tactility. When in the course of that first week my fingers "awoke" (a circumstance that stupefied and even angered the Lecouchant sages, experts in dementia paralytica, to such a degree that they advised you to rush me off to some more exotic and broadminded institution—which you did) I derived much entertainment from mapping my sensitive spots which were always situated in exact opposition, e.g. on both sides of my forehead, on the jaws, orbital parts, breasts, testicles, knees, flanks. At an average stage of observation, the average size of each spot of life never exceeded that of Australia (I felt gigantic at times) and never dwindled (when I dwindled myself) below the diameter of a medal of medium merit, at which level I perceived my entire skin as that of a leopard painted by a meticulous lunatic from a broken home.

In some connection with those "tactile symmetries" (about which I am still attempting to correspond with a not too responsive medical journal, swarming with Freudians), I would like to place the first pictorial compositions, flat, primitive images, which occurred in duplicate, right and left of my traveling body, on the opposite panels of my hallucinations. If, for example, Annette boarded a bus with her empty basket on the left of my being, she came out of that bus on my right with a load of vegetables, a royal cauliflower presiding over the cucumbers. As the days passed, the symmetries got replaced by more elaborate inter-responses, or reappeared in miniature within the limits of a given image. Picturesque episodes now accompanied my mysterious voyage. I glimpsed Bel rummaging after work amidst a heap of naked babies at the communal day-nursery, in frantic search for her own firstborn, now ten months old, and recognizable by the symmetrical blotches of red eczema on its sides and little legs. A glossy-haunched swimmer used one hand to brush away from her face wet strands of hair, and pushed with the other (on the *other* side of my mind) the raft on which I lay, a naked old man with a rag around his foremast, gliding supine into a full moon whose snaky reflections rippled among the water lilies. A long tunnel engulfed me, half-promised a circlet of light at its far end, half-kept the promise, revealing a publicity sunset, but I never reached it, the tunnel faded, and a familiar mist took over again. As was "done" that season, groups of smart idlers visited my bed, which had slowed down in a display hall where Ivor Black in the role of a fashionable young doctor demonstrated me to three actresses playing society belles: their skirts ballooned as they settled down on white chairs, and one lady, indicating my groin, would have touched me with her cold fan, had not the learned Moor struck it aside with his ivory pointer, whereupon my raft resumed its lone glide.

Whoever charted my destiny had moments of triteness. At times my swift course became a celestial affair at an allegorical altitude that bore unpleasant religious connotations—unless simply reflecting transportation of cadavers by commercial aircraft. A certain notion of daytime and nighttime, in more or less regular alternation, gradually established itself in my mind as my grotesque adventure reached its final phase. Diurnal and nocturnal effects were rendered obliquely at first with nurses and other stagehands going to extreme lengths in the handling of movable properties, such as the bouncing of fake starlight from reflecting surfaces or the daubing of dawns here and there at suitable intervals. It had never occurred to me before that, historically, art, or at least artifacts, had preceded, not followed, nature; yet that is exactly what happened in my case. Thus, in the mute remoteness clouding around me, recognizable sounds were produced at first optically in the pale margin of the film track during the taking of the actual scene (say, the ceremony of scientific feeding); eventually something about the running ribbon tempted the ear to replace the eye; and finally hearing returned—with a vengeance. The first crisp nurse-rustle was a thunderclap; my first belly wamble, a crash of cymbals.

I owe thwarted obituarists, as well as all lovers of medical lore, some clinical elucidations. My lungs and my heart acted, or were induced to act, normally; so did my bowels, those buffoons in the cast of our private miracle plays. My frame lay flat as in an Old Master's Lesson of Anatomy. The prevention of bedsores, especially at the Lecouchant Hospital, was nothing short of a mania, explicable, maybe, by a desperate urge to substitute pillows and various mechanical devices for the rational treatment of an unfathomable disease. My body was "sleeping" as a giant's foot might be "sleeping"; more accurately, however, my condition was a horrible form of protracted (twenty nights!) insomnia with my mind as consistently alert as that of the Sleepless Slav in some circus show I once read about in *The Graphic*. I was not even a mummy; I was—in the beginning, at least—the longitudinal section of a mummy, or rather the abstraction of its thinnest possible cut. What about the head?—readers who are all head must be clamoring to be told. Well, my brow was like misty glass (before two lateral spots got cleared somehow or other); my mouth stayed mute and benumbed until I realized I could feel my tongue—feel it in the phantom form of the kind of air bladder that might help a fish with his respiration problems, but was useless to me. I had some sense of duration and direction—two things which a beloved creature seeking to help a poor madman with the whitest of lies, affirmed, in a later world, were quite separate phases of a single phenomenon. Most of my cerebral aqueduct (this is getting a little technical) seemed to descend wedgewise, after some derailment or inundation, into the structure housing its closest ally—which oddly enough is also our humblest sense, the easiest and sometimes the most gratifying to dispense with— and, oh, how I cursed it when I could not close it to ether or excrements, and, oh (cheers for old "oh"), how I thanked it for crying "Coffee!" or "*Plage!*" (because an anonymous drug smelled like the cream Iris used to rub my back with in Cannice half a century ago!).

Now comes a snaggy bit: I do not know if my eyes remained always wide open "in a glazed look of arrogant stupor" as imagined by a reporter who got as far as the corridor desk. But I doubt very much I could blink—and without the oil of blinking the motor of sight could hardly have run. Yet, somehow, during my glide down those illusory canals and cloudways, and right over another continent, I did glimpse off and on, through subpalpebral mirages, the shadow of a hand or the glint of an instrument. As to my world of sound, it remained solid fantasy. I heard strangers discuss in droning voices all the books I had written or thought I had written, for everything they mentioned, titles, the names of characters, every phrase they shouted was preposterously distorted by the delirium of demonic scholarship. Louise regaled the company with one of her good stories—those I called "name hangers" because they only *seemed* to reach this or that point—a *quid pro quo*, say, at a party—but were really meant to introduce some high-born "old friend" of hers, or a glamorous politician, or a cousin of that politician. Learned papers were read at fantastic symposiums. In the year of grace 1798, Gavrila Petrovich Kamenev, a gifted young poet, was heard chuckling as he composed his Ossianic pastiche *Slovo o polku Igoreve*. Somewhere in Abyssinia drunken Rimbaud was reciting to a surprised Russian traveler the poem *Le Tramway ivre* (. . . *En blouse rouge, à face en pis de vache, le bourreau me trancha la tête aussi* . . .). Or else I'd hear the pressed repeater hiss in a pocket of my brain and tell the time, the rime, the meter that who could dream I'd hear again?

I should also point out that my flesh was in fairly good shape: no ligaments torn, no muscles trapped; my spinal cord may have been slightly bruised during the absurd collapse that precipitated my voyage but it was still there, lining me, shading my being, as good as the primitive structure of some translucent aquatic creature. Yet the medical treatment I was subjected to (especially at the Lecouchant place) implied—insofar as now reconstructed—that my injuries were all physical, only physical, and could be only dealt with by physical means. I am not speaking of modern alchemy, of magic philtres injected into me—those did, perhaps, act somehow, not only on my body, but also on the divinity installed within me, as might the suggestions of ambitious shamans or quaking councilors upon a mad emperor; what I cannot get over are such imprinted images as the damned braces and belts that held me stretched on my back (preventing me from walking away with my rubber raft under my arm as I felt I could), or even worse the man-made electric leeches, which masked executioners attached to my head and limbs—until chased away by that saint in Catapult, Cal., Professor H. P. Sloan, who was on the brink of suspecting, just when I started to get well,

that I might be cured—might have been cured!—in a trice by
hypnosis and some sense of humor on the hypnotist's part.

3

To the best of my knowledge my Christian name was Vadim;
so was my father's. The U.S.A. passport recently issued me—
an elegant booklet with a golden design on its green cover
perforated by the number 00678638—did not mention my ancestral title; this had figured, though, on my British passport,
throughout its several editions. Youth, Adulthood, Old Age,
before the last one was mutilated beyond recognition by
friendly forgers, practical jokers at heart. All this I re-gleaned
one night, as certain brain cells, which had been frozen, now
bloomed anew. Others, however, still puckered like retarded
buds, and although I could freely twiddle (for the first time
since I collapsed) my toes under the bedclothes, I just could
not make out in that darker corner of my mind what surname
came after my Russian patronymic. I felt it began with an *N*,
as did the term for the beautifully spontaneous arrangement
of words at moments of inspiration like the rouleaux of red
corpuscles in freshly drawn blood under the microscope—a
word I once used in *See under Real*, but could not remember
either, something to do with a roll of coins, capitalistic metaphor, eh, Marxy? Yes, I definitely felt my family name began
with an *N* and bore an odious resemblance to the surname or
pseudonym of a presumably notorious (Notorov? No) Bulgarian, or Babylonian, or, maybe, Betelgeusian writer with
whom scatterbrained *émigrés* from some other galaxy constantly confused me; but whether it was something on the
lines of Nebesnyy or Nabedrin or Nablidze (Nablidze? Funny)
I simply could not tell. I preferred not to overtax my willpower (go away, Naborcroft) and so gave up trying—or perhaps it began with a *B* and the *n* just clung to it like some
desperate parasite? (Bonidze? Blonsky?—No, that belonged to
the BINT business.) Did I have some princely Caucasian
blood? Why had allusions to a Mr. Nabarro, a British politi-

cian, cropped up among the clippings I received from England concerning the London edition of *A Kingdom by the Sea* (lovely lilting title)? Why did Ivor call me "MacNab"?

Without a name I remained unreal in regained consciousness. Poor Vivian, poor Vadim Vadimovich, was but a figment of somebody's—not even my own—imagination. One dire detail: in rapid Russian speech longish name-and-patronymic combinations undergo familiar slurrings: thus "Pavel Pavlovich," Paul, son of Paul, when casually interpellated is made to sound like "Pahlpahlych" and the hardly utterable, tapeworm-long "Vladimir Vladimirovich" becomes colloquially similar to "Vadim Vadimych."

I gave up. And when I gave up for good my sonorous surname crept up from behind, like a prankish child that makes a nodding old nurse jump at his sudden shout.

There remained other problems. Where was I? What about a little light? How did one tell by touch a lamp's button from a bell's button in the dark. What was, apart from my own identity, that other person, promised to me, belonging to me? I could locate the bluish blinds of twin windows. Why not uncurtain them?

> *Tak, vdol' naklónnogo luchá*
> *Ya výshel iz paralichá.*
>
> *Along a slanting ray, like this*
> *I slipped out of paralysis.*

—if "paralysis" is not too strong a word for the condition that mimicked it (with some obscure help from the patient): a rather quaint but not too serious psychological disorder— or at least so it seemed in lighthearted retrospect.

I was prepared by certain indices for spells of dizziness and nausea but I did not expect my legs to misbehave as they did, when—unbuckled and alone—I blithely stepped out of bed on that first night of recovery. Beastly gravity humiliated me at once: my legs telescoped under me. The crash brought in the night nurse, and she helped me back into bed. After that I slept. Never before or since did I sleep more deliciously.

One of the windows was wide open when I woke up. My mind and my eye were by now sufficiently keen to make out the medicaments on my bedside table. Amidst its miserable population I noticed a few stranded travelers from another world: a transparent envelope with a non-masculine handkerchief found and laundered by the staff; a diminutive golden pencil belonging to the eyelet of a congeric agenda in a vanity bag; a pair of harlequin sunglasses, which for some reason suggested not protection from a harsh light but the masking of tear-swollen lids. The combination of those ingredients resulted in a dazzling pyrotechny of sense; and next moment (coincidence was still on my side) the door of my room moved: a small soundless move that came to a brief soundless stop and then was continued in a slow, infinitely slow sequence of suspension dots in diamond type. I emitted a bellow of joy, and Reality entered.

4

With the following gentle scene I propose to conclude this autobiography. I had been wheeled into the rose-twined gallery for Special Convalescents in the second and last of my hospitals. You were reclining in a lounge chair beside me, in much the same attitude in which I had left you on June 15, at Gandora. You complained gaily that a woman in the room next to yours on the ground floor of the annex had a phonograph playing bird-call records, by means of which she hoped to make the mockingbirds of the hospital park imitate the nightingales and thrushes of her place in Devon or Dorset. You knew very well I wished to find out something. We both hedged. I drew your attention to the beauty of the climbing roses. You said: "Everything is beautiful against the sky (*na fone neba*)" and apologized for the "aphorism." At last, in the most casual of tones I asked how you had liked the fragment of *Ardis* I gave you to read just before taking the little walk from which I had returned only now, three weeks later, in Catapult, California.

You looked away. You considered the mauve mountains. You cleared your throat and bravely replied that you had not liked it at all.

Meaning she would not marry a madman?

Meaning she would marry a sane man who could tell the difference between time and space.

Explain.

She was awfully eager to read the rest of the manuscript, but *that* fragment ought to be scrapped. It was written as nicely as everything I wrote but happened to be marred by a fatal philosophical flaw.

Young, graceful, tremendously charming, hopelessly homely Mary Middle came to say I would have to be back when the bell tinkled for tea. In five minutes. Another nurse signaled to her from the sun-striped end of the gallery, and she fluttered away.

The place (you said) was full of dying American bankers and perfectly healthy Englishmen. I had described a person in the act of imagining his recent evening stroll. A stroll from point H (Home, Hotel) to point P (Parapet, Pinewood). Imagining fluently the sequence of wayside events—child swinging in villa garden, lawn sprinkler rotating, dog chasing a wet ball. The narrator reaches point P in his mind, stops—and is puzzled and upset (quite unreasonably as we shall see) by being unable to execute mentally the about-face that would turn direction HP into direction PH.

"His mistake," she continued, "his morbid mistake is quite simple. He has confused direction and duration. He speaks of space but he means time. His impressions along the HP route (dog overtakes ball, car pulls up at next villa) refer to a series of time events, and not to blocks of painted space that a child can rearrange in any old way. It has taken him time—even if only a few moments—to cover distance HP in thought. By the time he reaches P he has accumulated duration, he is saddled with it! Why then is it so extraordinary that he cannot imagine himself turning on his heel? Nobody can imagine in physical terms the act of reversing the order of time. Time is not reversible. Reverse motion is used in films only for comic effects—the resurrection of a smashed bottle of beer—

"Or rum," I put in, and here the bell tinkled.

"That's all very well," I said, as I groped for the levers of my wheelchair, and you helped me to roll back to my room. "And I'm grateful, I'm touched, I'm cured! Your explanation, however, is merely an exquisite quibble—and you know it; but never mind, the notion of trying to twirl time is a *trouvaille*; it resembles (kissing the hand resting on my sleeve) the neat formula a physicist finds to keep people happy until (yawning, crawling back into bed) until the next chap snatches the chalk. I had been promised some rum with my tea—Ceylon and Jamaica, the sibling islands (mumbling comfortably, dropping off, mumble dying away)—"

CHRONOLOGY

NOTE ON THE TEXTS

NOTES

Chronology

1899   Born Vladimir Vladimirovich Nabokov on April 23 (April 10 Old Style) at 47 Bolshaya Morskaya Street in St. Petersburg, first child of Vladimir Dmitrievich Nabokov, b. 1870, and Elena Ivanovna Nabokov, b. 1876. Christened in Orthodox ceremony in late spring. Father is a lecturer in criminal law at the Imperial School of Jurisprudence, and an editor of the liberal law journal *Pravo*. Family lives in plush Morskaya Street home with many servants and spends summer on the three neighboring estates of Rozhdestveno and Vyra (maternal grandfather's) and Batovo (paternal grandmother's), about 50 miles south of St. Petersburg. (Grandfather Dmitri Nikolaevich Nabokov, b. 1826, married Baroness Maria Ferdinandovna von Korff, b. 1842, in 1859. Grandfather became a member of the State Council and served as a liberal minister of justice from 1878 to 1885. Grandfather Ivan Vasilievich Rukavishnikov, b. 1841, a wealthy landowner and magistrate, married Olga Nikolaevna Kozlov, b. 1845, a daughter of the first president of the Royal Academy of Medicine. Mother was privately tutored in the natural sciences by a university professor. Parents were married in November 1897 and had a stillborn son in 1898.)

1900   Brother Sergey born in March. Nabokov speaks, and learns numbers, at an early age.

1901   Grandfather Rukavishnikov dies in March and grandmother Rukavishnikov dies in June, both of cancer. Mother inherits Vyra estate and uncle Vasiliy "Ruka" Rukavishnikov inherits Rozhdestveno. Doctors advise mother to go abroad for her health, and she takes Nabokov and Sergey to Pau and Biarritz in the south of France (father remains in St. Petersburg to teach).

1902   Nabokov and Sergey learn English from Rachel Home, first of a succession of British governesses. Spends summers at Vyra, enjoying the company of both sides of large extended family whose estates dot the area. Mother tells him to remember details they admire on walks in country, and reads him fairy tales and adventure stories in English at bedtime.

751

1903   Sister Olga born in January (brothers and sisters will be reared separately within household; Nabokov remains the favorite of parents). Father becomes a member of the St. Petersburg City Duma (council). After major pogrom at Kishinev in April, he writes article for *Pravo* charging government with tacitly encouraging pogroms. Family travels abroad in autumn and visits grandfather Nabokov, now senile, in Nice. In St. Petersburg Nabokov toboggans and takes long walks with new English governess; reads English juvenile magazines *Chatterbox* and *Little Folks* (has not yet learned to read Russian).

1904   Japan attacks Russia in February. Attends opera, which he does not enjoy, and theater with parents. Plays chess and cards with family. Grandfather Nabokov dies on March 28 in St. Petersburg. Father takes family to Rome and Naples for three weeks and then Beaulieu for the summer; there Nabokov falls in love with a Romanian girl. Family returns in fall to Russia, where setbacks in the Russo-Japanese War have increased pressure for political reform. Father plays active role in first national congress of zemstvos (local assemblies); congress, whose final session is held in the Nabokov home, calls for a written constitution, a national legislative assembly, and guaranteed civil rights, and effectively launches the 1905 (or First) Russian Revolution. Father, told his political activities are incompatible with his post at the Imperial School of Jurisprudence, resigns.

1905   Tsarist troops fire on a peaceful demonstration in St. Petersburg on January 22 ("Bloody Sunday"), killing more than a hundred people. Father denounces killings in the St. Petersburg Duma and is deprived of his court title. Advised to remove family from strife, father takes them in February to Abbazia (now Opatija, Croatia), where they stay with paternal aunt Natalia de Peterson and family. Nabokov misses Vyra and nostalgically traces details of the estate on his pillow with his finger. Father called back in October to Russia, where general strike spreads throughout country. Father goes to Moscow for founding sessions of Constitutional Democratic (CD) party; remainder of family moves to Wiesbaden, where Nabokov becomes friends with his cousin, Baron Yuri Rausch von Traubenburg, son of paternal aunt Nina.

1906   Family returns to Russia, but remains at Vyra through winter. Swiss governess Cécile Miauton arrives (she will be part of the household for seven years). Miauton tutors Nabokov and Sergey in mornings and in afternoons reads children her favorite French novels, poetry, and stories, beginning with Corneille and Hugo. Nabokov soon becomes fluent in French and memorizes passages from Racine. Sister Elena is born in March. Father, as leading speaker of the CDs, the largest party in the First State Duma, challenges Chief Minister Ivan Goremykin's rejection of the Duma's reform program in May: "Let the executive power submit to the legislative!" Nabokov is now taught to read and write in Russian over the summer by the village schoolmaster, Vasily Zhernosekov, a Socialist Revolutionary. Begins to catch butterflies (lepidopterology will become a lifelong passion). After Duma is unexpectedly dissolved by Tsar Nicholas II in July, father signs Vyborg manifesto (calling populace to civil disobedience) in protest and is stripped of his political rights; he becomes editor of *Rech'*, St. Petersburg's leading liberal daily and unofficial CD newspaper.

1907   Has severe bout of pneumonia, and loses his prodigious capacity for mathematical calculation. Studies books on Lepidoptera and specimens brought by mother while convalescing. Begins regular lessons with a succession of Russian-speaking tutors. Studies drawing and painting and learns tennis and boxing. Family travels to Biarritz in August, where Nabokov falls in love with Serbian girl, Zina.

1908   Father serves three-month prison sentence for signing Vyborg manifesto. Nabokov masters the known butterflies of Europe. Is permitted to stop going to church after telling father that he finds services boring.

1909   Sees father stop to chat with Leo Tolstoy during a walk. Becomes infatuated and spends much time with nine-year-old girl, Claude Deprès, during fall vacation at Biarritz. Though he still enjoys English juvenile magazines and *Punch*, Nabokov reads widely in his father's library, which contains 10,000 volumes. Early favorites include Jules Verne, Conan Doyle, Kipling, Conrad, Chesterton, Wilde, Pushkin, and Tolstoy.

1910   Continues friendship with cousin Yuri; they provoke each
            other to repeated tests of courage. Translates into French
            alexandrines Mayne Reid's *The Headless Horseman*, rears
            caterpillars, keeps notes in English on the butterflies he
            collects, reads entomological journals, and "dreams" his
            way through A. Seitz's *Macrolepidoptera of the World*. Af-
            ter fall family vacation in Germany, Nabokov and Sergey
            stay in Berlin with tutor for three months while under-
            going orthodontic work; reads Tolstoy's *Voyna i mir* (*War
            and Peace*).

1911   Begins classes at elite but liberal Tenishev School, helped
            in studies by tutors at home. Rankles at conformity of
            school life but copes easily with courses, which include
            history, geography, geometry, algebra, physics, chemistry,
            Russian, French, German, Scripture, and woodworking.
            Plays soccer, always as goalkeeper. Closest school friends
            are Samuil Rosov and Samuil Kyandzhuntsev. Brother
            Kirill is born in June. Father publicly challenges editor
            of conservative newspaper to duel for personal insult in
            October; Nabokov, in agony of apprehension, imagines
            father's death, but an apology averts the duel.

1912–13   Miauton returns to Switzerland. Nabokov begins two
            years of drawing lessons with leading St. Petersburg artist
            Mstislav Dobuzhinsky (who will later call him his most
            hopeless pupil). Begins reading new Symbolist, Acmeist,
            and Futurist poetry along with works of Pushkin, Poe,
            Browning, Keats, Verlaine, Rimbaud, Gogol, Chekhov,
            Dostoevsky, Shakespeare, Tolstoy, Flaubert, and William
            James.

1914   H. G. Wells, whose work Nabokov admires, dines at Na-
            bokovs' home during his tour of Russia. School report in
            spring describes Nabokov: "zealous football-player, excel-
            lent worker, respected as comrade of both flanks (Rosov-
            Popov), always modest, serious and restrained (though not
            adverse to a joke), Nabokov creates a most agreeable im-
            pression by his moral decency." Composes what he later
            calls his first poem in July and becomes prey to "the numb
            fury of versemaking." Germany declares war on Russia
            August 1; father, a reserve officer, is called up on August
            3 and leaves with his regiment for Vyborg while mother

volunteers as nurse in hospital for wounded soldiers. Nabokov continues to write poetry almost daily. Evgenia Hofeld, governess for Elena and Olga, arrives (will remain with family for many years and become closest companion of mother in her last years).

1915   Confined to bed with typhus in early summer. After recovering, begins love affair with Valentina "Lyussya" Shulgin, who is vacationing with her family near Vyra; writes many love poems to her. Father is transferred in September to the General Staff in Petrograd (as capital has been renamed). Nabokov is taught Russian literature by poet and critic Vladimir Gippius, whose verse he likes but whose pressure towards social concern he resists. Often skips classes throughout school year to meet with Lyussya. Smokes heavily. In November co-edits the school journal *Yunaya mysl'* (*Young Thought*), which contains his first publication, poem "Osen'" ("Autumn"). Translates Alfred de Musset's "La Nuit de décembre," dedicating it to Lyussya.

1916   Translation of "La Nuit de décembre" appears in *Yunaya mysl'*. Publishes at own expense *Stikhi* (*Poems*), collection of 68 love poems; another poem appears in leading literary journal *Vestnik Evropy* in July. Sees cousin Yuri, now in the army. Uncle "Ruka" Rukavishnikov dies in France in fall, leaving Nabokov 2,000-acre Rozhdestveno estate and manor. Is compelled to take extra lessons, having received "not satisfactory" grade in algebra at end of spring term. Affair with Lyussya ends and Nabokov begins what he later describes as "an extravagant phase of sentiment and sensuality." By end of year he is conducting affairs with three married women, including his cousin Tatiana Segerkranz, Yuri's 27-year-old sister.

1917   Sick with pneumonia, then measles. While recuperating at Imatra resort in Finland in January, begins romance with Eva Lubryjinksa. In Petrograd on March 12 soldiers refuse to fire on demonstrators and then mutiny, leading to the collapse of the Tsarist regime. Father becomes head of chancellery in the first Provisional Government. Nabokov has his appendix removed in May; writes "Dozhd' proletel" (later translated as "The Rain Has Flown"), the earliest poem he will include in his collected poems. Selects verses he will publish with schoolmate Andrey Balashov in *Dva puti* (*Two Paths*; printed 1918). Begins album of verses dedicated to Eva Lubryjinksa. Bolsheviks seize power in Petrograd in coup on November 7. Father sends family to Gaspra, estate outside Yalta in the Crimea, before being imprisoned by Bolsheviks for five days in December; after his release, he joins family in Crimea. Nabokov plays chess with him nightly and composes his first chess problems.

1918   After the Bolsheviks seize the Yalta area in late January, father adopts "disguise" of medical doctor. Nabokov writes first short verse play, "Vesnoy" ("In Spring"). German army occupies Crimea in April. Father begins to write his memoir *The Provisional Government.* Nabokov hunts butterflies, sees Yuri while he is on leave in Yalta. Family moves to Livadia, nearer Yalta, so that Sergey, Olga, and Elena can attend school. Nabokov studies Latin with tutor, continues writing poetry; publishes two poems in CD newspaper *Yaltinsky golos.* Meets poet Maximilian Voloshin, who suggests reading Andrey Bely on metrical patterns in Russian verse. Applies Bely's method to classics of Russian poetry and his own works; finds his poems metrically featureless and for about a year constructs his new verse to yield arresting Belian diagrams. Tutors favorite sister, Elena. After German troops withdraw in November, father becomes minister of justice in the Crimean Provisional Regional Government, civilian regime organized by CDs and Tatars.

1919   Writes "Dvoe" ("The Two"), 430-line riposte to Aleksandr Blok's "Dvenadstat" ("The Twelve"). Considers enlisting in White Army commanded by General Anton Denikin when cousin Yuri visits. Yuri is killed in battle soon after returning to the front; Nabokov serves as a pallbearer at his funeral in Yalta on March 14. Red Army begins advance into Crimea on April 3. Family sails from Sebastopol on April 15 aboard Greek freighter and arrives in Athens on April 23, then goes in late May to London, where they rent house in South Kensington with money from sale of mother's jewels. Nabokov spends time with other Russian emigrés including old schoolmate Samuil Rosov; renews romance with Eva Lubryjinksa. Enters Trinity College, Cambridge, on partial scholarship, in October. Studies Modern and Medieval Languages (French and Russian) and Natural Sciences (zoology). Shares room with Russian emigré Mikhail Kalashnikov. Writes poetry in Russian and plays goal for Trinity soccer team. Buys Dahl's four-volume Russian dictionary and reads in it every night, jotting down verbal finds. Writes first entomological paper, "A Few Notes on Crimean Lepidoptera" (published in *Entomologist*, Feb. 1920). Also reads Housman, Rupert Brooke, and Walter de la Mare and writes a few English poems.

1920   Spends time with brother Sergey, now at Christ's College, Cambridge, and becomes friends with Prince Nikita Romanov. Drops zoology to leave time for verse, women, soccer. Family moves to Berlin and father helps found liberal daily emigré newspaper *Rul'* (*The Rudder*). Nabokov receives advance from emigré publishing house Slovo for Russian translation of Romain Rolland's *Colas Breugnon*. Moves into lodgings next to Trinity with Kalashnikov in October. Argues with George Wells, son of H. G. Wells, about politics. Poem "Remembrance" published in *The English Review* (November).

1921   Three poems and story "Nezhit'" (later translated as "The Wood-Sprite") appear in *Rul'* on January 7 under name Vladimir Sirin, pseudonym adopted to distinguish himself from father (Nabokov will retain the Sirin pseudonym for his Russian writings into the 1960s). Begins regular contributions to *Rul'* of poems, plays, stories, chess problems, crossword puzzles, and reviews. Completes *Nikolka Persik*, translation of *Colas Breugnon* (published Nov. 1922). Spends summer in Berlin, where he falls in love with Svetlana Siewert, Kalashnikov's cousin. Visitors to family's house in Wilmersdorf include poet Sasha Chorny, Iosif Hessen, head of Slovo, cousin Nicolas Nabokov, Konstantin Stanislavsky, and actors from Stanislavsky's Moscow Art Theater. Returns to Cambridge and becomes friend of Count Robert de Calry, English student of Russian ancestry. During winter ski trip to Switzerland with de Calry visits Cécile Miauton in Lausanne.

1922   Father is shot and killed on March 28 while struggling with one of the monarchist gunmen attempting to assassinate fellow CD leader Pavel Milyukov. Nabokov attends funeral

in Tegel, near Berlin, then returns to Cambridge to study
for exams. Writes mother: "At times it's all so oppressive
I could go out of my mind—but I have to hide. There
are things and feelings no one will ever find out." Graduates with second-class honors B.A. degree in June. Returns to Berlin and becomes engaged to Svetlana Siewert.
Takes job in bank but leaves after three hours. Receives
advance of $5 from Gamayun publishers to translate *Alice's
Adventures in Wonderland*. With several writers including
friends Gleb Struve and Ivan Lukash, forms literary circle
they name Bratstvo kruglogo stola (Brotherhood of the
Round Table). *Grozd' (The Cluster)*, collection of poems
written 1921 to 1922, published by Gamayun in December.

1923   *Gorniy put' (Empyrean Path)*, collection of poems written
1918 to 1921, published by Grani in January. Engagement
to Svetlana is broken off by her parents, who object to
Nabokov's not having steady job. *Anya v strane chudes*
(translation of *Alice's Adventures in Wonderland*) published by Gamayun in March. At masquerade charity ball
on May 8 Nabokov meets Véra Evseevna Slonim (b. 1902),
formerly of St. Petersburg, daughter of a Russian Jewish
emigré businessman. Works briefly as film extra, then for
three months as agricultural laborer in south of France;
writes verse plays. Returns in August to Berlin where he
courts Véra Slonim; begins writing stories regularly. Hoping that theatrical work will earn more money, writes
sketches with his good friend Ivan Lukash. Mother goes
with Elena and Olga to find apartment in Prague, where
she is eligible for a pension. Nabokov takes Kirill and Hofeld to join them in December; while in Prague, writes
five-act verse play *Tragediya gospodina Morna (The
Tragedy of Mr. Morn*; still unpublished). Evsey Slonim's
businesses fail in hyperinflation.

1924   Meets Russian poet Marina Tsvetaeva. Returns to Berlin
and takes room at 21 Lutherstrasse. Pantomime "Voda
zhivaya" ("Living Water"), written with Lukash, is performed at emigré cabaret for more than a month. As center of Russian emigration shifts to Paris, Nabokov remains
in Berlin (later attributes decision in part to his fear that
his Russian would atrophy if he lived in a country whose
language he knew well). Becomes engaged to Véra and
begins to earn living tutoring in English, French, tennis,

and boxing (tutoring will be his major source of income until 1929 and continue sporadically until 1941). Works on scenarios for cabarets and theater alone or with Lukash. Publishes nine stories in emigré journals and newspapers and begins contributing poems, chess problems, and crossword puzzles to new *Rul'* Sunday supplement, *Nash mir* (*Our World*).

1925   Marries Véra in civil ceremony on April 15. Nabokov acts as private tutor to two Russian Jewish schoolboys; he has them read and discuss Proust and Joyce's *Ulysses*. Increased income allows him to send more money to his mother. Often visits with Slonim family. Takes Véra to meet his family in Prague in August; they go to Konstanz, Germany, for a week before returning to Berlin, where they move into two rooms at 31 Motzstrasse. Writes novel *Mashen'ka* (later translated as *Mary*), September–November. Joins literary club organized by Raisa Tatarinov and critic Yuli Aykhenvald (will remain a member and contribute talks until 1933). Publishes six stories during year.

1926   Forms close friendships with George Hessen, son of *Rul'* editor Iosif Hessen, and Mikhail Kaminka, son of his father's CD and publishing colleague and best friend, Avgust Kaminka. Gives reading of *Mashen'ka* at local literary club where Aykhenvald proclaims: "A new Turgenev has appeared"; novel is published by Slovo in March to good reviews. Writes play *Chelovek iz SSSR* (later translated as *The Man from the USSR*) for new emigré Group Theater. Continues publishing stories. Composes 882-line Pushkinian poem, "Universitetskaya poema."

1927   *Chelovek iz SSSR*, performed in April, is well received. Poem "Bilet" (*Rul'*, June 26), about returning to a Russia freed from Communism, is printed in *Pravda* on July 17 along with a reply by Soviet poet Demyan Bedny ("Bilet" will be Nabokov's only work published in the Soviet Union in his lifetime). Has idea for *Korol', dama, valet* (later translated as *King, Queen, Knave*) while acting as chaperone with Véra for three boys at Baltic beach of Binz in summer. Goes with Véra to Misdroy, Germany, where he hunts moths; on return to Berlin they move into rented rooms at 12 Passauer Strasse. Nabokov becomes poetry reviewer for *Rul'*; continues publishing stories and poems, doing some translations with Véra, giving readings, and tutoring, though he has fewer pupils.

1928   Signs agreement in March with major newspaper *Vossische Zeitung* for serialization in German of *Mashen'ka*. With Véra begins attending Poets' Club, whose members include Raïsa Blokh and Vladimir Korvin-Piotrovsky. Véra's father dies in June and her mother dies in August; Véra takes job as secretary in French embassy to pay their medical bills. *Korol', dama, valet* (written January–June) published by Slovo in September to good reviews. Sells German rights to Ullstein publishing company for 7,500 marks. Aykhenvald, the first major critic to hail Nabokov, is killed by a streetcar as he returns from party at the Nabokovs' on December 16.

1929   Goes with Véra to the Pyrenees, February–June, where he hunts butterflies and begins novel *Zashchita Luzhina* (later translated as *The Defense*). Buys a small lakefront property in Kolberg with Anna Feigin, Véra's cousin; completes novel there in August and it is serialized in *Sovremennye zapiski (Contemporary Annals)*, leading emigré literary review published in Paris, October 1929–April 1930. (All Nabokov's remaining Russian novels will be published serially in the journal, which pays better than emigré book publishers.) Moves with Véra into furnished rooms at 27 Luitpoldstrasse. *Vozvrashchenie Chorba (The Return of Chorb)*, collection of stories and poems, published in December by Slovo.

1930   Completes novella *Soglyadatay* (later translated as *The Eye*) in February. Begins novel *Podvig* (later translated as *Glory*) in May; later that month goes to Prague, where he visits his family, counsels Kirill on his poetry, and gives public readings. Economic depression in Germany causes further decline in numbers of Berlin emigré community and viability of *Rul'*, but Nabokov's publication in *Sovremennye zapiski* provokes high praise from some writers like Vladislav Khodasevich and Nina Berberova, and attacks from others, like Georgy Adamovich and Georgy Ivanov, associated with new rival journal *Chisla (Numbers)*. Véra takes job as secretary in a firm of German Jewish lawyers. *Zashchita Luzhina* is published as book in September and

Soglyadatay appears in *Sovremennye zapiski* in November. Completes *Podvig*.

1931   Writes novel *Kamera obskura* (later translated as *Camera Obscura* and as *Laughter in the Dark*) between January and May. *Podvig* is serialized in *Sovremennye zapiski* (Feb. 1931–Jan. 1932). Writes "Les Écrivains et l'époque" (*Le Mois*, June–July), his first French article. Continues publishing stories. *Rul'* fails in October. Joins soccer team of Russian sports club as goalkeeper.

1932   Writes appeal for assistance for the unemployed in emigré paper *Poslednie novosti* (*The Latest News*). In severe financial straits, Nabokov and Véra take a room in a crowded family apartment on 29 Westfälische Strasse. Meets Hollywood director Sergey Bertenson, a Russian emigré; offers him *Kamera obskura* but Bertenson pronounces it unsuitable for filming. Visits family in Prague; is delighted with nephew Rostislav Petkevitch, infant son of sister Olga. *Kamera obskura* appears in *Sovremennye zapiski* (May 1932–May 1933). Writes first draft of *Otchayanie* (later translated as *Despair*) between June and September. Moves with Véra into apartment of Anna Feigin on 22 Nestorstrasse in the Wilmersdorf district in July. Travels to Paris in fall where he gives highly successful public reading and explores opportunities for work. Sees brother Sergey and cousin Nicolas Nabokov, who live in France. Meets Vladislav Khodasevich, Nina Berberova, Mark Aldanov, Jean Paulhan, Gabriel Marcel, and Jules Supervielle. Visits with *Sovremennye zapiski* editors. Completes *Otchayanie*. Gives reading in Antwerp before returning to Berlin. *Podvig* is published in book form in November by Sovremennye zapiski.

1933   Adolf Hitler is appointed chancellor of Germany on January 30. Nabokov begins gathering materials on Nikolay Chernyshevsky and on Russian naturalist-explorers of Central Asia for projected novel *Dar* (later translated as *The Gift*). Is sick with neuralgia intercostalis for most of winter. Véra loses her secretarial job when law firm is forced to close in March and begins working as a free-lance stenographer, tourist guide, and interpreter. Nabokov writes Gleb Struve, now at the University of London, asking for help arranging English translations of his works. Applies for teaching position in Switzerland, but is rejected. Reads Virginia Woolf and Katherine Mansfield for story "Admiralteyskaya igla" ("The Admiralty Spire"). At invitation of emigré publisher, writes to James Joyce in November, offering to translate *Ulysses*: "the Russian language can be made to convey in a most subtle way the musical peculiarities and intricacies of the original." Sees Ivan Bunin, who has just been awarded the Nobel Prize, and speaks at meeting in his honor. *Kamera obskura* published as a book in December by Sovremennye zapiski.

1934   *Otchayanie* is serialized in *Sovremennye zapiski* (Jan.–Oct.). *La Course du fou*, translation of *Zashchita Luzhina*, is published in France. Continues working on Chernyshevsky chapter of *Dar*; writes Khodasevich that it is "monstrously difficult." Son, Dmitri Vladimirovich Nabokov, is born May 10. In June, begins anti-totalitarian novel *Priglashenie na kazn'* (later translated as *Invitation to a Beheading*), which he completes in December. Continues publishing stories in journals.

1935   Helps care for Dmitri; calls it "a mixture of hard labor and heaven." Continues publishing stories. In June, begins new chapter of *Dar*. *Priglashenie na kazn'* published serially in *Sovremennye zapiski* (June 1935–Feb. 1936). Writes in English autobiographical piece, "It Is Me" (later lost), about his English education. Contacts Gleb Struve about possibility of teaching Russian or French literature in England. Dissatisfied with Winifred Roy's translation, *Camera Obscura* (published in England by John Long in 1936), Nabokov translates *Otchayanie* into English as *Despair*, September–December.

1936   Makes successful reading tour of Brussels, Antwerp, and Paris in January and February; "Mademoiselle O," memoir in French of Cécile Miauton written for the tour, is especially well received. In Brussels, sees brother Kirill, who is studying at Louvain University. Shares a reading in Paris with Khodasevich, whom he considers the greatest contemporary Russian poet. *Otchayanie* published as book by Petropolis (Berlin) in February. Véra is fired in May from her job with an engineering firm because she is Jewish. Nabokov learns that one of his father's murderers,

Sergey Taboritsky, is deputy secretary in new Reich department of Russian emigré affairs and begins search for work in England or America. By August, begins final consecutive composition of *Dar*. Avoids government's registration of emigrés.

1937   Leaves Germany on January 18 for reading tour of Brussels, Paris, and London, planning to find employment in France or England, while Véra winds up their affairs in Berlin. Visits Kirill in Brussels. In Paris is pleased to see James Joyce in audience during a reading. Begins four-month affair with Russian emigré Irina Guadanini in February; plagued by guilt, develops severe psoriasis and comes near suicide. Goes to England late in February; gives readings in London, visits Cambridge, and unsuccessfully seeks work. Returns to France and obtains permits for him and Véra to stay there. In April *Despair* is published in London by John Long and first chapter of *Dar* appears in *Sovremennye zapiski*. Meets Sylvia Beach, Adrienne Monnier, and Henry Church. Receives free radiation treatments for psoriasis from emigré physician. Véra and Dmitri leave Germany for Prague in April to visit Nabokov's mother, who has not yet seen her grandson; Nabokov joins them in May (last time he sees mother) and on June 30 returns with them to Paris. Sells French rights to *Despair* to Gallimard, then settles with Véra and Dmitri in Cannes, where it is cheaper to live. Tells Véra of his affair with Guadanini. Cherynshevsky chapter of *Dar* is turned down by *Sovremennye zapiski* in August; Nabokov protests political censorship but, needing money, agrees to continue publishing novel in the journal (remaining chapters appear Sept. 1937–Oct. 1938). Signs contract with New York publisher Bobbs-Merrill for *Kamera obskura* and begins translating and rewriting it under title *Laughter in the Dark*. Moves with family to Menton in October; works on *Dar* and writes three-act play *Sobytie* (later translated as *The Event*) for new Russian theater in Paris.

1938   Completes *Dar* in January. *Sobytie* is successfully produced in March and appears in *Russkie zapiski* in April. *Laughter in the Dark*, published in New York by Bobbs-Merrill on April 22, receives some good reviews but does not sell well. Moves with family to Moulinet, above Menton, in July, and captures what seems to be his first new species of butterfly (after Nabokov's death it proves to be a hybrid). Redescends to Cap d'Antibes in late August where he writes play *Izobretenie Val'sa* (published by *Russkie zapiski* in November and later translated as *The Waltz Invention*). Receiving only small remuneration for his works, requests monthly support from Russian Literary Fund in the U.S.; they send him $20. *Soglyadatay* (*The Eye*), collection of 1930 novella and other stories, published by Russkie zapiski. After receiving official identity card, moves with family to Paris in October and rents small apartment at 8 rue de Saigon. Often sees friends, including Khodasevich, George Hessen, Mark Aldanov, and *Sovremennye zapiski* editors Ilya Fondaminsky and Vladimir Zenzinov. *Priglashenie na kazn'* published in book form by Dom Knigi, emigré house in Paris. Continues publishing stories in emigré papers and journals. In December begins novel in English, *The Real Life of Sebastian Knight*, completing it the following month.

1939   Asks Lucie Léon Noel to check his English in *The Real Life of Sebastian Knight*. At Paul Léon's home, meets James Joyce. Moves with family to larger apartment at 59 rue Boileau. Financially desperate without a work permit in France, travels to England in April in unsuccessful search for literary or academic work. Mother dies in Prague on May 2. Seeks work in England again in June. Khodasevich dies of cancer on June 14. Publishes "Poety" ("The Poets") over pseudonym "Vasily Shishkov" to catch out influential critic Georgy Adamovich, who has regularly condescended to Nabokov's and Khodasevich's work. Adamovich enthusiastically announces arrival of major new talent; Nabokov obliquely discloses hoax in story "Vasily Shishkov." Summers with family at Fréjus on the Riviera. Germany invades Poland on September 1 and France declares war on Germany September 3. Fearing Paris will be bombed, sends Dmitri to stay with Anna Feigin in Deauville. Fails to find publisher for *Sebastian Knight*; with no other work to sell, begins accepting 1,000 francs monthly from Samuil Kyandzhuntsev, old Tenishev friend, which he supplements by tutoring. Aldanov, who has been offered a job teaching summer course in Russian literature at Stanford University in California, recommends Nabokov in his place. Nabokov receives and accepts

Stanford offer and applies for U.S. visa. Writes novella *Volshebnik* (posthumously published as *The Enchanter*), October–November, about a man who desires a 12-year-old girl. Dmitri returns to Paris in December.

1940   Writes lectures on Russian literature over spring and summer in preparation for teaching in the U.S. Begins Russian novel, *Solus Rex* (never completed). Germans begin offensive against France and the Low Countries on May 10. With help of the Hebrew Immigrant Aid Society, given in appreciation of Nabokov's father's championing of Jews in pre-revolutionary Russia, Nabokov, Véra, and Dmitri sail for New York aboard the *Champlain*, arriving on May 27 with $600. Meets Sergei Rachmaninoff, who had twice sent him money in Europe. Unsuccessfully seeks employment and receives small grant from Russian Literary Fund. With Véra and Dmitri vacations at Vermont summer home of Harvard professor Mikhail Karpovich, then rents New York apartment at 35 West 87th Street; begins tutoring in Russian and seeking ways to bring Anna Feigin and other emigré friends to the U.S. Abandons *Solus Rex* after realizing his English prose style can develop only if he renounces composing in Russian. Through cousin Nicolas Nabokov, meets Edmund Wilson, acting literary editor of *The New Republic*, and is soon writing literary reviews for the journal; also writes reviews for New York *Sun* and *The New York Times*. Sees old friends including Roman Grynberg, Mstislav Dobuzhinsky, Aldanov, and Zenzinov, meets Max Eastman, and becomes friends with Wilson and his wife, Mary McCarthy, and Harry and Elena Levin. Receives final terms of offer from Stanford to teach Modern Russian Literature and Art of Writing in summer of 1941. Begins preparing full set of lectures on Russian literature in fall. Researches Lepidoptera at American Museum of Natural History. Receives advance from Wilson to translate Pushkin's "Mozart and Salieri" for *The New Republic* (published April 21, 1941).

1941   Tutors privately in Russian, writes two papers on Lepidoptera, and establishes himself on lecture roster of Institute of International Education. Has eight teeth extracted and dentures fitted. Receives $750 and bonus for two weeks of extremely successful lectures at Wellesley College in March. His frank anti-Sovietism particularly appeals to

Wellesley president Mildred McAfee. Begins translating Pushkin and other Russian poets in April for Stanford course. Through Wilson, meets Edmund Weeks, editor of *Atlantic Monthly*; "Cloud, Castle, Lake," translation of 1937 story "Ozero, oblako, bashnya," appears in June (the first of many Nabokov stories and poems published in *Atlantic* over next two years). Is appointed to one-year position at Wellesley College as Resident Lecturer in Comparative Literature, with salary of $3,000. In late May Dorothy Leuthold, whom Nabokov has tutored in Russian, drives Nabokov, Véra, and Dmitri to California for Stanford course. During stops Nabokov hunts butterflies and moths and on June 9 discovers new species on rim of Grand Canyon; names it *Neonympha dorothea* in Leuthold's honor. Meets Yvor Winters and Henry Lanz over summer. In July, learns that *The Real Life of Sebastian Knight* has been accepted by James Laughlin for New Directions on recommendation of reader Delmore Schwartz. Returns east by train to begin position at Wellesley College, renting house at 19 Appleby Road in Wellesley, Massachusetts. Translates three poems of Khodasevich (published in *New Directions in Prose and Poetry*) and translates Gogol, Pushkin, Lermontov, and Tyutchev for teaching. Begins traveling regularly to Harvard's Museum of Comparative Zoology in Cambridge, where he volunteers to set the Lepidoptera collection in order. Writes poem in English, "Softest of Tongues" (*Atlantic Monthly*, Dec.). *The Real Life of Sebastian Knight*, published by New Directions December 18, receives mostly good reviews but sells poorly. Begins writing a new novel (later titled *Bend Sinister*).

1942   Commissioned by New Directions to write volume of verse translations of Pushkin and Tyutchev and critical book on Gogol. Despite faculty backing and student enthusiasm, is not reappointed at Wellesley through opposition of president Mildred McAfee, who now disapproves of Nabokov's hostility toward the Soviet government (U.S. is now allied with the Soviet Union in World War II and McAfee has entered government service as head of the Women's Naval Reserve, WAVES). Appointed in June to part-time position as Research Fellow in Entomology at the Museum of Comparative Zoology for 1942–43 academic year at salary of $1,000 (over next four years will spend more time researching and writing on Lepidoptera than in writing fiction). "The Refrigerator Awakes," first of his poems published in *The New Yorker*, appears June 6. Long poem "Slava" (later translated as "Fame") published in New York emigré journal *Novy zhurnal*. Spends most of summer with Mikhail and Tatiana Karpovich in Vermont, where Nabokov works in attic for eight to ten hours a day on Gogol book. Rents apartment at 8 Craigie Circle, Cambridge, where he and his family remain until 1948; often sees Harry and Elena Levin, and Edmund Wilson and Mary McCarthy. Undertakes lecture and reading tour for Institute of International Education, traveling to colleges in South Carolina, Georgia, and Tennessee in October and in Illinois and Minnesota in November. Begins friendship with Florence Read, president of Spelman, college for black women in Atlanta. Gives Dmitri lessons in Russian grammar while Véra is hospitalized with pneumonia in December. Completes book on Gogol.

1943   Writes first story in English, "The Assistant Producer" (published *Atlantic Monthly*, May) and begins teaching noncredit course in elementary Russian at Wellesley College. Awarded Guggenheim Fellowship of $2,500 to complete new novel. Visits emigré friends in New York, including George Hessen and Anna Feigin, whom he helped bring to America; on return to Cambridge writes story "That in Aleppo Once . . . " (*Atlantic Monthly*, Nov.). Continues writing poems in Russian for *Novy zhurnal*. Dictates book tentatively titled *Gogol Through the Looking-Glass* to Véra (she types all Nabokov's works for publication) and sends it to New Directions. Travels with Véra and Dmitri to Wasatch Mountains in Utah, where he hunts butterflies and moths and captures several new species. In fall, resumes teaching noncredit course at Wellesley and receives $200 salary increase on new annual contract at Museum of Comparative Zoology (museum appointment will be renewed annually until 1948). Responding to Laughlin's complaint that the Gogol book needs more factual information, Nabokov adds a chronology. Publishes "The Nearctic Forms of *Lycaeides* Hüb." in *Psyche* (Sept.–Dec.). Has upper teeth removed and a dental plate fitted in November. Corresponds regularly with Wilson and often visits him.

1944   Persuaded by Véra to devote more time to new novel,
       soon completes four chapters under working title *The Per-
       son from Porlock* (later retitled *Bend Sinister*). Gives lecture
       on Russian literature at Yale in March and a reading at
       Cornell in May. Through Katharine White, an admirer of
       his *Atlantic* stories, signs first reading agreement with *The
       New Yorker* in June (agreement will be maintained over
       three decades); White also arranges a $500 advance, having
       been informed by Wilson that Nabokov is short of money.
       Devises system for studying butterfly markings and their
       evolution by counting rows of scales on wings, and writes
       major paper revising the neotropical Plebejinae. Vacations
       with Véra near Wilson and McCarthy in Wellfleet, Mas-
       sachusetts, and, after Dmitri returns from summer camp,
       spends August with family in Wellesley, often playing ten-
       nis with poet Jorge Guillén. *Nikolai Gogol* published by
       New Directions August 15. Writes story "Time and Ebb"
       (*Atlantic Monthly*, Jan. 1945). Dmitri enters Dexter School
       in Brookline, Massachusetts, in fall and Nabokov begins
       appointment as lecturer in Russian at Wellesley College
       on year's contract for $800 salary, teaching elementary
       Russian.

1945   Lectures at St. Timothy's College in Maryland and Smith
       College in Massachusetts. *Three Russian Poets*, verse trans-
       lations of Pushkin, Lermontov, and Tyutchev, published
       by New Directions in February. *The New Yorker* accepts
       first story from Nabokov, "Double Talk" (published July
       23), paying $817.50, the most he has ever received for a
       story. After suffering heart palpitations, gives up smoking
       on doctor's advice in spring and begins "inhaling" mo-
       lasses candies (gains 60 pounds over the summer). Na-
       bokov and Véra become American citizens on July 12.
       Begins teaching a second course, intermediate Russian, at
       Wellesley, with salary increased to $2,000. In September
       learns in a letter from Kirill, who is working as an inter-
       preter for American occupation forces in Germany and has
       traced him through *New Yorker* story, that Sergey died
       from malnutrition in a German concentration camp after
       being arrested as a "British spy" for criticizing Nazi Ger-
       many. Also hears from sister Elena Sikorski and Evgenia
       Hofeld, who is caring for nephew Rostislav Petkevich;
       sends them money and packages and seeks a way to bring
       them out of Czechoslovakia.

1946   Meets W. H. Auden; compliments him on work of Conrad Aiken, with whom he has confused him. Third course, on Russian literature in translation, is approved for the next academic year at Wellesley; anticipating its demands, Nabokov hurries to complete novel and submits it under provisional title *Solus Rex* to Allen Tate at Henry Holt in June. Suffering from exhaustion, goes with family to Newfound Lake in New Hampshire, then to town of Wellesley for August. Rereads Tolstoy and Dostoevsky in preparation for new lectures. Begins research for monograph on nearctic *Lycaeides* (completes research in spring 1947, having examined 2,000 specimens). Continues seeking a permanent job; is passed over for positions at the Voice of America, Harvard, and Vassar. Just before novel goes to printer in November, settles on title *Bend Sinister*. Earns extra money by speaking to women's clubs.

1947   Begins planning autobiography and a novel about "a man who likes little girls." Finishes first draft of *Lycaeides* monograph in May. *Bend Sinister* published June 12 to mixed reviews; since Tate has left Henry Holt, it is poorly promoted and does not sell well. Loses 20 pounds hunting butterflies and climbing with Dmitri and Véra in and around Estes Park in Colorado during summer. Writes autobiographical essay "Portrait of My Uncle" (*The New Yorker*, Jan. 3, 1948). Dmitri begins at St. Mark's boarding school in Southborough, Massachusetts, in fall. Nabokov resumes work at Museum of Comparative Zoology and Wellesley on new annual contracts. Receives offer of a permanent position teaching Russian literature at Cornell University at $5,000 salary, which he accepts after Wellesley refuses him a permanent appointment. Helps obtain position for Elena Sikorski at United Nations library in Geneva; continues sending money to Hofeld and Rostislav and writes affidavit in unsuccessful attempt to bring Rostislav to America. *Nine Stories* published by New Directions in December.

1948   Story "Signs and Symbols" published with minor editorial intervention by *The New Yorker* (May 15) after Nabokov tells Katharine White planned alterations are unnecessary and in some cases "murderous." Seriously ill throughout spring from broken blood vessel in lung. Véra reads his lectures at Wellesley and takes students through final exams while Nabokov writes in bed three additional chapters of autobiography (published in *The New Yorker* July 1948–Jan. 1949). Completes "The Nearctic Members of the Genus *Lycaeides Hübner*" in June (published as whole issue of *Bulletin of the Museum of Comparative Zoology*, Feb. 1949). Moves to Ithaca, New York, in July and settles with Véra and Dmitri into furnished house at 802 East Seneca Street. Still convalescing, prepares lectures and completes "First Poem" chapter of autobiography (published in *Partisan Review*, Sept. 1949). Becomes close friend of Morris Bishop, who initiated job offer from Cornell. Dmitri enters Holderness School in New Hampshire, with tuition costing about a third of Nabokov's salary. Buys eight-year-old Plymouth that Véra drives (Nabokov never learns to drive) and takes in lodger to help pay rent. Teaches two surveys of Russian literature (one in Russian). Translates medieval heroic poem *Slovo o polku Igoreve* (*The Song of Igor's Campaign*) for classes. Véra acts as his teaching assistant, drives him to school, continues typing up his writing, and begins conducting most of his business correspondence in her own name.

1949   Teaches seminar, Russian Poetry 1870–1925, in spring term, holding classes in his home, in addition to the two survey courses. Writes two more chapters of autobiography. Publishes negative review of Sartre's *La Nausée* and its English translation in *The New York Times Book Review*. Drives with Véra in May to New York City for reading from his Russian works and visits with emigré friends and relatives. Travels west in summer in newly purchased 1946 Oldsmobile. Conducts classes at University of Utah Writers' Workshop in July, where he enjoys company of Wallace Stegner and son Page, Theodore Geisel ("Dr. Seuss"), Martha Foley, and John Crowe Ransom. Hunts butterflies in Utah and Wyoming with Véra. Returns to Cornell where he teaches Russian literature surveys and seminar on Pushkin. Katharine and E. B. White visit in October. Submits "Student Days" chapter of autobiography to *The New Yorker*; cannot agree to changes suggested by White and withdraws it (published as "Lodgings in Trinity Lane," *Harper's Magazine*, Jan. 1951).

1950   Needing money, lectures at University of Toronto for $150 during semester break. Meets Harold Ross at *New Yorker* party in March and sees Edmund Wilson for first time since Wilson went to Europe in 1948. Hospitalized in April for two weeks with severe pain, eventually determined to be from intercostal neuralgia; has relapse and is unwell until May. Véra conducts classes during his absences. Finishes autobiography, *Conclusive Evidence*, in May and in June has his remaining six teeth extracted in Boston; while returning to Ithaca with Véra, captures specimens of rare *Lycaeides melissa samuelis*, which he had been the first to classify. Under pressure to teach larger classes, spends summer writing lectures for new Masterpieces of European Fiction course on Austen, Dickens, Flaubert, Tolstoy, Stevenson, Proust, Kafka, and Joyce. Begins novel under title *The Kingdom by the Sea* (later, *Lolita*). Dissatisfied, decides to burn the manuscript but is dissuaded by Véra.

1951   *Conclusive Evidence*, published in February by Harper and Brothers, receives excellent reviews but sells poorly (book is published in England as *Speak, Memory*). Receives National Institute of Arts and Letters award of $1,000 at ceremony in New York City on May 25. Dmitri is accepted by Harvard without scholarship. Nabokov borrows $1,000 from emigré friend Roman Grynberg, explaining: "I can't write stories for money . . . and something else has me, a novel . . ." He and Véra sell their furniture and piano and move out of rented house before going west for summer. Works on *Lolita* in car and motels; catches first female of *Lycaeides argyrognomon sublivens* in Telluride, Colorado, where Dmitri joins them, then hunts butterflies in Wyoming and Montana. Moves with Véra into a professor's home for fall semester at Cornell (will live in homes of absent professors throughout remaining time there). Does research on schoolgirls for *Lolita*. Suffers from severe insomnia while writing story "The Lance" (*The New Yorker*, Feb. 2, 1952). Reads and lectures at Nabokov evening staged by Russian emigré community in New York City.

1952   As visiting lecturer for second semester at Harvard, teaches courses on Russian modernism, on Pushkin, and on the novel, including *Don Quixote*. With Véra, often sees Dmitri, Harry and Elena Levin, Alice and William James (son of the philosopher), and old Wellesley friends, as well as

Edmund Wilson and his fourth wife, Elena. Meets Richard Wilbur and May Sarton. Reads in Morris Gray Poetry Series; gives reading at Wellesley and lectures on Gogol at Dartmouth. In April, *Dar (The Gift)* is published for the first time complete by Chekhov, Russian publishing house in New York. Agrees to do a Russian version of *Conclusive Evidence* for Chekhov and receives $1,500 advance. Receives second Guggenheim award, which he plans to use to write an annotated literal translation of Pushkin's *Evgeniy Onegin*. Goes to Wyoming with Véra to hunt butterflies in summer. Resumes Cornell teaching in fall and works on *Lolita*.

1953   Takes unpaid semester's leave from Cornell to do research for his *Eugene Onegin* in Cambridge. Hunts butterflies with Véra in Arizona in spring and Oregon in summer; writes story about Professor Pnin as first installment of novel he can publish as sketches (four chapters are published in *The New Yorker* April 23, 1953–Nov. 12, 1955). Chiefly through efforts of Morris Bishop, Nabokov's Cornell salary is increased to $6,000 in fall. Completes *Lolita* on December 6 and while in New York to record talk for BBC on translation gives typescript to Pascal Covici of Viking. Plans to have the novel published anonymously to avoid scandal that would endanger his position at Cornell.

1954   Viking turns down *Lolita* for fear of prosecution. Second chapter of *Pnin* is rejected by *The New Yorker* as "unpleasant." In February and March, rushes to complete *Drugie berega (Other Shores)*, expanded and revised Russian translation of autobiography (published by Chekhov). Records reading in New York for BBC program and lectures for three days at University of Kansas. During summer in New Mexico with Véra and Dmitri, works on notes (never completed) for projected Simon and Schuster edition of *Anna Karenina*. Simon and Schuster rejects *Lolita* in July as "pure pornography." Returns to Cornell and works intensely on *Eugene Onegin*. Gives paper, "Problems of Translation: *Onegin* in English" (published in *Partisan Review*, Autumn 1955), at English Institute conference at Columbia University. Sends *Lolita* manuscript to Edmund Wilson, who reads half of it and responds that he likes it less than anything of Nabokov's that he has read (Nabokov later urges Wilson to read the whole work carefully; tells Wilson that it is "a highly moral affair"). *Lolita* is turned down by New Directions, Farrar, Straus, and in December by Doubleday, despite editor Jason Epstein's support of it. Philip Rahv of *Partisan Review* counsels Nabokov that publishing the book anonymously will destroy its best defense.

1955   Convinced that he will not find an American publisher for *Lolita*, Nabokov sends typescript to literary agent Doussia Ergaz in Paris. Maurice Girodias, founder of new Olympia Press, agrees to publish it on condition that it carry Nabokov's name. Dmitri graduates cum laude from Harvard and enrolls in Longy School of Music in Cambridge, where he concentrates on singing. Epstein visits in June and arranges for Nabokov and Dmitri to translate Lermontov's *Geroy nashego vremeni* (*A Hero of Our Time*) and for Nabokov to translate *Anna Karenina* (his translation is never completed). Nabokov is hospitalized for eight days during summer with attack of lumbago. *Lolita* is published in Paris in September in Olympia's Traveler's Edition, a line consisting mostly of pornographic books aimed at English-speaking tourist market. Nabokov receives copies of the book in October and discovers that copyright has been assigned to Olympia Press as well as to him. Pnin novel, provisionally titled *My Poor Pnin*, is rejected as too short by Viking and then by Harper and Brothers. Nabokov is distressed when Katharine White moves from editorial to general policy department at *The New Yorker*. Graham Greene names *Lolita* one of the three best books of 1955 in London *Sunday Times* Christmas issue.

1956   On sabbatical for spring semester, conducts final research for *Eugene Onegin* in Cambridge. Meets John Dos Passos. Scandal begins to break around *Lolita* when John Gordon attacks Greene for praising it and denounces the novel as "Sheer unrestrained pornography" in the London *Sunday Express*. After *The New York Times Book Review* reports on the dispute and cites letters praising the quality of *Lolita*, Nabokov receives offers for rights from several American publishers. *Vesna v Fial'te i drugie rasskazy* (*Spring in Fialta and Other Stories*) published by Chekhov in March. Nabokov records reading from his *Eugene Onegin* for BBC. In June U.S. Customs seizes, and then releases, copies of *Lolita* (it will do so again in November). Travels with Véra to Utah, Wyoming, Montana, Minnesota, and Michigan, hunting butterflies and working on translation, *A Hero of Our Time*. In New York in October discusses with Epstein, Fred Dupee, and Melvin Lasky, editor of *Anchor Review*, plans to publish excerpts from *Lolita* in the magazine to test public reaction to it. Writes afterword, "On a Book Entitled *Lolita*." The French Ministry of Interior bans *Lolita* and 24 other Olympia titles in December and Girodias sues to have the ban lifted (he wins the case in January 1958).

1957   Harvard University, seeking a new Russian professor, almost appoints Nabokov; opposition to him is led by Roman Jakobson, who comments during faculty meeting: "Gentlemen, even if one allows that he is an important writer, are we next to invite an elephant to be professor of zoology?" *Pnin*, published March 7 by Doubleday to extremely favorable reviews, goes into second printing in two weeks. Begins work on novel (later *Pale Fire*) but puts it aside to complete *Eugene Onegin* and stays in Ithaca over summer. *Anchor Review* publishes nearly a third of *Lolita* in June, with Nabokov's afterword and critical commentary by Dupee. Nabokov contracts with publishers in Italy, France, Germany, and Sweden for translation rights to *Lolita*. Doubleday and then MacDowell, Obolensky, withdraw their offers for American rights when Girodias demands up to 62.5 percent of Nabokov's royalties. In December completes revisions of *Eugene Onegin*.

1958   *A Hero of Our Time* published by Doubleday in March. Hunts butterflies in Montana, Alberta, and Wyoming with Véra in summer. Hears from George Weidenfeld in England and Gallimard in France that they want to publish as many Nabokov works as possible. Putnam's works out contract for *Lolita* in March, assigning to Nabokov royalties of 7.5 percent and the same to Girodias. Published on August 18, *Lolita* sells 100,000 copies in three weeks, the fastest sales for an American novel since *Gone With the Wind*. *Nabokov's Dozen*, collection of 13 stories, published in September by Doubleday. Nabokov contracts with Harris-Kubrick Pictures in November for film rights to *Lolita* for $150,000 plus share of profits. Is awarded a year's leave of absence from Cornell, and searches for replacement so that leave can commence in February; finds novelist Herbert Gold to fill the position.

1959   Delivers last Cornell lectures on January 19. Makes first notes for "Texture of Time" (later a part of *Ada*) and stores belongings before leaving with Véra for New York City on February 24. Is interviewed by major American and English publications, meets George Weidenfeld, and sees Anna Feigin and Dmitri. Reworks translation, *Song of Igor's Campaign*, and begins preparing annotations. Hunts butterflies in Tennessee and Texas in April, then in Arizona, where he revises *Invitation to a Beheading*, Dmitri's translation of *Priglashenie na kazn'*. Asked to write *Lolita* screenplay, travels to Los Angeles with Véra in late July for discussions with director Stanley Kubrick and producer James Harris; cannot agree to changes they propose and soon rejects offer. Persuaded by Véra that the combination of teaching and writing is too burdensome for him, resigns from Cornell and sails to Europe on September 29 to visit sister Elena and brother Kirill, planning to return in a few months. Spends two weeks in Geneva with Elena, a UNESCO librarian, and Kirill, a Brussels travel agent, then goes with Véra to Paris for reception at Gallimard where Nabokov encounters Girodias, but fails to realize who he is. Gives numerous press interviews. Asks to meet Alain Robbe-Grillet, whose work he admires, and is interviewed by him. In London, meets Graham Greene and appears on *The Bookman* television show. Delivers lecture in Cambridge, then returns to London for November 6 Weidenfeld and Nicolson publication of *Lolita*, which immediately sells out. For next two months travels with Véra in Italy and Sicily; when he can elude the press, works on *Letters to Terra* project (later a part of *Ada*). Begins giving interviews in groups. Kubrick cables request that Nabokov write *Lolita* screenplay, with more artistic freedom. In Milan for reception by Mondadori, arranges audition for Dmitri with singing teacher Maestro Campogalliani. Spends Christmas holidays in San Remo, joined by Dmitri and Elena and nephew Vladimir Sikorski. Dmitri begins translating *Dar* as *The Gift*.

1960   During stay in Menton, Nabokov accepts offer of $40,000 for writing *Lolita* screenplay, plus an additional $35,000 if script is credited solely to him. Dmitri begins studying with Campogalliani. Nabokov turns down membership in the American National Institute of Arts and Letters, writing "all my thinking life I have declined to 'belong' " (will continue to reject all offers of honorary degrees and memberships). Arrives in Los Angeles with Véra in early March. Finishes screenplay July 9; told that it would take seven hours to run, produces a shorter version by September 8. Rostislav Petkevich dies in Prague of the effects of alcoholism. *Song of Igor's Campaign* published by Vintage. Nabokov hears that Dmitri has won first prize among basses in international opera competition in Italy. Returns to Europe in November to be near him, settling with Véra in Nice; works intensively on *Pale Fire* over winter.

1961   Completes *Pale Fire* poem February 11 and begins work on prose portion of novel. Attends Dmitri's operatic debut in *La Bohème* in Reggio, in which Luciano Pavarotti also debuts, then sees Dmitri in *Lucia da Lammermoor* (Nabokov and Véra try to see each of his new roles). In Stresa in May, revises Dmitri's translation of the first chapter of *Dar* (*The Gift*). Hunts butterflies in Valais, Switzerland, in August, then goes to Montreux, where he finds atmosphere conducive to writing. On advice of Peter Ustinov, who lives in the Montreux Palace Hotel, Nabokov and Véra take rooms there in October, planning to stay until spring. Completes *Pale Fire* on December 4.

1962   Corrects French translation of *Pnin* and Michael Scammell's English translation of the last four chapters of *Dar* (*The Gift*). Regularly reads New York *Herald Tribune* and American magazines and literary journals. Hears from agent Irving Lazar in February that Harris and Kubrick have extensively reworked *Lolita* screenplay. *Pale Fire* published by Putnam's in April. Sails aboard *Queen Elizabeth* with Véra for premiere of *Lolita* in New York. Sees film at screening a few days before attending opening on June 13 and praises the director and cast; conceals his disappointment that little remains of his original screenplay. Gives numerous interviews before returning to Montreux in late June. Featured in cover story in *Newsweek* (June 25) and in July hears that *Pale Fire* has made the bestseller list. Visited by former schoolmate Samuil Rosoff, whom he has not seen since 1919, and Elena. Moves with Véra into sixth-floor apartment of Montreux Palace, facing Lake

Geneva. Dmitri becomes ill with painful swelling of joints; in October, while in remission, he begins racing car in competitions. During visit by George Weidenfeld, Nabokov plans reissue of *Speak, Memory* and projected *Butterflies of Europe*, complete illustrated catalog of all species and main subspecies with notes by Nabokov on classification, habitat, and behavior. Compiles index for *Eugene Onegin*. Dmitri's illness recurs and is diagnosed as Reiter's syndrome.

1963   Dmitri is hospitalized in January and February, and again in summer. Nabokov revises *Eugene Onegin*, begins translating *Lolita* into Russian, and goes over *The Eye*, Dmitri's translation of *Soglyadatay*. Interviewed by Alvin Toffler in March for *Playboy* (published Jan. 1964). *The Gift*, translation with Michael Scammell and Dmitri of *Dar*, published in May by Putnam's; reviews stress the extent and achievement of Nabokov's work. Hunts butterflies with Véra in Valais and in Vaud, Switzerland, where they are joined by Dmitri; visitors include George Hessen, Raisa Tatarinov, Elena, Anna Feigin, and Véra's sister Sonia Slonim. Writes introduction for Time-Life reissue of *Bend Sinister* (published 1964).

1964   With Dmitri well enough to resume singing lessons in March, leaves with Véra for publication of *Eugene Onegin* in New York. Goes to Ithaca to retrieve some papers from storage and to visit with Morris Bishop. Gives reading at Harvard (his last public reading), where he meets graduate student Andrew Field. Kirill dies of a heart attack in Munich on April 16. After April 21 reception for *Eugene Onegin* (published by Bollingen in June), returns to Switzerland. Véra is hospitalized for several weeks of tests in May and has appendix removed. Makes revisions in *The Eye* for *Playboy* (published March 1965). Hunts butterflies at Valais in summer. *The Defense*, translation with Michael Scammell of *Zaschita Luzhina*, published by Putnam's in September. Works on *The Texture of Time* while awaiting British Museum's response to his queries for *Butterflies of Europe*. Resumes translating *Lolita* into Russian in December.

1965   Begins extensively revising *Despair* (1936 translation of *Otchayanie*). Composes first chess problem in years. Completes Russian translation of *Lolita*. During construction work at Montreux Palace Hotel in spring, travels with Véra to Gardone, then St. Moritz, for butterflies, taking side trip to Milan to research paintings for projected work *Butterflies in Art* (never completed). Is relieved to learn that Dmitri will give up car racing to concentrate on singing. Reads Edmund Wilson's harshly critical review of *Eugene Onegin* for *New York Review of Books* (July 15) and writes immediate response (letter appears Aug. 26); the controversy draws in writers including Anthony Burgess, Robert Lowell, and George Steiner. Unable to endure publishing uncertainties about ever-expanding *Butterflies of Europe* and finding his creative energies being drained, cancels project despite Weidenfeld's offer of a $10,000 advance. *The Eye* published by Phaedra in early fall. Interviewed and filmed by Robert Hughes in and around Montreux in September for New York Educational Television. Writes new afterword for Russian *Lolita* about difficulties of translating from English to Russian. Extensively rewrites parts of *The Waltz Invention*, Dmitri's translation of *Izobretenie Val'sa*. Over winter revises autobiography as *Speak, Memory: An Autobiography Revisited*. Agrees to allow Radio Liberty to publish some of his works for free clandestine distribution in Soviet Union, under imprint Editions Victor (they will publish *Priglashenie na kazn'* in 1966 and *Zaschita Luzhina* in 1967). In December has first detailed flash of a section of *Ada*.

1966   Completes work on *Speak, Memory*. "Nabokov's Reply," article on *Eugene Onegin* controversy, appears in *Encounter* (Feb.). Writes "*Lolita* and Mr. Girodias" (*Evergreen Review*, Feb. 1967), refutation of Girodias' "*Lolita*, Nabokov, and I" (*Evergreen Review*, Sept. 1965). Begins composing *Ada* at a rapid rate. *The Waltz Invention* published by Phaedra in February. Visited by cartoonist Saul Steinberg. Revised *Despair* published by Putnam's in May. Explores Italian galleries for butterflies in art project in spring and summer; continues working on *Ada*. Véra flies to New York to discuss Nabokov's publishing future with Putnam. Dissatisfied with Putnam's response concerning advances and advertising, Nabokov seeks another publisher. Stops work on *Ada* in November to revise *Eugene Onegin*, making translation still more literal. Extensively revises *King, Queen, Knave*, Dmitri's translation of *Korol', dama, valet* (completes revisions in March 1967).

1967 *Speak, Memory: An Autobiography Revisited* published by Putnam's in January. French court rules agreement between Olympia Press and Nabokov canceled as of December 1964. Nabokov spends April to August with Véra in northern Italy, working intensively on *Ada*; they are joined in Camogli by Dmitri and Elena, and visited by Peter Kemeny of McGraw-Hill. Russian translation of *Lolita* published by Phaedra in August. Véra flies to New York in November to settle with McGraw-Hill final details of contract for 11 books at $250,000 advance. Andrew Field, who is updating and expanding Dieter Zimmer's Nabokov bibliography for McGraw-Hill, visits in December.

1968 Visited by Irving Lazar, who discusses film rights for *Ada* and a *Lolita* musical proposed by Harold Prince, and by Alfred Appel, who goes over notes for his *Annotated Lolita* with Nabokov. Véra brings Anna Feigin, now 80 years old and ailing, from New York to live near her and Nabokov in Montreux. *King, Queen, Knave* published by McGraw-Hill in April. Nabokov agrees to Andrew Field's request to undertake his biography. Hunts butterflies in Vaud and Valais, Switzerland, from May to July. Receives from sister Olga in Prague about 150 letters he had written to his mother. Completes *Ada* in October and begins choosing and translating Russian poems for collection (later titled *Poems and Problems*).

1969 Joseph Papp stages Russell McGrath's adaptation of *Invitation to a Beheading* at New York Shakespeare Festival in March. Film rights for *Ada* are bought by Columbia for $500,000 (film is not produced). *Ada* published by McGraw-Hill on May 5 to initial critical acclaim and strong sales. Summers with Véra in Ticino and Bernese Oberland, Switzerland; enjoys visit from Carl and Ellendea Proffer, who are setting up Ardis Press to publish Russian works. Writes "Notes to Ada by Vivian Darkbloom" (published in 1970 Penguin edition in England). Gives numerous interviews to Italian journalists in Montreux for Mondadori translation of *Ada*. In October, begins writing *Transparent Things*, but makes slow progress.

1970   Completes compilation of *Poems and Problems* in January.
            Drafts notes for inclusion in *Tri-Quarterly* issue devoted
            to his work (published Winter 1970). Visits Vatican Mu-
            seum for *Butterflies in Art* project. Goes with Véra to
            Sicily in spring and Valais during summer for butterflies.
            Transparent Things "bursts into life" on June 30. Visited
            by Alan Jay Lerner to discuss musical of *Lolita*, and by
            Alfred and Nina Appel for five days in November. With
            Dmitri now singing in North and South America, Véra
            completes the translation of *Podvig* (*Glory*) while Nabokov
            revises the translations. *Mary*, translation by Nabokov with
            Michael Glenny of *Mashen'ka*, published in September by
            McGraw-Hill. Field arrives December 31 for month's stay
            in Montreux to discuss Nabokov biography.

1971   Musical *Lolita, My Love* staged unsuccessfully in Philadel-
            phia and Boston. Nabokov starts translating Russian sto-
            ries with Dmitri in spring for McGraw-Hill collections.
            Poems and Problems, collection of 39 Russian poems with
            translations, 14 English poems, and 18 chess problems,
            published by McGraw-Hill in March. Flies to Portugal
            with Véra for spring, but finds few butterflies and soon
            returns. Cuts short butterfly hunting in France in summer
            when Véra is hospitalized for reaction to antibiotics; reads
            her Solzhenitsyn's *Avgust chetyrnadtsatogo* (*August 1914*)
            while she recovers. Vacations near Gstaad with Véra, Dmi-
            tri, Anna Feigin, Elena, and Sonia Slonim in August; hunts
            butterflies and hikes with Dmitri. Receives reply to a re-
            cent letter to Wilson, first friendly exchange since their
            Eugene Onegin quarrel. Soon after, Nabokov receives copy
            of passage about him in Wilson's *Upstate* and writes letter
            to *The New York Times Book Review* (Nov. 7) refuting
            statements "on the brink of libel." After five-month pause,
            begins intensive work on *Transparent Things*. *Glory* pub-
            lished by McGraw-Hill in December.

1972   Completes *Transparent Things* on April 1; published by
            McGraw-Hill in November to mixed reviews, it sells
            poorly. In spring and summer hunts butterflies in France
            and Switzerland. Edmund Wilson dies on June 12. At re-
            quest of Edmund White, Nabokov writes article, "On In-
            spiration," for *Saturday Review of the Arts* (Jan. 6, 1973)
            Nabokov issue. Revises Dmitri's translations of stories for
            collection *Tyrants Destroyed and Other Stories*.

1973   Anna Feigin dies on January 6. Véra is hospitalized in mid-
        January with two slipped discs; Nabokov writes that the
        "feeling of distress, désarroi, utter panic and dreadful pre-
        sentiment every time V. is away in hospital, is one of the
        greatest torments of my life." In January and February
        reads and corrects manuscript of Andrew Field's *Nabokov:
        His Life in Part*, distressed by its inaccuracies. Begins writ-
        ing *Look at the Harlequins!* In April, starts translating
        stories with Dmitri for *Details of a Sunset and Other Sto-
        ries. A Russian Beauty and Other Stories*, translations with
        Simon Karlinsky and Dmitri, published by McGraw-Hill
        in April. Gives Elena a list of details to check for his *Look
        at the Harlequins!* on her summer trip to Leningrad.
        Spends June and July with Véra in Italy hunting butter-
        flies. During August and September reads and corrects
        revised manuscript of Field's biography, strongly disap-
        proving of it; beyond a letter asking him to acknowledge
        corrections, will never communicate directly with Field
        again. Learns that he has won National Medal for Liter-
        ature prize of $10,000. *Strong Opinions*, collection of
        interviews and other public prose, published by McGraw-
        Hill in November.

1974   *Lolita: A Screenplay*, published by McGraw-Hill in Feb-
        ruary, sells very poorly. Writes letter welcoming Solzhe-
        nitsyn to West after his expulsion from the Soviet Union.
        Signs new agreement with McGraw-Hill for six books over
        next four years. Goes over Edmund Wilson's letters for his
        widow, Elena, who is preparing a book on Wilson's cor-
        respondence; writes her that it is "agony" to go over the
        exchanges from the "early radiant era of our correspon-
        dence." Spends eight days revising German translation of
        Ada. Composes chess problems in April. Begins writing
        letters on behalf of Soviet dissidents. Has new novel (even-
        tually called *The Original of Laura*) "mapped out rather
        clearly for next year." Works on revisions to French edi-
        tion of *Ada* during summer butterfly expedition to Zer-
        matt, then travels on with Véra for a week with Dmitri in
        Sarnico. Visited by Viktor Nekrasov and Vladimir Maxi-
        mov. Is distressed when Solzhenitsyn fails to arrive for visit
        due to a miscommunication. *Look at the Harlequins!*
        published by McGraw-Hill in August to mixed reviews.
        Mashen'ka and *Podvig* are reissued in November by Ardis

(Ardis will republish all of Nabokov's Russian fiction over next decade).

1975   *Tyrants Destroyed and Other Stories*, translated with Dmitri, published by McGraw-Hill in January. Names J. D. Salinger, John Updike, and Edmund White as his favorite American writers in interview for *Esquire*. After completing revisions to French *Ada ou l'ardeur* in February, exhausts himself checking proofs to meet May publication deadline. Goes to Davos in June for butterflies and in late July has severe fall on mountainside. Continues to feel unwell and has tests that disclose tumor on prostate, found to be benign after October operation. Returns to writing *The Original of Laura* in December. Revised translation of *Eugene Onegin* published by Princeton University Press.

1976   Suggests that McGraw-Hill bring out a volume of the Nabokov-Wilson correspondence with Simon Karlinsky as editor (*The Nabokov-Wilson Letters, 1940–1971*, is posthumously published in 1979). *Details of a Sunset and Other Stories* published by McGraw-Hill in March to good reviews. Suffers concussion from fall on May 1 and is hospitalized for ten days. Lumbago attack forces postponement of summer butterfly excursion and an infection causes fever. Readmitted to hospital, semi-conscious, in June and remains until September, delirious much of the time, then undergoes two weeks of convalescence and physiotherapy in Valmont Clinic with Véra, who had damaged her spine attempting to support him after fall. Selects poems for collection *Stikhi* (*Poems*) for Ardis in autumn; weak, with almost no sleep, can write out little of *The Original of Laura*.

1977   Has last interview with BBC Television in February. Develops high fever during bout of influenza and is hospitalized in Lausanne from March 17 to May 7. Reenters Nestlé Hospital in Lausanne when fever returns on June 5 and is placed in intensive care on June 30 with severe bronchial congestion. Dies at 6:50 P.M. on July 2, with Véra and Dmitri at bedside. After cremation at a non-religious funeral service in Vevey attended by a dozen family members and friends, ashes are interred in Clarens cemetery on July 8.

Note on the Texts

This volume presents three novels by Vladimir Nabokov: *Ada or Ardor: A Family Chronicle* (1969), *Transparent Things* (1972), and *Look at the Harlequins!* (1974). The texts presented here incorporate revisions and corrections Nabokov noted in his own copies and, in a few instances, revisions entered with Nabokov's permission by his wife, Véra, and his son, Dmitri.

Nabokov began making notes for "The Texture of Time," a work exploring the nature of time, early in 1959, and later in the same year he also began making notes for "Letters to Terra," a novel influenced by themes from science fiction. After putting both projects aside to complete *Pale Fire* and work on *Eugene Onegin*, Nabokov resumed work on "The Texture of Time" and "Letters from Terra" in the early 1960s. However, in December 1965 Nabokov envisioned a scene in what would become *Ada* (Van Veen's visit to the ruined Villa Venus in Part II, Chapter 3), and by February 1966 he had begun intensive work on the novel, using *Ada* as the title and incorporating both "The Texture of Time" and "Letters to Terra" into it. Nabokov completed the writing of what became his longest novel in October 1968 and read galley and page proofs in January and February 1969. *Ada or Ardor: A Family Chronicle* was published in New York on May 5, 1969, by McGraw-Hill Book Company. The novel initially received good reviews and sold well. Nabokov wrote the afterword, "Notes to Ada by Vivian Darkbloom," in the autumn of 1969. The notes were published in 1970 in the English Penguin edition but were not added to any other edition in Nabokov's lifetime. The text of *Ada* printed here is that of the first McGraw-Hill printing; the text of "Notes to Ada by Vivian Darkbloom" is taken from the first Penguin printing. Both texts incorporate revisions and corrections made in Nabokov's own copies.

Nabokov began writing *Transparent Things* early in October 1969 but soon put it aside because of the demands of other projects. He returned to the novel in 1970 and worked on it intermittently until November 1971, when he began a sustained period of composition that continued until the completion of the manuscript on April 1, 1972. *Transparent Things* was published in New York by McGraw-Hill International in November 1972. The text printed here incorporates revisions and corrections made in Nabokov's own copies, some of which were entered with his permission by Véra and Dmitri Nabokov.

Nabokov began writing *Look at the Harlequins!* in February 1973 and completed the work in early April 1974. He read proofs during June and July, and the book was published in New York by McGraw-Hill Book Company in the fall of 1974. The text printed here is that of the first edition, incorporating the revisions and corrections marked by Nabokov in his own copies.

This volume presents the texts of the original printings chosen for inclusion here, but it does not attempt to reproduce features of their typographic design, such as display capitalization of chapter openings. The texts are printed without change, except for the correction of typographical errors and the incorporation of revisions and corrections made by Nabokov and his family in his own copies. Spelling, punctuation, and capitalization are often expressive features, and they are not altered, even when inconsistent or irregular.

The following three lists record by page and line number revisions and corrections (other than corrections of typographical errors) incorporated into the text of this volume; in each case the reading of the present text comes first, followed by that of the first edition.

Ada
20.14–15, Durmanov] Veen   97.23, Speke] Stanley   109.9, clean-living] clean-leaving   129.31, If . . . the] If the   302.37, *du monde*] *au monde*   407.29, when an] than an   413.4, (forget it, what's] what's

Transparent Things
491.25, (but too] and too   491.25, group),] group,   529.4–5, for instance] such as   535.23, does, after all,] after all   535.23, have claims] has certain claims   551.3, it glided] glided   560.6–7, being driven] driven

Look at the Harlequins!
571.5, confirmed] confined   725.16, *sharlatany*] *sharlatanchi*

The following is a list of typographical errors corrected, cited by page and line number: 8.26, down; 10.27, indentified; 11.28, great-grandmother.; 12.2, this; 19.8, extending,; 21.22, shows; 23.30, expensive,; 24.21, ardor—to; 24.33, *yami*; 34.16, parasol;; 41.28, dinner over; 53.5, secretely; 58.4, lirodendron; 66.2–3, arrived to; 73.5, *faire*)"; 77.5, isn't?"; 85.13, almost,; 91.32, arrived to; 92.18, *apofeos*; 93.4, "*Eshcho*; 108.35, even; 109.5, ten-year old; 113.40, dark,; 127.35, *xlic*; 130.21, line,"; 145.29, womens'; 152.22–23, downstairs.; 153.36, arcobatics; 156.37–38, "obmanipulations'; 165.9, She; 168.14, foliage; 173.22, palor; 178.2, of raising; 178.8, carved,; 180.16, but the; 180.30, ORHIDEYA; 195.20, Lowden).; 195.21, Demon; 201.31, Praslin's; 207.28, *gout*;

207.29, politicians; 223.29, *asssez*; 234.18, T'is; 250.26, of his; 266.15, of having; 273.10, mirages,; 273.11, terrace,; 294.34–35, much-to say; 308.29, children; 312.24, libelulla . . . ulla; 314.7, taps,; 322.26, daughter); 334.29, Ada,; 337.38, follows;; 344.5, "Permanent"; 345.40, informed of:; 347.22, P.M.; 347.24, Avenue,; 351.36, *affascinati*; 361.15, stayed); 374.9, tone.; 375.5, make; 382.1, *konskie*; 386.40, Van,; 398.18–19, pokonchila soboy; 411.13, hour; 412.5, 1893; 412.26, marks; 412.27, hand; 418.7, presence).; 418.18, "*I* . . . grubs!"; 419.24, wondered; 420.26, path; 420.27, staunchily; 421.9, *neopravdanny a*; 431.17, temper,; 439.22, Synesthetia; 451.10, positions'; 453.18–19, to sleep; 457.22, Time).; 459.2, detumify; 467.29, Vineland-born; 468.23, described; 469.22, Phineas; 470.26, braques; 470.40, Joe's; 474.31, *vendage*; 476.5, to done; 476.41, *qui dis-je*; 477.5, is dangerous; 477.35, *Klubsessel* . . . ; 477.36–38, By chance . . . ; 479.7, *ne sais*; 479.15, *marais noir*; 480.35, *coigner*; 568.24, "brillant; 569.26, and,; 572.10, *kotishsya*; 572.18, lees; 578.4, WC; 585.21, abreast,; 585.37, said; 587.4, New; 593.26–27, recolections; 593.30, if; 632.22, tourch; 632.25, appeal; 634.37, be ginning; 634.39, ledger; 636.25, *oskandalisya*; 643.32, Ivanova; 648.36, Blagovo; 651.34, marked . . . whatever [duplication of two lines at 652.2–3]; 654.20, rasing; 659.9, snork'; 659.14, think,; 687.18, Duchess' "; 690.22, latter; 692.20, 'A; 693.17, daughter.; 696.24, perfoms; 702.39, childrens'; 732.35, meet my; 736.12–13, centimers; 742.33–34, over such.

Notes

In the notes below, the reference numbers denote page and line of this volume (the line count includes titles and headings). No note is made for material included in standard desk-reference books such as Webster's *Collegiate*, *Biographical*, and *Geographical* dictionaries. Quotations from Shakespeare are keyed to *The Riverside Shakespeare*, ed. G. Blakemore Evans (Boston: Houghton Mifflin, 1974). For further background and references to other studies, see Brian Boyd, *Vladimir Nabokov, The Russian Years* and *Vladimir Nabokov, The American Years* (Princeton: Princeton University Press, 1990 and 1991), *The Nabokov-Wilson Letters, 1940–1971*, ed. Simon Karlinsky (New York: Harper & Row, Publishers, 1979); *Vladimir Nabokov: Selected Letters, 1940–1977*, ed. Dmitri Nabokov and Matthew J. Bruccoli (San Diego and New York: Harcourt, Brace, Jovanovich / Bruccoli Clark Layman, 1989); Vladimir Nabokov, *Strong Opinions* (New York: McGraw-Hill Book Company, 1973); Bobbie Ann Mason, *Nabokov's Garden: A Guide to Ada* (Ann Arbor: Ardis, 1974); Brian Boyd, *Nabokov's Ada: The Place of Consciousness* (Ann Arbor: Ardis, 1985); and Brian Boyd's chapter-by-chapter notes in the ongoing series "Annotations to *Ada*" in *The Nabokovian* (1993–).

The publishers thank Dmitri Nabokov for his cooperation and assistance in the preparation of this volume and Glenn Horowitz for generous access to Vladimir Nabokov's personal copies of his books.

ADA
The "Notes to Ada by Vivian Darkbloom," written by Nabokov in 1969, are on pp. 469–85 in this volume.

7.6   transfigured . . . R. G. Stonelower] Cf. critic George Steiner, "To Traduce or to Transfigure: On Modern Verse Translation" (*Encounter*, Aug. 1966); see Darkbloom note.

7.10   *Detstvo i Otrochestvo* (*Childhood and Fatherland*)] Leo Tolstoy's autobiographical novellas are *Detstvo*, *Otrochestvo*, and *Iunost* (*Childhood*, *Boyhood*, and *Youth*, 1852–57). "Fatherland" is *Otechestvo* in Russian.

7.21   Estoty] Also Estotiland, name used in the 16th and 17th centuries for northeast Labrador.

10.33–34   *en regard*] On the opposite page.

11.15   *Compliquaria compliquata*] Complications complicated.

13.12–14   trashy ephemeron . . . famous Russian romance]   A garbling of Aleksandr Pushkin's novel in verse, *Eugene Onegin* (1823–31), on which Tchaikovsky's opera is based (see Darkbloom note to p. 408).

13.17   *cabinet reculé*]   Back room.

14.12   sharovars]   See Darkbloom. *Sharovary* are wide trousers.

14.17   *kurva* or "ribbon boule"]   See Darkbloom; Robert Lowell rendered *kurvu-Moskvu* ("Moscow the Whore") as "Moscow's ribbon of boulevards" in his translation of "Net, ne spriatatsia mne ot velikoi mury" ("No, I won't hide behind the great nonsense"; 1931) in *The New York Review of Books*.

15.36–37   "Eugene and Lara" or "Lenore Raven"]   Cf. Pushkin's *Eugene Onegin* (in which Larina is the surname of the sisters Tatiana and Olga) and Edgar Allan Poe's poems "Lenore" (1831) and "The Raven" (1845).

16.11   *dackel*]   Dachshund.

17.4   Douglas d'Artagnan]   Douglas Fairbanks played d'Artagnan in the 1921 movie *The Three Musketeers*.

18.4   Lolita, Texas]   See Darkbloom note; still the name of the small town between Houston and Corpus Christi.

19.26   *bien rangés*]   Well-ordered, steady.

22.32   *garçonnière*]   Bachelor apartment.

23.9   *appenzeller*]   Breed of mountain dog from Appenzell canton, Switzerland, a black and tan short-haired mastiff.

24.5   my lad . . . pity]   See Darkbloom; cf. *A Shropshire Lad* (1896), poem V ("Oh see how thick the goldcup flowers"), line 31.

24.6   *flou*]   Fuzzy, woolly, hazy.

24.13–15   in Florence . . . St. Zeus]   The story of the elm is in the legend of Zenobius, a 5th-century bishop of Florence. The Colonna di San Zanobi, a speckled marble pillar, was erected in 1330 opposite the Battistero to commemorate the removal of the saint's relics to the Duomo.

26.6   Sex Rouge]   Mountain in the Swiss canton of the Valais.

26.13   *hier geld*]   Here money.

26.40   dracunculi]   Little dragons.

27.31–35   purple pill . . . hunting season.]   Cf. *Lolita*, Pt. I, ch. 27.

28.33   landparty]   German, "excursion, country outing."

29.7   *Princesse Lointaine*]   See Darkbloom; play (1895) by Edmond Rostand.

30.39–40   Bronzino's Cupid . . . bower)]   *Venus, Satyr and Cupid* (1550–55).

38.37   Pavel . . . Paul-minus-Peter]   Tsar Pavel I (1754–1801) was rumored to be the son of Catherine the Great by someone other than her husband, the grand duke Peter.

39.11   ("*mimo, chitatel'*,"]   In Turgenev's novel *Dym* (*Smoke*; 1867), ch. 19: "Strashnaya, temnaya istoriya . . . Mimo, chitatel' mimo!" ("A dark, terrible story . . . Past, reader, get past!")

41.6–7   *nature morte* by Juan de Labrador]   Juan Fernandez "el Labrador," also known as Juan Labrador (d. circa 1600), Spanish still-life (*nature morte*) painter.

41.23   anatomical term . . . middle]   *Ojo* means "eye," *cojon* means "testicle."

42.11   *klubnika*]   Hautbois or green strawberries.

43.4   "soubret . . . frissonnet frill"]   *Soubret*, "coy, reserved"; *soubrette*, "coquettish maidservant"; *frisson*, "emotional thrill, shiver."

43.20   "Cendrillon"]   Cinderella.

44.25   stamnos]   Wide-mouthed vase with handles set horizontally on the shoulders.

45.13   *rond-point*]   Meeting-point of two or more paths.

47.25–26   Joyce's . . . washerwomen?]   I.viii, the "Anna Livia Plurabelle" section of James Joyce's *Finnegans Wake* (1939).

49.19–20   Cattleya . . . Proust)]   In Proust's *Un Amour de Swann* in *A la recherche du temps perdu*, the cattleya (a tropical American orchid) is the favorite flower of Swann's mistress Odette and *faire cattleya* (to do a cattleya) becomes their private term for love-making.

50.5   *Nymphalis carmen*]   An invented nymphalid of the genus *Nymphalis*. In *Lolita*, "Carmen" was Humbert's pet name for Lolita.

50.8–10   Odettian . . . guermantoid]   Odette (see note 49.19–20) becomes by the end of *A la recherche du temps perdu* the mistress of the Duc de Guermantes.

50.12–14   *Antocharis* . . . *A. prittwitzi* Stümper]   Invented butterfly of the genus *Antocharis*, the Orange-tips. Max von Prittwitz commanded the German Eighth Army in East Prussia in August 1914. After suffering a minor defeat on August 20, von Prittwitz panicked and was relieved of his command; under new leadership, the Eighth Army decisively defeated two Russian invading armies. Stümper means "bungler."

53.9–10   Bourget's "*monologue intérieur*"]   Bourget introduced the term in his novel *Cosmopolis* (1893).

53.12   Lyovin]   A nobleman who sometimes works in the fields with his peasants in *Anna Karenina*.

55.17   "*Je vous . . . enfants!*"]   Please, children!

57.4   *à neuf ans*]   At nine years old.

57.4   Gilberte Swann]   Gilberte is the young girl with whom Marcel, the narrator of Proust's *A la recherche du temps perdu*, falls in love as a boy.

58.4   imperialis]   Paulownia.

58.12   oystering]   Dutch *Oosters*, "Eastern, Oriental."

59.33   *tout ceci, vsyo eto*]   All this (in French and Russian).

61.13–14   lampad]   Lamp or candlestick, usually only with reference to the seven lamps of fire in Revelation 4:5.

61.40   lucifers]   The lucifer hummingbird, *Calothora lucifer*, of southwestern North America, bronze-green and fork-tailed.

62.11   orchal]   Of the testicles.

64.9   wick]   Corner, especially of eye or mouth.

64.18   *jour de fête*]   Birthday.

65.6   Shattal]   Nabokov noted in his own copy of *Ada*: "invented = Eden = Tigris & Euphrates." The Tigris and Euphrates are traditionally associated with Eden; they join to form the Shatt-al-Arab channel in southeast Iraq.

68.23   burn]   Brook or rivulet.

68.32   Tarentine sail]   In Nabokov's own copy, glossed "brown sail." Tarentum (now Taranto) was a Greek city of ancient Italy.

68.35   bilboquet]   Cup-and-ball (a toy).

70.15   Jew's eye]   Something of infinitely great value (from the torture used to extort money from Jews in the time of King John).

70.33   Cyrillitsa]   Russian, "Cyrillic alphabet."

71.36   Parnassian]   Butterfly of the genus *Parnassius*.

75.3   *arrière*]   Great-.

75.27   *taksik*]   Little dachshund.

75.33   Barabbits]   In Nabokov's own copy of *Ada*, glossed "follower of Barabbas."

76.12   Ségur's]   Anatole-Henri-Philippe Ségur wrote *Fables* (1848); he was the second son of Sophie Rostopchine, Comtesse de Ségur (1799–1874), author of French children's novels.

76.14   monologue . . . king]   *King Lear*, V.iii.309: "Never, never, never, never, never."

76.23   *energichno*]   Energetically.

76.30   sullow]   Plough (now only dialect).

77.21   skybab]   In Nabokov's own copy of *Ada*: "Kaibab (in Arizona)." The Kaibab Plateau is in Grand Canyon National Park.

78.15   *l'ardeur . . . canicule*]   The heat of the dog days.

80.14   ardilla]   Spanish, "squirrel."

80.28   *avournine*]   Anglo-Irish, "sweetheart."

81.30   *ensellure*]   French, "curve of the back."

83.3   *Ophrys*]   Genus of insect-mimicking orchids, which are fertilized when male insects attempt to copulate with the flowers. The species names are invented.

86.35–39   *Mon enfant . . . douceur*]   See Darkbloom. Chateaubriand's "Romance à Hélène" (c. 1802) includes the lines (13–14, 25–26): "Ma soeur, te souvient-il encore / Du château que baignait la Dore . . . Oh! qui me rendra mon Hélène, / Et ma montagne, et le grand chêne" ("My sister, do you still recall / The castle that the Dore bathed . . . Oh! who will give me back my Helene, / And my mountain, and the great oak"); Baudelaire's "L'Invitation au voyage" (1855) begins, "Mon enfant, ma soeur, / Songe à la douceur / D'aller là-bas vivre ensemble!" ("My child, my sister, / Think of the sweetness / Of going there to live together!").

88.25   codetta]   A short connecting link between the pairs of entries of the theme in the exposition of a fugue.

90.25–26   Marmoreal Guest . . . ghost]   From Pushkin's *Kamennyy gost* (1830; *The Stone Guest*), a verse-drama adaptation of the end of the *Don Juan* story: the arrival of the marble statue of Donna Anna's dead husband frightens Don Juan to death.

93.37   telegas]   Russian wagons, four-wheeled, rude, and springless.

94.16   Rob Roy]   A kind of short, light, flat-decked canoe for river cruising.

94.25   break]   A four-wheeled, straight-body, high-swung pleasure carriage, usually accommodating six or more persons besides the driver and footman.

94.31   ignicolists]   Fire-worshippers.

95.25   "Tartuffe"]   The villain in Molière's play of that title (1664).

97.23   Nile . . . Speke]   See Darkbloom; John Speke (1827–64) telegraphed the Royal Geographic Society in 1862 after his visit to the point where the White Nile flows out of Lake Victoria: "Inform Sir Roderick Murchison that all is well, and that the Nile is settled." Speke first reached the lake in 1858, but his claim that it was the source of the Nile had been disputed.

97.32–33   Think and dream . . . in French]   *Songer* (verb).

97.33–35   *douceur . . . rhyme*]   See note 86.35–39 and Darkbloom note to p. 86.

101.12   "*midinette*"]   Parisian shop-girl.

103.18–21   Their fall . . . blood.]   Cf. *Matin d'Octobre* ("October Morning"; 1874), second quatrain. (Lines 3–4 of the sonnet are accurately translated; lines 1–2 literally translate: "Their fall is slow. One can follow them / With the gaze, recognizing.")

106.16–17   Shastras . . . Nefsawis]   Nabokov noted in his own copy of *Ada*: "erotic works: Kama Shastra (or sutra) and Nefsawi (or Nefzawi)." Richard Burton (1821–90) formed the Kama Shastra Society of London and Benares, which from 1883 to 1888 issued English translations of Indian and Arabic erotic classics including the treatise *Kama Sutra of Vatsyayana* (1883; transl. by Burton and Foster Arbuthnot) and *The Perfumed Garden of the Sheik Nefzaoui or the Arab Art of Love, sixteenth century* (transl. from a French version by Burton; 1886). Sanskrit *Kama* means "love, pleasure, sensual gratification" and *Shastra*, "scripture, doctrines."

106.38   breloque]   Charm (for watches or bracelets); trinket.

107.18   bubas]   Buba, "yaws."

107.26   lepidosis]   Any scaly skin disease, such as ichthyosis or psoriasis.

108.1   *donc*]   Therefore.

109.36–38   Begouri . . . footnote]   A footnote by Burton in *The Perfumed Garden* (see note 106.16–17) reads: "In vulgar Arabic, this manner of enjoying a woman is called *begouri*, that is to say, after the fashion of a bull."

112.6–7   *Ma soeur . . . la Dore?*]   See Darkbloom and note 86.35–39.

113.23   Brantôme]   A village in France and the name of Pierre de Bourdeilles, Seigneur de Brantôme (c. 1540–1614), whose "le fruit de l'amour mondain n'est autre chose que la jouissance" (*Receuil des Dames* Pt. II, Discours II; "the fruit of worldly love is nothing other than orgasm") Nabokov quotes in *Eugene Onegin* (commentary to IV.v.8).

116.25   exactly twenty-eight]   Degrees Réaumur (95 degrees F.).

118.13   finding . . . plain]   Robert Browning, "Memorabilia" (1855), lines 1–2, 13–15: "Ah, did you once see Shelley plain, / And did he stop and speak to you"; "For there I picked up on the heather / And there I put inside my breast / A moulted feather, an eagle-feather! / Well, I forget the rest."

119.1–8   "Here, said the guide . . . side."] Nabokov wrote to Bobbie Ann Mason: "The poem *Peter and Margaret* is of course Nabokov's own composition . . . it is a stylized glimpse of a mysterious person visiting the place, open to tourists, where in legendary times (legendary in Antiterra terms) a certain Peter T. had his last interview with the Queen's sister. Although he accuses the old guide of being a ghost, it is he, in the reversal of time, who is a ghostly tourist, the ghost of Peter T. himself." In 1955 Princess Margaret, sister of Queen Elizabeth II, was prevented from marrying R.A.F Group Captain Peter Townsend (1915–95) because he was divorced.

119.22   "*minirechi*"] Russian *rechi*, "speeches."

121.11   camel driver—shamoes] Pun on French *chameaux*, "camels," and shamoes as a variant form of chamois.

124.7   Leman Lake] French name for Lake Geneva.

126.5–6   cedrat] Citron.

126.22   dalk] Cavity or depression in the ground.

127.11–12   The winds . . . *désert*—"] Cf. the Abbé Jacques Delille (1738–1813), *Les Trois Règnes de la Nature* (*The Three Natural Kingdoms*, 1808), V: "Tel un sauvage lis, / Confiant au désert le parfum qu'il exhale, / Cache aux vents indiscrets sa beauté virginale" ("Thus a wild lily, / Entrusting to the wilderness the perfume it exhales, / Hides its virginal beauty from the indiscreet winds").

128.3–4   Kuznetsova . . . *Onegin and Olga*] Russian soprano Maria Kuznetsova (1880–1966) played Tatiana (Olga is Tatiana's sister) in the opera *Eugene Onegin* by Tchaikovsky (the correct transliteration would be "Chaykovsky" or "Chaikovsky"); see also Darkbloom note to p. 408.

128.9   *Nymphalis danaus* Nab.] An invented species in the real genus *Nymphalis*. The viceroy is the American nymphalid *Limenitis archippus*, which mimics the monarch, *Danaus plexippus*.

132.19–26   Tiltil . . . Louis Pierre] Tyltyl and Mytyl, her brother, are characters in Maeterlinck's fairy play *L'Oiseau bleu* (*The Blue Bird*; 1909). Mytilene is another name for the island of Lesbos, the home of the Greek poet Sappho (c. 610–580 B.C.). French novelist and poet Pierre Louÿs (1871–1925) published *Chansons de Bilitis* (1894), prose poems about Sapphic love purported to be translations from the Greek.

132.27   "garbotosh"] Cf. Greta Garbo.

133.16   la Rousse] *La rousse*, "the redhead"; *Larousse* is a popular French dictionary.

135.30   *amour-propre* . . . *sale amour.*] See Darkbloom; *amour-propre* means "self-love," but *amour propre* could mean "clean love"; *sale* means "dirty."

136.30   "tonic bar"] In his copy of *Ada*, Nabokov noted: "soft drinks only."

138.2   volitations] Flights.

138.24   *shuler's*] Russian *shuler*, "cheat, card sharper."

141.20–22   Russian . . . minus the umlaut] See note 138.24; German *Schüler* (schoolboy).

141.32–33   Rosy aurora . . . Laborious old Chose] See Darkbloom; "Le Crépuscule du matin" ("Morning Twilight"; 1852), lines 25–28: "Dawn shivering in pink and green dress / Was advancing slowly over the deserted Seine, / And somber Paris, rubbing his eyes, / Grasped his tools, industrious old man."

143.19   drew only gee-gees] *Dada* means in French hobby-horse, from the children's word *dia dia* (English gee gee, "horse").

145.4–8   *The Ranter . . .* Rantariver] Cf. *Granta*, Cambridge University magazine founded 1894 and named after the River Granta (another name for the Cam).

146.15   "ondulas"] Little waves.

147.11   *burka*] A coarse cloak worn especially in Russia.

148.37   Karaite from Chufut Kale] Schismatic Jewish sect that was centered in the 15th to 18th centuries in the now-ruined Crimean town of Chufut Kale.

156.6   "Bilitis,"] See note 132.19–26.

156.37–38   'obmanipulations'] Russian *obman*, "deception."

157.16–17   a certain Venetian] Giovanni Casanova.

157.28   dorean] Made of dorean, a striped Indian muslin. In Nabokov's own copy of *Ada*, glossed as "golden silk."

159.6   Silesian river] Oder.

160.21   raccommodated] French and Italian *raccommodare*, "to mend."

160.34–35   *zucchero*] Italian, "sugar."

165.28   nuque] Nape.

167.16   cochlea] Winding stair.

168.14   *raimée*] *Ramée* means "green foliage," *raimée*, "woman loved again."

172.16–17   Babylonian willows] The weeping willow *Salyx babylonica*.

173.3   Scheher . . . his Ada] Cf. Shahryar and Scheherazade, his storyteller, intended victim, and ultimate bride in *The Thousand and One Nights*.

174.36   "winslow"]   In Nabokov's own copy of *Ada*, glossed as "caress."

177.20   Baron Klim Avidov]   Anagram of "Vladimir Nabokov."

177.20–21   saffian]   A leather made of goat- or sheepskin tanned with sumac and brightly dyed.

177.24   Jurojin]   In Japan, one of the Seven Gods of Luck.

177.40–178.1   Minsk-born Pat Rishin . . . Wilson]   See Darkbloom; Norman Podhoretz, "Edmund Wilson, the last patrician" (*The Reporter*, Dec. 25, 1958, Jan. 8, 1959). During the dispute over Nabokov's *Eugene Onegin* translation, Wilson wrote (*New York Review of Books*, Aug. 26, 1965): "I have heard Mr. Nabokov insist on the superiority of the Petersburg pronunciation to that of Moscow, and am rather surprised to find him recommending the pronunciation of Minsk." Cf. the passage concerning Minsk and chess in ch. 6 of *Speak, Memory*, p. 472 in *Novels and Memoirs 1941–1951* (Library of America, 1996).

178.8   Lalla Rookh]   Cf. Thomas Moore's *Lalla Rookh: an Oriental Romance* (1817), verse tales connected by a prose story. The "Lalla Rookh" theme was fashionable in Russia in the early 19th century.

179.5   Ozhegov]   S. I. Ozhegov's *Slovar russkogo yazyka* (*Dictionary of the Russian Language*; 1949, rev. eds. 1952, 1960).

179.7   Edmundson]   Cf. Edmund Wilson's "My Fifty Years With Dictionaries and Grammars" (*New Yorker*, April 20, 1963), his criticism of Nabokov for his "dictionary words" in his harsh review of *Eugene Onegin* (*New York Review of Books*, July 15, 1965) and Nabokov's response: " . . . what does Mr. Wilson mean by implying I should not use words that in the process of lexicographic evolution begin to occur only at the level of a 'fairly comprehensive dictionary'? When does a dictionary cease being an abridged one and start growing 'fairly' and then 'extremely' comprehensive? Is the sequence: vest-pocket, coat-pocket, greatcoat-pocket, my three book shelves, Mr. Wilson's rich library? . . . And how does the harassed translator know that somewhere on the library ladder he has just stopped short of Wilson's Fairly Comprehensive and may safely use 'polyhedral' but not 'lingonberry'?" (*Encounter*, Feb. 1966).

179.7–8   Dr. Gerschizhevsky's]   See Darkbloom; in his review of Nabokov's *Eugene Onegin*, "A Manufactured Monument?" (*Modern Philology*, May 1966), Alexander Gerschenkron defended Dmitri Chizhevsky, whom Nabokov had attacked.

179.9   four-volume Dahl]   Vladimir Dahl (Dal'; 1801–72), *Tolkovyy slovar' zhivogo russkogo yazyka* (*Interpretive Dictionary of the Living Russian Language*; 1863–66).

179.29   Benten]   In Japan, the only female among the Seven Gods of Luck, with the serpent as her messenger.

179.33   *spektrik*]   Russian, "little spectrum" (because there are seven tiles to arrange on it).

183.22–23   larch plantation . . . Mansfield Park]   From the wood at Sotherton in Pt. 1, ch. 9, of Jane Austen's novel (1814). Nabokov wrote for an interview, "Without a visual perception of the larch labyrinth in *Mansfield Park* that novel loses some of its stereographic charm" (*Strong Opinions*, Interview no. 14).

184.7   "Berenice"]   Tragedy (1670) by Jean Racine.

185.16   Kachalov . . . Seagull Theater]   Vasily Kachalov (1875–1948), from 1900 in the troupe of Stanislavsky's Moscow Art Theater, played in *Gore ot uma* (*Woe from Wit*; literally, *Grief from Mind*) in 1906 and 1914. The theater's emblem was a seagull, after Chekhov's play.

189.21   yacs, and yoickfests]   In Nabokov's own copy of *Ada*: "yoick = hunting cry, yac = Cadillacs." (Cadillac is pronounced "Cad-ee-yak" in French.)

189.26   *gornishon*]   Russian *gornichnaya* means "maid"; French *cornichon* and Russian *kornishon* mean "gherkin."

189.37   oeillet]   French, "carnation; eyelet."

191.2–4   Kitty . . . Lyovka Tolstoy]   See Darkbloom. For *Anna Karenina*, Tolstoy drew on his relationship with his wife, Sofia, for that of Lyovin and Kitty and on the aristocratic name Obolenski for the name of Stepan (Stiva) Oblonski, Kitty's brother-in-law.

191.16–17   shaftment]   Distance from the tip of the extended thumb across the breadth of the palm.

191.18–19   Hump . . . Life]   In palmistry, the Mount of Venus (ball of thumb) indicates one's love-life and the line parallel to the fingers along the middle of the palm, longevity.

191.27–28   *château que baignait la Dore*]   See p. 112.7, 9 and note 86.35–39.

192.31   amerlocks]   French slang, *amerloque*, "American, Yankee."

193.27   solanders]   Boxes in the shape of books.

193.36   tittery]   Gin.

195.2   *seins durs*]   Literally, "hard breasts"; see Darkbloom.

196.4–6   "*Lorsque . . . pi-ano*]   Cf. Coppées "La Veillée" ("The Vigil"; 1878), lines 1, 3, 7.

196.26   snagrel]   The Virginia snakeroot, a type of birthwort.

196.35–197.9   *Leur chute . . . glow*]   See page 103.18–21 and note.

198.28   battants]   Leaves.

199.4   "subbetuline,"]   Birch trees are of the genus *Betula*.

199.15   pinacoteca]   Italian, "picture gallery."

200.26–27   condemned doors]   French *portes condamnées*, "blocked doors."

202.17   *à quatre mains*]   (Piano piece) for four hands.

202.37   sander]   A pike perch of central Europe.

202.38–39   asparagus . . . Proust's After-effect]   In the Combray section of *Du côté de chez Swann* (*Swann's Way*), the narrator describes the asparagus his family ate almost every night one summer as: "rainbow effects which are not of this earth. It seemed to me that these celestial shades betrayed the delightful creatures who had amused themselves by being metamorphosed into vegetables and who, through the disguise of their firm, edible flesh, allowed one to perceive in these nascent colors of dawn, in these sketched rainbows, in this extinction of blue evenings, this precious essence that I would recognise again when, all night after I had eaten them, they played, lyrical and gross in their trickery like the fairies in Shakespeare, at changing my chamberpot into an urn of perfume."

203.6   *chelovek*]   Man.

203.40   *moi, qui vous parle*]   *I* (emphatic), I myself.

204.35   gemel]   Twin.

207.8–9   saucisson d'Arles . . . *asperges en branches*]   Arles sausage . . . asparagus spears.

207.15–18   reformed "sign . . . Russians]   The reform of Russian Orthodox church texts and ritual introduced at the 1654 synod of Moscow resulted in the *Raskol* or Great Schism; the Raskolnik or *starovery* (Old Believers) were excommunicated and persecuted. The reforms included signing the cross with three fingers rather than two.

207.19   Great . . . Slaves]   Cf. Canada's Great Slave Lake. The word *slave* derives from the medieval Latin *sclavus*, "Slav."

207.21–22   Vengerov . . . Pushkinist]   Vengerov (1855–1920) edited a series called *Pushkinist*; the last volume (1923) was edited by Nabokov's friend Nikolay Yakovlev.

207.25   unfinished canto]   Pushkin appended parts of the fragment, *Onegin's Journey*, to his verse-drama; cf. xxvi.5–8 in Nabokov's translation: "What news of oysters? They have come. O glee! / Off flies gluttonous juventy / to swallow from their sea shells / the cloisterers, plump and alive."

208.31   "*A l'eau!*"]   Literally, "To the water!"

210.11   thirty-seven and seven]   Degrees Celsius; 99.9 degrees F.

214.5   Nabok]   "The founder of our family was Nabok Murza (*floreat* 1380), a Russianized Tatar prince in Muscovy" (*Speak, Memory*, ch. 3).

214.21   *colazione*]   Italian, "light meal."

216.12–13   '*Ombre Chevalier*,']   European freshwater saibling, a kind of trout. The separate meaning of *ombre* is "shade" and of *chevalier*, "knight."

216.15–16   philosopher . . . *une acte gratuite*]   Nabokov wrote to Jason Epstein (April 22, 1957) that in his essay "The Dyer's Hand: Poetry and the Poetic Process," W. H. Auden had written "acte gratuite" instead of "acte gratuit."

216.17–18   '*je me regrette*' . . . '*je regrette*']   "I'm sorry for myself" . . . "I'm sorry."

217.26–31   Dorn . . . question]   See Darkbloom; from the closing of Chekhov's play (1896), where Dorn is trying to steer Trigorin aside to tell him that Treplyov has shot himself.

218.34   macchie]   Italian, "thickets, maquis."

219.15–16   Cardinal . . . collection]   Cardinal Carlo de Medici (1596–1666); after his death his large collection of paintings was distributed among various Florentine galleries.

220.15   omoplates]   Shoulder-blades.

229.4   florula]   Flora of a small, restricted area.

230.7   *zaychik*]   Reflection of a sun ray.

231.9–10   broke . . . butterfly on the wheel]   Cf. Alexander Pope, *Epistle to Dr. Arbuthnot* (1732), lines 307–8: "Satire or sense, alas! can Sporus feel? / Who breaks a butterfly upon a wheel?"

231.24   "Malbrough"]   "Malbrouk s'en va-t-en guerre," old French folk song probably about a crusader, confused in the 18th century with the campaigns of the Duke of Marlborough.

232.1–2   pogonia]   Small genus of terrestrial orchid of the North Temperate Zone.

232.29–31   "*Mon page . . . beau page*]   See Darkbloom; stanza 6 of "Malbrouk."

233.23   bergamask]   A kind of rustic dance; cf. Paul Verlaine's poem "Clair de lune" ("Moonlight") collected in *Fêtes galantes* (1869).

235.11   *Mais . . . allemand*]   The German musician, of course.

237.8   in bloom (blue! bloom!)]   Cf. *Ulysses*, ch. 11: "Blew. Blue Bloom is on the. and Bloom. Old Bloom. Blue bloom is on the rye."

240.9–10   "Malbrook" . . . *guerre*]   See note 231.24.

240.34   *L'arbre . . . d'or*]   The tree with forty golden écus (a coin): a French name for the ginkgo (or gingko), for the color of its leaves in the fall.

245.12   saffian]   See note 177.20–21.

247.24   Dormilona]   The plant *Mimosa pudica* whose leaf-stalk droops and leaves close when touched; in Spanish, "sleepyhead."

247.39–248.1   Sorrows . . . Veen.]   In Goethe's *The Sorrows of Young Werther* (1774), the hero shoots himself because he cannot have Charlotte, who is married to another.

248.22   *chervonetz*]   Ten-ruble gold coin.

250.30   sparver]   Canopy of a bed.

251.20   greater *serratus*]   Muscle linking the eight upper ribs and the edge of the shoulder blades near the spine.

252.12   Onegin's coachman . . . *priehali*]   In a canceled draft of Pushkin's *Eugene Onegin* I.lii.11.

252.21   he be *tvoyu mat'*]   See Darkbloom; *ebi* means "fuck."

255.4   Pisang]   The plantain *Musa paradisiaca*, a kind of banana.

255.36   *Flèche*]   Arrow.

257.17–37   old Tartar . . . daughter with pitcher]   Cf. Tolstoy's "Kavkazkyy plennik" ("The Captive of the Caucasus"; 1872). A *beshmet* is a kind of quilted coat.

258.15   viatically]   In terms of travel.

258.20–21   *Arrêtez près . . . le* store *pour messieurs*]   Stop near . . . the men's store.

259.13   Varangian]   Scandinavian tribe that founded a dynasty in Russia in the 9th century

260.3   *tribadka*]   From "tribade": "lesbian."

262.20   randonnies]   Cf. *randonnées* (trips, excursions).

263.15   *girlinière*]   Cf. *garçonnière*, bachelor apartment.

264.5   *cottage orné*]   Literally "decorated cottage," an artfully rustic building, as constructed in the late 18th and early 19th century in England.

265.13   pisang-green . . . albergo]   See note 255.4. Italian *albergo*, "inn."

266.5   paleotropical]   Of the tropical and subtropical regions of the Eastern Hemisphere.

266.5   "mimotypes"]   A type of animal life resembling that of a different geographic region but not closely related to it.

266.32–33   *je . . . verge*]   Anglo-French: "I am on the verge"; (French *verge* means "rod, wand, shaft" and "penis" but not "brink").

267.14   early Thargelion]   The 11th month in the ancient Greek calendar, May–June.

267.28   drill-jar]   A device used in deep-well boring to allow the drill to be given a sharp loosening blow or jar when jammed in the rock.

269.18   *érable*]   Maple.

270.14   Counterstone]   In Nabokov's own copy of *Ada*, glossed: "Anti Einstein." *Stein* is German for "stone."

271.8   Sig Leymanski]   See Darkbloom note; anagram of Kingsley Amis (1922–95).

271.26   funest]   Fatal, dire, doleful.

273.24   Voltemand]   A letter-carrier in *Hamlet*, I.ii and II.ii.

273.29   *lapochka*]   Little paw.

273.32   Grombchevski]   The traveler Bronislav Grombchevski (1855–1926), responsible for the geographical exploration of much of the Russian Empire.

274.1   *The Possessed* by Miss Love]   Cf. *By Love Possessed* (1957) by James Gould Cozzens.

274.2   *The Puffer* by Mr. Dukes]   Cf. Saul Bellow's *Herzog* (1964) (*Herzog* is German for duke). In Nabokov's own copy of *Ada*, noted for translators: "to puff, to push a book by means of publicity etc."

274.23   *Terre à terre*]   Commonplace, unimaginative, pedestrian in style.

274.31   (*The Village Eyebrow*)]   Cf. the New York newspaper *Village Voice* and *The New Yorker*, whose emblem, the dandy Eustace Tilley, is usually portrayed with a raised eyebrow.

274.33   Goluba University]   *Goluba* is Russian (and *columba*, Latin) for dove; cf. Columbia University.

274.38   Ben Sirine]   Abu Bakr Muhammad ibn Sirin (654–728/9). Sirin, Nabokov's Russian pseudonym, is "Sirine" in French transliteration.

275.25   "The Weed . . . Flower"]   Herman Melville, "The Ravaged Villa" (1891), line 6: "The weed exiles the flower."

275.40   Witch (or Viedma]   Viedma, a town in Rio Negro province, south central Argentina; Russian *vedma*, witch.

276.34   Deuil]   French, "mourning, sorrow, affliction."

278.7   Shell Pink Book]   Cf. *Guide Rose* (*Pink Guide*), an annual guide to the higher-class Paris brothels in the mid-20th century.

278.34 "Art redeemed Politics"] In Nabokov's own copy of *Ada*, glossed: "Bertrand Russel[l]'s idea."

279.25–26 Vulner's . . . *Architecture*] The 1965 Penguin revised edition of the book by Peter Kidson, Peter Murray, and Paul Thompson is in the Pelican series. Vuln ("wound"; from Latin *vulnare*) is a heraldic term; in heraldic representation, the pelican vulns its breast to produce blood to feed its young.

279.28–29 El Freud . . . Dudok] E. L. Freud is noted in the Pelican edition (p. 311) as having built a close of houses influenced by Dutch municipal architect Willem Dudok (1884–1974).

279.28–29 great-necessity houses] French *chalet de necessité*, "outhouse."

280.18 *bautta*] Italian, "domino" (the garment).

281.14–15 clickies] Glossed in Nabokov's own copy of *Ada* as: "girls (very vulgar)."

281.32 Lalage] A courtesan repeatedly mentioned by Horace.

281.38 mollitude] Softness. Nabokov used the word in his translation of *Eugene Onegin* (see his commentary to III.vii.10).

282.6 Theban fresco] In the tomb of Nakht in Thebes.

282.35 empasmed] *Empasm*, a perfumed powder to mask the odor of sweat.

284.2–3 line that Seneca . . . composed] Line 4 of the eight-line poem *Omnia tempus edax depascitur, omnia carpit* ("Greedy time consumes all, plucks up all").

287.15–16 kneeling . . . Marmlad] See Darkbloom; cf. *Crime and Punishment* (1866), end of I.ii.

288.9–10 Dunne . . . "reverse memory"] John William Dunne, in his *An Experiment with Time* (1927).

288.15–16 Osberg's little gitana . . . Ramera] See Darkbloom note to p. 64, referring to Jorge Luis Borges (1899–1986). Spanish *gitana* means "gypsy" (Humbert as narrator refers to Lolita as *gitanilla* in *Lolita*, Pt. 2, ch. 22), *el motel* means "the motel," and *ramera*, "whore."

291.6 "*nertoros*,"] Lower; the dead.

292.16 prasine] Of a leek-green color.

292.28 "All . . . wives."] Cf. Swinburne's "Dolores" ("Notre-Dame des Sept Douleurs," 1866), lines 157–60: "Time turns the old days to derision, / Our loves into corpses or wives; / And marriage and death and division / Make barren our lives."

293.8   pommette] French, "cheekbone; small knob, as on the end of a sword-hilt or cane."

293.24–25   spontaneous . . . bleak house] In Dickens' *Bleak House*, ch. 32, Krook dies of spontaneous combustion.

296.19   "Pah!"] Cf. Russian *pakh*, "groin."

296.32–33   *poule* . . . *puella*] French *poule*, "tart"; Latin *puella*, "maiden."

297.32–38   right hand . . . *that's* the solution!] Cf. Immanuel Kant, *Prolegomena to Any Future Metaphysics*, para. 13: "What can be more similar in every respect and in every part more alike to my hand and to my ear, than their images in a mirror? And yet I cannot put such a hand as is seen in the glass in the place of this archetype; for if this is a right hand, that in the glass is a left one, and the image or reflection of the right ear is a left one which can never serve as a substitute for the other. There are in this case no internal differences which our understanding could determine by thinking alone. Yet the differences are internal as the senses teach; for, notwithstanding their complete equality and similarity, the left hand cannot be enclosed in the same bounds as the right one (they are not congruent); the glove of one hand cannot be used for the other. What is the solution?"

299.18–19   *pour cogner une fraise*] See Darkbloom; in French, the phrase actually means: "to thump a strawberry."

300.3   Sterva] Russian, "whore."

301.11   *dans ton petit cas*] In your little case.

301.16–20   "state" . . . *Humaine*] André Malraux's *La Condition humaine* (1933) has been translated as *Man's Fate* (1934) and *Man's Estate* (1948). French *pompier*, "conventional, commonplace" (of a work of art).

301.22   *Koulak* . . . *hollandaise*] "Rich Tasmanian peasant of Dutch origin." Tasmania was once called Van Diemen's Land.

302.6   myrrherabol] *Herabol myrrh*, true myrrh.

302.38–40   adieu, . . . Hamlet] Cf. II.ii.122–24.

304.1   *c'est . . . famille*] It's in the family.

305.28   *Slat Sign*] Advertising sign in which slats are painted to reveal one of three images, depending on the angle from which the sign is viewed. In Nabokov's own copy of *Ada*, he noted for translators: "see Webster 1960 p. 2360 a changing luminous advertisement."

305.34   *bergères* and *torchères*] Easy chairs and candlesticks.

306.8   Sustermans] Flemish portraitist Justus (also Joost) Sustermans (1597–1681), court painter to Cosimo II de Medici.

306.10   *rovesciata*] In Nabokov's own copy of *Ada*, glossed: "bicycle kick." A soccer kick executed when the footballer, with his back to the opposing team's goal, kicks the ball toward his shoulder while flipping backwards to get out of its path.

306.38   *The Ugly New Englander*] Cf. William J. Lederer and Eugene Burdick, *The Ugly American* (1958).

307.9–10   the Pioneers . . . Pyogenes] In Nabokov's own copy of *Ada*, glossed: "my American genes vanquished the microbes" (the illness caused by *Streptococcus pyogenes*).

307.15–16   literal French . . . *en regard*] Herondas (also, Herodas, Herodes; 3rd c. B.C.), *Mimes*, ed. J. Arbuthnot Nairn, trans. Louis Laloy (1928), in the Budé series. See also note 10.33–34.

307.31–34   "*O dear . . . window*] Cf. *Hamlet* II.ii. 120, IV.v.178, 181–82 ("herb of repentance" is a name for rue), 50.

308.28   (*quatre à quatre*)] Four by four.

310.29   Arshin] Russian unit of distance, equal to 28 inches.

312.24   libellula] A family of dragonflies, comprising in older classifications all the dragonflies.

313.4   vison] The American mink.

314.30   Cranach crayons] In his own copy of *Ada*, Nabokov glossed: "pastels."

315.24–25   Almehs] Egyptian singing and dancing girls.

315.30   "*N'exagérons . . . sais*,"] Let's not exaggerate, you know.

315.36   *pas petite moi*] Not little me.

316.16–17   first vowel *à la Russe*)] Russian *ebat*, to fuck.

316.19   *viola sordina*] Viola with mute.

318.31   *Quercus ruslan* Chât.] Nabokov wrote to Bobbie Ann Mason: "The specific name of this invented tree alludes to the beginning of Pushkin's long poem *Ruslan and Lyudmila* (1820) where there is a cat (*chat* in French) walking on a golden chain around a fairytale oaktree. The oak in *Ada* is supposed to have been described by a botanist named Châtel (or Châtelet or Château-Lafite) abbreviated to Chât. after the specific ruslan. The distorted shadow of Chateaubriand should not interfere with the flash of the Ruslan-oak-cat recognition."

319.38   *tsigans*] Russian *tsigan* (pl. *tsigany*), "gypsy."

320.4–5   Domenico Benci . . . Brina] Florentine painters Domenico Benci, or Beceri (fl. 1565), and Giovanni del Brina, or Brini (d. 1599).

320.17 "lidderons"] Obsolete word for "scoundrels, rascals."

320.34 caruncula] Naked fleshy excrescence.

321.22 satyrion] Old name for orchid, once considered an aphrodisiac.

322.27 'automobile'] German, *Wagen*.

323.20 March Hare] March is the rutting season for hares.

324.4 magnanery] *Magnanerie*, establishment where silkworms are raised.

324.19 Price, Norris, and Ward] Mrs. Norris and Mrs. Price are two of the Ward sisters in Jane Austen's *Mansfield Park* (the third is Lady Bertram).

324.36 Lord of Erection.] The lord of a temporal lordship created by the secularization of an ecclesiastical benefice during the Reformation.

324.36–37 Marvel's Melon] See Darkbloom note to p. 128.

324.39 *la force des choses*] Literally, "the force of things."

325.2 Romany clips] Obsolete, "embraces, hugs, grips." In Nabokov's own copy of *Ada*: "gypsy holds in wrestling."

325.17 *foute*] See Darkbloom; French *foutre*, "to fuck."

325.18 Carte du Tendre] See Darkbloom; the *Carte de Tendre* is in Madeleine de Scudéry's romance *Clélie* (10 vols; 1654–60).

325.35 *Souvenance*] French, "Remembrance."

326.21 dimidiated] Cut in, or reduced to, half.

327.35 *Gwen de Vere* and *Klara Mertvago*] Cf. Tennyson's "Guinevere" and "Lady Clara Vere de Vere" and the Lara of Boris Pasternak's *Doctor Zhivago* (see Darkbloom note to p. 47).

327.38 racemosa] Nabokov's proposed English equivalent for the Russian *cheryomukha* ("bird cherry"), the tree *Padus racemosa* (*Eugene Onegin*, commentary to VI.vii.9).

328.27 *uha*, the shashlik, the *Ai*] Fish soup, kebabs, and a champagne of Ay, France.

328.31 *tsiganshchina*] See Darkbloom and note 319.38.

328.31 Grigoriev] The musical setting of Apollon Grigoriev's "Dve gitary" ("Two Guitars") mimicks a gypsy song.

329.13 the long sobs . . . violins] First lines of Paul Verlaine's "Chanson d'automne" ("Autumn Song"; 1866).

329.35 *Siyala noch'*] Usually translated "Night was shining" (1877).

330.3–8 Glinka's . . . *passion!*] "Somnenie" ("Doubt"; 1838), words by N. Kukolnik (1809–68).

330.10 "The tender . . . forgotten,"] Words and music by Anatoly Lenin.

330.10–11 "The time . . . sprouting,"] Lines 1–2 of Alexey Tolstoy's untitled poem "To bylo ranneyu vesnoy."

330.12–13 "Many songs . . . gladness,"] Opening of "Dubinushka," a revolutionary song written down by V. I. Bogdanov and revised by A. A. Olkhin that was often sung by Fyodor Chaliapin before 1917.

330.15–16 *There's a crag . . . highest*] Opening line of A. A. Navrotsky's "Utyos Stenki Razina" ("The Cliff of Stenka Razin"; c. 1864).

330.19–20 *In a monotone . . . bit*] "Odnozuchno zvuchit kolkolchik," words by I. Makarov, music by A. Gurshlev.

330.22–23 *Nadezhda . . . riot*] Cf. line 1 of "Sentimental March" by poet and singer Bulat Okudzhava (b. 1924): "Nadezhda, ya vernus togda, kogda trubach otboy sygraet" (Nabokov's genuine translation reads: "Speranza, I am coming home the day the bugler sounds retreat"; *Nadezhda* means "Hope").

330.24–26 Turgenev's . . . *coverings*] "On the Road" (1843), turned into a gypsy song by V. V. Abaza.

331.4 declansh his masher] French *déclancher*, "dislocate", *mâchoire*, "jaw."

331.18 *Uzh . . . ogni*] See Darkbloom; poem by Konstantin Romanov set to music by Tchaikovsky.

331.20 bugler's sharp elbow] "Sentimental March" (see note 330.22–23), line 2: "When to his lips he brings the bugle and backward his sharp elbow turns."

331.31 ensellure] See note 81.30.

331.34 rizzom] A straw (of grain); a particle; the least bit.

332.19 boudery . . . manger] Cf. boudoir and *salle à manger*, dining room.

332.31 *estanciero*] Ranch owner.

333.3–4 philtrum] The vertical groove between upper lip and nose.

333.37 menald] Speckled, variegated.

334.2 delphinet] The dolphin was an attribute of Venus.

334.19 "Oh-de-grâce."] *Eau de Grasse*; Grasse is the perfume center in the French Alpes-Maritimes.

334.23–26 "*Mne snitsa . . . rival!*"] From Glinka's "Doubt."

335.37   Acrasia]   Intemperance; the fair witch of the Bower of Bliss in Spenser's *Faerie Queene* (1590–96), II.xii.

336.3   *vue d'oiseau*]   Bird's-eye view.

336.35   separatum]   Offprint.

337.11   lycaenid]   One of the *Lycaenidae* family of butterflies.

337.23   Perwitsky]   A polecat of eastern Europe and northern Asia.

338.3   *Esmeralda*]   Gypsy dancing-girl in Victor Hugo's *Notre-Dame de Paris* (1831).

338.36   Pardus and Peg]   The leopard, as sacred to Bacchus and drawer of his chariot, and Pegasus.

340.11–12   "backfish."]   Teenager.

340.27   *The Beau . . . Butterfly*]   Cf. the dandy Eustace Tilley, emblem of *The New Yorker.*

344.9–10   Pension . . . Nice]   Chekhov lived at this address in 1901 while his *Three Sisters* was in rehearsal.

349.33   Backbay]   Back Bay, an elite residential section of Boston.

350.2   The picture]   Bosch's *Last Judgment.*

351.7   Bronze Riders]   Cf. Pushkin's *The Bronze Horseman* or *Rider* (referring to a statue of Peter the Great).

351.35   Jeroen Anthniszoon van Äken]   Dutch name of Hieronymus Bosch.

351.35–36   *molti . . . arte*]   "The many fascinating aspects of his enigmatic art"; from Mario Buscagli's *Bosch* (Florence, 1966), p. 3.

351.38–39   bequeathed . . . catheter.]   Cf. Shakespeare's will, in which he added to his first draft, "Itm̄ I gyve unto my wief my second best bed wth the furniture" (i.e. bed furnishings), and chapter 9 of Joyce's *Ulysses* (1922).

352.22   Nuremberg Old Maid's]   The Iron Maiden or Iron Virgin, an instrument of torture in the old castle of Nuremberg.

355.39–356.1   Boris Godunov . . . gravity]   Near the end of Pushkin's play *Boris Godunov* (1824–25) Boris says to his son, as he is dying: "Ty muzh i tsar'; lyubi svoyu sestru, / Ty ey odin khranitel' ostayosh'sya" ("You are a man and a tsar; love your sister, / You alone will remain a refuge for her").

357.11   pterion]   In the skull, the juncture of the frontal, parietal, and temporal bones; it is just above and to the front of the top of the ear.

359.14   Eberthella]   A genus of bacteria occurring in the human intestines, usually associated with inflammation.

359.15   "baptism of desire"] The Roman Catholic and Orthodox churches recognize the validity of "baptism of desire" in those animated by a perfect love of God who wish to be baptized but die before the sacrament can be administered.

360.34   ambon] Pulpit or reading-desk.

361.1–2   Bouches-Rouges-du-Rhône] Red-Mouths-of-the-Rhone; cf. the Bouches-du-Rhône department of southeast France.

365.3–4   The Veens . . . dogs.] Cf. John Collins Bossidy (1860–1928), "On the Aristocracy of Harvard": "And this is good old Boston, / The home of the bean and the cod, / Where the Lowells talk to the Cabots, / And the Cabots talk only to God."

367.13–14   Sween . . . Milton Eliot] The title of T. S. Eliot's *Sweeney Agonistes* (1932) is taken from Milton's *Samson Agonistes* (1671).

367.23   rue des Jeunes Martyres . . . Ovenman] Cf. Henri de Toulouse-Lautrec's poster *Le Divan japonais* (1892–93), which advertised the cabaret of E. Fournier (French *four* means "oven") at 75 rue des Martyrs in Paris, and the photographed modern-dress version of the poster, with the original in the background, that appeared in a Barton and Guestier wine advertisement that ran in *The New Yorker* in the 1960s. Nabokov told Bobbie Ann Mason that the photograph "is meticulously described by Van . . . and should be looked up by all admirers of Lucette."

368.31–32   got *le paquet*] *Donner le paquet* means "to give (someone) a piece of one's mind."

368.34–35   lautréamontesque . . . lautrecasqueque] An attempt at "lautrec-esque"; cf. French poet Comte de Lautréamont (1846–70), real name Isidore-Lucien Ducasse.

369.12   Ausonian] Poetic word for "Italian."

369.26   Heinrich Heideland] German *Heide*, "moor": Henry Moore.

370.34   *est un peu snob*] Is a little snobbish.

371.13   ganch] To execute by impaling on a stake.

371.28   sheeing] Skiing. The Norwegian and Swedish pronunciation, "shee," is often used, especially in England.

374.18   chromesthesia] Sensitivity to color.

375.2   metabasis] Change of disease or symptoms.

378.9   *bautta*] See note 280.18.

378.24   Screepatch] Glossed in Nabokov's own copy of *Ada* as: "[Russian] Skripach: fiddler" (violinist).

380.40   *pozharskiya kotleti*]   Grilled chops or cutlets.

381.34   Spring in Fialta]   Title of Nabokov's long story "Vesna v Fialte" (1936); Fialta combines Yalta on the Black Sea, Fiume (now Rijeka) on the Adriatic, and the Russian word for violet, *fialka*.

382.11   Herb . . . painter]   Nabokov noted in his own copy of *Ada*: "déjeuner sur l'*herbe*" (Édouard Manet's painting *Picnic on the Grass*).

382.12   his last duchess]   Cf. Robert Browning's "My Last Duchess" (1842).

383.1   "*merde.*"]   Shit.

383.17   *kto siya pava?*]   Literally: "who's this peahen?"

384.5   *michman*]   Russian, "midshipman."

384.6   Gavaille]   Russian transliteration of Hawaii (Gavaii) retransliterated into French.

385.2–3   I love . . . tenderly.]   See Darkbloom note. At this point of the poem, Eugene pompously rejects Tatiana's offer of love.

385.17–18   Mademoiselle Condor . . . pun]   Glossed in Nabokov's own copy of *Ada*: "Con d'or = Cunt of gold."

385.21   "For the sweet . . . sweet,"]   Cf. *Hamlet* V.i.243: "Sweets to the sweet, farewell!"

387.20–21   *Insiste . . . fortiter*]   See Darkbloom; *Confessions*, 11.27.34.

391.12–15   *gitana* . . . Osberg's novella]   Dolores is the real name of Lolita in Nabokov's novel; see note 288.15–16.

391.21   *qui n'en porte pas*]   Who's not wearing any.

391.39   *gitanilla*]   Little gypsy (female).

392.19–21   Donna Anna . . . Stone Cuckold's revenge]   See note 90.25–26.

393.4–5   Father Sergius . . . member]   In Tolstoy's novella *Father Sergius* the would-be saint chops off his finger to resist the temptation roused by a woman who enters his cave and undresses.

396.11   Oceanus Nox]   See Darkbloom. Cf. Virgil, *Aeneid*, II.250 ("et ruit Oceano nox," "and night rushes from the Ocean"); Victor Hugo used the phrase for his poem "Oceano nox" (1840), a lament for sailors drowned at sea.

400.30–31   *mauresque*]   Moorish.

401.10–11   *The Artisan*]   Cf. *Partisan Review*; it began as a monthly.

401.17–20   And o'er . . . shone]   See Darkbloom; in Lermontov, "Tacit" is "Kazbek" and Mount Peck, "Caucasus."

401.31   petite fille modèle]   Model little girl; cf. the Comtesse de Ségur's
novel *Les petites filles modèles* (1858).

402.9   *Blackrent*]   A synonym of "blackmail."

402.13   "Sale Histoire"]   Dirty Story.

402.15   *libellula*]   See note 312.24.

403.22   *maussade*]   Sultry, sullen.

404.7–10   Sween . . . *The Waistline*]   See Darkbloom note to p. 9.

404.19–20   Kirman Lavehr]   The highest quality of Persian rug woven in
Kerman, characterized by elaborate fluid designs, floral, animal, and figural.

405.13–15   obscure figure . . . Unbeloved]   Cf. Dorothy Emmett's fore-
word to Samuel Alexander's *Space, Time and Deity: The Gifford Lectures at
Glasgow, 1916–1918* (1966): "Alexander continued to live in Manchester, until
his death in 1938, a beloved figure around whom legends collected, both in
the university and city." Alexander (1859–1938) held the Sir Samuel Hall Chair
of Philosophy at the University of Manchester.

405.24   Les Trois Cygnes]   The Three Swans.

406.14   *rez-de-chaussée*]   Ground floor.

406.28   Vrubel's wonderful picture]   *Demon* (or *Demon Seated*; 1890,
Moscow, Tretyakov Gallery), one of a series of paintings of Lermontov's
Demon by Mikhail Vrubel (1856–1910).

406.33   Sex Noir]   A mountain west of Sex Rouge (see note 26.6).

408.19–20   *belle-soeur*]   Sister-in-law.

409.11–12   *What Daisy Knew*]   Cf. Henry James's *Daisy Miller* (1878) and
What Maisie Knew (1897).

409.37   naric]   Of a nostril.

411.22   fast little Unseretti]   Cf. car racing champions Bobby Unser and
Mario Andretti.

414.26   *muirninochka*]   See Darkbloom; Irish *muirnín*, "sweetheart,
darling."

414.38–39   Dr. Swissair of Lumbago]   Swiss is "Schweitzer" in German.
Albert Schweitzer's hospital was at Lambaréné in Gabon.

416.26–27   the Vane sisters]   Title of a Nabokov story (1951) that ends in
an acrostic woven into the final paragraph.

417.7   alberghian]   Italian *albergo*, "inn."

417.8–9   Aleksey . . . here)]   See Darkbloom; in *Anna Karenina* Vronsky
and Anna stay in a small-town hotel in Italy.

417.18   Rufomonticulus] From Latin, "small red mountain": Mont Roux.

417.25   platbands] Flowerbeds.

420.17   *hohlushka*] Crested.

424.18   "*Ne ricane pas!*"] Don't sneer!

424.28   "*Perestagne* (stop, *cesse*)!"] French transliteration of Russian *perestan*, "stop."

426.20   Goreloe] A real village near Tambov in Russia, its name means "burnt up."

427.11   flyback] A stopwatch whose hands may be made to fly back to zero.

428.40–429.1   Somethingsoprano] Vicosoprano, south of Ardez.

429.4–12   Aurelius Augustinus . . . prayer] St. Augustine's discussion of time is in *Confessions*, Bk. 11.

432.4–5   assassin pun . . . Verlaine] See Darkbloom; "Art poétique" ("The Art of Poetry"; 1874), lines 17–18: "Fuis du plus loin la Pointe assassine, / L'Esprit cruel et le Rire impur" ("Fly furthest from the murderous Epigram, / Cruel Wit and base Laughter"). Nabokov replied to a query about the pun: "In a poem about poetry as he understands it, Verlaine warns the poet against using *la pointe assassine*, that is introducing an epigrammatic or moral point at the end of a poem, and thereby murdering the poem. What amused me was to pun on 'point,' thus making a pun in the very act of prohibiting it." (*Strong Opinions*, Interview no. 10.)

432.40   the specious present] The time span of immediate consciousness; the term was coined by E. R. Clay (see note 439.39) and popularized by William James, *The Principles of Pyschology* (1890), Vol. 1, ch. xv: "But *the original paragon and prototype of all conceived times is the specious present, the short duration of which we are immediately and incessantly sensible.*"

433.7   Venus sign] A solid-black and upside-down version of the Venus sign is a symbol on road maps for a church or monastery. The Venus sign is believed to derive from a handmirror.

433.10   pilcrow] The paragraph mark.

433.16–19   "Space . . . *Universe*] The quotation is from lines 215–16 of Shade's poem in *Pale Fire*. The mathematician and philosopher Martin Gardner quoted the lines in his *The Ambidextrous Universe* (1964), p. 167, and listed Shade, but not Nabokov, in the index. Gardner noted in his 1979 revised edition that Nabokov here returned the joke.

433.26   (Guyau in Whitrow)] Jean Guyau's *La Genèse de l'Idée de Temps* (1890) is discussed on pp. 51–53 of G. J. Whitrow's *The Natural Philosophy of Time* (1961).

433.26–29   The indistinguishable inane . . . Time.] Cf. John Locke, *An Essay Concerning Human Understanding* (1690), II.vii.10: "Nor let any one think these too narrow bounds for the capacious Mind of Man to expatiate in, which takes its flight further than the Stars, and cannot be confined by the limits of the World; that extends its thoughts often, even beyond the utmost expansion of Matter, and makes excursions into that incomprehensible *Inane*."

433.31   S. Alexander] See note 405.13–15.

434.12–15   Engelwein . . . time.] Cf. Paul Langevin (German *Engel* and *Wein* are *l'ange* and *vin* in French; in English, "angel" and "wine"). In 1911 at Bologna Langevin presented a paper (published as "L'Evolution de l'espace et du temps," *Revue de Metaphysique et de Morale*, XIX, 1911) suggesting that someone traveling on a projectile could live two years in space while 200 years passed on earth.

434.30   minimus] Little finger.

434.36–37   He defined . . . yet] *Confessions*, Bk. 11, 14: "There are therefore two times, the past and the future, but in what sense, when the past no longer is and the future is not yet?"

435.16   arollas] Swiss pines.

435.17   *éboulements*] Cave-ins; collapsings; falls; debris.

439.28   the Umbrail . . . Furka] High mountain passes in Switzerland.

439.39   Clay . . . "Specious Present."] In *The Alternative*; see also note
432.40.

442.36   "deperishing"] French *dépérir*, "to waste away."

442.39   Acrazia] See note 335.37.

443.35   anthophobia] Fear of flowers.

444.8   sourdine] Muted, subdued.

444.27   ackers] Patches of ruffled water.

445.6   *entrain*] Liveliness, high spirits.

445.13   Laputa] Name of the flying island in Jonathan Swift's *Gullivers Travels* (1726), Bk. 3.

446.37–38   Verglas] Glazed frost.

447.28   ascended . . . Cartesian glassman] Cf. Nabokov's description of toys at a St. Petersburg fair in *Speak, Memory*, ch. 12: "Cartesian devils called *amerikanskie zhiteli* (American inhabitants)—minute goblins of glass riding up and down in glass tubes filled with pink- or lilac-tinted alcohol as real Americans do (though all the epithet meant was outlandish) in the shafts of transparent skyscrapers as the office lights go out in the greenish sky."

450.16   platch]   To splash, besmear.

450.39–451.2   Morzhey . . . mermaid's message)]   See Darkbloom; Russian *morzhey*, "of walruses," also "of penises"; English morse, "walrus."

451.6–10   British . . . different positions.']   From the article "Space-Time," mostly written by Albert Einstein, in editions of the *Encyclopaedia Britannica* from 1929 to 1970: "Space denotes the property in virtue of which rigid bodies can occupy different positions."

457.13–14   native girl . . . Master]   Cf. Paul Gauguin's painting *Ea haere ia oe* (*Où vas-tu? Where Are You Going?*).

459.11   *en regard*]   See note 10.33–34.

459.11   Griboyedov]   See page 185.4.

459.12   John Shade]   See note 433.16–19.

460.15–16   "Whitehead's Bright Fringe"]   Alfred North Whitehead's Tarner Lectures, delivered in Trinity College, Cambridge, in November 1919 (published in *The Concept of Nature*): "The passage of nature leaves nothing between the past and the future. What we perceive as present is the vivid fringe of memory tinged with anticipation. This vividness lights up the discriminated field within a duration."

460.25   Victor Vitry]   Cf. Russo-French film director Sacha Guitry (1885–1957).

461.30–31   Siegrid Mitchel . . . Margaret Undset]   Cf. Sigrid Undset (1882–1949) and Margaret Mitchell (1900–49).

462.22–23   the comedian Steller]   Cf. British actor Peter Sellers (1925–80); he played the part of Clare Quilty in the 1962 movie *Lolita*.

462.32   breloques]   See note 106.38.

463.6   distant Atomsk]   In *Speak, Memory*, ch. 13, Nabokov refers to "Tomsk or Omsk (now Bombsk)."

464.17   Emile says]   Emile Littré (1801–81), French lexicographer, in *Dictionnaire de la langue française.*

464.34   *sanglot*]   French, "sob"; cf. Stéphane Mallarmé's poem "L'Après-midi d'un faune," whose line "Sans pitié du sanglot dont j'étais encore ivre" ("without pity for the sob with which I was still drunk") was a motif in Nabokov's *Bend Sinister.*

465.24–25   John Shade's famous poem]   "Pale Fire"; see note 433.16–19.

466.19–20   the one . . . balustrade]   Cf. "Pale Fire," lines 576–79 ("And, also blond, / But with a touch of tawny in the shade, / Feet up, knees clasped, on a stone balustrade / The other sits") and 585–86 ("And she, the second love, with instep bare / In ballerina black").

466.37   constate]   Evidence positively, establish, verify.

467.22   Babes . . . Woods]   Probably *The Babes in the Wood*, an anonymous English ballad illustrated by Randolph Caldecott (1846–86).

467.35   Count Tolstoy's reminiscences]   See note 7.9–10.

TRANSPARENT THINGS

490.33   *en face*]   Face-on.

491.24   *belle chambre au quatrième*]   Nice fourth-floor room.

492.34–35   when pencil lead was discovered]   An unusually pure deposit
of graphite, thought to be a type of lead, was discovered in Borrowdale, England, in 1564. German Swiss naturalist Konrad von Gesner first described how
it could be used in a wooden holder for writing in 1565.

494.8   *rez-de-chaussée*]   Ground-floor.

496.2–3   *Confections . . . soldes.*]   Ready-made (clothes). Our triumphant
clearance sale.

497.8   dingdong bell]   Cf. *The Tempest*, I.ii.396–405: "Full fadom five thy
father lies, / Of his bones are coral made: / . . . Sea-nymphs hourly ring his
knell: / Ding-dong. / Hark now I hear them—ding-dong bell."

497.17–21   The masculine ending . . . daring attitudes]   With the French
word "osées" substitued for "ose" the sign could be read: "3 Photos osées"
("3 daring Photos"); "Poses osées" would mean "daring Attitudes."

498.16   the Boston strangler]   The deaths of 13 women in the Boston area
beteen June 1962 and January 1964 were attributed to a murderer known as
the "Boston Strangler"; Alberto DeSalvo later confessed to the crimes.

499.14   *homard à l'américaine*]   Lobster American-style.

502.29–30   Anacreon . . . "wine's skeleton"]   Anacreon was said to have
choked to death on a grapeseed in his wine.

502.31–32   Alyokhin . . . dead bull.]   Alexander Alyokhin (1892–1946,
world chess champion, 1927–35, 1937–46) died in Portugal; according to the
autopsy, he choked on unchewed meat.

503.2   Atman]   In Hinduism, the innermost essence of each individual, or,
often, the supreme universal self.

503.3–6   footnotes as: / The cromlech . . . masculine.]   In John Fowles'
The French Lieutenant's Woman (1969), Chapter 3 contains the phrase "Crom-
lechs and menhirs" and some of the novel's footnotes are Freudian. Reviewers
frequently compared Fowles' novel with Nabokov's *Ada*; both books were
published in 1969.

506.25–26   *La particule . . . prénom.*] "The particle (*de*) would have clashed with the last syllable of my first name." I.e., she thinks her mother's Russian nobility would entitle her to call herself "de Chamar" in French.

506.27   'chamar,' . . . "peacock fan,"] "Chamar" could mean a fan used as a mark of royalty or in temples on the Indian subcontinent; it can also mean a member of a low Indian caste whose caste occupation is leatherworking.

506.30   in those *parages.*] Thereabouts.

507.8–9   *Ouvre . . . mon bûcher.*] Cf. Alfred de Musset's poem *A Julie* ("To Julie"; 1832), lines 35–36: "Ouvre ta robe, Déjanire, / Que je monte sur mon bûcher" ("Open your dress, Dejanira / that I may mount to [be burnt at] my stake").

507.20   *Parlez-moi de son*] Tell me about his.

507.22   *Mais au contraire*] No, quite the reverse.

507.23   *lui*] He.

507.25–26   *grain de beauté*] Mole.

508.13   *chasseurs*] Hotel porters.

508.25–26   dummy . . . landlady] In "The Empty House" (1893; *The Return of Sherlock Holmes*, 1905).

509.20   Nocturia] Excessive urination at night.

512.18   garland-brief days] Cf. A. E. Housman, "To An Athlete Dying Young" (*A Shropshire Lad*, 1896, poem xix—about an athlete who has died in a foreign war), last line: "The garland briefer than a girl's."

514.29   "*Alors . . . maison,*"] Then let us go into the house.

515.27   *voyeur malgré lui*] Voyeur in spite of himself.

515.35–36   girl . . . Lutwidgean] Charles Lutwidge Dodgson (pen-name, Lewis Carroll) photographed naked young girls.

516.24–25   Denton mount . . . bird-wing] A plaster of Paris mount for exposing a showy butterfly, decorative but scorned by scientists. Birdwings are large and mostly brilliantly colored butterflies in the genus *Ornithoptera*.

517.33   *à sept heures précises*] At seven exactly.

519.26–31   *rafale de neige . . . sugrob*] The French for snowdrift can be *congère* or *amas de neige*; *rafale de neige* would mean "snowstorm." In Russian, *sugrob* means "snowdrift" and *metel*, "snowstorm."

521.24   *je t'aime* in Russian] *Ya lyublyu tebya* (I love you).

522.16   tempo turns] Parallel turns.

524.14   "*godilles*" and "*wedeln*" (rom?)]   An oscillating movement of the body in skiing that involves short quick turns straight down the fall line. The technique, developed in Austria in the 1950s, was just filtering into English dictionaries in the 1960s, hence the "rom?" (a proofreader's query: roman, or italics?).

525.3   Mondstein]   Moonstone.

525.25   *buvette*]   Refreshment room.

526.36–37   "*Grüss Gott,*"]   Greetings.

530.32–33   *Roches étonnées*]   Fissured or flinty rocks.

530.34   (*écarquillages*)]   *Écarquiller les yeux* means to open the eyes wide.

534.12   Chudo-Yudo]   A marvelous monster in Russian folklore; cf. also Russian *chudo* ("wonder") and judo.

539.28   *anide*]   Anidian, formless, lacking differentiation (of an embryo or fetus).

540.13–14   Condom . . . Pussy in Savoie]   The places are real.

541.21   "rimiform"]   In botany, shaped like a slit (from Latin *rima*, "narrow furrow").

541.21   balanic]   Balan- or balano-, a combinative form, glans penis.

541.25   kew tree]   Ginkgo.

541.25   nebris]   Faun skin; in classical art, worn by Dionysus, satyrs, etc.

541.27   "Adam von Librikov"]   Anagram of Vladimir Nabokov; possibly also "Man of butterflies" (*librik* is Estonian for "butterfly" and *ov* the Russian plural genitive inflection; *von* is German for "of"; *adam* is Hebrew for "man").

544.24   "Pouce"]   French, thumb.

546.21   *fegato*]   Liver.

549.17–19   (Person . . . saint)]   Cf. French poet and diplomat Saint-John Perse (1877–1975).

549.38–39   *Est-ce que . . . Madame*]   Do you know, Madame.

550.27   Carte du Tendre . . . Torture]   Pun on *tendre* as noun ("tenderness") and verb ("to stretch"); see also note 325.18.

551.13   gullies . . . ridges]   French, *couloirs . . . arêtes*.

551.22   *more* (sea)]   *More* is Russian.

551.39–40   large white butterfly . . . wings]   A Parnassian, probably *Parnassius mnemosyne*.

552.32–33   either raining . . . all]   Cf. Wittgenstein's *Tractatus Logico-*

Philosophicus (1921; trans. D.F. Pears and B.F. McGuiness, 1961), 4.461: "For example, I know nothing about the weather when I know that it is either raining or not raining"; *Philosophical Investigations* (1953; trans. G.E.M. Anscombe, 1963), para 356: "One is inclined to say: 'Either it is raining, or it isn't—how I know, how the information has reached me, is another matter.' But then let us put the question like this: What do I call 'information that it is raining'? (Or have I only information of this information too?)"

553.27   *père . . . fils*]   Father . . . son.

554.4   "Dust to dust"]   *The Book of Common Prayer*, Burial of the Dead: First Anthem.

554.18–20   A search for lost time . . . *je suis né*"]   The French translates the opening of Thomas Hood's "I Remember, I Remember" (1827): "I remember, I remember, / The house where I was born." Goodgrief combines Hood ("Good" in the Russian transliteration) and the surname of C. K. Scott Moncrieff, the translator of Proust who changed the title of *A la recherche du temps perdu* (*In Search of Lost Time*) to *Remembrance of Things Past* in order to keep to Proust's R—T—P— pattern and to echo Shakespeare's sonnet 30: "When to the sessions of sweet silent thought / I summon up remembrance of things past . . . "

555.32   "Beau Romeo"]   In Stresa there is a hotel Borromeo.

556.5–7   Monsieur Wilde's English . . . intonation.]   Nabokov commented that George Steiner "absurdly overestimates Oscar Wilde's mastery of French" (*Strong Opinions*, Article 7, "Anniversary Notes"—"George Steiner").

556.12–13   "One talks . . . years ago]   Cf. Oscar Wilde's *The Ballad of Reading Gaol* (1898), I.1.5–6, I.7.1.

558.24–25   The lady with the little dog]   Title of Anton Chekhov's story of an adulterous affair, "Dama s sobachkoi" (1899).

559.22   kix]   The husk or case of a chrysalis; hence, a protective covering.

559.32–33   (sericanette)]   Seric, archaic, "Chinese." In a "Words" file Nabokov kept, he marked off as used in *Transparent Things* "Sericana, region of SW China (in Milton)."

560.6   Amilcar]   The Carthaginian general Amilcar (or Hamilcar) was the father of Hannibal.

560.16   *gousset*]   Gusset.

LOOK AT THE HARLEQUINS!

565.11   *Parandrus*]   A mythical stag able to change color like a chameleon.

571.34–35   last aurochs . . . John III (Sobieski)]   The auroch, or urus, the extinct European wild ox, was known to have survived in Jaktorow forest in central Poland until 1627. Stefan Czarniecki (1599–1665; Charnetski is the Russian transliteration of the name) was a Polish general appointed commander in chief in 1665. John Sobieski (1624–96), who had learned the art of war under Czarniecki, succeeded him as commander in chief and in 1674 was elected king of Poland, as John III.

572.9–10   "And whither . . . (*yablochko*)?] Véra Nabokov wrote to Dieter Zimmer (Feb. 10, 1962): "A Bolshevik soldier song of the time of the revolution. The 'little apple' was meant to mean a bourgeois." The chastushka in full: "Hey, little apple, / Where are you rolling? / Bump into the Cheka [secret police], / And you won't come back!"

574.16   ara] Macaw.

574.31   *salle d'eau*] Toilet.

575.29   Nina Lecerf] Flighty vamp in Nabokov's *The Real Life of Sebastian Knight.*

578.31   *casse-tête*] Puzzle.

579.29   *partie de plaisir*] Party, outing.

580.12   *homme d'affaires*] Agent, lawyer.

580.19   *plage*] Beach.

580.23   listened to me like Desdemona.] Cf. Othello I.iii.128–70.

580.31   Wells has a 'Mr. Snooks'] In "Miss Winchelsea's Heart" in *Twelve Stories and a Dream* (1905).

581.1–5   *The Passionate . . . flies.'* "] Cf. the beginning of Chap. 7 in Wells' novel (1922).

581.15   I had seen . . . plain.] See note 118.13.

582.22   Marevo] Russian, "mirage."

582.36   their rodential Gadara.] Cf. Mark 5:1–20.

583.1   Tauchnitz] German publisher of continental editions of British and American novels.

585.25–26   *accroche-coeur*] Spit, or kiss, curl (literally, "heart-hook").

585.40–586.1   naked-neck. . . Brooke] Sherril Schell's photograph (1913), reproduced as a second frontispiece to *The Collected Poems of Rupert Brooke* (London, 1921), shows Brooke in profile, the line of his neck emphasized by its being thrust forward and shirtless.

586.1   *a-houri-sang*] French *ahurissant*, "flabbergasting."

586.12–13   Pushkin . . . feet.] *Eugene Onegin*, I.xxxii–iv, especially xxxiii.2–6, in Nabokov's translation: "how I envied the waves / running in turbulent succession / with love to lie down at her feet! / How much I longed then with the waves / to touch the dear feet with my lips!"

586.21   "nymphet."] Word introduced in this sense in *Lolita*, Pt. I, ch. 5.

586.26   Cannice-Matin] Cf. *Nice-Matin*, the main regional newspaper of the French Riviera.

587.26   Mirana Palace] Humbert Humbert's father's hotel in *Lolita*.

587.38–39   *caleçon de bain*] Swimsuit.

588.17   *repoussé*] Embossing.

588.26–27   (*Du côté . . . chez Swann*)] *Swann's Way* (1913), the first volume of Proust's *A la recherche du temps perdu*.

588.28   Moïse] French *Moïse*, "Moses," *moïse*, "small wicker cradle."

588.34   chromodiascope] Viewing apparatus for color transparencies.

588.38   "*Hora?*,"] Spanish for "hour" (but with a silent *h*).

590.35   tremendous olive-green . . . flush] The sphingid moth *Celerio galii*, the Bedstraw Hawk.

591.12   "Pandora"] The butterfly *Pandoriana pandora*, the largest European fritillary.

591.16   Nieder-Österreich] Lower Austria.

591.19   Psyche] Goddess of the soul, often represented with butterfly wings to signify the lightness of the soul.

591.34   Small White] A butterfly of the species *Pieris rapae*.

591.34–35   Mann's White] A butterfly of the species *Pieris manni*.

592.2   Ergane] A butterfly of the species *Pieris ergane*.

595.21   *ce qu'on appelle*] What is called.

596.12   *Dors, Médor!*] Sleep, Médor!

597.32   *rastaquouères*] Flashy adventurers.

598.6   '*Si c'est riche.*'] If it is rich.

602.21   *maire*] Mayor.

602.37   Serov] Valentin Serov (1865–1911).

603.28   *bifsteck pommes*] Steak with french fries.

603.29   *Novosti emigratsii*] *News of the Emigration.*

603.30   *chambre garnie*] Furnished room.

603.40–604.1   16th *arrondissement*] Center of the Russian emigré community in Paris.

604.14   *nansenskiy pasport*] Nansen passport, issued by the League of Nations for stateless persons.

605.25–26   fierceness of Pushkin's . . . luck)] In Pushkin's story, "Pikovaya dama" ("The Queen of Spades"; 1834), the obsessive Hermann learns from the spirit of the Countess the secret of which three cards to draw, but a slip of the hand makes him select the wrong card on the third draw; he loses all, and goes mad.

608.32   "Prostakov-Skotinin,"] The surnames of the heroine and her brother in the comedy *Nedorosl'* (*The Minor*; 1782) by Denis Fonvizin.

609.34   *à la ronde*] To all around.

611.11–12   (Plenilune)] Full moon.

612.29–30   *crime passionnel*] Crime of passion.

612.33   *kak pozhivaete . . . do svidaniya*] How are you . . . good-bye.

614.7   "*fairelamourir*"] *Faire l'amour*, "make love"; *mourir*, "die."

615.4   *vaw-dutch-ka*] Rough phonetic pronunciation of *vodochka*, vodka (diminutive).

615.14   "Paon d'Or,"] Golden Peacock.

615.21   "putty saw-lay"] *Petit salé*, "pickled pork."

617.35   *faits-divers*] News-in-brief, human-interest stories.

619.30–31   Heine's month of May] The untitled poem "Im wunderschoenen Monat Mai" ("In the wonderful month of May"; 1822–23).

620.13   "*J'ai froid*,"] I'm cold.

621.13–14   Avenue Koch? . . . general] Avenue Foch, after Ferdinand Foch, marshal of France and in 1918 commander in chief of the Allied forces on the western front in World War I.

621.26   portrait *en pied*] Full-length portrait.

621.32   Ivan Shipogradov] A version of Ivan Bunin (1870–1953).

621.39   Vasiliy Sokolovski . . . "Jeremy"] A version of novelist and critic Dmitri Merezhkovski (1865–1941).

622.17   line from Keats] Cf. *Endymion* (1818), line 1: "A thing of beauty is a joy forever."

623.21   *à quatre mains*] Four-handed.

624.5   St. Supplice] Actually St. Sulpice (*supplice* means "torture").

624.19   *hors-concours*] Beyond competition.

626.3   *Zdraste*] Hi!

627.3   Yablokov's] From *yabloko*, "apple," and Nabokov: tribute to American critic and friend of Nabokov, Alfred Appel Jr. (b. 1934), editor of *The Annotated Lolita*.

630.24   "Passy na Rousi"] Passy, the most Russian district of Paris; *na Rusi*, in Russia.

631.5–8   oxman . . . lab!)] In H. G. Wells' science-fiction novel *The Island of Dr. Moreau* (1896), an Ox-Boar man and Swine Men are among the creatures that Moreau forms from animals. A puma escapes from his laboratory.

631.11   Boyan] Ancient Russian bard, invoked as precursor by the author (unknown) of Russia's medieval masterpiece, *Slovo o polku Igoreve*; Nabokov discusses Boyan in his translation, *Song of Igor's Campaign*.

632.7–8   "Boyan" . . . "Bronze Horseman,"] Cf. publishers Slovo (based in Berlin; see preceding note) and Petropolis (in Berlin, then Paris), whose logo was the statue of the bronze horseman (Peter the Great) that inspired Pushkin's 1833 poem of that name.

632.11   *hôtel particulier*] Town-house.

634.35   Azef . . . double agent] Evno Azef (1869–1918) was an agent of the Tsarist secret police who led the Battle Organization of the Socialist Revolutionary party from 1904 until 1909, when he was exposed as a double agent. An advocate of revolutionary terrorism, Azef organized a number of spectacular assassinations, including that of Minister of the Interior von Plehve in 1904, while betraying other revolutionary plots to the police.

635.17   *Geroy nashey ery*] Cf. the title of Mikhail Lermontov's *Geroy nashego vremeni* (*Hero of Our Time*; 1840).

635.24   *Prime Numbers*] Cf. the Russian emigré literary review, *Chisla* (*Numbers*; 1930–34), which attacked Nabokov and Khodasevich and was attacked by them in return.

635.29–30 *Princess . . . Tamara.*] *Princess Mary* is a section of Lermontov's *Geroy nashego vremeni*; *Mashen'ka* (*Mary*; 1926) is Nabokov's first novel, and "Tamara" is the name Nabokov gave in his autobiography to the girl with whom he had the love affair commemorated in *Mashen'ka*.

635.31   Lermontov's or Rubinstein's] Tamara is the heroine of Lermontov's poem *Demon* (*The Demon*; 1829–39), made into an opera, *Demon* (1871) by Anton Rubinstein.

636.12–13 Onegin . . . Lenskis] Cf. Pushkin's *Eugene Onegin*.

636.27–28 Varlamov . . . Mayor] Konstantin Varlamov (1848–1915) acted at the Alexandrinsky Theater in St. Petersburg, 1875–1915; he first played the role of "Town Mayor" in Gogol's *Revizor* (*The Inspector General*; 1836) in 1887 and continued to appear in the role into his later years.

637.5–6   Demon. Vrubel . . . diamond eyes]   See note 406.28.

638.2–4   a dozen . . . *Paradise Lost*]   Nabokov spent about eight years translating *Eugene Onegin* into English (and then more time retranslating it) and used as the epigraph to his translation Pushkin's comment on Chateaubriand's translation into French of *Paradise Lost*.

638.8   "V. Irisin"]   Cf. V. Sirin, Nabokov's Russian pen name.

638.33–34   "in the lonely . . . night,"]   From the opening of stanza 4 of "Sred' shumnogo bala, sluchaino" ("Amidst a noisy ball, by chance"; written 1851, pub. 1857) by Aleksey Konstantinovich Tolstoy (1817–75).

639.22–23   General Pudov-Usurovski's]   Russian *pudov* means "very heavy," and Latin *usura*, "interest, usury".

640.9–10   Turgenev . . . New York]   Cf. Chekhov Publishing House, New York.

641.18   "Chernolyubov and Dobroshevski"]   Cf. Nikolay Chernyshevsky (1828–89) and his fellow-radical Nikolay Dobrolyubov (1836–61). Nabokov's *Dar* (*The Gift*) includes a biography of Chernyshevsky.

645.6–7   en fait de démence]   In terms of madness.

645.36   *shapochka*]   Little hat.

646.33–647.1   butterfly . . . nettlefly]   The *Aglais urticae* or nettlefly is one of the commonest butterflies of the Old World.

647.31   "inflammation . . . lungs"]   Literal translation of Russian *vospalenie lyogkikh*, pneumonia.

649.8   *grasseyement*]   Rolling (uvular burring) of the *r*.

650.31   James Lodge]   Cf. James Laughlin of New Directions, publisher of some Nabokov works including *The Real Life of Sebastian Knight* in 1941; Nabokov vacationed at Laughlin's Alta Lodge in Utah in 1943.

651.22–24   Andalusian playwright . . . Boiteux]   Playwright Luis Velez de Guevara (1579–1644) wrote *El diablo cojuelo* (1641), which suggested the title and structure for Alain-René Le Sage's *Le Diable boiteux* (1707; *The Lame Devil*).

652.12   (Adam Atropovich . . . leader)]   A version of Georgy Adamovich (1894–1972), leader of the modish Parisian emigré critics; Greek *Atropos*, "inflexible," is the name of one of the three Fates.

652.20   *empressés*]   Eager, zealous.

652.33–34   *faux bonhomme*]   Sly customer.

652.40   *The Mother*]   Vsevolod Pudovkin's film *Mat'* (1926), an adaptation of Gorky's 1906–7 novel.

654.6   *doigté*] Fingering.

654.31–32   René Clair's new film] *Break the News* (1938), filmed in Britain.

654.35–37   transformation . . . beetle] Cf. Kafka's *Die Verwandlung* (*The Transformation* or *Metamorphosis*; 1915); in his Cornell lectures, Nabokov identified Gregor Samsa's transformation as a "beetle" (Samsa is commonly said to have become a cockroach).

656.7   from brevier to long primer] Type sizes (8 point to 10 point), roughly footnote size to main text size.

656.10   *biographie romancée*] Romanticized or novelized biography.

658.31–33   Neochomsk . . . linguistics!")] Russian *ni o chyom*, "about nothing"; Noam Chomsky, a linguist and philosopher of language.

659.10–11   Gogol's . . . *The Carrick*] "Shinel" (also known as "The Overcoat"; 1842).

659.12   an amiable opera basso] Partly a tribute to Nabokov's son Dmitri, also an opera basso fluent in Italian, English, French, and Russian.

659.28   (*simbolizirovanie, mortidnik*)] Symbolization; "deathnik."

660.17   *The Beau and the Butterfly*] See note 340.27.

660.19   *Kingdom by the Sea*] The phrase, from Edgar Allan Poe's poem "Annabel Lee" (1849), occurs in *Lolita* and was Nabokov's working title for the novel.

661.40   *My govorim . . . togda*] We speak Russian. Do you speak? Let's speak then.

663.17   Hero of Toil] The high Soviet award, *Geroy sotsialisticheskogo truda*, Hero of Socialist Toil.

664.28   *Dr. Olga Repnin*] Prince Pyotr Repnin's illegitimate son was Ivan Petrovich Pnin (1773–1805), a poet. Nabokov used his truncated surname for the title character of *Pnin*.

668.29   *Krasnaya Niva* ("Red Corn")] Cf. *Krasnaya nov* (*Red Virgin Soil*), a major Soviet literary magazine, established 1921, and *Niva* (*The Cornfield*), a popular illustrated family periodical of the pre-revolutionary period.

669.31   *cahiers*] Exercise books.

671.19   Big Peter] Cf. the hearty Pierre, the extrovert-cum-executioner in Nabokov's *Priglashenie na kazn'* (*Invitation to a Beheading*).

672.17   eoan] Dawning.

676.21   *En français . . . texte.*] In French in the text: used in translations into French to mark any passages in the original that were already in French.

679.12   Bellargus sedan]   Cf. the butterfly *Lysandra bellargus*, a European lycaenid of a vivid sky blue. In *Lolita*, Humbert travels through America in his "Melmoth."

679.15   *Mes Moteaux* as Verlaine]   "My Motels." In *Lolita*, Humbert also echoes Verlaine by exclaiming "*Mes fenêtres!*" in parody of Verlaine's auto-biographical prose pieces, with titles like "Mes hôpitaux" ("My Hospitals"; 1891), "Mes prisons" ("My Prisons"; 1893), "Ma Candidature" ("My Candidacy"; 1893).

679.37   Brunn's membrane]   That part of the lining of the nose which is sensitive to smell.

680.10   *dixi*]   I have said [it].

681.3   Audace]   French, "audacious."

681.4–5   ("*Bourreau . . . Liberté!*")]   Executioner, do your duty toward Liberty!

682.16   *Solus rex*]   Latin, "the king alone." The name for a kind of chess problem in which the white king is the only piece left on the board and the title for Nabokov's last, unfinished, Russian novel (1940).

683.12–13   Chute complète]   Utter failure, complete falling-off.

683.25–26   What did Emma . . . hat?]   In Flaubert's *Madame Bovary*.

685.32   Levitan's]   Russian landscape painter Isaak Levitan (1860–1900).

686.6   Tolstoy's *Death of Ivan*]   *Death of Ivan Ilich* (1886); Nabokov taught the work in his Masterpieces of European Fiction class at Cornell.

686.7   Stern's . . . sentimental]   In his Cornell lectures on *Mansfield Park*, Nabokov referred his students to Laurence Sterne's *A Sentimental Journey through France and Italy* (1768).

687.2–3   (*chudnyy . . . rozmarina*)]   The wonderful smell of rosemary.

687.9   *On se tutoie*]   French, "we will call each other thee" (French *tu*, Russian *ty*).

687.16–17   little golden sea snakes]   Cf. Coleridge's *The Rime of the Ancient Mariner* (1798), lines 272–81.

687.18   'My Last Duchess.']   Written by Robert Browning in 1842.

687.32   *The Black Widow* . . . George.]   Movie (1954) directed by Nunnally Johnson and starring Gene Tierney, Ginger Rogers, George Raft, and Van Johnson.

688.31   Goodminton]   Pun on badminton; by the late 1960s, Nabokov's relations with Walter Minton of Putnam had become strained.

688.37–689.5   Serov's . . . Hermitage]   Cf. Serov's *Devochka s persikami*

(*Girl with Peaches*, 1887; Moscow: Tretyakov Gallery), which depicts a dark-haired girl of about twelve at a sunny table handling a peach.

694.38–695.1   *like that . . . Canto One of* Onegin] *Eugene Onegin*, I.xxii.3–4, in Nabokov's translation: "still the tired footmen / sleep on the pelisses at the carriage porch."

695.2–5   *where under . . . fluff*] Cf. *Eugene Onegin*, I.xx, lines 1–2, 11–12 (describing the theater and the dancer Istomina), in Nabokov's translation: "The house is full already; boxes glitter, / parterre and stalls—all seethes // . . . and suddenly a leap, and suddenly she flies, / she flies like fluff from Eol's lips."

696.26   *A toi*] Yours.

697.25   "*Elles vous aiment tant!*"] They love you so!

698.11   *kegelkugel*] German, "skittle ball," used in ninepins.

699.17   *fadeur*] Insipidity

700.13   Strelitzia] *Strelitzia reginae* is the bird-of-paradise flower.

701.30–31   Charles Dodgson] See note 515.35–36.

704.4   *toupet*] Cheek, effrontery.

708.3   *isoletta*] Islet.

708.4   Gattinara] Dark red Italian table wine.

708.33   wicks] See note 64.9.

709.12   Klop] Russian, "bug, bedbug": a kind of Beetle (Volkswagen).

710.7   *cent fois*] A hundred times.

710.8–9   *Petit Larousse*] *Petit Larousse illustré*, a popular French encyclopedic dictionary.

710.27–28   *ci-devant*'s] Emigré's.

711.3   *clystère de Tchékhov*] Chekhovian clyster.

715.9   *clou*] Star (in the theatrical sense).

717.12   sharovars] See note 14.12.

717.31   *kotleta po kievski*] Cutlet, Kiev-style.

717.38   *liftyorsha*] Female elevator attendant.

718.18   (nobody . . . Gogol, knows)] Cf. Gogol's "Nos" ("The Nose"; 1836); the story, set in St. Petersburg, stresses the difficulty of knowing what is going on.

719.11–12   Gertsen Street] As the street of Nabokov's childhood home (Bolshaya Morskaya) was renamed in the Soviet era.

719.18–19   statue . . . ten years before] The statue, by M. K. Anikushin, was unveiled in 1957.

720.22   *tundrovyy*] In the tundra.

721.30–32   Tsarskoselski Statue . . . poems)] Tsarskoe Selo, near St. Petersburg, was renamed Pushkin in the Soviet era; in the park of the Eka-terinskiy dvorets (Catherine Palace) stands this statue-cum-fountain, an 1816 work by P. P. Sokolov. Pushkin wrote a four-line poem about it ("Tsarsko-selskaya statuya") in 1830.

722.33   Lola Sloan . . . lollypop] A photograph of Sue Lyon as Lolita, in heart-shaped sunglasses and sucking on a lollipop, was used to publicize Stan-ley Kubrick's 1962 film *Lolita* and for subsequent book jackets.

724.33   *"Et ce . . . tout!"*] And that's not all!

725.8   *Vraiment?*] Really?

727.12–13   French *malice* . . . "malice,"] The French word can also mean mischievousness; a dig (at someone), a trick, a prank.

730.29   *avait du bon*] Had some good in it.

732.36   *spartitraffico*] Traffic island.

733.11–12   in 1815 . . . Kaverin?] Pyotr Kaverin (1794–1855), "hussar, [and] man about town," to whom in 1817 Pushkin addressed a poem "advising him to go on leading a happy, thoroughly dissipated life. . . . Kaverin was able to stow away at one meal four bottles of champagne, one after the other, and leave the restaurant at a casual stroll" (in Nabokov's commentary to I.xvi.5–6, in *Eugene Onegin*.

739.1   Lecouchant] French, "setting sun, west."

742.12–13   Kamenev . . . *Slovo o polku Igoreve*] Kamenev was a minor poet under the influence of Ossian, a 3rd-century bard whose works were supposedly translated but in fact mostly written by James Macpherson (1736–96). Kamenev is not known to have had anything to do with the *Slovo o polku Igoreve* (see note 631.11). Nabokov accepted the authenticity of the text and discusses its history in his translation of the poem.

742.14–17   in Abyssinia . . . *Tramway Ivre . . . aussi*] Arthur Rimbaud abandoned poetry at an early age and became a trader in Abyssinia, where he died in 1891. The title of his "Le Bateau ivre" ("The Drunken Boat"; 1871) is fused with Nikolay Gumilov's "Zabludivshiysya tramvay" ("The Tram Off the Rails," or "The Crazy Tram"; c. 1919–20), with a French translation from the latter of lines 29–30: "V krasnoy rubashke, s litsom kak vymya, / Golovu srezal palach i mne" ("The executioner, in a red shirt, with a face like an udder, cut off my head too"). Gumilev (1886–1921) twice journeyed in Africa.

747.2–3   *trouvaille*] Find.

CATALOGING INFORMATION

Nabokov, Vladimir Vladimirovich, 1899–1977.
    [Novels. Selections]
      Novels 1969–1974 / Vladimir Nabokov.
          p.   cm. — (The Library of America ; 89)
      Contents: Ada, or Ardor: A family chronicle —
Transparent Things —Look at the Harlequins!

    1. Nabokov, Vladimir Vladimirovich, 1899–1977.
I. Title.   II. Series.
PS3527.A15A6   1996
813'.54—dc20   96-15255
ISBN 1–883011–20–5 (alk. paper)   CIP

THE LIBRARY OF AMERICA SERIES

1. Herman Melville, *Typee, Omoo, Mardi* (1982)
2. Nathaniel Hawthorne, *Tales and Sketches* (1982)
3. Walt Whitman, *Poetry and Prose* (1982)
4. Harriet Beecher Stowe, *Three Novels* (1982)
5. Mark Twain, *Mississippi Writings* (1982)
6. Jack London, *Novels and Stories* (1982)
7. Jack London, *Novels and Social Writings* (1982)
8. William Dean Howells, *Novels 1875–1886* (1982)
9. Herman Melville, *Redburn, White-Jacket, Moby-Dick* (1983)
10. Nathaniel Hawthorne, *Collected Novels* (1983)
11. Francis Parkman, *France and England in North America* vol. I, (1983)
12. Francis Parkman, *France and England in North America* vol. II, (1983)
13. Henry James, *Novels 1871–1880* (1983)
14. Henry Adams, *Novels, Mont Saint Michel, The Education* (1983)
15. Ralph Waldo Emerson, *Essays and Lectures* (1983)
16. Washington Irving, *History, Tales and Sketches* (1983)
17. Thomas Jefferson, *Writings* (1984)
18. Stephen Crane, *Prose and Poetry* (1984)
19. Edgar Allan Poe, *Poetry and Tales* (1984)
20. Edgar Allan Poe, *Essays and Reviews* (1984)
21. Mark Twain, *The Innocents Abroad, Roughing It* (1984)
22. Henry James, *Essays, American & English Writers* (1984)
23. Henry James, *European Writers & The Prefaces* (1984)
24. Herman Melville, *Pierre, Israel Potter, The Confidence-Man, Tales & Billy Budd* (1985)
25. William Faulkner, *Novels 1930–1935* (1985)
26. James Fenimore Cooper, *The Leatherstocking Tales* vol. I, (1985)
27. James Fenimore Cooper, *The Leatherstocking Tales* vol. II, (1985)
28. Henry David Thoreau, *A Week, Walden, The Maine Woods, Cape Cod* (1985)
29. Henry James, *Novels 1881–1886* (1985)
30. Edith Wharton, *Novels* (1986)
31. Henry Adams, *History of the United States during the Administrations of Jefferson* (1986)
32. Henry Adams, *History of the United States during the Administrations of Madison* (1986)
33. Frank Norris, *Novels and Essays* (1986)
34. W. E. B. Du Bois, *Writings* (1986)
35. Willa Cather, *Early Novels and Stories* (1987)
36. Theodore Dreiser, *Sister Carrie, Jennie Gerhardt, Twelve Men* (1987)
37. Benjamin Franklin, *Writings* (1987)
38. William James, *Writings 1902–1910* (1987)
39. Flannery O'Connor, *Collected Works* (1988)
40. Eugene O'Neill, *Complete Plays 1913–1920* (1988)
41. Eugene O'Neill, *Complete Plays 1920–1931* (1988)
42. Eugene O'Neill, *Complete Plays 1932–1943* (1988)
43. Henry James, *Novels 1886–1890* (1989)
44. William Dean Howells, *Novels 1886–1888* (1989)
45. Abraham Lincoln, *Speeches and Writings 1832–1858* (1989)
46. Abraham Lincoln, *Speeches and Writings 1859–1865* (1989)
47. Edith Wharton, *Novellas and Other Writings* (1990)
48. William Faulkner, *Novels 1936–1940* (1990)
49. Willa Cather, *Later Novels* (1990)
50. Ulysses S. Grant, *Personal Memoirs and Selected Letters* (1990)
51. William Tecumseh Sherman, *Memoirs* (1990)
52. Washington Irving, *Bracebridge Hall, Tales of a Traveller, The Alhambra* (1991)
53. Francis Parkman, *The Oregon Trail, The Conspiracy of Pontiac* (1991)
54. James Fenimore Cooper, *Sea Tales: The Pilot, The Red Rover* (1991)

This book is set in 10 point Linotron Galliard,
a face designed for photocomposition by Matthew Carter
and based on the sixteenth-century face Granjon. The paper is
acid-free Ecusta Nyalite and meets the requirements for permanence
of the American National Standards Institute. The binding
material is Brillianta, a woven rayon cloth made by
Van Heek-Scholco Textielfabrieken, Holland.
The composition is by The Clarinda
Company. Printing and binding by
R.R.Donnelley & Sons Company.
Designed by Bruce Campbell.